Birthright

Birthright

Copyright © 2020 J.R. Harris

Published by Leaky Pen Publishing

Printed in the U.S.A

Cover art by: Omarainahi
Cover art rear: DarkworkX
Bible quote: New International Version, Biblica, 2011, Biblegateway.com
Drop cap font designed by: Steffmann, Dieter
Map images: Joe McDermont, Star Raven, Lileya
Edited by: William Lovan

First printing February 2020

ISBN-13: 978-1-7321186-2-1
ISBN-13: 978-1-7321186-3-8 (e book)
ISBN-10: 1-7321186-2-0

Library of Congress Control Number: 2019900887

JRHARRIS.NET
Wickedly Clever Fantasy
LeakyPenPublishing@Gmail.com
WWW. Facebook.com/JRHarris

Acknowledgments

This book is dedicated to my wife, Traci, who always offered words of encouragement even in the darkest of times, and to my beta readers; R. Harris, B. Lovan, P. Lovan, T. Koch, P. Harwood, L. Fowlston and S. McColloch. Your critiquing and suggestions were invaluable.

Notable Works

World of Icearaus Trilogy

~Icearaus Flight~

"SOMETIMES THE STRONGEST AMONG US ARE THE ONES WHO SMILE THROUGH THE SILENT PAIN, CRY BEHIND CLOSED DOORS, AND FIGHT BATTLES NOBODY KNOWS ABOUT."

~UNKNOWN

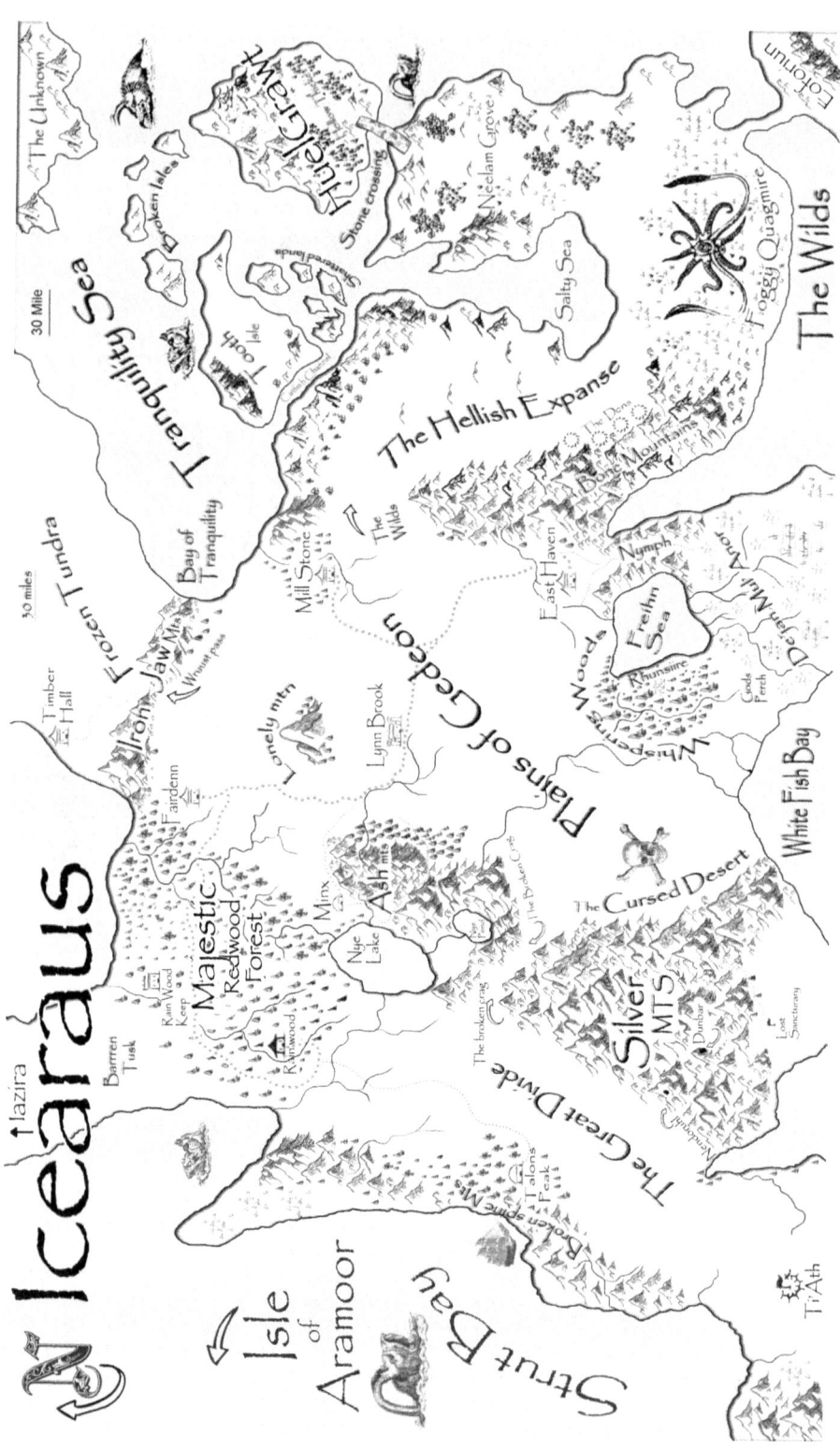

Birthright

J.R. Harris

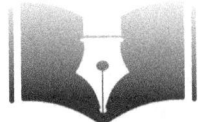

Leaky Pen Publishing

Daedric Alphabet

= A	= H	= O	
= B	= I	= P	= V
= C	= J	= Q	= W
= **D**	= K	= R	= X
= E	= L	= S	= Y
= F	= M	= T	= Z
= G	= **N**	= U	

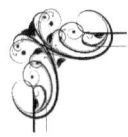

Chapter 1

he old man never felt threatened, even with the weight of a hundred glares pressing down on his frail bone-thin body. Glancing upward, he cursed the glowing orb as it spilled out rays of oranges, reds, and yellows like a toppled pot of molten lava. Having spent the last few decades deep underground in a world immune to the elements, he had forgotten the harsh realities of the surface. Wiping away the sweat that streamed down his face, the pains of the surface world haunted him.

Swiftly moving through the ruble, his pupil-less eyes darted left, then right surveying the environment. To either side, the skeletal remains of ramshackle buildings stood like wounded soldiers from a long bygone war. A war he began but failed to finish. A war envisioned by the Dark Master—his father. Satisfied his direction was accurate, his thin blackened lips squeezed into a narrow smile.

Winding his way through the rubble, he stopped when he happened upon a graveyard of bones from a recent battle. Something happened here, something devastating and unplanned. Choosing a large gray bone, possibly a femur, he held it to his nose and took a long whiff. It was indeed human, and through what little marrow remained a vision formed in his mind. Cries of pain rang out like thunder, the clash of steel shattering, of raw untamed magic being unleashed, and terror from the sky. A great battle took place here and the assassins greatly outnumbered their opponents yet they were still defeated.

This will not be the case next time, he thought, then discarded the bone. *Next time they will face an enemy much deadlier than anything which walks this land.*

Following the road, he worked his way around toppled stone walls, twisted steel, and splintered timbers. Eventually, he arrived at a large intersection ringed by four enormous dilapidated buildings. The air had grown uncomfortably warm, and the faint breeze did little to ease his suffering. Peering down each road as if he'd lost his way, he eyed a stone bench in the shade under the remains of a toppled statue. Loosening his cloak he allowed the faint breeze to cool his hot skin as he sat.

High above the city perched on a ledge obscured by shadows, Vexacion knelt. His keen vision had spotted the intruder long before he entered the Lost Sanctuary, and he continued to watch his every movement. *Who is this old man and how did he come to be here?* he thought. The Lost Sanctuary was not a town in the middle of the mainland easily accessed. No, it was a hidden city surrounded by treacherous mountains with a dark past none would enter, willingly.

Regardless of this man's reasoning, the job to prevent detection and intrusion now fell upon his shoulders since the untimely passing of Lord Rayne. He was now Lord of the Brotherhood, a position appointed to him by King Karayan.

Vexacion considered his options. He could either have him killed or captured but something told him to do neither. Instead, he leaned back resting against the stone wall and watched.

Malvo snatched a large black beetle which climbed up his leg. Holding it up he watched the six thin black legs kick at the air trying to escape, then opened his mouth and swallowed it whole. *Why won't they come*, he pondered. He could taste their presence like a foul piece of pork. Kicking around a few stones trying to locate more bugs, he decided more drastic measures would be necessary to draw out the assassins.

Vexacion's vision was trained on the old man as he darted through the rubble. This man seemed to know exactly where he was going and did nothing to conceal his approach. It was only when he was less than a block away from the entrance to the hidden compound did he draw concern.

Kill or capture, Vexacion thought. It would be nice to know how this man came to know the location of the brotherhood.

From his vantage point, he flashed the signal to capture rather than kill the intruder.

Detaching from the crumbling structures and rundown buildings, assassins materialized from the shadows. Clothed entirely in black they all appeared identical, down to the double-edged daggers which were coated with a slimy green residue.

The old man stepped back appearing startled, then spun on his heels. Retreat was impossible as the road became clogged with warm bodies. Quickly assessing the numbers, at least two dozen assassins arrived for his capture. This number was crucial when it came to deciding which spell would be used to dispatch his adversaries. One too weak might allow a few to escape and give warning while a stronger one would be wasteful. Having selected one he felt appropriate, he began to clap enthusiastically.

One assassin stood out from the rest, but only because of his blood red mask. "By order of Lord Vexacion Le Torneau, you are hereby under arrest for the unlawful intrusion upon brotherhood land. Surrender peacefully and Lord Vexacion may grant you a merciful death," he said with a childlike voice. From the folds in his cloak he produced a set of glossy black shackles which emitted a faint yellow glow.

An eerie silence hung in the thick stagnant air as the man pulled back the hood of his tattered robe. Thin wisps of white hair clung to a bald head filthy with dark brown spots.

Every assassin stepped back startled by the mans aged appearance.

The old man released a menacing laugh which echoed through the ruins. He had no desire to surrender. He came here to become Lord and make the brotherhood his own. There was only one way to accomplish this task and that would be to make an example out of these men. Mumbling the spell through his pursed lips, his presence was about to be known.

"Stop what you're doing, NOW!" the red-masked assassin screamed.

Having finished the chant, the old man released an eardrum-busting scream. Immediately afterward he raised his arms, stomped his feet, and appeared genuinely possessed. Immediately, the ground trembled and ruble danced as a massive vortex formed.

It was only now the real horror of the situation became evident as hundreds of skeletal arms topped with clawed hands broke through the ground. Whipping and thrashing, they targeted nearby assassins and latched on with a grip of steel.

Slashing at the arms with razor-sharp weapons bone fragments filled the air, but the magical enchantment could not be dispelled or defeated.

The attack was vicious and with such onset not one assassin escaped. Controlled by a single mind, each arm began to retract back into the hole from which it came dragging the victim with it. Screams rang out like a choir as each man neared his death.

Each arm never slowed as bones snapped like dried twigs, skulls were crushed to powder, and skin was stripped free and left to dry in the mid-day sun. Within seconds, every man who came for his capture was gone leaving behind only a stark reminder of their existence. A boot here, glove there, an occasional tooth, and every dagger lay unbloodied.

Vexacion stood and mopped the sweat from his face. He was no stranger to death, but what he witnessed sent an icy chill up his spine. Two-dozen highly trained assassins destroyed without drawing a drop of blood from their opponent was impossible. Regaining his composure, he sent the signal for all who remained within the vicinity to retreat.

The ground rumbled and burped. Blood blew back up through the holes spraying into the air like a geyser then fell like rain. Everything near was doused in blood except for the man who initiated the carnage.

Malvo's vision drifted over the ruins. He knew out there somewhere this man known as Vexacion watched and waited.

Vexacion's hand was forced. He had to do something, but he didn't know what. To do nothing though was not an option as it is a sign of weakness, cowardice, and his men which remained would no longer follow his lead. Shimmying down the building, he set to chase.

Vexacion had no problem following the path this man took after he entered the brotherhoods hideout. Most assassins sat with their backs against the wall with their knees pulled tightly to their chest sobbing. Those who chose to challenge him were left as blood splotches on the white marble walls.

On his way, Vexacion assured those who chose not to fight they would not be punished as this man was much more than he appeared to be. Eventually, the path led directly to the Lord's chamber—his chamber. Drawing a deep breath, he prepared to expect the unexpected. Throwing open the door he walked right in, studied the environment, then approached the old man who sat in his chair.

The old man stood, then extended his arm to greet Vexacion. "Welcome to the Brotherhood of the Dark Prince. You must be Vexacion Le Torneau?" he asked. "Your reputation as a callous, ruthless man has not gone unnoticed."

Vexacion stood silent refusing to shake hands with this man. "The blood of those men you destroyed rests on your hands. As lord of the Brotherhood I personally hold you responsible."

The old man drank in Vexacion's altered posture. He could tell the man was ready to spring quick as a viper if necessary. "No," the old man hissed. "And if you question me or my actions again, you will join them."

Vexacion went for his dagger.

The old man was faster though and snatched him by the neck. With strength not from this world he lifted the struggling man from the ground. "A lot of ignorant, unskilled, and ill-trained men died who were not worthy of being members of the Brotherhood of the Dark Prince. Weakness and bad decisions will be rewarded with death. I am here to make the brotherhood strong again. A force to be reckoned with. A force to rule the world."

"Those men were my brothers," Vexacion gurgled. In his mind he could picture himself cutting the tongue from this wretched creature once he escaped.

The old man threw Vexacion to the ground like a discarded rag. "Hopefully you will not make the same mistake. To underestimate the abilities of your opponent is something I will not allow within the ranks of the Brotherhood of the Dark Prince."

Vexacion rubbed his neck then wiped the water from his eyes. "What do you know of the brotherhood, old man?"

The old man slid the chair out and sat. Afterward, he studied a parchment with nothing on it. "The brotherhood is broken, divided, leaderless. I am here to amend the situation, to take command and reignite the brotherhood under a new banner."

"The brotherhood answers only to me. And I answer directly to King Karayan. To question me is to question him, an act I don't believe you wish to pursue. Your thoughts are noble and your abilities remarkable. Your actions though are dire, and you must be held accountable."

The old man laid the parchment down then crossed his hands. "So, you choose to follow the actions of a dead man?"

Vexacion listened to the words carefully. "King Karayan is a man of youthful vigor. A new ember burns in his eyes as he nears his goal of capturing the traitors who allowed the bearer to escape. It is through him we will rejoice when he cuts the beating heart from their chests and offers them to his savior."

Malvo laughed. "There is only one who can return him to his former glory, and she no longer resides in this world. From the very second she entered the portal his gift or immortality was stripped away. He may not know it yet, but he is dying and taking all those who follow down the same doomed path."

"You lie with a forked tongue. I saw Karayan not two days ago and he appeared vibrant as ever."

"Vexacion, time is a fickle thing. It may not reveal itself today, or tomorrow, or even the next. Eventually, it will reclaim which has been stolen. Don't be deceived, King Karayan is dying."

Vexacion scratched his chin. "And if I don't back down, surrender my rule?"

The old man's eyes narrowed to slits and he barred a full set of jagged teeth. "Then you will die. I will have control of the brotherhood and they will serve my purpose. You can either join me as my second or join those who challenged me."

Vexacion sensed the sincerity in the stranger's voice and understood he had no qualms about killing those who got in his way. "I will consider your words on a few conditions. First, who are you? Second, we must be allowed to continue our search for the traitors. I cannot allow those who slaughtered my brothers to roam unchecked. I want them held accountable for their actions. I want them strung up in the dungeon. What they did to Lord Rayne... I will not sleep until I get my revenge."

The old man listened to the demands. "My name is Malvo, Malvo Necrosyse—Founder of the Brotherhood of the Dark Prince under the guidance of the Dark Master. It is through him we will make Icearaus great again. Unfortunately, your other request cannot be honored at this time."

Where have I heard that name from, Vexacion thought, then he remembered Karayan said it a few times inadvertently. "And why is that?"

Malvo leaned back in the chair and interlaced his fingers across his chest. "Ellusia Daquell now lives within the elven community. Lady Alenia has taken her in as a daughter and thus placed her under the protection of the elves. Because of this protection, she's impossible to acquire. As we all know Averie is in the new world and only the Creator knows of her location—"

"What about Pegan? He's the one responsible for Lord Rayne's death."

Malvo thought for a moment. "You find Pegan and you will be no better off than Lord Rayne. Pegan is an anomaly. He shouldn't exist. Nobody knows where he came from or where he's going. His skills are unnatural, beyond comprehension. When he is aided by Elwrick he will match any threat with a fury this world has yet to see."

Vexacion crossed his arms. "You speak as if you know him personally."

"I have my suspicions, that's all," Malvo said. "There is one though who roams Icearaus. One who holds more responsibility than all others combined."

"Lilith?" Vexacion asked.

"Yes," Malvo answered. "We will track her down and destroy her."

"You did not come here to track down and destroy one woman," Vexacion said. "You have another goal in mind?"

Malvo released a noise which sounded something between a snarl and a laugh. "You're correct, and we will talk about it when the time is right. Now though, you must leave as I have pressing matters which must be addressed."

Vexacion tried to speak but discovered he no longer had control of his body. Guided by a demonic force his movements were jerky as he was led to the door. Once outside, the door slammed shut and whatever inflicted him left and he fell to the floor exhausted. From the crack beneath the door a bright red light appeared, and the pungent scent of burning sulfur filled his nostrils and left both eyes watering. Horrific piercing cries filled his ears, and then something heavy, but not solid hit the floor with a thud.

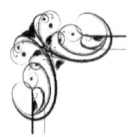

Chapter 2

Modern Day America

April 13th, 2018

5:27 a.m.

verie awoke lying on her back staring straight into a salmon-colored sky. Faint wisps of translucent clouds hung like marshmallows while a flock of dark-colored birds fluttered past. The air was crisp, and its chilling bite brought a shiver to her spine. Rubbing her arms, she could already feel the goosebumps forming on her exposed skin.

Sitting upright, she yawned then stretched as if woken from a winter's hibernation and observed her surreal environment. Lush green grass speckled with yellow and blue flowers gave way to a white picket fence. Beyond the fence a dirt road traced the edge of a dense forest. Each tree was a spectacle to behold with its thick bark, extreme height, and enormous girth. The branches near the top were woven together creating a latticework of foliage which kept the ground concealed in shadows. From somewhere within the darkness, she could make out the faint slapping of water against stone.

Struggling to stand she wobbled like a newborn fawn, then made her way towards the fence. Along the way her bare feet sunk into the sponge-like ground forcing her on more than one occasion to swing her arms to keep balance.

Clinging to the fence like a paper bag blown in the wind, she watched as the sun crested the trees in all its glory chasing away the chill and bringing hope to her dismal situation. The forest lightened and through the trees she could make out the shimmering surface of a large lake. The sounds of birds filled the air as they woke to start their day and the snap of twigs breaking told her food could be found, if she only dared to enter.

Rubbing her grumbling belly, she quickly remembered why she was here. Inside her she carried a child, a gift from the Creator. A child who would someday return to Icearaus while she would be forced to remain. The thought of that day brought a tear to her eye.

The rumbling came again, but this time much stronger and carried the hint of pain. She would need to find food soon. Checking to make sure the small sword she took from Jairo survived the journey, she would have no choice but to kill something.

Mooo...

Bock, bock, bock, bock, bock, begowwwwk…

Averie spun ripping her sword free expecting a fight. She swore an oath to Elwrick to protect this child, even offering her own life if needed.

Begowwwwk, cluck-cluck, begowwwwk, bock—

Mooo…

Oink, oink—oink, oink—

Averie's eyes widened, then the corners of her mouth curled upward ending with a devilish grin. She was not alone, abandoned in a wooded area far from civilization where she would be forced to forage, but on a farm. *Maybe she had not left Icearaus at all, only relocated to an undiscovered area outside of Karayan's rule*, she thought.

To the left was a never-ending pasture filled with a wide variety of cows. Most were white with black splotches but mixed in were larger cream-colored ones or much smaller dark brown ones. Inside the pasture was another area separated by a fence made up of steel bars that reminded her of the prison cell at the Lost Sanctuary. Contained within this separate area were pigs of every shape, size, and color. Most had their faces stuffed in a trough, but a few wallowed in a giant mud pit. Chickens roamed freely pecking at the ground while a plump orange colored rooster with black tipped feathers was perched on the fence.

Beside the pasture was an enormous red barn constructed from wooden planks. Large double doors were open revealing a cache of hay bales stacked from floor to ceiling leaving only a small passage between to enter. Along one side of the barn dirty windows looked out at the pasture.

What excited her most though was the leathery brown two-story cottage built upon a stone foundation nestled back in a grove of trees. Surrounding the foundation were beautiful bushes with purple leaves mixed with dark green shrubs with red berries. One area had a plethora of clay pots filled with yellow petal plants and bright green stems. Along the front of the cottage was a porch which spanned the entire length where a long wooden bench hung from thick chains. Large windows with their curtains tied back allowed the light to enter unimpeded and double doors with silver knobs could be seen off to one side.

Averie's racing heart relaxed. Even though she had never been here before, the house emitted an aura of welcoming and calmness.

Begowwwwk, cluck, cluck, begowwwwk, bock. The rooster took notice of the intruder and headed her way to investigate.

Averie smiled as she wondered if she was home.

Begowwwwk, the rooster growled, flapping its wings and fluffing up to show its dominance.

Averie doubled over. The sudden hunger pangs almost dropped her to her knees and she found it difficult to breathe. She was too weak to kill and butcher a pig or cow, and to chase a chicken would only wear her down. This left her with only one option, enter the cottage in hopes of finding food.

"Hopefully we can find some food here," she whispered to the fetus, then rubbed her enlarged belly.

Using the skills Pegan taught her, not a sound was made as she crept up the porch towards the double doors. Cautiously twisting the knob, it moved no more than a smidgen then stopped. The other knob netted the same results. On her knees she tried to peer under the door but found it perfectly sealed. *How is that possible*, she thought. Using the tip of her sword she poked it into the keyhole and tried to turn it only chipping away the shiny surface.

Flustered, she moved on to a window and peered inside. Directly in the center sat a large lustrous ornately carved wooden table surrounded by eight high backed wooden chairs. Down the center of the table was a long cloth with frayed ends which hung over the sides. On the decorated cloth sat a green glass bowl filled with fruit. Some she recognized such as grapes and apples, but there were other oddly shaped items as well.

Above the table hanging from the ceiling was a strange object heavy with hundreds of tear-shaped diamonds that sparkled as the sun reflected off the multi-shaped surface. The floor glistened while the walls were painted a light gray. Eventually, her eyes were drawn to a large painting on the far wall. The woman was beautiful with radiant skin flowing locks of auburn hair. The man reminded her of Pegan, sturdy, but caring. The younger boy appeared to have lost interest sometime earlier by his frown, probably from having to wait on the painter.

Sliding her finger along the edge, the entire piece of glass was void of any gaps. *There must be a way in*, she thought, then leaned closer to examine the window. To her surprise she discovered it was not a single piece of glass, but multiple pieces compressed together. Taping on the glass with her finger it emitted a strange harmonic thumping sound.

Averie leaned back against the porch railing and wished Pegan was here. He would know what to do. He could figure out a way to get inside. "This is going to be more difficult than I first thought," she grumbled as the hunger pangs returned. Feeling as if she might vomit she dropped to her knees and cried out. She would need to act soon before the fetus starved.

Forcing herself to stand she neared the window and pulled her sword free. Wedging the blade between the glass and wooden frame she gently pried.

Clink… chink… pop. A strange noise came from the glass as a small crack formed. It was hairpin thin, blue in color, and no longer than her finger.

Averie froze. The noise was not loud but had a piercing quality that made your hair stand erect. Time stood still as she looked around waiting for someone to appear. To investigate the strange noise but when no one arrived she decided to try again. Pressing the blade into the wood beside the window she pried harder.

Suddenly, the small crack accelerated and spiderwebbed reaching all corners. Moments later it exploded spewing fragments of glass sharp enough to cut on contact.

Chickens squalled, cows mooed, and pigs oinked. Averie was positive the noise was heard around the world.

Not knowing what to do, or if she should do anything, she did the first thing which came to her mind and ran. Across the yard and through an opening in the fence she vanished into the darkness of the woods. Branches slashed at her face, vines grabbed her feet. Swinging her sword as if she'd gone mad, she hacked and slashed at anything in her path. Continuing to run she stopped when she reached the water's edge. With nowhere else to go she turned to face her pursuers, but there were none.

Averie didn't want to go back and considered searching the forest for food, but the hunger pangs of a starving fetus forced her decision. She would return and confess to the cottage owner of her crime and beg for mercy and food. Regardless, she would get food or die trying.

Creeping like a cat on the hunt, she climbed the porch and bypassed the broken window on her way to the door. It was here she would confess her crimes and knocked. When no one came she hit harder. Still, no one answered. She didn't want to trespass, but she had to eat and returned to the window. All around the opening, inside and out, glass fragments sparkled.

Inside on the table salvation waited and her vision was focused on the fruit, not the dagger length shard which jutted out from the frame. Climbing through the opening the shard caught her near the wrist bone and sliced her clear to the elbow as she fell inside.

Averie cared none the less if she was discovered at this pointed and screamed. Pain raced through her arm clouding her mind as she watched the thin red line form. She would need to do something, and do it quick before she lost to much blood. Shoving the bowl aside she grabbed the towel and tightly wrapped her arm. Pressing the wounded limb against her side to keep the cloth from unraveling she now concentrated on the food. Saliva dripped from her mouth as she grabbed a bright red apple and bit down with the force of a monster. To her shock she discovered the apple was hard as stone nearly breaking her teeth and tasted like candle wax. Discarding it for another she discovered all the apples were inedible, the oranges could not be peeled, and the grapes were spongy like rolled up slugs.

Disgusted, and still hungry she moved to the next room. One wall was lined with an array of different sized cabinets with a white marble top laced with blue veins. In the center of it was a black basin separated into two sections. Above it built into the wall was a large window like the one she broke. Lining the opposite wall were more cabinets but they were separated by two boxes. One box had a bunch of knobs and a glass surface, the other was much taller with two doors that spanned the entire length of the front. Inside the small box was a gaggle of pots and pans, metal sheets, and one big silver spoon.

The taller box was made up of two distinct sections. One was cold as ice and everything inside was frozen. Still, she removed each item and scrutinized it before placing it on the floor and moving on. When that side was empty she moved to the next. The other side was much warmer but still cold to the touch. Inside it were jugs, clear containers, boxes, and glass jars. Pulling out each item she tested them by either taking a bite or cutting off the top and taking a drink. Some things made her lips pucker and she quickly discarded them while other items she enjoyed and ate it all. A few items she recognized such as eggs and bacon and knew they had to be cooked first so she placed them aside unmolested.

With the hunger pangs now resolved, she focused on things which she would need for survivability in the wild and began searching the house. To her surprise she discovered the upstairs desolate as if no one lived there. Downstairs, she located a coat that was much too large but would protect her from the elements. In an adjacent closet she found boots with fur around the top which would protect her feet. Hanging on the back of the closet door she located a hat that covered her ears and thick gloves to protect her hands. Everything else she examined which she could not use or didn't know what it was she organized by size or neatly folded the items on the bed. She was not here to ransack the cottage, only take what she needed.

Unsure where to go, she made her way to the barn having decided it would offer the best refuge. Not only would it offer protection from the cold, but it also allowed her to stay hidden. Still, she could not be sure it was unoccupied and approached cautiously. Removing her sword, she carefully entered and waited for her eyes to adjust to the darkness.

It was a typical barn the same as you would find on Icearaus containing nothing but feed for the animals. Near the back she found a room that was surprisingly clean. Located inside was a large wooden table with a vice-like mechanism fastened to the top. Behind the table on the wall was a large shelf that held numerous small totes. Inside each were small copper projectiles. On the opposite wall was a much larger wooden shelf that held translucent bins. Inside those bins were brass tubes the length of her finger. One large bucket placed by itself in the corner was full of coarse black powder. On a third wall was a window hidden behind a thick brown curtain. From here she could see the front of the cottage.

At the desk was a large chair which she found quite comfortable but unfit for sleeping. She would have no choice but to gather hay and make a bed.

As she completed the chore her focus quickly went to her throbbing arm. Removing the blood-soaked towel, she could see the wound was deep, but not life-threatening and would heal leaving behind an ugly scar as a painful reminder.

With her bed made and heavy eyes she laid down to rest but found little. Her mind drifted back to Icearaus and she envisioned herself wrapped in the arms of Pegan. "I love you, Pegan Rhoe," she whispered. Smiling, her hand gripped the necklace Elwrick gave her and she drifted into a silent slumber.

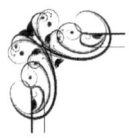
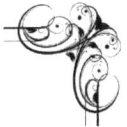

Chapter 3

ester nervously waited outside the elaborate double doors and viewed his reflection in the polished mahogany wood. Content with his appearance, he knocked, paused, then knocked again when it didn't open. Leaning against the wall he considered leaving, but one word rang clear in the message he received—*immediately*. Sliding his dagger free he flipped it in the air and caught it by the blade. Delighted with his skill of a blade he smiled, then rapped again on the door with the pommel of his dagger. Performing a few practice slashes and jabs, the blade vanished back into its sheath then he adjusted his tunic. *Why would King Karayan wish to see me*, he thought. In his forty-plus years, this was the first time he had ever been summoned to a private meeting, in Karayan's private chamber no less. Normally this pleasure was only afforded to women.

Jester paced the length of the hallway pondering the note he received as he considered King Karayan's sudden change. Lately, the King had not been his angry, bitter, hateful self. He'd become distant, rarely leaving the palace, less vocal, and often sending his servants to do his bidding. The few times King Karayan did make an unannounced appearance, his once mighty demeanor and commanding presence had waned. He was not the only one who noticed King Karayan seemed lost in a strange fogginess or drunken stupor as rumors of his appearance grew from the darkened recesses of the slums. His words lacked authority, and his once daunting glare which could drive a man insane had lost its bite.

Stopping at the door, he considered the note and the words printed on it. He needed to talk to the King or risk torture and death, something he didn't want to experience. Curling his fingers into a tight fist he pounded his hand against the door, then stepped back.

The blade hissed free from the sheath as King Karayan spun to face the door. It was the only thing separating him from the enemy, and he would not go down without a fight. Out there somewhere he knew Malvo lurked plotting his revenge, devising a dastardly plan to get even for being held underground for decades. Cautiously approaching the door, he peered through a small hole drilled into the wood which afforded him a view of whoever waited on the opposite side.

Tossing the blade aside he relaxed realizing it was Jester, one of the few men he still considered trustworthy. *Why is he here though?* Karayan thought, then the memory of the note crept back into his mind.

Karayan quickly relocated to the opposite side of the room near a large desk.

It was here he felt most comfortable as there was also a secret passage allowing him to escape if needed behind an immense floral tapestry. "Enter," Karayan firmly stated.

Jester twisted the dagger-shaped ivory handle and the door swung silently inward. Gathering his wits, his mind rifled through a hundred different reasons why he had been summoned, yet none of them made sense. There would only be one way to know for sure, and he entered.

"Close the door," Karayan said. "This conversation is for your ears only."

Jester paused from the sight of King Karayan. The Kings once youthful appearance had faded, and thick wrinkles now creased his leathery face. His black flowing mane which he often described as a symbol of power and honor, now revealed faint streaks of ghosting and his sturdy posture had visible flaws.

After closing the door Jester performed a gracious bow. "My King, what honor do I have this day to grace your presence?"

King Karayan studied Jesters movements searching for the slightest hint of treason. Having discovered none, he pointed to a chair opposite the desk. "Sit, we have much to discuss."

Jester glanced at the chair, then back at the closed door.

"Sit," Karayan repeated. "I can see it in your eyes, and your actions, you're concerned why you've here. I can assure you; you have done nothing wrong. Had you, we would be having this conversation in a room more accustomed to having blood spilled on the floor."

Jester slid the chair slightly back and at an angle allowing him a direct path to the door if needed.

Karayan eased into his seat moments after Jester sat.

Outside the window, lightning lit the darkened sky and rain pounded against the glass.

"There's a storm brewing," Jester said. "Odd for this time of year."

Karayan leaned back in the chair, his vision focused on the ceiling. "Yes, very strange indeed, almost unnatural I would say." Karayan glanced at the glass and caught his own reflection then quickly turned away. The sight of his face made him sick. "There's something I need accomplished," Karayan said after a long delay. "I have invested a great deal of time and energy considering who would be the best man to see its completion. I need someone who is both sharp with their mind, and masterful with a blade. In the end one name rose to the top, yours."

Jester's eyes widened and his breath quickened. His patience and planning were about to pay off. This would be his opportunity to prove to the people of Icearaus he was the best man to take Karayan's place once the King took his final breath, which wouldn't be long judging from his current appearance. "My King, might I enquire about the task?"

From a drawer in the desk Karayan removed a rolled-up map and placed it on the desk. Carefully unrolling the delicate parchment, he placed a jade figurine in each corner. "I need you to go here." He pointed to a well-known landmark on the map.

"Rain Wood Keep?" Jester asked.

"Yes. Deep within the catacombs you will discover a secret chamber. It is there I need you to recover a tome of significant value."

Jester rubbed his chin, then laughed. "My King. I have been there but never inside. Rumor is there are leagues upon leagues of tunnels many layers deep. It would take months of searching before this secret chamber is located, if ever. Besides, those halls are filled with all manner of vile creatures who now call it home. There is a great possibility they have ransacked this chamber destroying everything, including this elusive tome."

"I have no doubt creatures have ransacked the keep, but this tome they will avoid. You will recognize it by the unique black demon hide leather binding. The cover will be bordered with rune words written in obsidian black ink and a pentagram drawn of virgin blood. Inside the Pentagram will be an image of a goat's skull with piercing red eyes which seem to be alive."

Jester shivered at the thought of finding this tome. "You wish for me to enter this abandoned keep, fight my way through hordes of monsters who wish to suck the marrow from my bones, find this secret chamber, and recover a tome hidden somewhere within—alone?"

"Do you honestly believe I'm that stupid?" Karayan asked. "I'm prepared to send with you a small force to deal with the vile beasts that call it home, along with a man named Johnathan Barrett."

Jester eased back in the chair relieved he would not be going alone. "I have heard that name before."

"Yes, you have. He is the man who designed this palace and is also responsible for Rain Wood Keep. He knows every passage, every hallway, every tunnel. He can lead you directly to this secret chamber as he oversaw its construction. Once there, it will be YOUR responsibility to recover this tome. All you must do is keep him alive long enough to get in and get out. After that I care little for his, or the others return." Karayan leaned forward resting his elbows on the desk. "No others must know you have this tome, not even the men who join you."

"My King, keeping this a secret will complicates matters—"

"What are you saying, I have chosen the wrong man for the job?"

Jester grinned. "I will think of something to ease their questioning."

"Now make haste," Karayan said. "Each minute I sit here doing nothing, the enemy grows stronger."

"My King, I will gather my men and leave at first light," Jester said.

"Did you not hear me? Time is of the utmost importance. Delaying this by even an hour could cost me greatly. Perhaps you don't understand the importance of this mission."

"My King, I will see it done immediately." Afterward, he gave a quick bow then abruptly departed.

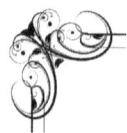
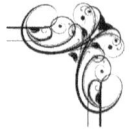

Chapter 4

verie heard the wretched creature long before it reared its ugly black and white head. Red and blue eyes clashed against the starry sky and a piercing cry came from a mouth of glistening steel. Moving like a banshee, the beast left a trail of fluttering dust as it roared past.

Averie covered her mouth careful not to breathe, for it may alert the beast of her presence.

Releasing a grinding growl, the behemoth stopped near the cottage then to her horror spewed out a living man.

No longer could she witness the terrible acts the beast had planned and closed the curtains. All she waited for now was to hear the screams of the family being devoured.

Sarah waited by the door until Mike climbed the stairs. "Really, lights and sirens?"

"Hey, when my little sister gets robbed I hold nothing back," Mike told her.

"Well… I really wouldn't say we were robbed," Tom said as he joined them.

"Sarah told me—" Mike started to say.

"I know what she told you, but she panicked," Tom interrupted. "I can honestly say I have never seen anything quite like this before. Hell, I've never even heard of anything like this, ever, not even on television."

Mike's nose wrinkled with confusion. "What's going on?"

"Over here," Tom said. "Let me show you where they broke in."

Mike studied the broken window as he wrote down notes on a small pad before following the trail of blood to where the waxed fruit lay. On each piece were visible bite marks. From there, the blood trail led him to the kitchen where he nearly dropped the notepad. "This is how you found it?"

"Exactly!" Sarah said. "I told Tom not to touch a thing until you had a chance to examine it."

Mike removed his brown, wide-brimmed hat and placed it on the counter. Afterward, he rubbed his forehead in confusion as he debated his options. "What about the rest of the house?"

"That's what puzzles me the most." Tom had a baffled look on his face. "Everything in the house was searched, but nothing was stolen."

"Besides your hunting coat and my winter boots, hat, and gloves," Sarah corrected him.

"And you double checked your guns, all of them?" Mike asked.

"Double and triple checked them. Here is where it gets bizarre. Each gun was placed on the bed sorted by length. The ammo too was dumped out then organized by size. From what I can tell not one round was stolen."

"You keep count of your ammo?" Mike asked.

"Remember I reload my own, so I know exactly what I have in stock."

"Not only the ammo and guns. Whoever did this, did the same thing with the clothes and Billy's toys," Sarah told Mike.

Mike snatched his hat then walked back out to the porch. "I'm going to take a look around, you both wait here."

Twenty minutes later Mike returned shaking his head. "I couldn't find a single trace of someone ever coming here or leaving. It's as if they magically fell from the sky then floated away."

Following Sarah inside, Mike sat on the couch and broke out his notepad. "Let me get this straight. Someone breaks in and removes all your stuff from the fridge, rifles through all your belongings, steals only a few, non-valuable items and everything else they neatly fold and organize?"

"That about covers it." Tom looked out the broken window into the darkness.

Mike busted out in laughter. "Wish they would visit my house next."

"This isn't funny," Sarah scolded him. "Something serious happened here and I want to know who violated our home?"

Mike shook his head in disbelief. "I'm sorry but…" he said with a chuckle. "I've been the sheriff for fifteen years now and thought I'd seen it all, but this here is a first."

"There must be something you can do?" Tom asked.

"Luckily, whoever did this cut themselves and judging from the amount of blood it looks quite severe. Let me check the hospital to see if anyone has shown up with a good-sized cut. I'll also ask Jennifer if anybody stopped by the clinic needing stitches. In the meantime, I'll get a blood sample and send it to the lab, but it will take months to get the results. If you want I can try and recover a few fingerprints as well, but it probably won't be much use. Remember, Willowdale is a small community with limited resources. We don't have the funds to launch a major investigation. If someone got killed it would be different."

"Do you think they will ever get caught?" Sarah asked.

"Honestly, I don't know," Mike finally admitted after reviewing the evidence once more.

"Thanks for stopping by," Sarah said, then hugged him.

"What big brothers are for?" Mike smiled, then started to leave then abruptly stopped at the door. "Hey Tom, you still have all those hunting cams?"

"Yeah, why?"

"Place a few of them in inconspicuous areas near the house. If they return, perhaps we can catch them on the camera."

"I'll do it first thing in the morning," Tom said.

"You'll do it now," Sarah corrected Tom.

Mike winked at Tom. "Sounds like the misses has spoken, you better get right on that."

Averie woke to the crash of thunder. Scrambling to her feet she peered out

the window as the first drops of rain speckled the glass. Some time through the night angry thunderheads rolled in obscuring the moon and blotting out every star. Across the way the house sat dark except for a single light burning on the front porch.

Rubbing her grumbling belly, the fetus was letting her know it was hungry by sending pains careening across her abdomen. She would have no choice but to challenge the weather in search of food.

At the barn door she waited until her eyes adjusted to the darkness before venturing out. Near her the rooster perched atop the coop appearing to be sleeping, but she knew from experience the bird was aware of his surroundings and quite alert. To catch him in her condition and with a damaged arm would be impossible.

Oink… oink…snort…wee… oink.

"Pigs," she whispered. An adult pig would be too difficult to kill, but she remembered observing a few piglets. Trapped in the pen there would be nowhere for them to run, and easy targets. Creeping through the shadows like a phantasm in search of lost souls she neared the pigs unobserved.

Lightning ripped apart the sky and the clash of thunder was deafening. From the east an ill wind blew rattling trees and bringing life to inanimate objects.

Wiping the water from her face she examined the locking mechanism. It was unlike anything she had ever seen. First, she pulled, then pushed, but it held fast. It was only after she discovered a rod had to be pushed in and a lever lifted did the gate open. Forced by the wind it slammed against the fence drawing the attention of all inside.

Each pig squealed and squawked climbing over the other trying to place distance between them and the intruder. Nobody had to tell them a woman standing there with a sword would end well. Before daybreak, blood would be spilled.

Averie studied each piglet deciding on a small pink one with white splotches. It was cute, and she didn't want to hurt the creature, but food was a necessity. Besides, *it was only one piglet*, she kept telling herself.

Oink… oink… squeal… the pigs screamed as they trampled across the pen searching for an escape. Clang, the noise tore through the night as the metal trough slammed against the steel bars before becoming dislodged and spilled its contents. Alerted by the noise cows mooed and the pounding of their hooves sounded like one long beat of thunder as the herd vacated the area. *Cock a doodle doo*, the rooster screamed from the coop.

"What in the world," Tom complained as he scrambled from the bed. Grabbing a flashlight and the shotgun he bolted out the front door. "Who's there?" he screamed into the rain and thunder.

Averie panicked. She needed to get away quick but slipped in her haste and fell face down in the mud. Scrambling like an eight-legged octopus up a mossy rock she crawled her way to the side of the cottage and took refuge behind a dense bush. Covering her mouth, she dared not breath a sound.

Tom bolted past observing the pigpen and the gate wide open. There was nothing he could do now as every pig was on the loose. He would have to wait until morning before collecting them.

Averie remained hid until the house was dark again before venturing back to the barn. Regardless of the pain, food would have to wait for another night.

"Billy," Tom screamed.

Averie woke from the noise then peeked out the window. The wind had died down, but a steady drizzle fell from an ashen gray sky. Near the cottage a man paced the length of the house.

"Billy, get out here," Tom screamed again, then reached down and snagged a piglet as it tried to bolt past.

Averie smiled as she took in his features. He was a tall man with dark hair cut short at the top while his face was stern with high cheekbones, narrow nose, and beady eyes. In those eyes she saw a man hardened by work yet deep with compassion. Dawning a thick yellow coat and leather gloves, his knee-high black boots made a slurping sound with each step.

"Yeah," Billy answered. His face was permanently frozen in a yawn as he walked out.

This was no doubt his son, she thought. In the child she could see all the features of the man waiting to come out.

"You never closed the pig pen as I asked, now every pig has escaped except the one I'm holding."

"I did too."

"Hmmm," Tom grumbled as he watched another piglet dart past.

"What's going on?" Sarah asked after she came out holding a steaming cup of coffee.

Averie made an *OHHH* sound as her mouth shaped into a circle. This woman was beautiful. Prettier than all others she had seen except Lady Alenia. Her auburn hair new held faint streaks of blonde that glistened in the porch light. Cascading down past her shoulders, the ends frolicked on the gentle breeze. Pastel colored skin high-lighted her rose-colored lips, and her perfectly shaped cheekbones supported the brightest blue eyes she had ever seen.

In the distance, the faint sound of thunder rolled, and the wind increased slightly.

"Somehow the pig pen got opened last night," Tom said.

Between them, a piglet zipped past, ears tucked down, running for his life. Behind it, the rooster was cackling and heavy on the chase.

Sarah sipped on her coffer giggling as a piglet ran between Toms leg's. "You know, it was blustery last night, perhaps the wind blew the gate open."

"Doubtful," Tom said. "There was a rock placed in front of the gate to prevent it from closing."

Sarah's face went deathly pale. "Do you think whoever broke in could be out there watching us? Waiting for you to leave so I'll be home alone?"

Tom looked towards the woods. "I hope not. Regardless, I need to get the back fifty acres cleared and ready if we still plan on ordering that additional cattle."

"I'm going somewhere then. I won't stay here alone while you're so far away, not with some freak on the loose."

Tom spit on the ground. "You would think this far out of town and away from the main road we'd never see another living soul, yet here we are dealing with trouble."

"Did you look at the cams yet?" she asked.

"Not yet, we need to collect these pigs first before they wander too far, and coyotes get em'."

"Billy, help your father, I'll get breakfast started."

With the morning chores finally complete, Tom sat down at the computer with a handful of sim cards. On one of them he hoped to discover something. One after another revealed nothing, that is, until he slid the last card into the machine.

"What in the hell," Tom said as he replayed the clip.

Hunched low to the ground, a darkened shadow crept past. At one point it glanced directly at the camera revealing catastrophic golden eyes before vanishing into the darkness.

The sound of glass shattering sounded like a siren as the coffee cup slid from Sarah's fingers and hit the floor. "I'm moving," was all she could muster.

Tom rewound the video and watched it again. "Wonder what the hell it is?"

"I don't know," Sarah said. "But I'm not staying here as long as that thing is lurking around."

"Relax, will you," Tom said. "For all we know it might be an endangered animal that's wounded. Why don't you invite Mike and Jennifer over for dinner. In the meantime, I still got a fence to install."

"The hell you do. You're not leaving me alone with that monster out there on the loose," Sarah complained.

"The thing is obviously nocturnal," Tom explained to Sarah. "It's probably sleeping in the woods right now."

"I don't care if it's hibernating right now, you're not going nowhere," Sarah snapped back.

As the sun set Averie made her way from the barn to the cottage. Through the window she could see many people all sitting at the table. She could hear the laughter, smell the food, and feel the love.

Mike held up the images Tom printed from the video. "Never seen anything like this in all my life. Was there anything else on the video?"

"No. Only this brief glimpse, and this is the best picture of it as well," Tom answered.

"I want it dead," Sarah interjected her opinion.

"Calm down," Mike told Sarah. "First let's figure out what it is."

"I think we should stay here tonight," Jennifer said. "This way if it does come back you and Tom can be ready for it."

"Me," Tom complained. "Mike is the law around here. He can deal with this demon thing."

Mike laughed. "Don't worry, if it rears its ugly head I'll deal with it."

Averie knelt for a long while watching them oblivious to the red light in the corner of the porch watching her. How she wished to be with a family again, to feel wanted, loved, not alone, or hungry and afraid like she was now. Unsure why, she gripped the necklace and thought of Pegan and for a moment, she believed she felt a faint heartbeat. Tomorrow at first light she would reveal herself and hope these people would show her mercy.

Tom slept little that night. Tossing and turning vivid dreams assaulted his mind. Finally, he had no choice but to rise or risk waking Sarah who soundly slept. Splashing his face with cold water he made his way to the porch only to discover Mike sitting on the steps.

"Couldn't sleep either?" Mike asked. In his hand he held his Glock and beside him were two fully loaded magazines.

"No," Tom said. "I have a strange feeling about this, something's wrong."

Mike cocked his head. "What do you mean?"

"You couldn't see it in the pictures, but in the video, I saw something in those eyes. I can't explain it."

"Well try," Mike said.

Tom took a deep breath then slowly let it out. "It's like they could see through flesh and blood clear down into your soul. Mike, I don't want to sound like an idiot but it's like that creature is from another world."

"Well, I can't tell you where she's from, but I can tell you where she's been hiding."

"What?" Tom's eyes opened wide.

"As we speak she's hiding in your barn, your reloading room to be exact."

"She… what do you mean she?"

Sitting here in the dark I watched her peer out that window a few times. Having noticed me she quickly closed the shade only to look again a few hours later. Not too long ago she came to the door but retreated into the shadows. I would guess she's hungry and waiting to sneak out unobserved."

"Why didn't you—"

"What? Go look for her?"

"Yes."

"She'll come out when she's ready. Why go in and risk injury to either her or me?"

"Because you're the sheriff, that's what you do," Tom said.

"I enforce the law," Mike answered. "I don't bust in and traumatize women who may be suffering from a mental condition. I figured I would wait here until either she came out or Jennifer woke. She has training on how to deal with mentally unstable people."

"If you're not worried then why are you so heavily armed?" Tom noted the extra magazines.

"I didn't say I won't defend myself. I know from the pictures she's armed with a sword."

"We have to do something?" Tom said.

"Why don't you have a seat and watch?" Mike suggested. "The minute you act like you're not watching you'll catch a fleeting glance of her peeking out. She's quick though so you have to be fast."

Tom did as instructed and soon noticed movement in the shadows of the barn. Golden eyes watched them as much as they watched her.

"Did you see her?" Mike asked.

"I saw something," Tom said. "I won't go as far as to say it's a woman. In fact, I would not—"

"Don't move," Mike whispered.

From the shadows of the barn Averie cautiously walked out into the open. Not far, but enough to be noticed while still leaving the option to flee if needed.

Mike stood while holstering his weapon in one fluid movement. He knew the intruder was a woman, but not one riding on the edge of giving birth. There was no way he could point his firearm at her regardless of her actions, even if he were being stabbed. Unsure what to say, he said the first thing which came to his mind. "Easy now, we only want to talk with you."

Averie stopped and looked at them as if she didn't understand the language.

Mike put his hands out in a gesture of peace. "We know you're hungry and injured. We want to help you."

"She's a criminal," Tom whispered.

"Shut up," Mike whispered back. "What has she done beside steal a few useless items and clean your house?"

Tom knew Mike was right. Really, what has the woman done.

"I know your arm is cut and I'm sure it's painful. My wife is a doctor, she can help you. All I need is for you to put the sword down."

Averie looked down at her sword. "No," she hissed. "I will not surrender my only form of protection. I come here in peace and offer no ill-will towards your kind."

"What do you mean, our kind?" Mike asked.

Tom looked at the woman, then Mike. "What do we do now?"

Mike cautiously moved down the stairs.

Averie backed away as the man approached, then crouched and drew the sword. She tried to replicate the stance she had seen Pegan do many times, but her swollen belly made it hard for her to breath.

"I want to help you," Mike softly whispered. "But I can't as long as your holding that weapon."

Averie tried to stand but fell back slamming her wounded arm into the barn door. Crying out in pain she kept a white-knuckled grip on the sword.

"Please, drop the weapon," Tom begged her.

Averie knelt first, then leaned back against the barn door. Her grip slackened allowing the blade to slide free barely missing her leg as it stuck in the ground. "I'm sorry," she whispered hoping her unborn child would understand. She tried to survive but this world was too difficult. Glancing skyward her vision faded into darkness as her eyes closed. "I'm sorry Elwrick, I failed."

Mike's years of training kicked in and without realizing it he had his pen out writing the name down on his hand. It could prove useful in finding the man who may have been responsible for her condition.

Slumping sideways she let the hunger pangs flow through her body like an evil poison and she released a scream which destroyed all logical thinking and brought on an immediate emotional response.

Sarah's heart stopped. The scream was the kind only a mother would recognize from the loss of a child. Scrambling from the bed she was only partway dressed as she bolted through the front door nearly taking them off the hinges.

Jennifer followed nearly running Sarah over from her much longer stride.

Mike knelt beside the strange woman.

"Do you think the baby is coming?" Tom asked Mike.

"What the hell did you two do?" Sarah screamed as she ran carelessly towards them.

"Nothing," Tom tried to explain but Sarah shoved him out of the way before he could finish.

Jennifer went straight to Mike. "If you did nothing then why is she curled up crying… and who the hell is she?"

"We didn't do anything," Tom argued back. "This is the woman who broke into the house—"

Sarah looked at the woman and tried to imagine her climbing through the window. "Yeah, right."

"Look," Tom pleaded. "You can see she has on the stolen items."

Jennifer knelt beside the woman and stroked back her mud-soaked hair. "Do you have a name, sweetie?" she whispered.

Sarah grabbed Tom by the shirt. "If you hurt her I swear…"

Averie never answered. Instead, she gripped her abdomen as blood trickled down her chin from a bit lip.

"You need to relax," Jennifer said. "Can you tell me where it hurts?"

Averie held her abdomen in a death grip while trying to remove the cloth which was now stuck to her arm by dried blood. In the end all she accomplished was barfing up a smelly black vile on Jennifer's hand.

"That's disgusting," Mike said as he turned away.

Jennifer looked around, then focused on Tom. "Get me something so we can carry her inside."

"Put her in my room," Billy excitedly said.

Averie didn't remember much about the trip from the barn to the cottage. All she could think about was the growling that came from inside her stomach, and the pain of her stomach slowly digesting itself. The few times the pain did wane her arm felt as if it was set on fire igniting a whole new series of pain receptors. Sweat dripped down her pale face pooling in both recessed eye sockets. *Death could not come soon enough*, she thought.

"I'm going to have to ask you all to leave," Jennifer said. "I don't know who this woman is, but she is still afforded a right to privacy while I do a cursory examination."

"What if she—" Mike started to argue.

"What if she does what? For God's sake the woman can't even stand," Jennifer snapped back.

"Okay," Mike agreed, "But I'm going to be waiting right outside."

When the door closed Jennifer looked at the strange woman and softly spoke. "I'm not going to hurt you, I want to help you."

Averie panicked, she had heard those very words before by Jairo, and began to whimper. Pegan and Saress were not here to save her now, and she was in no condition to fight. Besides, she had lost her only weapon by the barn.

"My name is Jennifer. Do you have a name?"

Averie hesitated. A lot could be learned from a person by their name. *This could be an agent of Karayan searching for her*, she thought.

"Sweetie," Jennifer said. "I want to help you, but I need you to talk to me."

Averie appeared beyond frightened. "My name is Averie," she whispered.

"That is a beautiful name," Jennifer said as she put a cloth in a bowl of warm water. "I need to get you cleaned up so I can do an examination. I promise you I won't hurt you."

As time passed and the door remained closed, Mike and Tom ventured out to the barn.

"What do you make of this?" Tom asked.

Mike glanced into the loading room. "Of," he confusingly said.

"This whole thing?" Tom said.

"Well, she said a name and I wrote it down. I believe it's a good place to start." Mike examined the items Averie collected she felt might be useful someday. "I don't see any clues about where she came from. No cell phone, no ID. Nothing but a strange woman who seemed to have fallen from the sky."

"Do you think she's mental? Perhaps we should call a few of the hospitals," Tom suggested.

"No, I don't think so, but Jennifer will know for sure. Right now, I suggest we keep this on the low until I can get her name and look her up in the database. She may have fled a bad relationship. I've had to arrest men before who were searching hospitals for women they abused, I don't want to put her in that situation."

"To be honest," Tom said as he picked up the sword. "It's not the woman that bothers me. It's those piercing eyes."

Mike nodded in agreement. "They do have a way of cutting you straight to the bone."

Flipping the blade this way and that Tom examined the exquisite carvings down the blade. The pommel had finely engraved rune words and the piece was perfectly balanced. Plucking a piece of straw from a nearby hay bale, he held it out and the blade cleanly sliced the straw in half. "That is one damn sharp weapon."

Hours passed before Jennifer opened the door allowing the others to enter. In that time, she had convinced Averie to get undressed and put on clean maternity clothes Sarah went and purchased, washed and combed her hair, and had the wounded arm cleaned and bandaged. Two plates of food had been devoured, three glasses of milk drank, and a bunch of grapes delivered by special request.

"Did you all want to come in and meet Averie?" Jennifer asked.

Sarah was the first one in and was stunned by the woman's appearance. At first, she would have questioned if it was even the same woman, but her eyes confirmed it was. Even in the bright room they glowed bright gold.

Averie watched them all gather around her as if she was a campfire.

Sarah spoke first. "Well now that you're feeling better, would you mind telling us where you came from, and why you're here."

"She doesn't talk much," Jennifer said. "It took me forever to get more than a few words out of her at a time."

Mike sat down in a chair beside the bed. "Averie, if you're in trouble I need to know. You said a name when you were outside. Did he hurt you?"

Averie shook her head, no.

Jennifer patted Averie on the leg. "Did I lie to you about helping you?"

Averie shook her head no.

"We only ask you these questions because we want to help you," Jennifer continued.

"I'm here because this is where the portal sent me," Averie finally said, then covered her mouth.

"Portal?" Mike asked.

Averie didn't want to say anymore, but what choice did she have at this point. These people brought her into their home, cleaned and fed her, healed her arm, and seemed legitimately concerned about her well-being.

"Averie," Sarah said. "We need to know how you got here?"

Averie looked up at the ceiling. Hanging from it was a strange device which spun and pushed the air. Closing her eyes, she relaxed as the breeze caressed her warm skin.

"Maybe we should let her rest for a bit," Sarah suggested.

Averie opened her eyes and drew in a deep breath. As she exhaled, her words were barely audible. From her came a tale which could have only been conceived in the mind of a fantasy author. She weaved a story of pain and suffering, death and destruction, and lost love. She spoke of reptiles, creatures in the night, and dark magic beyond comprehension."

"Where does Elwrick fit into this?" Mike asked.

"Elwrick is the Spiritual Guide who told me my unborn child is a gift from the Creator. Eventually he will return to Icearaus."

"Icearaus?" Billy asked.

"Yes, that is where I am from."

"Well, you look exhausted," Sarah said. "You should sleep here tonight in an actual bed and in the morning, we can talk over breakfast."

"That's a good idea," Jennifer agreed. "I need to run into the clinic anyway and get some antibiotics for her arm. I'm sure it feels much better cleaned but that won't stop the infection."

"I believe her," Billy said as they gathered at the kitchen table.

"Believe she's a nutcase," Tom said. "Probably harmless, but really should be in a home."

"And those eyes," Sarah said.

Jennifer remained quiet for some time listening to the others banter about Averie, then raised her hand to silence them all. "I think you're all wrong. I want to show you something I took during the examination." From her purse she removed a small purple pouch pulled tight with a red drawstring. Opening the pouch, she dumped out a cache of golden coins.

Tom's eyes nearly exploded from his skull. "That's enough for all of us to retire."

"Wherever she came from, whoever sent her here wanted to make sure she would be financially set for life."

"That's not all," Mike added. "I've examined hundreds of slashing weapons, but I have never seen anything this refined, this sharp, this light, or this dangerous. I can guarantee you this was not made in China, or America for that matter. The skill used to create this blade is beyond anything we possess in this world."

"I believe her," Billy said again.

Sarah poked at the pile of coins with her finger. "Regardless whether she's an alien or not. I'm no goddamn thief, these coins belong to Averie and I'm returning them first thing in the morning."

Tom leaned back in the chair. "What's the chance we have a real, true to life alien in our house?"

Every head turned at once as if controlled by a single brain to the door down the hall where Averie slept.

Chapter 5

egan's mind diminished with each passing day since Thathra's funeral. Surrounded by friends did little to ease his troubles. With each breath he sank deeper and deeper into an abyss of utter darkness no light could penetrate. Most days he roamed aimlessly lacking sustenance and nights he would forego sleep and stare blindly at the heavens watching the stars twinkle. Tonight, though, he did neither and sat in a darkened nook of the dining hall, his eyes glowing like a wild animal as he stared into the unknown.

Saress sat across the way watching him through squinted eyes. Unlike the elves who knew little of Pegan, she had grown to love the man and could sense things no others could. She could sense his pain, his anger, his hatred. She knew he bore the weight of Thathra's death upon his shoulders. She also knew his heart was destroyed the moment Averie went through the portal.

When the last elf departed Saress made her way to the nook and sat beside Pegan. "Thathra's death isn't your weight to bear. He knew death was possible when he accepted Elwrick's request. If anyone should bear the weight it should be me as he saved my life, yet I could not do the same for him," she whispered.

"It is my weight to bear?" Pegan snapped back. "Had I never accepted this quest from Elwrick Thathra would still be alive, and Averie would still be here."

"You're partially right," Saress said. "Thathra would be alive. Averie though would be dead, but only after being tortured beyond imagination."

Pegan went to speak but Saress stopped him. "You must remember the link Elwrick placed on me never waned. Up until the moment she left I could always feel her fears. Averie loved you very much and it hurt her more than you can ever imagine leaving you, but she had to. Think of the joy she brought to your life and the experiences you both shared. Those memories you'll have forever until the day you die. No one can take that away, ever."

Pegan closed his eyes and remembered the day when they exited the cave. The way she danced and spun, the sun glowing off her smiling face and how happy and excited she was to see the surface again. Then the image faded to horror as Phlorax's skeletal face filled his mind and began laughing at him.

Saress placed her hand on Pegan's arm. "Inside you Pegan resides another entity who sometimes takes control of your subconscious mind and allows you to do things, impossible things. Elwrick is aware as well but isn't sure exactly what to do. After our return from the island I told him of the things you did. I fear as time progresses and we remain here you are losing your mind as this thing inside you needs to hunt, not sit dormant."

Pegan eyed her suspiciously.

"We need to find the dwarves. You know it and I know it," Saress said.

"Why?" Pegan mumbled. "Why are the dwarves so important? What is their purpose? What will finding them accomplish when there is nothing left worth saving. As far as I can see, all is lost."

Saress came to her feet sending a bench sailing with her tail. "No! Nothing is lost, yet. It will be though if we continue to sit here and dwell on something which could not have been prevented. Look around. All these elves need you," Saress hissed. "All these children look at you as their savior. You're their only hope, Pegan Rhoe."

"Hope is nothing more than a fleeting fallacy which we hold onto with a death grip for no better reason than to prolong our own suffering," Pegan yelled at Saress.

"They need you, we all need you," she snarled.

"Me," Pegan grumbled. "Why me? Why not Elwrick, he's the man who put this in motion. Had it not been for him I… No, you cannot put all their lives upon my shoulders. I've already failed once. I will not allow it to happen again."

Ellusia heard the yelling partway across the bridge and came running. "Pegan," she yelled as she entered.

"I need to go," Pegan said as he started to walk away.

"Listen to me," Ellusia screamed as tears streamed down her face. "Don't believe for a second you failed."

"That's easy coming from the one who saved her. Had it not been for you—"

Ellusia reared back and slapped him across the face. Afterward, she backed away and put her head down. "I'm sorry," she whispered. "I didn't save her, you didn't save her, Saress didn't save her. Together, all of us saved her because none of us could have done it alone. Elwrick knew this and that's why he gathered the very people he did. Thathra's death was something which could not have been prevented regardless how many times you replay the battle in your mind. There was nothing you could have done to prevent it. There was nothing any of us could have done."

Pegan never made a sound as he neared the door.

"Pegan, please. Talk with Gleia. She helped me deal with his loss, she can help you too."

Pegan had an evil twisted look on his face. "Not you, nor Gleia can help me. No one can." Moments later he vanished into the darkness.

Saress looked at Ellusia. "No one can help him because what he desires is impossible."

"Averie's return?" Ellusia questioned.

"Yes," Saress said, then took to chase after Pegan.

Nearing the outskirts of Rhunsiire Pegan encountered a thick fog that rolled off the shores of the Freihn Sea. Massive swells of white erased everything in the distance making navigation nearly impossible. Glancing at the moon and stars Pegan continued onward, he needed no physical path to follow. He was trained in the outdoors, survivability was second nature to him so when he arrived at what he believed to be Thathra's grave was instead a small hut with a single window glowing bright, frustration set in.

How can I be so far off, and I don't remember there ever being a hut on the grassy knoll where Thathra was laid to rest, he thought? As he neared the door swung open inviting him inside.

Peering inside, the small hut was empty, yet something beckoned him to enter. Stepping back, he looked the way he'd come and was greeted with an impenetrable wall of haze which left him dizzy. Less than fifty feet around him now, the wall of haze quickly engulfed him. He should have been able to run through it, to continue onward but this haze had a strange tangible property which forced him inside.

—*WHAM*. The door slammed shut with an ear-drum busting bang trapping him inside.

Pegan jerked on the handle yet the door seemed solid as stone. Jerking his weapons free he hacked and slashed sending blue sparks sailing yet nary a mark was made.

Gasping like a fish dropped in poisonous water, the air thickened and the heat intensified until large beads of sweat streamed down his face. Loosening his tunic, he rubbed his throat trying to coax air to enter his lungs. Outside the window what remained of the forest was quickly devoured by this monstrous fog. Fighting for air his vision clouded and then darkness engulfed him. His legs grew weak and he struggled to stand. Eventually, he gave in to the demands of the hut and collapsed into unconsciousness.

The messenger arrived at first light to notify Saress she had been summoned to a private meeting with Lady Alenia. Upon her arrival she noticed two additional elves standing with the Queen.

"Thank you for arriving so quickly," Lady Alenia said. "As you know getting Averie to the portal was only our first leg of the journey, now we must prepare for the second."

"Discovering the dwarves," Saress said.

"Yes," Lady Alenia agreed. "For this quest I am sending two of my most trusted allies. Don't let their youthful appearance fool you, they have stood beside me for ages and I would willingly place my life in either of their hands."

"I am Glorandial," the lady elf said as she reached out with her hand in a welcoming gesture. She was not beautiful, but far from ugly and her voice was charming. Smaller than most elves by a good foot, even if she stood on her toes, yet she carried herself as if she were a giant. Flaming red hair curled down past her green leather chameleon armor which changed its appearance depending on where she stood affording her a transparent appearance. On each hip curved scimitars swung keeping perfect rhythm with each step. "And this is my husband, Filaurel," she continued. "He doesn't say much until you get to know him then he won't shut up," she giggled. Unlike Glorandial, he was taller and more muscular. Blonde hair rimmed his perfectly accentuated face and highlighted his mesmerizing pale blue eyes. Unlike her armor, his moved perfectly with each step as if it were a second layer of skin. Over his shoulder a bow was slung and from his hip a sword dangled.

"I don't believe Pegan will be joining us," Saress said. "He left sometime during the night and I don't suspect he will return. I tried to follow him, but he is like a ghost and untraceable when he chooses."

"I already know," Lady Alenia informed her. "My scouts followed him out of Rhunsiire as well to a grassy knoll where his trail ended. It's almost as if the hand of the Creator reached down and snatched him. His future, whatever that entails, now resides within his own hands. Regardless, we cannot let his sudden departure prevent us from doing what must be accomplished."

A knock at the door alerted them someone waited.

"Enter," Lady Alenia grumbled, obviously irritated by the interruption.

The runner was red faced and breathing heavy. "Two representatives of the reptiles sent by King Hulradeeh have arrived. I felt it best to have them brought here immediately."

Saress smiled when the realization sunk in she would not be the only lizard going.

The scrape of claws and heavy footfalls informed them a monster waited outside.

"Enter," Saress said in reptilian.

Glorandial stepped back as the monstrosity splintered the door frame entering. This thing, this creature had to be the largest carnivore to ever roam Icearaus. Moss green and made up of a million armor-plated scales, it moved by powerful legs thick as tree trunks and clawed feet left large scars in the decorative, highly polished wood floor with each step. As it breathed, the scales expanded then contracted exposing underlying muscles while large yellow eyes with pitch black crescent-shaped pupils scanned them all, as if trying to decide which one to eat. Snapping its maw, large swatches of drool hung from the glistening white serrated teeth.

"Heidhantynth," Saress said as she pushed the table out of the way and ran to hug him. "And who is joining you?" she asked.

"My sister, Airriossalth."

"We have been truly blessed," Saress said. "These two are the best fighters we have in the brood."

"Welcome," Lady Alenia said. "It is an honor to have you here."

Saress looked out the door. "Where's Airriossalth?" she asked Heidhantynth.

"Who knows. Probably frolicking in the river or sniffing wildflowers. You never know with her," Heidhantynth sneered.

Glorandial chuckled.

"I've never seen a lazier reptile," Heidhantynth continued. "There was twenty in our brood and I'll give you one guess who hatched last. If not for our mother, she would probably still be in her shell trying to talk our brothers and sisters into feeding her."

"Oh, she's not that bad," Saress said.

"Knowing now that we have more members going than first expected, perhaps we should wait until all has arrived before I explain what must be accomplished. We will meet here again tomorrow at first light," Lady Alenia advised them.

Birthright

Pegan woke staring at a wooden floor and a pounding headache. Blood dripped from his nose and his body ached as if he'd been stretched beyond humanly possible. When he glanced up a light brighter than any he could imagine burned through the lone window. *Where am I?* he thought.

"You're in the Realm of Light," Elwrick said. "And as long as you remain within this room you will be immune to the devastating effects it would wreak upon your body."

The hut appeared much larger now and was finely furnished with an oil hand rubbed circular oak table surrounded by four chairs. Not far from where he lay a couch with thick cushions sat unoccupied.

"And as far as I can tell you don't really have much of a choice as I am the only one who can let you out."

Near the door Pegan caught sight of Elwrick. His featureless glowing form of light fibers was mind-boggling.

"How is this possible?" Pegan asked with broken words from where he lay.

"I have known this spell for some time now but have never tested it as the results could be fatal. Regardless, let's get you up where I am sure you will be more comfortable."

Pegan never resisted as Elwrick guided him to the couch.

"Why did you bring me here?" Pegan asked as the dizziness cleared.

"You're here because I have something to give you, and I think we should talk where we won't be interrupted by whatever dwells inside you."

"Give me what?" Pegan eyed the Spiritual Guide suspiciously. *Last time he gave him something it resulted in more pain than he ever dreamed possible*, he thought

Elwrick sat beside Pegan. "Hold out your hand."

Pegan cocked his head sideways to better view the intertwined streaks of lights.

"Pegan, I will not force you to take this as I did Fel-Strike. You must willing accept this gift."

Pegan cautiously uncurled his fingers exposing his palm. On it, the scars remained from his battle with the chasm demon.

Elwrick reached into his pocket and removed a small crystal-clear piece of glass. When he held it up to the light two separate colored mists became visible. One was blue and the other pink. After a few moments the pair began a dance like two viper snakes at a mating ritual. "Do you know what this is?" he asked.

"Some kind of mystical glass?"

"No," Elwrick said in a tone that could drive fleas off a cat's back. "This is part of one of the most powerful stones in the world. In fact, there is only one that is more powerful, and its existence is unknown. This is a sliver taken from a soul stone."

"What does this have to do with me?" Pegan cocked his head sideways as he asked.

"Pegan, contained within this sliver is the essence of Averie. More importantly, it also contains the essence of you. When you put that soul stone around her neck you somehow called forth a part of her soul and placed it within that soul stone. Afterward, I am assuming you did the same to yourself.

Standing at the altar when she made the commitment I saw what had been done and broke away this piece to give to you. Because both of your souls are now contained within that stone you have literally became one entity. You will feel her fears, feel her triumphs, and she will do the same of you. In time this bond will strengthen allowing you to communicate directly. I only hope she will understand what is happening."

The color drained from Pegan's face.

"What you have done as far as I know has never been accomplished before, not even by the greatest wizards."

Pegan squeezed his hand around the tiny shard and within it a faint red light started to beat as if it grew a heart. Through his veins flooding his mind he could feel her. She was relaxed yet nervous and in tremendous pain. "I can feel her," Pegan whispered. "She's hurting."

"She's hurting the same way you're hurting. You both need each other more than you can ever imagine at this moment."

Pegan's eyebrows shot skyward. "What are you getting at?"

"Pegan, what I'm going to say might frighten you more than you can ever imagine. Because your souls are now linked. If one dies, so will the other."

Pegan looked down at his feet in thought.

"That's why I brought you here."

"You knew I was going to terminate my existence."

"Yes," Elwrick softly said. "And by doing that you would have accomplished Karayan's goal."

Pegan stood and paced the room. "Had you let me sneak in and assassinate him as I wanted, we would not be having this conversation."

Elwrick rose. "What you fail to understand is Karayan can make a thousand mistakes, but you can only make one. If something went wrong before the assassination and you were killed, Karayan instantly regains his power." Elwrick sat back on the couch. "There is more I think you need to know." From a drawer on a nightstand beside the couch Elwrick removed a thick black tome. Flipping through the pages he stopped on one covered with strange writing. "This writing is in an ancient language forgotten by all but a very few. Let me read what I believe applies to your situation—*It will be then, when what is hidden is revealed, lion and lamb live together, broken hearts bring forth a time of serenity.*"

Pegan pondered what Elwrick said. "I don't understand."

Elwrick carefully closed the book and placed it back in the drawer. "I don't either. Often, we don't fully realize what a prophecy means until it has come to pass. As with most, we decipher them the best we can going off our beliefs and interpretations."

"And what do you believe?" Pegan asked.

"I believe when what is hidden is revealed has to do with the dwarves' discovery. The Lion and the lamb I believe are you and Averie. If what I believe is true, this is only possible through her return."

"Are you saying you can bring Averie home?"

"No," Elwrick said. "What I am saying is you can."

Pegan sat back down on the couch, his eyes glazed over with tears.

Birthright

Pegan did nothing to mask his appearance as he walked down the center of Rhunsiire. From high above lanterns sparked to life as elves stuck their heads out windows and peered through cracked doors. They had all heard the rumors Pegan abandoned them to die at the hands of Karayan. Even though they had a well-trained army. Most elves were peaceful and never held a weapon. Climbing down rope ladders or descending stairs they followed him all the way to the forge where he sat at a large grinding stone.

"I knew you would return," Lady Alenia said as she stepped from the shadows. "You're a good man who would never leave those who cannot defend themselves to die."

Blue sparks lit the night sky as Pegan began to sharpen his blades.

"In the morning your companions will be gathering to depart. I take it you will be joining them?"

When he finished, Pegan stood and looked out over the gathering crowd. "No," Pegan said.

You could hear the air being ripped from the lungs of those who gathered.

"I will not meet them in the morning. I leave in an hour with or without them."

"And where do you plan to go?" Lady Alenia asked.

Pegan looked evil when he spoke. "The location doesn't matter. I will scour every inch of this land until I find a clue which leads me in the right direction."

Lady Alenia placed her hand on Ryul's shoulder. "Send word to all those who are going to be at my private chamber immediately."

"Consider it done," Ryul said.

One by one, they gathered until only one was missing.

"Where's Airriossalth?" Saress asked Heidhantynth.

"She was hungry and went to a nearby pond to collect a fish. She should be here shortly."

"She better," Lady Alenia said. "I've had a hard-enough time keeping Pegan here as it is."

Saress glanced at Pegan who nervously twitched the pommel of Fel-Strike with his finger.

"Is that her coming now?" Glorandial asked.

Coming up the path was a reptile not much taller than Glorandial. She was olive colored with a bright yellow underbelly. Directly down the center of her head were an erect set of scales like the dorsal fin of a fish. Her movements were sporadic as she darted here and there sniffing flowers, looking at trees, or leaping through the air snapping her maw at passing butterflies.

"Get your butt over here, NOW!" Heidhantynth screamed in reptilian.

Airriossalth stopped and looked in their direction. They could see her eyes narrow as she released an angry hiss. There were sights to see and smells to admire. None of which she may ever experience again.

"Welcome," Lady Alenia said when the final member arrived. "As you know our goal is to find the dwarves which is going to be quite difficult without some clue as to which direction they went. As you know, Icearaus isn't the only

31

landmass on this planet. All around us lies unexplored terrain. It could take centuries of searching before a single clue is located."

"What choice do we have," Pegan snarled. "I will—"

"Allow me to finish, please," Lady Alenia said. "When I slew the chasm demon on the Isle of Aramoor, I felt something I had not in a long time. The presence of a very evil and vile monster. A monster who goes by the name of Malvo Necrosyse. I only felt it for a brief second, but long enough to determine the source and it radiated from somewhere beneath the Rain Wood Keep."

"That Keep is nothing more than dilapidated ruins. I have been there on multiple occasions and there are no catacombs," Pegan informed her.

"My senses do not lie. Somewhere beneath Rain Wood Keep you will find a hidden chamber."

"Why would this man know the location of the dwarves?" Saress asked.

"I don't know for sure that he does," she admitted. "It's believed this man Malvo Necrosyse, self-proclaimed necromancer who can travel between Icearaus and hell began the Great War by corrupting the dwarves. If that rumor is indeed true he would have had more than one defector who would have told him of the dwarves' plans. More than likely he would have wrote that information down somewhere, probably in a journal for later use."

"If Pegan could not find this chamber, what makes you believe we can?" Filaurel asked.

"Because I'm sending another man with you who is highly skilled in this area. Raestmond is a master at construction and can spot details other would miss."

"No," Pegan said. "Tanara has lost her mother and brother. I refuse to take her father."

"He has agreed to go, he understands the consequences," Lady Alenia said. "I'm not forcing him to do this."

"Then it's decided. We leave for Rain Wood Keep," Saress said.

"Not so hasty," Lady Alenia said. "To save you days of travel I can open a portal which will place you at the portcullis. Be advised though once you leave here, nowhere is safe as my scouts have informed me Karayan has been spewing his filth turning all against us."

Saress mumbled a strange mix of words and a silver arrow formed where an arrow should be sitting. "Then let the Creator have mercy on those unfortunate souls who try and stop us."

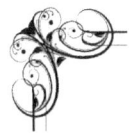
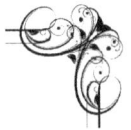

Chapter 6

alvo knelt with his head bowed. Above him, a crimson colored swirling vortex spun counter-clockwise. From it spewed droplets of plasma which rained down leaving long streaks of yellow goo running down the walls. Cracks in the floor grew and up through the fissures blood percolated turning the stone to a turbulent sea of coagulation.

Screams filled his ears as the female sacrifice dangled by a barbed chain. Great care had been taken when the hook was inserted up through her back to prevent damage to any vital organs. That's how the Dark Master liked them, alive and fresh.

Raising his hand's, he allowed the plasma to wash over his naked form. To feel its energy coursing through his body, giving him the strength required to complete the demonic summoners chant. Violently shaking, he appeared possessed as the words escaped his mouth.

From the vortex, a black mist swirled outward like a coiled snake and tore through the blood smashing into the walls. The room trembled as the screams of the damned followed.

Coiling around the sacrifice the rattle of chains ensued followed by muffled cries. The feeding seemed to last for hours, followed by an eerie silence as the black haze slithered away leaving behind nothing more than a twisted chain and mangled hook. From the hook dangled a few scraps of flesh and a single eye.

Diving into the coagulated blood the black haze vanished only to return in the shape of a man. "Much time has passed since our last encounter," the Dark Master hissed. "So much I was beginning to think you abandoned me."

Malvo kept his head bowed. "Father, I could not communicate because of the immense power you granted Karayan. I was kept underground like a worm held in a dungeon. It was only the company of the chasm demon which kept me from going insane. That time though has now passed. With the bearer—"

The misshapen shadowy haze screamed a hiss. It was not the name which bothered him. It was the fact the bearer carried a child placed there by the hand of the Creator, his most hated adversary.

"With her gone and Karayan's power stripped away, I am now able to continue with my mission."

"Excellent," the Dark Master snarled.

"You will be enthralled to learn though I have claimed the brotherhood and placed it under a banner of your name," Malvo continued. "It's through them I will take control of Icearaus issuing in a new era."

"How many more decades will pass before I see your plan come to fruition?"

the Dark Master asked.

Malvo released a comforting sigh as torturous screams flowed from the vortex. "Father, you have been around since before time existed. The life of man is but a blink in your eye. We must not hasten our actions. Karayan must be allowed to carry out this foolish war. It is then when he fails, and the world falls into chaos the hearts of man will fail, and they will throw themselves at my feet sealing their fate."

The Dark Master laughed wickedly. "It is then I will claim Icearaus."

"Yes, Father," Malvo said. "For all your suffering now, you will be justly rewarded."

The shadow lifted Malvo's head by the chin until their eyes met. "Do not become a stranger again," the Dark Master snarled. "I must return to my Realm before my presence is detected by that wretched Elf Queen and that meddlesome Spiritual Guide."

"Yes, Father," Malvo said, then graciously bowed.

Malvo woke the next morning as if in a drunken stupor. Anger flooded his mind and he had a sudden desire to hurt someone or something. Removing a small knife from the drawer of a nearby cabinet, he slowly pressed the blade under his fingernail. A smile formed across his blackened lips as he watched the blood flow down the edge and drip from the blade staining the floor. Each drop pounded like a drum bringing on a pain-filled euphoria and he began to relax.

Tap… tap…tap…

A rapping at the door brought Malvo back to reality. Removing the knife and tossing it on a nearby table, he pulled the cowl down over his eyes concealing the gratification which still flowed through his veins. "Enter."

"My Lord," Vexacion said upon entering. "The men wish to know more about you. I highly recommend you make an appearance to appease the recent rumors."

Malvo eyed him with disgust. "My arrival was not enough to prove I am the right man for the job?"

"A few of the men have said they heard King Karayan talk about you. Saying you're nothing more than a weak necromancer who deals with magical trickery and dark illusions."

"And what do you believe?" Malvo asked.

"I believe there is more to you than what you're revealing. Judging from my research, I would say you're more along the lines of a Warlock, that is, if any still exist."

Malvo moved next to Vexacion and whispered. "Let me tell you a little secret. If Warlocks did exist, they would cower at my feet."

Vexacion stepped back placing some distance between the two.

"I will address this rumor later. As of now, I require your services."

The lump in Vexacion's throat was visible as he swallowed.

"It is time for the first objective of the Brotherhood of the Dark Prince to be set in motion. Word has reached my ear Karayan has devised a plan to eradicate the brotherhood from existence. This abomination cannot be allowed to occur."

"I assume you wish for Karayan to take a tumble down a long flight of stairs."

"I like you're thinking, but no," Malvo said. "Karayan must not be harmed. In fact, we need to make sure he can initiate this war against the elves. With each passing day he grows weaker and soon one of his Royal Guards will question him. This cannot be allowed to occur and the only way to prevent it is with their destruction."

Vexacion tilted his head sideways confused by the order.

Malvo handed Vexacion a small charred piece of parchment. "Study these words and remember every one of them. Afterward, eat the parchment thus destroying all traces of its existence. Follow those words precisely and report back to me once the mission has been accomplished."

"Yes, my Lord," Vexacion said as he read the note, then swallowed the parchment.

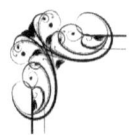 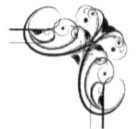

Chapter 7

 **arah looked like a reincarnated dishrag as she stumbled** from the kitchen towards the recliner. Dark circles ringed her eyes while her face drooped like a crayon left in the July sun. Lying back, she sunk into the comfy cushions allowing her mind to wander. The coffee cup she carried grew heavy and soon dangled by a single finger.

Tom tip-toed across the living room and carefully pulled the cup free trying not to wake her.

"Uh, what happened?" Sarah asked, one eye remained slammed shut.

"You nearly dropped the mug." Tom placed the mug on the end table. "You're exhausted, go lay down."

"I have to wait for Jennifer," she explained. "Averie is going to need the antibiotics."

"Well, you missed her by about two hours. She already dropped off the antibiotics and made sure I wrote down the directions."

Sarah rubbed the sleep from her eyes then glanced at the clock. To her shock it was nearing midnight. "I should go check on her."

"I already have and she is sound asleep."

Sarah released a ragged breath. "It's so weird," she said after a few minutes.

Tom could see her wheels spinning, but she wasn't going anywhere.

"Where do you think Averie came from?" Sarah asked. "She didn't wander here, I know that much."

"I don't know," Tom finally admitted after a few minutes. "We're both exhausted though so let's get some sleep and perhaps in the morning we can make some more sense of this."

Averie could have slept a lifetime had it not been for the child inside her kicking her in the ribs demanding food. "Ten more minutes, please," she whispered while rubbing her belly, but the baby wasn't having any of it, and kicked harder. Rubbing her stomach again, she tried to fall back asleep when the pains started. They were faint, barely discernible, but she knew the demon they would become if she waited.

She had no idea how long she had been asleep, minutes, hours, or even days as she lay there. Wiping the sweat from her face, she slowly opened her eyes. The curtains had been drawn and the door partially closed masking the room in shadows. From somewhere she could hear the muffled voices of people. "Hopefully they will give me some food," she whispered to her unborn child. Kicking away the covers, she groaned as she rolled on her side, then stood on wobbling legs. It was only now she noticed the throbbing in her arm and she suddenly felt dizzy. Gripping the bed for balance, she remained there for a length of time before venturing out.

Tom nearly spit his coffee across the room as Averie materialized from the shadowed hall. She reminded him of some exotic creature on display at a freak-show circus. Her fine hair floated like a halo while her overly large shirt was partially tucked in. One pant leg rode up past her knee while a sock managed to get tangled around her big toe and dangled like a worm on a hook.

Sarah came from the kitchen to see what all the laughter was about and barely maintained her composure. "Did you get enough rest?"

Averie rubber her eyes confused why they were laughing at her. "Can I please have some scraps of food? Anything, my baby is hungry."

"You don't have to beg," Sarah told her. "I already have a plate prepared for you. Have a seat on the sofa and kick your feet up while I warm it up. I also have your antibiotics to kill the infection in your arm."

Tom slowly lost interest and went back to reading a farming magazine.

"Okay, now here is how we're going to defeat this Lich," Billy said into the mic which was built into the headphones.

Averie suddenly bolted upright and her vision became fixated on the computer monitor.

Tom lowered the magazine and watched Averie. Her sudden movement caught him by surprise.

Averie pointed at the computer monitor. "Elwrick, Elwrick, I'm here."

Tom looked at the computer monitor and noticed Billy's character. He had dressed him to resemble Gandalf with a long flowing white robe, pointed hat, and a full-length beard. "Billy, can you turn that off please?" Tom politely asked.

"Dad, where at the very end of the Godless Crypt. Any moment now we're going to fight the Lich Lord Beetle Grub, and his maggot minions. If I leave now they won't have a healer and it will be a total wipe. You want me to have that on my conscious?"

Averie watched with wide eyes as the robed character began performing spells placing blue auras on those who wore plate mail armor.

"Elwrick," Averie screamed as she partially stood up from the couch.

"Billy, I said turn it off NOW," Tom yelled.

Sarah came from the kitchen to see what all the commotion was.

Suddenly, all hell broke loose on the computer as the Lich Lord appeared. From his fingers came flaming red balls and silver lightning. Screams, booms, and chants filled the air.

The robed figure healed those who had been injured, then returned a spell which bathed the Lich Lord in electricity.

Two men in plate armor and another who wore leather charged the Lich Lord. Behind them, two men launched a barrage of arrows.

The Lich countered sending the man in leather to a fiery death.

"NOO," Averie screamed as she watched the man fall. Flailing her arms and kicking her legs, the coffee table flipped over sending a vase sailing which shattered upon finding the wall. Climbing up the couch she reached for her sword should have been.

Tom bolted from the chair sending the magazine fluttering like a butterfly.

The couch wobbled then flipped over launching Averie against the wall. Crawling on her knees she tried to escape, but there was no escaping. On her hands she could feel the jagged stone floor of the sacrificial chamber. Around her she could see the Din'Jin dancing, hear their disgusting chants, smell their filth. Her mind flooded with visions of what they intended to do to her child and what they had planned for her. The pain in her calves returned as the hooks were slowly pressed through the muscles. An ear-drum busting scream tore from her throat as each needle was inserted into each fingertip until it drilled into the joint between the knuckles. Tears marred her face as the excruciating pain of being hoisted up and the clank of the chain returned.

Tom never slowed as he tore past snatching Billy by the collar. The computer chair spun three times before it came to a rest near the front door. "I said turn it OFF!"

Sarah tossed the table aside as if she suddenly had super-human strength and fell to her knees wrapping Averie in her arms. "It's going to be okay," she kept whispering.

Outside the window the sound of screeching gravel could be heard. Moments later the door banged open knocking a nearby picture to the floor. Mike bolted in brandishing his pistol. Behind him, Jennifer held a small bat with a white-knuckled grip. They had heard the screams clear out on the highway with the windows up and the music playing.

Mike quickly surveyed the situation, then joined Tom in Billy's bedroom where all the yelling was coming from.

Jennifer sat beside Averie who held onto Sarah with a vice-like grip. "You need to calm down and tell us what happened," she said as she brushed back the hair which covered Averie's face.

Averie's words were meaningless as they were tainted with heavy sobs.

"Take a deep breath and calm down," Jennifer told her again. "I can't understand what you're saying."

Averie pointed to the computer screen which was nothing more now than ghosts standing by grave markers. "L, L, Lich," she managed to whisper.

"Averie, it's only a game Billy plays, nothing more. It isn't real," Sarah said.

Averie looked at Sarah, then back at the computer. "It is real," she demanded. Releasing her death grip, she showed them the scars on the ends of each finger where needles had been inserted. "A Lich Lord named Phlorax, and his acolyte Tavok did this to me to drain my yellow blood. His minions shoved hooks through my calves and left me to hang. It was Elwrick who fought the Lich Lord so Pegan could save me."

Jennifer examined the scars. "My God," she said, shaking her head in disbelief.

"My world is much different than yours. Evil, pure evil thrives among us."

"We have evil too, only in different ways," Jennifer told her. "What you're describing is sadistic and barbaric."

Birthright

Later that evening Averie sat on the couch eating pumpkin pie smothered in whip cream. She had never tasted anything quite like it. Solid, yet soft and the white topping was smooth as silk. Having finished two plates, she laid back in the recliner and closed her eyes. Outside, the orange sky revealed the sun was setting and soon it would be dark.

"Averie." Sarah called her name.

Averie groggily looked at Sarah.

"When you arrived here, the stone necklace was dull. Now it has a faint red beat. Do you know why?"

Averie held it up and studied the stone. "I don't know," she whispered. "I only know Elwrick told me never to take it off."

From across the living room Billy watched Averie even though Tom had informed him to leave her alone. The risk of a spanking was worth the reward of knowing if she was a real live alien. Slowly meandering his way to the couch, he sat beside Averie and smiled at her.

Tom eyed the boy suspiciously. Years of experience told him Billy was up to no good.

"Are you really an alien?" he whispered hoping his parents didn't hear. "I mean you don't look like an alien covered in slime with long tentacles that slurp the brains out of your victims."

"Billy, that's enough," Tom scolded him.

Averie looked at her arms and legs. "I don't have tentacles," she answered with widened eyes.

Sarah sat up, her face red as ketchup. "One more comment like that and you'll wish you had tentacles so you could crawl away, as you won't be able to walk. Do I make myself clear?"

Billy gulped. To be spanked by Tom was one thing, but his mother would hold a grudge for months and occasionally remind him of his errors with the back of her hand.

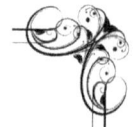

Chapter 8

egan studied the shimmering doorway as if it were an enemy. On it he could see his own reflection and reached up and touched his face. Running his fingers through the coarse hair he suddenly realized, since Averie's departure, he had yet to shave.

"She is going to be fine," Saress whispered into his ear.

Pegan gripped the shard and held it to his lips. Through it he could feel she was in no danger. "I know," he whispered, then stepped into the portal.

Lights brighter than the sun flashed by in long streaks, then there was only darkness. In less than the blink of his eye, he was spit out into the unknown.

Saress materialized beside Pegan and immediately fell to her knees. Reptiles had a much harder time with portal travel due to an enlarged cerebellum to control their tail. Gasping for air she made a sound like a dead man waking, then barfed out the contents of her stomach on the hard-packed weed-infested ground.

The two elves appeared next holding hands as if they were out on a moonlit evening stroll.

Raestmond emerged next. On his face he bore a look of concern.

Heidhantynth came through landing hard on his back. Lashing out violently at anything nearby, he scrambled to his feet then spewed out his contents on Saress's back.

Airriossalth came last and burst out laughing upon seeing her companions in such sad shape. For some odd reason she was unaffected by the quick rate of travel.

Within minutes, the sickness passed and they all stood looking at the menacing structure in the distance. Ragged, uneven, cold stone walls were partially hidden behind remnants of banners that hung like tortured skeletons. The rusty bars of the cock-eyed portcullis were overgrown by weeds with dagger length thorns, while the partially crumbled crenellations left a jagged scar against the pastel colored sky. From somewhere deep with the dilapidated structure came a low moaning howl that made their hair stand erect.

Drip…

The sound of each drop hitting the floor lingered on the warm stagnant air as if frozen in time. The painful rhythm and volume neither increased nor decreased, regardless of where they traveled.

Drip…

At first it was only a minor annoyance, but now, it manifested into a nausea-inducing thump which raced through their innards and brought on the urge to vomit.

Drip…

Behind them, the scrape of claws on the stone floor told them they were not alone.

Jester spun, looking down the hall they recently traveled and held out his torch chasing away the gloom. In his other hand, his blade sparkled. Wrinkling his forehead, his eyes narrowed as he spun back nearly striking his companions with the torch. "How much further?" he asked Barrett.

Barrett knew the exact location of the entrance and could have taken them they're within minutes, but he had no desire to die a gruesome death. He had personally witnessed the quick aging ward Karayan placed on the room. All those who entered uninvited would begin to age at an advanced rate and within minutes their skin would turn to dust leaving behind only their bones. Instead, he led them through leagues of abandoned subterranean tunnels until he knew they were thoroughly confused. Eventually, he would lead them to King Karayan's private library and claim it as the secret chamber where there were thousands upon thousands of tomes to be searched. Eventually, they would be forced to return unsuccessful on their endeavor. "Less than an hour from here," Barrett said, then took a long swig from his waterskin. "You didn't think it would be simple, did you?"

"Let's continue," a guard grumbled. "I grow tired of this disgusting building, and the filth which dwells here."

Another hour passed before Barrett led them to a large room. "Here we are."

Jester held his torch high forcing the darkness to flee into the many nooks and crevices. Dusty bookshelves stood in formation like ancient sentries waiting to go to war. The ground was littered with torn pages and books had been strewn from wall to wall. Intermingled with the pages were gnawed on bones and rubble which fell from the crumbling ceiling.

Kicking his way through the clutter, Barrett led them to the back of the room where he pulled on a lever disguised as a book. A rumbling came deep from within the keep and a stone door partially opened. "The mechanism must have failed due to lack of oil but there is still enough room for us to enter the secret chamber."

Jester looked to his men who appeared haggard. "Perhaps we should return to the tents and get some rest. Now that we know the location and have killed everything on the way, we can make better time and begin our search tomorrow."

The men agreed.

"Lead us out of here," Jester ordered Barrett.

Pegan ventured out alone. Using the shadows of passing clouds the man faded out of existence. Working his way to the Keep he arrived at the portcullis and quickly performed a cursory search. He could tell by the ground a group of men had recently passed and tried to conceal their footprints. Satisfied nobody was watching, he struck his blades together creating a blue spark, the designated signal for the others to come.

One by one they darted across the clearing until they all gathered at the portcullis.

"A group of men have recently passed," Pegan whispered.

Glorandial slowly slid her swords free careful not to make a sound.

"Can you tell how many?" Saress asked.

"Five, maybe six. One is lighter than the rest so either a child or a woman."

Carefully working their way through the vines, Pegan led them down a narrow breezeway then took a quick right down a darkened passage. He followed it for some distance then took a sharp left. In the distance they could see an arched doorway which led to a large courtyard.

"Do you know where you're going?" Filaurel asked Pegan.

"Where approaching the basilica, the center of the Keep," Pegan mumbled. "From here we'll need the services of Raestmond to locate the hidden chamber."

Pegan brought them to an abrupt halt at the doorway. To their surprise located in the North-West corner was a small camp consisting of six tents. Near the tents was a large pit thick with glowing red coals. Above it a pig cooked on a spit. From one of the tents the singing of a woman could be heard.

"Shall we see whose home?" Glorandial asked.

"My pleasure," Filaurel answered.

Pegan stopped them before they could venture out. "We need to be cautious. We don't know who, or what could be watching."

The singing grew louder as a woman emerged holding a pot.

Heidhantynth tore his sword free and anger dripped from his eyes in the form of tears. He had waited years to get even with those responsible for the slaughter of his father. Tonight, the thirst of retaliation would be quenched. Knocking Pegan to the ground as he bolted past, he charged with a lust fueled rage for revenge.

"About time you all ret—" the woman began to say then screamed and dropped the pot.

"No," Pegan screamed from where he lay. He could see the woman was unarmed and no threat.

Catching the woman outside the ring of tents Heidhantynth leaped through the air swinging his blade with all his hate-fueled strength. No sound was made as steel found flesh and the head slid free as the body continued for some distance before crumbling. Blood spurted from the neck like a fresh mountain spring ringing the body.

Pegan leaped to his feet and stood there in horror. For all he knew this was a homeless family whose boys were out hunting and suddenly became motherless.

"What are you doing?" Airriossalth hissed.

"She was going to warn the others." Heidhantynth tried to justify his actions.

Pegan approached with a look of disgust on his face. "Warn who? We don't even know if they're the enemy."

Heidhantynth realized he had done wrong but his thirst for revenge clouded his judgement. Lowering his head, he walked away in shame.

"Search the tents," Pegan ordered the others. "I need to talk with

Heidhantynth, alone."

Saress put her hand on Pegan's shoulder. She knew Heidhantynth had did wrong but also understood his anger. "Pegan," she said. "You have to understand. For years we have been hunted for our skins. How he tolerates you I have yet to understand. His father was captured, and rumor has it he was skinned alive and became items to barter with. Is that all were worth?"

"No," Pegan said as he looked into her yellow eyes. "I would rather have you at my side than any man who walks Icearaus. I still need to talk with him though."

"Be easy on him, please, for me," Saress whispered.

Pegan made his way to Heidhantynth who stood alone. "I know how you feel," he said. "I have killed hundreds of innocent people for no better reason than to line my pockets with gold. It took the death of an elf to teach me the difference between right and wrong."

With the tents searched the others joined Pegan and Heidhantynth.

Pegan climbed on a stump where he could be seen by all. "We don't kill everything we come across, there are still good people in this world. We only kill those who oppose us and try to prevent us from completing out task. If we kill like the enemy, think like the enemy, we become the enemy. From this moment forward unless we are threatened we capture and interrogate."

Filaurel dropped a few papers on the stump where Pegan stood. "From what I can decipher from these papers, these people where sent her by Karayan to recover something."

"I'm sorry," Heidhantynth said.

Pegan patted him on the shoulder. "I know, all I ask is that you control your anger."

"Shall we try and track down these men?" Glorandial asked. "Discover why Karayan has sent them here."

Pegan thought for a moment as he examined the shadowed hallways. "Before we begin I need to know that you all are with me to the end. No questions, no arguments. Even if you disagree with my actions. I will not go through what I experienced with Lorandrail, I have too much to lose." Pegan gripped the stone and closed his eyes allowing the feeling to flood his veins.

"You know I will," Saress said.

Pegan stopped Heidhantynth as he started to kneel. "I am not asking you to swear allegiance to me like I'm a king because I'm not. I only need to know if you're with me to the end?"

"Until the end," they all said in unison.

"For Averie," Pegan whispered, but they all heard.

"For Averie," they all cheered.

Pegan pondered his options. "We're not going to track them. We're going to hide in their tents and wait. This place is enormous; if we venture out we may never find them."

"They may be watching as we speak and already fled," Glorandial said.

"Possible." Pegan looked at the tents. "If they did then our camp has already been made, but something tells me they're still here."

Through holes in the tents they watched and waited. The sky darkened and shadowed lengthened when the group of men emerged from the darkened recesses of an arched hallway.

Pegan stepped from his tent and crossed his arms. "Good evening gentlemen. What brings you all out here today?" He kicked the severed head out of the way.

They all froze for a moment, then realized it was only one man.

Jester laughed as he stepped to the forefront of his men. In his hand he wielded a menacing looking long sword still red with blood.

Pegan showed little concern for the man, or his weapon. All he cared about was that his companions did not kill them before they could be questioned.

Heidhantynth tore his way through the tent, bent at the waist, then released a wicked hiss. His bright pink tongue flapped like a flag in a windstorm. Long strings of drool hung from his chin and in both eyes, the fires of hate burned.

Saress had no choice but to react. She refused to leave the pair out there easily outnumbered.

"Kill them," Jester screamed. "I want his skin."

His men rushed past drawing their weapons.

One man fell instantly. Gurgling and gasping he fought to close the massive tear in his throat by the arrow Filaurel fired.

"ᚤᚨᛈᚥᛁᚤᚱ ᚲᚱᚱᚢᚢ," Saress hissed as she drew back the string on her bow. She had spent the last few weeks perfecting the rune words Elwrick taught her to activate the magic contained within. Depending on the combination of words the bow would create different projectiles. Never again would she run out of arrows. This combination she spoke would create a magical arrow which ignored the protection afforded by armor. Releasing the string the lightning blue arrow sizzled through the air leaving a trail of glowing red sparks.

Horrid screams and the smell of fear filled the air as another fell to his knees then crumbled as the magical arrow pierced the plate mail armor and blew out the back obliterating the heart. Saress grinned a half-hearted smile. "Thank you, Pegan Rhoe," she screamed out as she tore her way through the side of the tent.

Jester backed away then darted into the shadows of a nearby hallway. There was no need to remain and watch his companions get slaughtered. Two had already fallen and it was obvious the others would soon follow.

Airriossalth carefully removed the short stick she carried from her belt and snapped it hard with both hands expanding it into a full-length staff. Affixed to one end was a pulsating blue heart shaped orb.

Lost in confusion, the other men panicked and began searching for an escape route but there was movement all around them.

Heidhantynth lowered his shield and charged directly at them.

Pegan closely followed.

Airriossalth circled the basilica in long strides. Her clawed feet tearing up weeds and roots as she looked for a position which would give her the best opportunity to strike.

Glorandial circled the other direction twirling both blades. There was no need to follow Heidhantynth or Pegan into the fight as the proximity could lead to her injuring one of their own.

Barrett fell to the ground and covered his head screaming for mercy.

Heidhantynth slammed into the group sending one sailing as if he'd been launched by a catapult. The remaining two jumped to either side narrowly missing being crushed.

Pegan anticipated the reaction and was there before the guard could react and slammed the pommel of his dagger against the guard's skull leaving him unconscious.

Observing the man fall but not dying, Heidhantynth took to flight landing on the skull with his massive clawed foot pulverizing the skull into dust.

Pegan sighed. He purposely kept him alive to be questioned later.

Shaking the cobwebs from his mind, the guard who was launched came to his senses and began crawling away, abandoning his sword where it lay.

Glorandial observed this from across the basilica and met him near a doorway. Coming down with both blades she punctured both lungs leaving him to drown in his own blood.

Gathering his bearings and making a quick note of the closest escape route, the guard made a break for the safety of a nearby opening in the stone wall. Bolting for freedom his feet were suddenly swept out from under him and he crashed hard into a gaggle of thorny weeds which tore into his cheek and punctured one eye.

Airriossalth quickly pounced upon the man and began beating him with her staff. The grotesque snapping of ribs breaking echoed off the bare stone walls.

Heidhantynth quickly surveyed the battlefield, then made the decision his sister may need help disposing of the one she was mercilessly beating.

Pegan was in utter shock at the carnage he observed. He thought he made it clear they were to keep some alive yet all around him rivers of blood formed, and the dead lay scattered like dry leaves tossed in the wind. If he didn't do something quick, the last remaining guard beside the man who lay cowering would be beaten into the ground.

Heidhantynth ran with all the intent in the world of crushing the man who lay there screaming for mercy.

"Keep him alive," Pegan screamed as he bolted across the battlefield.

Airriossalth realized she had lost control and stepped back. If she didn't stop soon there would be nothing left to question.

Heidhantynth skidded to a halt placing his blade against the throat of the semi-unconscious man. The two elves quickly had Barrett bound at the wrist by the time the wounded man was dragged back to camp by his ponytail.

"Well, at least we saved two," Pegan chuckled.

"One escaped," Filaurel said. "The direction he fled neither I nor Saress had a shot and it was not worth the risk on hitting a companion."

Pegan scratched his chin.

"Shall I chase him down?" Filaurel asked.

"No," Pegan said as he glanced at the two prisoners Airriossalth guarded. "We'll discover why Karayan sent them here soon enough and be on our way."

Filaurel un-nocked his arrow and placed it in his quiver. From the dead he recovered the arrow he spent.

Pegan approached the prisoners but his vision remained focused on Airriossalth. "Does your staff always glow like that?"

"Only when I wish it to."

Saress tapped Pegan on the shoulder. "Airriossalth was without thermal vision has no thermal vision and is blind in the dark tunnels of the lair. As you know most species abandon those who are crippled but not us. Nobody knows for sure where the staff came from, it simply arrived one day and King Hulradeeh presented it to her as a hatchling. If you ask me I think a Spiritual Guide we all know was probably involved with its creation."

"Amazing," Pegan said. "It would have been a shame for someone like her to be cast out because she has no thermal vision. She seems like such a wonderful lady."

"She's the best. A wonderful friend and a dedicated mother. Not to mention because of her sight deficiency her hearing has advanced well beyond all ours combined."

Pegan glanced at Airriossalth.

Airriossalth smiled back. "Now I see why Saress speaks so highly of you."

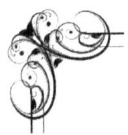

Chapter 9

verie bolted upright and gripped her stomach. **Something** was dreadfully wrong, and she didn't know what. She had come to recognize the pain caused by hunger, but this was different. Inside her it felt as if something was swimming, large bubbles bursting, or a kaleidoscope of butterflies fluttering. The sensation slowly faded, but quickly returned as a violent turning or rotation sensation near her sternum, followed by a sharp kick to the rips which knocked the breath from her lungs. "Help me," she cried out.

Half blind and mumbling incoherently, Sarah stumbled down the hall as if her feet were too heavy to lift.

Jennifer too heard the call and fumbled her way down the stairs nearly falling having missed the last step.

Ripping the curtain free of the rod Averie frantically fought with the window. The darkened room was rapidly closing in, suffocating her.

Jennifer placed her hand on Averie's shoulder. "Calm down."

Large beads of sweat rolled down Averie's face. "I can't breathe," she hollered through struggled gasps.

Sarah flipped the lock lever and the window glided opening allowing the fresh crisp air to flood the overly warm room. Outside she could see the faint pinkish glow on the horizon, and the rooster strutting his way to his preferred fence post. The morning had arrived quicker than expected and with events none of them expected.

Averie haphazardly sunk into the couch cushions, dripping with sweat, the look of fear plastered on her face.

"What's wrong with her?" Sarah asked Jennifer. "Is the baby coming?"

"Can you tell me what happened? Do you hurt anywhere?" Jennifer asked.

Averie proceeded to explain the events which woke her.

Jennifer poked, pushed, and prodded but couldn't find anything wrong. "I think you felt the baby move, that's all. To be sure though you better come down to the clinic today so I can do an ultrasound. This way we know exactly what is happening with the fetus. If something is wrong it would be better to know sooner, than later."

"Do you think the shell broke?" Averie asked.

"You mean your water?" Jennifer returned a puzzled look.

"Water," Averie whispered. "My baby is inside a protective shell, like an egg. It had to be that way to protect the fetus during the portal here. After my baby is born, I have to break the shell."

"If it has broken, the ultrasound will show," Jennifer said.

"Any idea what she's talking about?" Sarah whispered to Jennifer.

"I don't know, but if this fetus is inside a shell like a chicken then that pretty much confirms what we all already believe. Averie is from another world," Jennifer whispered back.

"What time should we be there?" Sarah asked Jennifer.

"Around noonish, I have a few appointments before that."

Averie rubbed her belly, and as she did, she could feel movement deep inside her again. It wasn't painful, more like being tickled on the inside by a feather. It took a movement for the realization to sink in, inside her was a living breathing entity. Any day now she would be responsible for the life of another. Averie's face went deathly pale. "What's going to happen to me?" Averie asked.

"Eventually you're going to have a beautiful baby and get to experience all the joys of being a mother," Jennifer said. "Something I never got to do because of a rare congenital disability."

From the twisted look Averie offered the answer Jennifer gave was not correct. "What happens after the baby comes, where am I to live? I know nothing of your world and have no money." Averie looked at her reflection in the window. "I don't want my baby to die here."

Sarah came from the kitchen holding a large glass of milk and handed it to Averie. "I already told you, you can stay here as long as you want. We have plenty of room and to be honest, I could use the company while Tom works the farm."

"You say that now, but those who don't contribute to the family are soon removed and… and I don't understand any of this. How am I to do my part?"

"What you need to remember is this isn't Icearaus. In our world women who are pregnant are treated differently. You won't be expected to do chores beyond what you feel you're capable of doing."

"I feel so worthless—"

"That's enough," Sarah scolded her. "You're not worthless, your pregnant and due any day now. What do you think we're going to do, make you go work the fields?"

Averie opened her mouth to speak but stopped when Tom arrived half-dressed and groggy.

"I heard what you said about having no money. You have more money than you can even imagine, but you can't use them in their current form. We have to exchange them for dollars."

Averie looked at Tom confused.

"You have a bag of gold coins more valuable than anything we own. If you want, I could sell a few."

"I already told you those coins belong to her and were not taking them," Sarah snapped.

Averie's eyes lit up like someone stuck a flashlight in her ear. "You can have them," she eagerly said.

"I don't want all of them, only a few," Tom told her. "Hold on to the rest as a keepsake from your home."

"You think that's a good idea? I thought we agreed to keep her a secret for the time being," Sarah said.

"I'll take Mike with me and go to Frankfort. How big that city is none would even remember us and besides. They probably see old coins daily."

Averie rose holding on to the couch to gather her bearings, then wobbled her way down the hall to Billy's room. It was here she had left her coin purse on the dresser. Returning a few minutes later she handed the bag to Tom who removed two coins then returned the bag.

"Keep the rest, you'll get enough money for these two to last a lifetime," Tom informed her.

Averie hoped this time would never arrive, but it did and much sooner than expected.

"Are you ready to go?" Sarah asked as she snatched her purse from the back of a kitchen chair.

Averie suddenly felt cold, her skin clammy. The open front door looked more like the entrance to hell than the outdoors.

"You're going to be fine," Sarah said as she waited by the front door. "There's not a pregnant woman alive today who hasn't had an ultrasound."

"Is, is Jennifer going to be there?" Averie asked.

"Don't be silly, you know she is. She did mine when I was pregnant with Billy."

Averie's eyes sparkled as an escape plan formed. "What about Billy, he can't stay here alone. He's much too young. It would be wise for me to stay here with him while you go."

"Hmmm," Sarah mumbled rubbing her chin. "I could be wrong since I'm no expert, but I don't think it works that way. Besides, Billy is plenty old enough to stay here alone."

"What about Tom and Mike? What if they need more coins and I'm not home to give them more?"

Sarah held up her cell phone. "They both know my number and can call me if an emergency arises."

Averie had a concerned look on her face.

"I don't believe for a second Mike will let anything happen to Tom in Frankfort. They'll sell the coins and be home later this evening."

Averie looked to the ceiling for help finding another reason why she should remain here.

"You're stalling," Sarah said. "Now come on, we can't keep Jennifer waiting, she is a busy woman."

Averie made her way to the porch where she froze. It was not the outdoors that frightened her, but the monstrous beast which was only feet away from the stairs. Its big glossy glass eyes watching her every movement and the growl which came from behind steel teeth waiting to taste her.

Sarah popped the lever and the door swung silently open. "Come now, I need to get you buckled in."

Averie reluctantly came leaving long skid marks in the gravel. On her way she looked at the forest and considered fleeing, but where would she go after that.

"Once we leave you'll see cars everywhere."

"And my baby won't be hurt?"

"I promise. You and your baby won't be hurt."

Averie flashed her a suspicious look.

"Have I ever lied to you?"

Averie thought for a moment and realized none of them had. Drawing a deep breath, she quickly sat and adjuster her position to where she was comfortable. Watching Sarah as she carefully placed the seat belt under her belly, she tried to smile, but her tense muscles and rigid frame exposed the façade.

"You need to relax. You're going to have a heart attack before we leave the driveway."

Before they even made it to the blacktop, Averie's eyes slammed shut and her nails dug into the armrests.

"Open your eyes and watch, there is a whole world out there waiting to be discovered."

Averie did as Sarah asked and soon a smile replaced the growing trepidation. Much faster than a horse and carriage they covered great distances in the blink of an eye. Occasionally, she would tense up expecting to die as another beast came directly at them only to pass without touching.

"We live on the outskirts of Willowdale." Sarah pointed to the welcome sign as they drove past. "When we get to town you'll see a whole new world."

Again, Sarah told the truth as Averie watched with widened eyes.

Taking it slow Sarah took the time to explain about traffic lights and fast food restaurants. What mom and pop stores were versus the big chain stores and how she preferred the earlier explaining how she wanted to do her part to support local businesses. Down the main road they passed a row of antique stores and slightly used merchandise shops where she liked to shop for unique items found nowhere else.

Passing one behemoth structure overflowing with cars Averie's jaw fell open and all she could do was point.

"That's the Willowdale Mall," Sarah explained. "Inside it contains about a hundred stores, most of them clothes."

Averie watched with wide eyes as it faded from view.

Sarah glanced at the clock on the radio. "It's about that time. We should get going to the clinic."

Not far from the mall Sarah pulled into the parking lot of a large brick building painted white with red trim. Near the top a large sign read Willowdale Live Well Clinic.

Waiting by tinted glass double doors Jennifer waved as the car rolled past.

"Welcome," Jennifer greeted them, then exchanged hugs with each. **"And** how was the trip?" she asked Averie.

Averie hesitated to answer.

"It was excellent," Sarah said. "She was a bit nervous at first. After we got going she picked up on everything and was soon telling me what stores where. She's a very bright girl, that's for sure."

"Fantastic," Jennifer cheered. "Are you ready to see your baby?"

Averie nodded her answer.

"Great, let's get you back to the examination room." Along the way she explained the process and what was to be expected.

At the end of a long hall Jennifer opened the door and the room magically brightened revealing white tile with gold inlays. Against the far wall was a stainless-steel bed frame which supported a blue plastic mattress. Across the mattress was a brilliant white sheet of paper. Beside the bed was a wooden table with a black box which sprouted a network of lengthy tentacles. Pale gray cabinets hung on one wall while a counter contained a plethora of glass jars, plastic bottles, and boxes.

"Please, come in and have a seat on the bed," Jennifer said.

Averie froze at the door and gripped the handle draining the color from her knuckles. "No," she angrily hissed. She had seen this before with Jairo and had no intentions of being delivered directly to Karayan for disposal. "I will not allow my child to be destroyed."

Jennifer looked at Sarah, then to Averie. "I have no intentions of destroying your child. I am a woman of medicine and dedicated my life to saving people."

"You lie, I have seen this before. You plan to deliver my child to Karayan."

"I plan to do no such thing," Jennifer snapped back growing frustrated from the false accusations. "If I wanted to do something involving your baby why would I have waited until now. I could have easily taken the child that day outside the barn had I wanted."

"You have to believe us," Sarah said. "We only have you and your baby's best interest in mind."

"And you won't steal my child and give him to Karayan?"

"Why would I do that?" Jennifer asked. "This Karayan guy sounds like a complete jerk."

Averie released her death grip on the knob but remained hesitant even as Sarah helped her to the bed.

"Now lie down and relax. The procedure isn't painful. To be honest it's quite exciting. Where else can you see another life inside you?"

"What are you going to do again?" Averie asked as she lay on the bed.

"I put this slimy gel on your belly and move the transducer around and it creates an image of your baby. By doing this I can see how healthy it is."

Averie closed her eyes as the cooling sensation raced up her spine forcing an involuntary shiver to come.

"Open your eyes," Jennifer said as she began to move the transducer around.

Averie slowly did and the frightened look on her face fled, replaced by a smile and a giggle. On the black box she could see the outline of a curled-up baby.

Taking more time than she would have with any other patient she explained every inch of the ultrasound. "Do you want to know what the sex is?"

"I already know I am having a dominant male."

Jennifer moved the transducer around taking a second look at the fetus. "Well, I don't want to burst your bubble, but you're having a girl. A girl who is very healthy and quite active which is why you're feeling so much movement."

Averie's eyes narrowed. "You lie. I was told I would carry a male, a dominant male to rule Icearaus."

"I would never lie about this," Jennifer told Averie.

"Are you positive?" Sarah asked. "Is there a chance the machine could be broken?"

"Sorry," Jennifer said as she moved the transducer around some more. "I have a clear image of the fetus and I am one-hundred percent positive it's a girl."

Averie's head slumped, and a single large tear came from one eye. "How is this possible?" she asked. "It's not supposed to be like this."

Jennifer shook her head. "I don't know. I don't make them, I only tell you what you're having and if they're healthy."

Averie covered her face with both hands and wept. "This can't be. I'm a failure."

"You're not a failure," Sarah told her.

"Yes, I am," Averie screamed. "Pegan will never accept me back now. And what about all those who put their trust in me that my son would save Icearaus. I failed them all."

"I would appreciate it if you didn't talk like that," Jennifer said. "You're not a failure. You're a mother who is carrying a beautiful baby girl who is healthy. That's what's important, not the sex."

Averie looked at Jennifer through swollen eyes. "My baby is supposed to be a strong male, not a weak submissive female."

"Whoa," Sarah snapped. "What's all this talk about submissive. I don't know about your world, but here, women are equally as powerful as men."

"If not more," Jennifer added.

Averie closed her eyes and laid her head back deep in thought.

"Look here, I want to show you something?"

Both Averie and Sarah looked at the screen.

Using the eraser end of a pencil, Jennifer traced the edge of something on the screen. "Right here is that protective shell you told us about. I have never seen anything like it before. It seems rigid yet pliable. It moves as the fetus moves."

Averie smiled a told-you-so smile.

"Well," Sarah said. "Since the boys are in Frankfort. How about us girls go out for lunch?"

"Sounds good to me," Jennifer agreed. "I'm about starved to death. There is one problem though, what do we do about Averie's eyes? There bound to draw attention."

"We'll think of something along the way and if we don't, screw the people, let them talk," Sarah said.

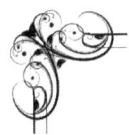
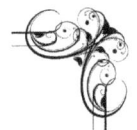

Chapter 10

he soldier looked at Barrett who had his head lowered as if he'd already accepted defeat. He, on the other hand, had no desire to die at the hands of these ruthless thugs. "By the orders of King Karayan I demand you release us, NOW!"

Pegan ignored the demand, his attention remained focused on Fel-Strike as he carefully cleaned the dirt out from under his fingernail.

"Release us now and I will see to it you receive your weight in gold," he continued. "I personally see no reason for King Karayan to know about the others," he stuttered. There had to be something he could say to spare his life.

Pegan finished with one hand then diligently worked on the other. Afterward, he held his hand up to the diminishing light to examine his work.

"Are we going to question them, or not?" Heidhantynth hissed as the repeated thump of his foot reverberated like a war drum off the cold stone walls.

Pegan glanced at the elves. They had positioned themselves to either side of the prisoners. Behind the elves, Airriossalth was on all fours with her nose inches away from a bright yellow dandelion. Licking at it with her bright pink forked tongue she was busy examining every detail of the wildflower.

Saress remained in the shadows some distance away keeping an ever-watchful eye on the basilica incase the one who escaped returned with friends.

Raestmond worked the fire pit with a long stick sending embers flying. "It sure would be a shame for this beautiful pig to go to waste," he chuckled.

Pegan had a sadistic smile on his face as he approached Glorandial. "If either one of these men move more than what's required to breathe, kill them slowly."

Glorandial purposely pressed her blade against the sheath as she slid it free creating a prolonged earsplitting squeal. "It would be my pleasure."

"Heidhantynth, come with me," Pegan said as he nodded.

Heidhantynth did as instructed and followed Pegan across the basilica.

"Listen to me," Pegan said.

Heidhantynth went to speak but Pegan raised his finger stopping him. "I understand you're hatred towards man, and I am sorry about your father. In your eyes the best route to success is with pain and bloodshed, and sometimes it is. There are other times when a delay is more effective than the torture. Many times, people have told me everything I wish to know long before blood was ever spilled."

Heidhantynth nodded, even though he would have much rather started chopping off fingers and toes from the beginning.

"Listen to Pegan," Airriossalth yelled from where she studied a larkspur. "He's skilled at gathering information."

The prisoner who demanded his freedom drained of color. He had never met Pegan before but recognized the name instantly. Pegan Rhoe was world-renowned as the best at extracting information and worked directly with King Karayan killing the bearers, this was, up until he suddenly vanished.

Filaurel made his way to the fire pit and cut off a piece of meat. "The pork is amazing. Excellently spiced and basted to perfection." Cutting off a few slabs he brought them to his companions.

"No thank you," Pegan said. "I prefer to question the prisoners on an empty stomach. It makes me less compassionate and often times those who've eaten vomit from observing my work."

Filaurel looked at his pork with disgust, and tossed what remained on the ground. The others did likewise.

The guard dreamed all day about sinking his teeth into that pork, and now it lay before him on the ground. The smell made his mouth water and stomach growl. "What kind of man starves his prisoners?"

Barrett kept his head lowered; vision fixed on the ground. He knew in time they would get tired of his companion's mouth and extract their anger upon him.

Glorandial drew her arm back then followed through with her intentions. The smack sounded like a raw steak hitting a stone counter as the back of her gloved hand connected with the side of the prisoner's face. "Don't speak until asked."

Pegan knelt before the prisoner who received the slap. "How humiliating getting slapped like that from a woman. I would be—"

"Karayan will hear of this treasonous act and will no doubt take pleasure in removing your skin one inch at a time," the prisoner interrupted.

Barrett looked away. He had no desire to see what was about to come of his companion.

Pegan grabbed the prison by the neck lifting him to his feet. "Don't ever mention his name again within my presence or you'll be cut into so many pieces not one will be big enough to feed a crow."

"I'm not afraid of you," the prisoner sneered. "You, and your band of thugs attacked us by surprise. In a fair fight the outcome would have been much different."

Pegan took a step back and examined the prisoner. "You're right, we did. Filaurel, bring this man his sword and untie him. This man wants a fair fight, he shall have one. You can choose any one of us to fight. The rest of us will only observe. If you defeat whomever you choose, then you're free to walk away with your pride and warn your King. Lose though and…" he let the words trail off allowing the prisoner's mind to fill in the rest.

Filaurel returned dropping the sword at the prisoner's feet, then released the bindings.

The prisoner looked at the weapon but made no movement towards it.

Saress remained in the shadows, ready to draw the bowstring at a moment's notice if he tried to flee instead of fight.

"Pick it up," Pegan demanded. "You wanted this fight and I have afforded it to you."

The prisoner looked at the weapon again, then placed his hands behind his back and knelt. "King Karayan is—"

Glorandial slapped him again.

"We will get no useful information from this one," Pegan said. "Heidhantynth, if he speaks again without being asked remove his tongue."

Pegan moved on to the other man who had remained quiet with his head bowed since his surrender. "What's your name?" Pegan asked.

"Barrett Solve—"

"Silence you fool, they're the enemy," the prisoner hissed.

Pegan looked at Heidhantynth. "What are you waiting for?"

Heidhantynth removed a small serrated dagger from a concealed sheath.

Pegan stopped Heidhantynth before the blade found flesh. "Not like that, it's too easy. Prove to me how strong you are, rip it from his mouth."

Heidhantynth was salivating with the thought. How sweet revenge would be and now he had the approval of Pegan to do it.

The prisoner slammed his mouth shut. The thick muscles that lined his jaw protruded under the skin.

"Airriossalth," Pegan said. "It seems this man has a problem opening his mouth. Will you kindly assist your brother?"

Oblivious to her surroundings, Airriossalth spun a purple flower by its bright green stem.

"Airriossalth," Pegan said louder. "I know you heard me."

Airriossalth looked at Pegan. "I'm sorry but I did not. The color of this flower is captivating don't you think?"

Pegan shrugged his shoulders and released a long-winded sigh. Afterward, he repeated his earlier words.

"Will you please hold this?" Airriossalth asked Filaurel as she handed him the flower.

Pegan backed away into the shadows to stand beside Saress. "Are you sure she's killed before?"

"Yes," Saress assured him. "She does it politely and with compassion."

Pegan laughed so hard he almost chocked. "I see."

"Pegan." Saress suddenly turning serious. "You must remember she's never been out of the swamp so everything she sees, and smells is new to her. Don't do anything to embarrass her."

"I would never embarrass her. She just seems too nice to be a killer."

"When needed, she can be vicious.," Saress informed him. "Right now, she doesn't sense a threat."

Pegan patted Saress on the shoulder. "I find it wonderful she can still find beauty in all this mess. It's women like her—"

A scream shot through them like shards of glass sending a shiver to every fiber of their being.

Pegan turned to see what occurred, and what he saw, frightened him.

Airriossalth had a hold of the prisoner's chin with one hand while gripping his forehead with the other. Forcefully prying open his mouth, the grizzly tearing sound of muscles being ripped free from their bones soon followed. Adjusting her hold she pried harder until the tendons failed creating loud pops and curling into small balls. Pulling harder the screams that came this time were purely inhuman.

Pegan cringed from the sheer brutality.

The crack of the jawbone breaking brought a shiver to Pegan's spine and he stood there with his mouth agape and eyes wide from what occurred next. Both lips of the prisoner ripped at the commissure and tore clear to the neck. Blood spewed from either side cascading down his cheeks and painted his chest a ghastly crimson.

Heidhantynth decided now was the time to perform the procedure and forced his hands into the opening.

Pegan moved closer to get a better view. In all his years of performing tortures, he had yet to see a tongue forcefully ripped from a mouth. In all honesty he was not sure it was possible having witnessed people hung by their tongue's, yet the muscles always held.

Heidhantynth grabbed the bright pink muscle and jerked fully expecting the muscle to tear free, but it held fast.

The scream the man rent was horrific. Not the kind you would expect from pain, but the kind that made your blood run cold and question your own sanity.

Frustrated with his failure, he jerked harder ripping the head from Airriossalth's grip forcing one of her long black claws to puncture the eye of the prisoner. "Gross," she hissed. Removing her claw from the eye socket she flicked her wrist launching the eye somewhere across the basilica.

"Hmmm," Heidhantynth snarled. He peered into the mouth to see exactly how the tongue was fastened. "Ah, I see now," he said with a smile. Reaching in again he gripped the tongue and jerked up, not out. The tissue at the frenum was no match for his strength and easily tore away. Satisfied with the results he began to twist the tongue as if he were wringing out a rag until it began to tear free of the hyoid bone. Moments later, a loud pop like a wagon axel breaking echoed as the last ligament failed, and the entire tongue slid out in one piece.

Pegan stood there in amazement. He never believed it was possible, and still wouldn't had he not seen it. "Show it to the other prisoner then toss it on the fire." Pegan watched Heidhantynth walk away then focused on the man who was nearing the point of unconsciousness. "Airriossalth, I need you to keep his head tilted forward. I wish for him not to drown in his own blood. He still may be of use to us."

"How do you come to that conclusion?" Glorandial asked. "I don't see him doing much talking anymore."

Pegan looked at Glorandial startled by her question. "He still has hands to write with."

"Now, shall we continue," Pegan said as he forcefully turned Barrett's head so he could see his companion drenched in blood. "Why did Karayan send you here? What is so important in this old Keep?"

Barrett vomited from what he saw. "Are you going to kill me?" Barrett asked.

"Maybe, maybe not," Pegan answered. "Depends on your willingness to give us the information we seek."

"My name is Barrett Solventine. I have no weapons nor am I a fighter. I'm a builder by trade."

Barrett's companion tried to say something, but the words came as a jumbled incoherent mess.

Pegan looked at the prisoner who tried to speak, then to Airriossalth. "What of this man. Was he armed?"

"Oh yes," she answered with a soft feminine voice mixed with a slight hiss. "This man is very dangerous; he had knives and swords. Many were nicked and scared from use."

"Heidhantynth," Pegan address the big lizard. "Throw him on the bed of hot coals. I've grown tired of his mouth and wish for him to no longer be within our presence. Airriossalth, if he tries to crawl away smack him a good one with your staff."

Moments later a crash was heard, and embers fluttered like glowing butterflies. Pegan cringed as he watched the man kick and flail. Each time he tried to work his way out, Airriossalth was there beating him with her staff. Eventually the thrashing ended, clothes caught fire, leather smoldered, and the acidic smell of burnt skin and singed hair filled their nostrils.

Pegan turned back to Barrett. "Now that we won't be interrupted anymore, why are you here?"

Barrett weighed his options and decided it was best to speak the truth. After all he held no loyalty to Karayan. He was only here as a guide, nothing more. If he did get out of here with his head attached, he would flee somewhere never to be seen again. "I designed and oversaw the construction of this Keep many decades ago. I was brought here by a man named Jester to reveal the location of a secret chamber deep underground. Jester never told me why he sought this secret chamber."

"Jester... Jester," Pegan whispered. "I've heard that name before. Regardless, we too are here for this elusive chamber. Perhaps we can work together. You reveal to us its location and I will throw a good word in to Lady Alenia upon our return."

"You're taking me to the elves, even after I gave you what you wanted?"

"You won't be safe anywhere else?" Pegan said.

Barrett had a sudden change of heart knowing what was to become of him afterward. "And if I don't take you there, then what?"

Pegan looked to Raestmond, then at Barrett. "We have a builder ourselves so in time we will discover the location. All your services will do is hasten our time inside this dilapidated structure and keep yourself alive."

Barrett looked at the smoldering corpse. "Fine, but I think there are some things you should know. The room to the secret chamber is filthy with wards and all who enter will perish."

Pegan thought for a moment. *If Karayan created the words they would have dissolved immediately upon his power being removed.* "We'll cross that path when we get there," Pegan said as he looked up at the stars and thought of Averie. "We leave at first light."

"Pegan, can I talk with for a moment?" Saress asked. "Something has been

bothering me as of lately."

Pegan could tell she was deeply troubled by something.

"As you know my reptilian friends lost their father to men and now, they feel you're purposely taunting them by saying their birth names incorrectly."

"Oh no," Pegan said. "You know I mean no Ill will towards them, but I cannot pronounce their given names. The same as I could not say yours. I will talk with them."

"I understand," Airriossalth said from across the way. "You should have told us, instead of having us believe you were mocking us. In your language my name translates into Ameria, and Heidhantynth is Dinko. We would much appreciate it if you could use them."

"Consider it done," Pegan said. "Now how about some of this pork. No need having it go to waste."

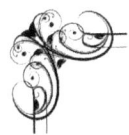
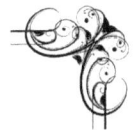

Chapter 11

om turned the radio down and they drove in silence for some distance.

"Alright, what's bothering you?" Mike asked.

Tom veered off the road into a rest stop that overlooked the valley and put the car in park. "I'm not going to sell the coins," Tom admitted. "I only used that as an excuse to get away. I'm going to Frankfort to check the local mental hospitals, mainly the psychiatric wards to see if they have any missing patients."

"Why?" Mike asked.

Tom turned the engine off. "I don't know… I just don't know. I find it hard to believe that someone would be here from another world. That's the kind of stuff fantasy movies are made from, it's not reality. I don't think she's dangerous which is why I had no problem leaving her with Sarah. Perhaps she was abducted from a hospital and abused until she became pregnant then whoever took her dropped her off."

Mike took a drink from his Pepsi. "And this guy, whoever he is, picked your house two-hundred and fifty miles away. And, not to mention you can't even see it from the highway. If you blink you miss the turn off. Hell, even you've missed it on occasion."

"I know it sounds far-fetched, but there has to be a reasonable explanation. Someone simply doesn't appear from thin air."

Mike rolled down the window letting the fresh mountain air in. "I can tell you this much. I don't know where she came from, but it's not from Earth."

"You talk as if you believe she is an alien."

Mike scratched his chin. "Tom, I want to tell you something I haven't told another living soul, not even Jennifer. In fact, when I took the call I damn near dropped the phone."

Tom cocked his head waiting to hear what Mike had to say.

"Yesterday I got a call from the lab—"

"That was quick," Tom interrupted.

"Yeah, I wasn't expecting it either, and, I damn sure wasn't expecting what they told me. The lab tech was puzzled wondering where I retrieved the blood. I told him it was evidence left behind from a crime scene. He had the audacity to call me a liar and was highly pissed saying I wasted his time, and the states money with this prank. I told him it was no prank and didn't appreciate being accused of such a heinous act. For a moment the phone went deathly silent to the point I believed he hung up. That's when he told me the blood was not of human origin. In fact, they couldn't link it to anything living."

"How is that possible?" Tom asked.

"There is only one reasonable explanation. Averie isn't from this world and has spoken the truth since we found her."

"Wow," Tom said. "Wasn't expecting this."

Mike had a distant stare. "There's more and I think it explains her strange eye color. A normal person has forty-six chromosomes, twenty-three pairs. Averie has forty-seven. Twenty-three pairs and a single abnormal chromosome that is chemically bonded to chromosome number fifteen."

"And?" Tom confusingly asked.

"Chromosome fifteen is where your eye color originates from. I don't want to bore you with the details as I don't fully understand them myself, but the tech said this chromosome seemed to be constructed from some kind of strange gold metallic mineral."

"How is that even possible?" Tom asked.

"I don't know. The lab tech said it was as if someone made a chromosome of pure gold and implanted it inside her DNA. He had no logical explanation hence why he accused me of facilitating this prank."

Tom fired up the car and put it in drive. "I wish you would have told me this sooner. Now I have to cancel the appointments I made at the mental hospitals so we can sell these coins. Averie is going to need money and who knows how long ET is going to be living with us?"

The derelict building was little more than a shack sunk back between two large bushes and a broken stone retaining wall. The orange fluorescent neon sign which read *Flying High Pawnshop* was lifelessly dim while a glowing open sign flickered as if running on fumes. Through the filthy wall-to-ceiling windows, movement was obscured.

Tom let his vision drift over the apocalyptic image, then to Mike who let the slide slam forward on his Glock resulting in a high-pitched metallic ping. Flipping off the safety he jammed it in his coat pocket. It appeared his best friend was getting ready for some secret government co-op rescue mission straight from a Tom Clancy novel. "Are you sure about this?" Tom asked. "Perhaps we should go to a pawnshop on the nicer side of town."

On the sidewalk a homeless man passed pushing a shopping cart loaded with grossly overstuffed garbage bags. The clack of each wheel hitting the cracks sounded like gunfire.

"I'm not a hundred percent positive, if that's what you're asking," Mike said as he watched the homeless man search though an overflowing garbage can. "I contacted an old confidential informant who told me this is the place to unload hot items."

"How does it work?" Tom asked as if he were a child.

"It's easy. No paperwork of the transaction ever takes place, and everything is on a cash only basis. In truth, I would stake my paycheck on it that the pawnshop is nothing more than a front to launder money from other illegal activities such as drug dealing and gun smuggling which takes place after the store closes."

"And the police allow this to occur?"

"It all has to do with politics," Mike said. "That's one of the reasons I left here and accepted the position in Willowdale. I don't think it's right, but one man can't change the minds of a dysfunctional and corrupt police force. Had I not conformed to their way of thinking I would have either been setup and charged with a bogus crime or forced to resign."

"And to think we rely on the police to uphold the law."

Mike laughed. "Shall we get this over with before the homeless man comes back and steals the wheels off the car?"

Tom looked at the building again and shook his head in disgust. "The place looks shady as hell. I'll be happy to escape with my life, let alone the wheels."

The door creaked like an old sarcophagus being opened for the first time in centuries.

"Can I help you?" a lady asked from the back standing behind a glass counter. She was aged but wore it well. Tall, pale skinned, and wearing black leather pants that appeared painted on. The white tank top barely covered the northern hemisphere which was obviously not a gift from God but created in the mind of a sick monster. Both arms were heavily tattooed but still revealed the faint pink pinprick from today's high.

Mike surveyed the environment noting every detail. To the right were rows of garden tools, lawn mowers, weed eaters, trimmers and edger's, multiple chain saws and a large pressure washer on wheels. To the left were steel racks burdened with televisions, blue ray players, x-boxes and play stations, computers and stereo equipment. At the end was a glass shelf loaded with DVD and blue ray movies. Decorating the walls were a mixed bag of musical instruments along with hunting bows and other items that were being displayed at unreasonable prices.

The door behind the counter swung open and a monster of a man stepped into the room. His long black greasy hair was pulled back in a pony tail and his exposed chest was ripe with muscles and covered with prison ink. Behind two bushy eyebrows were beady eyes that could strike fear into the hearts of even the hardiest of men.

Mike gripped the Glock resting his index finger on the trigger. His muscles tensed, and he was ready to react in a moment's notice if needed.

"She asked you a question," the man growled. His voice was raspy, like coarse sandpaper dragged over a granite stone.

Tom cautiously approached the counter and removed the two coins from his pocket. "I've run on hard times and need to sell a few rare coins from my collection."

"Stole them more likely," the man mockingly chuckled.

"No," Tom argued. "These coins were passed down from generation to generation in my family. What you—"

"I don't need your whole goddamn family history," the lady hissed in a voice that sounded like the squeaky wheel of a vacuum cleaner. "If you want to sell them, let me see em'."

Tom was expecting to be shot seconds after laying the coins on the counter.

The lady snatched the coins and held them up to the light, then bit each one. Satisfied they were gold she grabbed a magnifying glass to examine the intricate detail carved into each. "Who's Karayan?"

Tom paused. He never considered what to say if he was asked about the coins. "He was an Inca King."

Mike rolled his eyes. *That's the best you could come up with. Were both going to get shot before this day ends*, he thought.

"I may have been born at night, but not last night," the lady said. "Regardless it matters not to me as the value is in the gold, not the name. Five thousand each, nothing more."

"They're worth five times that and you know it," Tom argued.

"Then take them to a different pawnshop where the legitimacy, proof of ownership, and a police check of stolen property will have to be completed before you ever receive a dime. Here, I take all the risks and you walk away with cold hard cash in your pocket."

It crossed Tom's mind to tell the lady to pound sand, but ten thousand would last Averie a long time. He wanted to get her something though and a large diamond ring on display caught his eye. "Ten K' and that diamond ring. Figure if you're going to screw me you might as well put a ring on my finger first."

The lady looked at the ring and pulled it from the case examining the small tag attached to it. "Deal," she said, then handed Tom the ring. "Tiny, go in the safe and get me two loafs of bread."

Tom examined the ring. It was beyond beautiful and he was positive Averie would love it. Afterward he set it on the counter and waited.

The man quickly departed through the door he came from, only to reemerge minutes later holding two bundles of cash neatly wrapped with bank bands and handed them to Tom. "Do you want to count it?"

"I don't believe that's necessary," Mike answered. "I don't see a reputable company like this cheating its customers. If you did and word got out, which it would, it would probably come back to haunt you."

"Thank you for your time," Tom said as he stuffed the cash in the inside pocket of his coat and started to leave.

"Don't forget the ring," Mike said.

"Almost forgot." Tom snatched the item and tucked it neatly away.

The moment the door closed the lady nodded to Tiny giving her approval. Scurrying to the door Tiny waved at the homeless man across the street and gave him a hundred-dollar bill upon his arrival.

Reaching into his pocket the homeless man produced a small scrap of paper. On it was the vehicles plate number, make, model and color along with the vehicle identification number.

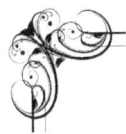

Chapter 12

he sun was sinking behind the Ash Mountains setting the sky ablaze with flaming reds and molten oranges. In that orange Vexacion could barely discern the faint twinkle of newborn stars. Soon, night would rule the world, a time when he was most comfortable. Kneeling behind a dilapidated wagon abandoned near the road he melded into the shadows and faded from existence. It was painfully obvious from the rickety wagons and the bone thin horses which pulled them, life had become difficult for those who lived within the quaint town. A problem he planned to fully exploit. Watching each wagon slowly roll past he observed the driver. Most were men coming from the fields with what rations they could salvage hoping to make a coin at the market. Waiting patiently, eventually, the right wagon would come along and when it did he would pounce.

Slipping through the darkness like a wisp of smoke blown on the subtle breeze Vexacion materialized nearly on top of his victim. She tried to scream but he was quicker and covered her mouth. Behind her riding in the back were two small children dressed in ripped clothes and covered in dirt.

"Quiet," he whispered into her ear then removed his gloved hand from her mouth. "I only wish a moment of your time. Steer the cart away from the gate to that bramble of trees off in the distance. We need to talk where prying ears cannot fall on our conversation."

The woman looked at the stranger through frightened eyes. On him, she could see the glint of steel from the multiple daggers he wore. To do anything beyond what he requested would more than likely result in all their death's, so she did as he asked.

Vexacion kept a close watch for any who may have followed them.

"Please don't hurt my children," she said with a quivering jaw when the wagon came to a rest under a large bushy tree.

Vexacion looked at the two in the back who coward away from him. "I'm not here to hurt you, I'm here to help you."

The lady eyed him suspiciously. In her mind any time a man pulled a woman away he had dastardly thoughts. "What do you want from me?" she asked.

"I need a job completed inside the walls of Lynn Brook. It won't be easy and there is great risk to you and your children. In return you will be paid handsomely. Enough for you to move away from here and give your children a better life."

She looked at her children huddled together. In their eyes she could see desperation. There was nothing in this town since the escape of the bearer. The quality of life had diminished to the point more vagrants roamed the streets begging than those who held legitimate jobs. She would have left a long time ago but the cost to move was well beyond her capabilities. Considering the cost to move to Fairdenn and locate another residence would be at least a couple gold, an amount she would probably never see in her lifetime. "I can do it, but I will need at least three gold pieces?"

Vexacion grinned, then leaned back on the wooden seat. "You do as I ask, and I will pay you ten gold pieces."

The woman's eyebrows raised until they vanished into her bushy brown hair. With ten gold she could buy a fine plot in East Haven, a much nicer and safer town not yet ravaged by Karayan's anger. "What must I do?"

"First, you need to get me inside under the guise of a different name, perhaps your husband or brother. Afterward, I need you to visit every tavern, every business, every place people frequent and whisper into every ear that will listen the Royal Guards are planning to assassinate King Karayan."

"Is that true?" the woman asked.

"No, but I need you to convince as many as you can that it is."

"Nobody will believe me," she said. "King Karayan is considered by all to be immortal."

"Most wont and will become angered by what you whisper. More importantly though, a few will believe you and once the seed has been planted it will fester among the masses."

"When do I get paid?"

Vexacion removed ten silver pieces from his pocket and placed them in her hand. "I will give you this now, so you can feed and clothe your children. As for the rest, I will pay you after a week has passed. Near the center of town is a rickety well which has not seen water in decades, do you know the one."

"Phifer's well?" she answered.

"Yes," Vexacion said. "Go there on the fifth night when the moon is at its highest point and in the bucket will be your coins. Speak nothing of this conversation and after you receive your payment I recommend you flee Lynn Brook never to return."

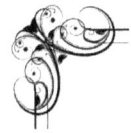

Chapter 13

arrett was good with his word and as the sun rose, he led them into the bowels of the Keep.

"Tell me more about this chamber?" Pegan asked. "How did it come to be?"

Barrett stopped at the base of a wide set of marble steps that arched upward. He knew the room, knew the horrors that waited. Wiping the sweat from his upper lip his words came in broken whispers. "The chamber you search for is no secret, but common knowledge. It's fear that keeps it a secret."

"Fear of what?" Filaurel asked.

Barrett appeared hollow-eyed. "Fear of what lives there. I have seen the corpses dragged up from the depths. Words cannot describe the torment permanently etched on their faces. Bodies twisted in unimaginable positions. Bones ripped free then rearranged to fit the suitor. Some were gutted missing their entrails, while others were half eaten, or had their limbs chewed off. Almost always, their face was devoured."

Raestmond looked at Pegan. "Do you think he speaks the truth?"

Pegan thought back to the battle with the demon, and how it feasted upon Thathra's face. "Possibly at one time, but the creature has been destroyed. All that remains now is a haunting memory of a horrid past."

None spoke another word, each lost in their own thoughts as Barrett led them through crumbling corridors and hallways clogged with broken furniture and other debris. At each turn new stairs took them higher and higher into the Keep. It was only when they entered what appeared to be the defunct kitchen, did they stop to rest.

Filaurel went to a large window which afforded a beautiful view of the Rain Wood Forest. Enormous majestic trees with glistening green leaves spread out as far as he could see. Beyond that he caught a faint glimpse of the shimmering waters of the ocean. "You said these bodies were dragged up from the depths, yet you take us higher and higher. I'm beginning to think you're leading us astray waiting for an opportunity to escape."

Barrett crossed his arms. "The doorway is at the top."

Filaurel looked confused by the answer.

"What you fail to understand is the stairs were built first, then the Keep was constructed around them. As far as I know it is the only one in existence."

Pegan rubbed his chin carefully listening to Barrett's explanation. "Why did you build it that way?"

Barrett smiled. "Simple, anyone looking for the chamber would go down thus never finding it. Who would believe the entrance is at the highest point."

From the abandoned kitchen Barrett led them down a few more halls, one long wide corridor heavy with shredded tapestries, up a few more staircases before arriving at a small windowless room. Directly in the center were crumbling stairs that spiraled upward into a hazy, dust infested darkness. "I must warn you the stairs were dangerous when first built, now, there downright treacherous. One slip can be fatal."

Pegan ran his hand along the icy slick smooth surface. Each step was covered with a slippery moss created from an unknown water source that dripped from somewhere above.

"I'll never fit," Saress complained.

"Nor will I," Dinko added.

Ameria raised her staff allowing the glow to chase away the darkness.

"There is no other way to get there, but up these stairs," Barrett said.

Pegan eased his way up a couple steps. His feet sliding out from beneath him with each step. "If I must, I will go alone."

"That won't be necessary," Saress hissed. "I will find a way up those stairs, even if I have to chew my own arm off. How far do we have to climb?"

Barrett looked at her confused by the question. "All the way to the top."

Saress raised her hand to smack him but decided a simple look of disgust was sufficient. "If I'm to fit I will have to rid myself of these." Unlatching multiple belts and straps a plethora of weapons fell free which Pegan quickly gathered.

Dinko did likewise except the elves acquired his gear.

Saress, Dinko, and Ameria placed themselves at different intervals in the group and dug their claws into the stonework. It was the only way those lacking claws could climb without tumbling back down to their deaths. It felt like hours passed and they were each drenched in sweat and every muscle burned from exhaustion when they arrived at a large landing with a single window. From here they could see all the way to Fairdenn. Across the landing and masked in a shadowy gloom stood a large rough-cut wooden door bound in steel.

"No amount of torture can make me go in there," Barrett said. "I know what awaits us if we do."

Dinko snatched Barrett by the neck and hoisted him off the ground. "I'll carry you if I must."

Barrett flailed his arms and legs while gasping for air.

Pegan ignored the scuffle and focused on the opposing obstacle before them. The door stood proud, bold, unrelenting. "If this door was alive, imagine the unspeakable horrors it had witnessed," he whispered. Carefully guiding each step. he moved silently across the landing and placed his ear against the door. Afterward, he ran his hand around the entire perimeter of the door searching for something. Looking back to the others who waited near the stairs Pegan smiled, then his hand found the basalt stone fanged shaped knob and with a flick of his wrist, it turned.

Saress drew her bowstring back and a blueish silver bolt materialized dropping into place.

Pegan leaped back quick as a cat as the door swung outward. Landing in a crouch both daggers came free becoming extensions of his arms.

Rrrriiinnnggg, **the phone screamed.**

"Can you answer that Billy, it might be your father," Sarah yelled.

Billy groaned and complained as he searched for a safe spot to camp his character. "Umm, hello," Billy said into the receiver peeking around the corner keeping an eye on the computer screen.

"Let me speak with you mother," Tom said.

"Mom, it's dad," Billy said as he set the phone down then scurried away.

"Hi honey," Sarah said. "Did you sell the coins?"

"Yep, there sold. I wanted to give you a heads-up. Jennifer is coming over tonight, both I and Mike have a confessions to make."

"Is everything okay?" Her voice began to break.

"Everything is fine. Really, it's all Mike's fault for keeping this a secret."

"What secret, what are you talking about?"

Static filled the phone as the connection was lost.

"Is something wrong?" Averie asked.

"I honestly don't know." The dishrag she carried slipped from her trembling fingers and fluttered to the floor. "He said something about a secret then the phone lost connection."

Headlights through the window lit up the living room alerting everyone inside Tom and Mike had arrived.

Sarah and Jennifer waited at the door. Both relieved their husbands were home yet upset about this untold information which kept them both sick with worry.

Averie watched from the kitchen the scolding Tom was receiving. She even giggled when Tom tried to place all the blame on Mike, yet Sarah was having none of it. Jennifer was there too giving them both a piece of her mind.

"Now get in here and tell us what's going on. You know I don't like secrets," Sarah snarled at Tom who entered looking like a whooped puppy. Mike was right behind him with his head lowered as well.

Jennifer crossed her arms. "Well, I'm waiting."

Tom started to explain but paused to watch Averie stagger past. Both hands holding tight to a plate loaded with pumpkin pie smothered with whip cream. Arriving at the couch she flopped down like a beached whale and groaned. "This thing is never going to come out."

"Not if you keep feeding it like that," Tom chuckled.

"Am I eating too much? Should I stop?" Averie asked.

Sarah knew exactly how Averie felt. When she was pregnant with Billy all she wanted to do was eat everything she saw. "Don't listen to Tom, you eat as much as you feel you need to." Afterward, she playfully kicked Tom in the shin.

"I'm still waiting," Jennifer said, her arms still crossed and foot taping to an imaginary rhythm.

"Let me begin," Tom said, then he told them about his original intention which brought fire to both Sarah and Jennifer's face. "I didn't know," he pleaded. "None of this makes sense."

"Guess now is as good as time as any to spill the beans," Mike said, drawing a stern look from Jennifer.

"Were you involved in this fiasco as well?" Sarah growled.

"With the hospitals, no. But I did withhold information."

"Go on," Jennifer said. "This oughta be good."

"You remember Melvin at the lab?" Mike asked Jennifer.

"Yes, he's a fine lab tech."

"We'll anyway. He called me and told me he finished the lab work on the blood—"

"That was quick. Normally it would take months," Jennifer said.

"Please don't interrupt me," Mike said. "He called me and asked where I got the blood because it was not of human origin. What troubled him more was he couldn't link it to anything from this world."

Neither Sarah nor Jennifer looked amused when Mike finished.

"It appears Averie really is a woman from another world," Tom said.

"We already know this," Jennifer said. "I did the ultrasound today and confirmed the fetus is indeed incased inside an egg-like shell to protect it. She has told us no lies."

"What do we do now?" Tom asked.

"What do you mean by that. I already told her she can live with us as long as she likes, even after the child is born," Sarah said.

Oblivious to the recent conversation, Averie walked past with the empty plate only to return with a large glass of milk.

Ameria released a nausea-inducing hiss as a gust of air blew past.

Saress readied her aim waiting to strike the first thing to emerge, but nothing did.

"Something evil dwells here," Ameria slowly hissed as the scales on her head stood erect.

Pegan looked to the others. "I don't fear evil, for he and I once slept in the same bed." Leaning into the wind he charged into the unknown.

Saress never hesitated and followed. They had already been through hell together, what could be inside this room that would be worse.

Ameria was on the heels of Saress and Dinko followed keeping hold of Barrett preventing him from fleeing. The entire time the prisoner was screaming how they were all going to die.

The elves came next while Raestmond clearly had second thoughts about volunteering and hesitated at the doorway.

The room was ripe with chaos. Furniture lay broken and scattered while the glass from a lone window lay strewn from wall to wall. Blowing through the gaping hole the wind thrashed the curtain leaving it flapping like a thousand angry snake tongues. Opposite the door they entered was another door and before it lay a skeleton bone pile ravaged by small critters. Near the center was a strange object which seemed immune to the ravages of time. Built upon two intricately carved wooden goat shaped feet was an oval frame which held tight to a lustrous sheen. Painstakingly carved into the frame were thousands of faces each stuck in a perpetual state of torment. Within the borders of the frame work a bluish green hue swirled searching for a way to escape.

As a craftsman, Raestmond was immediately drawn to the strange device. The detail was beyond anything he ever dreamed possible. "What an odd-looking mirror," he said, then reached out to touch the exquisite frame.

Pegan tore across the room slapping away Raestmond's hand. "It's not a mirror, but a magical doorway you fool. None of us here know what kind of dark magic was used to create this device and to touch it could destroy you."

Ameria opened her mouth revealing a row of jagged teeth, then released a low rumbling growl which turned into an ear-piercing hiss. The entire time her staff remained pointed directly at the strange object.

"A doorway," Raestmond said. "Perhaps it leads to the secret chamber?"

Pegan shook his head then pointed towards the closed door. "No, that one leads to the secret chamber."

"When we leave we are taking this with us so it can be destroyed," Dinko said as he pointed at the magical doorway.

Ameria never moved. Her body remained rigid while low growls continued to escape her partially open maw.

"Pegan!" Averie's scream tore through the darkened house. She could feel him as if she was part of him. Inside of him, wearing the same skin, sharing the same soul. Through him, through her, a strange magic raced.

Sarah stumbled from the bed and into the hall. Bouncing off the wall her elbow punctured the sheetrock and pictures fell from their hooks. Gaining her bearing, she bolted down the hall to where Averie should have been sleeping.

Averie screamed out words in a foreign tongue and her body convulsed. The pulsating light coming from the necklace set the room ablaze.

Unsure exactly what to do, Sarah grabbed the phone and frantically dialed.

Averie's fingers curled into fist burying her nails into the meaty section of her palms smearing blood on everything she touched.

"Keep her from falling off the bed." Sarah yelled at Tom as Averie began flopping like a fish out of water.

Billy stood in the doorway his eyes wet with moisture. "Is she dying?" he cried out. He'd never seen anyone die before except on television and it never looked this painful.

"You need to relax," Jennifer calmly said into the receiver. She wasn't sure what was happening but from all the yelling she could tell it wasn't good. Mike was at work, so she grabbed her cell phone and texted him to go to Tom's house immediately. "Now tell me what's happening," she calmly said into the receiver.

"What's happening to me?" Averie screamed again. The magic raced through her and she saw into different spectrums. Life was like a kaleidoscope with twisting and twirling colors clashing together harassing her mind. Her tone made all their hairs stand erect. The pulsating necklace intensified until they could see her bones through the skin.

"I'm on my way," Jennifer screamed into the receiver.

Pegan's eyes glossed over like frozen puddles and he spoke in a tone which sounded more dead than alive. "It can't be destroyed," Pegan hissed. "Magical doorways are created in the bowels of hell by tortured souls and delivered to our world by carrion crawlers. To destroy it will unleash the dark magic contained within having devastating effects."

Saress cocked her head sideways. "How do you know all this?"

Cocking his head in an unnatural position he appeared inhuman. "Don't question me," he snarled. Drool hung from his chin and his fingers flexed with each breath.

Glorandial reacted haphazardly ripping the curtain free of the rod and in one single motion it fluttered down covering the magical doorway.

Pegan stumbled as if waking from a drunken stupor then fell. Crawling on the ground he snarled and hissed appearing to resist the temptation of some unseen monster.

Mike arrived with lights blazing and sirens screaming. From the way the lights flashed through the closed curtain it appeared he arrived at a disco night club, not his sister's house. Busting through the door he made his way down the hall towards the screams.

"I don't know what to do?" Sarah cried out as Averie continued to convulse.

As quick as it began, it ended. Averie released a long-winded gasp of air then went silent. It was only the rise and fall of her chest which proved she was still alive.

"What the hell is going on?" Mike asked.

Tom stood there with his mouth agape debating where to begin. Luckily, he didn't have to as the grinding of gravel outside let them know Jennifer had arrived.

Sarah dropped to her knees beside the bed and began to wipe away the sweat that ran down Averie's face.

Jennifer wedged herself between Tom and Mike and went straight to Averie After a few minutes she questioned Sarah, who told her everything she could remember, but it all happened so fast she had a hard time trying to decide what was real or imagined.

"I think she had a seizure," Jennifer suggested after analyzing the information she was told.

Tom disagreed. "I don't think so. She was clearly talking to something or someone."

"You better head back to work," Jennifer told Mike. "I'm going to stay here for the night in case she has another episode."

Pegan crawled his way to the wall then used it for support to stand. Shaking the cobwebs from his mind he looked at them as they all watched him. "Did something happen?" he asked.

"You were talking…" Saress let her words die off. Telling him what had occurred would do nothing. She had seen this before and each time it happened Pegan had no memory of the incident. "You were telling us that you believe the door there is the entrance to the secret chamber."

Pegan eyed the door. "Yes, I believe so and we wasted enough time in this room."

"I showed you to the door," Barrett said. "I would rather take my chances on my own than being judged by the elves."

"No," Ameria said. "You will stay with us and be judged by Lady Alenia."

Beyond the door they followed a wide set of steps that lead them directly down into the bowels of hell. The mercury rose until the thermometer busted and the air grew heavy. On their shoulders they could feel the weight of the world bearing down. Eventually, the stairs gave way to a large cavern where double doors hung by twisted hinges.

Saress instinctively let her vision fall into the thermal spectrum. This ability would allow her to see if any warm-blooded creatures were located inside or passed recently. "Nothing lives here, or has recently.".

Ameria entered and raised her staff lighting the room.

Pegan turned in a circle taking in the room. It was not square, or round, but oval and empty except for a large obsidian pedestal near the center. Surrounding it were scattered chunks of a strange, glass like substance with a reflective luster. Each piece was twisted and contorted in gruesome shapes. Near the pedestal the cold stiff half-eaten body of a strange looking man lay undisturbed.

Ameria growled as she neared the pedestal. On it she could sense the taint left behind by the hellish creature it once contained. "Something evil lived here," she hissed.

"The demon, the one we fought on the island was kept here," Pegan said.

"Are you positive?" Glorandial asked.

Pegan's pale eyes flashed silver in the staff's light. "I can still see it."

"See what?" Filaurel quietly asked.

Pegan shuffled his way to the pedestal and placed both hands on the cold stone. His words were mesmerizing as he told of what occurred at this very spot. He spoke of the room opposite the closed door and the secret chamber and how to access it. As he finished Pegan's face distorted and twisted with pain.

"We need to leave this room, NOW!" Ameria hissed to Saress. "Nothing but evil derives from this place."

<hr />

Malvo bolted upright in his bed as an icy chill crawled up his spine. He felt the very feeling many decades ago. Only one person had the capabilities to warrant such a feeling. A creature created by the Creator to battle his father's pets. A creature destined to be the mother of his child. Sprinting from his bed to the spiraled horned goat head skull which sat in a small pentagram on the desk he fell to his knees and began to whisper. The words he spoke would grant him infinite vision of the room where the feeling derived from.

<hr />

Averie's eyes clinched tight. An unspeakable evil crept through her veins, Pegan's veins. "Leave him alone," Averie whispered, but in the still of the early morning light it sounded like a howl.

"Here we go again," Tom grumbled from the recliner.

Sarah and Jennifer sprinted down the hall to Averie's room.

Averie clutched the pulsating red diamond necklace with both hands.

Both women arrived and waited patiently beside the bed.

"I'm here, I'm here," Averie screamed as her body twisted. "Be strong, don't succumb to this heathen."

"What do we do?" Sarah yelled at Jennifer.

"Saress, watch over Pegan as you did me, protect him from this evil which floods his body," she whispered.

"Shhh," Jennifer said. "Tom's right, she is talking to someone. She is talking to Pegan and he must be fighting something very wicked."

Saress panicked for a moment not sure what to do, then she sprang into action. Darting across the room she snatched Pegan around the waist and bolted for a tall wide door on the other side of the room. Ameria was right, this room had evil intentions.

Averie's breathing quickened then her eyes shot open and she looked in all directions at once.

"What happened?" Jennifer softly asked. She could see the woman was uninjured, but highly confused as if she experienced a sudden stroke.

Averie held tight to the stone. "I, I can feel Pegan within me. I felt his fears, felt his joys." She paused to lick her dry lips. "I felt an unspeakable horror moving in to destroy him."

Jennifer bit her lip not sure what to say. What can you say to a woman who is speaking to the man she loves who is worlds away?

"You don't believe me?" Averie whispered.

"I do believe you," Jennifer said. "I'm not sure how to respond to it though."

"I do," Tom said as he leaned against the door frame. "You said an unspeakable horror moved in to kill him, did it succeed?"

Averie shook her head no. "Moments after I whispered for Saress to protect him, the evil, foreboding feeling left him. I can't explain it," she softly said. "I can still feel him though as if we are one, as if we share a single soul."

"Thank God," Tom said.

"What do you mean by that?" Jennifer asked.

"Think about it," Tom said as he entered and sat on the foot of the bed. "Averie has lost so much. Torn from her world and planted in ours. Everything she knew and understood was replaced in less than the blink of an eye and the only thing she has left is the man she loves, and he gets killed. What would that do to her. In this world one of the few things we all have in common is hope."

Malvo curled his fingers into a fist and slammed his hand against the desk. The feeling faded before he could complete the spell. Regardless, he knew now he was being sought after. Possibly for revenge.

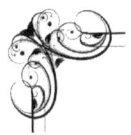

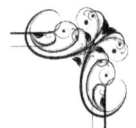

Chapter 14

 ilaurel's heart skipped a beat as he entered the enormous octagon shaped chamber whose ceiling was made of dust infused darkness. It was the largest library he had ever seen. His life, plus his children's life would pass long before Malvo's journal would be located within the thousands of shelves. If they were to succeed, a different plan would need to be devised.

Raestmond ran his hand along the multitude of tomes at eye level sending dust fleeting. Everything ever written must have originated form this room. From the floor extending well into the darkness, every shelf was burdened with tomes of different sizes. Some were impossibly thick requiring two hands to carry while others were only a few parchments. Most were bound in black leather with strange writing while the floor was barely visible beneath a thick layer of loose pages haphazardly strewn.

In the center on a dais of carved lava rock was a pedestal of bones bound by sinew. Sitting on the pedestal was a large tome opened to a page depicting weird diagrams and symbols. Beside it was an unidentifiable skull with enormous fangs and the remnants of a black candle.

Glorandial slowly spun in a circle baffled by the sheer number of tomes. She had explored the elven library on many occasions with Lady Alenia and believed it to be quite vast. This though was beyond comprehension and had no reason to exist.

"The journal isn't here," Pegan whispered. "It will be where Malvo performed his dark rituals, not where he studied."

"And where would that be?" Filaurel asked. "There are no other doors."

"I don't know," Pegan whispered.

"Let me help," Barrett said. It was obvious these thugs had no intentions of releasing him so he might as well help. Perhaps the Elf Queen would show mercy on him, but he highly doubted it. She had a reputation as a ruthless torturer, and there were rumors she had a pet which could penetrate your mind revealing your deepest thoughts. "It's one of the burnt-out lanterns, but I don't remember which. To many decades have passed since I've been down here."

Twisting, jerking, and pulling on every lantern, a subtle click was heard and one wall rumbled as a door partially opened before falling from its iron roller. Dinko and Saress aided it the remainder of the way.

Ameria poked her staff into the hallway and released a snarling growl. The stale air had a fowl, tomb-like funk and the smell of decay stung their nostrils. "The living are not welcome here," she hissed. Her heightened senses pushing her brain into overload.

"We have no other choice," Saress said. "If this is the way to the journal then our path has already been determined."

Pegan drew his daggers then waded into the darkness.

"Why does he do that?" Filaurel asked all who would listen. "His reckless actions are going to get us killed."

"Because he is driven by the love of a woman who no longer resides with us. He believes he can bring her home and will allow nothing to stand in his way, even death," Saress said as she walked past into the darkness after him.

The hallway was unusually wide and abnormally tall, as if to allow creatures not from this world easy passage. In the dim light and abysmal conditions, they lost track of time and distance while wandering aimlessly through cobwebs thick as thread. Eventually, they emerged into a chamber carved in the shape of a giant pentagram. One of the points held a large black cauldron and beside it was a wooden table holding a large tome. The second point was separated by a tattered curtain. Beyond the curtain rested the remnants of a wooden bed and straw mattress. Beside the bed built into the wall was a small door built for a child. The third point contained an enormous shelf loaded with bottles, boxes, tubes, needles, chunks of steel, a few pure gold bars, a bundle of human hair, skins hung up to dry, a large jar full of eyes, teeth lined up in a row by size and a box full of eyelids. The fourth point held a graveyard worth of bones. The last point was obviously where victims were brought for dismantling. A large bird cage hung from a rusty chain and shackles were embedded into the stone wall. On the floor were chains with iron shackles still holding tight to dried skin. Built into the wall was a shelf were a wide variety of blood-stained knives lay covered in dust. Beside the knives were pliers, saws, a large device designed to rip open the chest cavity, spoons for digging out entrails, one long rusty needle and a spool of coarse thread.

"What is this place?" Glorandial mumbled.

Pegan leaned against the wall for support. "A place where great suffering occurred.".

"Where should we begin?" Saress asked Pegan.

Pegan's vision made Barrett take a step back and reconsider his future. "Do you know its location?"

Barrett shook his head no. "I only built the room. I didn't tell him where to hide his journal."

"I guess we'll tear this room apart," Dinko hissed as he kicked over a small desk splintering it.

"No, wait," Raestmond demanded. "If it's in here and we destroy the place we may never find it. We have to do this methodically and systematically."

Dinko looked at Raestmond as if he grew a second head.

"What I mean is we need a method to our search," Raestmond explained. "We each take a section and examine every inch. If we run wild, we'll end up missing the journal believing the area was already searched." Raestmond explained in terms the lizard's brain could understand.

Engrossed in their assigned areas none noticed Barrett back away into the gloom. Once clear of the room, he bolted for freedom. Through the library he sprinted into the oval room and quietly closed the door. Not far from there a hidden alcove held a large steel wheel. When cranked, a complex transaction occurred inside the door and inch-thick hardened steel shafts expanded on all sides driving deep into the granite stone walls.

Laughing like a madman, he made his way through the darkness and fled.

Pegan finished his area then paused to look at the others to see if they were having any better luck when he realized Barrett was gone. "Where's Barrett?"

Everybody stopped in unison and looked to one another.

"That was your job to watch him," Filaurel accused Dinko.

"No," Dinko angrily hissed.

"Yes, it was." Filaurel jerked his sword free of its sheath.

"No! it wasn't," Dinko snarled, then slid his sword free.

"It was all of our jobs," Pegan said as he stepped between the two. "Saress, track him down, now."

Saress sprinted down the hall fading into the shadows.

Raestmond rubbed his chin as he overlooked the complex. Looking over each inch his vision was drawn back to a stone he examined earlier. It was near the cauldron above the desk and seemed out of place. He pressed and pulled on it earlier and it felt solid, yet here he was once again pondering this strange object.

Saress returned with a frown on her face and worry in her eyes.

Raestmond placed his palm on the stone and instead of pushing, he twisted his wrist and the stone slowly began to turn and a rattling could be heard from somewhere above. As he turned it faster, a skeleton fastened to a rusty chain lowered into view. Both of its hands were fixed together holding a small black tome. "There is your journal," he whispered.

Filaurel carefully slid the journal into a black satchel and tied the cord.

"Hopefully the journal will explain how to get out of here," Saress said. "The door to the library has been secured, effectively trapping us down here to die."

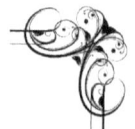

Chapter 15

p and at em' sleepy head," Sarah said as she gently nudged Averie on the shoulder.

Averie slowly opened one eye, then the other. She remembered lying down on the couch and the warmth of the electric blanket and nothing more.

"It lives," Tom chucked when he saw Averie. Her hair looked like a coughed-up fur ball and a line of dried drool marred her cheek.

Averie tried to smile but every muscle was stiff and refused to function.

Sarah was nodding her head yes as she spoke. "You really need to take a shower. You look like something the cat drug in."

Averie groaned and her joints popped as she scurried down the hall to the bathroom. She had come to enjoy the feeling of the hot water and how it soothed her muscles and aching bones.

"Oh, I forgot to tell you," Tom said as he poured another cup of coffee. "Jennifer called while you were in the shower. She is bringing over an outfit for Averie. She sounded rather excited. Did you two have something planned today you somehow neglected to tell me?"

"Wwwweeelllll," Sarah slowly said. "We were thinking of taking Averie to the mall. Baby Dayz is having a store wide clearance sale and soon we're going to need a crib and other items."

"Not sure I'd call it a mall. More like a collection of run-down stores all struggling to survive. Still, they do have Bud's Gun Shop and Hunting Supplies. Count me in.".

"Count you in?" Sarah grumbled. "We we're planning on this being a ladies' only trip. Not some male bonding moment why you both drool over the latest guns that do the exact same thing your guns do now."

"Wait a dang minute," Tom argued. "My gun collection. What about the mountain of shoes you have in the closet?"

"I wear every one of those," she argued. "When was the last time you shot one of those old relics? Or are you waiting for Mike to serve the spiders living in them eviction notices."

Tom laughed so hard he choked on his coffee. "My guns are kept pristine and oiled on a regular basis. There are no spiders living in them. And, it just so happens I have a fifteen percent off coupon for the gun shop."

Sarah took a deep breath then slowly let it out. There was no way she was going to win this fight. "Well, if you're going you might as well invite Mike. Lord knows his feelings will get hurt if he found out you went to the gun shop without him."

Tom danced his way to the phone grinning from ear to ear with his hard-earned victory.

"Men are such big babies," Sarah said as Tom relayed the good news.

Tom stuck his tongue out at Sarah in retaliation.

Mike and Jennifer arrived earlier than expected each carrying a large box. "I picked up a few odds and ends for Averie at the consignment store. The lady had a few nice items specially for expecting mothers, and they were about her size, so I picked them up. This way she can feel normal when we go out." Jennifer dropped the box on the coffee table.

"A few things," Mike argued as he imitated his back breaking. "We dang near had to rent a Hyster to load the Jeep."

Sarah chuckled hearing her brother complain. "Quit your whining, it's for a good cause. Anyway, Averie just got out of the shower. Let's go show her what you picked up?"

Less than an hour later Averie emerged from her room looking like she came from the Hollywood Walk of Fame. Strutting her stuff down the hall she wore a classy black dress with transparent sleeves and flowing ruffles. Her blonde hair hung loose yet slightly curling at the ends. On top of her head she sported a wide brimmed Black Lanzom hat which seemed to hover like a halo. The final touch was a pair of silver rimmed rose colored glasses.

"Wow, you look amazing," Tom said. "Are you sure she's going to want the kind of attention this dress is going to attract?"

"If anybody asks we'll tell them she is an old friend from Europe who came to visit, and her name is Vivian," Sarah said. "Besides, who she is, is none of anybody's business."

With all the current sales happening they knew the mall was going to be crowded, but this was ridiculous. Each time Tom stopped to look at something he was pushed along like a cow being herded out to pasture. Averie though had no problem as men shoved their wives out of the way yelling—*move it, pregnant lady coming through*—allowing her ample room to pass.

"Excuse me, pardon me, excuse me," Sarah repeated as she wiggled through the quickly closing gaps.

"Hey, watch it," a man screamed at Sarah as she bumped into him knocking the bag from his hand.

"Sorry," Sarah pleaded as she set to chase after Averie.

Averie found a spot on a raised dais where people were setting that allowed her a spectacular view of the mall. She had never seen a market of this magnitude. Sure, Icearaus had a market but it was different. There, most people had their wares which consisted of pots, pans, utensils, and other miscellaneous items laid out on the ground while the richer people had stalls where pigs and chickens hung. Here, every store was enormous, and each vendor was selling thousands of items.

"I take it you're having a good time?" Sarah asked.

Averie splayed her arms and spun like a ballerina. "I wish Pegan were here to see this."

"Hopefully some day you can explain it to him," Jennifer said.

"Shall we continue on," Sarah suggested. "We have to meet Tom and Mike at the food court in fifteen minutes."

Averie looked at each store and the items they had on display, but one captivated her attention. Floor to ceiling windows glowed faint blue and a small waterfall fed a steam that wound its way across the marble floor to a large pond which spewed a faint mist. Above the door an elegant red neon sign read Sandy's Perfume Palace. Averie looked at Sarah. "Can I go in here?"

"If you want," Sarah said. "I normally avoid it like the plague as perfume drives my sinuses into a tizzy, and the owner, Samantha, is a real cactus."

Averie's eyes opened wide. "The owner is a cactus? How is that possible?"

Jennifer laughed. "She's not a real cactus like you would find growing in the desert. It's another way to say she's rude."

Averie smiled as if she understood but they all saw through the rouge.

"Hmm," Jennifer said. "All the years I've lived here and never met her. How about I take Averie in while you run over to Twisties and get us three pretzels," Jennifer said. "No salt on mine."

"Got it," Sarah said and sprinted off through the crowd.

Once inside, Averie was mystified by the sights, smells, and sounds. Glowing shelves made of crystal held all manner of vials filled with different colored liquids. Along the walls were paintings of men and women in various stages of dress and the aroma of hypnotic fragrances flooded her senses. Meandering her way through the isles she crossed a wooden bridge and watched the gold colored fish for a few minutes before moving to a section with highly polished, hand rubbed, wooden shelves were loaded with salves and bath oils. There was one scent that attracted her more than all the rest though, and it was hers to discover.

"Hello there dear, I'm Samantha. How can I help you?"

Averie looked at the lady. She was middle-aged but carried herself quite elegantly. Dirty blonde hair accentuated her unusually narrow, yet stern face and perky nose. Around her pelican-shaped neck hung a string of captivating pearls. "I need to find that scent in the air."

"Oh, you must be smelling the Versace Bright Crystal. A customer was not in here five minutes ago spraying it." From behind the counter Samantha retrieved a classy heart shaped bottle with a crystal stopper. Contained within the glass was a pinkish fluid. "This is one of my favorites. It as a heavenly floral fragrance with a touch of fruit. Perfect for wearing on an evening out with your man." Spraying some on a thin strip of paper she handed it to Averie.

"It's wonderful," Averie said, then held it up for Jennifer to sniff.

Jennifer did all she could to keep from gagging. "I personally think it smells like Pine Sol but that's just me. I prefer Obsession myself."

"Obviously this woman has a much more refined palette," Samantha said. "Obsession is considered by most as one step up from Febreze and can often be found in the medicine cabinets of finer trailer parks."

"Now wait a damn minute," Jennifer snapped. "I happen to own the

Willowdale Live Well Clinic and am a highly educated woman so where—"

"I never said you were poor or uneducated," Samantha backtracked.

"I must have taken the trailer park wrong then?" Jennifer asked.

"Should I not get it?" Averie asked Jennifer.

Jennifer's face was beat red, and her fingers curled into clubs. "It's not for me. If you like it, get it."

Samantha grabbed a much larger box from under the counter and returned the sample bottle. "Most women of your status purchase the eight-ounce size."

Sarah wedged her way between Jennifer and Averie. "Thank you, but I'm sure the two-ounce bottle will be more than plenty." Then shoved the bottle back.

"Why don't you let her decide," Samantha growled. "She's not a child and judging from her appearance, obviously much more sophisticated."

"Samantha, you know damn well eight ounces is more than she'll ever need," Sarah snarled back. "She isn't going to bathe in it like you."

"You haven't changed a bit," Samantha hissed.

"Well if that isn't the pot calling the kettle black," Sarah snapped.

Averie trusted Sarah and Jennifer with her life. Had it not been for them she would have died by now. "I will take the smaller one," Averie said as each woman paused to take a breath. "Is this enough?" Averie reached into her purse and pulled out the two stacks of cash Tom gave her and laid them on the counter.

Samantha's eyes lit up like she stuck her finger in a light socket. "I'm sure that will cover the cost."

In a single hectic movement Sarah snatched the money with one hand while rearing back with the other. "Reach for it again and I will slap you right here in front of God and everybody."

"What in the hell is going on?" Mike asked as he entered. Close behind him Tom followed.

"What the hell is wrong with you," Jennifer screamed at Samantha.

"She tried to steal Averie's money?" Sarah explained to Mike as she stuffed the cash back in Averie's purse.

Samantha looked at Mike and knew he was the sheriff. This was the last thing she needed. "I did no such thing. I was going to count what was needed and return the rest."

"You liar." Jennifer was fuming with anger.

"Calm down," Mike said. "I'm sure it was all a misunderstanding."

Sarah looked at Samantha with her eye's squinted. "You ever—"

"Sarah, that's enough," Tom scolded her.

Sarah opened her purse and dropped a twenty on the counter. "There, that should cover it. Keep the change."

Jennifer took Averie by the hand. "Let's get out of here, this place has left a foul taste in my mouth."

Samantha watched them leave. "I'll get you for this, just you wait and see," she whispered.

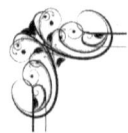 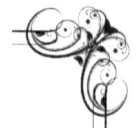

Chapter 16

 egan got tangled in the curtain ripping it from the wire where it hung. "We need to get this small door open. Inside there must be a lever or switch to open the library door."

"We've already tried, it won't budge," Glorandial informed Pegan.

Saress latched onto the small knob then propped her foot against the wall and heaved releasing a deep grunt. The sound of metal snapping echoed in the stagnant environment as the handle broke free. From the inside, the faint ping sound followed as the inside knob hit the stone floor then rolled around.

Raestmond studied the wooden obstacle. He had built hundreds of doors, but this one struck him as odd—it had no hinges. "We're going about this wrong," he said. Sticking his finger inside the hole he felt for the latching mechanism but there was none. Next, he traced the edge of the door until he found a chiseled groove in the stone the exact size of the knob. "It's a pocket door," he whispered.

"A pocket what?" Pegan asked.

"The door slides into the wall," Raestmond said. Sticking his fingers in the knob hole he struggled to move the door an inch.

"Allow me," Dinko said, then dug his claws into the wood and tore it open in one angry swipe of his arm.

The doorway was too small for the reptiles, so Ameria poked her staff inside lighting the way for Pegan. Raestmond followed close behind.

A small bed made of straw was in one corner, and beside it was a rustic table thick with melted wax. On the walls were tattered tapestries, the images they once held would forever remain a secret. In another corner was a hole in the floor surrounded by a knee-high wall of stone. On the wall sat a wooden bucket fastened to a length of thin rope. Pegan lowered the bucket until he heard the splash, then raised it. The water was crystal clear and tasted good on his dry throat.

Glorandial and Filaurel entered to help with the search but no levers, switches, or mechanisms were discovered which would unbolt the library door.

Back at the library Raestmond grabbed a parchment and slid it between the gap in the door and the framework. Sliding it up and down he marked where each bolt was located. There was twenty in all—six on either side and four on top and bottom.

"How long will your staff glow?" Pegan asked Ameria.

Ameria cocked her head sideways, unsure of the question.

"It will glow as long as she wishes. It has no fuel source," Dinko answered for his sister.

"And we have water, there is a well in that smaller room," Pegan said.

"Eventually we're going to run out of food," Filaurel advised them as he sat his satchel down.

Raestmond all but got leveled as Dinko bolted past throwing himself against the door. They all felt the bone-crunching impact as the big lizard stumbled back, then fell to his knees shaking the stars from his brain.

"The door is indestructible," Raestmond advised Dinko. "It's built the same as a strong box. Steel plates riveted together then encased in an outer layer of wood for appearance. You would have to destroy this entire Keep to level it."

Dinko pulled his sword free and attacked the inanimate object, effectively destroying his weapon. Frustrated, he walked some distance away then turned and threw the mangled piece of steel at the door. "There must be a way," he hissed.

Ameria grabbed Dinko by the shoulders. "Stop that. All your doing is making a ruckus."

Glorandial had a look of defeat on her face. "It was secured after Barrett escaped, so we know the mechanism resides on the other side."

"If our paths ever cross again…" Dinko allowed his angry hiss to fade away.

Filaurel patted the big lizard on the shoulder. "This time I'll hold him down, not your sister."

Pegan paced the room. "This don't make sense. Why would Malvo build a chamber designed to imprison himself?"

Raestmond sat with his back against the door. "Malvo didn't order its construction, Karayan did."

Filaurel rubbed his forehead. "This was built to hold Malvo as a prisoner."

Raestmond looked at Pegan. "Barrett knew the location of the mechanism to secure the door. He was only biding his time waiting for the chance to escape. Once we provided that opportunity by focusing on the journal, he did exactly that. Now, were the prisoner, not Malvo."

"It can't end like this," Pegan whispered. "There has to be a way."

Filaurel wiped the dripping sweat from his chin. "Unless you have some unforeseen magic to portal us free of this place, over the next few days we're going to get a lot skinnier."

Pegan looked around the library, and then at his companions. On their faces they each bore a look of disgust, and their eyes dripped with defeat. "Malvo escaped, and we will also!"

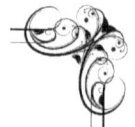

Chapter 17

iny placed the gold coin on its edge then flicked it with his finger. Glinting as it wobbled like an out of round tire it came to rest lying flat. Picking up the abnormally heavy coin, he repeated the process multiple times as the smelting pot heated up.

Sheba snatched the coin as it wobbled and examined it under the magnifying glass. "I think we should wait?"

"Wait for what?" Tiny asked. "It's useless as it is. When we combine them both into one large nugget, we'll double our money."

Sheba flipped the coin over and on the backside under the stamped impression of a man's face were the numbers *YAK 16*. "Wonder what *YAK 16* means. Do you think these coins were stamped in the sixteenth year?"

"Before Christ, or after?" Tiny answered with a question of his own.

Sheba took a drag off the joint and handed it to Tiny to kill off. "I'm serious here. What if this coin is damn near two-thousand years old?"

"What do you want to do then?" Tiny asked.

"What about that guy over at the college. Occasionally he's on TV. I can't remember his name, but he is supposed to work with old relics and crap like that. Let's go see him. Perhaps he can enlighten us on these coins."

Tiny unplugged the smelting pot. "I think we're wasting our time, but if it takes someone with a fancy degree to tell you the coins aren't worth crap unless there melted down, then so be it."

That evening as class was getting dismissed the old beater pulled into the Frankfort University parking lot rattling like a tin can full of marbles. The noxious smoke trail obscured the vision of those who watched and stung the eyes of those to close. Students and faculty alike scattered as the two heathens climbed from the rusty hulk and made their way towards the red brick building.

"May I help you?" A security guard wearing an overly starched baby blue uniform asked as he stopped them at the sidewalk. He was the only one brave enough to approach the pair, probably because he had a firearm on his hip.

"Um… yes. I'm Tiny, and this is my wife, Sheba," Tiny said as he read the security guard's name tag before continuing. "Mr. Shriver, if possible, we would like to see the man who teaches the class dealing with metals."

Mr. Shriver sneered as his eyes did a cursory search of them looking for weapons. He knew they each probably had something illegal, but without undeniable proof, he couldn't prevent them from entering the facility. "The welding class is around back in a sheet metal building. You can't miss it."

Tiny looked in all directions making sure nobody was within earshot. "Not welding. We need the man who can tell us if the gold coins we received at our pawnshop are real."

"You want Mr. Middleton then, the metallurgist?"

"I guess," Sheba answered. "Is he the one who can tell how old the coins are as well?"

"I'm not sure if he could tell you that, he's not a coin expert."

Sheba sighed. "But he can tell us if their real coins, not fake?"

"Most certainly," Mr. Shriver answered. "Mr. Middleton is a world-class metallurgist whose done extensive work for NASA. He's the one who discovered the metal composition that allows spacecraft to withstand the sun's devastating effects while in orbit and not burn up on reentry. He's also been on countless television shows and documentaries about rare metals. I know he has done more, something in the medical field as well but this is all I can remember. Did you have an appointment scheduled?"

"No," Tiny answered. "We received the coins a few days ago and instead of melting them down for the gold, we decided they may be rarer than we first thought and wish to have an expert in the field examine them."

"He's a busy man and normally won't see visitors unless they have a scheduled appointment. But since you're here let's see if he's willing to work with you. Follow me."

Entering the school through a secluded side door, they followed Mr. Shriver down a narrow hall lined with doors on either side. Tiny wiped the sweat from his chin as his mind raced back to his time at San Quintin. Halfway down the hall they turned down a much wider hall lined with lockers before climbing a series of faux marble stairs. Winding their way through a maze of more hallways and corridors they stopped at a pair of wooden double doors with frosted glass. On it was etched—Room 108 Metallurgy Prof. Frank Middleton. Tapping on the glass with his knuckle, Mr. Shriver stepped back and waited.

"Come in," Mr. Middleton announced.

"Wait out here," Mr. Shriver told them. "Let me see if he's available."

"Mr. Shriver," the professor said with a smile. "Fancy seeing you here. Considering giving up your job in security and taking a few classes."

Mr. Shriver blushed apple red. "No sir. I am leaving though. Starting on Monday, I'm taking a new job."

"Really," Mr. Middleton said. "Where at?"

"The DMV, state job, better retirement and benefits. With my wife just having our second child insurance costs are killing me?"

"Well good for you," Mr. Middleton said as he rose from his swivel chair and took Mr. Shriver's hand with a firm grasp. "You've done a hell of a job here and I'm sure you'll do even better there. In fact, I'm going to talk to your boss and see if we can't get you a leaving bonus for your excellent work. By the way, what can I do for you?"

"I have a couple waiting outside who wishes to talk with you about a few rare coins…" then proceeded to tell him what he knew.

"Interesting," Mr. Middleton said. "We'll show them in and let's get this over with."

Mr. Middleton cringed as the pair entered. He could all but taste the heavy scent of marijuana. The last thing he wanted to do was deal with some druggies trying to pawn off a few fake coins to buy their next high. He considered asking them to leave, but he did tell Mr. Shriver he would see them and decided to hold up his end of the bargain. "Can I help you?"

"I hope so," Sheba said. "We need some advice. I received two pure gold coins at the pawnshop I own. What I am trying to figure out is how old they are and their value?"

"I hate to tell you this," Mr. Middleton said as he leaned against his desk. "There is no such thing as a pure gold coin. Gold is too soft and must be combined with other metals to keep its shape."

"We were scammed?" Tiny grumbled. "I knew those two guys were up to no good."

A strange feeling deep inside told Sheba there were more to these coins than what meets the eye. "Can you take a look at them at least? Maybe we won't lose too much. I can pay you for your services."

Mr. Middleton took a deep breath and slowly released it. He had no desire to work with these street thugs, but if telling them the coins were fake and they got scammed would get them to leave peacefully, he was all for it. "Sure, why not. I have a few minutes."

Sheba removed the coins from her purse and placed them on the desk. The resounding thud told them all they were heavier than what they appeared.

Mr. Middleton slid on his frameless spectacles and picked up one coin and held it to the light. On it he could see the name Karayan and the lettering *YAK 16*. He had heard that name before but couldn't place where. The second coin was duller in color meaning it was probably older, and the *YAK* number read *3*.

From a desk drawer, Mr. Middleton removed a small pointed device and poked one coin, then the other but the device refused the penetrate, or even mare the surface. Placing one coin on the electronic scale followed by the other, both weights were precisely the same down to the thousandth. "Mind if I scratch off a smidgen? It's the only true way to determine the composition."

"That's fine," Sheba said. "By the way, any idea what the *YAK* number means?"

The professor scratched his wrinkled forehead as he thought. "I'm not a hundred percent positive but I think these coins are old, really old. Probably thousands of years old. I have never seen one, but it is believed that before kings understood dates, they stamped coins with how long they have been in power. If I had to take a guess, I would say the YAK stands for Years as King." He held up one coin. "This coin would have been minted in his third year as king and probably the more valuable of the pair."

Sheba's chin nearly bounced off the floor.

Mr. Middleton removed a small file from his drawer and fought like hell with the coins failing to remove a single flake of gold dust. "I'm going to have to put these on the scope to get a better analysis, follow me." He cared little now for the people who brought in the rare coins. All he wanted to know was their true identity and how they came to be within their possession. Extremely rare items like these were not handed off at pawnshops but put on display at the Smithsonian.

The room next door held an enormous, futuristic-looking machine. Covered with knobs, gadgets, and levers, it would take a degree to figure out how it operated. Flipping a few switches, the two computer screens roared to life and the light under the translucent glass was so bright it nearly blinded them. Placing both coins on the glass, he adjusted a massive crank and the entire top of the machine lowered until it was less than a hairs width away from the coins. Afterward, he messed with a different series of dials, adjusted this lever, flipped a long-knobbed switched, and then cranked a small wheel which brought the image into focus. Looking through another device which resembled divers goggles the image was magnified even greater. With one hand he continually adjusted the machine while his other worked feverishly writing down everything he saw. When he finished and removed the goggles, his face was deathly pale. "Where did you get these at?" Mr. Middleton sounded like a father scolding his son who was caught looking at pornography.

Tiny looked agitated. "I already said how we acquired them.".

Mr. Middleton wiped the sweat from his upper lip. "Somehow I don't believe you. These coins are extremely rare."

"What do you mean?" Sheba asked.

"The coins are made up of gold, that you already know. What you don't know is the metal which gives it it's strength doesn't exist."

"Say what?" Tiny asked. "Your million-dollar machine must be broken."

"The machine is fine," Mr. Middleton assured him. "The molecular structure of the infused materials are not something found on this planet, or any meteorite as far as I know. I believe the metal is beyond the far reaches of the Milky Way Galaxy."

Sheba smiled. "If I were to sell them, would a hundred K be asking too much?"

"If they were my coins, I would never sell them as they're irreplaceable. If I had to though, I would ask a hundred times that amount."

Sheba carefully placed the coins back in her purse. "Thank you for your time professor."

"I sure wish you had the name of the guys who sold them to you. I would like to know where they acquired them?"

"Unfortunately, we can't divulge that information," Tiny said. In his eye, he held a glint of sarcasm.

Mr. Middleton watched them both leave.

"Are they real?" Mr. Shriver asked.

"Not only are they real, there extremely rare and very valuable. Excuse me if you don't mind. I have a phone call to make."

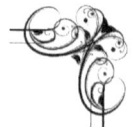

Chapter 18

he woman's work was worth twice what he paid. Word spread at an alarming rate reaching every ear from Lynn Brook to East Haven; as far north as Timber Hall and west to Talons Peak. Karayan's servants would have certainly heard the false rumors and from different source making it all-that-much more believable. All he had to do now was wait for the cover of darkness too set the wheels turning.

Sitting on the basin of a large water fountain in the palace garden, Vexacion's vision jumped from balcony to balcony until arriving at the largest and highest built into the polished smooth stone. It would be here he planned to make his intrusion as the doorway led directly into Karayan's private bedchamber.

The light of day would have significantly reduced the chance of falling to his death, but the risk of detection was too great. He had to get in unseen and unheard. As the sun kissed the peaks of the Silver Mountains painting the sky the color of rich marmalade, he slipped on gloves embedded with curved hooks and set out. Sprinting across the palace garden's he blended in to the shadows of a bushy tree near the palace wall. He would need every minute to reach the first of many balconies before morning.

As night fell, Vexacion crept from beneath a bushy tree and darted across the narrow clearing undetected to the eastern wall. Vines thick as his wrist clung to the stone growing into the mortar. Testing a few he determined they would support his weight and began his ascent. Higher and higher he climbed until the ground was lost in darkness and the vines thinned and broke away leaving him clinging to the smooth stone. From here he would have no choice but to scale the wall.

Slowly moving horizontal, he was meticulous with his calculations always knowing where he planned to grab next by looking for the tiniest of ridges made during the tower's construction, or cracks from where the mortar had failed. Falling from this height would not bode well for his health so he quickly devised an alternative route if something went wrong.

Using the moonlight to guide his direction he heaved his way upward inches at a time. The higher he went, the harder the wind blew. A few times he was left dangling by one hand as a gust rocked his body. Struggling to regain his grip, he flattened himself against the stone until the wind subsided. To try and do anything else was foolish.

Hours crept passed, and every inch of his muscular body was covered in sweat. Both arms were numb from exhaustion and his toes were on the verge of breaking. Glancing about, his destination was less than fifty feet above him.

Grimacing in pain, he forced his body to continue until he was close enough to grab the railing and pull himself onto the balcony. With his back against the wall he slid to a sitting position enjoying the much-needed rest. From the ground where he began to here, it was much higher than first anticipated. Forcing himself to continue before he was ready, he unwrapped a thin rope from around his waist and attached a small three-pronged hook.

He would need to hurry as the moon was nearing its apex. If he waited too long, morning would arrive leaving him exposed and vulnerable. Swinging the hook by the rope, he let it sail and watched it wrap around the railing of the next balcony. Testing its hold, he scurried to the next balcony. The process repeated itself until he arrived at Karayan's doorway.

Vexacion initially planned to arrive before Karayan and use the time to recover his strength, but this was not to be. Karayan was already there sitting at his desk feverishly working a quill drawing large sweeping arcs across a map of Icearaus. Dressed in a robe it was obvious Karayan was not expecting company. His obsidian-colored armor rested on its rack and his two-handed sword hung on the wall.

Quietly testing the knob on the glass door, he discovered it was locked—a mere inconvenience for a man of his skill. From a deep pocket in his trousers he removed a small pouch and dumped out the tools in his hand. Selecting the perfect combination, he feed them into the keyhole and slowly twisted watching the lever on the other side turn until it clicked open.

Returning the tools to the pouch, he waited until the wind was nonexistent then slipped inside undetected and melded in with the shadows of the four-post bed.

Karayan tapped a section of the map. "I have to get the rock giants and cave trolls to swear their allegiance to me," he mumbled.

Vexacion stepped from the shadows. "My King," he said, then performed a gracious bow.

Karayan leaped to his feet knocking over the chair. Instinctively, he reached for his sword but found himself weaponless. "Vexacion," he forcefully said. "How did you get…" he let his words trail off as he spotted the partially open door. "Should you not be attending matters elsewhere than inside my bedchamber?"

Vexacion leaned against the bedpost and picked something from his teeth. "I am here because I couldn't take a chance of the information which crossed my ears going astray."

"And this information could not wait until more favorable conditions? Such as in my throne room during the light of day. Not minutes before I planned on sleeping."

"If I waited until morning, you may not be alive to hear what I have to say." Vexacion covered the distance across the room at break-neck speed to stand inches from Karayan. "It seems one of your men, possibly more, are planning your assassination," he whispered.

Karayan laughed. "My men are loyal to the death. None of them would ever contemplate what you propose."

"Therein lies the issue. You trust those who should not be trusted. The Royal Guards know the truth. Your veil of power has been stripped. No longer are you indestructible. Given enough time, one, or more will strike you down and take your place."

Karayan cocked his head sideways. "And you know this, how?"

"The brotherhood has eyes and ears everywhere. We see the unseen and hear the unheard. Whispers in the night speak of you as weak, vulnerable, no longer fit to lead Icearaus. Men who visit the tavern and filled with liquid courage laugh at how you were defeated by a mere child, a female child none the less."

"Why should I believe you? Perhaps you're here to strike me down. To advance your position from the Lord of the Brotherhood to the King of Icearaus."

"If what you say is true, we would not be having this conversation." Vexacion adjusted his cloak revealing a row of deadly weapons. "By now, your corpse would have been tossed over the railing and a servant cleaning up the blood."

Karayan paced the length of the room. He knew Vexacion was correct. He had heard similar reports from his servants. Weeks earlier he would have destroyed all those who spoke such blasphemy. Now, he had no choice but to ignore the rumors. Any injury, even a simple scrape, cut, or puncture could lead to infection and his eventual death. Each move he made now was calculated by the risk of injury. He had to be alive when the bearer's child returned so it could be sacrificed to the Dark Master and have his power restored. "Why would the brotherhood be concerned with my death? What do you want in return?"

Vexacion returned to the balcony and watched the lights of Lynn Brook twinkle. When he turned back to Karayan his voice was cold, remorseless. "As Lord of the Brotherhood I have taken a key interest in your survival for one reason, the survival of the brotherhood. If you were to be assassinated, none of us know if your replacement will agree with the brotherhood and implement change, changes we can't allow to come to fruition. Therefore, by offering you aid in your time of need, the favor will be returned ten-fold once the child is destroyed and your power restored."

Karayan smiled. "You plan to destroy those who would challenge me?"

Vexacion knew the rumors the woman started had reached all the right ears. Karayan was thick with fear and was ripe for the plucking. "I could, tonight if I chose but this won't solve your problem. Others will step up to fill the shoes of those I kill and challenge you. You must be the one to make a statement. You must be the one to destroy those who challenge you. If I destroy those who would challenge your rule, it only confirms the rumors you are weak."

"How do I know which of the Royal Guards are questioning my rule?"

"You don't. Therefore, they all must die."

"And how would you suggest I kill fifty of the best swordsman to grace Icearaus?"

Vexacion flashed Karayan a half-crooked smile, and his eyes narrowed. The victory was his for the taking. "Sit, and allow me to explain."

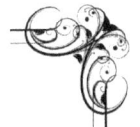

Chapter 19

ave leaned back in his chair and rubbed his tired eyes until he saw spots. Normally, his lab coat was pressed to perfection, black shoes polished to a high shine, and his face perfectly shaven. Tonight, his lab coat had more wrinkles than a pug, his shoes weren't even on his feet and his five o'clock shadow started yesterday.

In front of him was a bank of computer monitors six wide and four high. Most were dark except for a thin green line which ran horizontal across the screen. Occasionally a small spike would occur then it quickly returned to a flat line. Two computers though shared the same image of a distant galaxy in an array of dazzling colors.

Sandy watched Dave from the doorway fully expecting the man to tumble over backwards any moment and die right on the spot. Over the last few days he'd been working on something he wouldn't discuss and neglecting his sleep, which was beginning to rear its ugly head. "Why don't you go home and get some rest? You look terrible," she said. The clack of her heals against the concrete floor echoed against the bare walls.

"I wish I could." Dave closed his eyes then scrubbed his forehead.

"If you're going to stay, at least tell me what you're working on. I'm your partner for God's sake. Remember, me and you against the world when I first started."

Dave looked at the computer screens. More importantly the strange blip which kept repeating itself. "I'm going to tell you something very few know. Those of us who do are forbidden to talk about it or risk prosecution."

Sandy sat down in the chair beside him and focused her attention on every word he said.

"Long before I started working here a strange phenomenon occurred. Those who worked here at the time didn't understand its significance and failed to investigate. It's not totally their fault as they didn't have the technology we do today. By the time it was over eleven good men lost their lives, including the man who mentored me."

"What happened?" Sandy asked.

"Aliens," Dave boldly said. "A mother and a child."

Sandy rolled her eyes and released a laugh. "You don't honestly expect me to believe that, do you?"

Dave's face lacked any sense of amusement.

Sandy leaned back in the chair and looked at the ceiling. On it, someone had painted a beautiful mural of the Milky Way. "Dave, I'm your partner and have been for ten years now. Tell me the truth, what really happened. What is the agency trying to hide?"

Dave focused on the blip once more ignoring Sandy.

Sandy rose and went to the coffee maker and poured two cups and brought one to Dave. "Here, I think you need this. I made it exactly how you like it. Loaded with creamer until it looks like milk and heavy with sugar."

"Thank you kindly." Dave eagerly accepted the cup. "Liquid energy to keep me going for another eight hours while I try and trace this down."

Sandy repositioned herself in the chair and removed her dark-rimmed glasses then ran her fingers through her mud colored hair. "You're serious about this?"

"Sandy," Dave said, his eyes were dark and desperate. "Let me fill you in on something I have not told another person, not even my mother and I tell her everything. Not long ago the computers picked up an anomaly entering our galaxy—"

"It could be anything," Sandy interrupted. "Sound waves, thermal blast from a failed star, galaxies colliding, even solar wind. There are a number of things that will throw the computer into a fit."

"Please, let me finish," Dave said lifting his hand. "This anomaly was not a sound wave, blast of energy or solar wind. It was a disruption of space and time. Something solid entered our galaxy."

"And?" Sandy asked showing a bit more interest. "Perhaps it was a meteorite?"

"Here, watch this," Dave said as he pointed at the computer screen. "The computer traced the trajectory of the object as it crossed the Milky Way in less than a tenth of a second."

"Impossible," Sandy exclaimed. "Even at the speed of light it would take six hundred years to cover that distance." Sandy examined the computer screen.

Dave wiped the sweat from his forehead. "If that has you baffled, here's what's really going to bake your noodle. I was able to trace its place of origin by the trajectory, it came from here." Dave pointed at the screen showing a distant galaxy.

Sandy's mouth opened wide. "The Constellation Draco?".

"Yes, but more precisely this Tadpole Galaxy."

"Your joking, right?" Sandy asked. "That galaxy is four hundred and twenty million light years from earth."

Ring, ring… the phone leaked out a scream.

Dave looked at the phone. "Here we go again, another one calling wanting to know something about Area 51, or who knows what. You want to hear it as well? We can both have a good laugh afterward," Dave asked Sandy as he hit the speaker button. "Center for the Investigation and Research for Extraterrestrial Intelligence. Dave speaking, how may I help you?"

"Dave, Dave Nelson?" The voice flowed from the speaker.

"Possibly," Dave laughed. "All depends on how much money I owe."

"Thank God. I've been trying to get ahold of someone for the last hour who knows what in the hell is going on."

"So why the hell did you call me?"

Sandy covered her mouth to keep from being heard laughing.

"Originally, I was looking for Loren Sparks, but was told he retired a few years back and you took his place. I was hoping I could get his number if you have it? I have a few questions for him."

"I did know Loren and worked under his guidance for a few years before his departure. He was a brilliant scientist whose discovers changed how we view the world. Unfortunately, I don't have his number. Is there anything I can help you with, Mr…?"

"Middleton, Frank Middleton, professor of Metallurgy at the University of Frankfort."

Dave's face drained of color. "Mr. Middleton. Loren spoke highly of you."

"Thank you," Frank responded. "I have a few questions then for you. Hopefully you can help me out. Before his retirement, did Loren ever mention the name Karayan?"

Dave nearly dropped the phone.

"Hello, hello," Frank said as the phone went quiet.

"Mr. Middleton," Dave said. "I know you and Loren were very close, almost like brothers from the way he talked, so I think it's only right you know the truth. Loren never retired. He took his own life."

Sandy's jaw nearly bounced off the desk. In all her years working there she never knew.

"Bull," Frank snapped. "He would never do such a stupid thing. Something went seriously wrong and the government is hiding something—"

"Mr. Middleton," Dave stopped him. "He isn't the only one. Every person associated with the Karayan incident has now died, and in similar ways. They each complained of voices in their heads and became increasingly psychotic. Eventually, they put a gun to their heads and pulled the trigger. Loren though was slightly different. He mumbled crazy things about wanting to save the world and destroyed everything he had on the computer, the hard drive, and shredded his paperwork."

"Why didn't he ask for help. I would have done anything for him?" Frank asked.

"Only he knows the answer to that question, and he took it to his grave. With that said I have a few questions for you." Dave adjusted his position in the chair. "The name Karayan has never been spoken outside these walls and all evidence of it has been destroyed. How did it come to reach your ears?"

Frank took a breath and slowly let it out. "When I was a young man, I made a monumental discovery and Science Today did an article labeling me as the greatest metallurgist of our generation. Decades after that article was printed Loren approached me with a small knife believing it was from beyond the stars. At first, I thought he was crazy but after doing numerous experiments I believed he was right. I asked him where he got it, but he would never tell me. One night after a few shots of tequila he let it slip that he received the knife from a boy named Karayan, even showed me a picture of him and his mother. They looked normal yet had the brightest golden eyes I had ever saw. Damn near bore clear through into your soul."

"That was a long time ago, why are you bringing this up?" Dave asked. "Why the sudden interest today?"

"Because I had two people show up in my classroom earlier wanting me to identify two gold coins. They both had similar properties to the knife, and each had the name Karayan clearly stamped on them. I wanted to find out if he knew anything about the coins and if these people stole them? Knowing now about his death, perhaps these two were involved."

"I can tell you without a doubt the boy didn't have any coins and shortly after they were brought to the research center, the boy vanished without a trace. The mother died months later but not before saying her son went home to a world called Icearaus."

Frank rubbed his chin. "All I know is there are a lot of unanswered questions bouncing around inside my head right now. Questions I want answers to."

"You and me both," Dave said, then turned off the speaker. "You and me both."

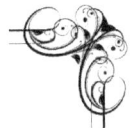

Chapter 20

 s dawn broke, the sun burned bloody red, and the air was thick and heavy. The usual sounds of birds chirping, and dogs barking were nonexistent as if they knew what lie ahead. On the foyer to the throne room fifty men waited. Each dressed in armor polished to an impeccable shine, each sporting a purple plume from the helmet.

Karayan smiled with delight. He was not sure how the assassin had accomplished such a complicated task in such short order, yet here stood every one of his most trusted men—those who would be willing to lay down their life for him. Now, the only thing left was for him to cause a delay to allow enough time for the piping to be installed.

Karayan swung wide the double doors allowing the light to flood the room. "Welcome Gentlemen," Karayan said. "I'm delighted to see you all could make it on such short notice."

A few of the guards looked at each other with suspicion. Through-out their careers they had yet to see Karayan be this nice.

Greeting each one by name he had a scribe mark off each name on the attendance sheet. He had to be proof positive every Royal Guardsmen where here. As the last one entered he thanked the scribe for his work then closed the door. Waiting there for a few minutes, he collected his thoughts as the Royal Guards fell into rank and file.

Karayan was stealthy quiet as he made his way to the dais. Taking up a position beside his throne he leaned against the backrest. "Most of you are wondering why I have summoned you here on such short notice."

A few men nodded.

Karayan eyed those men who nodded wondering if they were the ones responsible for the rumors. The ones spreading talk of Karayan suddenly vanishing without a trace. "I have brought you here because no longer can the truth be denied. The bearer has escaped and has moved on to her new world. Even though she lives she is dead to us. No longer can we deny the facts and therefore we must plan for future events and what must occur once the child returns."

"Karayan, Karayan…" the men cheered his name.

From where he stood Karayan could see the cracks in the double doors being filled with a foam substance designed to seal any air from escaping. Pacing the length of the dais he folded his arms behind his back and lowered his head as if lost in thought. "Unfortunately, we cannot begin the process of rebuilding the future until we address the past. The only way to do this properly is to make the past so painful it is never forgotten by the future."

The men looked at each other not sure where Karayan was going with this.

Karayan summoned for his servant to bring him a drink. He was not thirsty but needed to buy more time. A few minutes later the scantily dressed woman returned holding a crystal glass and a bottle of dark liquid. Handing him the glass, she slowly poured out the contents of the bottle careful not to spill a drop. When the glass was full she backed away then quickly went to the corner and waited for further instructions.

Karayan sipped on the glass of wine as he looked over his troops.

When the glass ran dry he held it straight out then released it watching it tumble until it hit the stone floor and shattered. His demeanor suddenly changed, and he grew viciously angry. A fit of anger fueled by the thought of having his immortality stripped away in a single breath—driven by the idea Lilith betrayed him—intensified by the thought of how Pegan aided the bearer to escape. Making his way to the front of the dais he addressed his men once more.

"It is I who must first accept failure for her escape, which I have come to terms with because I am only one man. What I cannot come to terms with is the fact that you have failed me, because you are fifty strong. Bring me the bearer was all I asked. A task which seemed simple enough, yet not one of you could complete. Instead, you allowed one of your own to be bought out with a few coins and allow her to walk right out the portcullis never to be seen again."

"My King," a Royal Guard said. "The man responsible for that treasonous act suffered greatly for his blunder and has long since perished."

The fluttering of a tapestry caught Karayan's eye which only mean one thing. The steel tube was being inserted into the wall. Any moment now he expected to receive the signal the device was ready, and he would have to take his leave.

"Yes, he has," Karayan agreed. "But his bloodline lives on and in it flows deception."

"My King," a Royal Guard pleaded. "I am not responsible for my brother's actions. His disgrace of our family name has surely been enough punishment."

Karayan eyed the man suspiciously. "If I'm not mistaken, you're his elder?"

"Only by one year.".

"And as his elder are you not responsible for teaching him right from wrong?"

"My King—" he started to plead but stopped when a second servant entered.

"King Karayan," she said then approached and whispered into his ear.

Karayan slapped the woman knocking her to the ground. "Why did you wait to inform me of this matter."

Little to the servant's knowledge, she was the signal and the message was a lie only known by him and the man who waited outside. "I must attend to this matter immediately," Karayan said. "I will leave it up to your fellow guardsman if you should face punishment for your brother's action. Upon my return if no decision has been made on your behalf, then I will decide." Karayan bolted out the back door taking his two servants with him. Not that he cared if they died, he had no desire to train their replacements. Securing the door with multiple locks he was positive it would hold from the pounding he knew it was about to receive.

Birthright

Karayan sprinted outside to where the large wagon waited. In the back was an iron drum with three enormous pipes sprouting at different angles. The first pipe was short and came out of its side. The second pipe looked more like a chimney except it had a valve about a foot up from the drum and was topped with a pointed roof to prevent water from entering if it rained. The third pipe contained a large valve where it joined the building. Near the wagon stood a shriveled up old man, his toothless grin stretched from ear to ear. "I see Vexacion delivered on his promise."

The old man looked confused by what Karayan said. "I've been set up and ready for two days. All I had to do was install the flue pipe."

Karayan looked at the contraption. "How does this work?"

"It's like a regular stove, except for a few modifications to keep those nearby safe," the old man said. "You load the wood in here through this door and the straight pipe allows air to enter through a one-way valve. The pipe with the roof works like a regular chimney while you get the fire burning. Once you are ready to add the ingredients you close the valve on the chimney and open the other valve allowing the noxious fumes to enter the chamber."

Karayan wanted to slap the old man. "I understand that. How does it KILL!"

"Oh," the man laughed. "Once you have a bed of glowing coals you drop in these chunks of Bitumen and Sulfate Crystals through this tiny door. The fumes created are highly poisonous and cause blood vessels to burst while preventing the lungs from functioning."

Karayan nodded his approval. "Let's not tarry any longer."

The old man motioned for his two associates to begin. Quickly they loaded the drum with dried wood then doused the contents with lantern oil. Tossing in a burning torch the door was closed and almost immediately black smoke rolled from the chimney. It only took minutes before a glowing bed of coals formed.

Satisfied the drum was ready, the old man removed a small pouch containing the toxic ingredients. Motioning for his two associates to take their places at each valve, he opened the small lid and was about to dump in the components when Karayan stopped him. "Wait. I want to open the valve to the chamber." Shoving the guy out of the way Karayan gripped the valve.

With everything ready, the old man dumped in the entire contents and quickly closed the lid. As the chimney valve closed, Karayan opened the other.

Within seconds pounding was heard on the double doors followed by screams of terror. Hoarse coughing and gasping drowned out the sound of metal slapping against wood as they tried to chop their way free. The crashing and clanging of steel armor hitting stone soon erupted and then there was a deathly silence only found in a tomb.

Across the way high up in a tree Vexacion watched. With this complete Karayan would be utterly alone when Lord Necrosyse felt the time was right to destroy him. Releasing a laugh, he slithered down to begin his next objective.

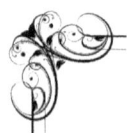
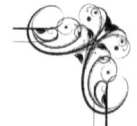

Chapter 21

lwrick was not sure how long it had been since his meeting with Pegan. His mind was still trying to fathom how Pegan transferred part of his soul, and Averie's into a stone constructed to hold one, and what kind of immense power that took. He knew Pegan didn't create the soul stone as it was discovered in Ti'ath amongst a pile of bones. The same bones that kept Windsong, the magical bow he gave to Saress hidden for decades. "How is it possible," he whispered to himself, trying to understand how Pegan accomplished the impossible. The most powerful creature he knew, Lich Queen Vhathialox, didn't have the power to combine two souls effectively making them one person.

Elwrick left his home following a dirt path that followed a slow flowing stream. The weather was beautiful, the air warm, and the sky was an endless sea of turquoise. A slight breeze carried a refreshing sweetness like honey and made the densely leafed trees dance. In the distance, enormous white-topped mountains ringed the valley of his home except to the south where he caught a faint glimpse of the shimmering surface of Lake Evermore.

At a pace no faster than a snail, he strolled through his gardens. Awe inspiring flowers of magnificent proportions and every color imaginable bloomed. Hours passed, and he had yet to come to an end because there was no end. The entire Realm of Light belonged to him, and it was all a garden with flowing streams and gorgeous waterfalls, ponds and streams, and grassy knolls.

Following the trail, it climbed sharply then traced the edge of a steep drop-off. As it snaked its way higher and higher his mind wandered, wondering what to ask when he reached his destination, the Alter of Knowledge. Should he ask about Pegan and the stone? Perhaps understanding Pegan will help him understand the prophecy. "No," he mumbled as he watched a deer leap past. It too was made like him, a creature of light and designed to bring a bit of normalcy to his existence.

Passing a small pond filled with silver fish he considered his options again. If he asked about the prophecy, the answer may reveal insight into both questions plaguing his mind.

As night fell and the sky filled with magical lights the trail guided him to a stone mound with an altar that resonated a faint silver hue. Made of perfectly pure marble not one flaw was visible. It was flat on the top while the corners were carved to resemble twisted pillars. Between the pillars carved into the stone were kneeling winged angels with their heads bowed. On the ground before the altar was a spot worn smooth from previous uses.

Falling to his knees he closed his eyes and placed both hands on the altar becoming one with the stone. His entire body felt as if it was being pulled in a thousand different directions and lights brighter than the sun flooded his mind. Screaming in pain he considered the option to return but it was too late. Once the process started, he was beyond the state of return. Only the Arch Angel Raphael, the angel of knowledge could send him home.

Elwrick found himself standing in a room without walls, a floor or a ceiling. In every direction he looked all he saw was pure darkness except for directly in front of him. A tall ornate golden candleholder floated in the darkness and on it burned seven silver candles. He had been here before and knew it was not the afterlife, but a realm somewhere in-between where angels and those from the mortal realm could interact. Dropping to his knees before the candleholder he folded his arms across his chest and focused on one of the single flames. *"Is the prophecy of damnation being fulfilled?"* he asked.

He didn't need to physically speak the words as angels were capable of reading minds and already knew the question he was going to ask. Still, before they would consider answering, he had to mentally ask it.

Elwrick trembled with fear when he felt a warm hand on his back. It was an unusual feeling as he never trembled from the touch of an angel. When he opened his eyes, an old man wearing a white robe and brown worn sandals waited. He had a long flowing gray beard and wrinkled tarnished skin. Elwrick shivered again. It was not an angel but the manifestation of the Creator.

"My son," the old man said. "The prophecy for which you speak isn't determined by me when it is to come to fruition."

"Then by who?" Elwrick pleaded.

The old man placed his palm on Elwrick's forehead.

Elwrick wanted to rear back and run away but found himself immobile. Screaming out, his vision clouded and when it cleared, he saw a bone-thin sheep. The sheep was meandering through an enormous pasture scattered with hundreds of dead sheep, their bodies rotting in the sun and festering with flies. Sprinkled across the pasture were patches of Milkweed, Hemlock, Larkspur, the Darling Pea Plant and the occasional Forb.

Elwrick woke gripping the stone. The sun was barely visible over the mountains and the air held a refreshing crispness. The walk home would go much faster than his journey here with his mind racing with thoughts about the vision.

Opening his front door, he made his way to the living room and sat in his favorite chair and closed his eyes. In his mind he relived the vision. Everything in that vision meant something. All he had to do was determine what and he decided to call on the aid of the woman he loved.

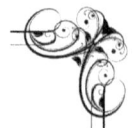

Chapter 22

ester rode like a wild man as he passed through the Majestic Redwood Forest. The trail was easy to navigate, and he made excellent time stopping only when the horse needed to rest. Days passed in a blur, and the sun had yet to rise when the gray, lifeless stone walls of Lynn Brook materialized through the thick fog. Spurring his horse onward, he rode with a revitalized determination when two burning lights came into view. It signified the location of the portcullis; a haven for the troubled, a warm bed for the tired, food for the hungry, and his home.

His days of travel did not go without worry. The majority of his time was spent scheming up a hundred different scenarios as to why he returned without the journal, and not one of them seemed plausible. He knew the King's policy exceptionally well since he had written the majority of it.

—*To abandon your comrades in battle is a sign of cowardice and will be meet with swift retribution.*

The guardsman at the gate stood rigid, one hand raised in a salute.

Returning the salute, Jester skillfully guided his mount through the partially closed portcullis then continued towards the palace where he knew Karayan would be eagerly awaiting his return.

Dismounting at the stable, Jester jogged his way to the throne room where two ragged-looking men greeted him. They each wore plain clothes and wielded rudimentary weapons. The Royal Guardsmen regularly posted here were nowhere to be seen.

"Halt," the larger of the two yelled as he drew his sword. "By the King's orders, none are allowed inside."

Jester looked past the two men at the double doors and saw them bolted shut. "Listen here maggot," Jester snarled. He had ridden hard and covered many leagues the last few days and the only thing stopping him from a warm bath, hot meal, and his bed were these two ill-trained men. "I could be wrong but if King Karayan discovered you two were the ones responsible for preventing the much-needed information I carry from reaching his ears…" He paused to let them reconsider their actions. "It would not surprise me to see both your heads atop a pole before the sun sets… tonight."

The other guard stepped up, his hand resting on the hilt of his sword. "King Karayan informed us he was expecting no one and was not to be disturbed."

Jester nodded. "Then you have sealed your fate, and that of your children and their children."

One guard nervously looked to the other. "What should we do?" he mumbled.

The guard looked around as he kicked the ground. "I think King Karayan only meant these doors. The rear entrance lies unguarded. You could go that way, and none would be any the wiser."

"Then I guess I will take my leave and go in the back entrance."

Jester expertly navigated the darkened halls of the palace still considering his options up until the moment he reached the double doors of Karayan's bedchamber. Catching his breath, he twisted his armor and made it appear as if he'd recently experienced a horrific battle. Happy with his appearance, he knocked.

"Who's out there?" Karayan demanded of his servant.

The woman left the bed to look through the peephole. "It's Jester."

Karayan stood and quickly dressed. If what he believed to be correct, Jester should have the journal. Hopefully, he could decipher something which would return him to his former glory. "Enter," Karayan demanded.

Jester drew a long-winded breath and did as instructed.

"Leave us," Karayan hissed at the servant as Jester entered. "Wait in the hallway until I call for you."

Jester bowed showing his respect to the King.

"What news do you bring?" Karayan asked.

Jester sighed. "Not good. Upon are arrival we were ambushed by a large group of elves and reptiles. More importantly, the man leading them was none other than Pegan Rhoe. We fought like blood-thirsty animals, yet we eventually succumbed to their numbers. As my comrades fell, I had no choice but to flee. To warn you not to send more men as they're walking into their deaths."

"What did you say?" Karayan growled. The fire in his eyes could melt steel.

Jester stumbled back placing some distance between him and Karayan. "The elves are interested in the Keep, or the secrets held within as well. If you wish to discover the missing journal, it's going to take a much larger force than six men."

"You said reptiles?"

"Yes," Jester said. "There was a small force of reptiles aiding the elves."

Karayan scratched his chin. "Why would either race be interested in the Keep?"

"Perhaps they are interested in the journal?"

"No," Karayan said. "There must be another reason. Malvo's location was a secret. I will send a small force to capture one, and then I will discover their true intent."

"You wish me to return and lead a small force?" Jester asked.

"No, I have other plans for you, much more important plans." From a desk drawer he removed a map and unrolled it on the table placing a gold figurine in each corner. Rubbing his chin as he studied the map, he pointed to an area deep in the Ask Mountains. "I need you to take a few men and visit King Hazgrag and convince him to swear his allegiance to me."

"The Stone Giants?" Jester asked.

"Yes, and after that head south to the Misty Ravine and visit King Ulgra and do the same."

"Sir," Jester's voice was no more than a newborn kitten's mew. "Both races neither like nor tolerate man. To convince them—"

"Perhaps I have the wrong man for the job?"

"No sir," Jester said as he stood proud. "I will see it done regardless of the cost."

Karayan pointed to a different section of the map. "After you finish this task, head to God's Perch. I will have a group of men waiting for you with further instructions on what is to transpire."

Jester looked at the map.

"Heed my warning. Do not pass the Whispering Woods in the light of day for the elves have scouts everywhere. Travel only in the dark of night and trace the edge of the Cursed Desert. It is detrimental to our mission that your passing goes unnoticed."

"Why God's Perch?" Jester confusingly asked. "Can you inform me of future events you have planned?"

"The reptiles are to be destroyed by a force who will enter the De'jan Mul' Anor from the Nymph Pass. They will have no other choice but to flee the same as they did from the Cursed Desert. This time though we will be waiting for them and as they begin the climb, they will be easy pickings for archers."

Jester smiled with the thought of those filthy creatures finally becoming extinct.

"By then my army should be moving in to destroy the Whispering Woods and the elves. You will head north following the bank of the Freihn Sea and come in from the rear catching them by surprise."

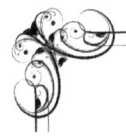
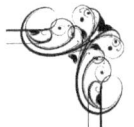

Chapter 23

he library lay in disorder. Every bookshelf was toppled and stacked creating stairs allowing those trapped beneath the surface to reach the ceiling. Ameria followed close to Raestmond providing light as he examined every inch of the perfectly smooth surface.

"Not a single crack, chip, or nick," Raestmond groaned, then slammed his fist against the ceiling. "It appears this room was meticulously carved from the inside of a giant slab of basalt."

Filaurel wiped the sweat from his face. "The temperature must have risen twenty degrees."

Glorandial picked up the water skin and took a sip. Drenched in sweat her hair clung to her face. "I never dreamed it would end this way. I always pictured myself dying at the hands of an enemy's sword or a stray arrow. Not of starvation underground in a filthy rat hole."

"Not starvation," Filaurel corrected his wife. "But suffocation and dehydration." Loosening his cloak strings, he massaged his sweaty neck coaxing the air to enter. Over the last few hours the air had grown stagnant and the well had run dry.

Pegan paced the length of the room mumbling incoherently. He hadn't eaten or drank for days, or weeks for all they knew. In the underground time meant nothing. Stumbling to his knees he quickly gathered himself and stood. His appearance had grown ugly since the last time his companions saw him in the light. Both eyes were recessed into the skull like rotten fruit and his cheek bones protruded outward stretching the skin.

"You need to eat something," Saress told Pegan.

"There's nothing left unless you want to eat the leather satchel," Filaurel told Saress.

"It can't end this way," Pegan hissed as he started pacing once more.

"We'll find a way to escape," Saress reassured them. "Malvo did."

"I don't think so," Raestmond said from atop a bookshelf where he sat. His mouth remained opened creating a large O and sweat dripped from his chin. "I've checked every inch of this room and the other. There is no way out. We're going to die here."

Ameria dimmed the light basking the room in a warm glow. "Should I extinguish it allowing us to fade away in our own thoughts and dreams? In any way we seem redeemable."

Averie giggled, then flat out burst into laughter.

Sarah smiled as she peeked around the corner. "You know that coyote is never going to catch that bird no matter what he does?"

"Yes he will, yes he will. He's almost got him." Averie leaned forward on the couch as if she was there running beside the coyote.

Tom lowered the paper and began to watch. He never really cared for cartoons, but her enthusiasm was bleeding off onto him and he began to cheer for the coyote as well.

Sarah shook her head in amazement, then went back to making breakfast.

Billy had seen this episode a hundred times and knew the outcome. "Nah, he isn't going to catch the bird, he never does."

"Averie, how do you like your eggs?" Sarah asked.

Averie never heard the words as her eyes slowly closed and she appeared to be drifting off to sleep.

Sarah peered around the corner, "Averie?"

Tom looked at Averie who swayed side to side. "The woman can't be tired," Tom jokingly said. "She slept sounder last night than road kill. In fact, I think we all did for a change." Over the last few days normalcy seemed to have replaced chaos.

"Remember she's pregnant, and tiny. I'm sure it's taxing on her," Sarah informed Tom. "Lay her down, this way she doesn't hurt herself. We don't want her falling over."

"Fine," Tom grumbled as he flipped the handle lowing the foot rest.

Averie's mind flooded with visions of horror. Pegan was dying and he was keeping it contained deep within himself to protect her. She could feel it now as his body withered. No longer did he have the strength to keep it under control and she was instantly sick with pain.

Tom jolted to a halt halfway to the couch when Averie slowly opened her eyes. They no longer looked human, but dead, and her face began to wither. Jagged wrinkles formed on her perfectly smooth skin and she seemed to be suddenly aging at an alarming rate. Her hair faded to gray and every fingernail turned black as the polish flaked off.

"Oh my God," Billy screamed as he stepped back stumbling over the computer chair.

Averie's lips curled back exposing her teeth and she hissed something awful.

Sarah came running from the kitchen hearing the commotion.

"Save yourself," Averie pleaded to Pegan. Gripping the glowing diamond, it pulsated at an alarming rate.

Tom wasn't sure what he should do, so he did nothing.

Averie released her grasp on the diamond and held her stomach. Beneath her, a river of blood leaked.

Sarah screamed a horrid scream and she was brought back to the very moment she had a miscarriage with her daughter.

"Save my baby!" she screamed, then her dying eyes slammed shut.

Birthright

"I will not allow you to destroy my child," Pegan hissed as he turned to face his companions.

Saress stumbled backwards falling over a bookshelf. Something now lived within Pegan that was not from this world. Both eyes were no longer white, but piercing orbs of glowing silver and his face twisted with an unsavory thirst for revenge. Moving at an alarming rate he bolted across the library colliding with the pedestal ripping it from the base. The tendons in both hands bulged as he flung it against the wall pulverizing the twisted bones pedestal to a fine powder.

Filaurel nocked an arrow not sure if Pegan was possessed by a demon or lost his mind and would attack them next.

Pegan put his hands to his head and screamed in defiance. The noise made the entire room tremble and drove all things living to their knees. Throwing his head back like a baying wolf, his blackened lips parted, and he howled something in an archaic language.

Saress wept, when this entity in Pegan came out bad things were about to occur.

Breaking through the stone ground a spiraling beam of light bore into the ceiling sending chunks of smoldering stone falling like rain. Those around him had no choice but to flee or be pelted. Crackling with energy, the beam of light branched out like lightning anchoring itself to the walls.

Falling to his knees he continued to scream things which made no sense to his mortal companions.

Small holes and fissures formed in the stone floor and up through it came a dense haze obscuring himself from their vision.

"What is this madness?" Glorandial screamed.

"She's dying," Sarah screamed into the receiver.

The terror in Sarah's voice made Jennifer's blood run cold. Grabbing her purse, she sprinted for the Jeep and put the petal to the floor. Passing cars like the last lap of the Indy 500 she ran an older Buick off the road as the sound of grinding metal filled the air when the sides of their vehicle's met. "I'm sorry," she screamed out the window barely maintaining control of the Jeep as it veered across all lanes of traffic. Never taking her foot of the gas the jeep twisted onto two wheels as she rounded the corner and merged onto the highway. From here it was a straight shot to Sarah's, and she planted her foot to the floor. Behind her a trail of smoke followed as the fender rubbed against the tire.

Pegan heard the call of his mate. He could feel her dying along with her child and only he could save them. Calling on the magic that coursed through his very core at that moment he flung his arms upward and screamed a horrific cry. Coming from the beam of light an oval-shaped pulsating blue portal spitting silver sparks formed. Ripe with energy it began to act like an enormous vacuum slurping up everything Pegan desired, and a few things he didn't.

Fighting to resist the enormous pull, his companions clung to anything they could grasp but miserably failed as their fingers were pried loose and they flew like paper dolls caught in the wind into the portal. Behind them book shelves, books, dust, dirt, debris, the iron door, chunks of the glossy stone from the oval room, pieces of the stone stairs leading there, and the magical doorway from upstairs were all pulled inside. Satisfied his work was complete he looked back through the open doorway. The steel bolts were bent and twisted like broken ribs exploding outward from a cadaver. Smiling in victory he stepped into the portal.

Moments later the portal collapsed in on itself then exploded outward blowing all four walls outward allowing the ceiling to crumble. Moments later, the entire Keep imploded leaving the once magnificent structure nothing more than a smoldering heap of rubble.

Averie slumped over in the couch, her breath nothing more than ragged gasps. Still clutching her belly, she could feel life re-enter her body. Pegan had succeeded.

Tom held a gaggle of towels. He knew he should place them on her to stem the flow of blood but felt guilty, as if he was violating her privacy by doing so. Lifting her dress he closed his eyes and tossed the towels underneath and was going to begin pressing them down when he heard a rumbling and grinding noise coming down the driveway. Looking out the window the remnants of a smoking Jeep formed. "Thank God Jennifer's here," he hollered. Now she could do the things that may be involve with having to see her nude.

Jennifer brought the smoldering hulk to a stop ignoring the flame that dripped off the rear tire. The vehicle could be replaced. Averie, not so much. She was the only one of her kind. Sprinting inside she never hesitated as she passed Sarah and knelt beside Averie.

Averie looked at Jennifer and faintly smiled. Her chest was covered in blood and she could feel the baby moving letting her know it had survived.

Tom was walking in circles mumbling to himself still not sure if Averie was dead or alive.

"What happened?" Jennifer calmly asked Sarah. It would do none of them good if she panicked as well.

Sarah wiped away her tears then relayed what she could remember, but it happened so quick she was positive she forgot a few of the essential details.

Averie released a long-winded gasp then relaxed.

Elwrick sat on the bed holding Lady Alenia's hand with both his. He took great care in explaining to her the vision he saw. He hoped between them they could figure out the meaning of the sheep and the pasture.

Lady Alenia stood and paced the room whispering the words Elwrick told her. "Averie has to be the sheep, there can be no other meaning."

"Let's not jump to conclusions so quickly. The sheep could be the bearer's child, or all of humanity. It's hard to say without a doubt the sheep represents a single woman," Elwrick informed her.

"No," Lady Alenia said. "I am positive, the sheep signifies Averie."

"If that's is true, then all the dead sheep must be the bearers before her," Elwrick concluded.

"But why are they all—" Elwrick suddenly sprang to his feet as if he'd been pricked by a hot poker.

"What in the world?" Lady Alenia confusingly asked.

"Something's wrong," Elwrick quickly said. He could feel a disruption in the natural balance of life. Magic, extremely powerful magic the likes of which he never sensed before was being performed all around them. Casting a protection spell first on the woman he loved he immediately did one on himself next.

"What's wrong?" Lady Alenia pleaded as a purple hue formed inches from her skin and surrounded her.

Elwrick bolted for the door snatching Lady Alenia by the wrist. "We have to get out of—"

In the exact center of the room a pulsating blue portal opened with such force it blew the ceiling off the tree and sent it sailing somewhere over the Whispering Woods. Lady Alenia was ripped from Elwrick's hand and thrown back into the room. Elwrick was launched the other direction sending him through the closed door leaving it hanging by a single mangled hinge. Landing on the ground far below his body left an impression in the soft ground. Furniture splintered and every window shattered outward sending shards of deadly glass sailing for leagues in every direction.

The explosion reverberated through all of Rhunsiire out onto the Plains of Gedeon reaching the walls of Lynn Brook. Waves blew across the Freihn Sea pushed by the subsonic force of the concussion. To the south, God's perch shook so violently it was only the hand of the Creator which kept it from crumbling into the 'Anor.

Elwrick stumbled to his feet. Luckily, the protection spell absorbed the majority of the blast or he would have been instantly vaporized, as well as the woman he loved. "Don't go in there," Elwrick screamed at the approaching elves who neared with their weapons drawn.

Bolting back up the stairs Elwrick only had one thought on his mind, did Lady Alenia survive. From the doorway he could see the pulsating blue portal spitting sparks igniting everything they touched. Black smoke billowed upward in hellish swirls and flames leaped into the air. In the corner he could see the mangled corpse of Lady Alenia lying partially covered in debris. Blood streamed from her nose and mouth and one leg was unnaturally bent with the bone protruding through the skin. Running into the nightmare he refused to allow Lady Alenia's body to be taken back to hell by some demonic creature.

The portal began to make a low rumbling, growl sound like an angry cat.

Elwrick turned to face the demonic device. The first thing which emerged he planned to destroy.

His reactions was sluggish compared to the blistering speed of the portal and something large, green, and screaming was belched out flattening him to the ground. Fighting to kick the hideous thing off he was hit again from a different angle sending him stumbling backwards out the door and tumbling down the stairs. From the ground lying flat on his back he could hear the sound of many solid objects hitting what remained of the room's interior followed by screams of terror.

Growing in size and intensity the portal collapsed in on itself creating a loud *WHOOSHING* sound as it slurped up all the smoke and extinguished the flame.

Elwrick's mind refocused on the woman he loved. *He could not allow her life to end this way*, he thought. and with his hands glowing bright green and ready to launch a barrage of spells he charged back up the stairs and into the nightmare thirsty for revenge.

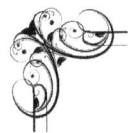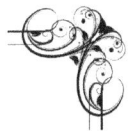

Chapter 24

verie woke in her bed to a semi-dark room. **Through the** window, she could see the full moon glowing bright accentuated by a million twinkling stars. Trying to get up she fell back releasing a horrid moan. Her entire body ached as if she'd been flogged by a hose filled with sand. Closing her eyes, she licked her dried lips. Outside the door, she could hear the hushed whispers of a mild argument.

Rubbing her belly, Averie felt the baby more now than ever. Twisting and turning the fetus appeared to be searching for a way out of the living tomb. "I'll get you food," she whispered, then forced herself upright until she rested on her elbows. Drawing a haggard breath, she didn't realize how weak she was until now.

"You need to rest," Jennifer told Averie as she helped the exhausted woman lie back down and pulled the covers up to her neck. "You lost a lot of blood and whatever you experienced left you near dead."

Averie watched Jennifer closely as she unhooked a bag hanging from a sliver pole and replaced it with a new bag. Almost instantly, she could feel a cool sensation creep into her arm. "What are you doing to me?" It was only now she realized the bag was connected to her arm through a long clear tube.

"This is a bag of Saline. It's helping replace the fluids you lost, that's all," Jennifer informed Averie as she pattered her patient's leg. "You went through quite an ordeal. Can you tell me what you were experiencing?"

"Pegan was dying," Averie whispered.

"Why would that affect you? You're worlds apart," Jennifer asked as she removed the stethoscope from around her neck and listened to Averie's heart one more time, then checked her temperature and blood pressure.

Averie held up the stone and watched the faint pulse of light. "I was dying, my baby was dying. I pleaded to Pegan to save himself and my baby. Almost instantly I felt life re-enter me. No longer was their pain. I felt nothing. I don't understand what is happening to me."

Jennifer sat on the edge of the bed. "I don't know either. The good news is while you slept, I checked on the fetus and she appears perfectly healthy. You also appear to be returning to normal at an alarming rate."

Sarah walked in and quietly closed the door. "How is she?"

"She's dilating quickly. If I had to guess I would say the baby will come any day now."

Averie's eyes opened wide hearing what Jennifer said. She wanted the child out, but she wasn't ready to be a mother.

"Are you about ready to be a mother?" Sarah asked Averie.

Averie shook her head yes, but her eyes said no.

"It's okay if you're scared, were going to be with you the whole time. I have a feeling you're going to do wonderful."

Averie tried to get up again, but Jennifer ordered her to stay put. "I'm not going to tell you again. Next time I'm going to strap you down. You need to rest. Your body is a train wreck."

Averie quickly laid back down. She had no desire to be strapped down to a bed. Bad things happened to people who were strapped down.

"I'm going to stay here through-out the night and check on you about every fifteen minutes," Jennifer said. "You need your rest. In the morning if you're feeling up to it, we'll let you walk around a bit."

"Okay," Averie said in a meek voice.

Sarah didn't need to ask if Jennifer was exhausted, she could see the blackish bags under her eyes growing bigger with every passing minute. "Why don't you get some sleep, you're going to kill yourself."

Jennifer eased back in the recliner and kicked her feet up. Mopping her face with both hands, she released a groan that sounded more like a hog snorting than something human.

Sarah sat beside her on the new plush black leather sofa. Pushing the button beside the built-in cupholder she watched the footrest rise. There was no saving the other couch as it appeared a murder took place on it. "Are you going to be okay?" she asked Jennifer.

Jennifer focused on something outside. "I only wish I knew what she was observing."

Sarah looked to where Jennifer watched the rooster. "In the morning perhaps she can explain more."

Tom entered through the back door. His face was covered in soot. "The old sofa has now been reduced to nothing more than ash and buried a good ten feet below ground. We'll long be gone from this world before there is any chance of her DNA being discovered."

"Now go shower before you touch anything, especially my new sofa." She ran her hand down the arm of the couch.

Snoring from the recliner informed Sarah she would be the one supervising Averie tonight.

Sarah managed to remain awake checking on Averie every fifteen minutes until the sky lightened, and the rooster voiced his opinion. Wiggling into the covers, she curled up beside Tom and kissed his cheek. "I love you," she whispered.

Tom mumbled something, slapped his gums, then responded with a long, drawn-out snore.

Averie's eyes sprung open and cold beads of sweat ran down her face. Something was wrong. She could feel it deep inside her body like tiny uncomfortable hugs which were quickly preceded by the sensation of being harassed by an annoying fly.

She tried to get up, but her body failed to function.

The pain faded but quickly returned sharper and more consistent.

She arched her back, trying to find a position to alleviate the pain yet nothing worked.

Her lips puckered as she gasped for air. A faint whimper escaped her lips. She tried to keep it in, to not wake the others but failed.

The pain subsided once more but returned with a burning angry hatred. A shocking pain erupted in her back as if her spine was being ground into flour on volcanic rock. A blood-curdling scream tore through her throat and tears cascaded down her cheeks.

Sarah leaped from her bed and ran down the hall towards the noise.

Jennifer shot from the sofa tripping over the table and landing hard on her chest knocking the wind from her lungs.

Averie screamed again. She felt as if her abdomen was inside of a hot vice and a thousand evil demons cranked the handle. "Help me," she cried out. She felt as if every organ below her neck was experiencing a catastrophic failure.

Sarah bust through the door nearly taking it free of the frame and sent the handle smashing through the sheetrock. Averie lay on the bed, arched back, and drenched in sweat. "What do I do?" Sarah repeatedly screamed.

"I'm on my way," Jennifer yelled as she scrambled to her feet, a large red rash forming down the side of her face where she slid on the carpet.

Billy's face was ghost-white pale when he looked in the room. "What's wrong?"

"Nothing," Sarah yelled. "Go back to bed."

Averie screamed again and arched her back further then twisted. She would have fallen from the bed had Sarah not been there to grab her.

Tom and Jennifer collided as they tried to enter the room. Stumbling backward, Jennifer grabbed the wall ripping pictures free and breaking off two fingernails.

Averie's head jerked left, then right and her eyes strained as if she was looking for something invisible.

Jennifer finally arrived looking ragged as all hell and seething in pain. Her hand throbbed but she would deal with that later. "I'm here to help," Jennifer said as she stroked Averie's forehead and she could see the wet sheets from where her water had broken. "You need to calm down. You're going to be fine. You're simply doing something women have done for thousands of years."

Sarah looked at Tom; a sigh of relief escaped her lips. "How does she stay so calm?"

Tom shrugged. "It's what she does."

Averie screamed as if she'd been set on fire.

Jennifer glanced back at Tom. "Take Billy into town, take him anywhere, I don't care. He doesn't need to see this."

"You heard the Dr.," Tom informed Billy, who stood stiff-legged with opened eyes.

"I'll call you in a bit," Sarah said. "Oh, and pick up a pumpkin pie, with extra whip cream, Averie's going to want something when this is all over."

"Can do," Tom said.

Jennifer waited until she heard the door close then pulled the blanket back. "Bring me a bowl of warm water and a bunch of rags. The baby's coming now whether we like it or not."

It all happened so quickly, and within an hour, Averie lay on the bed soaking in the slime. Refusing to be cleaned, she sat there holding the translucent egg. Inside, she could make out the shape of an infant floating in a strange, multicolored fluid.

Jennifer reached out and touched the shell, expecting it to be pliable, but firm. She was shocked to discover her finger easily sunk into the outer layer, and the entire object wobbled like Jell-O.

All the pain Averie experienced was now gone, replaced with joy. "I need to break the shell," she whispered. "But it's not ready yet." She spoke out of instincts, not from experience.

Within moments, the shell began to solidify and turned a glistening white. Taping on the shell a small crack formed and she picked away small chunks at first. Another crack formed running clear to the bottom, then the entire structure failed. Fluid the consistency of pancake batter poured over the sides and hung from the mattress in long strands.

Jennifer stripped away her clothes and climbed into a pair of sweats and a T-shirt offered by Sarah.

Sarah handed her a cup of coffee. "Here, drink this, you look terrible."

Jennifer took a sip. The warmth of the fluid and shot of caffeine flowed through her veins. "I've never seen anything like this," Jennifer said, shaking her head in confusion. "I have delivered hundreds of babies, but this is a first."

Sarah busted out laughing. "Think about it. You're the only woman on earth to deliver an alien baby."

They both released a hearty laugh.

Ring, ring, the phone screamed.

"Hello," Sarah said.

"Did she have it?" Tom excitedly asked.

"Well, yeah, kind of. You can come home now."

"Are you okay?" Tom asked. "You sound startled."

"Yeah, I'm fine, we're all fine."

"Was it just like Averie said?" Tom asked. "Was the baby in an egg?"

"Exactly, it—"

"That's crazy," Tom interrupted. "Who would ever think a woman from outer space would have her child in our house. Bet that would be a first for the tabloids that line the supermarket shelves."

Sarah chuckled as the image filled her mind.

"Oh, and I wanted to let you know I ran into Mike at the Glowing Doughnut. Of all places he could be, the doughnut shop. No wonder cops have a bad name."

"Did you tell him to bring some doughnuts home?"

"Yup, he's going to grab a dozen. Anyway," Tom said, then took a sip of the soda he held. "He said he was there finishing up paperwork which meant he was destroying the receipt."

Sarah laughed so hard she buck snorted.

"He had to make one more stop and then he would meet us at the house. He wants to see the new baby as well."

Tom, Mike, and Billy entered the house to the sound of a crying baby.

Sarah stuck her head from the bedroom and told them to wait a few minutes. Jennifer was busy teaching Averie what breastfeeding was and how to do it.

Tom made a funny face. "Thank God you warned me, that's the last thing I want to see."

An hour later they gathered around the bed, the baby asleep in Averie's arms while she gorged herself on a large piece of pumpkin pie smothered in whip cream.

"Have you thought of a name yet?" Tom asked.

Averie shook her head. "It's tradition for the father to name the baby," Averie responded.

"Well, I don't think that applies in this situation," Jennifer advised her. "I believe it would be okay for you to break it just this once."

Averie thought for a moment. "Well, she did arrive in an egg. I'm going to name her Robyn."

"Robyn," Sarah said. "Robyn, what a precious name."

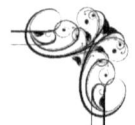

Chapter 25

ady Alenia lay unconscious covered with a silky-smooth blanket. Both arms were wrapped in bandages and her face and right shoulder were heavily bruised. One eye was swollen shut and the other was froze over like a winter puddle. The subtle rise of her chest and the gurgling sound she created was the only sign of life.

Elwrick tip-toed into the medical ward not wanting to wake those who rested. Across the room he could see Lady Alenia and tears instantly flowed. She looked so helpless. In an instance, the strength she carried so proud was wiped away.

Gleia rubbed Elwrick's back comforting him.

"How bad is she?" he asked Gleia.

"A few broken bones; cuts, scrapes, some bruising—"

"I want her healed. I want her healed NOW!" Elwrick demanded, his voice caused a few patients to stir in their beds.

"Elwrick," Gleia called to him. "You need to be quiet. We have injured elves here who need their rest. She was not the only one injured in the fiasco."

"I'm sorry, I'm sorry," he repeated. "I'm just so angry."

"She's going to be fine, but it's going to take time."

Elwrick lowered his head. "I feel so worthless right now. I need to do something for her." Elwrick looked at the ceiling.

"Elwrick." Gleia's tone grew harsh. "You did what you could do. YOU sensed the magic. YOU put the protection spell on her. Had it not been for that there would be nothing left to heal."

Elwrick curled his fingers into a fist. "Sitting here doing nothing—"

"What are you going to do? We both know you can't heal a mortal when the wounds were caused by a mortal. It's one of the ways the Creator prevents you from interfering in the affairs of man. Allow me to do my job while you do yours. Guide us in the right direction to survive the evil we face."

Elwrick smiled. He did trust Gleia. Her skills were remarkable.

"Give her some time and she'll be back to her good old ornery self," Gleia said. "I do fear she will have a permanent limp though. Her leg was twisted in ways I never dreamed possible without removing it from the body."

Elwrick tried to speak but Gleia stopped him. "I want you to know that Ellusia was the first one to arrive and handled the situation perfectly. It was her quick assessment and early treatment which prevented any serious trauma."

Elwrick looked bitter when he spoke. "Where's Pegan? I believe it's time he and I had a discussion about this strange ability he has when the need arises."

Gleia knew Elwrick would be furious and ordered Pegan taken to her private bed chamber to heal. "He is on the mend as well as his companions. His injuries were mostly caused from starvation and dehydration."

"That's not what I asked. Where is he?" Elwrick demanded again.

"I won't tell you, not while you're so angry. Elwrick, I don't believe Pegan had any intentions of injuring anybody. He did what he had to do to save the lives of his companions."

"I don't want to destroy him. I only wish for him to reveal what lurks inside his body which allows these strange events to occur," Elwrick said. "If we can identify it, perhaps we can find a way to control it."

"I already asked him," Gleia said as she motioned for Elwrick to join her outside the ward. "He doesn't remember anything except looking at Ameria as she recommended turning off her light so they could all die in peace. His vision faded to darkness and the next thing he remembers was waking up here."

"I need to see him," Elwrick demanded once more. "Even though he may not remember. His subconscious mind will if we can get to it soon enough."

Gleia stepped away. In his words she could hear the urgency. "I will take you to him, but first, I will have your word he will not be harmed."

"You have my word. That is, unless whatever's inside Pegan has sinister intentions."

Pegan woke releasing bouts of frightful screams. Inside, he felt like a sharp-toothed creature was eating its way out while debilitating pains pierced through his mind and brought strange, flashing colors to his vision.

"Easy," Elwrick said as he rose from the chair. He had been watching Pegan for some time wondering when he would wake. "Pegan, time is of the essence if were to figure out what this thing is inside you. You must allow me to relive your life with a mind trace spell to identify what occurred down in that hole."

Pegan's vision drifted around the room as confusion set in. "Mind trace?"

Elwrick rested his hand on Pegan's shoulder. "Yes. It's different than all other spells I have done to you. All others where I read your mind was a simple memory restoration. This spell puts me in your body and makes you relive the past for as long back as I wish. I must warn you though you will experience everything as if you're reliving the situation again. Any and all pain you felt before, you will feel again."

Pegan thought for a moment, then looked at Elwrick. "Will Averie suffer again as well?"

"No," Elwrick explained. "It's a very complex spell and I will only relive your life, not hers. She will never know I was inside your mind."

Pegan rubbed his throbbing head. "If you believe it will help."

"I believe it will not only help you, but the woman your soul is bound to." Placing his palm against Pegan's sweaty forehead, he traveled back through time reliving his last few weeks. By doing this he hoped to catch a fleeting glance of this strange entity which lives within the man. Light faded to darkness and he entered a hellish environment. He could sense the demonic forces tugging at his soul. As if he was there that day sweat dripped from his forehead, his lips dried and cracked and both eyes recessed back into his skull. He was there when they entered Malvo's library searching every detail they may have missed. Everything Pegan saw and felt that day, he experienced.

Dropping to his knees he felt like vomiting when he heard the cries of the damned in Malvo's sacrificial chamber. Even though Pegan couldn't see into the past, he could, and the atrocities he witnessed left him stricken with grief. "No," he cried out as he watched Barrett slip away into the darkness.

Elwrick lowered his head as he clutched the bedsheets. Trapped in Malvo's chamber he watched their feeble attempts to escape knowing they were doomed. An army of a thousand men couldn't have broken down that door. As they gathered, he heard the words Ameria spoke when she asked if she should dim the staff's light and let them perish in peace and instantly Pegan's mind went horribly dark, as if his soul died. There was no recollection, no history, no beginning or end. There was only darkness, a horrible void of nothingness.

"Elwrick," Pegan whispered when he woke for the second time.

Elwrick's face flushed of color. *How is this possible*, he thought. Pegan radiated no magic, yet this creature was strong enough to topple an entire Keep. Transport all of his companions safely here along with a magical doorway located in a different location, yet block itself from detection.

"What did you discover?" Gleia asked when she saw life reenter Elwrick.

Elwrick faced Gleia. "Nothing. During the portals creation his mind was void of all thoughts, for a moment I thought he died. There was no heartbeat, no brain activity… nothing."

Gleia shook her head in confusion. "Yet Pegan appears unscathed beyond being excessively exhausted and thin from hunger."

Elwrick appeared deep in thought. "None of this makes sense."

Pegan looked to Elwrick for help. "What's happening to me?"

"I don't know," Elwrick whispered.

Pegan tried to rise. He wanted to stand, to ask Elwrick if the others had survived but when he moved, pain ravaged his mind and he fell back to the bed like a crumbling statue.

"He needs to rest," Gleia told Elwrick. "In a few days he will have regained much of his strength."

Pegan kept his eyes closed as he reached out to Elwrick and took the Spiritual Guide's hand in a weak grasp. "Averie had the baby," he whispered. "She did it, they survived."

"Are you positive?" Elwrick asked.

"Yes. Her name is Robyn."

"Her," Elwrick said, then turned to face Gleia. "Are you sure Pegan's not delirious. The bearer has never had a female."

"Elwrick," Pegan said. For a brief second his strength returned, and his eyes flashed bright silver. "She had the child, and the child is a female."

Elwrick stepped back and his face drained away every ounce of color. "Regardless, the child lives. Karayan will not be happy if the news reaches his ears. I must take my leave immediately. There are questions which must be answered." Elwrick sprinted to the door then turned back. "This information about the bearer's child isn't to leave this room."

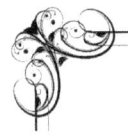
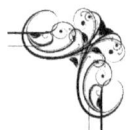

Chapter 26

orry, but I'm not interested," the coin collector said as he slid the coin back shaking his head side to side.

"On the phone—"

"I know what I said on the phone. I was under the assumption you had the entire collection for the price you were asking, not two coins."

"How do you know there's a collection?" Sheba desperately asked. "Perhaps these are the only two years he made them."

The man flashed her a—*don't be stupid*—look. "This King, this man named Karayan would not wait until his third year in power to stamp his first coin. He would want the world to know he was in power instantly."

Sheba went to speak then stopped as the coin expert raised his finger.

"And why would he wait thirteen more years to stamp his next series. I hate to tell you this, every year new coins are stamped with the King's name authorizing it as legal currency. The real question is how many years was he in power, that we don't know. Regardless, if I had one through sixteen there would be a substantial increase in their value."

"I don't understand why it matters?" Tiny asked.

"Let me explain it to you again. When it comes to extremely rare old coins the value lies in a complete set, not the material composition. Alone, these coins aren't worth a Chinese nickel."

"So, without an entire set they're worthless?" Tiny snarled.

"In a sense, yes. You see, the base metal which gives it its hardness, we don't know what it is. Therefore, you can't melt it down without destroying the gold value. More than likely the man who sold these to you understood this and played off your ignorance. You should have checked with a coin expert first, not a metallurgist who looks at the value of the extremely rare composition, not the coin."

"I knew those two were shady as hell," Tiny grumbled. "Ten K' down the toilet."

"Let me get this straight," Sheba asked as she leaned on the counter. "If we had the collection, THEN you would be interested?"

"If you had the collection you would be walking out of here a very rich woman."

"How rich?" Sheba asked.

Removing a Canary Yellow Sticky Post-It from his desk he scribbled down a number and slid it across the table.

Sheba almost fell over looking at all the zeros, then peeled the page free. "I'm going to keep this as a reminder for when we return."

The man removed his glasses and laid them on the desk and rubbed his temples. "That number is only valid after I have verified the coins are real. Being in the business for over thirty years I can spot a fake in a heartbeat. Try and scam me and you'll never do business in this town again."

"Thank you for your time, sir. We'll be in contact." Sheba smiled.

"I'm open until five."

Tiny's mouth came unhinged and he found it hard to speak. "Five million dollars? With that kind of money, we can move to Mexico and live the life of luxury."

"Are you thinking what I'm thinking?" Sheba asked.

"Yup, time to pay your sister a visit."

"We're going to have to be smart about this. Debbie won't give up the information easily."

"She will if we offer her a cut of the pie."

"I don't know," Sheba said. "Debbie's a do-gooder. If she does help, I can guarantee she won't get the information for us. She'll want no part of this in any way, shape, or form. Her kids are her life; she would never risk anything to go to prison and not be able to see them."

"And I'm fine with that," Tiny said. "All I need is for her to get me in the door, I can do the rest."

Days later, the old beater sputtered as it glided through the empty, well-lit parking lot. From the passenger's seat, Tiny cased the building through the floor-to-ceiling windows. The words Frankfort DMV in big bold white letters glowed brightly in the moonlight. Inside, the plastic green and white chairs were stacked and slid to one side allowing the janitor to sweep and mop. The wooden counter which spanned the back was wiped down and polished to a high luster and each computer monitor ran a screen saver program. In the upper right-hand corner hiding partially hidden behind a faux palm tree was a tiny red light signifying the camera was recording.

Tiny took a long drag off the joint which looked more like a twisted twig from a sick tree then closed his eyes to relax. Inside his chest, he could feel the noxious fumes merging with his blood. Holding his breath until he neared unconsciousness, he belched out a puff of smoke filling the car. "You're sure the code from your sister will turn the alarm system off?" he asked in a raspy voice.

Sheba pulled the car into the darkened alley behind the laundry mat and parked beside a row of big brown steel dumpsters. "Positive. You saw how her eyes lit up when I told her she'd get a hundred K' for doing nothing."

"Remember, according to Debbie you have forty-five seconds to type the code after you enter. Otherwise the cops are going to swarm this place like a doughnut shop having a two for one bake sale."

"You make sure to get the plates switched before I get back," Tiny coughed. "I won't be long."

"Don't worry about my part," Sheba snapped. "You make sure you get the damn address." Thoughts of a sunny beach and a fruity drink with an umbrella floating in it filled her mind.

With no headlights visible, Tiny climbed from the heap and tossed the spent joint on the ground. "Now looks like as good a time as any." From his pocket he removed a nylon stocking and dragged it over his head. Sprinting across the street he darted down the sidewalk and slipped behind a dense bush. Waiting a few minutes to make sure he was not seen he hugged the wall as he made his way to the employee entrance located in the back.

Minutes later, the door swung silently inward and he vanished inside. Beside the door built into the wall exactly where Debbie told them was a glistening white box with a small green screen. Below the screen was three glowing red lights. Flipping down the plastic cover he typed in the number on the keypad then hit the pound sign. Moments later the three red lights turned green and a sexy electronic voice croaked—*alarm disabled.*

"Sweet," he said, then danced down the hall to the bank of computers.

The cushioned chair groaned as Tiny flopped down. Resting his feet up on the counter he slid the keyboard onto his lap and used the hacked code to access the system. In the silence of the night, each keystroke sounded like a hammer falling against an anvil.

Following the written directions from Debbie he navigated his way to the identification page and typed in the VIN number of the vehicle. Waiting patiently as a small wheel spun in the middle of the page signifying the machine was working, he checked the drawer, but all the money was already removed.

-*Bling*- the computer made a sound and on the screen was all the information on Tom.

Snatching a pen from the bear-shaped mug he wrote down the required information and stuffed the page in his pocket, then logged off.

"Get on the ground," Shriver screamed. He'd been employed here less than two weeks, and this was his first night alone. In one hand he held his pistol and the other a long black Mag Flashlight. "Get on the ground," he snarled again.

Where in the hell did he come from, Tiny thought.

"Are you deaf," Shriver yelled. "I said get on the ground."

"I'm moving," Tiny answered as he knelt. Almost instantly he recognized the guard's face from the college and decided to use the man's inexperience against him. Lowering himself slowly, he casually removed the pistol from his boot holster keeping it hidden in the shadows.

Setting the flashlight on the counter Shriver grabbed his mic. "10-31 in progress—"

Bang, the shot rang out and the flash momentarily blinded both of them.

Stumbling backwards, Shriver dropped the mic and grabbed his chest. He could feel his warm blood seeping through the uniform.

Tiny scrambled to his feet and bolted for the back door.

"10-71," Shriver gurgled into the mic then fell backwards slamming against the wall and sliding down into a sitting position. Spitting up blood his vision faded.

Sprinting across the parking lot Tiny leaped inside. "Go," he screamed.

Tires squealed as the car lurched into motion. Blowing through the stop sign she held her foot to the floor. "What in the hell happened in there?" she screamed over the roar of the engine.

"There was a guard—watch out," Tiny yelled as Sheba never slowed for the red light nearly T-boning a bright silver thunderbird.

"I heard gunfire; did you shoot him?"

"I had no choice. I'm not going back to prison."

The next morning Sheba sat staring blindly at the television with a lost look on her face.

"Hello and good morning." A professional dressed lady wearing makeup to mask her age said. "*We're live at the Frankfort DMV Eastside, where a robbery and murder occurred. Details are still…*"

Sheba turned the television down as Tiny walked in and sat beside her. "The guard you shot died. Oh man, I didn't plan on this. What are we going to do?"

Tiny finished packing the dragon-shaped bong. "Calm down; nobody knows we did it. I was covered the entire time. We'll give it a few days to cool off then we'll borrow your sister's car and go get the rest of the coins. Hopefully within a week we'll be in Mexico living the dream."

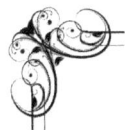 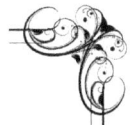

Chapter 27

he hour was late when the derelict building rose up out of the mist and fog. Filthy windows glowed dim and the stone chimney coughed up bouts of black smoke. Near the entrance she could see two men standing guard. Luckily, she knew the location of an often-forgotten rear door and assumed it would be easily accessible. Hiding in the darkness of a large bushy tree Lilith waited until an ominous dark cloud drifted past obscuring the moon and casting the land in shadows.

She didn't have much time and had to reach the building before the cloud drifted away. Her name was widely known across Icearaus and carried a handsome reward—rather it was attached to the body or not.

Hobbling her way down the path as fast as her twisted legs would move, she arrived at the back door. Placing her ear against the rough-cut wood she listened for any sign of life. Hearing none, she slowly turned the knob careful not to make a sound and entered. The hall was long and dimly lit by a few sputtering lanterns. At the end was a large wooden door rimmed in steel which opened to the tavern. Beyond the door she heard loud voices, men cheering, and the clank of glasses. Luckily, the stairs she needed were on this side.

Staying in the shadows Lilith snuck partway down the hall then climbed a narrow set of wooden stairs that creaked with each step. Near the top she paused and watched a drunk stagger past in search of more ale. In his current state he probably wouldn't have recognized her anyway.

Navigating the hallway, she arrived at a narrow, rickety staircase that didn't look fit for use. Waiting for another drunkard to pass she quietly scaled them.

Reaching the landing the long straggly hairs on a clump of warts on the back of her neck stood erect. Every lantern sat cold and the only light came from a single candle at the far end on a small table in front of a dirty window. *Only my nerves*, Lilith told herself, then went to the last door on the south side and retrieved a small silver key from the pouch she wore around her waist.

Vexacion almost gagged revealing his location when he saw the woman enter. She was the ugliest thing he'd ever encountered. Huge festering warts covered her face and matted hair hung in mangy clumps reaching her waist. Tattered robes hung on her bone-thin frame and she reeked of raw sewage.

Lilith quickly surveyed the room. It was minimally furnished with a single bed, a table, and a broad chest. On the table a single candle flickered. Softly closing the door, she flipped the latch locking out the world that wanted her dead. It would feel good to rest, to take the weight off her tired legs and give her bare feet a chance to heal.

Releasing a sigh, she laid down and wiggled her twisted toes which refused to fit in any shoe she found. Hopefully soon, Viktor would arrive and with him a cure for the liches curse.

"You're late," Vexacion said from the shadows. With her capture he would now be able to return home. Still, he had to make sure it was the right hag. To return with the wrong subject would not bode well for his current position within the ranks of the brotherhood.

Lilith cocked her head sideways. In the dim light only half her face was visible, but both eyes glowed like flaming daggers.

"It crossed my mind to leave; my patience was growing weary."

"Viktor, you don't know how long I have dreamed of hearing your voice again. Too long have my travels been with nobody at my side. Come; sit with me. Let me feel your touch and gaze into your beautiful eyes." She patted the bed with her frail three-fingered hand.

Vexacion released a grossly exaggerated laugh as he stepped from the shadows.

Lilith tried to rise when she saw the figure, but she was pulled back down onto the bed from behind.

"Bind her," Vexacion snarled. "This is the hag we're searching for."

Lilith tried to resist, but she was no match for the enemy's strength and both hands were forced behind her back and shackled at the wrist "Move and I'll cut your throat." She heard a creepy voice from the darkness whisper into her ear.

With the lantern now glowing, Lilith got a good look at her abductor. "Vexacion Le Torneau," she hissed.

"Yes, it is I," Vexacion said, then performed a gracious bow.

"Where is Viktor, you fool?"

"Oh, around," Vexacion mockingly said. "Do you wish to see him?"

"If you've harmed him—"

"I don't believe you're in a position to be making threats," Vexacion laughed.

Lilith became nauseous when a spine with the head still attached was placed on the bed. Both eyes had been gouged out and every tooth forcefully removed. The dried leathery skin was still purple from the merciless beating he had taken. "You will burn in hell for this."

"Enough," Vexacion growled "Let's get down to why we're here, shall we."

Lilith spat on him.

Vexacion raised his hand to slap her, then lowered it. "You're lucky," Vexacion hissed as he wiped away the spit. "The orders I received are very specific. No harm shall come to you until after your meeting. Then you're mine to do with as I please."

"And who issued these orders?" Lilith asked, wondering which assassin acquired the coveted position as Lord of the Brotherhood.

"A man whose powers are beyond this world."

"So powerful you fear his name?"

Vexacion thought for a moment. "Fear, no. Respect would be the proper word. His name is Malvo Necrosyse., Lord of the Brotherhood of the Dark Prince."

"Malvo is dead you fool," Lilith snarled as she fought with the shackles.

"Dead," Vexacion said. "I believe you're sorely mistaken. Lord Necrosyse is very much alive and is patiently waiting for your return. It appears you and he have some unfinished business."

Lilith thought back to her baby and how she abandoned him. "And what will that be, to rape me until I carry his child?"

"I'm not sure what Lord Necrosyse has in store for you. My guess is it has something to do with your head and the high value placed upon it."

"I'll destroy myself long before he has—"

"No no, my dear," Vexacion interrupted. "Lord Necrosyse has already accounted for this and informed me you're to remain bound and constantly watched until directly delivered to his hands."

"You're a fool for aiding this man," Lilith said. "I have seen the future of Icearaus and it drove a stake of fear straight through my heart. Why do you think I risked everything to escape? Now you, like me, are stuck here and we will soon become fodder to the war machine the Dark Master is amassing."

"Silence," Vexacion said, then raised his hand threatening to slap her. "You know nothing of which you speak and spread lies to try and save your neck. Lord Necrosyse is a good man who only wishes to see the brotherhood flourish."

"To use the brotherhood to push his sinister—"

"Gag and blindfold her," Vexacion hissed to the others. "I've heard enough from her filthy mouth. We leave for the Lost Sanctuary shortly."

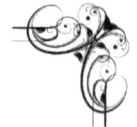

Chapter 28

 amantha tried to put the incident behind her, yet the memories still burned in her brain like a never-dying ember awaking an ugly past. All through middle school and partway through high school her and Tom were inseparable. In her junior year she had visions of a grand wedding, children, and the white picket fence. All that changed though at the beginning of her senior year when Mike moved here taking the position as deputy sheriff. Sarah, his little sister followed wanting to get out of the crime and corruption that flourished in Frankfort.

Samantha didn't think much about it until one day she waited outside the school for Tom to arrive and noticed he was giving Sarah a ride to school. Questioning him, Tom said it was nothing, that her car broke down and he was too much of a gentleman to make a lady walk. As weeks and months drifted away and winter turned to spring it all came crashing down. Outside Nancie's House of Ice Cream, he told her he was planning to ask Sarah to the senior dance, not her.

Decades had passed since then and she kept telling herself to forget about it and move on, but she couldn't. Like a parasite, the thought of Tom and that skank lying together at night left her fuming with anger. And now, all these years later she dares to embarrass her, in her own damn store no less.

Gripping the steering wheel until her nails dug into the soft leather covering, she kept replaying the incident like a bad movie stuck on an endless loop. They say revenge is best served cold. Today though, it would be delivered steaming hot and on a platter of designer sheets.

Parking down the road in a vacant veterinary parking lot she waited until the black Cadillac Escalade rumbled past. Driving it was a dashing woman oblivious to her husband's deceit. When the taillights faded Samantha put the Jaguar XJS in gear and pulled in behind the Mayor's Mansion. The mansion was nothing new to her; she had visited it many, many times when she needed something done such as a parking ticket dismissed, or a failed building inspection to vanish. The Mayor, on the other hand, called her over each time his wife left town for business, or if he wanted to do something he was to ashamed to ask his wife.

Seductively, she popped a few buttons loose on her blouse, freshened up her makeup in the rear-view mirror, then dabbed on a bit of perfume. Satisfied with her—take me—appearance she skipped her way to the back door which she knew would be conveniently left unlocked.

Tony Donaldson lay sprawled out on his king-sized bed partially covered by a red satin sheet. The curtains were drawn blocking out the light except for a small sliver which scared the adjacent wall. Built into the wall, a large screen television was perfectly angled for his viewing pleasure. On the screen the salacious movie sat frozen in time.

Samantha didn't need directions to the bedroom; she knew the layout of the mansion better than the woman who lived here. Stopping to glance at a family picture hanging on the wall, she was shocked to see how much Tony had changed. His once raven black hair was now gray and his neatly trimmed mustache was gone. His eyes though still held the same mesmerizing gaze of his youth.

Tony pulled back the comforter as Samantha entered and patted the mattress. In the glow of the television, his mocking grin almost looked evil.

Samantha strutted across the room exaggerating the sway of each hip with every step as she made her way to the plush, winged-back Victorian chair located beside the bed. Crossing her legs, she peeled away one high-heel shoe and dangled it from her big toe. "I don't think I can do this today," she said in a broken voice.

Tony rolled to his side resting his head on the pillow. "Is everything okay? You sound like someone kicked your dog."

Samantha glanced up at the television allowing the anticipation build. "They may as well have," she whispered. Trying to squeeze out a tear, she miserably failed.

Tony sat up in the bed. "What's going on?"

Samantha wiped away the only tear she managed to create. "I'm so damn humiliated. All I want to do is cry and hide in shame," she whimpered. "They came into the store, threatening to slap me around, breaking stuff, ran off customers…"

Tony climbed from the bed ignoring his nakedness and sat beside her. "Who did this to you? Did you call the sheriff?"

"What good would calling the sheriff do when he was the main instigator. With him was another woman hanging on his hip who appeared all strung out on something. If I had to guess, I would say it was his wife." Samantha knew Sarah was good friends with Mike. To hurt Sarah was one thing, but to destroy Mike's reputation was even sweeter.

Tony looked shocked. "Mike, Mike McCullaha and his wife Jennifer?"

"That's her name?" Samantha asked. "The woman who owns that atrocity known as the clinic downtown is his wife?" Samantha decided to take here scheme a bit further and destroy the entire family forcing them into bankruptcy.

"And your positive—" Tony started to say.

"I told the sheriff I was going to report this, and he told me if I did, he would run my name through the wringer so bad I would never do business again this side of the Mississippi."

"They had Sarah with them as well as a pregnant lady who I had never seen before. Probably bringing her into the clinic to do an abortion, we all know she performs them, but nobody will stop her from killing babies."

"Are you sure?" Tony asked. "I know both of them personally, and Mike has always been on the up and up. Each time I've had to go to the clinic, Jennifer's always been very respectful. Don't know much about Sarah except her and Tom run the Fischer Farm. Seems like every year though they donate beef to the needy without asking for anything in return. Your positive this was not a case of mistaken identity?"

"You don't believe me, fine," Samantha growled. "I guess that saying is true that the cops take care of their own."

"I do believe you. It just seems so out of character for a woman who practices medicine and a man who upholds the law."

"Drugs can make people do crazy things."

Tony leaned back in the chair and put his arm around her shoulder resting his hand on her chest. "I'm not sure exactly what I can do about it right now? Tomorrow I will talk with Mike and get his side of the story. I'm sure it was nothing more than a miscommunication."

"I want him fired—"

"It's not that easy," Tony explained. "There has to be an investigation, witnesses questioned, videos watched—"

"Sounds to me like you're trying to protect them. I thought I meant something to you."

"You do, but I can't fire him without knowing the facts."

"Fine, then put him on administrative leave without pay while you perform your investigation."

"That would only leave us with two officers. That's not enough to keep crime from coming to Willowdale."

"Well then hire another one while you do your investigation."

Tony rubbed his head in confusion. "I will see what I can do."

"We need to do something about that abortion clinic Jennifer is running as well," Samantha continued.

"It's a clinic—"

"It's an abortion center disguised as a clinic. You don't hear about the awful things they do in there to pregnant women seeking help and advice. I work at the mall and hear all the latest news. Only last week a woman went in there having stomach pains and the next thing she knows her child had to be aborted costing her insurance thousands. Women go in there expecting a simple procedure only to discover they may never have children again. Worse yet, I heard they sell parts of the fetus to research centers. Now I understand how Mike can afford that house. Hell, its nicer than your mansion."

Tony rubbed his eye's until he saw spots. "Again, it's not that easy."

"Sure, it is," Samantha said as her hand worked up his thigh. "All you have to do is make a few phone calls and nothing changes between us. If not, I don't believe our relationship can continue to flourish." Rising from the chair she allowed her skirt to flutter to the floor as she made her way to the bed.

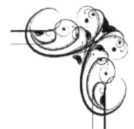

Chapter 29

he assassin was disgusted with his current job assignment. A man of his skill should have been doing something more assassin-like, not intermingling with a gaggle of slobs. Grumbling the entire way from the Lost Sanctuary to Lynn Brook he tried to justify the reasoning of his station but could find none. He only hoped the reward would be worth the humiliation. Staggering into the stable, he bumped into a stall dropping the flask he held, then entered the stall to relieve himself. He wasn't drunk but had to play the part to fit in with the rest of Karayan's men if he was to keep an eye on Karayan at all times.

Climbing up on the stall he sat in the shadows trying hard not to laugh as Karayan's new entourage gathered at the stable. Not one of them was fit to ride a horse, let alone wield a weapon. Resting his hand on his concealed dagger, he considered slicing the King's throat and ending his suffering, but his orders from Lord Necrosyse were bloody clear. King Karayan was to remain alive and in power until said time Lord Necrosyse authorized his execution. If Karayan were to die before his time, he would take the Kings place when punishment was handed out.

When all had gathered he filtered in unrecognized and mounted his horse. Doing his best to fit in his garb was tattered and the sword hanging at his hip was rusty brown. Across his chest was a deadly longbow resembling a tree branch strung with a frayed string. He would ride with them this morning out of the city to Timber Hall. He didn't know why, but he would soon find out.

Men, women, and children scattered as the parade of horses tore through the streets of Timber Hall without slowing. Navigating the narrow streets they arrived at the summit where a large hut stood proud against the frigid background. The only thing living was the guard posted at the front gate.

"Halt," the guard yelled, then pointed his spear directly at Karayan who led the ragged looking bunch.

Karayan ignored the request, and with a wave of his hand, twenty arrows took to flight. The majority of arrows missed the target except one which hit the barbarian's heart, killing him instantly. The assassin placed his bow back over his shoulder and smiled.

Dismounting before the horse came to a complete stop, Karayan stumbled nearly falling face-first in the snow. Ripping his sword free, he raised it high then let it fall offering a hearty grunt. The neck bone and tissue offered little resistance as the sharpened blade passed cleanly through burying into the ground.

Surrounded by men, Karayan entered the abode carrying the severed head by the hair.

Emperor Haumlell knelt upon observing the King. "My King. What pleasure do I have being blessed with your presence this fine day?"

Karayan looked out the window viewing the city. "It appears Timber Hall has flourished since your return."

"Only because of your guidance."

Karayan tossed the head at the Emperor's feet. "Perhaps your city has flourished to well and your men feel you have grown beyond my reach. Perhaps they now view you as my equal, if not stronger."

"My King," Emperor Haumlell pleaded. "I don't know what came over my guard, or why he acted in such a hostile manner. I can assure you it will never happen again."

"Make sure it doesn't," Karayan hissed. "Next time it will be your head I remove and one of my men will take your place." Karayan kicked the head out of the way then gripped Emperor Haumlell by his fur coat and jerked the sniveling barbarian to his feet. "Time has come for you to prove your worth."

"What is it you wish of me?" the Emperor asked.

Karayan removed his riding gloves and placed them on the desk. Afterward, he interlocked his fingers and stretched until each knuckled made a sickly popping sound. "Where's your servant? The ride was long, and I've developed quite a thirst."

Emperor Haumlell called for his slave who was forced to live in a room no bigger than a closet. "Bring me a drink, NOW! The very best the house has. Nothing is too good for our King."

Karayan's vision followed the scantily dressed girl as she left the room. "War is coming to Icearaus."

Emperor Haumlell's eye's opened wide.

The squeal of the door notified them the girl had returned. In one hand she carried two glasses and in the other a bottle.

"Rose Velvet Wine," Emperor Haumlell said. "There is no finer wine in all of the Frozen Tundra."

The woman set the glasses on the table then carefully filled each making sure not a single drop spilled. Afterward, she handed a glass to the Emperor and then the King.

Emperor Haumlell swished the glass watching the wine paint the interior a sunset red. "The berries to make this wine are only found in the farthest regions of the north in the Tramulatarian Ice Caves. Many good men die each year trying to recover but a handful of these."

Karayan looked at the glass, then handed it to Emperor Haumlell. "Sip mine first."

Emperor Haumlell did as instructed then handed it back.

Karayan watched for any sign of poison. Observing none, he drank the entire contents in one gulp then handed the glass back to the waiting slave. "Good slaves are hard to come by. When I leave, she rides with me." Karayan raised his eyebrows waiting for an objection.

"As you wish," Emperor Haumlell whispered.

Dismissing the girl back to her quarters, Karayan continued where he left off. "As I said before, war is coming to Icearaus and it is time for you to play your part in the future of Icearaus."

The assassin listened carefully to each word. He would have to remember exacting details to pass back to Lord Necrosyse.

"It appears the filthy reptiles of the 'Anor have joined forces with the elves from the Whispering Woods. Together, they have decided to rid the world of man and claim it as their own."

The assassin squinted—none of this made sense. Perhaps Karayan would reveal more of his plans as time passed.

Emperor Haumlell stroked his long beard. "My King. If the reptiles believe they can defeat you in open war, they have indeed grown bold and must be dealt with."

"I'm delighted to see you feel this way. It will be the job of the barbarians to enter the 'Anor and destroy them."

Emperor Haumlell's shoulders slumped. "My King, the 'Anor is a wretched place and we all know the reptiles live underground in a vast network of tunnels. Of all those who have ventured in, not one has returned. We will be slaughtered fighting underground in the bleakest of conditions."

"That is the beauty of my plan. The method of the reptiles destruction has already been created, and not one man will have to enter their filthy lair. All your army must do is protect my men long enough for the device to be put in place."

What kind of device could destroy an entire race? The assassin thought. This new information discovered was crucial and must be sent to Lord Necrosyse immediately upon his return.

Emperor Haumlell smiled at the thought of not having to enter the subterranean network.

"Take your army and gather at the mouth of the Nymph Pass. It will be there you will enter the 'Anor."

"My King, how much time do I have to prepare?"

Karayan squinted. "Your army should always be prepared. Those who are not constantly ready for war are bound to die by it. The enemy does not deliver a messenger informing you of when and how the attack will occur. Regardless, you're young and still learning. I will give you sixty days to ready your army then every able man over the age of twelve should be ready to travel."

"My King, that is a very generous timeframe."

"Indeed, it is. I do not wish to see my young Emperor fail. Therefore, I've given you plenty of time to equip and prepare your Barbarian force for war."

Emperor Haumlell smiled. Now would be the time to prove his worth. To forever engrave his name in the history of Icearaus and be remembered as the greatest Emperor of all time.

"Emperor Haumlell," Karayan called out. "Your role in this is crucial; do not fail me."

"I will make you proud."

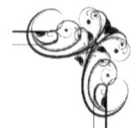

Chapter 30

he smell of roast beef, twice baked potatoes, and collard greens saturated the kitchen like a new coat of paint. Frank turned the dials down to simmer then carried two China plates to the kitchen table. From the shelf he retrieved a bottle of wine and buried it in a metal tub full of ice. Striking a match he finalized the elegant evening by lighting three candles. Any minute now his guest should arrive.

Frank watched the grandfather clock strike six, then six-thirty. When it dinged seven times, he became worried something was drastically wrong. Grabbing his phone he hit the speed dial.

"Hello," Gina answered.

Frank made a confused face. In the background, he was positive he heard the sound of an outboard motor slowing down. "Is everything okay?" he asked.

"Everything is fine. Why do you ask?"

"Because we had plans for dinner tonight—"

"We did?" Gina interrupted. "I remember you were talking about it, but I figured you were telling me what you were planning on making. Not that we had a dinner date. Had I known I would have told you I had plans."

Who is that? Frank heard a man ask in the background.

Oh, nobody, just a friend from college. He heard Gina answer.

"Nobody," Frank mumbled. "I thought we had something more?"

"More than what?" Gina asked. "I never agreed to a monogamous relationship."

"What about the cruise, and the vacation to Australia?" Frank pleaded.

"Look, I'm sorry," Gina said. "You're a good friend and a nice man but nothing more. On Monday we can talk about it if it will make you feel better. I never meant to hurt you."

"This doesn't make any sense," Frank said.

"Look, I already said I'm sorry. I have to go now. We can talk about it on Monday."

Frank looked at his phone as the line went dead, then he threw the phone across the room busting it into a thousand pieces.

Looking around his house it no longer felt like a home, but the waiting room at the mortuary. Turning off the stove and oven he had no desire to be here. The thoughts of Gina and the things they'd done haunted his memories. Grabbing his jacket and keys, he made for the door and slammed it on the way out knocking her picture from the wall.

Birthright

Lightning fired across the sky giving forewarning of a brewing storm. In the distance he could see thick, dark, thunderheads forming. Scanning through the radio it seemed as if every DJ knew of his pain and played sad songs forcing tears from his eyes. "How can she do this to me?" he cried. This was the first time he realized how much he loved her, and how much it hurt losing her.

Scanning through the stations a few more times it stopped on some heavy metal punk rock song where he couldn't understand the words and his pain turned to anger. "Three goddamn years," he grumbled, then slammed his fist into the steering wheel forcing the car to veer nearly striking a parked Mercedes. "Three years," he screamed at the headliner of the car and pounded his fist against the dash keeping rhythm with the pounding drums.

As the song ended his head pounded and his bruised fist hurt like hell. Spinning the knob until the radio turned off he merged onto the highway and put his foot to the floor. Where he was going, he had no idea, but it wasn't here.

Less than five miles later flashing lights in the rearview mirror caught his attention.

Easing the car into the emergency lane, he flipped on the interior light and waited.

"Good evening sir," the officer said as he leaned against the car. "Can I see your driver's license, insurance, and registration please."

Frank quickly found said items from the glove box and handed them to the officer.

"Do you know why I stopped you?" the officer asked.

Frank shook his head no.

"We've had reports of a vehicle matching this description swerving through town, and then you blew by me on the highway going one-o-five in a sixty-five. Hang tight while I go run your information then we'll get you out of here."

Frank sat in the Corvette festering. Here he was getting a ticket, probably going to jail while Gina was on a boat drinking a cold beer and having a good time."

The officer quickly returned and handed him back his information. "Frank Middleton. The same Frank Middleton who teaches the Metallurgy class at Frankfort University?"

"As far as I know there's only one," Frank answered.

"Would you kindly mind telling me what's going on inside your mind. My son took your class a few years back and had nothing but good things to say about you. From what I can remember this appears out of character for you."

Frank sighed, then told him about Gina.

The officer shook his head, then rested his elbows on the doorsill. "Let me tell you what happened to me and you won't feel so bad."

"I don't need a lesson," Frank said.

"You can either hear me out or receive a hefty ticket? The choice is yours."

"If it saves me from a ticket, go ahead," Frank groaned.

"I thought my marriage was sound," the officer said as he thought back to the night it all went bad. "Come to find out she had a thing going with my sergeant. While I was on mandatory overtime working the beat, he was over at my house with my wife, in my bed. The only way I found out was I stopped by to see how she was doing and walked in on them about three in the morning. Took all I could to keep from shooting both of them. Then to add to insult when I went through the divorce she received half of everything. The car she bought with the overtime I worked, he's now driving."

"So, what is my lesson from this?" Frank asked.

"The lesson is women are nothing but trouble and what their selling, I'm not buying. There are too many fish in the sea to get tied down to one catch. When I meet a woman now, she pays for everything herself, all the way from a pack of gum to a dinner. Women wanted equal rights, by golly, they're going to get it."

"I don't want women thinking I'm a prick," Frank explained.

"Then plan on living your life in misery because that's where your headed. Women don't care about you; they don't care about me. All they care about is what they can get out of us. If all you want is a little slap and tickle there's too many places to get it for free, just check your emotions at the door if you know what I mean. Start living for yourself, not others. Find the next new discovery, create a new metal, design a spacecraft. Your smart, you can do that. Don't throw your life away because of a skirt."

"You know, you're right," Frank said as he thought about the coins. In the morning he would find that pawnshop and offer to buy the coins and break them down into their finer components. Make himself feel useful again instead of teaching snobby kids' things they don't care about. They only needed the class so they could graduate.

"Learn from me," the officer said. "Now that it's all in the past, my life is so much nicer."

Frank smiled. He already felt better.

"You have a good night and drive safe," the officer said.

Frank drove to the Northside of Frankfort where the hotels were a thousand bucks a night, and a suit and tie was required to enter. Although he was not dressed for the occasion he was known well enough he should be able to talk his way inside. Parking next to a fire-engine red Dodge Viper, he knew the owner to be a well-to-do man who made his money in trading stocks and bonds. He was known to frequent the more elaborate areas flashing his money and always had a woman who appeared only months over the legal drinking age hanging on each arm.

"Frank," the maitre d' excitedly said when he saw his old friend enter.

Frank greeted the man with a handshake. "Joe, how's it going?"

"Good. You?" Joe looked past Frank. "Where's Gina?"

"I'm flying solo tonight," Frank answered. "Heading to the lounge for a few drinks and watch the game. Might want to book me a room as well in case I have one too many. Can't risk a DUI."

"The top floor as usual overlooking the city and the lake?" Joe asked.

"No, not tonight. I want a different room, any one available except for the one I normally get."

Joe nodded. He could tell from the way Frank spoke it was probably over between Gina and him. "I'll have them start you a tab."

The morning arrived with the crash of thunder and a torrential down-pour. No desire to get up Frank lay there sprawled out on the bed watching the news waiting for room service to arrive with his breakfast.

Rap...rap came a tapping at the door. "Room service."

"Come in," Frank said as he sat up in the bed and turned down the television.

The elder woman smiled as she entered pushing a silver cart. Behind her smile, Frank could see decades of wisdom in her wrinkles. He guessed in her younger years she was a lover, wife, mother, and breadwinner of the family. Now, she worked whittling away the days when she wasn't watching the grandkids. Looking at the television as she crossed the room, she paused. "Such a shame about that security guard," she said with the sweetest voice.

"Yes," Frank said. "What makes it even worse is he was a good friend of mine. He worked at the university and took the job there for better pay and benefits."

The woman shook her head in disgust. "What is wrong with people these days?"

Frank turned the Television up so they both could hear the latest hoping they had someone in custody.

"The police are asking for your help," the news lady said. *"With no new leads they decided to release the video from the DMV with hopes someone would come forward. Crime Stoppers has offered a ten-thousand-dollar reward for information leading to an arrest and you can remain anonymous if you choose."*

They both watched the video and Frank's chin nearly hit the floor. "I've seen that guy before."

"Are you positive?" the lady asked.

"Pretty positive. Don't know for sure because his face is covered, but he carries himself the same as a man who was in my classroom not too long ago."

"You need to report this," the woman said as she took the lid off the platter.

"What if I'm wrong? An innocent man could go to jail."

"Or a killer could walk free," she spat back.

Frank drove around town his mind lost in thought. If he did report it and it was the guy from the pawnshop he may never get a chance to buy the coins. Perhaps he should buy them first, then report what he knows. If he did buy them first, could he be linked someway to the crime. It was Saturday evening; he may have to wait until Monday anyway.

As evening fell on the street and the police headquarters within sight, he pulled into the mostly vacant parking lot. Waiting for a lull in the rain he battled the blustering wind to the front door. To his surprise he found it open and a young lady wearing a police uniform sitting at the receptionist desk.

Startled by his sudden appearance, she nearly dropped the pen she employed. "Can I help you?"

"Hmm, I hope so," Frank said as he approached the desk looking in all directions to see if anyone was within earshot. "I may have some information about the DMV murder.".

The lady's eyebrows crawled up her forehead. "Please, have a seat. I believe Detective Weaver is still in the building."

Before Frank's butt found the hard-plastic chair, he was ushered back by a young man wearing a rusty brown twill suit. On his belt hung a silver badge and on his hip a holstered pistol. Led down numerous hallways designed to confuse, they arrived at what looked like a prison tier with rows of doors on either side. The very last door on the right-hand side was propped open.

Inside Frank felt more like a prisoner than a witness. Bleak stone walls with no windows and a single table with two chairs. In the upper right-hand corner the red light glowed from a camera.

"Sorry for the accommodations," Detective Weaver said. "Normally, I would have this conversation at my desk, but we can't risk any information getting out to the public."

Frank sat in the closest chair to the door.

"Can I get you something to drink, soda, water, coffee?"

"No thank you.".

Detective Weaver sat across from him and rested his hands on the table. "Diana at the front desk said you have some info on the DMV murder?"

Frank leaned back in the chair. "I hope I'm doing the right thing. I don't want an innocent man go to prison."

"Don't worry. Anything you say will be fully investigated first."

Scratching his chin, Frank relayed the entire incident at the college.

Detective Weaver scratched his forehead. "Exactly how does this tie into the murder?"

"Because I saw the video on the news and the guy in the video had the same build and carried himself in the same way. I know it doesn't mean much, but it might be something."

"Give me one minute." Detective Weaver left then returned holding a laptop. On it he replayed the video. "Do you see anything else that may identify him?"

Frank watched the video a few more times. "It's so hard to say because he's covered. The way he carries himself though reminds me so much of the man at the school."

Detective Weaver closed the laptop. "This is the first real lead we have to go on. Do you remember which pawnshop they were from?"

"They didn't say, but since they had no paperwork, I assume it's one of those dirty establishments on the south-side of town."

Detective Weaver took a slow sip from his coffee mug then stood up. "Well, I would like to thank you for your time and information. If I can get your number, I will be in contact if we need anything else."

After providing his information, Frank was led out by the receptionist while Detective Weaver vanished deeper into the brick building.

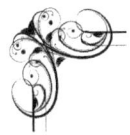

Chapter 31

ith each passing day, Sandy watched Dave become more deeply engrossed with the phenomena of this supposed alien. Studying charts, creating graphs, he spent his nights reading about the cosmos instead of sleeping. Finally, she couldn't take it anymore and as she watched his tail lights leave the parking lot for lunch, she picked up the phone and dialed a number she hadn't dialed in many years.

"Hello," a man on the other end of the line said.

"Mark, it's me, Sandy."

An awkward silence formed between them.

"I told you never to call me!".

"The divorce happened over ten years ago. I let it go years ago. It's about time you did the same."

"You betrayed me in my time of need," Mark hissed.

"I stuck with you through your alcoholism," Sandy hissed back. "All the nights you were out drinking, I stayed home with the kids making excuses to protect your image. I'm sorry, but when I found out you were having an affair with your secretary, I couldn't do it anymore. You left me with no choice."

"Fine, whatever. What do you want?"

"I know you have access to all the records of everything ever recorded on the computers from the investigation department. I want everything you got on the Karayan case."

"That case is sealed," Mark hesitantly responded.

"Don't play me as being stupid. I know you have a way to get them," she fired back.

"Talking like that you know you're going to get us both fired."

"Why do you think I used my phone and not a government one. Nobody is to know of this, ever."

"This is risky," Mark mumbled. "I've recently remarried. To get caught I will lose everything."

"Mark, after the divorce I asked for nothing. No alimony and no child support. I could have taken you to the cleaners but I'm not a cold-hearted bitch. You owe me this."

"Fine, I will see what I can do," Mark grumbled.

"One more thing," Sandy said. "I need them ASAP, like yesterday if possible."

"Jesus Christ," Mark snarled. "You want the fillings out of my teeth as well?"

"If it relates to the Karayan case then yes," she answered unapologetically.

The phone was silent for a minute and she was about to hang up when Mark spoke. "You know the Sea Hag Restaurant down on Marine Drive?"

"The one with the big sailfish mounted on the roof?"

"Yeah, that one. Meet me there in two hours and I will have everything I can find. After this, don't ever contact me again."

"Deal," she said, then hung up the phone.

On the way out the door she met Dave. "I'm heading out to run a few errands, shouldn't be gone long."

"Grab me a Coke while you're out," Dave said. In his hand he carried a huge book titled *Astronomica*.

Traffic was terrible, and she was all but certain she was going to be late when the restaurant came into view. Whipping her car into the turning lane she pressed on the pedal flying by the gridlock. Observing a slim opening in the on-coming traffic she cut off a semi as she angled the steel machine into the driveway scarping the muffler in the process. In the back parking lot, a maroon-colored SUV flashed its lights at her.

Pulling up beside the unknown vehicle she put the car in park.

The driver rolled down the black tinted window barely enough to slide out a thick bright yellow envelope bound with a string. "Everything on the boy has been destroyed. This is all he could recover."

Snatching the envelope, she tried to see who the delivery boy was, but the driver quickly rolled up the window allowing her to see only his midnight black sunglasses.

Stepping on the gas the SUV sped out of the parking lot with lights and sirens blazing. She tried to get the license plate, but they had been removed. Merging in with the traffic the SUV cut across three lanes and blended in with the traffic and was gone.

"Damn him," she whispered, then undid the string and slid out the manila folder. On the front was a black and white polaroid picture of a younger dark-haired woman fastened with a paper clip and the words TOP SECRET stamped in big red letters. In the upper right-hand corner was the name Avicia Karayan.

Opening the cover was like looking into a time capsule. I better save this for Dave, she thought, and slid the folder into the envelope and tied the string.

"I thought you forgot about me," Dave said as he used a ruler to draw a straight line from one point on the map to another.

Sandy was pasty white from the few paragraphs she did read.

"Is everything okay?" Dave asked as he dropped the pencil.

Sandy raised the envelope and dropped it on the desk. When it hit it sounded like it contained a led weight. They both stared at it for a minute. "I recovered this for you. It's all the information that remains on the Karayan case," Sandy whispered.

Dave slowly untied the string and slid out the manila folder and looked at the picture for a few minutes. "She looks perfectly normal to me."

Opening the cover, Dave leaned back in the chair and began to read. Page after page faded away and outside the daylight gave way to darkness. Still the pages came as he read a complete history of Icearaus, the portal and how it came to be, about Elwrick and his fantastic horse named Midnight which could be summoned with a thought, the island of Aramoor and the beautiful gardens. Captain Royston and the boat which could move without wind. More pages told of a race of elves from the Whispering Woods and reptiles that could speak from the 'Anor and the barbarians from the Frozen Tundra. Still the pages continued about the underground cities beneath the Silver Mountains and the dwarves that once lived there.

The last pages though were the most interesting as they told of her encounters on Earth and the horrors she faced. The family who accepted her tried to keep her a secret, but a nosey neighbor found out she was an alien and contacted a local paper and sold the story for untold wealth. The CIA was reached, and she was forcefully removed from their residence. The family who took her in were arrested for espionage and conspiracy against the government. Avicia and her child were brought here, and this is where…

Dave wiped a tear away, then broke down sobbing.

"What did you discover?" Sandy softly asked.

"Avicia was brought here and every day she had experiments performed on her. Things no woman should ever have to endure. Loren, the man I idolized, was one of the biggest contributors to the research performing many of the experiments."

Sandy took the folder and when she finished reading the page detailing the things Avicia experienced, she dropped the folder and ran to the bathroom to vomit.

"They killed her," Dave snarled, then threw his Coke across the room. "They goddamn killed her because she was different. She didn't die of natural causes like Loren said. That son of a bitch, if I—"

"Now hold on," Sandy interrupted as she dried her mouth. "I thought it was this agencies job to disprove aliens exist?"

Dave shot her an evil eye. "You don't destroy life to hide its existence. My God, don't tell me you agree with what they—"

"No, I don't agree," Sandy screamed. "I think what they did is downright sickening. We can't go acting all crazy though. Upper management will suspect something, and I need this job."

"I'm sorry, I can't be part of an organization that terrorizes people in such a perverted way. Nowhere did I read in her file that she ever threatened them."

Sandy released a deep sigh. She knew where this was going and spoke first. "We couldn't save Avicia, perhaps we can save this one."

"Now you're thinking straight," Dave grumbled, still furious about the lies Loren told him. "All we have to do is find her before someone reports her."

"What about work?" Sandy asked.

"I already have a plan. It seems the stress of the job is to much and we both need a mental break for a few weeks. That should be enough time to locate the subject."

Sandy smiled at the thought of meeting a real live alien. "I think we can do it. With modern technology we can trace damn near anything. I bet we can pinpoint exactly where she came down."

Dave appeared more determined than ever as he splayed open a map on the desk and fired up all sixteen computer monitors. Starting the program, he began plotting points on the map.

"Before we do anything, I think we should talk with the professor that called you. I would bet my paycheck he knows more than what he's telling us."

"Call Delta Airlines and book us two seats to Frankfort first thing in the morning. Make sure its first class as I don't want to be disturbed while I continue my research."

Sandy had a smirk a mile wide. "I guess we'll see exactly what Mr. Middleton has to say."

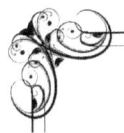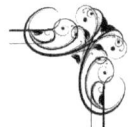

Chapter 32

arlock," Elwrick said. "Impossible," was the next words to roll off his tongue. He must have missed something, somewhere in the Compendium of Creatures—a tome which held vast knowledge of every known creature to exist on the Mortal Realm.

Starting back at the beginning, he read through all four thousand five hundred and twenty-seven pages a second time, and the results were the same. A Witch or Warlock was the only known species to have silver eyes.

Elwrick carefully closed the extremely rare book and slid it partway across the table. Inflicted by grief from the trauma of watching the woman he loved inches from death, his eyes must have deceived him. Perhaps in the candlelight he caught the reflection of the silver candleholder. That had to be it, he told himself. To believe anything else was foolish. The way of the Witch and Warlock died out over three-hundred years ago when an angry mob destroyed the last known family. An angry mob whipped into a crazed frenzy by a necromancer named Malvo Necrosyse. The same necromancer whose journal they now held within their possession.

Placing the book back on the shelf, he went to the bedroom where he laid down and closed his eyes. He wasn't sleeping though. Beings of light needed no rest, and he only had a bedroom so he could lie down while he pondered future events. His mind drifted back to the sheep and Averie. *If she was the sheep, what was the meaning of all the dead sheep? Was she destined to die as well? Were all bearers destine to die?* He thought. I'm overthinking this. The answer is simple and staring me right in the face.

When his eyes opened, the sun shone brightly through the window and a slight breeze tickled the curtain. To decipher the vision, he would need to travel back to the Mortal Realm to Talons Peak. It was the only community he remembered where there was an abundance of sheep. It would be here the answer would come to him, and he thought of *Talons Peak,* and shimmered out of existence.

The weather here was horrid forcing all inhabitants to seek shelter. In the center of town, the remains of Rufus's house stood like burnt matchsticks and beside it was a grave marker where Rufus was laid to rest.

Elwrick knelt beside the grave and offered a prayer. From his eyes came tears consecrating the muddy ground.

Meandering through town, he found himself on the outskirts looking at the Broken Spine Mountains. From here he could see the trail Pegan led Averie down to escape, and his mind drifted back to that very day. It was similar to this storm except nastier and influenced by a liches disciple. With each passing memory, his face twisted with anger. The things she had to endure to survive the journey, and now, she was facing death again if what Lady Alenia believes true about the sheep.

Eventually Elwrick arrived at the corner post of a large pasture. Inside were hundreds of sheep doing what sheep do. "Damn you," Elwrick screamed as he looked up into the bleak sky. "She carries your child and all you provide is a meaningless vision," he shouted into the falling rain.

"Can I help you?"

"I don't believe so," Elwrick answered in a startled voice as he turned to put a face to the soft voice. It was a young man whose face had yet to see a razor, but the dirt was proof he had more experience at life than most grown men. A wide-brimmed hat deflected the water away from his lean body while canvas coveralls and knee-high boots protected him from the elements.

"I'm Jacob," the boy said as he propped his foot up on the lower rung of the rough wooden fence. "Who might you be?"

Elwrick ran his fingers through his drenched beard. "I'm Elwrick."

"Ah yes, now I remember. The lizard healer."

Elwrick laughed. "I guess you could call me that."

"I wasn't here to see it, but the stories are astounding." The boy pulled a piece of straw from his hat and began chewing on it. "What brings you out on a day like this?"

"I need to watch your sheep for a bit."

"Why, have they wronged you?" Jacob asked.

"No, no," Elwrick answered. "There is no need to trouble you with things beyond your grasp."

"Try me," Jacob said with a smile. "You might be surprised. My mom says I'm the smartest person she knows."

What did he have to lose, after all, this boy was a sheep farmer, Elwrick thought, then told Jacob of the vision in excruciating detail. "Now do you understand. I wish to watch your sheep hoping they will reveal a clue to the vision so I can save a woman in trouble."

Jacob scratched his chin as he looked out over the pasture. "Don't know what it means, but I would never allow my sheep in that pasture," Jacob said.

"Why's that?" Elwrick confusingly asked.

Jacob looked at Elwrick, then started laughing. "You're kidding, right?"

Elwrick sighed. "I'm standing here in the rain watching sheep who seem to be enjoying themselves in this blasted storm. Do I look like I'm joking?"

Jacob waited for a minute watching a sheep walk to within a few feet of them and graze on a large green plant. "Because Milkweed, Hemlock, Larkspur, and the Darling Pea Plant are deadly poisonous to sheep. The Forb is the only thing edible in your vision."

Elwrick suddenly went cold. "Thank you. Thank you for the information," Elwrick said, then realized the boy was gone. In the ground were no footprints of Jacobs arrival or departure. Spinning in a circle, he looked in all directions, but the boy had vanished.

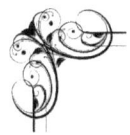
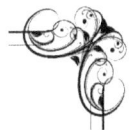

Chapter 33

lanting a big ol' wet sloppy kiss on Jennifer's lips as she slept, Mike quietly snuck out of the house before the sun rose. His pants were pressed to perfection with a razor-sharp crease, shoes spit-polished to a mirror sheen, and his silver badge rubbed until it sparkled like a diamond. Today was the day he had waited for all his life and to be late was unacceptable.

Turning on the radio, he made it no more than a mile then turned it off and rolled down the window. The sound of the wind was much more calming than some overrated sixteen-year-old pop star eating on the mic as they sang.

Mike could have left home at eight-thirty and still arrived in plenty of time for his nine o'clock appointment with the Mayor, but he didn't sleep a wink after receiving the official letter the day before by certified mail.

Over the last few years he watched the chief growing ever closer to retirement, and he stepped up taking on all the duties. Now, his hard work was about to pay off as he accepted the coveted position as Chief of Police.

Looking in the rear-view mirror he rehearsed his acceptance speech and how he planned to send the current chief off in grand fashion. The man had taught him so much over the years and propelled his career to where it was today.

Driving through town, he observed all the stores with their lights off and doors locked. All the owners were still home asleep in their warm beds oblivious to what was about to occur. Making his way to Badger Hill where he proposed to Jennifer, he watched the sun rise spilling its colors like an artist starting a new painting on a blank canvas.

Standing at the railing overlooking Willowdale as the town came alive, he repeated his speech for the entire world to hear. Later tonight at the grand ceremony, his wife and friends would gather and hear it for the first time.

Back in the car and cruising down the winding road back to town, the time had come for him to accept his new position and he made his way for town hall.

Jennifer arrived at the Fischer Farm bright-eyed and bushy-tailed. In her hand she carried a large envelope.

"Come in," Sarah mumbled as she opened the door.

Jennifer's eyes opened wide. "You look like a sloth that fell from a tree."

"Don't start with me," Sarah snapped as she fought with the coffee pot. "Think I got three and a half seconds of sleep last night."

"Oh, is everything okay?"

"Robyn was fussy last night. Wanted the bottle, didn't want the bottle, wanted to be held, didn't want to be held… no matter what we tried that little girl would not go to sleep."

"You should have called me," Jennifer said.

"You need your sleep too. We can't call you every time Robyn's cranky."

Jennifer laid the envelope on the table. "Is Robyn better now?"

"Sleeping like a baby."

Jennifer laughed. "Guess her work is done."

The look Sarah shot Jennifer made her think twice about her next joke and she quickly changed the subject. "Is Averie awake?"

"She's in the shower," Sarah said as she finally got the coffee pot working.

"Look what I have," Jenifer said as she opened the envelope and pulled out two forms and handed them to Sarah.

Sarah quickly scanned each page. "Citizenship applications?"

"Yup."

"How do you plan to pull this off?" Sarah mumbled as she pulled the creamer from the fridge.

Jennifer grinned. "I have a friend in the business who owes me a huge favor."

Mike strutted into the headquarters, nodded at the receptionist, then made his way to the Mayor's office. Stepping back after knocking on the door he checked his uniform making sure not one wrinkle was visible.

"Come in," Tony said as he stood up from his plush leather chair and placed his hands on the oil-rubbed mahogany desk.

Mike entered, then hesitated. There was no congratulation banner, no smiling Chief, and no cake. There was only him, and the painful silence of rejection.

"You mind closing the door," Tony said as he sat back down.

Mike slowly closed the door. The entire time his mind lost in thought about what in the world was going on. Suddenly, none of this made sense.

"I've put off having this meeting for a few days so that I could gather the facts," Tony said as he pulled a file out from the drawer.

"Do you mind telling me what in the world is going on?" Mike asked as he sat in the high-backed leather chair opposite Tony.

Tony flipped open the file. "I've known you for a long time Mike, and you've always been an upstanding citizen and excellent officer."

"I'm getting passed over for the promotion to Chief?" Mike asked.

"Promotion?" Tony's face scrunched.

"Isn't that what this letter's about?"

Tony looked down at the official letter Mike removed from his coat pocket. "What made you think that?" Tony asked.

"Never mind then about the letter," Mike growled as he crumbled it up and tossed it in the trash can beside the desk. "What is it about then?"

Tony cleared his throat. "It's about your performance lately. It seems you haven't been yourself. I really can't explain it beyond you appear lost in a strange fogginess or stupor."

Mike's eyebrows climbed his forehead like a frightened caterpillar. "What are you getting at?"

"This isn't easy to ask," Tony said as he leaned back in his chair and placed his laced fingers on his chest. "Have you been doing drugs lately?"

Mike came unglued as he shot out of the chair knocking it over. "I've never done a drug in my life and you know it."

"Mike, I'm your friend. If there's something going on you need to tell me."

"Something? Like what?" Mike was flabbergasted by the accusations.

Tony cocked his head sideways. "Then how do you justify slapping around a helpless woman and destroying her store. Then when she threatened to call the police you said, and I quote, 'I am the police and if she said anything she would never do business again in this city,' end quote."

"Excuse me?" Mike asked as he almost fell over.

Tony rifled through the pages of the report. "I didn't believe it either. Not until numerous witnesses came forth with similar stories."

"And exactly who made these accusations?"

Tony looked at Mike funny. "You know as well as I do I can't tell you due to confidentiality laws."

"Fine," Mike grumbled. "Whoever made these accusations is a liar."

From the file Tony removed a plain white envelope and slid it across the table. "What's that for?"

"It's your final paycheck plus a recommendation letter. After talking with the Chief, he decided it would be in the city's best interest if we parted ways."

"Am I being terminated?"

"Mike," Tony said as he stood. "I'm still your friend. I talked with the Mayor of Meyer County and he has a job waiting for you. I told him you put in your resignation letter for personal reasons, not that you were being terminated. Inside your file I put in a resignation letter as well."

Mike slammed his fist on the desk knocking a picture over. "I didn't do a damn thing, and you know it. I'm the most professional officer on the force. My record over the last fifteen years has been impeccable."

Tony repositioned the picture then pushed the envelope closer to Mike. "I'm sorry. You can turn in your uniforms tomorrow. Now if you will excuse me I have an important city council meeting to attend."

Mike looked down at the envelope. "Keep your GODDAMN blood money."

Tony followed Mike out to his car. "Don't do anything stupid. Think of Jennifer and what it would do to her if you got locked up."

Mike never heard a word as his foot hit the gas pedal and he sped away leaving behind a cloud of dust.

Averie dragged herself down the hall and flopped down in the recliner. Under both eyes were bags which appeared to be made from concrete.

"Didn't get much sleep either?" Jennifer asked.

Averie shook her head, no.

"Maybe Mike and I should stay here tonight so you both can get some sleep."

Tom entered the house covered in dirt and grumbling something about how miserable his life currently was. "No Mike today. I thought he had Tuesdays off."

"He has a meeting with the Mayor."

"That doesn't sound good," Sarah said as she poured Tom a cup of coffee.

"How's the field going?" she asked Tom.

"Going to be a lot of work if we want to get that back fifty acres ready for cows. It's in worse shape than I thought."

Sarah turned to face Jennifer. "What's going on with the Mayor?"

"Mike's been expecting a promotion. He believes this may be his lucky day."

"Well if I don't see him, tell him congratulations for me," Tom said as he exited out the front door with his coffee cup in hand.

Jennifer pulled out a chair at the table and sat. "Averie, can you come?"

Averie stumbled her way to the dining room rubbing the side of her face. Both eyes had yet to open fully.

"Are you ready to become a citizen?" Jennifer asked.

Averie's eye's widened and her mouth opened to speak, but then it shut quicker than a bear trap.

"It's okay, all it means is the United States will become your official home," Sarah informed Averie.

"I hope you don't mind," Jennifer said as she glanced the page over one time for accuracy. "But I took the liberty of filling it out. All I need is your last name."

Averie thought long and hard staring at the ceiling. "My last name is Fischer."

"That's my last name dear. We need your last name," Sarah said.

Averie became rigid, distant, and her breathing slowed. "That name is dead to me. My last name is Fischer."

"Why can't she use our last name?" Billy asked. "She's part of the family."

"I thought she would like to use her Father's name to remember him," Jennifer answered Billy.

"Remember my Father," Averie said. "My Father kept me locked in a dirt floor room where I was forced to eat slugs and worms. Every day he would beat and terrorize me."

"That mother…" Jennifer covered her mouth before she could finish. "I knew you went through hell, but I figured the Keeper was a guard, not your Father."

"I think you should use it," Sarah said. "To show your Father that your stronger than he will ever be. To show Robyn that you're a survivor, not a victim."

"Have you lost your mind?" Jennifer asked Sarah. "You really want Averie reliving her past?"

"My Father is dead," Averie whispered. "The night I was rescued Pegan put a blade to my Father's throat and sliced it from ear to ear."

"I like that man more and more every day," Jennifer said.

Sarah covered her mouth with both hands, and her face went pale.

Averie watched the chickens peck the ground through the window. "SnowBriar," Averie said, catching them all by surprise. "My name is Averie SnowBriar."

"That is a beautiful name and one you should never be ashamed to bear," Sarah said.

"Well Miss SnowBriar. Would you like to sign your paperwork, so that you can become a member of our society?"

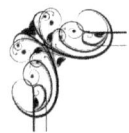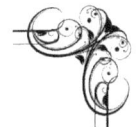

Chapter 34

ady Alenia tried to rise, but her body ached in places she never knew existed and she fell back on the bed.

"Easy now," Elwrick said as he brushed her hair away that blanketed her face. "You've been resting a long time."

She reached up and stroked his face. "What happened?" she whispered, her throat was dry and parched making the words scratchy.

Elwrick sat on the bed and held her frail hand, then told her of the incident.

"How is that possible?" she asked.

Elwrick shook his head. "I don't know. For a minute I thought Pegan was a Warlock."

"Warlock? Their time on this planet ended long ago."

Elwrick patted her good leg and smiled. "Last time I saw Pegan his eyes flashed the brightest silver I had ever seen. Only for a moment, but they were silver."

Lady Alenia licked her dry lips. "Would a Warlock possess that kind of power?"

Elwrick rose, then paced the length of the medical ward stopping at the closed window. "I went to the Keep to see the destruction. No mortal has the power to do what he did." Elwrick flipped the latch cracking open the window allowing fresh air to enter. "I didn't recognize the Keep at first. It looked like it was dropped from the heavens."

"That bad?"

"It was obliterated. Stones thick as your bed scattered like leaves tossed in the wind. Timbers were splintered, steel beams twisted and mangled in demonic tortured shapes and the smell of death was heavy from within."

Lady Alenia thought back to why Pegan went there to begin with. "The journal. Did they recover the journal?"

"Yes. Raestmond discovered its hiding location. I put it in the artifact room along with an extremely rare and quite strange magical doorway."

Lady Alenia propped herself up in the bed. "A magical doorway. That indeed is rare as they are constructed in the deepest pits of hell. How did it come to be here amongst us mortals?"

"That is the mystery," Elwrick said. "I talked with Saress and she informed me Pegan explained to them exactly what it was when they were in the room with that demonic creation—things way beyond a mortal's understanding. Details only someone whose been to hell would know."

"Is," Lady Alenia stopped to reconsider her words. "Is Pegan a demon yet to be identified?"

"I don't believe—"

"Is he EVIL!" Lady Alenia interrupted.

"I don't believe so. Dark magic, or evil magic is a manifestation inside the mind. It cannot be hidden or concealed and is easily detectable. This thing, this entity which has entered Pegan is neither of the body, or the mind. I fear it has woven itself around his very soul and only reveals itself when the need arises."

"There must be a way to communicate with it. We must find a way before it destroys us all."

Elwrick pondered her words. "I don't believe this thing has any animosity towards us. It's a parasite and acts only to ensure its host will survive."

Lady Alenia looked confused.

"From my understanding it only rears its ugly head each time Pegan is on the brink of death."

That evening as the sky darkened Lady Alenia walked from the Medical Ward with the aid of a beautiful cane Raestmond painstakingly crafted. With his arm around her waist, Elwrick accompanied the Elf Queen. At the base of the stairs, elves cheered when they saw their Queen emerge.

Lady Alenia waved to them and thanked them all for their support.

"Speech, speech, speech," the elves chanted.

Lady Alenia raised her hand to silence them. "I would like to thank you for your support. As of now there are more important matters which must be addressed than a speech to make you feel good while evil thrives outside our borders. I want each and every one of you to know though your survival is my highest concern, and I will face the deadliest enemies to ensure the survival of the elven race against the evil which wishes to destroy us."

The crowd parted creating a path for them to pass. Along the way she exchanged handshakes, kisses and hugs. What she really wanted at this very moment though was to be alone with Elwrick in her new home which she was told was an engineering marvel.

Carrying her up the stairs the door magically opened as Elwrick neared.

Lady Alenia's mouth formed into a circle and an *ooohhh* sound escaped her mouth. *This place is beautiful,* she thought. Lavishly decorated with exquisite furniture and every lamp was polished to a magnificent sheen. Tables were made from the finest exotic woods and paintings hung on every wall. From the main room was a bedroom with an oversized bed made for two and six pillows. A dresser topped with a huge mirror was perfectly placed so the light through the oversized window shown perfectly on the bench in front of it. On a second dresser was a large porcelain bowl filled with cool water and beside it was a stack of clean towels.

Elwrick lowered Lady Alenia onto the bed and propped her wounded leg up on a pillow. "Gleia said you need to keep it elevated for a few more weeks."

"Lay with me," Lady Alenia whispered to Elwrick.

Elwrick did as she asked, then placed his arm around her as she rested her head on his chest.

In his arms, Lady Alenia felt safe and her eyes slowly drifted closed.

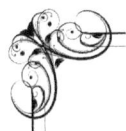
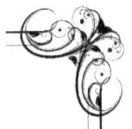

Chapter 35

ike drove the streets of **Willowdale lost in a foggy haze.** "How is this even possible?" he kept repeating. One minute he was planning on running the small police force, and now he was unemployed. *How am I going to tell Jennifer? Without my pension we'll never be able to retire.*

Easing the Impala to a stop at a red light, he unfastened his badge and looked at it. Five days a week for the last fifteen years he proudly wore it. Volunteering to work Christmas, Thanksgiving, and the Fourth of July so the other officers could spend time with their kids. None of that mattered to the Mayor, or the Chief. Each time they called him to run security at a special event, he was there regardless of what he had planned. None of it mattered.

The honk of a car horn caught his attention. Who knows how long the light had been green.

Pulling into a parking spot, he dug through the glove box and found a fine-tipped permeant marker. Across the front of his badge he wrote the initials E.O.W. then tossed it on the passenger's seat. "Oh, what the hell," he grumbled and took off his uniform top and wadded it up throwing it next to the badge.

The ringing of his phone broke the eerie silence inside the vehicle. "Hello."

"How did it go?" Jennifer asked.

"We need to talk."

"You sound—"

"What? A little pissed," Mike interrupted.

"To say the least," Jennifer hesitantly said. "Did you get passed over for the promotion, again?"

"I'll be home shortly," Mike said. "I need to be alone for a bit to clear my head."

"Well don't go to the house. I'm at Sarah's. I told her we would stay here tonight to watch Robyn. Neither of them got a minute of sleep last night."

Mike hung up the phone and put the car in drive. Not far from there was an ice cream shop and it just sounded right.

Hours later, Jennifer and Sarah watched Mike as the car slowly rolled down the drive. They both could see something went dreadfully wrong by the vacant expression on his face.

Jennifer greeted him with a hug and a kiss. "Don't worry about the promotion. You're still the best officer and they know it."

Mike looked down the driveway. "I was terminated."

"How? What? Why? Are you joking?" Jennifer stumbled on the words.

Mike repeated the conversation verbatim between Tony and him.

"Fine," Jennifer hissed as she crossed her arms. "All their doing is losing the best officer they have on the force. The clinic is doing great, no worries."

Mike sighed. "That's garbage, and you know it."

"What do you mean?" Jennifer asked.

"We both knew when we bought the house it was going to take two incomes to make ends meet. On the months the Clinic is slow we struggle to survive."

"Then we'll give back the house. What are they going to do? Arrest us. Truth be told I'm tired of making the *thirty-five hundred dollar* a month payment anyway. We don't need a six-bedroom colonial. I would be perfectly happy in a two-bedroom ranch."

"Remember, that's what I said when we were looking, but you had to have it."

Jennifer raised her hands in defense. "Okay, so I wanted the house. I screwed up, fine, is that what you want to hear. I screwed up."

"Nobody screwed up," Sarah interrupted. "And it's nobody's fault."

Averie looked almost like a ghost as she watched them talk. She could see events playing out the same as on Icearaus. "This is my fault," she finally said.

Sarah cocked her head sideways. "Excuse me."

"Don't you understand. On Icearaus, everywhere I went trouble followed. Now, it appears to have followed me here. Perhaps I should leave before death finds all of us."

"It's not your fault," Jennifer said.

"I never want to hear you talk like that again young lady," Sarah snapped. "This has nothing to do with you."

Averie stood there looking pale.

"It's not your fault," Billy whispered.

"Come inside and let's talk about this like adults. Besides, I have an idea. Your firing may be a blessing in disguise."

Tom stood there shell-shocked when he heard. "You know who's behind this, don't you?"

"No," Mike said as he shook his head.

"I guarantee you it's Samantha," Tom said.

"Why would she—"

"Because she hates it when things don't go her way, or she gets embarrassed."

"She was the one responsible for getting Ron's Tire Shop shut down for supposedly selling defunct tires, yet every person you interviewed who bought tires there never had a single problem. Eventually, the truth came out Ron denied her credit and she was humiliated. Debra's House of Pancakes, and that toy store…" Tom started snapping his fingers. "What was the name again?"

"Toy World?" Sarah said.

"That's the one," Tom said. "Behind all the closures where two people, Samantha and Tony. Now we have a fourth victim. Those two are out of control."

"It still doesn't help me with a job," Mike said.

"That's why I called Tom in from the field," Sarah said. "Tom, you always say good help is hard to come by and you and Mike are best buds. I know you could use the help on that fifty acres and it will make it so much easier to run the farm with a good farmhand. Why don't we put him on the payroll?"

Tom shook his head. "Unfortunately, I can't hire Mike. I'm sorry."

"I understand," Mike said. "The Mayor did say that Meyer County would hire me as a deputy. Perhaps I will go there."

Sarah's mouth came unhinged and the gasp she made sounded like an asthma patient having an attack. "Tom Fischer—"

"I'm sorry," Tom interrupted. "I won't have a man working for me who beats women."

"You don't believe this garbage, do you?" Sarah hissed at Tom.

"Of course not," Tom said, then busted out laughing. "You should have seen the look on your face though."

Sarah kicked Tom in the shin putting an abrupt end to the laughter.

"Still, I refuse to be your boss," Tom said as he stuck his hand out. "What I will do is allow you to buy half the farm, fifty-fifty partners."

Mike stepped back. "I appreciate the offer, but we don't have the cash to buy-in. All we need is enough to make sure we can pay the bills and get by."

"I didn't ask for cash right now. We'll write up a contract and you can pay me a percentage of your monthly earnings."

"Fantastic," Jennifer cheered. "See, everything is going to work out."

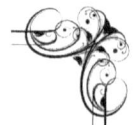

Chapter 36

ave stood at the carousel and watched the belt slowly chug along in a jerking wheezing motion. Suitcase after suitcase passed only broken by the accessional duffel bag.

"There's mine." Sandy pointed at a bright pink suitcase on the verge of exploding as it broke through the transparent curtains.

"I was thinking we may want to keep this trip a secret," Dave said as he watched more luggage slowly pass.

"Why is that?" Sandy asked, then moved out of the way so a younger lady could grab her backpack off the conveyor.

Dave reached down and grabbed the bright pink suitcase and stood it up beside them. "I don't know. A gut feeling I guess."

Sandy pointed at the mangled piece of luggage hanging half-way off the conveyor. "I think that one is yours."

"Jesus, what'd they do to it, drag it behind the plane?"

"I only hope the wheels are still on it. Otherwise, you're going to have to carry it," Sandy said as she started laughing.

Dave snatched the monstrosity and somehow managed to get it balanced on the three remaining wheels while extending the handle. "Customer service is going to hear about this," Dave grumbled as they followed the signs to the car rental station.

Later that evening at the hotel Dave had a detailed map of Kentucky rolled out on the desk. On either side of the map was a laptop, each running different tracing programs, but in a continuous loop. On a second table was a map of Frankfort.

Sandy circled the location of Frankfort University then used a highlighter to plot their course from the hotel to the college.

"I think it came down right here." Dave pointed to a small dot on the map beside the name Willowdale.

"It?" Sandy cautiously asked.

"Well, do you know what it is?"

Sandy shook her head, no. "From the size of the dot though my guess is it shouldn't take much to find IT," emphasizing it.

Dave laughed. From his suitcase he removed another laptop hoping it still worked properly.

"Jesus, did you bring the whole lab?" Sandy asked.

"I brought just enough to ensure I could complete my task," Dave answered. Firing up the laptop he accessed a secret government website with up to the minute city maps taken from passing satellites. Once the image was downloaded, he sent it through an untraceable server where it overlaid perfectly with the trace program. "The laptops are much slower than the mainframe systems at the lab so it's going to take a few days to recreate the trajectory. If it works though, the computer should be able to tell us within a quarter-mile of where it landed."

"A quarter-mile. If it came down in the middle of the town, that could be the entire town," Sandy complained.

"I'm using the latest state of the art equipment. What more can I do?"

"I guess a quarter-mile is better than if we only knew the state," Sandy sighed.

"Maybe we'll get lucky and Frank knows more than what he's saying."

Dave looked out the window to the glowing sign across the street—Bartholomew's Steakhouse. "How about we go get something to eat. You like steak?"

"Love it, but the price might be a little steep judging from how the building looks.".

Dave held up the state credit card. "Tonight is on me, let's enjoy ourselves."

The next morning at nine, Dave and Sandy entered the administration building and located the receptionist.

"Can I help you?" the young man sitting at a desk loaded with papers and folders asked. On his monitor were a thousand sticky notes and a bank of phones besides the desk blinked in a series of bleeps.

"If possible, I would like to arrange a meeting with Professor Frank Middleton," Dave said with a professional tone.

"I'm afraid that won't be possible. Professor Middleton has taken a leave of absence for personal reasons."

"Any idea how long he's going to be gone?" Sandy asked.

"Unfortunately, even if I knew I couldn't tell you because of legal reasons."

Dave released a heavy breath. "Thank you for your time.".

Sandy leaned against the car's fender and watched the students come and go. "Now what?"

Dave looked around. "Not sure yet. He's a popular man. Someone has to know where he lives."

Sandy smacked herself in the forehead with her palm, then started laughing. "I feel like an idiot." Using her cellphone, she quickly Googled the name Professor Frank Middleton, Frankfort Kentucky.

"Bingo," Dave cheered when an address materialized on the screen.

Dave typed the coordinates into the GPS, and almost immediately, an electronic voice began barking directions.

Halfway across town they arrived at what many would consider a small mansion with perfectly manicured bushes, golf-course green grass, a large fountain supported by four lions, and a cobble stone walkway straight out of the Wizard of Oz. Coming down that walkway was a man sporting a designer suit. "Well, here goes nothing." Sandy swung the door open and climbed out.

"Hopefully he'll help us."

Frank met them at the car. "Can I help you?"

"Professor Frank Middleton?" Dave asked.

"Are you from the police?" Frank answered with a question of his own.

Dave looked at Frank like the man had three eyes. "No. Why would we be from the police? We're the scientist from Florida?"

"Florida?"

"Remember, you called looking for Loren?"

"Oh, yes, yes, that's right. What can I do for you?"

"We wanted to know if you knew anything more about those strange coins?"

"I already told you everything I know on the phone. Now if you'll excuse me, I have a very important meeting which requires my presence." Frank started to walk away.

Dave thought for a minute. *He had to get something more out of this man. He could tell by Franks reluctancy to talk he had more to give.* "One more question?" Dave pleaded. "I thought all pawnshops were required by law to collect paperwork from the seller. This way they could make sure the item was not stolen. Out there somewhere, there has to be a paper trail back to the pawnshop and the original owner."

Frank lurched to a stop. "There's one pawnshop on the south…" *What if these two where here to buy the coins,* he thought. *It's obvious they were sent here by the government and had unlimited resources, money to them was no object.* "Only on items with serial numbers." Frank told an ugly lie. "If I had to guess I would try one of those out of the way pawnshops located on the outskirts of Frankfort. Now if you'll excuse me I'm running late.'"

"Thank you for your time," Sandy said.

Frank watched them drive away then sped off in the opposite direction. He had spent the last few hours making phone calls to other pawnshop owners describing Tiny and Sheba. One name kept floating to the top—*Flying High*.

Not a mile down the road Dave pulled into a gas station and parked.

"You thinking what I'm thinking?" Sandy asked.

"Yup, he's lying through his teeth."

"What now, there's probably a hundred pawnshops in town. And we already know Franks no help."

"And the sad thing is he could be saving his own life, but I fear it may already be too late."

"What do you mean?" Sandy asked.

"I know you didn't read the file as I did, so let me explain. Not only did the scientist who experimented on Avicia die. All those who held a negative position with her experienced some form of grief in their lives—"

"So let me get this straight," Sandy interrupted. "Everyone who was involved with the last incident experienced hell, and now you dragged the both of us right into the mix? We may want to reconsider our future actions very closely."

"There's more if you let me finish," Dave snapped. "Honestly. I don't think we have anything to worry about. I once believed the family who helped her were arrested and never heard from again. Reading the folder again on the flight I discovered I skipped over a few paragraphs where it explains the disposition of the original family. It appears they were released and given new names and now flourish, living in Southern California on the beach."

"Why didn't we go there and talk with them?" Sandy asked.

Dave looked at Sandy like she was stupid. "Did you not hear what I said. We were already on the plane. I don't think the pilot would have changed course because I told him I needed to go somewhere else. Besides, what can they tell us?"

Sandy raised her hand to smack him a good one. "Don't treat me like that."

"I'm sorry," Dave whispered, trying to restore the peace.

Sandy bit her finger as she thought. "Are you talking about some kind of curse, like you would find on an Egyptian tomb were all those who open it die from some foreign disease which has no cure?"

Dave raised his hands in the air. "Honestly, I don't know what the hell I believe anymore. All I know is the last time an incident like this happened a lot of people's lives changed, and most were for the worse. All I'm trying to do is prevent an innocent life from being lost. I honestly don't care about those who perish because of their own ignorance."

"Tonight, I want to see that file so I can read it in its entirety," Sandy complained. "Tomorrow, I may be on a plane back to Florida."

Dave started the car. "Let's head back to the hotel and check on the computers. If where lucky its finished the trace program, but I doubt it. Afterward, well get a bit to eat then go hit a few pawnshops and ask a few questions. When I talked with Frank on the phone that day he let a few details slip on what the owners looked like. Perhaps someone will know the pawnshop."

Frank pounded on the steering wheel. "Damn it all to hell," he cursed. The *Flying High Pawnshop* was closed for a week due to a family emergency. He knew exactly what the emergency was. Tiny and Sheba were probably out of town trying to sell the coins. All he could do know was bide his time and check every day hoping they returned early and with the coins.

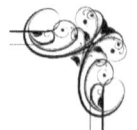

Chapter 37

he days blurred into a kaleidoscope of dense trees, towering mountains, and deadly cliffs.

Raising his fist high in the air Jester signaled for his two companions to stop as he neared the edge of a steep drop-off. Frustrated with the abysmal conditions, he climbed from his horse to stretch, then plot a new course. They should have been well on their way home by now, if not already within the walls of Lynn Brook. The weather though had other plans. Torrential rains washed away every known path and destroyed the once easily traveled trails while gale-force winds toppled trees and clogged the few passages they managed to locate.

Remfrey climbed from his mount and sunk ankle-deep in the muddy ground. Beneath his stained brown leather armor enormous muscles rippled threatening to bust each seam. Swiping the water and mist from his face, he shielded his experienced eyes with his gloved hand while he surveyed the mountainous terrain. The shrouded moon did little to light his path as he sloshed through the slop while a hurricane-force wind pushed him at a pace slightly faster than a walk. Nearing Jester, he cupped his hands around his mouth to amplify the sound. "How much further?".

Jester's darkened silhouette glowed as a lightning bolt tore through the sky. "I'm not positive," he admitted. "The path to the ravine is destroyed. We'll have to find a different route."

"I only hope Chieftain Ulgra is as agreeable as King Hazgrag," Remfrey said.

Jester thought back to their meeting with the Stone Giants and how eager King Hazgrag was to place his stamp on the allegiance agreement. "He understands the importance of this victory, even willing to put aside his distaste for the cave trolls to see it accomplished."

Derric, a skinny, clean-shaven kid who had yet to experience combat beyond the training grounds spurred his horse urging it forward until he looked down at Jester. "Did you get us lost out here to die?" the kid sneered.

"I know exactly where we're headed," Jester hissed as he pointed at a stone spire jutting upward like a broken tooth. "See that stone spire to the west; it signifies the entrance to the ravine. We only have to discover a suitable route without breaking our necks, or the necks of our mounts."

"Perhaps we should seek shelter for the night and allow the storm to pass?" Derric suggested. From his wide-brimmed hat, a river of water flowed.

"NO!" Jester snapped, his glare could have set flame to steel. "We've been gone too long as it is."

Remfrey looked at Derric, then shook his head in disgust. "If you're going to make it in the King's army, better get used to operating in less-than-favorable conditions." Tapping Jester on his shoulder to draw the commander's attention, Remfrey revealed his experience of the area by pointing to the west at a high ridge. "Perhaps Dagger-Tooth Pass has avoided the ravages of the storm?"

Jester nodded his approval. "Perhaps. As of now I see no other option." Jester quickly mounted his steed, then spurred the beast and jerked on the reins guiding him up a steep trail created by a mudslide. Slipping and sliding the horse somehow maintained its balance enough to merge onto an adjacent path which traced the edge of a harrowing cliff. From there he took a switchback which climbed high into the Ash Mountains before merging with a trail which appeared at one time to have possibly been a road.

The road was easily traveled, and their pace increased before splitting off onto a harrowing trail clogged with dense ferns and clingy vines. The clay ground turned icy slick as they crested the Broken-Blade Ridge then followed the path which snaked it way down into a misty ravine. Following a roaring stream, the trail turned north and led them out through a series of twists and turns where death lingered only one slip away. At one section Jester had no choice but to cut a new path between trails as the one they followed was gone by way of the storm.

Three more hours would pass before they stood at the base of the tall stone spire.

"Gentlemen, welcome to *Uscara Vrogaa*, or Home of the Bottomless Ravine in cave troll tongue."

From the abyss, bouts of mist and steam rose up through the gloomy, damp air. The roar of water muffled the thunder while lightning blistered the sky.

From his pack Jester removed three torches and handed one to each. "The path down is treacherous even in the best of weather. With the storm fast at hand well be lucky to survive the descent."

Derric looked about while Jester searched through his pack looking for the vial of oil he brought. "It'll be light soon. Perhaps we should wait until then to enter."

Remfrey examined the path which traced the edge of the jagged cliff. "I have to agree with the kid on this one. For one, we don't know what we're walking in to. Second, the cave trolls are extremely aggressive towards man, it's possible a fight will occur."

Jester looked at his two companions with disgust dripping from his eyes. "Have you both lost your backbone along the journey?"

"I can't explain it, but the rising hair on my neck tells me we should wait," Derric said as he clung to his horse to prevent being blown free.

Jester's fingers curled inward forming fists.

Lightning tore through the sky briefly illuminating the land and leaving them all momentarily blind.

"We've come too far to quit now," Jester growled.

"The kid gives sound advice," Remfrey said. "I don't believe he is suggesting we quit, only that we wait until morning when the situation can be better assessed. Even in the gloom and shrouded mist, cave trolls have superior vision. If things go bad, I would prefer to fight them on an even battlefield."

Jester let his eyes dart back and forth and finally settled on the kid. "Fine. Not too far back we passed a small cave in the face of the mountain. We'll camp there until dawn breaks." Jester snatched the torches and stuffed them back in the pack. "We'll be needing these later," he grumbled."

The cave penetrated deeper than first thought, and it turned into a rather cozy environment. Near the back dried wood was located and a fire quickly constructed. It would be light in a few hours, but they each welcomed the warmth and a hot meal.

"What do you think? Is King Karayan going to win this war?" Derric asked Remfrey.

Remfrey thought for a moment. "I don't know. I do believe Karayan underestimates his enemy. The elves are cunning, and they have Pegan Rhoe on their side."

"He's only one man. Yes—he's an assassin, but he's still a man. He'll bleed and die just like the filthy elves," Jester intervened.

Remfrey ran his fingers through his hair then rung out the water from the strands. "I don't think he can die. I've heard others speak about his past and what little of it is known, is quite troubling. I mean, he defeated Arlin Brack. That alone should have been impossible."

"To fear the name is a sign of cowardice," Jester hissed. "I've never met the man, but I question the things he's done, and believe them as lies."

"Someday we'll find out." Derric pulled off his hat allowing his curly blond hair to career past his shoulders. Loosening his cloak, he allowed the heat to penetrate his tunic.

Jester rested his back against the stone wall. "Well, when he's strung-up by his toes, and his skin is slowly being peeled off his back, you can ask him if they're true."

As the sun rose, the sky cleared and the howling wind calmed to a breeze.

Jester walked out and stretched taking in a deep breath of the freshly washed air. He didn't want to admit it, but the kid was correct. The morning sun warmed his skin, and instantly, he felt revitalized. "Smells like a good day to make the trolls join the crusade."

The ravine looked much different in the light. The darkened mist was now smoke gray and on the far wall of the gorge, a broken glimpse of a shimmering waterfall emerged. Moss grew in random places along with grasses, and little yellow flowers with broad green leaves flourished. Far below, mist obscured their vision making the path fade away after a few hundred paces while the churning of the waterfall sounded like the starving belly of a hungry beast.

Carefully maneuvering their mounts down the icy slick path, they made it no more than a few yards before each horse locked their knees and refused to advance, even after being spurred and whipped. They would rather be beat, than tumble to their deaths over the side.

"Guess we'll walk from here," Jester said as he hopped down. His feet though had no grip and shot out from under him like a greased pig. "*OOOPH,*" a groan shot from his lungs as he landed flat on his back then slid partway down the path. Swinging his arms wildly, he tried to grasp anything before careening over the edge.

The laughter from his companions echoed into the gloom.

Holding onto their mounts for support, the other two carefully dismounted.

Jester looked like an octopus trying to climb a ladder as he righted himself.

Holding onto to exposed roots, jagged stones, or using their weapons as anchors, they worked their way down a series of switchbacks. In a few locations, they were forced to climb over rubble as the path was chocked full of debris washed down from above. None knew how far they had gone as the mist enveloped them like a wet blanket. Before long they were each covered in sweat and smelled like swamp water when the path transformed into a series of stone steps much larger than any man could effectively use. Carefully navigating the enlarged steps they were each covered in mud and slime when the stairs widened out to a large landing littered with splintered timbers, cracked boulders, gnawed on bones, and discarded furs.

Jester scrambled his way to the river's edge and washed the mud from his face and hands. "This river splits the ravine in two."

"How do we cross?" Derric confusingly asked as he used a long stick to try and determine the depth of the water."

"You're wasting your time with that stick," Remfrey told him. "Rumor is the river so deep I could drop a stone in it, and you would die of old age before it found the bottom."

The kid's eyes grew as large as wagon-wheels.

"Near the center of the ravine is a log bridge," Jester told him.

Following the rocky bank, it was nearing noon when a wide, arched bridge constructed of hastily debarked logs bound together with thick twine broke through the haze. Testing the structure, Jester crossed first and waited for his men on the other side. Not far from there a foul funk worse than their own cut through the gloom. Animals were strung up in various stages of being butchered and were smothered with flies. The meat wiggled and squirmed as if it were still alive.

Jester slid his sword free and jabbed the carcass. To their surprise thousands of larvae fell free painting the muddy ground.

"That's disgusting," Derric whispered while holding back his vomit.

Cave trolls are filthy disgusting creatures," Jester said. "I'm surprised Karayan ___ in his army. If it were me, I would slaughter them and let the ___ ing corpses. But, I'm here to follow orders."

___ e here to do and be done with it," Remfrey snarled.

___ hem southwest until their necks burned from the sun.

___ ey eventually arrived at a crude dais built of boulders,

___ Upon it, a hastily constructed throne of woven tree

___ thicker limbs and crude stones sat empty.

___ surveying the area.

than a few

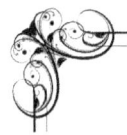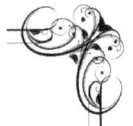

Chapter 38

sing the testimony from **Professor Middleton and the DNA** found on the Marijuana joint near the crime scene, Detective Weaver believed he had enough circumstantial evidence to land a search warrant on the *Flying High Pawnshop*. That was not to be the case though as he watched all the color bleed from Judge Diana Burgers face onto the page in the form of a big red stamp which read DENIED.

Judge Burger slid the search warrant towards the detective with a baffled look in her eyes. "Would you kindly explain to me why you're here wasting my time? I put three cases on hold because you had to get this taken care of ASAP."

Detective Weaver seemed lost as he searched the ceiling for an answer. "I thought there—"

"Listen," Judge Burger interrupted as she splayed her arms out wide. "What do you hope to discover with a search warrant. From my understanding nothing was stolen which could link the owners of the *Flying High Pawnshop* to the murder. Besides, in the paperwork you don't even list the owners, only the pawnshop."

"I planned on drawing up arrest warrants on the owners after I discovered more concrete evidence at the pawnshop," Detective Weaver calmly explained.

Judge Burger leaned back in her chair and studied Detective Weaver. "I understand this is your first case as a detective and I applaud your eagerness to get the man who did this off the streets before he kills again. But," she raised her finger in the air to make a point. "We cannot circumvent the laws and infringe upon the rights of the people so you can begin a vicious witch hunt."

Detective Weaver bit his lower lip as he thought. "Instead of crucifying me for trying to do something good. Why not give me some advice. You were a very successful detective for many years before taking the bench."

Judge Burger leaned forward resting her elbows on the desk. "Here's the best advice I can give you. Go back to the DMV and search every nook and cranny. Every killer leaves a trace; all you must do is find it. Trust me. If you look hard enough, you will find something linking the killer to the crime scene. You do that, and I will issue you an arrest warrant no questions asked."

Later that evening Detective Weaver met a state official at the DMV and had the door opened. Standing there for an extraordinary length of time he let his eyes drink in the entire scene. The words Judge Burger told him still fresh in his mind—*there is always something left behind.*

Pacing the length of the DMV waiting room like a death row inmate moments before his execution, his eyes focused on the floor, and the bloodstain which now appeared black. "Why would a man rob the DMV?" he whispered, then ran multiple scenarios through his mind. *There was no money to be stolen. The computers were old and outdated worth little to nothing. The furniture was nothing more than plastic chairs... Why would he be here?*

Opening his laptop, he replayed the video of the deadly night, then watched it again looking for the slightest detail he might have overlooked.

"Damn, nothing," he grumbled.

"Detective Weaver?" An older lady wearing a classy business suit holding a briefcase asked.

Detective Weaver looked up from the laptop. "Yes?"

"I'm Janet McNeely from the Special Crimes Unit, Motor Vehicle Commission. I was assigned to this case a few days ago, but only got around to reviewing the specifics earlier today. I called Police Headquarters to see which detective was assigned to the case and was given your name. I figured tomorrow we could meet and compare notes after I did my preliminary investigation, but since you're here we might as well kill two birds with one stone."

"SCU," Detective Weaver mumbled. "Why would they get involved? It was a robbery gone bad, not a crime against the DMV."

"I would not be so sure of that," Ms. McNeely said as she laid her briefcase on the counter. Flipping the latches, the top sprung open. From inside she removed a few pages and spread them out on the desk. "I watched the surveillance video numerous times and I don't believe the killer meant to kill anyone. He was here searching for information and encountered the newly hired security guard by accident, and the killer wasn't working alone."

"The video only shows one man besides the security guard who surprised him."

Ms. McNeely looked at Detective Weaver like he was stupid. "Are you a rookie?" she asked.

"I am," Detective Weaver aggressively answered. "This is my first case. We all have to start somewhere."

"I'm sorry," Ms. McNeely answered as she blushed bright red embarrassed by what she said. "I thought they would have put a more experienced detective on such a high-profile case."

"You're not the only one," Detective Weaver slowly answered. "So, what do you have?" he asked, now that introductions were complete.

"The system is hard-wired, and all codes that are entered are sent instantly to the alarm company to keep as a record. I got those records and discovered the code used is from a current employee. But they won't tell me who without a subpoena to protect the individual's rights."

"It was an inside job then?" Detective Weaver asked.

"Don't jump to conclusions so quickly. I have yet to get the name of the employee and talk with them. They could have been held hostage and forced to give it up. They could be another homicide victim for all we know."

"I also know the killer accessed the computer system illegally."

"Why would they do that? What would he hope to gain?"

"Usually, a breach to the system involves credit card fraud and the criminal is

"Guess we'll walk from here," Jester said as he hopped down. His feet though had no grip and shot out from under him like a greased pig. "*OOOPH,*" a groan shot from his lungs as he landed flat on his back then slid partway down the path. Swinging his arms wildly, he tried to grasp anything before careening over the edge.

The laughter from his companions echoed into the gloom.

Holding onto their mounts for support, the other two carefully dismounted.

Jester looked like an octopus trying to climb a ladder as he righted himself.

Holding onto to exposed roots, jagged stones, or using their weapons as anchors, they worked their way down a series of switchbacks. In a few locations, they were forced to climb over rubble as the path was chocked full of debris washed down from above. None knew how far they had gone as the mist enveloped them like a wet blanket. Before long they were each covered in sweat and smelled like swamp water when the path transformed into a series of stone steps much larger than any man could effectively use. Carefully navigating the enlarged steps they were each covered in mud and slime when the stairs widened out to a large landing littered with splintered timbers, cracked boulders, gnawed on bones, and discarded furs.

Jester scrambled his way to the river's edge and washed the mud from his face and hands. "This river splits the ravine in two."

"How do we cross?" Derric confusingly asked as he used a long stick to try and determine the depth of the water."

"You're wasting your time with that stick," Remfrey told him. "Rumor is the river so deep I could drop a stone in it, and you would die of old age before it found the bottom."

The kid's eyes grew as large as wagon-wheels.

"Near the center of the ravine is a log bridge," Jester told him.

Following the rocky bank, it was nearing noon when a wide, arched bridge constructed of hastily debarked logs bound together with thick twine broke through the haze. Testing the structure, Jester crossed first and waited for his men on the other side. Not far from there a foul funk worse than their own cut through the gloom. Animals were strung up in various stages of being butchered and were smothered with flies. The meat wiggled and squirmed as if it were still alive.

Jester slid his sword free and jabbed the carcass. To their surprise thousands of larvae fell free painting the muddy ground.

"That's disgusting," Derric whispered while holding back his vomit.

Cave trolls are filthy disgusting creatures," Jester said. "I'm surprised Karayan even wants them in his army. If it were me, I would slaughter them and let the carrion feast on their rotting corpses. But, I'm here to follow orders."

"Let's do what we came here to do and be done with it," Remfrey snarled.

From here, Jester led them southwest until their necks burned from the sun. Keeping a steady pace, they eventually arrived at a crude dais built of boulders, tree trunks, and bones. Upon it, a hastily constructed throne of woven tree branches reinforced with thicker limbs and crude stones sat empty.

Jester spun in a circle surveying the area.

"Where are these filthy creatures?" Derric asked.

"Deep underground in their homes," Jester suggested as he picked up a stick and examined the bite marks on it. "Cave trolls are nocturnal and only come out in the daylight under dire situations. We'll have to venture into the caves to find them."

"WHAT!" Derric complained.

"I suggest we wait here for nightfall when they emerge from their dens. To go underground would put us at their mercy, and no way to escape if something goes wrong," Remfrey explained.

Jester handed each a torch. "You wanted to wait to daylight to come here. Now you have to reap what you sow. Light them up. We're going inside."

Each grumbled as flint sparked and flames came to life. Not far from the throne they discovered the entrance to a large cave hidden behind a row of tall trees and stacked logs.

Squeezing through a tight gap discovered in the stacked logs, Jester held the torch high to light the way. The ground sloped steeply downward and narrowed the farther it went. Water dripped from the ceiling and tree roots sprouted out like straggly hairs. Clumps of moss and fungus grew on various stones and the air held a warm, swampy stagnation which instantly drew sweat to their skin. From somewhere below the reek of filth assaulted their senses and made their eyes water and noses run.

"This is insane to encroach upon their lair," Remfrey explained as if he'd been here before.

"The quicker we get this over with, the quicker we can get home to a warm bed and a soft woman," Jester said as he led the way venturing further into the tunnel. Choosing each step wisely they quickly arrived at a spiraling set of stairs which led down to a large chamber littered with Stalagmites.

"This is the main gathering hall," Remfrey whispered. "We can't see them in the darkness, but from here individual tunnels lead to each of their homes."

Half of Jester's face was hidden in shadows as he glanced at Remfrey. "How do you know this?"

"I read a book written by an assassin named Demetrius when he was searching for a legendary place known as Dragon's Down. How it came to be in Karayan's possession I don't know, but I found it very interesting. This man, Demetrius, went into great detail about the cave trolls and their caves. Apparently, he explored every inch of it and came out alive."

Jester's teeth glinted in the torchlight. "Then we shall as well."

"Why are you here?" The deep, gravely, and barely understandable voice cut through the darkness.

Jester moved farther into the enormous cavern and held the torch out trying to see who spoke. "I wish a meeting with the Chieftain, and then we shall be on our way, nothing more."

"Leave now—"

"Step into the light so I can see who I talk TO!"

"Leave at once and never return," the voice boomed.

"All I ask is for the Chieftain to hear me out. It will take no more than a few looking for financial information. I don't have access to the system, but my Information Technologist will be here shortly, and he will get us into the system and discover exactly what the killer was searching for."

"Maybe he can shed some light on the case," Detective Weaver grumbled. "None of this is adding up."

"It will in time," she told him. "I've been doing this for twenty years, and when it's over, you'll discover there's a motive behind everything."

An hour later, a young kid with pop-bottle thick glasses and dark hair resembling a wore-out mop missing the handle entered. "Got the warrant signed. Give me ten minutes and I'll tell you exactly what the guy was searching for and how he cracked it."

"Charles, you are the man," Ms. McNeely said.

The man removed a small laptop from his backpack and hooked it up to the computer and started a program that ran at a blistering pace. Instantly the screen filled with letters, numbers, and symbols. As time passed, digits disappeared until only an eight-digit code remained. After that he typed in a series of commands and every page the killer looked at was printed off.

Detective Weaver watched patiently as the techie did his thing.

"It appears either the killer received the password from a current employee or used a HASH program to crack their password. Regardless, the man only went to a total of three pages and researched only one family using the VIN from a vehicle registered to Tom and Sarah Fischer. No credit card information was stolen."

"Was the credit card information not taken because he was interrupted by the security guard?" Detective Weaver asked Charles.

"Doubtful. It appears once the killer got the information he logged out. My guess from how the alarm system was disabled and the computer getting hacked he wanted to get in and out without leaving evidence a crime occurred. If the guard didn't get killed, none of us would be sitting here today because not one red flag was sent out."

Detective Weaver took the pages from the printer.

Tom and Sarah Fischer
4114 Old Oak Rd.
Willowdale, KY, 99423
(859) 473 - 1192

"Willowdale, that's four-plus hours away. Why in the world would the killer be looking up their address?" Detective Weaver asked Ms. McNeely.

"Before I went to work for the SCU, I did a few years as a detective in homicide. Crimes like these are usually done to get information on someone who needs to be rubbed out, so they can't testify in court. If I were you, I would notify them immediately. Hopefully, they're not already dead."

Using his cell phone, Detective Weaver dialed the number and waited.

Each time it rang he got more and more worried he may be too late.

"Hello," Sarah grumbled. In each hand she held a pan while trying to balance the phone on her shoulder.

"Mrs. Fischer?" Detective Weaver asked, releasing a sigh of relief.

"Yes?" she answered in a cautious tone, not recognizing the voice.

"This is Detective Weaver with the Frankfort Police Department. Is Mr. Tom Fischer available?"

"May I ask what this is concerning?" Sarah asked.

"An incident which occurred at the Frankfort Division of Motor Vehicles."

"Oh my God, there wasn't an accident?" she asked.

"No ma'am. I only need to ask your husband a few questions."

"One moment, let me get him," Sarah said, then covered the receiver. "Tom, it's a detective from the Frankfort Police Department, he wants to ask you a few questions. Think it has to do with the coins? Maybe I should tell him you stepped out for the moment."

Tom looked baffled as he entered the kitchen. "I haven't done anything wrong. Here, hand me the phone."

Sarah did but remained close enough she could hear the conversation.

"This is Tom Fischer. How can I help you?"

"I'm Detective Weaver with the Frankfort Police Department, Homicide Division and I'm currently investigating a murder which occurred at one of our DMV facilities."

"How does that affect me?" Tom asked.

"I'm worried that you and your wife may be in danger. The killer searched for your address using the DMV database from the VIN he recovered from your vehicle."

"Excuse me?" Tom said. "Why would he do that?"

"That is the million-dollar question," Detective Weaver said. "Knowing what we know now, have you or your vehicle been to Frankfort anytime recently where the killer may have acquired the VIN?"

"I was there a while ago to pawn a few items. Beyond that, I have not been there in ten years, and no one has burrowed my vehicle."

"Where did you pawn the items?"

"A shady establishment named the *Flying High Pawnshop*."

"I could have guessed that," Detective Weaver said. "Were you alone at the time you pawned said items?"

"Why is that important?" Tom asked.

"If you had a friend with you, is there a chance he could have wrote it down and sold it. Druggies will do all sorts of crazy things."

"I had my good friend Mike McCullaha with me, and I know for a fact he doesn't do drugs."

"I hate to ask this of you, and I will make the trip worth your while. Would it be possible for you to come down to the station? I have some questions I would like to ask you in person. We may be able to tie this whole thing together and bring this man to justice before someone else gets hurt."

"I'd rather not. It's a long drive and I have a farm to maintain."

"Mr. Fischer," Detective Weaver said. "This man killed a security guard to get your address. Is not wanting to drive down here worth your family's life? Let's get this man put away before he can act on whatever he plans to do."

Tom looked at Sarah, Billy, and Averie who all waited patiently. "I'll leave first thing in the morning and I'm bringing my family as well. If this psycho is out there, I'm not leaving them here alone."

"I don't blame you one bit," Detective weaver replied. "Bring your friend as well, this Mike McCullaha. I may have some questions for him as well."

"We'll see you in the morning," Tom said, then hung up the phone.

"Wwwweeellllll?" Sarah asked, rubbing her fingers together like a mad scientist.

Tom didn't answer. Instead, he picked up the phone and called Mike. "Can you come over right away and bring your pistol," then hung up.

Sitting around the kitchen table, Tom told them all at once about the phone conversation.

"If he tries to come in here he'll leave in a body bag," Mike said as he carefully loaded a magazine with hollow-point self-defense bullets.

Sarah closed the normally open drapes. "If he's out there I don't want him watching us."

"Do you think he will come here?" Tom asked Mike who had years of experience in law enforcement.

"It's hard to say," Mike answered. "One thing we do know is the guy killed someone to get your address, that's never a good sign."

"That does it, tomorrow at first light we leave for Frankfort and go meet this detective," Tom said.

"No," Sarah complained. She had a bag out and was collecting clothes. "We're going to get a hotel in the next town over. I won't get a wink of sleep if we stay here."

"I think Sarah's right," Mike said as he peeked out the curtain towards the barn. "The killer could be outside waiting for us to turn off the lights."

Averie was pale as a ghost. "He will only be the first of many," she whispered.

"What?" Mike asked Averie.

"On Icearaus, many people lost their lives because of me. I fear before this is over there is going to be a graveyard worth of bodies piled high."

"I already asked you not to talk like that. This crime has nothing to do with you," Sarah snapped. There was a heated frustration in her voice.

"Everybody, calm down," Mike said. "If we start fighting amongst ourselves, we'll end up doing something stupid. Tom, grab your shotgun and let's check the area around the house before Averie brings the baby out. Afterward, we'll load up and go get something to eat and get a hotel room."

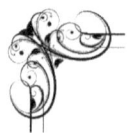
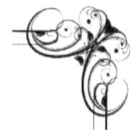

Chapter 39

ires burned, thousands of them in all directions.

Lady Alenia stood on the observation platform watching Karayan's army gather. It appeared every man, woman, and child from every town, city, or village came to participate in their destruction.

At the edge of the Whispering Woods, the elven army gathered. They were outnumbered a hundred to one but had one thing Karayan's army lacked. Knowing if they lost it was the end of their race, which would make them fight that much harder.

In an instant, the two armies collided out on the Plains of Gedeon and as quick as it started, it was over.

The battlefield lay quiet except for the rustle from a mournful wind which descended from the Ash Mountains and cooled the unburied corpses. The crash of steel was now silenced, the screams of the dying faded, the cheers of the victor hushed.

Arms lay scattered in the rain-soaked ground, their hands still gripping the broken hilt of their swords; helmeted heads with their tearful eyes frozen open in death searched for their bodies.

Neither side could claim victory for both took heavy losses. More would come. They would always come until the elves were extinct.

Lady Alenia awoke in a fit of rage fighting with her pillow. Gripping the material with pure fear her long nails dug in, and she ripped it apart throwing the carcass across the room. Feathers floated in an array of directions caught on the breeze which entered through the open window.

Her chest glistened with sweat and her silk gown clung to her body like a second layer of skin. Bolting upright, she squealed as the pain from her leg found her brain. Scanning the room for the enemy, she discovered she was alone. Elwrick must have left sometime earlier. Grabbing the cane, she hobbled her way to the washbasin and splashed cold water on her face. "We need more men," she whispered at her reflection in the mirrored surface of the water.

Quickly changing into more appropriate attire, she departed. Along the way she met many who wished her a quick recovery and if she needed anything all she had to do was ask. Wishing them well then exchanging hugs she politely told each she had essential matters which needed addressing. She wanted to sprint to the artifact room but hindered by her leg, she moved more at a snail's pace, and it seemed to take forever. As evening approached, she arrived at a massive tree deep in the Whispering Woods and stood there in horror. The door to the artifact room had been breached and now stood wide open.

Cautiously approaching, she was prepared to strike in case Malvo was here to claim what was his. Her heart relaxed though when she saw a white robe with gold thread glowing in the darkened environment. There was only one man who wore such elaborate attire even though it still bore the scars of his encounter with the Lich Lord. It was Elwrick, and he stood in the farthest recesses of the room and appeared deep in thought. The Spiritual Guide had come to help with the book which she would gladly accept. She didn't want to admit it, not to herself, not to anyone, but she could feel her magical ability slowly draining away with each passing day.

As she neared Elwrick came alive and moved at a flash preventing her from entering. "Stay away," he hissed.

Lady Alenia's eyes widened as she stepped back. She had never seen Elwrick take such an aggressive position against her.

Elwrick placed his hands on her shoulders. "I beg you; please stay away."

She had never heard Elwrick sound so desperate. Something inside that room brought out a fear in him she had never seen.

"I beg you," he whispered again. "Please return home."

She looked past Elwrick and into the room. What she saw made her legs weaken. The stump the book rested on was deathly sick, and black veins grew from the book leaching into the wood. Bloody sap seeped through the bark and trickled down the surface thickening at the base. The entire room reeked of decay and sulfur, and you could hear the muffled cries of the condemned weeping from the pages.

"It isn't safe for you, or any mortal to be here," Elwrick demanded. "The book is created from the skin of condemned souls and is bound to its Master's soul. The book is calling for help. It wants to go home."

"Where is home?" Lady Alenia asked. She could not look away from the pure evil that thrived within her realm.

Elwrick's eyes had a glossy stare. "Hell."

Lady Alenia clutched her chest and stepped back pulling away from Elwrick. "Get it out of my realm, NOW!" she hissed. "Destroy it. We will find another way to locate the dwarves."

"It cannot be destroyed, at least not by me. The power used in its construction is well beyond my grasp of understanding. The last few hours I have been pleading to the Creator to send aid, to protect those who he created. I only hope he has heard my cries of help."

Lady Alenia bit her finger as she pondered what to do. "Seal the door and neither of us is to return, ever. If we must, the elves will leave the Whispering Woods for a new home."

"No," Elwrick told her. "This book must be dealt with."

"By who?" she asked. "If neither you nor I have the power."

Elwrick shook his head not sure how to answer the question. "Knowing what I know now. It should have never been recovered; but left to rot down in that filthy hole."

Lady Alenia suddenly grew angry. "You said it was a journal of his past dealings. Not a book created in the darkest pits of hell."

"I didn't know?" Elwrick pleaded.

Lady Alenia hobbled to a nearby log and sat. When she looked up, her eyes were moist with tears. "What are we going to do?"

Elwrick sat beside her. "I'm not sure. I know I will not allow it to harm you, or any mortal for that matter. If I must, I will return to the Library of the Ancients and seek a path for its destruction before its malice can spread beyond the artifact room."

"I can destroy it?" A voice cut through the darkness.

Elwrick looked up to see a cloaked man standing there with glowing silver eyes.

"I can see its creation," Pegan said in an emotionless tone. He was no longer himself. He was this entity that lurked inside his soul.

Lady Alenia fell over backward trying to escape.

Elwrick cautiously backed away taking Lady Alenia with him. This is the first time he experienced what Saress had been trying to describe. On the air he could sense magic. Old magic from a forgotten time when the world was still young. Magic more powerful than any creature currently possessed. Magic beyond Elwrick's capabilities to understand. It was beyond the power of a Warlock, beyond that of a Witch. It was not from their world and it terrified him to the core.

Lady Alenia's eyes rolled back; then she fainted falling into Elwrick arms.

Pegan moved with the agility of a demon as he entered the room.

The book could sense the intrusion and released an eardrum-shattering scream.

Elwrick cradled Lady Alenia cupping her ears to keep the drums from bursting. The Queen had experienced so much hardship lately. The last thing she needed was to end up deaf on top of it. As the screech stopped, he whispered a protection spell on them both and instantly a faint purple aura surrounded them.

Pegan snarled something at the book in an ancient dialect then repeatedly slammed his fist onto the blackened cover. The muffled cries of tortured souls could be heard as blood splattered the walls, the floors, the ceiling, and himself. Gripping the veins, he tore them from the wood and blood pumped freely flowing from the wounds.

Malvo crumbled from his chair gripping his chest. He suddenly felt as if his heart was being ripped free from his body. Spitting up blood, his vision faded, and he nearly lost consciousness.

Flipping open on its own, the book formed into a sharp-toothed mouth and snapped at Pegan trying to devour him.

Pegan avoided each bite and knocked out a few of its jagged teeth with well-placed jabs before grasping the book on each end. Grunting and snarling like a wounded animal he began to pry it in half splitting it at the binding.

The book howled and snarled trying to free itself from his grasp.

Elwrick tried to see what was occurring inside the room, but smoke and steam filtered up through the floor obscuring his vision.

Malvo's breathing became hoarse, his knees buckled, and blood ran from his eyes. He would have no choice but to break his soul link to the demonic book or be destroyed. Whatever creature held it had equal power to himself and was relentless with the assault.

Pegan could feel the soul link fading and began to chant in an ancient tongue.

> *"Break the curse; let it die.*
> *Reveal to me which lay inside.*
> *Protection gone; protection lost.*
> *Protect these pages now with frost."*

From his fingertips shot a stream of pure frost crystallizing each page. Satisfied the book was harmless he picked it up and tossed it out of the room. Bouncing around it came to rest with frost dripping off the ruffled pages.

Elwrick laid the Queen on the grass and approached the book. He could feel the evil it once bore had been destroyed. No longer was the book a danger to anyone. As the haze cleared, he found Pegan lying unconscious slumped over the tree stump. His heartbeat was faint, and he gasped for air. No longer was his eyes sliver but their usual brown.

"What are you?" Elwrick whispered.

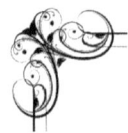
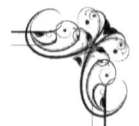

Chapter 40

he lights of Willowdale still twinkled when Tom urged them all to rise.

"What's the rush?" Sarah groggily grumbled as she pulled the pillow over her head. "You called the detective and told him we wouldn't arrive until dinner. We have all day to make the drive."

"I want to show Averie something?" Tom answered as he nudged Sarah again.

"What?" Sarah's muffled words filtered through the pillow.

"Get up and go shower. It's a surprise." Tom nudged her for the third time.

"Fine," Sarah snarled as she scampered from the bed into the bathroom.

Averie entered the bathroom moments after Sarah. "Why did he get us up so early?" She complained to the shower curtain.

"I don't know?" Sarah answered. "Alrighty, your turn," Sarah said as she stepped out and grabbed a towel off the rack.

Tom had Robyn bundled up and ready to go by the time Sarah and Averie emerged. Mike and Jennifer leaned against each other on the couch; their eyes slammed shut, while Billy swayed like a sapling in a windstorm on the bed.

"Okay, I think we're ready," Tom said as he opened the door.

Easing the van onto the highway, Tom brought it up to eighty-five then set the cruise. "We got a late start, so I have to make up some time."

The only one to answer was Mike, and that was with a long-drawn-out snore.

An hour later, Jennifer woke to a grumbling belly and an angry bladder. "I need to use the bathroom," she complained. "And I'm hungry."

Sarah never opened her eyes as she spoke. "I think we're all starving."

"We're almost there. Another fifteen minutes, I promise." Tom pressed on the pedal until the needle hit ninety and they started to climb the mountain. In the rear-view mirror, he could see the sky getting lighter.

"Don't get a speeding ticket," Sarah growled as she rubbed the sleep from her eyes. "Are you doing okay back there?" she asked Averie, then looked back to find four glowing golden eyes looking at her.

"A bit bouncy, but where fine.".

"I told you we should have got a rental van, the shocks on this thing are shot." Sarah gripped at Tom.

"Do you know how much it would have cost to rent a fifteen-passenger van. Besides, there is nothing wrong with our work van. It has plenty of room for all of us to stretch out."

Sarah ignored Tom's reasoning for taking the death trap. "She's growing so quickly and has your contagious smile."

"Not to mention your eyes as well," Jennifer added.

"I think she's wonderful," Billy said, then reached over the seat and tickled Robyn's toes making the child laugh hysterically.

Tom guided the van into the parking lot of the Mockingbird Restaurant and positioned the vehicle so they could see the valley below. "Watch," he said. "This is the exact spot I proposed to Sarah, and right about this time as well."

Within moments the sun broke over the horizon releasing a breathtaking array of radiant colors. Dazzling streaks of reds, pinks, and oranges glistened against the early morning dew making the valley shimmer like the surface of a magical lake.

Averie never once took her eyes off the picturesque scene. The view reminded her of the sun rising when Pegan led her out of the Ash Mountains. "It's beautiful," she whispered as a tear dripped down her cheek.

Sarah wiped away the tear. She knew without having to ask Averie was thinking of home, and suddenly, she didn't feel so hungry.

Mike, on the other hand, was an emotionless slug. "Yes, it's amazing. Can we eat now?" he moaned.

Inside, the atmosphere was relaxing yet warm and inviting. Most of the tables were empty with the silverware sparkling on virgin white napkins, and coffee cups flipped over as if mourning the loss of a good friend. Those who were there picked at mostly empty plates; sipped on coffee or chatted in private conversations.

Averie moved like a guided missile to a large, rough-cut table near an enormous crystal-clear window which over-looked the valley. From here she could continue to watch the sunrise, and her mind drifted back to Pegan. *I wonder what he's doing now? Perhaps he is high up on a mountain ridge watching the sunrise as well.* Gripping the diamond, she closed her eyes and whispered, *"I Love you, Pegan Rhoe."*

"Averie," Tom called her name. "Do you know why we're going to Frankfort?"

"Because a man was killed?"

"Yes, but the real reason is the killer was searching for our address. We believe it might be the guy at the pawnshop. We told the guy the coins were from our collection. If the detective asks anything about the coins, let me answer them, please. Detectives are good at prying out information you don't want them to know. Can you do that for me?"

"I'll handle the detective," Mike said. "Averie, you just sit there and look pretty."

<hr />

I love you. The soft words of Averie resonated through Pegan's brain, and he bolted upright expecting her to be beside him. Surrounded by darkness; he had no idea where he was or how he got there. Griping the shard until his palm bled, he focused on nothing but Averie, and he could feel her as if she was in his arms. She was happy and content and in no threat of danger. Laying back down, he did nothing to stem the flow of tears that flowed from his eyes as he placed

the shard against his chest. In time, he began to speak to it as if she was lying beside him, not this inanimate object.

"I'll drive from here," Mike offered.

"Shotgun," Averie screamed. She didn't know what it meant, but each time she heard it yelled, he who yelled it rode in the front seat.

"Sorry dear, but it looks like Averie beat you to it fair and square, guess you're riding in the back with me. Now maybe you'll reconsider trading in this old heap while we're down here and get something new," Sarah told Tom.

"There's nothing wrong with the van. It doesn't even have a hundred K' on the clock yet," Tom argued.

Back on the highway, the miles melted away as Averie watched the terrain pass. Long bridges spanned vast spaces while flowing rivers traced the edge of the road. Soon, the constant sway of the vehicle took its toll, and she found her eyelids too heavy to lift and her head nodded forward.

Sarah reached over and carefully pulled the lever lowering the seat back to a reclining position. Twenty miles later, she became the next victim to the swaying.

"I love you," Averie heard Pegan say. Instantly, her mouth formed into a smile, and her left hand rose until it found the diamond. From the stone, an incredible loving warmth radiated.

Mike turned the radio up trying to drown out the snores which sang him an out-of-tune chorus.

"Pegan," Averie thought and gripped the stone tighter until the edges dug into her skin.

Mike looked down at the speedometer. It said he was only going seventy-five. "Oh great, here comes a ticket," Mike complained. Glancing at the side view mirror he realized there was no cop on his tail, yet the flashing grew brighter and instantly a shiver ran up his spine. There was only one device that could make such a radiant light, and each time it pulsated with such intensity, something always went wrong. Easing his foot off the gas pedal, he aimed the vehicle like a dart heading straight for a rest-stop off-ramp.

Tom felt the vehicle slowing and opened one eye. "Is something wrong with the van?"

"We need to check on Averie," Mike said.

"Huh, what?" Sarah groggily answered, half asleep.

"I love you more than life itself." Pegan was talking to her. *"I will never stop loving you even though we are worlds apart. I long for the day our hearts will beat as one. The day I can take you in my arms and carry you away to be with me forever."*

The voice was faint, but she knew it could be none other than the man she loved. There was no other man who made her feel that way. Her right hand slowly curled around the door handle. She longed for his presence. The grip of his masculine hand's as he gently caressed her body; his hot breath against her neck as he whispered the words I love you into her ear. The magic created when their lips touched. The crashing of their bodies becoming one in a ritual of fiery passion. She would sacrifice anything and everything to be with him again.

The pulsating grew with such intensity Mike lost sight of the road through the windshield. "Jennifer," Mike screamed again as he guided the van into the rest stop scraping the guardrail sending sparks flying.

"I need you Pegan," Averie screamed as she jerked on the door handle like a pilot ripping the ejection lever of a wounded jet fighter.

"What are you doing?" Sarah screamed as she tore her seatbelt off and wrapped her arms around Averie, pinning her to the seat. Even at the reduced speed, if she got the door opened, the results could be catastrophic.

"STOP," Jennifer screamed as she fought with her seatbelt.

Tom ripped his seatbelt away and wedged himself between the seats and latched onto Averie's leg. The only way she was getting out now was to take him with her.

"Pegan," Averie screamed again. The snap of the door handle breaking sounded like dynamite exploding.

The van came to a screeching halt drawing the attention of a couple who waited by the restrooms.

As quick as it started, it was over. The bright flashing faded to a dull throb and the stone cooled.

"Are you okay?" Sarah asked cautiously releasing her grip.

Averie looked around as if she had no idea where she was. Sweat dripped from her face, and both hands trembled. "Pegan came to me. He needs me, and I need him."

Jennifer took a much-needed breath. "I don't know why, but someday I fear you and Robyn are going to be snatched away and sent home. The distance between you two is only a mere obstacle you both will conquer."

Sarah looked at Tom, who still held tight to Averie's leg. "Thank god for auto-locking doors."

Jennifer climbed over the three rows of seats and kissed Mike on the cheek. "Thank you for realizing something was wrong and slowing down before something bad happened."

"Averie," Sarah said. "We love you too much to see you get hurt. Why don't you ride back here with me? We can play *tic-tac-toe* or *hangman* on the phone."

Mike climbed out and looked at the long scrape down the side. "Sorry," was all he said.

"Don't worry about it," Tom said. We've been thinking of getting rid of it anyway."

A few hundred games later they passed an enormous sign labeled welcome to Frankfort.

Frankfort was nothing like anything Averie ever dreamed possible, and she watched the city pass with her head on a swivel. A vast network of wide and narrow streets separated buildings whose peaks pierced the baby-blue sky and glass windows glowed orange in the evening sun. Clogging the roads were mobs of people who moved like a swarm devouring everything in their path. Cars screamed at those who blocked their progress with an electric voice and belched noxious fumes making the warm, stagnant air barely breathable.

"I was hoping to avoid downtown and all the congestion, but the detective wishes to meet at the Olive Wok, not at the station," Mike told them.

"That seems odd," Sarah said.

"I thought the same thing as well," Mike said.

"Sounds fishy to me," Jennifer added.

"If it does turn bad and this is a setup, I brought my pistol. I'll gladly smile for my mugshot to protect the people I love," Mike said.

Ten minutes silently passed while three miles clocked on the odometer when Mike pulled into a heavily congested parking lot. Unable to locate an empty spot, he circled the lot when to his luck a Mercedes was backing out. Waiting patiently for the car to leave, a Screaming Yellow Corvette would have snatched the spot had Mike been a second slower on the pedal.

"Loser," Sarah whispered under her breath as the Corvette sped away hoping to steal another spot.

Averie carefully bundled a blanket around Robyn, then slid on her rose-colored glasses to shield her eyes.

"Let me take her," Tom said as he lifted the car seat out. Luckily, Robyn was fast asleep. Regardless of what they tried, nothing could hide the glow of her eyes as they burned with the intensity of the sun.

Taking a few minutes to get situated, they moved like a mob to the front entrance.

Near the door, a man wearing business attire patiently waited. Around his neck dangled a gold badge from a black strap.

"Detective Weaver?" Tom asked upon nearing.

"Yes?" he answered.

"I'm Tom, Tom Fischer and this is my wife, Sarah. You wanted to meet with us?"

Mike stood off to the side, his hand resting on his pistol in case this detective was the killer in disguise.

Detective Weaver looked Tom over. "I'm sorry," he pleaded. "When you told me that you're a farmer, I was expecting someone in coveralls and—"

"And what, married to his sister and having five teeth between the family?" Sarah hissed.

I'm an idiot, Detective Weaver thought as he blushed bright red. "I should be horse-whipped," he said. "I wasn't expecting such an elegant, professional-looking family. When you hear farmer, the first thing that comes to mind is the Beverly Hillbillies."

"It's alright," Tom said with a laugh. "Because on the farm I do wear coveralls and rubber boots clear up to my knees. I tried to marry my sister once, but she's already engaged to my cousin and the four chickens I offered her wasn't enough to break off their engagement."

Detective Weaver laughed while holding his belly. "At least you have a great sense of humor. Let me make it up to you by picking up the tab for dinner." There was no need to inform them he already had permission from the department to pay.

"Fantastic, steak and lobster for everyone," Sarah cheered.

"I hope you don't mind, but we are going to be joined by another gentlemen who also has information about this case."

"And who might that be?" Mike suspiciously asked.

"Mr. Frank Middleton. He's a metallurgist professor at Frankfort University. An extremely brilliant man who has done extensive work for NASA and the advancement of space exploration. He's the one who came forward with information that led me to the *Flying High Pawnshop*."

Mike nodded his approval. "Sounds fantastic."

"How about we go in and get situated while we wait for his arrival," Detective Weaver said as he opened the door. "I took the liberty to reserve a conference room in the back so that we won't be bothered."

The conference room was functional but not elegant. To one side sat a barge-sized oval desk which glistened in the artificial light. Surrounding it was an army's worth of leather winged-backed push-button armchairs neatly pushed in and evenly spaced apart. The carpet was warm with a tasteful design but not overbearing. The peach-colored walls were split horizontally down the center by a foot-wide strip of wallpaper depicting mallard ducks in various poses while elegant paintings of magnificent landscapes hung in designer frames and pleasantly positioned for the eye.

"Sit anywhere you like," Detective Weaver advised them.

A young lady entered and passed out menus. "What can I get you all to drink?" she asked.

Averie looked at Sarah for advice.

Sarah patted Averie on the shoulder. "Pick anything you want; Detective Weaver is picking up the tab."

Averie studied the menu like it was an undiscovered species. Afterward, she opened her purse and began to count her money.

Sarah suddenly realized Averie had no idea what they meant by picking up the tab. "Sweetie, you can put your money away, Detective Weaver is going to pay for us," she changed her wording.

"Can I get a Root Beer?" Averie asked the lady who waited patiently. Since her first introduction to soda, Root Beer has been her go-to choice.

Detective Weaver removed his coat and draped it over the back of the chair. "By the way, call me Ron. This is an informal meeting only to gather information, not a court hearing."

"What do you know so far?" Mike asked as he relaxed in a chair which afforded him a view of the doorway into the room. A habit he acquired from his years on the force.

"I would rather wait for Mr. Middleton to arrive first as his story is where the ball gets rolling."

The waitress returned with their drinks. "Love your eyes," she whispered to Averie. "Where do you get those contacts?"

"There not contacts," Jennifer intervened. "She has a rare eye condition which has altered the cones of her eyes, making them appear to shine. It occurs about one in five million."

"Wow," the waitress said. "You should go buy a lottery ticket."

"Trust me," Jennifer told the waitress. "It's not a gift. Everywhere she goes, it draws attention—sometimes negatively."

"Well I think their beautiful," she said, then quickly departed.

"They are different," Ron said, noting the piercing glow behind the rose-colored glasses.

"We're not here for her eyes, we're here to put this killer behind bars," Mike said to change the subject.

"Your right, but they are unusual," Ron said again.

Unsure why, they all stood when a man wearing a white polo shirt, green khaki shorts, and brown leather sandals entered.

"Sorry I'm late," Frank said as he looked at his watch. "I would have been here on time, but some idiot driving a beat-up old blue van cut me off and I had to park farther down the street and walk here."

"Idiot?" Mike whispered. "I'll show him who's an idiot." He planned to put his foot so far up Frank's butt the man would have toes for teeth, but Jennifer grabbed Mikes wrist and squeezed until he released a barely audible yelp. Not from the pain of her grasp, but from the hairs she was forcefully removing.

Detective Weaver met Frank halfway across the room with a handshake. "Glad you could make it. I have the Fischer family here, the ones who sold the coins to the *Flying High Pawnshop*. Between all the information gathered today hopefully Judge Burger will issue me an arrest warrant for the owners."

What luck, Frank thought, *knowing the owners of the rare coins were here, he may not have to deal with those slime-balls at the pawnshop after all. All he needed to do now was figure out which one was the owner and convince them to sell him the rest.* Greeting each with a handshake, he paused at Averie. It was painfully obvious who the alien was. She had the same piercing glare as the picture Loren showed him of the alien woman. Taking Averie's hand in his he gently kissed the backside. "*Votre très beau*," he whispered.

Averie's blush matched the color of her glasses. The language sounded so exotic, so sexy.

Jennifer whispered in Averie's ear. "That's French; he says your very beautiful."

The waitress returned holding a pad. "Are you ready to order?".

It was only now they realized not one of them had looked at the menu. "Give us a few minutes," Ron said.

Averie slowly flipped through the menu stopping on the last page.

Mr. Middleton purposely sat across from Averie and opened his menu. "I highly recommend the Taco de Pescado; it's to die for."

Averie looked over her menu at him.

Franks gaze fell on Averie, and the world around him faded. "By the way, call me Frank."

"What about the rest of us? What should we call you?" Jennifer asked.

Mike's eye's narrowed until they appeared closed. "I have a few choice words—"

Jennifer kicked Mike's shin under the table.

"I believe she can order for herself," Sarah informed the professor.

"All I was doing was recommending a dish, is that a crime?" Frank spat back.

"Can I get the spaghetti?" Averie asked.

"There's spaghetti here?" Tom asked as he flipped through the pages. "All I see is raw fish and something that looks like it came from under my lawnmower."

"The last page has American food," Sarah informed him.

With dinner ordered, Ron stood and positioned himself so they all could see him. "Since we're all here, why don't we begin this operation."

"I agree," Sarah said.

"Will you please tell us about the incident at the college," Ron asked Frank.

Frank slid his chair back and stood. Collecting his thoughts, he began to pace while he told them of the incident at the college. When he finished, he snapped his fingers at the waitress to gain her attention. "Bring me a chardonnay on the rocks." Afterward, he sat in a position where he had an unobstructed view of Averie's eyes.

Averie looked at Sarah for help.

"Must you continually stare at her. It's painfully obvious you're making her uncomfortable," Sarah told Frank.

"I'm sorry," Frank said as he looked away. "I can't seem to take my eyes off of her eyes. They're so exotic, so mesmerizing. Like looking into a dream you don't want to wake up from."

Sarah rolled her eyes, "Now I've heard everything," she said.

"Oh, you weren't here for that part. Averie has a rare condition which causes her eyes to glow," Ron explained. "After a while, you get used to them."

As the chatter calmed, Mike broke the awkward silence. "Excuse my ignorance, but I don't understand how the incident at the college relates to the murder?"

"Is she getting proper medical care?" Frank asked, changing the subject back to Averie.

Jennifer nearly came up out of the seat. "I'm her caretaker and she is getting the best medical care available."

"Okay, I've heard enough," Sarah screamed. "If we're not going to talk about why we're here then we're wasting our time."

"Sarah's right," Ron said. "We need to remain focused on why we're here, and that's the murder of an innocent man, not her eyes."

Mike rested his elbows on the table. "I don't want to sound like a jerk, but you seem awful inexperienced for a detective?"

"This is my first case as a detective," Ron admitted.

"First case," Mike mumbled. *Why would they put a rookie on a case of this importance, unless they didn't want it solved, at least not by him*, Mike thought. "You're going to have an uphill battle," Mike explained. "It appears they want you to fail so I'm going to go the extra mile to make sure you prove them wrong."

"I appreciate it," Ron said. "It seems like no one wishes to help me, not even the judge."

"Well let's see if we can't make them look like idiots when you land a conviction," Mike said as he scratched his chin. "Both Frank's and Tom's involvement stem from the coins. The question lies though how do the two coincide?" Taping his finger on the desk, he thought harder. "There's a piece of the puzzle missing here, all we have to do is find it and the answers will come."

Ron retrieved a laptop and placed it in the center of the table where they all could view it. "You pawned the rare coins at the *Flying High Pawnshop*. The owners visited Frank to determine the value. Frank told them how much they were worth, and suddenly, someone is searching for your address. I believe it's all too coincidental to be anyone else besides them."

Mike watched the video, then watched it again in slow motion. "You don't have much to go on, but there are clues."

Frank could care less about the dead man anymore. His entire interest was now on Averie. "After the meeting, would you care to have a drink with me in a more relaxed setting?" Frank whispered to Averie.

Averie's eyes opened wide as if asking for help.

Sarah didn't hear what was said, but she knew it wasn't appropriate by the look on Averie's face. "That's it, we're out of here," Sarah snarled as she stood knocking the chair over. "I would rather deal with the killer coming to our house than this neanderthal making the moves on Averie every other minute."

"All I did was ask her if she was interested in getting a drink afterwards," Frank angrily hissed. "Is that a crime?"

"For a man who is twice her age, it usually means you only have one thing on your mind," Jennifer answered before Sarah could.

Ron's face flushed red with anger. "Mr. Middleton, I don't believe now is the appropriate time for this." He couldn't afford for them to leave. Mike seemed somewhat knowledgeable when it came to criminal investigations and what he had to say could blow this case wide open.

Mike watched the video again in slow motion. "Yup, I'm positive it's the same guy. He is wearing the same watch he wore the day we met him, and right here," he hit pause. "You can see what appears to be a tattoo. I can tell you that mark there is the tail of a dragon. Go to the crime lab and have them blow this screen-shot up and it will link it right to him."

"You remember the watch?" Ron asked.

"I worked in law enforcement for fifteen years. I learned over the years to look at every detail when I go somewhere. It could mean the difference between going home alive, or in a box."

"There you have it," Tom said.

"There's more," Mike said only to flaunt his expertise. "You can see here he stepped in blood. Check the vehicle at the pawnshop for blood traces. If it's there, there is only one way it got there. Check camera's located at nearby stores. Often the killer will remove his mask right after leaving the building. You might get a good shot of his face."

Frank wrote a note and slid it across the table towards Averie.

"What is that," Sarah asked as she intercepted the note.

"None of your damn business," Frank hissed.

"Fine," Sarah handed the note to Averie.

Averie unfolded it and read the words. "It's your phone number?"

"Yes, the offer still stands for a drink."

Averie lowered her head as if ashamed. "I'm in love with another man."

"There, are you happy now that you heard it straight from her," Sarah snarled.

Frank assumed she was talking about Tom. "A woman of your quality deserves fine wine and caviar, not a pig farmer. I can provide you with the finer things in life you could only imagine."

"I don't believe so," Tom hissed.

Ron didn't know what the hell to do. His meeting seemed to turn into a family brawl fit for the Jerry Springer show.

"Enough," Mike finally yelled. Someone had to take charge of the situation as the detective seemed to be out of his league. "I think it's time we should go. I've given you more than enough to land an arrest warrant. All you have to do is follow-up with what I told you."

"Whenever you're ready to give your daughter a better life, call me," Frank told Averie.

Tom clenched his fist to punch Frank in the mouth, then realized it wasn't worth it. People like Frank often fall victim to their own karma.

"We'll show ourselves out," Mike said as he picked up Robyn who silently watched everything unfold while slurping on her binky.

"Call me," Frank mouthed to Averie as she stood.

Averie momentarily closed her eyes as she gripped the stone wishing Pegan was here to protect her from this heathen. *Please give me the strength to resist him,* she pleaded to Pegan, and instantly a sense of energy flooded through her veins and she could feel him flowing through her. Removing her glasses her eyes burned with an unsavory flavor and her lips curled back.

Ron and Frank both stepped backward as her vision bore into their souls.

"Leave me alone," she screamed with such intensity the window behind Frank shattered and sent deadly shards of glass sailing clear to the street shredding anything in their path.

People came running from all directions to see what went wrong.

"We better go, now," Mike screamed as he grabbed Averie by the wrist, and they ran for the door.

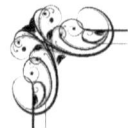
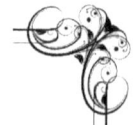

Chapter 41

he room was dimly lit by a single candle when Lady Alenia woke. She was not in her home; she was not in the medical ward. She had never seen this small room before. From where she lay though she could see Elwrick in his natural state sitting at a table. "Where am I?" she whispered.

"On the Realm of Light—"

"How is this possible?"

"I will explain to you later how I brought you here. Right now, I had to get you as far away from the Mortal Realm as possible."

Lady Alenia sat up in the bed. Her body felt weak, and her vision swooned. "What is happening?" she said in a broken, worried voice.

Elwrick crossed the room and sat beside her. Picking up her hand, he held it with his and gently squeezed. "While you slept, I read Malvo's book. He isn't a necromancer as we first believed; he isn't a man at all."

Lady Alenia's eyes widened.

"Malvo is much more vile and deadlier."

"Is he an agent of the Dark Master?"

"No," Elwrick said as he looked into her eyes. "If I'm not mistaken, Malvo is the Dark Masters child."

"His child?" she mumbled. "How can that be?"

Elwrick shook his head, "I don't know." Afterward, he stood and made his way to the window that looked out at the grassy plains. "The knowledge contained within that book answered many questions I had. And then it created a thousand more. Namely, why is he here, and what does he want?"

"That's why you brought me here; to protect me?"

"Yes, and no," Elwrick sighed. "I brought you here, so we can discuss future events which are to unfold without the worry of word reaching those we do not wish to hear. As the Dark Master offspring, Malvo has received every trait of his father, only not as potent because his mother was a mortal. One of his abilities is to enter the minds of any mortal who has sworn allegiance to the Dark Master."

"You mean become a spy?"

"Unknowingly, yes. Malvo can drift in and out of their minds at will if he chooses. He can see what they see, hear what they hear, even control their actions if necessary. To corrupt and control your actions would be devastating to the elves."

"What else did this book have to say?"

Elwrick sat down beside Lady Alenia. "The book speaks of a time before the creation of man, a time known as the Time of Creation," Elwrick told her. "In the beginning; the Dark Master was a beautiful Arch Angel, the Creator's greatest creation. His heart became tainted with anger and hate when he learned Icearaus was no to be his. In secrecy, he recruited a slew of angels, promising them whatever they wanted if they helped him destroy the Creator and he would rule the Heavens. A celestial war ensued and the Dark Master, along with his army was cast out to a dreadful place named Hades. The Realm of torment."

"He tried to defeat the Creator?" she asked.

"Yes," Elwrick laughed. "In our eyes the Dark Master is God-like. In the eyes of the Creator, the Dark Master is nothing more than a mosquito on the arm of creation waiting to be smack when his annoyance becomes too great. You must remember the Creator is all-powerful, all-knowing. He is both omnipotent and omnipresence. He is everywhere and knows our thoughts before we think them. There is no other like Him. He is the past, present, and future."

Lady Alenia went to speak, stopped, then started again. "He knew this was going to occur when he created the Dark Master? If he can destroy the Dark Master at any time, why does he not? Why does he allow this heathen to continue living?"

"I can only speculate on your questions and try to answer them the best I can," Elwrick said. "The Creator is a loving entity who believes in free choice. If he destroys the Dark Master and all that is bad becomes good, then he takes that choice away from us. You must remember only those who remain faithful are admitted to heaven. How can you remain faithful if you're never challenged."

Lady Alenia wiped away her tears. "We can't hide from him," Lady Alenia said after a few moments.

"Don't think for a minute I plan on lying down and dying like some rabid animal," Elwrick said as he sat back down. "We're going to fight this monster to the very end."

Lady Alenia gripped Elwrick's hand with a feather-soft grip. "Pegan, is he corrupted?".

"I don't believe so," Elwrick said. "It was through Pegan's actions Malvo's hold on the book was destroyed. He would have never allowed that if he was controlling Pegan. I am sure the Dark Master is currently removing the skin off Malvo's back at this very moment for allowing such an important artifact to be stolen."

"If Pegan could break Malvo's hold on the book, perhaps he can face Malvo in battle and win," Lady Alenia suggested.

Elwrick sighed. "Possibly, except for one problem. I have yet to determine exactly what Pegan is. We know what he isn't though, and that's corrupted by Malvo. With the vile nastiness removed from the book, I have been able to decipher part of the Dark Master plans."

"And that would be?" she asked.

"He plans to drive the world into chaos and confusion. How though I don't know. What I do know is our first goal needs to be to protect the elven race from Malvo's corruption, and it can only be accomplished through the process of sanctification."

Lady Alenia pulled back the blankets and stood on shaking legs. It was only now she realized how frail she was becoming. "Can you sanctify the elven community?".

"As a being of light and a Spiritual Guide, not only do I have the ability, it is my obligation to perform the ritual if asked. What I don't have is the ability to make the mortals of the world accept it. They can say with their mouths they believe. In their hearts though the truth will be revealed."

"If they believe they will be protected?" Lady Alenia asked.

"Protected from the mental intrusion of Malvo Necrosyse, yes, because darkness cannot grow where light thrives. Protected physically from those who have already succumbed to his demented ways, no. We still have a war to fight. A war we MUST win."

"Then we will begin the process immediately," Lady Alenia said as she sat back down. "He knows we have the book. He may already be plotting his revenge."

"I couldn't agree more. Time is of the essence. Afterward, I wish a meeting with all those who are trying to locate the dwarves. I may have accidentally discovered their location in my studies of the book."

Word reached every ear in Rhunsiire of the meeting. Extreme caution was taken not to allow the reasoning for the sudden meeting to be released in case Malvo was lurking inside an already corrupted elf.

At precisely three in the afternoon, every elf regardless of age gathered in the celebration clearing. All shops were to close; all work was to cease, all activities canceled. At the entrance, Ryul stood with two scribes who checked off each name as they entered. Every elf had to be accounted for, and any missing elves quickly located.

Upon confirmation every elf was there, Elwrick stood on the raised platform and addressed the whispering crowd. "We are gathered here today to discuss the war. Not the war we know is coming against Karayan, but a war you cannot see, smell or hear. It is a war for your very soul."

Whispers erupted through the crowd as most sounded confused by what they heard.

Elwrick was careful not to say Malvo's name as it may draw him there if he wasn't already. "This war cannot be fought with swords, axes, or arrows, but with belief. A strong belief in the Creator, and it is only through him life is allowed to exist."

An eerie silence filled the clearing.

"You will not be asked to fight this battle as you cannot win against the forces of darkness; none of us can. It is through our beliefs that we will be victorious as beings more powerful than us will take up this fight and watch over us. It is the Creators word that all who believe in him shall not perish to the darkness, but flourish in the light. It is today under the sun he created that we take up this oath of protection."

Elwrick was certain the cheer from the crowd could be heard clear to Lynn Brook. Raising his hand, it took a few minutes to silence the crowd when a young elf who could have been no older than five approached the platform and looked up. In the child's moist eyes, he could see the wonder, yet confusion of what he was hearing.

"Why?" the youngster asked.

The clearing went so quiet you could have heard a mouse tip-toe across a field of cotton as Pegan materialized through the trees and made his way to the platform and knelt beside the child. Even though it was a bright sunny day, his silver eyes sparkled.

The crowd gasped. Men drew their swords and woman hugged their children. Rumors flourished an entity possessed Pegan, an entity not from this world. *Was he here to devour their children, could anybody stop him?* thoughts flooded the minds of every elf.

Elwrick too stepped back and readied a spell of protection. Not for the child, but for Pegan. He had no idea if the elven warriors planned to attack him in retaliation as he was the cause of their Queen's near-death experience. Since that night, he had remained hidden and only visited by a few, namely Saress, Elwrick, Lady Alenia, Ellusia, and Gleia.

Pegan pressed his palm against the child's chest then spoke as if he was his mother in a way the child could understand. "Because inside you is a very special person, and it makes the Dark Master very angry when you're happy." Pegan held his rough hands out for the child to see. "He wants to hurt you in a way these hands or the weapons they hold cannot protect you. The only way you can be protected from this evil man is to believe with all your heart, the Creator is good and watches over you to keep you safe. It will be then he cannot come into your mind and hurt you."

One after another, the soldiers put their weapons away, and the entire elven community knelt in unison.

Elwrick smiled at Lady Alenia and held her hand tight. "I don't know what Pegan is, or what lives inside him, but he hears and sees things he should not. Neither I nor you discussed a single detail of this meeting, yet he knows much about things we discussed. It's almost as if he authored the tome."

It took her a minute as she adjusted her cane, but Lady Alenia knelt as well at Elwrick's feet.

Elwrick closed his eyes and splayed his arms wide. His voice was deep and spoken in a strange language. "Creator, I ask that you protect their minds. I ask that you set their minds on you and let them not conform to the darkness they are bound to encounter. Help them by the power of your spirit to focus on anything worthy of praise. I ask you now, let our minds dwell on these things." Elwrick fell to his knees and raised his hands higher, from his eyes, tears of light poured freely. "Let it be done this day, I call upon your glory to protect these elves, and all mortals far and wide who may not be here, yet believe in you," he screamed in their language.

Across the celebration clearing, a strange glow grew up from the ground, then quickly faded.

Elwrick looked about, but Pegan was nowhere to be seen. "It is done," he whispered. *I only hope Pegan believes,* he thought.

The next morning as the sun rose Lady Alenia and Elwrick met Pegan, Saress, Raestmond, Dinko, Ameria, Glorandial, and Filaurel at a secluded location outside Rhunsiire near the banks of the Freihn Sea.

Elwrick studied Pegan, his eyes were normal, the creature inside lay dormant.

Lady Alenia pressed her palm against a large tree and the outline of a door formed, then solidified. After a short time, the door opened allowing them to enter. Lady Alenia led them down a winding staircase to a large landing. From there a wide and tall hallway lit by magical lanterns directed them farther away from Rhunsiire to an enormous room. Once inside the door closed and faded from existence leaving only a wooden wall. There would be no escape until she allowed it. "I brought you here because no others know of it, and the chance of having our meeting fall on unwanted ears is minimal."

Pegan had a confused look on his face. "Everyone knows we are trying to locate the dwarves."

"Yes, this is true," Elwrick said as he took up a position beside Lady Alenia. "In my detailed examination of the tome, there was an entire section dedicated to the *Prophecy of Damnation* and what it read makes me believe it is coming to pass as we speak. If what I believe is true, the Dark Master will do little to stop you, even encouraging you to go as the version which has reached the eyes of mortal men has been manipulated and distorted to further allow the completion of the Dark Masters goal. If he knows we know the truth, which I am positive he will in time. He will send out agents to stop you every step of the way. Speed now is of great importance. We must find them to fulfill this prophecy."

"We still don't know which way we are heading?" Saress asked.

"East," Elwrick said. "Over the shadowed Mountains. Back to a time the world has forgotten. To a landmass known as *Huelgrawt*. The birthplace of life."

"The Wilds?" Saress asked.

"Yes," Elwrick told her.

"I do not fear the Wilds. When we relocated to the 'Anor, we fought many wicked beast, and we survived. We will survive this encounter as well."

Elwrick took a deep breath even though he didn't need too. "I don't know what lies and waits for you beyond our borders as my vision beyond the Shadowed Mountains are purposely clouded by the Creator. Once you go beyond those blackened stone peaks, you will be on your own. Don't let that knowledge though deter you from the cause. Finding them is our only hope to survive what Icearaus is soon to endure."

Lady Alenia moved away from them to the other side of the room. "To save time, I'm prepared to open a portal sending you to the peaks of the Shadowed Mountains. May the Creator watch over you and guide you on your journey."

Hugs and kisses were exchanged, and when they were ready, Lady Alenia waved her hand and an oval portal formed. When the mist cleared, a stone landing was visible.

"For Averie," Pegan whispered, then adjusted his weapons and stepped through; the rest followed.

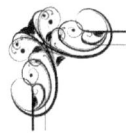

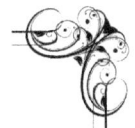

Chapter 42

alvo's bedchamber was altered from its original state into a sacrificial chamber for this exceptional event. In each corner of the room, a skull sat on a pedestal made of bone. Inside the skull, flaming black candles forced an eerie glow out the eye sockets. From the mouth of each skull, a burning incense stick jutted outward filling the room with the scent of burning sulfur. Rune words scribed in blood marred the walls while tuffs of hair dangled from strings thin as spiderwebs.

Malvo paced in a circle around his sinner which hung head down and naked by a barbed chain from a thick beam embedded in the ceiling. The sacrifice was vital for his success. If the man were loyal and faithful to the Creator, the doorway wouldn't open. It had to be a man destined for hell. In his hand, he gripped a unique ceremonial dagger; the only one of its kind in existence and required to complete the transformation separating his soul from the physical form. The handle was carved from the thigh bone of a virgin while the chipped basalt stone double-edged razor-sharp blade was constructed in the bowels of hell. Below the sacrifice was a giant pentagram, and inside the pentagram was a pit ready to devour whatever fell from the sacrifice. After the process was complete, the pit would become the celestial doorway to the damned, allowing him to hitch a ride as the doomed traveled to hell for eternal punishment.

Malvo closed his eyes and relished in the moment. This was the first time in decades he was going home. Home to a world no mortal could enter, at least not in physical form.

Inserting the knife millimeters below the skin at the navel, he carefully slid the blade down until it reached the metasternum. Smiling with delight, he soaked in every scream of the doomed. Twisting the knife, he redirected the motion until he reached the right nipple. Removing the blade, Malvo reinserted the tip at the metasternum and made a second slice coming to an end at the left nipple. Peeling open the skin he pinned the layers back using small hooks allowing him unimpeded access to the innards.

Screaming and thrashing the man begged for death.

"This is only the beginning of your torment," Malvo whispered into the screaming man's ear. Using the knife, he shifted around the guts until the liver was located. This organ was crucial to his travel, so extreme care was taken with its removal. Holding the darkish brown organ at eye level, he examined it in its entirety, flipping it at different angles. It would play the final part in his transformation, so he carefully placed it beside the pit to avoid damage.

Digging through the cavity the large intestine was removed and haphazardly placed around the rim of the pit like a garnish. Afterward, the small intestine was used to trace the bloody design of the pentagram. Each kidney was cutout and held over the pit and squeezed until every drop of blood was removed, then the dried-up sponge-like material was discarded. The bladder was removed and tossed to the side; it was not needed to complete the transformation and would only get in the way.

The pit filled with blood one drop at a time as the screaming sacrifice thrashed violently trying to ease his pain. The barbed chains relentlessly tightened burrowing the steel barbs into the ankle bones.

The gallbladder was removed and severed into many small chunks. Afterward, Malvo placed the pieces into the bloody stew, which was beginning to bubble. Following the gallbladder, the left eye was removed next with a spoon-like device and severed at the optical nerve. Dangling it above the stew, he released it and watched it dissolve, then repeated the process with the other eye.

Malvo spoke the phrase in an ancient version of Adamic. "*Body to spirit, spirit to soul. Allow me to travel with this doomed man home.*"

Moments before the host died, Malvo recovered the living liver and took a large bite from the organ allowing the blood to run down his chin and stain his black robe. By doing this, he was becoming one with the doomed. He would ride this soul to hell.

Instantly, Malvo was looking down from the corner of the room as a spirit. From here he could see his pale, lifeless body standing rigid at the sacrificial pit. His eyes were locked open and his mouth partly ajar as time ceased to exist freezing him in this position.

From where his soul floated, he could see the bubbling pit begin to swirl in a gurgling vortex. Hell was ready to accept another soul, along with a long-forgotten guest. From the pit, a demonic-shaped multi-fingered clawed hand jutted forth drawing the soul from the corpse. Now was his time. Latching on to the soul of the damned, he too was sucked into the palm and whisked away.

The Plaines of Hate was something the mortal mind couldn't fathom. Its ever-growing vastness had no end and resembled a giant furnace whose flames offered no light. Large holes ringed with brimstone covered the surface like festering wounds on a rotting corpse. From those holes, smoke and ash spewed clouding the blackened sky. Seeping up through jagged cracks in the crusty surface were the muffled cries of those condemned to eternal punishment. Spiritual fires licked at their formless bodies yet did not destroy the soul.

Malvo took great strides covering vast distances until he arrived at an enormous staircase which led to huge double doors built into a massive onyx stone wall. Beyond the wall, a behemoth citadel with towering spires grew to dizzying heights. To either side of the doors, grotesquely twisted demons with piercing red eyes stood guard.

Ascending the staircase in leaps and bounds, he stopped at the doors.

"Your appearance has been much anticipated," the demon said in common tongue. "Your Father will be excited to learn about your arrival."

"Take me to him," Malvo demanded. "I have urgent matters which must not be delayed."

"As you wish, my Lord," the demon replied, then knelt performing a gracious bow.

Inside the citadel, Malvo was guided down a series of corridors constructed from the living tissue of those condemned. In random spots holes in the floor allowed him a glimpse of those trapped below and the tortures they were forced to endure. Overflowing with excitement, he made a mental note to remember a few as new experiments on the Mortal Realm upon his return.

Climbing a wide arching staircase, he followed another hall then made a sharp right and nearly ran into the six-armed demon standing guard at a massive door which looked impossible to move. "Your father awaits," the beast growled through upturned lips.

Quickly ushered inside, the room was void of definition beyond a throne made of bone, and on it sat a man who appeared quite mortal. His long curls were raven black and both eyes were emerald green with the slightest hint of red. Muscles rippled under his tanned, leathery skin and he wore a simple cloth tunic, and matching trousers. A genuine grin crept across his face altering it from beautiful, to divine.

"My son," The Dark Master said in a gentle, caring voice. "Good to see you have found your way home."

Malvo knelt and lowered his head. There was no delaying this information even though he knew the punishment would be extreme. "Father, I come here not in time of celebration, but with concern. Due to unforeseen circumstances, my hand has now been forced. I have no other recourse but to put the next phase of my plan into action."

The Dark Master narrowed his eyes. "What unforeseen circumstances? You told me everything was going as planned."

"The book of knowledge was stolen from my grasp—"

"How is that possible?" the Dark Master hissed as he stood. From his mouth came a long forked black tongue which lashed out at his son.

"When I fled the Keep, it was forgotten. Now it lies in the hands of the elves."

The Dark Master rubbed his chin in thought, then started laughing. "They will never break its magic, and it will destroy everything within their realm it touches. Perhaps you have not failed me after all."

Malvo looked up at his father. "They have already defeated the protection placed upon it. We would be fools to believe they would not try and decipher the writings contained within."

The Dark Master rubbed his temples. "How could you allow this atrocity to occur. You should have died defending that book. I would have more respect for you dead than I do at this very moment."

"Father, the enemy will still fall as I have planned. I only need to begin the process earlier than expected with the Demon-Hyde Robes."

The Dark Master knelt beside Malvo and held his son's chin with an iron grip. "I have no desire to start my work anew. I will grant you the Demon-Hyde Robes, but it will not come without punishment. Let this be a lesson you shall never forget."

Malvo woke lying flat on his back and bound at the wrists and ankles with a searing hot cord that burned into his skin. All of his powers were gone. No longer could he brush away pain and it bore into him. He tried to scream, but a metal plate covered his mouth and was fastened to his face with coarse screws driven deep into the bones. Scrambling to his feet, he discovered he was confined within a tiny cell. The walls were constructed of a strange organ-like tissue which secreted an acid-like fluid. Severe, unimaginable pain ravaged his body and he felt as if a giant beast was digesting him.

Trying to escape, he threw himself against the narrow door. Having no luck, he glanced out the tiny window, but the steam and smoke obscured his vision and burned his eyes.

The screams that filtered through the cracks were horrendous and drove shivers up his spine.

To his surprise, the door slid silently open and a large scaly hand reached in and snatched him by the neck and dragged him from the cell. The multi-armed monster was enormous in stature. In his other hands, he carried new arrivals as well to begin their new life.

Malvo tried to close his eyes, but he had no eyelids. He would be forced to watch for all eternity.

Hung by his toes, he dangled over a pit which had an aorta-like valve. Around it smoke and steam seeped. When the valve opened searing hot acidic fluids belched upward coating his body.

Violently thrashing he wished for a death he knew would never come.

As the valve closed, his skin began to dissolve and slide free of his body until it lay in a heap beneath him like discarded clothing, and he was nothing more than a living skeleton.

Darkness flooded his mind and when he woke he was back in the small holding cell. His body was restored, and the pain started again. This time it was worse as he knew what to expect when the door opened and an enormous hand latched onto his face and dragged him out.

Malvo was relieved to discover he was taken in a different direction. To experience that again was unimaginable.

The demon carried Malvo down a vast hall then up a flight of stairs. It was there he was handed off to a smaller demon with green skin, elongated ears, and tiny eyes. "The Master wishes his return."

"Yesses," the demon hissed and latched onto Malvo's throat and carried him at breakneck speed through a series of tunnels. Eventually, they arrived at a large room with a pit which held a swirling vortex. Throwing him into the vortex, the demon then went back to work whipping those he felt needed to be whipped.

Malvo came to in the fetal position crying hysterically. His body was destroyed, his mind wrecked.

"This is only a taste of what you will experience shall you fail me again," the Dark Master said, then he reached out and touched Malvo and the pain faded.

"Father, I will not fail you again," Malvo pleaded.

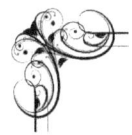
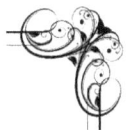

Chapter 43

he Prius silently glided over the highway.

"A Prius, really," Tiny complained. "You couldn't get your sister to rent us a Camaro or Mustang?"

"We're lucky she rented us anything after hearing about the murder," Sheba said. "Besides, our chances of getting pulled over are highly unlikely."

Tiny rolled the joint on his knee then fired it up. After taking a long drag, he reclined the seat to settle in for the long drive. "She should have told me the DMV had a pig."

Sheba accepted the joint and took a drag, then handed it back. "I don't think she knew,"

"Regardless, he's dead. There's no changing that."

"She's worried she's going to get tied into this and end up in prison."

Tiny dropped what remained of the joint in a beer bottle and watched it float. "We're going to be getting a lot of money for these coins. We'll give her a bit extra so she can skip town and go to Argentina, or something. We'll make it right with her."

"I only hope they have the complete collection," Sheba said, then lowered the window slightly allowing the smoke to leave.

"You heard the man as well as me. He's a coin collector. If need be, we'll take every goddamn coin he owns—"

"And any cash, but nothing else. I don't want anything traceable."

Daylight drifted into darkness when Sheba veered off the freeway onto a two-lane highway on the outskirts of Willowdale. "Keep your eyes peeled. From what I could tell from the internet the driveway is hard to spot in the daylight, and it's damn near invisible at night."

Tiny kept his head on a swivel as Sheba slowed.

"Damn, we missed it," Sheba growled when mile marker thirty-five came into view.

"How do you know?"

"Because it's between mile marker thirty-four and thirty-five," Sheba explained as she flipped a U-turn.

"Hit your brights," Tiny said.

Creeping down the highway at a snail's pace, Sheba stopped at what looked like a ditch. "I bet that's it right there."

"How far back is it off the road?" Tiny asked.

"A quarter mile or so."

"A few miles back there was that abandoned gas station. Pull in behind there and we will walk in. The last thing I want is to get trapped back in there and no way out." Tiny advised Sheba.

Doing as instructed, she eased the car to a silent stop and killed the lights. "It's dark out here. Hope we can find our way back," Sheba complained.

"Won't be a problem," Tiny said as he removed a revolver from the glove box.

"Jesus Christ, you don't plan on killing again?"

"Not if I don't have to." Tiny shoved the revolver in his pocket.

They walked for what seemed like hours in the dark when Sheba grew concerned they had gone in the wrong direction or taken the wrong driveway. "Perhaps we should go back and come back tomorrow night after we look at the map again?"

Tiny looked at his watch in the moonlight. "It's only been twenty minutes. It only seems like a long time because of the darkness and unknown."

Ten minutes later the road led them though an opening in a white picket fence. In the distance nestled back amongst the trees, a large farmhouse stood with a single porch light glowing.

"If luck goes our way, they're gone on vacation or something," Tiny said with a laugh.

"Well there's a car in the driveway, the same one that was used to sell us the coins so I doubt they're gone."

"Only one way to find out," Tiny said.

"Wait, let me go up and knock first. If anyone answers I will tell them the car broke down."

Tiny rested his arms on the fence. "And if they recognize you?"

"Hmm, didn't think of that. I'll worry about it then. You wait in the shadows on the grassy hill over there."

Bam, bam, bam, **Sheba pounded on the front door with her fist. Waiting a** few minutes, she pressed the glowing doorbell button. From outside she could hear the chime of the bell and still no one came. Satisfied luck had gone their way she waved at Tiny to come.

Unknown to her. In the upper right-hand corner of the porch, the trail cam flickered on and was recording everything.

Tiny sprinted across the yard and up the stairs. His speed never slowed as he leaped into the air slamming his foot into the door next to the deadbolt.

The sound of wood splintering caused the crickets to quit chirping.

"Quick, let's find what we came for and get out of here," Tiny said as he kicked the door again, leaving it hanging by a twisted hinge.

Splitting up they each took different areas.

"Look what I found," Tiny said as he came from the back holding up an assault rifle.

"I said we're taking nothing that can be traced," Sheba complained, then continued ripping drawers free of the dresser and dumping out the contents on the floor.

"Are you crazy, this is a custom made AR15. All I have to do is change the lower receiver."

Sheba paused to look at Tiny. Sweat dripped from her face and both hands shook nervously. "Fine, but you're not keeping it at the shop. Now get back to searching for the coins."

Moving through the house like a swarm of locust, they destroyed everything in their path.

From a room in the back Sheba screamed out a cheer of victory. Opening the purple pouch, she dumped out the gold coins on the bed and spread them out to observe. "Found them," she screamed out to Tiny.

Within seconds, Tiny was there beside her. For a moment, time stood still, and they almost forgot to breathe.

"Keep searching," Tiny said. "There might be more."

Minutes later Sheba released a second cheer when she located a stack of bills in the bottom drawer of the same dresser. "There's probably ten-thousand dollars here."

"If not, it's close to it," Tiny said as he looked at the bundles. "That stack there still has our strap on it."

Sheba shoved the bills into the purple pouch. "Let's get out of here."

"One minute," Tiny said as he recovered a short sword from the closet. The elaborate detail was nothing like he'd ever seen before. Perfectly balanced, it had an edge sharper than a scalpel.

"Something that elaborate will be easily identified," Sheba said as she looked at the weapon.

"Your right," Tiny agreed and discarded the sword on the floor.

Back at the front door, they waited for a few seconds to make sure no headlights were coming down the drive, then they bolted down the stairs and vanished into the darkness.

Seconds later, the red light of the trail cam dimmed, then clicked off.

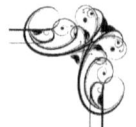

Chapter 44

exacion never felt so relieved when the torch lights of the Lost Sanctuary twinkled in the distance. His charge, Lilith, turned out to be the worst prisoner he had ever experienced. She fought the entire distance, regardless of the pain it brought.

Along the way Lilith grabbed at tree branches, fallen logs, large stones; anything she believed which might hinder their progress.

As time passed, the assassins were left with no choice but to bind her hands and feet and feed a pole through two loops and carry her the remainder of the distance.

Following the narrow trail down from the Silver Mountains, the small band of men emerged onto the rolling plains. The Lost Sanctuary was less than two hours away. Tonight, Vexacion planned to sleep in his bed, and he urged his men to pick up the pace to a jog.

Lilith woke when her back slammed against the cold stone ground.

Malvo looked down at Lilith, then to Vexacion. "I expected you days earlier."

"My Lord, she fought the entire distance. From the Silver Mountains until here we had no choice but to carry her like a pig."

Lilith twisted her head to get a better view of her environment. She was in a large room with crumbling walls. Debris littered the floor while the lack of a roof allowed the slight drizzle to enter.

An assassin dressed entirely in black separated from the group and approached Malvo. "Lord Necrosyse, are you sure this is the correct woman? You told us her beauty is legendary, yet you're presented with this abomination."

"She was in the correct location and clearly knew Viktor," Vexacion snapped at the assassin. "You wait until now to question me?" Vexacion started to slide his daggers free.

"I do not question you. I question if we were duped. If this woman is as smart as Lord Necrosyse says she is, perhaps she employed this hideous thing to take her place to make sure it was not a trap." Skylar Nightshade removed his mask then slid his weapons free as well. "If you wish to fight me, you will discover I am not a fledgling who cannot defend myself."

Vexacion stepped back and returned his weapons to their sheaths. He had no desire to fight Nightshade. The man spent years training with the notorious traitor Demetrius, who was now known under the name of Pegan Rhoe. "Skylar," Vexacion hissed. He hated this man like none other, and he was not sure why. Perhaps it was because who he trained with, but more likely, it was the knowledge Skylar's skills with a blade, rivaled his. "Why didn't you tell me you were joining me?"

"Why I joined you isn't important. What is important is if this is the correct woman we were searching for."

Malvo watched the two men bicker. "Enough! This is indeed the correct woman. She has only been disguised by an ugly encounter with a Lich Lord." Malvo pressed his thumb against Lilith's forehead and mumbled a few strange words and almost instantly, her body transformed back to her original appearance.

The men gasped at what they saw. She was indeed precisely as Malvo described.

Malvo looked at Vexacion. "You and your men will be greatly rewarded with her company after she and I have a friendly discussion. Take her to the chair."

Lilith screamed as she was lifted by her hair and dragged down a series of steps into the darkness.

Lilith opened her eyes when she heard the door slam closed. The room was empty except for a wooden chair fastened to the floor by metal brackets. Dragged closer, small teeth in the seat and arms pointing backward became visible.

Thrown into the chair with such force she nearly lost consciousness, she was fastened to the device with leather straps at every bendable joint rending her immobile.

"Welcome home," Malvo said upon entering.

Lilith tried to squirm, to do anything to get away from this heathen, but the metal teeth burrowed into the flesh forcing a whimper to escape her throat.

Malvo circled the chair looking Lilith over from head to toe. "You're a tough woman to track down, especially looking the way you did. I believe you would have never been discovered had you not tried to contact Viktor."

"What do you want?" Lilith hissed.

Malvo ignored the question. "Let me ease your troubled heart. Viktor didn't reveal your location, quickly. It took days to pry it out of him. Sure, I could have retrieved it sooner with a simple mind trace spell, but what sport is there in that. The joy I received in watching his eyes when he believed he was going to defeat my torture was… astounding."

"You disgust me," Lilith snarled.

Lilith spit up blood from the slap she received for that comment.

Malvo paced the length of the room. "In all regards, you're a lucky woman. Even though my men are loyal, I expected you to have been beaten, raped, and tortured long before your arrival. I can understand though why you were not having seen you upon arrival." Malvo moved in close and whispered into her ear. "You were not very pleasant to the eye, or the nose."

"What do you want from me?" Lilith hissed. She could feel his hot breath crawling down her neck.

Malvo grabbed Lilith by the hair and twisted her head until their eyes became one. "Lucinda, my dear, all I wish to know is why you betrayed me?"

"That name is dead to me.".

Malvo's finger's curled inward creating a giant fist, then he slugged her in the side of the face. The sounds which followed was like a pot shattering. Instantly, her right eye swelled shut and blood ran freely from her nose.

Coughing and hacking, Lilith spit out teeth before she choked on them.

"Shall we try this again?" Malvo asked as he pressed his finger into the side of her concaved face and began to twist his finger.

Lilith vomited as the pain ravaged her body. "I fled to Karayan—"

Malvo flicked her swollen eye with his finger forcing a tear to squeeze free and trickle down her cheek. "I could care less why you fled to Karayan as he was nothing more than a surrogate. A figure put in place by me, no by you."

"I had nothing to do with the rise of Karayan or his evil deeds. He was born evil, and evil he shall remain until he takes his last breath."

"Oh, but you did. Here is what you fail to understand. Karayan was never meant to be in power. Because of your ignorance and careless actions, you left me no other choice but to place him in power. This is, until the time is right and I no longer need him."

"Nobody can control Karayan, not even you. I'm tired of hearing your filthy lies, release me," Lilith demanded.

Malvo grabbed Lilith's pinky finger and jerked it back until the bone snapped and broke free of the skin.

Lilith nearly fainted as she refused to give him the satisfaction of hearing her scream.

Malvo grabbed Lilith by the chin and twisted her head until they looked directly at one another. "By betrayal, I mean, what did you do with my son?" He pushed her head away forcing it to flop as if attached by a spring.

"I never had a child," Lilith lied.

From the folds in his robe Malvo removed a short metal rod that ended in a point. Holding it out for her to see, the rod began to grow in length. Smiling the entire time he pressed it into the flesh between her index and middle finger until it drilled through the bone and pierced the Median Nerve. Flicking the metal rod, Lilith bit off a chunk of her tongue and spat it out. "Good, it appears my rod has found the correct nerve. Now I can continue with my questioning." Flicking the rod again, Lilith released a scream which could be heard throughout the Lost Sanctuary.

"Where is my son?" Malvo demanded.

"He's dead," Lilith screamed. "After I fled I aborted him so you couldn't sacrifice him to some demonic creature." Truth be told, she had no idea what happened to her son when she abandoned him on that cold rainy night in that alley on the Southside of Minx. He very well could be dead for all she knew.

"You lie! A mother would never abandon her child to die."

"I would rather live with the guilt of knowing I killed my son than the guilt of knowing he lives in the mind of some demonic creature who tortures him relentlessly. I told you what you wanted to know, now release me," she begged.

"*Hmm*," Malvo grumbled. "Your son was destined to become King of Icearaus, not a sacrifice," Malvo told her.

"I'm pleased to know my son died with honor as a child than to live as King promoting your disgusting beliefs," Lilith hissed. "It doesn't matter who is King. The bearer has reached the portal. Icearaus as we know it now, will never be the same."

Malvo laughed. "You have no idea how correct you are. I allowed the bearer to reach the portal; it was the only way to remove Karayan from power." Malvo walked around Lilith and ran his fingers down her neck forcing her to cringe. "My pet could have killed the bearer at any time, devoured her soul and mind, but he followed my orders to the letter. Had it not been for that whore of an Elf Queen, the great Elwrick would be dead."

"You never cease to amaze me with your lies," Lilith said, fully expecting to be punished for her words. "Had you wanted her to survive, you would never have sent your pet there to be destroyed."

"Silence," Malvo screamed, then began to beat her mercilessly until she no longer looked human.

Lilith fought and squirmed, but the jagged barbs tore into her muscle thwarting her attempts to avoid the abuse.

"I wonder if this is how my son felt? Was he alive when the carrion of the world picked out his eyes and ate the flesh from his bones?"

When he released his grip Lilith's head fell forward. She had long since faded into unconsciousness never feeling the last ten blows. "Wake her!" Malvo demanded of the two assassins who stood watch.

Lilith came to screaming.

Malvo grabbed Lilith by her head and twisted it, nearly snapping the neck bone. "Let me tell you why the bearer had to reach the portal. Karayan had an agreement with my Father giving him immortality as long as the soul of each bearer's child was offered to him on the sacrificial table. If only one was to escape the contract became null and void. It is now time to begin the next segment of the Fall of Icearaus, and unfortunately, his position is no longer needed."

From the coals in the brazier, a tiny flame jumped free and formed into a twisted little creature. "Your father wishes her alive and in the rack. She is much too powerful to remain on the surface."

"I already promised my men they could have her after I am done."

"Your Father cares little for the promises you made without consulting him first. After your blunder with the book, I would not press the issue," the little demon chuckled, then flat out laughed at Malvo.

Malvo looked at Lilith who was once again fading into unconsciousness. "Take her to the rack and remain guard until my Father comes. No one is to enter that room except me."

"Yes, Lord Necrosyse," they said in unison.

 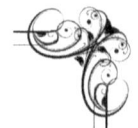

rank sure was interested in Averie," Jennifer said.

"He's after something," Tom advised them. "I don't know what or why, but I have a gut feeling we'll see him again."

"I think it's disgusting," Sarah complained. "The man is old enough to be her father."

"The way she shattered that window was pretty nasty. Hopefully Averie scared the wits out of him, and he'll leave her alone. I dang near loaded my drawers when it exploded," Mike confessed.

Averie was oblivious to the conversation happening around her. Instead, she stayed focused on her reflection in the van window. Removing the rose-colored glasses, she handed them to Sarah. "Thank you for allowing me to wear these, but I will no longer be needing them."

Sarah's mouth opened wide as she took the glasses. Her words were broken, and she started to cry. "Are you…" she couldn't finish the words as her cries became hysterical sobs.

"Before I left, Pegan told me never to be ashamed of who I am, yet here I sit hiding behind glasses. No longer will I hide in shame. I am Averie SnowBriar, child-bearer from Icearaus."

"Hell to the yes," Billy cheered from the back of the van and raised his clenched fist in the air.

Sarah dried her eyes. "I thought you were going to say you were going home. And Billy, where did you learn to talk like that?"

Averie's face lost all expression. "I can't go home."

Tom looked back at Averie. He could sense her pain. "You are home."

Billy waited until his father stopped speaking to answer his mother. "I heard it on a war movie where a rag-tag group of soldiers fought against insurmountable odds and won."

"I'm defending Billy on this one," Tom explained. "I didn't like the idea of her wearing them to begin with."

Sarah looked down at the glasses, then rolled the window down and tossed them out. Hugging Averie until they both could barely breathe, she finally let go. "I feel like such a fool. I should have asked you what you wanted to do, not forced on you what I believed was right."

"You have to remember it was my idea," Jennifer said. "That makes us both idiots."

Mike opened his mouth to say something, but the look Jennifer shot him forced his jaw to seize up and he knew better than to continue.

"What do we tell people who start to question—" Sarah began to say.

"To hell with the people," Mike interrupted. "Kids these days have pink, orange, green, blue, and purple hair and look like they fell face-first in a tackle box. If nobody questions them, I don't want to hear a single word about her."

Sarah broke out in a smile as a thought came to mind. "Are we in any rush to get home?" Sarah asked Tom.

Tom thought for a minute. "Before we left I gave the animals enough food to last a few days. I don't think so, why you ask?"

"Why don't we get a room and stay in Frankfort for the night. We could hit the mall, go see a movie—"

"They got Fast Tracks Go Kart Racing here as well," Billy interrupted. "I know Averie would love that."

"I don't know," Sarah said. "I'm kind of worried putting Averie behind the wheel."

"She'll do fine," Mike said. "If need be I'll ride with her. I spent a few years teaching driver's education. I can give her some pointers. Besides, what's she going to hit?"

"Sounds like a blast," Jennifer said. "I need to check in with the clinic first, make sure everything's running smooth."

"You can do that from the hotel," Sarah said.

Tom took the next exit and pulled into the parking lot of an ice cream shop. "Figured we could all get an ice cream cone and use the bathroom."

"Ooh, ice cream," Averie said. "What's ice cream?"

"You never gave this girl ice cream yet?" Jennifer asked Sarah.

"Well, um, no. She's always liked pumpkin pie with whip cream."

"I believe it's time to expand your palette," Jennifer told Averie.

At the hotel, Jennifer flopped down on the chair beside the bed and dialed the number to the clinic.

The phone rang three times, then an electronic voice answered. *The number you have dialed has been disconnected or is no longer in service.*

Jennifer looked at her phone, positive she dialed the right number, she tried again only to get the same results. Hmmm, looking through her list of contacts, she found Debra's phone number and called.

"Hello," a woman answered.

"Debra, it's me, Jennifer. What's going on at the clinic. I got a message saying the phone has been disconnected, is everything okay there?"

The phone went silent for a minute. "You mean you don't know?"

"Know what?"

"Two men showed up earlier today from the FDA with a cease and desist letter signed by a judge requiring all medical practices to stop. After the building was evacuated, the men chained and paddle locked the doors then posted no trespassing signs in multiple locations. I asked what was going on and he said the clinic is being investigated for performing illegal abortions and selling parts of the unborn fetuses for scientific research. I asked them if you had been notified and they told me they would be getting in touch with you shortly."

Jennifer's blood ran ice cold. "This has to be some kind of mistake. I have never performed an abortion or sold anything to research."

"That's what I told the agent, but he said his hands were tied, he's only the messenger. In a few days, the investigators are supposed to be here to start asking questions and searching through files. He hinted to the fact criminal charges may be pending, and it would look really bad if we suddenly skipped town."

"You know this is a lie," Jennifer yelled into the receiver.

"I need to know?" Debra asked in a tear-filled voice. "Have you been doing anything illegal? I have a two-year-old son. I can't go to prison over this."

"Debra, I'm telling you I have done nothing wrong, and they won't find a damn thing. This whole story is fabricated. I'll be home tomorrow and get this straightened out. You'll be back to work by the end of the day."

"I don't know," she said. "The one guy I talked to while the other was securing the building said they have some concrete evidence and it doesn't look good."

"Debra—" Jennifer started to say.

"I won't go to prison for you," Debra snarled into the phone.

Jennifer went to speak when the phone went silent, followed by a dial tone.

"Is everything okay?" Mike asked. He could see the confused look plastered on Jennifer's face.

"I'm not sure," she answered, then she told Mike about the phone conversation.

"That's a load of crap," Mike yelled. "You run that clinic on the up and up, and always have since the day you opened it."

"Well, tomorrow when we get home, the first thing I'm doing is going down there and finding out exactly what the hell is going on."

Sarah listened intently to the conversation. "I'm going to one-up you. I'm good friends with Robert at the FDA office as the farm gets certified each year and the livestock inspected for healthy living conditions. Tom may take care of the cows, but I'm the paperwork queen. I know the process better than anybody. Tomorrow before the rooster screams I'm calling him, and I'll get to the bottom of this. Nothing gets shut down without his approval."

"It's me," Averie said. "I'm the cause of all this. First Mike, now Jennifer. When is it going to end?"

Sarah mean-mugged Averie. "This is not your doing. Don't you believe that for one minute."

"Let's not allow this to ruin our night," Tom said. "We wanted to see a movie and ride the go-karts. We'll sort this out tomorrow when we get home."

The next morning Averie had to be woke up no less than six times. Between the movie, go-karts, mini-golf, the arcade, and walking what seemed like an endless mall, she was beyond exhausted.

"I'm driving," Sarah not so much said, but demanded. "Averie can ride up front with me since it's the only seat that lays back."

"What about the door handle?" Tom asked.

"The door can only be opened from the outside anyway since she ripped it off. There's no chance Averie will fall out."

Even though she didn't look it, Tom could tell Sarah was beyond livid with Robert, and he would hate to be in that man's shoes later today when they got home. Lowering his head, he climbed in the back and sat beside Billy.

Before they passed the Frankfort city limit sign, Averie was out cold.

Sarah never stopped to eat, bathroom breaks, or gas. By the time Willowdale came into view the van was running on fumes.

"Can you stop at the clinic?" Jennifer asked. "I want to see this paper they supposedly plastered on the door."

Across the street from the clinic, the van coasted into the gas station—the engine stalling out moments after the rig came to a stop.

"I'll walk from here," Jennifer said as she hopped out and jogged across the street. Moments later, she returned with a white sheet of paper. As the van filled with gas, she read the stop and desist letter out loud.

"Judge Mark Malone. Who the hell is Judge Mark Malone?" Mike asked. "There is no Judge Malone in Willowdale County."

"You're the sheriff—" Tom started to say.

"Was the sheriff," Mike corrected Tom. "Unless this guy started since I resigned, this whole thing is fabricated."

"We already know it's fabricated. This only adds fuel to the fire," Sarah hissed.

"Wait a damn minute here," Tom said, slapping his forehead. "Who submits the paperwork to the FDA, it would be the mayor after he received a few complaints. The same mayor who got rid of Mike's position. The process isn't quick, and with all the bureaucracy takes months to complete. There is no way this got pushed through this quick."

"I know Tony's involved in this scam, and once I can prove it. I'm going to go after him with everything I have until I draw blood," Sarah angrily snarled.

"Guess there is one positive to all this mess. I don't have to go to work today," Jennifer said with a laugh then tapped Mike on the shoulder. "You might want to ask Tom if he has any overtime you can do around the farm?"

Tom looked at Jennifer with a smile. "He doesn't get overtime. He's part-owner."

Mike shrugged his shoulders. "So goes the way with life."

"Has anyone checked on Averie lately?" Tom asked. "The girl has slept the whole way and is still sleeping."

"I've kept an eye on her; she's still breathing," Sarah said. "I think the go-karts whooped her soundly. She must have put a hundred miles on that yellow one."

"She was driving so slow. I passed her seventy-four times." Billy exaggerated.

"She never drove anything with a motor though either," Sarah told Billy. "I think she did great."

"She only hit a few things, you almost killed the poor attendant, made him jump right out of his skin when you lost control and came sliding in sideways, smoke rolling off the tires," Mike reminded Billy.

With the tank full and bladders empty, Sarah fired up the beast and headed home.

Less than a mile from home Averie bolted upright in the seat. "STOP," she screamed.

Sarah slammed on the brakes and veered off the road.

Averie's fingers curled inward as if she was frightened something might bite them. "Something's wrong," she whispered.

"The van is running fine," Tom said.

"Please listen to me. I don't know what, but I have a feeling something is dreadfully wrong," Averie pleaded.

"Wrong on Icearaus?" Tom asked.

Averie looked around as if searching for something. "No, here."

Mike removed his pistol and climbed from the van and opened the broken door. "Tom, you drive. Averie, please get in the back with Robyn. If you tell us somethings wrong, then something is wrong. I am not taking any chances, especially with a killer on the loose."

"Careful," Averie whispered as the van turned onto the driveway.

Tom slowed the van to a stop before reaching the white picket fence. The front window was cracked while the door hung by a single twisted hinge.

"Stay in the van!" Mike demanded.

"Please don't go in there," Averie pleaded.

"Mike knows what he's doing, he has experience in these situations most of us don't," Jennifer said to Averie. She could tell the woman was as nervous as a cat in a child's bounce house.

"You're not going in there alone," Tom said as he put the van in park.

Mike's look was all business. "Tom, this is no woman living in your barn. This man's a heartless, remorseless killer. There is no way I am letting you go in there. If something happened to you, I could never live with myself."

"The feeling is likewise," Tom said.

"Tom, I'm not going to tell you again, stay in the damn van. If you hear shots fired get the family the hell out of here. I can take care of myself."

"Maybe we should call the police?" Sarah asked.

"I was the police," Mike said. "Besides, after the heated discussion between Tony and I, I doubt he would send anyone out anyway. We're on our own for this one."

Mike was extra cautious as he neared peeking through windows to search for movement, then crawled on his knees below the window out of view to anyone who may have been hiding inside.

"POLICE!" Mike instinctively yelled as he tore the door open and quickly scanned the living room searching for suspects. The interior looked like a child picked up the house and shook it violently before discarding it to move on to another toy.

Tracing the wall for coverage, he entered the kitchen. Every pot and pan lay on the floor; dishes were scattered, glass littered the floor, and cabinet doors hung loose or were missing. Whoever had gone through here was searching for something quickly and didn't care what they destroyed in the process.

Stepping over a broken picture, he crept down the hall to the first

bedroom. The bed was flipped over, dresser destroyed, jewelry lay where it landed after being riffled through, nightstand broken, everything from the closet lay strewn like rubbish. Checking every inch, he moved on to the bathroom, then on to Billy's room which was utterly destroyed.

Searching through Averie's room, he picked up her sword. Sliding it back in the sheath, he shook his head in disgust. Why would somebody perform such wanton destruction for no better reason than to destroy what somebody else owns? From what he could tell, nothing was stolen, only destroyed.

Silently climbing the stairs, the rooms were easy to check as they had yet to be filled with furniture. Still, he had to make sure no one was hiding in a closet or the bathroom. Pulling the rope, he lowered the stairs to the attic and made a cursory check before closing it and sliding the lock closed. Afterward, he double-checked the lock to verify it was secured. If he did miss someone up there in the dark, that's where they would remain until they had to pound on the ceiling to get out.

"Please, please, please, don't let there be shots fired," Sarah begged.

They each drew an easy breathe when Mike finally emerged through the front door opening and waved for them to come.

Sarah broke down crying and fell to a sitting position when she saw her house. It was utterly destroyed.

Jennifer tried to comfort her and held her tight.

Averie looked around shaking her head. "Evil did this, pure evil."

"The good thing is whoever did this is gone," Mike said.

Tom picked up the family picture from the floor and looked at the cracked glass. "Damn them, damn them all to hell."

"If we all pitch in we can get this place somewhat organized in no time," Jennifer said.

"Make a list of everything that is broken for the insurance. I will submit it and sign it as the responding officer," Mike said.

Sarah, Averie, Jennifer, and Billy cleaned the house while Tom and Mike replaced the front door with a security door guaranteed to resist forced entry.

"Do your room first; mine can wait," Averie told Sarah. "I can sleep on the floor if needed."

"Hogwash," Sarah said. "We're going to do yours now, then ours."

Hanging up clothes and replacing the drawers the room was quickly coming together when Averie let out a blood-curdling cry and fell to her knees. "It's all gone, my whole life is gone."

"What's gone?" Sarah asked, then sat beside her.

"All my money is gone, how am I going to live?"

"That mother…" Sarah covered her mouth. "Tom, we have a problem."

Mike's face drained of color as he stood expressionless. "They stole her coins, didn't they?"

"They're all gone?" Averie whispered. "I have nothing."

"Sure you do, you still have us, and we're not going anywhere," Sarah said. "Besides. I'm going to pay you for the stolen coins. You put your trust in us, and we failed to protect them. I can't afford to pay you for them all at once though."

"It's not the money," Averie admitted. "Pegan gave them to me. At night I would hold them and think of him. Now they're gone."

Tom's fingers curled into a fist, and he slammed his hand against the wall cracking the sheetrock. "I swear to God I am going to kill the bastard that did this."

"Calm down," Mike told Tom.

"Calm down nothing," Tom hissed. "Averie's done nothing to anyone. She doesn't deserve this kind of crap. She's the most peaceful woman I know and deals with more crap... AHHH," he screamed.

"You're scaring Robyn," Sarah scolded Tom.

Mike grabbed Tom by the shirt and dragged him from the room and outside.

The inhospitable terrain of the Wilds leached the life out of everything which entered its domain. The ground under the towering peaks of sheer granite, marble, and basalt creaked and groaned while the bottomless ravines which dotted the abysmal landscape belched noxious fumes and croaked a dying moan. There were no trails, no paths, no roads; for nothing lived here to make them.

Seeking shelter from a blistering hot gale-force wind which whipped up from the valley below, Pegan led them into a small south-facing cave.

"We'll rest here for the night," Pegan said.

Standing at the edge of the cavern, Filaurel looked out into the pre-dawn gloom. It had been this way since their arrival. "Night," he grumbled. "There is no night; there is no day. There is only us, and a stagnant world time forgot."

"Perhaps a warm meal will do us good," Raestmond said as he gathered what small sticks he could find.

Pegan abruptly stopped Raestmond. "A fire will be nothing more than a beacon to all things that dwell in the Wilds of our location. Our passing must be quick and unnoticed for we are not welcome here."

Glorandial swiped the thick layer of dust away from an out-of-place bone-colored stone then sat. It was circular in shape, thick, and perfectly flat. "How did you know this cave existed?"

Sarah had a sudden revelation when she noticed the subtle pulsating of the stone around her neck. "Averie, you talk with Pegan through the stone, not the coins. That is what's important. Those coins were meant to be spent. In time you would have had to sell them anyway. Talk with Pegan now, tell him how much you love him. Tell him about the coins being stolen. I think you will find he won't care a whit. If he loves you, what will be important to him is that you're safe."

Jennifer slowly pulled the sword from the sheath and waved it in the air. "You still have this. It's more important than those coins. This is how you protect yourself."

Averie took the sword and held it to her chest. Through it she could feel Pegan as he taught her how to hold it properly. "Do you really believe he won't be mad?"

Birthright

"If he's mad then he really doesn't love you," Jennifer said.

Averie nodded. Then gripped the stone and closed her eyes. When she spoke, her voice was soft as summer rain.

—*Pegan, I love you with every fiber of my creation, and more. I long for the day when we will hold hands and walk beside the crystal blue streams again, lay on the grassy knolls and watch the stars twinkle. You must know the truth; I have failed us. If I return, we will have no money. The coins you gave me I lost—*

"Stolen," Jennifer said. "Stolen by a worthless heathen."

To hear her voice again was like magic. It was all around him; in the air, in his mind, in his soul. He had to find the source, he had to find her.

—*Averie*—Pegan screamed and fell to his knees, his eyes glowed like silver lasers.

Saress cocked her head sideways. The words were gibberish and meant nothing, but she knew the beast inside him had awoke when his silver eyes lit the caves environment.

Pegan dug until his hands bled and he unearthed an enormous stone which appeared to be part of the mountain's foundation. Slamming his fist against the stone, large cracks formed and the very mountain trembled.

Raestmond cringed. He knew, without a doubt, Pegan shattered every bone in his hand. There could be no other outcome as the impact was indescribable.

Pegan seemed unaffected as he gripped the stone as if to rip it free of the planet.

—*There was nothing you could do, the coins were stolen by creatures who worship the Dark Master. Besides, the coins mean nothing to me, it is you my heart belongs to. If it is the coins that make you happy I have a million more stashed away and will acquire a million more if that is what you desire—*

Averie gripped the necklace tighter when she heard his voice flood her mind. He wasn't angry with here and he knew they were stolen, how did he know?

—*I have a family, a good honest family who watches over me and provides for all my needs and wants and asks for nothing in return—*

Sarah dropped the sweeter she was folding to wipe the tears away from her eyes.

Pegan gasped as if he was losing unconsciousness.

—*Listen to the family who takes care of you. They seem both knowledgeable and concerned for your well-being. Someday I will find a way to repay them for their good deeds—*

"Look," Glorandial said as she pointed at Pegan. It was only know she noticed the pulsating shard in his hand.

"I bet he's talking to Averie," Saress said.

Jennifer smiled when Averie looked at her. She could see Joy on Averie's face that was not there only minutes ago.

—*I had the baby, I named her Robyn. She is the most beautiful girl I have ever seen, except*

Lady Alenia, whose beauty is beyond reproach. I hope you're not angry that I named her, Jennifer said it would be okay this one time to break tradition—

"Sure, throw me under the bus," Jennifer said with a laugh.

Pegan already knew she had the child, and the child's name but he didn't care. He would let her say it a thousand times to only hear her voice.

—The baby's name is beautiful and don't think for one minute I am upset that you named the child. It is foolish that the father should name the child, as the mother carries the baby inside her until birth—

Averie looked at Sarah who was crying hysterically.

—I have to go now, my family needs me. Tell Saress if you still see her that I love her like a mother. Please don't forget me and always remember in my heart you will remain until the day we fall into each other's arms—

Tears streamed from Pegan eyes when he heard she had to go. He needed her voice to calm the beast inside.

—Averie, I WILL always love you and will never stop searching for a way to bring you home, EVER—

When Averie finished, Sarah chocked on the words when she tried to speak. "True love like that can never be separated. I believe our God is a loving God, and sometimes he has to break your heart to save your soul. Perhaps this is the case."

Averie opened her hand and allowed the necklace to fall.

"Is he mad about the coins?" Jennifer asked.

"No," she shook her head. "He knows they were stolen. How does he know?"

"It doesn't matter," Sarah said. "What matters is his love for you."

Averie looked at Sarah. "He loves me, and I love him."

Pegan eyes were red and swollen when he looked up.

Saress knelt beside Pegan. She hated seeing her best human friend tormented by something none of them could see or understand. "Were you talking to Averie?"

Pegan nodded, yes. He already knew she had the child from a previous conversation and the coins meant nothing. It was her safety that was the utmost importance to him.

"Is she safe?" Saress asked.

Pegan sounded more determined than ever before when he spoke. "Her voice. It sounds so close to me, inside my head, inside my soul. If I could dig but a little further I can bring her home. I know I can."

Saress thought for a moment, then decided now would be a good time to confess. "Elwrick told me, told us about the shard and what you did. He asked us not to say anything as you would be living in a world of torment and pain none of us could imagine. He believed it would be best if we knew, don't be angry with him."

"I'm not angry with Elwrick, I did this to myself and I don't know why or how."

"You still have not answered my question, is she safe?" Saress asked him again.

Pegan nodded yes. "She also wishes you the best."

"At least she's safe," Filaurel said. "I'm all but positive the noise you created notified every beast between here and Hades of our arrival."

"Then I will fight every one of them," Saress hissed as she stood up. "Averie was my charge when she walked this world."

Filaurel backed away as Saress rose to her full height. For a moment, he thought he was dead as she looked like a mountain.

"Besides, I prefer an open fight instead of all this sneaking around," Saress continued.

"Filaurel is right. We should probably go," Pegan admitted.

Mike looked around in case the dirtbag was still in the area. Satisfied they were alone, he looked at Tom.

"What do you want?" Tom growled.

"You need to calm down," Mike said. "Look, it's not the end of the world. You have a beautiful family and an awesome home. Okay, so this creep broke in. They took what they wanted; they won't be back. Tomorrow we'll put in an alarm system… holy cow. Did you ever take down those trail cams?"

"No, I didn't."

Mike hollered out a scream of victory. "Quick, go get em'."

"Hope this works," Tom said as he flipped the switch on the computer. To their surprise, the screen came alive even though there was a crack from stem to stern and a permanent boot print on the white plastic edging.

Sliding in the SIM card he searched through the recorded video's until they found the one of the dreaded night.

Mike pointed at the screen. "Look, there's that woman knocking on the door, what's was her name again?"

"Sheba, I think," Tom answered.

Moments later, you could clearly see her look back as if she heard something. Seconds later, Tiny entered the screen slamming his foot into the door. Then he kicked it a second time breaking it from the hinges.

Fifteen minutes later, they were caught a second time on the camera exiting the residence. Sheba carried a bag while Tiny held a rifle.

"That looks like my AR," he complained. "I better go check," he mumbled as he sprinted down the hall to his room which still lay in ruins.

"Regardless, we have them on film. There is no denying it. Even if they can't get them for the murder, this case here is a slam dunk. Home invasion and robbery, they're both looking at twenty years plus. We'll never have to worry about them again," Mike said.

"See Averie, I told you it would work out," Sarah said.

Tom returned swinging a plastic sandwich bag. "The bastards may have stolen my AR, but not the firing pin. I always keep my guns stored without them in case we have visitors with children they can't be fired."

Mike thought for a minute. They never had children, so he never even considered this. "In the morning we'll call the detective."

"Morning my behind," Tom said. "I have his card with his personal home phone number. I'm calling him now and then were going to hop right back in the van and drive back."

"You really want to drive through the night?" Sarah asked.

"I'll drive through hell if I have to," Tom said. "If we can get there soon enough, perhaps we can get them arrested before they have a chance to dispose of the coins and returned to their rightful owner."

Pegan led them from the cave and down the side of a dark ravine were their pace slowed to a crawl. Each step was precisely calculated as one mistake would prove fatal. At the bottom, the ground leveled off, but was slick with stone chips which had flaked away from years of weathering. Pegan never slowed as they traveled east through the narrow maze created by jagged stone walls that jutted upwards to dizzying heights. In a few abnormally tight places, the reptiles were forced to endure excruciating pain as they were forced to squeeze between the passages ripping scales free.

On the far side, the stones were stacked like giant stairs which led to a large plateau overlooking the valley far below.

"Would it be easier to travel down there?" Raestmond asked, red-faced and exhausted.

Glorandial looked to where Raestmond pointed. "It appears to be rolling dunes edged by four circular craters. It seems as if something has passed recently. We might be able to find aid, they may know where the dwarves are."

"I wouldn't go down there," Pegan said. "The area is filthy with Sand Lurkers and those craters are the molten dens. The tracks you see are a mirage created by them to lure prey in to be quickly devoured."

"You talk as if you've been here before," Ameria said.

Pegan sat on a stone and looked out over the vast desert. " I have. A very long time ago, I came here searching for someone or something. I don't know who or what, but something kept calling me, and it was here within these mountains. I was a nomad lost in a foreign land and explored every inch. Clawing my way to the highest highs and slithering to the lowest lows, searching for the source."

"Then you know where we're going?" Glorandial asked.

"Sadly, no," Pegan confessed. "Whatever beaconed me led me to a great swamp. I refused to enter, burying the voice deep away inside my mind, and there it remained forgotten until recently. Once again it has awoken, and I hear its call. Eventually, I will have no choice but to enter that forsaken land and face whatever dwells within."

"Perhaps it is the dwarves calling you home," Filaurel said.

"Perhaps," Pegan said, but they all knew by the tone of his voice he had his doubts.

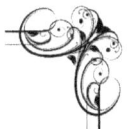

Chapter 46

on paced the long stark hallway flipping through a binder and mumbling what he planned to say when he faced the Judge. The elegant tap of his satin black oxford shoes keeping perfect rhythm with the faint music playing from the ceiling speakers. "C'mon, c'mon, c'mon," he groaned while looking at his watch. Time seemed to be moving backward.

"Relax," Nancy said as she studied the crossword puzzle. "I need a five-letter word for a creature from outer space."

"What the hell am I going to do if she refuses to give me an arrest warrant? How much more evidence do I need?"

"That's too many letters," Nancy giggled.

"You don't understand—"

"Listen," she suddenly became serious. "You have rock solid evidence for the home invasion and robbery. I also think your synopsis of the murder is spot on as well. You're getting all worked up over nothing."

"Nothing?" Ron snapped. "An innocent man lost his life, and it's possible the Fischer family could have been killed as well. You saw the pictures. They were remorseless as they destroyed the residence to get what they wanted. If they were home, there is no telling what they would have done to them to get those coins."

"The good thing is there is no denying—"

"Nine o'clock, let's go," Ron interrupted as he made his way to the door.

"You might want to…" It was too late, Ron was already through the door.

"Knock," Nancy finished.

"What the hell are you doing?" Judge Burger screamed as if she'd been caught doing something obscene.

"You told me to be here at nine," Ron stated.

"I didn't think nine… and one second," Judge Burger said as she pulled her hair back and fastened it in a tight bun. Slipping on her silver bracelet watch, she finished buttoning her black robe then fitted on a pair of Ray-Ban glasses which highlighted her bright hazel eyes.

Nancy peeked around the corner, fully expecting to find Ron dead on the floor.

"You may as well come on in," Judge Burger said when she caught Nancy's eye.

Nancy's pace was cautious as she entered. Judge Burger had a reputation of chewing up and spitting out all but the most experienced prosecutors. She, like Ron, was low on the totem pole of experience.

"Good morning prosecutor," Judge Burger said. "I see Ron has dragged you into this fiasco as well?"

"I was reluctant at first until we met the Fischer family and watched the video. Hearing their story, I think Ron has hit this one out of the ballpark."

Judge Burger leaned back in her chair placing her interlocked fingers behind her head. "Let's hear what you have since you felt the need to barge in on me in such glorious fashion."

Ron flipped through his papers until he found a document describing what he believed occurred, then he chocked under pressure. "I believe the man responsible for the murder is the same man who is guilty of a robbery which happened in Willowdale yesterday."

Judge Burger looked at him as if he suddenly turned stupid. "You might want to start making some sense before I hold you in contempt of court. I have a legitimate case to hear today. Not the garbage your spewing."

"Ron, take a deep breath and calm down. You have a solid case, you're nervous," Nancy told him.

Ron paced the room like a caged animal. Nancy was right, he was a smart man but the pressure finally got the best of him. Taking a deep breath he calmed down. "Please allow me to explain from the beginning."

"Please do," Judge Burger said as she looked at her watch.

"Tom Fischer pawned a few extremely valuable coins at the *Flying High Pawnshop*. During my investigation, I tracked down Mr. Tyler Shuwinski. A homeless man who resides in the area. It appears he records the license plate and VIN of all vehicles which visit the pawnshop in exchange for drugs. The owner, —Ms. Savannah Henderson—AKA Sheba, and her boyfriend Timothy Lunquest —AKA Tiny, sought out Professor Middleton to obtain their true value. After learning the coins were worth millions, it appears their lust for greed sent them to the DMV in search of the Fischer family residence. Oh, I forgot to mention. Hours ago, I received confirmation the code used to disable the alarm at the DMV belonged to Ms. Henderson's sister, Ms. Debbie Sniperton. I have not had a chance to speak with her yet about her involvement, but a quick search revealed she has an impeccable record and is married with two young children. Anyway, to get back to the subject. It appears Mr. Shriver, the security guard was using the restroom when Mr. Lunquest entered. Mr. Shriver upon leaving the restroom, surprised Mr. Lunquest and this was when the murder happened. A few days after the murder, Ms. Henderson and Mr. Lunquest traveled to Willowdale to the Fischer family residence and burglarized the residence in search of the remaining coins. We have this on video."

"Do you have a copy of the video?" Judge Burger asked.

"Yes." From his briefcase, Detective Weaver found a CD. On it was a burned copy from the SIM card.

Placing the CD in her computer, she watched everything unfold right before her eyes.

"Here are also the pictures of the damage they did inside the residence," while handing her a picture album.

Judge Burger looked through each picture shaking her head. "Okay, you win.

How do you wish to proceed with this?"

Ron loosened his tie and wiped the sweat from his chin. "After talking with Nancy, we decided the best course of action would be arrest warrants for the robbery. After we have them both in custody, we can start putting the pressure on Ms. Henderson. She has a clean record, not even a speeding ticket. After we start threatening her with hard time, I think she will crack to save her own skin. Mr. Lunquest, on the other hand is a career criminal with two stints in San Quentin, California. How he ended up here in Kentucky has yet to be determined. If he goes back now, it's going to be for good so he is going to be our problem child."

Judge Burger nodded her approval. "Come back this afternoon and I will have the arrest warrants for the robbery. I'm going to keep the murder out of the picture for now until you can get one of them to chirp."

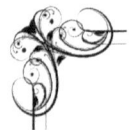
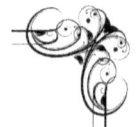

Chapter 47

 ave made a cursory search of the map of Willowdale trying to decide where the alien would have landed. If what he read was true about the Karayan case, the alien would have arrived near a residence away from the public eye. Zooming in to the point he could read address numbers, he went from yard to yard looking for any anomalies such as burnt grass, unusual broken trees, small craters, anything to signify a strange event had taken place.

Beside his laptop, another computer ran the tracing program, which chirped and clucked as it worked its way through the program calculating a billion points in the sky as it replicated the trajectory—Bling—the computer screeched and in the lower right-hand corner in big bold bright white letters coordinates materialized one digit at a time.

"Got it," Dave cheered as he scribbled down the numbers.

Closing out that map, he brought up another program which represented the earth and typed the coordinates into the search box. Within seconds of hitting the enter button, the globe began to spin, and the image grew as if you were arriving on the planet from outer space. First, the United States formed, then the state of Kentucky. Growing in proportion, the state map filled the screen then Willowdale emerged from under an electronically created clouded sky. To his surprise though the globe turned slightly east and a big red dot appeared on the outskirts of Willowdale.

This map lacked the fine-tuning capabilities of the other program, so Dave transferred that information to the other program and zoomed in. "Hmm," he mumbled as he leaned back in his chair and scratched his stubble-laden chin.

"Did you find the location?" Sandy yelled through the bathroom door. The constant go, go, go was wearing on her, and she decided a hot bath thick with Calgon was required.

"It did, but it's not what I expected."

"What do you mean?" she asked, closing her eyes and lowering herself chin-deep in the water.

"It appears whatever it was came down near an abandoned gas station on a deserted highway on the outskirts of town."

Sandy sat up in the tub. "Say what?"

Dave made his way to the door. "I said it appears whatever it was came down near an abandoned gas station. Not far from there, maybe a few miles is a farm but it seems too far away for the computer to make that kind of mistake."

"Oh, okay," she answered, then submerged herself once more.

Dave had his shoes off and was kicked back on the bed when Sandy exited the bathroom. In his hand he held the Karayan file. "After reading this for the third time, I'm starting to see a picture. It seems like only pregnant females are sent to other worlds."

Sandy flopped down on the other bed, an expressionless look on her face. "So, you think we're looking for a pregnant alien?"

"Possibly, but I'm not ruling nothing out. The only thing I know for sure is the fact that this file clearly states that Alicia told them all the women sent to other worlds have golden eyes. It's a trait only the bearer has, and it's passed on to her child."

"Interesting," Sandy agreed. "All we have to do is find the girl with the golden eyes and we have our alien."

Dave cocked his head sideways as he thought. "Sounds like the remake of a James Bond movie."

They both broke out in laughter.

"On a more serious note, we know Mr. Middleton is a waste of time and resources. Without his help, I don't think we have really any other choice but to drive out to Willowdale and look around. Eat at a few small diners, walk through the mall, perhaps we will overhear someone talking about a strange person they saw and then we can move in with some questions."

Sandy looked at the map. "We should explore that abandoned gas station as well. There may be more there than what meets the eye."

"Very true," Dave said as he flipped the light switch dimming the lights. "Let's get some sleep, I have a feeling it's going to be a long day tomorrow."

The next morning over breakfast, they discussed every possible scenario. What would they say if they encountered the alien? Was the alien aggressive? Where was the alien living? Did the alien already have the child?

Sandy sipped on her coffee as she read the file. "I think we're going about this wrong. I don't believe she will be aggressive at all. Judging from what I read here, it clearly says the scientist all agreed—Alicia was the most peaceful creature to ever grace their facility."

Dave drove while Sandy continued to read the file pointing out other details neither of them noticed on their first, second, or even third time reading it. To them, the document appeared to be alive, and each time they opened it, unknown information was revealed.

"We're here," Dave said as he took the exit onto a parallel highway and followed it for some distance before pulling off at the abandoned gas station. Getting out to stretch, he walked around the building looking through the dirty, cracked windows. Inside, the building was empty with only a small room in the back, which was probably the office at one time.

"Do you see anything?" Sandy asked as she wrapped her arms around herself searching for warmth. The temperature had dropped, and a brisk wind blew down from the north.

"Nothing," Dave answered. "I see no signs of anything living here."

"I'm getting back in the car, it's cold out here."

From the trunk, Dave grabbed the map. Down the road, a blue van heading their direction caught his eye. Only a van, he thought and unrolled the map laying it on the hood.

The blue van cruised past, then made an abrupt U-turn and pulled up alongside. Mike rolled down the window. "Are you lost or broken down? Need me to call someone for you?"

Dave looked down at the map, then up at Mike. "Well, we're kinda lost. We're from out of state and passing through. Willowdale sounded like a decent town to stop for the night, so I took the exit, but it must have been the wrong one."

"You wouldn't be the first," Mike explained. "You can either turn around and get back on the freeway and take the next exit, then a left. Or turn around and stay on the highway and take the scenic route into Willowdale. If you keep heading in the direction you're pointed there's not another town for forty miles."

Dave removed his wallet and pulled out a five and handed it to Mike. "You're a godsend. Thanks for the information."

Mike declined the offer. "No need. You may want to get to town though there's a storm brewing."

Dave leaned against the door of the van. "We'll thank you for the help. You and your family have a good…" Inside, in the back seat, he saw a pair of golden eyes that drove a shiver clear down into his soul. "Night and God bless you," he finished.

"You do the same," Mike said.

Tom put the van in gear and drove away.

Dave quickly climbed inside and sat down.

"He seemed like a very nice man"

Dave was deathly pale as he watched the van fade into the distance then take a sharp right-hand turn. "I saw her," he slowly said.

"Saw who?"

"The alien, she was in that van."

"And…"

"And I think I need a drink," Dave said as he put the car in drive and flipped a U-turn heading towards Willowdale.

They both sat in utter silence and watched the rain splatter against the window of the restaurant.

"Are you going to tell me what you saw, or what?"

"I can't," Dave admitted. "What I can tell you is the way the folder describes the eyes is nowhere near accurate. They have a mesmerizing characteristic to them as well. Even now, miles away, I can still feel them looking at me."

"Okay… okay," Sandy said. "We now know where she lives, and it is at that farm. What do we do from here?"

"I know what I'm not going to do and that's barge right in. I think tomorrow I will observe them from a distance, so I won't be noticed."

"How do you plan to do that?"

"I'll show you when the rain stops," he said, then held up his coffee cup to be refilled.

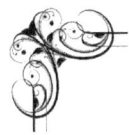
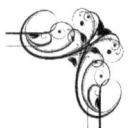

Chapter 48

ike sat on the front porch watching the chickens peck the soggy ground. In the distance, the darkened clouds glowed bright for a second as unseen lightning flashed across the sky. Moments later, thunder rolled and the rain fell in sheets.

Jennifer came out and sat beside him on the swing wrapped in a blanket. "Why don't you come inside? It's cold out here."

Mike scratched his head, then pulled his jacket tight against himself to block out the breeze. "What are we going to do?".

Jennifer looked confused. "What do you mean?"

"I don't have a job besides working here at the farm. The Clinic is shut down for who knows how long. If Tony was involved in it, you may never get your business license restored."

"We don't know—"

"Don't lie to yourself to make it sound better than what it really is, we're screwed. We have two vehicle loans, credit cards, utility bills, a mortgage on a house we never should have bought."

"What are you saying, it's my fault now?"

"You're the one who wanted that monstrosity," Mike barked.

"Okay, fine. I wanted the house, I'll find another job."

"Making the same kind of money? Even if you went back to work at the hospital you'll only make a third of what you did at the clinic. Our mortgage alone will sink us, which by the way is now overdue."

Jennifer watched lighting flash across the sky. "Damn."

"I don't think we have much of a choice. We may have to foreclose on the house, give back our vehicles, then move back to Frankfort."

"You can't be serious. You hate that city," Jennifer said.

"I know, but what choice do we have?"

"Let me talk with Sarah, see if she can give us a loan, just enough to pay our bills until you get your first check from the farm."

"You know I hate borrowing money from friends."

"Don't think of it as borrowing money, consider it more as a payday advance."

Later that evening as they gathered to watch a movie Jennifer asked Sarah if she could talk with her alone outside to avoid the embarrassment of everybody knowing their financial situation.

"What's that about?" Tom asked Mike as the two women walked outside.

Mike shrugged his shoulders, "Who knows, women."

On the front porch Jennifer broke down crying. "Mike is right, it's all my fault."

Sarah hugged her for a long time allowing her to release her feelings. "The first thing were going to do is go inside and talk about this like adults."

"Thank you," Jennifer sobbed.

Sarah had a raw look on her face when she entered. "Family meeting, now."

Tom and Billy knew better than to argue and they quickly went to the kitchen table.

"Mike, you need to come in here as well." Sarah's vision glanced to each participant. "We have a situation. Mike, you need to come clean and tell us everything. It's the only way we can help."

"What are you getting at?" Tom asked Sarah.

"Let me explain," Mike said as his shoulders slumped with embarrassment. Over the next hour he explained their financial situation.

Tom listened intently. "You're both my best friends and I'll be damned—

"Remember what Averie said," Billy chimed in. "Where she came from she was hated by all except for a few. Guess it will be the same way here. Even your good friend Debbie at the clinic believes you're a criminal. I have a few dollars in my penny bank you can have for helping Averie."

"Keep your money," Tom said. "We know their lying—"

"I haven't lied about anything," Averie said.

"Not you dear," Sarah said. "We're talking about Tony and the men who shut down Jennifer's Clinic."

Tom went to the kitchen and came back with his checkbook. "Write this for how much you owe on your vehicles and pay them off."

"I can't take—"

"I said pay off the damn vehicles. Considerate it an early Christmas present. I have an empty shop we can move all your belongings into and you both can move upstairs. Let the bank have the damn house."

"Are you sure?" Jennifer said.

"With Mike and I working the farm we can double the income."

"I don't know," Mike said. "I feel like I'm barging in. The third wheel."

"What do you have to lose?" Sarah said. "You're here more than you're at home anyway."

Tom looked around. "Everything we own is paid for and we work directly with the Federal Government across all fifty states. If they even tried to shut us down there would be hell to pay. Besides, even if they did we have a large enough clientele I would do business under the table and we would still be fine."

"It seems like everything is falling apart," Jennifer mumbled.

"This is what happened on Icearaus," Averie said. "My father was right, I am a disease."

Sarah was smoking mad when she looked at Averie. "I think Pegan would disagree with you on that one," Sarah said. "On Icearaus, did you lay down and surrender to the enemy?"

"No."

"And we're not going to here either. Tony wants a war, by golly, I'll give that man a war he will never forget," Sarah hissed.

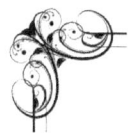 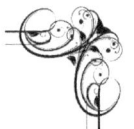

Chapter 49

ady Alenia sat on a carved wooden bench near the stairs that led up to her residence. The night was unseasonably warm, and the sky twinkled with a million stars. The rustle of the tree branches and the chirping of crickets the only sound.

Closing her eyes, she relaxed. There was no danger here. She could sense the presence of the elven soldiers carefully selected by Elwrick to be her protectors. He spent hours grueling them to make sure there was not the slightest hint of deception.

Across the way in the shadows of a large tree, Elwrick materialized into existence. He knew she was going through the change and had been for some time. Still, he didn't know how far her mind had degraded and wanted to test her senses.

Lady Alenia opened one eye when she heard the snap of a twig behind her. "Elwrick," she whispered.

Elwrick could sense the unsurety in her voice.

"I wondered when you were going to arrive," Lady Alenia said as she looked back to where more twigs were being broken upon his approach.

Elwrick released a heartfelt sigh. Her senses were still keen enough to detect his approach, but not much more. She should have sensed him instantly.

"Come, sit with me and enjoy the night," Lady Alenia whispered as she patted the bench.

Elwrick ran the back of his hand down her cheek following the jawline. From there he traced the outline of her neck with his finger. "You're looking as radiant as ever."

"I don't want you to stop, but you're going to get us both in trouble. As you're aware, numerous soldiers are watching your every movement."

Elwrick sat beside Lady Alenia and caressed her hand. "Sometimes, I wonder why the Creator created love. Is that wrong to say?".

"What do you mean?" She answered with a question.

"We are blessed with the gift to love and be loved. Yet here we sit very much in love and both knowing we can never be together."

Lady Alenia giggled then kissed his cheek. "This is because we are two different beings. You're a creature of light, while I am made of flesh, bone, and blood. Still, no laws prevent us from enjoying each other's company until the day the Creator calls me home."

"And once again I will be left here, alone, to suffer as I relive the past."

Lady Alenia snuggled close to Elwrick then rested her head on his chest. "You know the elves are going to talk about what they see tonight, and rumors are going to spread like fire through dried brush," Elwrick reminded her this time.

"There is no need for them to talk. If they can't see the feelings we have for each other, then they must be blind. From now until the end of days, I wish to remain wrapped in your loving arms and feel your warmth against me."

Elwrick sensed there was more to her sudden clinginess. They always had feelings for one another, but now she did nothing to keep them hidden.

For a long time, they sat there in silence enjoying the serene beauty of the night. Listening to the wind rustle the trees, the chirp of the crickets, a baying wolf, everything seemed to be in perfect tune.

"Lady Alenia," Elwrick finally said. "I sense there is more you wish to tell me."

"There is," she cautiously whispered. "But I lack the courage to find the right words."

Elwrick looked into her eyes. "You can tell me anything," he softly said into her ear, then kissed her cheek.

"Elwrick," she said as her eyes became moist. "I don't know how to tell you this, but I'm dying."

Elwrick tried to speak but she silenced him by placing her finger against his lips. "Elves don't age like other mortals. We keep our youthful appearance for our entire life then moments before we're called home, we age rapidly. Even now in your arms, I can feel it seeping into my bones like an evil wraith coming to claim what's been stolen."

Elwrick hugged her tight. He knew aging affected elves differently than man. "I already knew—"

"Allow me to finish, please," she interrupted Elwrick. "I'm ashamed, ashamed of the way I feel. I was once a mighty warrior, Queen of the Elves, Demon Slayer. That warrior has since died. No longer do I wish to wield a blade, no longer do I wish to wear armor, no longer do I have the will to fight."

Elwrick gripped Lady Alenia's hand. On it he could see century-old wrinkles forming. "You're telling me this now, but the warrior died in you long ago. Don't be ashamed of what you're becoming, embrace it. Mortals have yet to figure this out and I don't know why; time is an enemy which you cannot defeat."

"I don't want to appear weak."

"You don't look weak in my eyes, or in the eyes of those who follow you. You have fought things these elves could never even imagine. I have seen you stand your ground when all hope was lost. Had it not been for you, and of course Midnight, I would have perished during the Great War."

Lady Alenia stroked Elwrick gray beard. "You're the lucky one, you get to live forever and not face the fear of dying."

"You confuse living forever with immortality. Living forever is a curse where your forced to watch those you love slowly die. Immortality, however, isn't living forever, but living life to the fullest and doing things to enrich the lives of those around you. After your passing, your name will remain on their tongues. That is true immortality. Trust me, in the elven community, your name will remain forever on their tongues."

"I love you," she said, then snuggled closer and let her eyes slowly close.

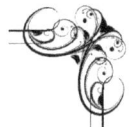

ack at the hotel Sandy's eyes couldn't grow any wider when she observed Dave remove a plain white box about the size of a dinner plate from a black bag labeled DJI-1. She already knew what it contained before he slid the lid free. "I better get used to dating women because we're going to jail for a long time once the agency discovers this thing missing."

"I officially signed it out," Dave sighed having heard her displeasure. "Besides, if anything goes bad you never knew I took it. All the heat will fall on me."

"It won't matter," she mumbled. "We're both going to fry."

"It's a beauty though," Dave said as he tossed the lid aside. Inside the box was the *DJI Mavic Pro Platinum, dual camera, full video, thermal infrared drone*. "This baby can fly up to forty miles per hour. It has a live video feed with audio and extremely advanced high zoom capabilities. We can read the ingredients on the back of a spaghetti sauce jar from a mile away if we want. With its night-vision camera we can observe the alien in day and night, in any kind of weather."

"We're going about this the wrong way," Sandy groaned.

"How so?" Dave asked.

"We're not investigating an organized crime syndicate where we could be discovered and taken into the woods and never seen again. We know where the alien lives. You talked to the man with her and he seemed like a respectable person. If we're caught sneaking around spying on them I think it will jeopardize our story when we tell them why we're here. I honestly believe it would be smart to walk right up and knock on the front door and introduce ourselves."

Dave looked down at the drone disgusted he may not get to play with the toy.

"If you would have told me about the drone before we left Florida, I would have said the same thing," Sandy continued.

"How about this," Dave said as he slid the lid back on the box. "Tomorrow we watch them from a distance. Not all day, a few hours in the morning, then again around lunch and a few hours in the evening. If they seem normal, the next morning we'll introduce ourselves."

"Deal," Sandy agreed. "But I still think we're wasting our time."

The first golden rays of the rising sun gently caressed the Fischer Farm when Averie woke. Outside the window, the glint of something blue caught her attention and she pulled back the curtain. Directly in front of the barn the van sat covered in dew, the big glass eyes on the front mocking her for her failures and her heart sank. Sarah and Tom had welcomed her into their home, gave her a room, fed her, provided for her needs, and what had she done in return?

Needlessly destroyed their possessions.

Bundling up Robyn with extra blankets she silently ventured out on a mission to right her wrongs.

The air held a crisp coolness and the stiff breeze blew down from the north promising a miserable winter.

Quickly crossing the driveway she sought the protection of the barn doors from the wind. Her fingers were already numb so she could only imagine the discomfort of Robyn whose lips we're turning blue. She would gladly suffer so her child would be warm. Satisfied Robyn was adequately protected, Averie located the big red dusty box near the back.

Searching through the toolbox she gathered everything she thought would help with the repair; screwdrivers, pliers, crescent wrench, hammer, and a few other oddities. Hopefully she would have the repair done and be back inside long before the family rose.

Sarah woke to the rooster crowing and an uncomfortable shiver. Wrapping herself tightly in her fire-engine red fleece robe she eased her feet into her furry bunny slippers with floppy ears then crept her way to the thermostat. "Thirty-seven degrees," she grumbled. "No wonder I'm shivering, it's freezing in here." Cranking the dial to seventy-five, she headed for the kitchen where the coffee pot was steadily calling her name.

Jennifer arrived before the first drip splattered against the glass pot. "My God it's freezing in here. Does this place have a heater?"

"I turned it on a few minutes ago," Sarah answered. "Not sure where the hell this sudden cold front came from."

"I'm going to go check on Robyn, make sure she's warm enough," Jennifer whispered.

"It won't take long for the house to heat up," Sarah assured her as she snatched the Mocha Creamer from the fridge.

Upstairs above the kitchen, movement could be heard.

"Mike must be waking up as well," Jennifer said as she glanced at the ceiling, then dematerialized into the shadows of the hallway.

Mike fumbled his way down the stairs still wrapped in a blanket. "I came down to start the coffee. Only way to warm up in this place."

"I already have a pot brewing," Sarah said as she removed four cups from the cupboard and placed them next to the pot.

The sound of someone running down the hall caught their attention then Jennifer slid around the corner on her socks nearly falling to the floor. "Averie and Robyn are gone," she cried out.

Sarah ran to Averie's room to see for herself, then to her room nearly throwing Tom from the bed. "Averie and Robyn are gone, get dressed NOW,"

Mike tossed the blanket down the same time Tom emerged from the bedroom holding the shotgun. "If that son-of-a-bitch did anything to her…"

They all knew Tom was talking about Frank.

"Hold on," Mike said as he grabbed Tom by the shoulder. "Before we go getting all crazy-like, let's check her room first. If anyone did snatch her they would have had to come through the window. We both know nobody was getting through the front door without the aid of a tank."

Sarah's heart sank and she burst out crying. "That why it was so cold in here. Someone snatched her and left the window open."

Tom spun a U-turn in the hall, Mike right on his heels.

Mike quickly scanned the room searching for clues about her sudden vanishing. Observing no signs of foul play he crossed the room in four leaps and jerked back the curtain fully expecting the window to be ajar, yet it was closed and securely locked.

"This don't make any sense," Tom said.

"Wait, wait, wait." Mike's words blended together as movement across the driveway caught his attention. Near the van he could see feet below the open passenger door. "She's at the van."

"Why would she be out at the van?" Sarah asked, but none answered.

They moved like a mob with a single purpose bumping into one another as they all tried to fit out the door at once. Upon their arrival, Sarah was the first to speak. "What are you doing out here?"

Averie was so focused on her work, she failed to notice their arrival.

Tom's jaw came unhinged and swung side to side. Somehow, Averie managed to get the door panel off and the window was now off track and cocked sideways.

Averie dropped the screwdriver to the ground. "I tried to fix it, and once again I've failed. Now the window will not move up or down," she whispered as she pressed the lever.

"It's freezing out here," Jennifer said as she picked up the car seat Robyn was bundled in.

"How about we go inside—" Sarah started to say.

"I have to fix this first. You and Tom have given me everything and I have done nothing in return." She picked up a pair of pliers and tugged on a wire that sent blue sparks flying when it broke free.

"Whoa, whoa, whoa," Tom said as he took the pliers from her. "If you want to help, that's fine. We have hundreds of things around here you're more than capable of doing, but not this. Hell, I'm not even sure it can be fixed, now," he added noting the octopus of wires hanging out from the skeletal frame.

Sarah flashed Tom an angry glance, then focused on Averie who was looking at a crescent wrench trying to figure out how it worked. "Averie dear," Sarah said. "Let's go inside and get you warmed up, your lips are blue and chapped. For all I care this old hunk of junk can rust into the ground."

Later that evening, Sarah's tongue hung from her mouth as she dragged the fine bristled brush across the coarse textured ham. Behind the brush, a glistening mixture of glaze and pineapple juice produced a glistening sheen. Delicately placing the pineapple rings slightly overlapping across the length of the ham, she coated it once more with her grandma's secret glaze, then slid it in the over and closed the door. Tonight, dinner would be to die for.

"Jennifer, you have a minute," Sarah called up the stairs. "I want your opinion on something."

"Sure, one second. Let me finish making the bed," she answered as she wiped the dust off the nightstand and adjusted a picture of her and Mike on their wedding day. All day long Mike, Tom, Billy, and Averie were making trips back and forth between the houses slowly moving everything over.

Sarah opened a few gravy packets and dumped them in the boiling water.

"What do you need?" Jennifer asked as she waltzed down the stairs.

"What do you think of this dress?" Sarah asked as she pulled a white dress from an unmarked box.

Jennifer rounded the corner then seized up like an engine lacking oil pressure. It was the very dress Averie wore upon her arrival to their world. "How did you—"

"No, it's not the same dress," Sarah informed her. "Before we left for Frankfort I had Suzy at the tailor shop look at the original one, but she couldn't repair it. She said she had never seen that kind of material before and swore it was made out of layered spiderwebs. So, I had her do the next best thing and make a duplicate out of silk and lace. I ran into town and picked it up a few hours ago while you were organizing the upstairs."

"She's going to love it," was all Jennifer could say as she ran her fingers down the silky-smooth material.

With dinner complete and the last plate sinking like a diving submarine in the kitchen sink, Sarah suggested they should go do something instead of sitting in front of the television watching re-runs.

Tom nodded in agreement. "I think it's a grand idea. Question is, what do we want to do?"

Averie's mind drifted back to the theatre and the smell of the popcorn. "Can we go to the movies?" she asked.

"I don't see why not," Tom said. Unfolding the paper, he opened it up to the entertainment section and laid it out for them all to see.

"How about that one right there?" Sarah asked as she pointed to a large add.

Jennifer looked to where Sarah pointed. "That's *Terminal Glory*. It's about a boy who has cancer and battles his way to victory. It's been labeled an all-time must see and rated five stars by Rotten Tomatoes."

"Sounds like a chick flick to me," Mike voiced his displeasure with her choice.

"And," Jennifer said with a disgusted tone.

"And it sounds like a darn good movie." Mike quickly altered his opinion.

"Then it's settled. Tonight, at nine we'll be going to the late showing," Sarah said as she pulled a plain white box out from a drawer. "By the way Averie, this came for you when you were out."

Tom eyed the box suspiciously, then realized there was no postage anywhere on it and knew Sarah was up to something.

"For me?" Averie excitedly asked.

"Yes, it's all yours," Sarah answered as she handed Averie the box.

Averie looked at it for a long time. She had never received a present before.

"Are you going to open it or what?" Billy asked. He seemed more anxious than Averie.

Averie carefully pulled away the tape, then slowly slid the lid open. Tears filled her eyes as the memories of Lady Alenia flooded her mind and the first time she looked at herself wearing it in the mirror. "How?" she whispered wiping away the tears.

"A while ago, I took the original to a tailor but they couldn't fix it so I had a replica made," Sarah explained to Averie.

"Replica?"

"It is a copy of the original," Tom tried to explain.

"Can I wear it?" Averie asked.

"It's yours to do with what you want." Sarah giggled observing the smile cross Averie's face.

"I'm going to put it on now," Averie told them.

"Hold on young lady. You need to shower and wash first. You're all sweaty and dirty from helping Mike and Jennifer move."

Averie played with the lever adjusting the temperature until it was spot on, then climbed in and allowed the water to cascade down her body. Closing her eyes, she laid her head back and relaxed. Time slowed and the sound of water draining faded. Swaying like a tree in a storm she began to sing.

"Listen," Sarah said. "I don't know the words, but it sounds amazing."

For a moment, time stood still and they all listened.

Later, Averie emerged from her room, danced down the hall, then did some strange jitterbug scoot as she crossed the living room floor and ended up twirling like a ballerina. The ruffles on her dress flung out wide like an open umbrella but what she did next left them all gasping with laughter. She stopped like a fashion model in a sexy pose at the end of a runway on a New York stage. "I think it's beautiful," she said after the performance.

"Your voice is amazing," Jennifer said.

Averie blushed bright red. "You heard me?"

"Yes, and it was mesmerizing," Mike said. "Something like you would hear in a medieval movie."

"I sang it for Pegan, I named it *Guiding Me Home*. When I was a little girl I would look in the mirror and picture one day singing to the world, but I'm not very good."

"Can we hear it in our language?" Sarah asked.

"*Umm*, sure. The words don't make any sense though," Averie said as she closed her eyes and began to perform a spectacular ballad.

"Stunning, simply stunning," Tom said. "The words hold a special meaning to you none of us will understand, but your voice... words can't describe how beautiful your voice is."

Dave came in hot and fast with the drone nearly crashing it into the car. "Do you understand now what I meant by her eyes?"

Sandy rubber her own eyes. "Yes, her eyes are unique, but it was her voice that touched me the most. It had a raw, medieval quality I can't place my finger on."

Dave carefully placed the drone in the box and slid the cover on. "I still can't believe we would destroy such a beautiful woman in the name of research."

"That's why we're risking everything now to prevent another tragedy," Sandy said as she climbed in the car.

Dave sat beside her and fired up the engine. "Let's go back to the hotel and change. Sounds like were going to see a movie tonight at nine."

"Sounds good to me," Sandy answered as she watched the video on the tablet the drone took of Averie. "We can see how she interacts with the populace."

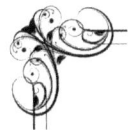

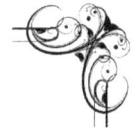

Chapter 51

he words Malvo spoke still haunted Vexacion's mind when Lilith collapsed partway to their destination—*if she dies before the Dark Master can feed, you will take her place.* He had seen the remnants of the corpses removed from that forsaken nightmare of a room and would rather appear weak in the eyes of his companions, than face that malevolent creature from the dark.

"Carry her the remainder of the distance," Vexacion ordered the two men.

Lilith's vision came in nauseating waves of faint grays, dull browns, and hazy reds. Marble walls and tiled floors passed in a translucent fog as if she was trapped in a nightmare dream from which she couldn't wake. Nothing seemed real or tangible. Both her arms lacked feeling, floating weightlessly adrift in a sea of pain and she was not sure if the screams were her own or that from another doomed soul.

"I hate this room," Vexacion said as he turned the knob and pushed the door inward.

"You don't like the torture chamber?" an assassin asked.

"I loved the torture chamber, and let's not forget many of the devices contained within were my creation. This though isn't a torture chamber, but something far more sinister."

"Meh," the assassin shrugged his shoulders. "To me, it appeared far more sadistic before Malvo cleaned it out."

Vexacion grabbed the assassin by the shoulder, and his focus was laser intense. "You've never seen it go through the change, I have."

Lilith viewed her new location when she was dropped to the stone floor. To her surprise, the room was empty except for a large circular device made of large bones bound together with braided ropes constructed from human hair. Dangling from the strange device were four chains, each ending in a steel clasp. Inside each clasp were gnarled, rusty teeth designed to penetrate both flesh and bone. Carved into the broken stone floor directly in front of the demonic-looking device was a pit filled with the entrails, body parts, brains, and coagulated blood of past victims. The movement of larvae as they swam kept the foul-smelling stew in a perpetual state of churning.

"Hurry," Vexacion demanded of his men. "Place her in the rack before Malvo comes, and be careful this time."

Lilith released a scream that fell on deaf ears as a clasp was fastened tightly to each wrist and ankle. Behind the device, all four chains were attached to a central chain which led to a large steel wheel. As the wheel was slowly cranked, each chain was pulled taut lifting her from the ground and forcing her nude body to float spread eagle directly in the center. Blood dripped from her wrists and ankles as the teeth buried into the bones holding her rigid.

The assassin looked around uneasy as the hair on his neck stood erect. "There, she's fastened to the rack. I'm leaving," the assassin grumbled.

"Not so fast," Vexacion snarled. Afterward, he carefully checked the assassins work. He could not afford a mishap like their last subject who exploded from the wheel being excessively cranked. Pulling on the chains, he wanted them tight, but not to the point of dislocating limbs. Satisfied she would live, albeit in extreme discomfort, the assassins departed securing the door behind them.

Lilith cautiously lifted her head when the sound of thunder reached her ears.

The room was going through a metamorphosis, becoming a literal hell for the living.

The ground changed first, becoming something more like an enormous scab growing over a festering wound. Geysers broke through the surface spewing noxious steam and yellow bile. Stone walls ignited in magical red flames forcing her to violently jerk from the searing heat which should have blistered the skin but left no marks. The ceiling became a sky of darkness that revealed no stars. Black, dense clouds floated past raining down blood. All around her, she was surrounded by the tormented screams of all those who suffered before her.

Driven nearly to madness, she looked up at the bleeding sky and wept. "Mother, help me," she cried out. No longer able to support her head, it fell forward, and her vision faded to darkness.

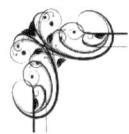
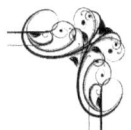

Chapter 52

o their surprise and shock, Averie sprinted to the van. Usually, she was reluctant to go near the monstrosity calling it nasty names such as *the Heathen*, and *the Nameless Beast*. "You all coming or what?" She hollered out through the half-cocked window.

"We need a new van," Sarah told Tom as he fastened the double locks on the front door.

Tom sighed. "I already have an appointment scheduled early next week to get the window fixed."

"I recommend we take two vehicles," Mike suggested. "If we take the van we'll freeze to death with the broken window."

"Sorry Averie," Tom said as he walked passed. "We're taking the car, and Mike is taking their Jeep. It's too cold to drive the van."

Averie sighed, she knew it was a ploy to get her out of the front seat, but she learned the game quick. "Shotgun," she yelled, then bolted past Tom towards the red Camry.

For Averie, it was a love-hate relationship. She loved observing the world. The sights, the sounds, the smells… each time they went somewhere, it was like seeing the world for the first time. The hate part came getting in the car. She still couldn't fathom something that moved on its own, even though Tom explained it to her a hundred and seventeen times precisely what an engine was.

Outside the theater, neon lights glistened against the darkened backdrop of a cloudy sky, and a line of people snaked clear to the street.

"I hope it's not sold out," Jennifer said.

"I'm sure it's not," Mike sarcastically said. "Anybody who's anybody is coming to see *Murder at Sunset.*"

Averie hopped out first and led the way.

Dave watched the pair of golden eyes dart across the darkened parking lot. "Here she comes," Dave said, taping Sandy on the shoulder.

Averie held the door open for the others; and an older couple who paused to take a lasting look. The older man with thinning gray hair shook his head in confusion. "Kids, what are they going to come up with next?"

"I agree," Mike said with a smile.

With the tickets purchased, Averie did exactly what they all suspected; she shot like an arrow straight to the concessions stand. Both eyes widened as she looked at all the choices. There were so many choices, but they lacked the one thing she craved.

"You need to pick something," Sarah whispered to Averie. "There's a line forming."

Averie looked back at the crowd, then back to the display case. "Popcorn," she finally blurted out obviously upset about the lack of popcorn. "I don't see any popcorn."

"That's because it's behind the counter," Tom reminded her.

Averie blushed red. "Oh," she looked past the clerk to the glass box. "I'll take a large popcorn and a large root beer."

"She acts almost like a child," Sandy whispered to Dave.

"Remember, she's not been here very long. I bet all this is new to her."

"She doesn't look pregnant?" Sandy suggested, noting the girl's hourglass figure.

"That's because she already had the child," Dave said. "That dark-haired woman is carrying the baby. Look, the baby has the same glowing eyes, except they burn even more intense."

Sandy agreed, having spotted the two glowing dots behind the blanket.

Remembering what Sarah taught her, she removed a small calculator from her purse and added everything up, then counted out the required amount to make the purchase. She had no desire to relive that moment in the perfume store.

"What a strange-looking necklace," Sandy whispered to Dave. In the dim light, they could see the faint pulsating of the stone under her white dress.

"Obviously she brought it with her from Icearaus," Dave said. "I bet she will be able to tell us some amazing stories."

"Should we go sit down?" Averie asked.

"Nah, not yet," Tom answered. "We still have some time, did you want to walk around and explore?"

Averie eagerly accepted the invitation. Holding a large bucket of popcorn in one hand, a drink in the other, and a wicked grin on her face, she set out like Columbus. Behind her, they followed not saying a word as she made her way down each aisle looking at the cardboard displays, posters, the highly decorative carpet, multi-colored lights, and more.

Mike abruptly stopped. "Did you see that, or am I losing my mind?" he asked Tom.

"See what?"

"I swear to God the couple sitting in the seating area are the same two we met at the abandoned gas station."

Tom glanced back and caught Dave's eye. "You know, I think your right."

Jennifer looked back as well. "So they came to the movies, what's the big deal?"

Mike scratched his chin. "I built my life around watching people. Call it an intuition or whatever, but them being here is no coincident. I have a feeling we're going to see them again."

"Really," Tom Sighed. "Think about it. How would they know we were coming here?"

Jennifer looked at the clock on the wall. "Shows starting soon, we better find our seats.".

"The tall guy with a shaved head recognized us," Sandy said. **"He** suspects something."

Walking to door number six, Sarah abruptly stopped. "Whoa, wait one damn minute." Her demeanor suddenly changed to that of a snake, and her focused eyes cut through the crowd and could have killed the man they landed on. "Go get the seats; I'll be there shortly," then darted off into the crowd.

"Oh no, this isn't good," Jennifer said as she spotted what caught Sarah's sudden interest.

"We better go too," Tom suggested. "When Sarah gets like this, trouble often follows."

They arrived just in time to see Sarah verbally assaulting Tony with words sharper than a sword. "You still screwing the floozy over at the perfume shop?" It was rumored he and Samantha were having an affair, but there was no proof, Regardless, Sarah didn't care. She was going on nothing more than a gut feeling at this point. "Or have you moved onto someone younger by now?"

"What is she talking about?" the woman—obviously his wife by the disgusted look on her face—screamed.

"I don't know?" Tony sputtered like a car running on fumes.

"What about all those movies I bought you?"

"I, I, I, I don't know what she's talking about honey. Donna, you have to believe me," Tony gasped in horror. All around him, his world was beginning to crumble as people started to gather.

"Oh, don't look so surprised now, each time I would—"

"Movies, what movies? What is this woman talking about?" Donna's face was blistering red as she interrupted Sarah.

A petite blonde stepped forward and stuck her finger right in Tony's face. "What about that time you offered to have that bogus speeding ticket dropped if I slept with you?"

"What? Sleep with him? You never told me about this." A man built like a fire hydrant stepped forward.

Sarah started an ugly storm of accusations as more women came forward with bad experiences.

"I still can't believe you dumped me for that hot mess," Sarah stomped her feet. "Oh, and by the way, I bought all those movies because you said your wife would find out if you used your credit card, and it would ruin your reputation as Mayor. I want them back, not tomorrow, not later, NOW!"

Tom damn near fainted, had it not been for Mike he surely would have hit the ground like a safe.

"Honey, I don't know what she or any of these women are talking about. This is a conspiracy to get me out of office. You have to believe me?"

Suddenly, it seemed as if every movie was put on pause as the real show was happening in the lobby.

"Let me tell you what he wanted me to do," an unseen woman screamed out from the crowd.

"Sure, you do. Why try and lie now?" Sarah remained on him like a pit bull on a pork chop. "You know, let's play copycat with the movie." She pulled out her phone and opened up the gallery, "I think I still have a picture of you wearing my underwear on your head like a mask, you know, WrestleMania."

Jennifer's mouth came unhinged, then she quickly covered Robyn's ears and walked away, she didn't want the child to be traumatized by the filth Sarah was spewing.

The lady heard enough and threw her drink in Tony's face. "After all these years, I can't believe it. I slaved to give you everything, and this is how you thank me, by having an affair," she screamed and walked past. The click of her heels sounded like cannons firing.

"Enjoy the show," Sarah told Tony, then vanished into the crowd like a rogue.

"Well that was interesting," Sandy said from where she sat observing the whole ugly scene play out.

"Let's pass on the movie," Dave said. "We'll go back to the hotel and gather our things and tomorrow morning head out to their house and meet her in person. Perhaps we will get the truth of what just happened here, and get to know her."

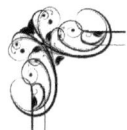 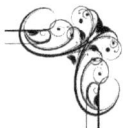

Chapter 53

alvo cautiously paced around the rack, his arms tightly folded behind his back. "You did well," he told Vexacion who followed in his footsteps. "Now wake her so we can finish our discussion."

Vexacion removed a pinch of Sal Ammoniac from the pouch he wore on his belt and rubbed it under her nose.

Lilith jerked violently as the powder assaulted her senses and burned her lungs.

Lifting her head, he looked into her one open eye; the other remained swollen shut. "I see my men are becoming very proficient at utilizing the rack. The first few times, well, let's say the subject didn't fare too well."

Blinded by pain, she recognized the voice instantly as Malvo Necrosyse. "What more do you want from me?" Lilith barely found the strength to whisper. "Have I not suffered enough for the death of our child?"

Malvo laughed. "You should consider yourself lucky. What you must understand is my father believes you're too powerful to remain in the Mortal Realm and must be sent to the underworld where you can be dealt with appropriately. I fear he is mistaken and you're nothing more than a broken hag holding onto life for no better reason than to be a thorn in my side."

Lilith tried to smile as if to tell him the words he spoke were true.

"My father's only requirement is that you must be alive upon his arrival for your soul to be snatched away and dragged down to Hades. Once there I'm all but certain you, and he, are going to have a delightful time. Until his arrival, though, you're mine to do with as I please."

"What have I done to you?" Lilith found the strength to scream at Malvo.

"What have you done to me," Malvo repeated what Lilith asked. "Because of you, I was forced to live underground like a rat for decades. Because of you, I forgot the warmth of the sun on my face. Because of you, I lacked the comfort of companionship."

"You lie," Lilith grumbled. "You're a demonic beast born in the fires of hell. You don't need to feel the sun on your face or the comfort of a woman."

"Your half right," Malvo spat back. "You must remember I am half-mortal and still enjoy some of the pleasures offered to those who dwell on the Mortal Realm."

Lilith tried to adjust her position, forcing the teeth to dig deeper.

Malvo removed a hot poker from a brazier. Holding it up to eye level, he examined the glowing red tip. "They say if you roll this along human flesh, it will peel the skin away causing excruciating pain. Perhaps I shall test out that theory on your thighs."

As he neared, she could feel the heat and fought with the chains.

Moments before the iron rod found flesh; a grotesque looking creature materialized up through the cracks in the floor. The thing was nothing more than a blob of rotting skin, gangly tentacles, two beady little red eyes, and an enormous mouth lined with razor-sharp teeth.

"What is that thing?" Vexacion asked as he stepped out of the way allowing it to slither past. Behind it, a glistening streak of slime and pus followed.

The thing ignored Vexacion and went straight to Malvo. "My Lord," it said in a gravelly voice. "I was sent here to inform you the first shipment has arrived. The Dark Master also wishes for Lucinda to be ready, for he plans to soon."

Malvo patted the creature on the head as if it were a dog. "This, my friend, is a Drargomus," he told Vexacion. "It can change its appearance to anything it wishes, living or dead. If it chooses, it can become anything from a treasure chest to a burning torch. The Drargomus are not dangerous, albeit, this one has taken on the appearance of something much sinister. They are the eyes and ears for my father on the Mortal Realm."

Vexacion eyed the ugly thing, then turned to Malvo. "If I'm to be correct, Lady Alenia and Elwrick can both detect the presence of a demon upon its arrival to our world. You're jeopardizing the Brotherhood's safety by allowing this thing to come here."

Malvo sneered at Vexacion's sudden ignorance. "The Drargomus are not demons; I know this much. Where they originate from is a mystery to all except my father."

"Beyond the disguise, how does it look?" Vexacion asked Malvo.

Malvo shrugged his shoulders. "Don't know. The Drargomus will never reveal its identity. It's this secrecy which has kept their race alive for, well, who knows how long, probably before the creation of man."

"Do you wish to return a message?" the Drargomus asked.

"Yes, tell my father I have received the shipment and will begin the process immediately. Also, inform him Lucinda is ready for his arrival. That will be all."

Vexacion watched the Drargomus dissolve back through the cracks from which it came. "That is one disgusting beast."

Malvo pulled his cowl up concealing most of his face. "Vexacion, assemble every assassin in the Great Hall tonight when the moon reaches the apex in the sky. Until then, I must take my leave and inspect that which has been delivered."

Vexacion ordered two assassins to stand guard inside the room and two more outside. "Watch her closely," he whispered to them. "We cannot allow a mishap."

Moments after the door closed, a swarm of flies flew up out of the churning pit of filth and attacked Lilith biting her relentlessly.

Nearing insanity, she fought with the chains tearing large gashes in her wrists and ankles. She didn't care if a hand was destroyed in the process; she needed to free a limb to swat away the swarm. The rattle of the chains forced the swarm away, but they quickly returned to continue with the biting. "Mother, help me," she cried out again

Malvo entered his bedchamber and found a box created from entwined bone waiting for him. Waving his hand across the iron latch it clicked open allowing him unfettered access. Opening the lid, the box hissed as the candlelight assaulted the darkness. Neatly stacked and folded inside were many robes.

Grabbing one, he held it up and it shimmered out of existence. Through the threads he could feel the dark magic pulsating, waiting to be unleashed upon its bearer. Folding it neatly back up he placed it back in the box then released a wicked laugh and cursed at the Creator. In his great wisdom, he had discovered a way to bring demons here undetected.

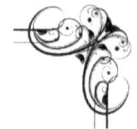

Chapter 54

ilith looked up at the scorched sky with her partially opened eye the very moment a blood-red lightning bolt branched out. The thunder rolled causing nauseating waves of pain to travel up her elongated spine. Her nude body appeared purple from the severe beatings she had endured since her capture and was now filthy with tiny red pinpricks that held an itch she couldn't scratch. "Mama," she whispered.

"Silence," one of the assassins screamed, then raised his hand to slap her, but thought better of it.

Lilith looked at him. For some unknown reason, he appeared unaffected by her horrendous conditions.

Near the door, a translucent woman appeared. She was beautiful but held a raw, animal quality. Behind the tangled mess of auburn-colored hair, two silver pools peered out digesting the situation.

"Mother," Lilith screamed.

"I said shut up," the assassin snarled. This time he made good with his threat of slapping her.

The lady walked through the assassin as if he were a mirage and stood before her daughter. "*What have you become?*" she asked. "*How can you allow them to do this to you? To humiliate you in such a perverse way?*"

"How can I stop them?" Lilith pleaded to the image.

The woman suddenly looked confused. "*You're the most powerful creature ever to walk this planet—*"

"The Lich Lord, he took—"

The woman slapped Lilith. "*Do you honestly believe that lich has power over you? Coursing through your body is all my magic, all your father's magic, and all your brother's magic. There is only one man stronger than you.*"

"Malvo," Lilith whispered.

The woman shook her head. "*No.*"

"This is a trick," Lilith screamed. *Malvo is playing tricks with my mind*, she thought. "You're DEAD," she screamed at the translucent woman. *He can't break me physically, so he decided to destroy my mind*, her mind continued to race. "Leave me you heathen and be gone from my mind."

The woman remained where she stood. "No, I am not dead. Not yet, anyway. As long as you live, I live inside you as does your father and your brother. We sacrificed ourselves so you could live because we know what the future holds. It was written in the prophecies."

Lilith thought back to when she was a child and a vision materialized. They lived peacefully in a small cave at the base of the shadowed mountains. It was here she learned her true identity. Someday she would become a powerful Witch. The people of Icearaus somehow discovered the family's heritage and surrounded the cave. Witches and Warlocks were demons from the underworld and had no place in the Mortal Realm. Hellbent on their destruction, people crashed down upon the cave with every weapon imaginable. The family fought hard but were eventually destroyed. Before that, Lilith was ordered to flee into the wilds and not return until she believed the time was right. "I saw you die. I saw your body stripped naked and hung from a tree. Beside you on that limb, my father hung as did my brother."

"What you saw was the destruction of our physical forms, not our souls. We could have destroyed all those who attacked us, but we knew what the future held, knew what had to be done. Through you though we live and always will. You never learned because you were too young to understand. Witches and Warlocks can leave their physical bodies and enter another Witch or Warlock and become a fold. Therefore, I live and will remain alive as long as you live."

"Father?" Lilith pleaded.

"I said silence," the assassin screamed.

"I *am* here as well," a deep voice said.

"Why have I never felt your presence?" Lilith asked, still not believing what she was being told.

"Because you're not a Witch, yet, you're a Witchling," the woman answered Lilith.

"A Witchling?"

"A young Witch who lacks the innate magical abilities gifted to you by the Creator. You must learn to unleash that power. It is then you will be able to call forth the powers of the souls who dwell within you."

"How?" Lilith asked. "How can I hear and see you now?"

"What you see is only in your mind. You can hear us because you have found the will and desire to call us forth. Otherwise, we would forever remain dormant."

"How can I call you when I can't free myself?"

The assassin slapped her again. "Another comment like that and I will slit your throat."

"In you resides a great power. You must find it and free yourself from these bindings. Once you're free, seek out the only man who can help you."

"Help me," she whispered.

"Seek out Elwrick, Spiritual Guide, Order of the First Flame. He will know what to do."

"That man is a heathen and responsible for our failed world," Lilith mumbled. "Help me, Mama, help me," she cried out once more.

"I cannot; you must find in you the power which has been obscured from your mind."

"Stolen," Lilith said.

"No," the woman screamed at her. *"A Witch's power can never be stolen. It is you. It is your life. Seek out Elwrick he is both wise and knowledgeable on the ways of the Witch, for we were once great friends."*

The image of the woman began to fade, and suddenly Lilith felt alone again. The voices in her mind were gone. Replaced by the buzzing of the flies and the scrape of the assassin's shoes as he paced, deciding what to do with the babbling prisoner.

Lilith forced her eyes shut and drifted back to when she was a child standing before an enormous boulder. The stone was vast and was sunk deep in the ground.

Move that stone; Lilith could hear her mother say.

Lilith pushed with all her might, but it never budged. Exhausted, she fell to her shaking knees.

Not with your hands, that is physically impossible. Use your mind, will that stone to lift in the air. Lilith could hear her mother's words. Focusing all her energy on the rock, it began to shake then slowly lifted, then crashed back down.

You're not trying, her mother scolded her. *Don't concentrate on the size; only the will to move it.*

Lilith closed her eyes and a mental image of the boulder flooded her mind. No longer did she feel its weight or mass as it silently rose light as a feather. Moving her hands in a swirling motion, she guided the stone to a new location then let it drop. Its sheer weight forced it to sink in the ground.

Lilith cheered, "Mother, I did it."

"Time to die," the assassin hissed as he showed her the jagged blade.

The scream Lilith released was that of a child experiencing sheer terror who needed the comfort of her mother's bosom. "MAMA!"

"Go ahead, kill her," the other assassin said. "And Malvo is going to do things to you far worse than what she's experiencing now."

The assassin slid his blade back in the sheath. He was right, the prisoner needed to remain alive. "Silence," he cursed at her.

"The magic is in you, find it and release yourself," the words of her mother came stronger than before.

Lilith focused every ounce of energy not into a scream, but a search of her soul. In it, she found a tiny spark hidden by a parasitic spell. Focusing on nothing but that spell, the spell the Lich Lord placed on her shattered and left her body in a dragon's roar. She could feel her magic once again flowing freely through her body. Touching every cell and fiber; she suddenly felt whole. Reunited with a soul she once believed stolen.

Lilith looked at the pestering flies and one by one they burst into flames and fell to ash.

"What are you doing?" The assassin screamed as he jerked his blade free.

The room suddenly became crystal clear. The magical mirage created by Malvo faded back to its original cold gray stone walls. Near her stood an assassin ready to strike with his blade. "No," Lilith hissed, and with a thought, the man exploded outward with such force, not one bone remained touching.

Screaming in horror, the other assassin slipped in his companion's blood as he bolted for the door.

Lilith lifted him from the floor with her mind and thrust him upward at a blistering pace. Upon impact the room violently shook, the sound of bones shattering filled the air, dust fell like snow, and rocks rained down marring the ground.

"What in the hell," an assassin outside the door said as he eased it open to peer inside. One assassin was etched to the ceiling, pale white and leaking fluids.

The other was gone.

Lilith looked at him and offered an evil grin.

He tried to slam the door, but an invisible force jerked him inside nearly snapping his neck. Behind him, the door slammed shut and the large wooden beam slid across preventing all others from entering.

The last assassin bolted away to inform Malvo something went drastically wrong inside the feeding chamber.

Winking her one good eye, all four shackles unlatched and she gently floated to the ground. Both legs trembled as they supported her weight.

Scampering to his feet, the assassin bolted for the door only to have his feet jerked out from beneath him moments before reaching it.

Lilith focused solely on the assassin and continued to weave her hands in a mesmerizing pattern.

"No, no, no, please no," the assassin begged Lilith.

Lilith motioned her hands towards the rack.

"PLEASE NO," the assassin screamed as he began to move. Clawing at the ground his fingernails were ripped free as he neared the rack. "PLEASE NO, I BEG YOU," he screamed again. Once there he was lifted by magical hands and placed inside the circular frame. Around each ankle and wrist, the shackles bit down into flesh and bone.

Lilith glanced at the steel wheel on the wall and it began to crank at a snail's pace until each joint dislocated, leaving him screaming in severe pain and vomiting uncontrollably.

Exhausted to the point of confusion, Lilith collapsed to her knees, her vision faded. Taking in a deep, ragged breath she screamed something in an archaic language then faded from existence. She was heading to the one place she might find salvation, and the one man who could fulfill her destiny, Rhunsiire.

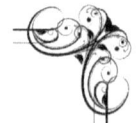

Chapter 55

t was two-thirty in the morning, and not one light was visible from Frankfort when Sheba pulled the car over. In the back, Tiny kept a tight grip on the homeless man's collar.

"Over there behind that clump of trees," Tiny told Sheba as he pointed with his other hand.

"You speak as if you've been here before."

Tiny answered with a smile.

When the car came to a stop for the second time, Tiny dragged the helpless, homeless man from the backseat and kicked him to the ground.

On his knees, the tattered man begged for his life.

"What the hell did you tell the police?" Tiny hissed.

"Not, noth, nothing, I swear—".

"Then why in the hell is my informant at the station telling me otherwise?" Tiny slapped him a good one.

"All I said—"

Tiny kicked him in the ribs forcing the rat to double over. "Damn you," Tiny snarled, then slugged him in the back of the head. The brass knuckles he wore tore open the scalp.

Covering his head to protect himself, the homeless man released a horrid scream.

Tiny was consumed by anger as he pulled a switch-blade knife out from his pocket.

Sheba's eyes widened. "Jesus, don't kill him."

"Punk needs to be taught a lesson about what happens to snitches." Tiny jerked the ear away from the man's head and in one swift motion sliced it off.

The man gripped the side of his head as he squirmed trying to escape.

Observing the man trying to flee, Tiny erupted with rage kicking him repeatedly. "Why in the hell would you tell the police about writing down the license plate and VIN of the people we stole the coins from?"

The bloodied man gasped for air as he tried to answer.

Tiny kicked him in the face rending him nearly unconscious. "Don't you know snitches get stitches?"

The man lay on his back, gurgling a raspy sound.

Sheba figured the lesson was over and they would soon be leaving back to Frankfort. "What do we do now?" Sheba asked. "The coin collector is on vacation to the Bahamas and won't be back for another ten days. I would assume by now we are the number one suspects in the murder."

Tiny retrieved a chain saw from the trunk of the car. "First thing I'm going to do is cut this sumbitch up into fifty pieces and drop the parts off at the dumpster behind Ricco's Butcher Shop. Let him get ground up with all the other cow parts and become fertilizer. Without him as a witness, they can't prove a damn thing."

"You can't be serious?"

Tiny looked at her, then ripped the cord firing up the machine.

"My God he's still alive," Sheba gasped in horror.

The new chain cut through flesh and bone like a hot knife through warm butter.

Sheba backed away, then backed farther away. Eventually, she had no choice but to turn around or barf. Blood sprayed out from underneath painting Tiny's legs bright red while the rattle of bone-chunks inside the chainsaw sounded like gravel trapped inside the hubcap of a moving vehicle.

Tiny kicked over the corpse then continued to carve until the body looked like a jigsaw puzzle dropped from the roof of a house.

Sheba could tell without having to ask this was not the first time Tiny used this device to rid the world of someone who had crossed him in the past.

Tiny tossed the saw aside and quickly located a box of kitchen-sized garbage bags. "Help me pick up the pieces."

Sheba froze, not sure exactly what to do. Chunks riddled the blood-soaked ground.

"Damn it, help me," Tiny snapped. "You know you're an accomplice to the murder even though you didn't pull the trigger, right. You think they're only going to prosecute me?"

Sheba held her breath as she picked up a hand and placed it in the bag and tied it off. "This is disgusting."

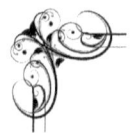
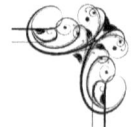

oth eyes bulged from their sockets, and his tongue turned sickly blue as the hand tightened around his neck. "How could you allow this to happen?" Malvo hissed.

"My Lord," he gasped as he clawed at an arm gifted with an unnatural strength. "I was outside the door—"

The assassin appeared more like a rag doll than a man when Malvo began thrashing him. Both leather boots flew in different directions, and long strands of drool hung from his chin.

"I don't want excuses, I want answers," Malvo snarled at the quivering mass of skin and bones.

"Lilith, she had a sudden, unexplainable power," the assassin explained from his knees as he massaged his throat. "Marcus was drug inside then the door slammed shut. As I fled I could hear Marcus screaming and pleading for Lilith to spare him."

"And you abandoned your companion?" Malvo hissed in an angry tone.

"You didn't see her; you would have fled too."

Malvo's hand shot straight out and his splayed fingers bore into each eye piercing the brain.

The body convulsed, then went limp.

Malvo lifted the assassin by the eye sockets and carried the corpse out to the main hallway for all to see. "Let him be an example to never call me a coward."

None spoke as the corpse slid free landing at Malvo's feet.

Malvo quickly departed the area and cautiously made his way towards the feeding chamber observing every shadowed crevice. If what the assassin said were true, Lilith must have discovered a way to break the Lich's spell and escaped. If she had, revenge would be first and foremost on her mind, and she was more than capable of destroying the entire Sanctuary. Witchlings were more dangerous than Witches as they lacked the necessary judgment to control the magic coursing through their veins—a skill only obtainable through centuries of training, training she never received.

The barred door was a mere inconvenience for Malvo as he waved his hand. On the other side, the wooden beam slid free then fell to the floor where it made an enormous crash.

Drawing a deep breath, Malvo started to enter and then abruptly stopped. Even though his magic was unworldly powerful, he was still half-mortal and would require protection against possible attacks if she was still in the room. Waving his hands in a swirling motion, his body slowly glowed with a bright orange hue.

Pulling his cowl down low over his eyes, he entered fully expecting an attack. Lilith very well could rise out of the churning pit or detach from a wall. Regardless of her approach, he would be ready.

Marcus was nearing unconsciousness when Malvo entered. "Help Me.".

Malvo looked to the ceiling, then to the puddle of blood. The destruction was fueled by pure rage.

"Get me down," Marcus begged, his breathing becoming haggard as his dislocated limbs struggled to keep his lungs from collapsing.

Malvo looked to the trapped man, then turned and walked out.

"You can't leave me like this," Marcus cursed at Malvo.

The thump of the door closing sounded like the dropping of a coffin's lid, and the assassin knew where his future lay.

Hours before the ceremony was to begin, Malvo walked behind the two men who carried the large box down the winding, dusty stairs which had not been used in centuries. "Careful," he hissed as the box bumped into a stone pillar.

Winding deeper underground until they were in complete darkness, black candles mounted on demon-shaped skulls embedded in the walls magically lit producing a red flame which guided their path. From the stone ceiling water dripped, and the smell of stagnation filled the hot musty air.

"How much further?" an assassin asked as he adjusted his slipping grip on the bone handle.

The stairs leveled off to a long wide hallway and at the far end were two enormous double doors. Engraved on the doors was a large pentagram outlined in rune words and centered inside was the face of a goat with large horns, massive fangs, and two glowing red eyes.

A shiver traveled up the assassin's spine, and his heart skipped a beat while the other stood locked in horror.

Malvo sidestepped the convoy and moved passed. Upon his arrival at the door, he placed his palm against the goat's forehead and spoke in an eerily demonic voice. Within minutes, the runes began to brighten one letter at a time. When all the words were glowing, the doors released a spine-tingling creak as they swung inward.

Beyond the door, the room was unlike anything any of them dreamed possible. A translucent red fog drifted through the walls and offered a faint glimpse of the blackened stone floor while the intense scent of sulfur mixed with burnt hair stung their nostrils. Near the ceiling on a ledge of jagged stone, granite gargoyles with outstretched wings and glowing green eyes gazed down upon the many rows of rough wooden benches. Across the room was an octagon-shaped dais constructed from basalt stone and accessed by three black marble steps heavy with red veins. On the dais was a wrought iron pedestal twisted and bent into a torturous position. On that pedestal rested a dense black book with strange red writing that glowed in the dimmed environment. Between the dais and the benches was a pool filled with churning blood accessed by four half-steps.

The main feature of the room though was a pentagram on the far wall highlighted with ashen gray rune words. Inside the pentagram was a large alcove roughly chiseled into the stone. Located inside, a disgusting creature whom naturally induced fear, sat silent. He had the body of a man, a goat's head and hoofed feet. The monstrosity sat with both arms stretched outward, palms turned skyward, and its mesmerizing gaze fell on all who entered.

Malvo directed the two men to place the box at the south end of the pool, then took his place on the dais behind the pedestal. "Leave me to prepare for tonight's ceremony."

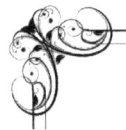
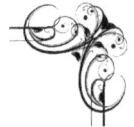

Chapter 57

ady Alenia sank back into the over-stuffed high-backed ornate chair on her newly constructed balcony. From here she could see the lanterns that lined the main road down the center of Rhunsiire come to life emitting a warm glow. She would have rather been with Ryul discussing battle plans and the future of Rhunsiire, but her leg was bothering her more than usual, and she chose to return home to rest. Placing her foot on a stool, she rubbed her knee and wondered what the future held for the elves once she was gone as her daughter revealed little interest in accepting the coveted position.

A smile came to her face as she watched elven families leave their homes and head out for the evening activities. They were living exactly how she intended. Since Elwrick informed Lady Alenia they were destined for war against Karayan, who by the way would stop at nothing to see their destruction to prevent the child from finding refuge, she held numerous meetings with the elven council, which in turn, told the citizens to continue with life as usual. Lady Alenia refused to allow Karayan to force them to live in fear.

Elwrick sensed Lady Alenia on the balcony long before he materialized in her bedchamber. He came here on purpose. Again he wanted to test her senses to judge how quickly her mind was diminishing.

Lady Alenia reached for her cane when Elwrick slid the glass door open.

"Please, don't get up on my account," Elwrick said as he softly closed the door. She should have detected him the moment he arrived yet she did not. Her mind was drifting farther and farther away with each passing day. He would give it not much longer than a few months before she would no longer grace their world. Elwrick moved to stand behind Lady Alenia and began massaging her shoulders.

Lady Alenia allowed her head to slump to the side, then closed her eyes. His hands felt strong enough to twist steel yet soft as silk as they worked each aching muscle. Melting like an ice cube left in the summer sun she became one with the chair. She wanted to remain here forever and have Elwrick caress every inch of her body. Reaching back, she rested her hand on his. "Elwrick, please don't leave me again. When you were gone, I was frightened. I think I'm losing my mind."

Elwrick lifted Lady Alenia from the chair and repositioned her in a different seat made for two on the other side of the balcony. "Are you comfortable?" he asked as he lifted her leg and slid the small stool under her foot.

"I would be comfortable in a dirt-floor shack with you by my side."

Elwrick smiled as two young boys ran past precisely navigating the rope bridge.

"You two be careful," the mother yelled as she led a young girl by the hand. Almost from birth elves were taught to walk amongst the trees. By the age of ten, they could navigate the trees better than the road far below.

It seemed like hours passed while they sat in silence watching the sky grow darker, and the stars flicker to life.

Lady Alenia squeezed his hand and smiled at him as he looked at her. "In your travels, have you learned any more about the riddle?"

"No," Elwrick answered her. "I believe you're correct. It has to do with Averie in her world, and there is nothing we can do to influence the tough decisions she's bound to face. All we can do is pray that she chooses the right ones." Elwrick knew without a doubt, the *Prophecy of Damnation* was occurring as they spoke, but why trouble her with events she couldn't control, so he chose to speak of other things he learned. "When I was out this time I was concentrating on the enemy, attempting to learn Karayan's plans."

"Did you learn anything which can help us in the looming war?" she excitedly asked and she looked into his eyes.

Elwrick sighed, "For the most part, no. What I did learn is Karayan sent men to every settlement notifying the inhabitants that every male over the age of ten must report to Lynn Brook to join his army. Those who don't will be considered deserters, an offense punishable by torture and death."

"Every male," she said. "Do you realize how big his army will be? There is no way we can fight an army of that size."

"Something else is happening as well, and I don't know what. I was in Lynn Brook by the wood mill and Karayan had carpenters there building huge bellows. I waited for a long time hoping they would discuss why but their lips are tight."

"And you couldn't make one of them talk?"

"You know I can't," Elwrick said. "As a Spiritual Guide, I am prohibited in interfering with the dealings of men, even if I know the outcome will be bad."

Lady Alenia sighed, then rested her head on Elwrick's shoulder. "Knowing this, I could send a spy to Lynn Brook and have them discover their purpose."

"I wouldn't risk the life of an elf right now, for I fear we are going to need every elf once Karayan launches his war. Karayan has placed watchers everywhere with only one purpose. The second they see anything resembling an elf to send out an alarm."

Lady Alenia watched an elf walk past. "What are we going to do?"

"As of now I don't think Karayan dares to enter the Whispering Woods, so we have some time. What I think our…" Elwrick allowed his words to trail off as he looked out over the main road at a pin-prick of light forming. "Is the watch still in place?"

Lady Alenia noticed the abnormality as well. "Yes. Since you departed, I doubled the number of soldiers as well."

Without warning, the light expanded outward creating a loud boom that shattered nearby windows and set the ground ablaze.

Children cried, women screamed, and men ran. War had officially come to Rhunsiire.

From every conceivable direction, soldiers appeared with weapons drawn ready to fight whatever emerged from the blinding green smoke.

Lady Alenia rubbed the blindness from her eyes. When she opened them, Elwrick was gone. Scrambling to her feet, she clung to the railing the moment Elwrick landed on the ground then bolted at a pace which made him appear more as a streak than a man. Collecting what energy she had left, she leaped over the railing and began falling at an alarming rate—the feather-light spell she cast fizzled. Her life would be over in seconds as the ground came at a rush.

Elwrick sensed her distressed instantly casted a slow-speed spell.

"I love you," Lady Alenia screamed knowing she was about to die.

Moments before impact she turned upright and landed on her feet soft as summer rain. Still, the jolt sent shockwaves of pain through her leg, but she was alive.

Two elven soldiers saw her struggling and lent aid.

"Stay back!" Elwrick screamed as he neared the smoke and dying flames. "We don't know yet what manner of beast has arrived."

As the smoke dissipated, on the ground was the ugliest creature ever to enter Rhunsiire.

Lady Alenia covered her mouth and looked away. No longer could she stare at the revolting beast.

Gleia appeared shortly after the beast's arrival expecting complete carnage, yet no fight was in progress. Instead, every elf turned away as the smell was horrific, and to look any longer would force them to vomit.

Elwrick knelt beside the beast. "This is no monster, but a woman," he whispered. She had been stripped nude and beaten beyond recognition. Limbs were broken and twisted while one eye remained swollen shut, the socket having been shattered from a devastating blow. The right half of her face was concaved like rotten fruit while every inch of her body was dark blue or purple from the horrendous thrashing she received. Both wrists and ankles were crushed and marred with nasty gashes where a clamping device held her.

Lady Alenia became hysterical swing her arms wide searching for an explanation. "Is this a message Karayan is sending to frighten us?" she screamed at Elwrick.

Gleia could do nothing but stare. She had never seen someone tortured so severe, yet remain alive.

A soldier slid his sword free and approached. "Shall I end her suffering?"

Lady Alenia nodded her approval.

"Stop," Gleia screamed. "What crime has this woman committed which warrants death?"

The soldier raised his sword. "It's not that she has committed a crime; it is the humane thing to do."

"You kill her and I will demand a trial with your head at stake," Gleia snarled.

The soldier lowered the sword, then slide it back in the sheath. Even though he was much older than the healer. She held a prominent position amongst the elves which could influence the council's decision.

Lady Alenia wept. She should have been the one to stop the soldier, but she panicked and her mind raced with fear.

Gleia began barking orders to have the woman carefully lifted and taken to the Medical Ward.

Once there, Gleia faced Lady Alenia. "Nobody is allowed to enter this ward except Ellusia, yourself, or Elwrick. Do I make myself clear?"

Lady Alenia sat on a nearby stool and wept again. Her time of Queen was coming to an end. No longer did she hold a position of authority where people respected her.

Gleia sensed Lady Alenia was troubled and knelt at her feet. "I know your mind is clouded and your time with us is coming to an end. Don't for one second be ashamed of your inability to make immediate decisions that affects life and limb. Any elves who question you, question me, and I am not one to be crossed. You're still my Queen until the moment you take your last breath, and I would follow you to Hades if you asked."

Lady Alenia smiled hearing the words Gleia spoke. There we're still a few who cared for her beyond Elwrick.

"What you need to do is spend time with the man you love. Not worry about this woman we're not sure yet deserves to live."

Elwrick took Lady Alenia by the hand and lifted her to her feet. "Shall we go for a long night stroll down by the river? We'll come back tomorrow and see how our latest arrival is doing."

Lady Alenia nodded.

After they departed, Gleia watched the lovers wind their way down the stairs and fade into the darkness before turning to the new guest.

"Do you think you can heal her?" Ellusia asked.

"There is something odd with this woman. She should not be alive, yet here she lays breathing."

"We're here to help you," Ellusia told the woman who appeared to be watching them with her open eye.

Gleia rubbed her chin deep in thought. "I must take my leave. Do everything possible to keep her alive."

"You can't leave me with her," Ellusia pleaded.

"You're the best healer to grace Rhunsiire since me. I believe you underestimate your skills."

Ellusia frowned, then rubbed the sweat away which suddenly percolated on her forehead.

With Gleia gone Ellusia remembered she still had the powder Elwrick gave her which saved Pegan. Quickly finding her medical bag she dumped out the contents and found the vile. Pouring the exact amount—which is precisely how much remained—into a tin cup she added water then stirred the contents until the powder dissolved. Carefully sitting the woman up, she held the container to the woman's purple lips. "Drink this if you can, it will make you feel better."

Lilith coughed between each swallow and as the last bit went down. Almost instantly, she suddenly became tired and closed her one eye. All she wanted to do was sleep as the pain that wreaked havoc upon her body slowly faded and she entered a dream-like state.

Ellusia retrieved a pale of warm water and began washing the patient when Gleia returned holding a thick black book.

"I'm not sure if I did the right thing or not," Ellusia confessed.

Gleia cocked her head sideways confused by Ellusia's sudden words.

Ellusia told Gleia about the powder and how she used it to save Pegan's life on the boat. "Now seemed like the right time to use what remained."

"You did great," Gleia congratulated her. "I think this woman is more important than any of us realize."

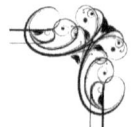

Chapter 58

he full moon crawled through a sky as dark as India Ink while an ill wind blew down from the Silver Mountains. Three O'clock in the morning had arrived gloriously. Malvo stood dressed in a blood-red robe with onyx black trim. The cowl was pulled low concealing his features except for his pale chin which supported a crooked smile.

Outside the door, assassins gathered waiting for the door to open. To be late for such an important meeting would prove costly to your health.

When the time was right, Malvo waved his hands and the doors emitted a spine-tingling squeal as they creaked open. "Enter, my brothers," Malvo ecstatically cheered.

Standing at the door, an exotic-looking woman waited. She wore a smooth basalt black dress with a sharp V-line exposing an unusual amount of cleavage. Around her waist was a gold-colored belt and from it dangled an exposed dagger with a serrated blade.

One by one, the assassins shuffled in and were greeted by the woman who informed them to sit anywhere of their choosing, as no seat was better than another. Vexacion entered last and decided to remain standing at the back of the room leaning against the stone wall.

Malvo raised both hands to the ceiling. "My brothers, tonight will be a night that will be remembered forever on the tongues of all who dwell on Icearaus. The birth of a new era is about to take place. The dawning of a new age is upon us."

The crowd's cheer was deafening.

"Tonight, we swear our allegiance to the Dark Master and take our proper place in the Brotherhood of the Dark Prince. Tonight, we take our blood oath in the Pool of Démonická Krv and receive our reward for faithful service—a gift offered by my Father."

"The Dark Master?" Confused whispers echoed in the darkness.

Malvo could see the concern on every eye when they heard the name. He knew the Dark Master was associated with hate and discontent. He would have no choice but to convince them and raised his hand drawing their attention. This moment was critical in his success. Each assassin had to willingly recite the pledge, voluntarily enter the pool of demon blood, then allow his blood to flow into the *Book of Eternity* without coercion or the robe's magic would fizzle. "Yes, my Father is the Dark Master, but I am no different than you. If you cut me, do I not bleed? If you strangle me, do I not choke? Simply because who my Father is the fact does not change, I remain devoted to the cause of watching the

Brotherhood of the Dark Prince rise to the glory it was meant to be."

A few assassins cheered.

Malvo remained expressionless as he looked out over the crowd. He would only need to convince Vexacion, and the rest would fall like dominos—which is why the woman was here. Malvo knew exactly the kind of companionship Vexacion loved and would use it to exploit the assassin's weakness. Glancing in her general direction, he nodded, letting her know it was time.

The woman slowly crept sideways until she bumped into Vexacion, then nonchalantly gripped his hand.

With the diminished light, it was only now Vexacion got a good look at her and time momentarily stopped. To say she was beautiful would be an insult worthy of death. This woman was gorgeous beyond comprehension. Everything about her from the way she batted her long black eyelashes to the way her hips swayed with each subtle movement made his heart flutter.

"Before we begin with tonight's ceremony I would like to introduce a special guest," Malvo said as he rested both hands on the pedestal. "She comes from a land far beyond our borders and is very near and dear to my heart. She goes by the name of Pennara and is my sister."

Every assassin looked back at the woman standing beside Vexacion.

The woman blushed bright red and turned away.

"Don't be fooled by her looks," Malvo continued. "Although she appears soft, I would challenge any of you to take her. She is both smart and cunning with a blade which would rival any of you. Besides, it appears she may have already discovered her entertainment for this evening."

"Sister," Skylar whispered to his long-time friend. "Something here is seriously wrong."

Vexacion gripped her hand. "Sister. He never mentioned he had a sister."

"No, we don't speak much of one another, but rest assured. We relish in delight when the other succeeds and grieve when they fail. The thickest chains of hell couldn't have kept me away from watching my brother create the greatest brotherhood in the history of Icearaus."

Vexacion playfully squeezed her hand. "And how long will you be staying?"

She thought for a minute. "I'm not sure. It depends on how I feel in the morning after I wake. If I like what I found, I see no need to rush back to my lonely house. My brother may have to get used to me being around."

Malvo purposely delayed the continuation of the ceremony to allow the Drargomus to work on Vexacion. The assassins would follow him to their graves if he asked.

"This is an exciting time we live in," Pennara whispered to Vexacion. "Think what it will mean to be a member of the brotherhood which is going to reshape Icearaus."

Vexacion's thinking was well beyond the ceremony. His thoughts were only on her and what it would mean for his future if he could convince her to take his name. For one, it would solidify his position of authority in the brotherhood. Two, she came from a distant land, perhaps he could travel there and create a brotherhood of his own and become Lord Vexacion.

Malvo could see from the expression on Vexacion's face the time was right to continue. "For the inauguration to be official, a witness must be present when you recite the pledge," Malvo informed them. "It cannot be any witness, but one sent directly from my Father to oversee the inauguration. Let it be known far and wide, my Father must wish us great success as he sent the Great Brorthrithus, a man of high position in his council. Brorthrithus, will you please come forward and introduce yourself."

The beast unfolded and climbed down from the alcove to stand beside Malvo. As he turned his head to gaze upon the crowd, his long gangly goatee swung from side to side. "Welcome one and all," he said in a deep, raspy voice while he spread his arms wide revealing long black fingernails. "Don't allow yourself to be fooled by Malvo; my role is a bit more complicated than he makes it appear. I have the responsibility to record every one of your names into the *Book of Eternity*, thus solidifying your station in the greatest brotherhood to ever walk Icearaus. After you're bathed in the Pool of Démonická Krv, Malvo will escort you to the Altar of Darkness. Upon your arrival, I will pierce your flesh then press your palm against the page allowing the *Book of Eternity* to rejoice in your pain. Only then do I have authorization from the Dark Master to offer you a remarkable gift the likes of which you never imagined possible. With this gift, you will defy sight becoming translucent at will and never feel the effects of exhaustion."

Malvo thanked Brorthrithus for being there, then dismissed him back to his position.

Vexacion began clapping. With the abilities afforded to him by this gift and his current skills, he would be unstoppable. When he finished clapping, he jogged down the center aisle to stand beside Malvo. "It is through you we will make the brotherhood untouchable," he cheered raising his fist in the air.

Malvo clapped Vexacion on the back. "You have no idea how true your words are."

Vexacion quickly departed back to stand beside Pennara.

It took a few moments for Malvo to silence the crowd. "As you're all aware by now, an incident occurred earlier which forced me to expedite this ceremony. Lilith has escaped from the feeding chamber, and her current whereabouts are unknown. She is a potent woman and could cause a substantial amount of damage to the brotherhood. I highly recommend you accept this gift from the Dark Master as Lilith will not be selective in who she destroys. It is through this gift you will find protection."

Skylar cocked his head sideways, then turned to his most trusted ally. "This meeting has not been expedited. It is occurring exactly when Malvo wished it to and has nothing to do with Lilith. Something here isn't right, and I don't know what."

"I feel the same," his friend whispered back. "I have been thinking it for a while there is more to this man than what we believe."

Malvo pulled back his cowl, his face partially hidden in the shadows. "At this time, I am going to ask each one of you to kneel and bow your heads and recite after me."

"Regardless, at this time we have no other course of action but to follow along," Skylar whispered again to his friend.

Every assassin did as Malvo asked.

Malvo opened the book on the pedestal then began to read out loud the pledge. "The Dark Master, Ruler of Icearaus, King of Darkness, and Creator of the World. I come before you on bended knee with my head bowed."

The assassins repeated everything.

Malvo waited until the chanting ended before continuing. "The Dark Master, I am nothing without you, but with you, I am everything."

The assassins repeated without question.

Malvo slowly turned the page then continued reading. "In starvation or celebration, in death or prosperity, loyalty with reward, dishonor with death."

Each assassin complied with the words.

"With this Oath completed, I willingly submit to the pool of Démonická Krv without the threat of harm or coercion."

Malvo turned the page as the assassins finished chanting the words. The last part was the most crucial for his success. They must willingly offer their blood to the *Book of Eternity.* "With my blood, I swear my allegiance to the Brotherhood of the Dark Prince, your Son." Malvo smiled as the word Dark Prince rolled off his tongue.

As the chant ended, Malvo removed a single black candle from its holder and held it straight out before him like a guiding beacon. His movements were sluggish as he cautiously took each step then entered the pool waiting on the first step. "Come, join me, my brother," Malvo said to Vexacion. "If you're to be my second, you must commit first as an example to all others the worthiness of our cause."

Pennara followed Vexacion holding tight to his hand. Upon his arrival, she stopped him. "You must be nude when you enter. There can be nothing between your flesh and the living blood."

Vexacion peered down at his weapons. They were what made him, him. Without them, he felt weak, vulnerable.

"It is the only way," she told him. "Don't worry; I will be right here waiting." Drawing a deep breath, he released the clasp and handed her his weapons belt. Afterward, he stripped.

Malvo took Vexacion by the hand and guided him into the waist-deep pool.

Vexacion's winced expecting the blood to be searing hot, but it was mildly warm and had a thick, velvety softness.

Malvo placed the candle in a holder which mimicked the head of a gargoyle on a black twisted iron stand. Instantly, two flaming eyes formed in the stone eye sockets and faint wisps of Sulphur smelling smoke puffed from the nostrils.

"The Dark Master has accepted your words. We can now prepare your body to receive the offering." Plugging his nose with two fingers, Malvo placed his palm against Vexacion's forehead and slowly lowered the body until it vanished below the foul fluid. When Malvo lifted Vexacion, the assassin's skin remained bright red even as the liquid drained away.

Vexacion gasped and spit out a mouthful. "I can't see, I can't see," he screamed as he reached out with both hands.

"Your vision will return shortly and much better than you ever dreamed possible," Malvo reassured him. "It is one of the effects of the pool."

Vexacion shivered as a sudden pain jolted his spine, and he found himself barely able to stand.

Malvo guided Vexacion from the pool to an alter which materialized right before their eyes. It was made of black stone and covered in blood-red rune writing. In each corner was a hole where a long pole jutted upward. On top of each pole were four different skulls with flaming eyes. Directly in the center on a stone platter carved to create a clawed hand was a large black book. On the opposite side of the altar, Brorthrithus waited.

"Hold out your hand," Brorthrithus instructed Vexacion.

Vexacion trembled, each muscle felt as if it had been ripped free of the bones and left to dangle. "Help me," he whispered. "I can't lift my arms."

"You must do this alone, you must discover the strength inside you," Brorthrithus ordered Vexacion.

Focusing on nothing but his arm, Vexacion managed to raise his arm waist-high.

Brorthrithus snatched Vexacion's hand as it neared and slashed his fingernail against the palm.

Vexacion screamed as the nail severed the flesh clear to the bone.

Brorthrithus cared little for Vexacion's discomfort as he twisted the arm forcing the palm against the open page.

Vexacion cried out as he fell to his knees pressing his forehead against the alter searching for relief.

The book drank up the blood and took the pain from him.

Vexacion scrambled to his shaking legs. His vision remained blurred and exhaustion filled his chest making it hard to breathe.

Pennara waited beside the altar near the bone chest. Upon Brorthrithus's approval, she carefully removed a neatly folded Demon-Hyde Robe and draped it over Vexacion.

Vexacion felt instantly warm, and his vision was restored immediately and quite astounding. He saw a kaleidoscope of colors and into spectrums the mortal eye could not. No longer would the darkness hinder him as the room appeared as bright as a sunny courtyard, and the tiredness which once filled his bones was now an endless supply of energy. Vexacion faced those who waited and clenched his fist in enthusiasm. "Next," he cheered.

PART II

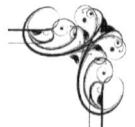

Chapter 59

he hour was early when Tatum Spire kissed her mother goodbye. Making her way from their humble, one-bedroom house built into the side of a large cavern, she skipped along a narrow path which wound its way around great pillars which supported the distant ceiling. Along the way, Tatum passed similar houses whose windows remained dark except for a few which held a faint glow shielded by heavy curtains. Humming a tune, she picked up the pace to a jog. In the distance, the glow from two enormous lanterns anchored to the granite wall caught her attention. Between the lamps was a thick, reinforced iron door. Near the door at a small building, she greeted the two guards with a wave.

"Leaving a bit early?" the guard asked.

Tatum smiled at the guard. "Jasmine's been out there all night. I wanted to give her the opportunity to visit her husband before he leaves for work."

The guard nodded his approval, then logged her name in the book. Everyone coming or going was documented; it had been this way since their arrival so long ago. On the wall was a giant steel wheel. As the dwarf cranked it, the door eased open.

Thanking the guard, Tatum squeezed out as she was not as petite as some would like to believe and took a deep breath of fresh air. The night sky still glistened with stars, and the horizon glowed with a silver streak—it would be another hour until the sun graced the world.

Using the moonlight to guide her passage, she navigated the narrow trail as it traced the edge of a jagged cliff. Eventually, the path turned east but continued to climb at an alarming rate before leveling off on a stone riddled plateau.

"You're early," Jasmine said without looking at Tatum.

"I know, I couldn't sleep," Tatum said, then placed her pack on the narrow bench hidden behind a house-sized boulder. "Figured if I arrived early enough you could spend some time with your husband."

"For as young as you are, you're amazing," Jasmine said, then handed Tatum the optical device.

Tatum took the instrument and placed it in her waist pouch while Jasmine dart off into the darkness. Alone and with nothing but the faint breeze and twinkling stars to keep her company, she searched through her pack and located a small bag of nuts and berries. Arriving this early, she would be hungry long before breakfast arrived.

When the first rays of sun painted the land with streaks of orange and cinnamon, it was time for Tatum to begin her job as city watch-woman.

Carefully removing the optical device, she held it up in the air and adjusted a few knobs to calibrate the instrument. Afterward, she checked it over for damage. It was a conical-shaped copper tube with large curved glass discs on either end. Below the main tube was a much smaller second tube affixed to the main tube with a semi-circular plate with numbers etched into the metal. A steel rod came from the large tube and passed through the secondary tube and was fixed to an arched cutout in the numbered plate which allowed the rod to slide back and forth to increase magnification.

Tatum was not positive how it functioned. All she knew was when she held it to her eye and slid the rod, not even a mouse on the valley floor could pass undetected.

Starting from the north, she slowly worked her way south adjusting the rod as she went looking over each area between the mountain and the bridge. She would repeat this same process every half hour for the duration of her shift.

"Beautiful morning," Tuzebelle said, her warm breath glowing in the early morning light.

"It's beyond beautiful, it's gorgeous.".

Making her way to the bench, Tuzebelle sat. "I hate it when you come up here this early."

"I know mother, but Jasmine never gets to see her husband. It's not fair."

"I know it isn't," Tuzebelle sighed. "With so few of us left. What choice do we have?" From her pack, she removed a plate wrapped tightly in a silver material to keep the food warm and in place. "I brought you breakfast. Thought you might be hungry coming out this early."

Tatum eagerly accepted the plate and peeled back the covering. "Smells delicious," she said as the aroma hit her.

"I made your favorite, scrambled eggs with bacon mixed in."

Tatum leaned back against the stone and placed the plate on her lap. "Mother, I'm not a child anymore. Last week I reached my twenty-fifth birthday. For years I've heard rumors this isn't our home and that we once lived under a great mountain in an enormous city with flowing rivers and a huge ball of light that mimicked the sun."

"I often wondered when your curiosity would get the better of you and ask." Tuzebelle looked off into the distance at a flock of birds.

"Where is our true home? Are we ever going to go home?" Tatum looked into her mother's big black eyes and saw a reflection of herself. The same curly auburn hair, flattened nose and pursed lips.

Tuzebelle closed her eyes in thought. She was only a youngster when the betrayal happened and remembered only faint details. "I don't remember much," she admitted. "I was maybe half your age when the attack occurred."

"Attack?" Tatum asked as her eyes grew wide.

"Let me start at the beginning," Tuzebelle told Tatum. "There was a dwarf, a great dwarf named Nümribelyn who designed Dünbar, a magnificent city under the Silver Mountains. The dwarves prospered there for centuries, but he knew a deep secret which he didn't reveal until the time was right. One night he called the dwarven council to a meeting and told them all to prepare because a strange event was about to occur. He called it the *Prophecy of Damnation* and the dwarves were on the brink of destruction and we needed to flee east."

Tatum never took her eyes off her mother.

"He told us to flee past the Shadowed Mountains, through the quagmire, then north to these mountains where we are to remain until his return. The council mocked him calling him an old man well beyond his time and did nothing to prepare."

"Then what happened?" Tatum asked after taking a bite.

"From what I am told life went on for many more years, and the city was growing in popularity. People came from all over Icearaus to gaze at its wonders. Because of this, we were amidst a great celebration with food, wine, and dancing—it was a great time to be a dwarf. And then the ambush happened. There were these creatures, ugly beyond words. They squeezed through the cracks in the walls and floors and came at us with fangs dripping poison and claws that cut clear to the bone."

Tatum stopped chewing to listen.

"We fought hard but eventually our numbers waned and then the dwarves from Nendorühl appeared. We thought help had arrived, but we were wrong. They joined the hideous beasts and killed many dwarves. Nümribelyn came, but there was nothing he could do, so he sacrificed himself and drew their attention off us, and then he fled into the darkness below knowing his head was the ultimate prize."

"Did he survive?" Tatum asked.

Tuzebelle ignored the question lost in hysteria. "Don't you understand? The council could have saved all of us had they only listened—"

"Mother, mother," Tatum interrupted. "Did he survive?"

"I don't know. Seeing our chance to escape, we fled with nothing but the clothes on our backs. The trip was long and tedious, and many dwarves died, but we endured."

Tatum hugged her mother. "Is that where my father died as well?"

Tuzebelle never told her how her father died thinking she was too young. "No, your father survived there only to die here. He went with a hunting party and never returned. They encountered the beast which has no name, and he sacrificed himself to save the others. Since that day, no dwarves are allowed across the bridge as the monster seems unable to cross it."

Tatum heard stories about the monster and how no physical weapons could harm it as it was an ethereal beast. "My father fought it?"

"Your father was a brave man and I could see him doing exactly what the others said upon their return. He told them to flee while he lowered his axe and charged directly at the beast."

Tatum had no desire to finish eating and wrapped the plate back up with the metal wrapper. "I'm so sorry," she whispered, then hugged her mother.

"It's not your fault," she whispered while wiping away her tears. "But you do need to get back to your job, and I need to go to mine."

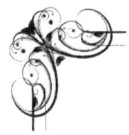
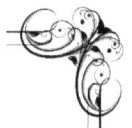

Chapter 60

arah woke to the strangest sensation. **The entire house** seemed to be vibrating as if experiencing a minor, never-ending earthquake that originated right outside their front door. "Six-thirty," she grumbled looking at the clock on the dresser. "Honey, there's a strange noise outside," she whispered to Tom and nudged his shoulder.

Tom groggily rolled over smacking his gums. "It's only the cows, go back to bed."

"Really, cows," she said. "It's coming from the living room?" She nudged him again.

"Maybe they're cold and wanted to come inside," he grumbled, rolling away from her.

"Great," she groaned, "There's the man of the house for you." *Guess I'll have to deal with whatever is going on*, she thought.

She was not the only one who noticed the unusual occurrence as Billy cracked open her bedroom door. "Mom, I think the mothership is landing to get Averie."

"Don't be silly," Sarah whispered to Billy. "She didn't come here in a ship, so why would they send one to pick her up?"

Climbing into sweats and a T-shirt, she grabbed the Louisville Slugger by the door then tip-toed down the dimly lit hall not wanting to wake the others. Nearing the living room, it suddenly grew bright as day. From outside, lights penetrated the glass, and the rumbling grew louder.

Sarah peered out the peep-hole to discover the largest dump truck ever to grace the planet sitting there idling. Climbing down from the cab, a man wearing a Chicago Cubs baseball cap backwards, grimy coveralls, and puffing on a cigarette turned her direction and was coming rather quickly.

Sarah opened the door and was slapped in the face by a bitter-cold gust of wind. "Can I help you?" she hollered out, her blue fingers gripping the bat.

The man first looked at the bat, then the woman. From his shirt pocket he removed a crumpled yellow sheet of paper. "I have an order for Tom Fischer. He purchased ten cords of wood, cut and split with delivery included. I need a signature and then show me where you want it."

Sarah looked at him like he had two heads. "I know it's cold, but do you mind waiting outside one minute while I wake my husband. I'm not sure what's going on."

"I understand ma'am," he nodded. "I'll be in my truck but remember; time is money."

Sarah returned to the bedroom where the shove she gave Tom nearly launched him to the floor.

"What, what's going on?" he squealed as he bolted upright.

"There's a dump truck in our front yard full of wood. Do you know anything about it?"

Tom rubbed the sleep from his eyes. "Already?".

"What do you mean, already?" Sarah snarled.

Tom quickly dressed. He knew if the truck was here for more than fifteen minutes, there was an additional charge. "I ordered ten cords of wood for the winter, but I didn't expect it to arrive so soon."

Averie poked her head into the bedroom. "There is a monster outside," she whispered.

"It's not a monster, it's a dump truck," Sarah told Averie, then turned back to Tom who was now searching through the closet for a thicker coat. "Why would you order wood? We spent a bundle putting in a new furnace because you were tired of wood and the mess it made."

"I decided to get the wood because I felt Averie would feel more at home with a fire. I doubt they have furnaces where she's from."

"Ooohhh, a fire," Averie said. "I can make a grand fire. Thathra taught me how."

"I'm going to go show him where to dump it before we get charged for an additional wait time. You mind starting some coffee?" Tom asked Sarah as he made for the hallway.

Sarah watched Tom walk out then turned to Averie. "Well, I guess you have a job to do. You'll be responsible for the first fire of the year."

Sarah was shocked to discover how hard a worker Averie was. Throwing on the leather gloves, she moved every bit as much as Tom and Mike when they stacked it in the back of the barn. Never once did she complain whine, moan, snivel, or cry. Tom told her she didn't need to help, but Averie wanted too and would not take no for an answer. Billy, on the other hand, tried every imaginable excuse possible even stating he needed to go feed Robyn to try and get out of helping. Tom was hearing none of it and threatened to tan Billy's hide on more than one occasion to get him moving again.

Once the wood was stacked, Averie went to shower while Tom discussed Billy's punishment with Sarah for his lack of participation.

"Why are we even discussing this," Sarah said as she looked at Billy. "Two weeks no video games and I'm going to add a few more chores to your already growing list."

"Mom, that's not fair—"

"You want to try for three? How about a month?" Sarah hissed.

Tom remained out of the line of fire. When it came to family matters, Sarah was always the judge, jury, and executioner.

Jennifer entered the kitchen with a concerned look on her face.

"Is everything okay?" Sarah asked.

Billy was relieved the heat was now off him, at least for the time being.

"I don't know," Jennifer finally said. "That was Robert on the phone, his wife Debra has fallen deathly ill."

"That was your head nurse at the clinic, right?" Sarah asked.

Jennifer nodded, yes. "Robert said he took her to the hospital and they found nothing wrong, so they sent her home. He wanted to know if I wouldn't mind coming over to look at her. Last time I saw her, she was fit as a fiddle. Don't understand her sudden change in health."

"If she's deathly ill, why would they send her home?" Sarah confusingly asked.

"That's another question which needs answering," Jennifer said. "Regardless, did you and Averie wish to accompany me?"

"While you're out, can you pick up lunch from the burger joint," Tom asked Sarah. "Mike, Billy, and I have work that needs to get done on the back forty before the cattle arrives."

"Don't forget we need an area for the dozen sheep we have coming," Sarah reminded Tom.

"I already have a plot picked out for them," Tom advised her.

"Sheep? What are you going to do with sheep?" Mike asked.

"Averie wants them for the wool, swears she's going to make clothes. Who am I to stop her."

"Well this outa be interesting," Mike said with a laugh. "Think I'll still buy mine from the store."

"TIMBER," Tom yelled as the forty-foot tree came crashing down.

"You know if we cut this up, next year we won't have to buy firewood," Mike said.

Tom shook his head no. "This baby is rotten clear to the core, probably wouldn't burn if you soaked it in gasoline and we'd have to clean the chimney daily from all the soot it would make. The only reason I brought it down is cows like to rub up against stuff if they have an itch. There's a chance it could fall killing a few."

"Ah, gotcha," Mike said. "What do we do with it now?"

Tom looked at his watch. "The girls should be back soon. Let's go back and clean up and get ready for lunch. We'll come back later with the tractor and drag it out to the edge of the property and let it finish rotting into the ground. Not good for anything else."

"Can I drive?" Billy asked.

"Sure," Tom answered. "You've worked your butt off since the chewing."

"Slow down," Tom told Billy. Near the house was a white Chevy Impala.
"Mike, do you know anyone who owns a white Impala?"

Mike looked at the car. "That's the same vehicle that was parked by that abandoned gas station a few days ago. I told you we would see them again."

Tom called Sarah on the phone. "Are you close to home?"

"No. Jennifer is still examining Debra. Why, are you hungry?"

"Look, you need to stay away until I call you. Mike was right. Those people from the theatre are now at our house, and we don't know why. I don't want

Averie around here."

"I'm getting Jennifer—"

"NO!" Tom said. "Stay away until we know what's going on."

Billy brought the Gator to a halt allowing Tom to take the wheel.

"Mike, do you have your pistol?" Tom asked before driving away.

"Is that even a question."

Tom rolled the Gator to a stop at the front porch stairs. "Can I help you?" he asked the man and woman standing by the door.

Mike was not so polite as he scrambled from the Gator. "More importantly, why in the hell are you following us?" Mike added to Tom's question.

Dave opened his mouth to speak, but Sandy interrupted him. "Now you wait just a damn minute young man. We didn't fly half-way across this country to be treated like we're some common criminals."

Tom looked at Mike for guidance. He always seemed to know what to do in these odd situations, but even he looked confused by this woman's sudden assertiveness.

"I'm sorry," Mike said. "We've all been on edge lately."

"And I know why," Dave said. "If you give me an hour of your time you'll understand."

"Can we talk inside? It's freezing out here," Sandy recommended.

"I don't even know who you are, why would I allow you inside my house?" Tom asked.

"Fair enough," the man said. "I'm Dave Nelson, and this is my close associate Sandy Long. Were from the Center for the Investigation and Research for Extraterrestrial Intelligence—"

"The agency that offers an enormous reward for anyone providing proof alien life exists," Mike interrupted.

Tom instantly flew off the handle. "Sorry, but we're not interested in what you have to say. You found your way in; you can find your way out." Tom pointed down the gravel driveway.

"I know how it sounds," Dave explained. "But you're basing your opinion off those stupid television commercials which is an agency not affiliated with us. They only say they are to sound more reputable. We've filed suit against them many times to get their ads changed, yet somehow they keep circumventing the system. What we do is try and disprove claims of alien life to keep the public from entering a state of chaos."

"And what happens if you discover an alien exist? They suddenly disappear, taken by men in long white coats?" Tom hissed.

"Calm down," Dave said. "Nobody is going to disappear. In fact, that's why we're here. If the woman living with you is an alien, we want to make sure she remains a secret."

"What do you mean remains a secret?" Mike asked.

"What woman?" Tom asked.

Sandy moved behind Dave seeking shelter from the stiff breeze. "Listen. I'm freezing. Will you please hear what we have to say. Afterward you can make a sound decision on what you want to do. If you don't want us around, fine. But I think you'll discover we're going to become pretty good friends."

"Listen," Dave calmly said. "We know about the woman and child. All I ask is that you hear us out."

"Sure," Tom said. "I'll hear you out since you went through all the trouble and expense to find me. I can tell you this much right now in case you have any funny idea's floating around inside your mind. You're not going to meet her until I am positive this is all on the up and up. She already had one bad experience with a man named Frank."

"Now there's a character," Dave said.

Mike became suddenly suspicious. "How do you know of Frank?"

"Again, it's a long story. We'll explain once we're inside," Sandy told them.

Sitting at the kitchen table Sandy spoke first. "I think it would be best if we start at the beginning."

"That's usually the best place," Mike said.

Dave took it from there and told them about the anomaly which occurred on the computer system then the strange phone call from Frank where they learned about the coins.

"That's how you know about Frank?" Tom asked Dave.

"Yes, but the rabbit hole goes much deeper than it first appears."

"How much deeper?" Mike asked.

"How about this," Sandy said as she produced the large yellow envelope from her handbag. "I can tell you're both tense and untrusting right now. I understand, believe me, I do. Perhaps it would be easier if I gave you this and you could read it for yourself at your own pace." She slid the yellow envelope across the table to Mike. "What I will tell you is you're not the first ones to have an alien living with you."

Mike opened the envelope and slid the file out. "Karayan," he whispered the name.

"You know the name?" Dave asked.

"Averie's mentioned him. He is the King of Icearaus and a very evil man."

Tom took a deep breath. "It was Karayan who tried to kill her before she fled."

Mike slid the envelope back to Sandy having never opened the file. "I don't think I should be reading this."

Sandy slid it back. "I think you should. The information is about her world, and when you finish, you'll understand more why we're here to protect you, as much as her."

Tom's face drained away every ounce of color. "What do you mean protect us?"

"All I can do is ask you to read it," Sandy said. "Everything you need to know is contained within that file. Especially if the saying is true that history always repeats itself."

Mike took the envelope. "How does this sound. Give us a few days to read and digest the information. Afterward, we'll talk with Averie. If she wants to meet you, then we'll arrange for it to happen. Otherwise, I would ask you to respect our privacy, please."

"Deal," Dave said. "If she doesn't want to meet us, that's all I need to hear. I have no desire to die like the others."

"Die like the others?" Tom slowly asked.

"It's all in the file," Sandy said. "All I ask is that you read it in its entirety."

Later that evening after Averie turned in for the night, Tom produced the large envelope and handed it to Jennifer. "You're the smart one here. Will you read this?"

Jennifer accepted the envelope with a confused look.

"Where did you get that?" Sarah asked.

Tom confessed the truth about the meeting.

"I knew you were lying. Those people weren't lost again," Sarah complained about his dishonesty.

"I didn't want to upset Averie if there was something inside there she doesn't need to know."

"I think Tom made a wise decision on his part," Jennifer agreed.

Opening the envelope was like exploring a time capsule. Jennifer didn't know what was going to come out. Looking at the picture she waited for a long time before speaking. "The woman is pretty. Has many of the same characteristics as Averie."

"Sandy said something about we're not the first ones to have an alien living with us. I need to know if it talks about the possibility of a community of aliens where she may fit it. Not that I want to see her go, but if she was among others like her she would probably be happier."

"Maybe the Amish people are aliens, and that's why they choose to live the way they do?" Mike suggested his opinion.

"We'll soon find out," Jennifer said as she opened the cover and began to read.

The sky revealed the first rays of the sun when Jennifer closed the file.

Sarah felt sick to her stomach. "There is no goddamn way in hell I'm allowing her to meet those people. Did you hear what they did to Avicia."

"More importantly, Averie is right when she keeps claiming that everything going wrong is her fault. If that file is true, everybody, and I mean everybody who crosses her is going to have a bad experience... oh my God," Jennifer suddenly changed her train of thought.

"What is it?" Mike asked.

"Debra, she was healthy as a horse. There's no reason she should be as sick as she is. Fever and chills, extreme weakness, abdominal pain, diarrhea, vomiting, and the blood vessels in her legs are rupturing. If I had to guess I would say it's a rare case of Bubonic Plague. I told Robert to take her back and have the hospital test for it. It is so rare now they probably never even considered it."

"What does that have to do with us?" Sarah asked. "She's never even met Averie."

"Because when we were in Frankfort she coincided with the people who shut down the clinic accusing me of doing illegal abortions, and now she is deathly ill."

Mike heard of the disease and knew how deadly it was. Getting up from the couch, he walked across the room placing as much distance between him and Jennifer. "Is it contagious?"

"You scum," Jennifer grumbled at Mike for leaving her like she was a walking petri dish. "That's what makes it even more coincidental. If it is the Bubonic Plague, it is almost impossible to spread from human to human. It transferred by fleas which feed off the infected blood of rats."

"So she would be the only one to get it, and no one else around her would get harmed." Sarah figured it out.

"Precisely," Jennifer concluded.

"It still don't add up," Mike said. "She never crossed Averie. This is all coincidental, that's all."

"Sure it does," Tom said. "She may not have crossed Averie. But the one section explained that all those who tried to harm or hold ill will against those who helped Avicia died of strange, UNNATURAL causes. Jennifer is aiding Averie, Debra crossed Jennifer, now Debra has the Bubonic Plague which in my mind is unnatural anymore considering todays vaccinations."

"What do we do now," Sarah said as she looked at the closed folder.

Jennifer slid the folder back into the envelope. "I think we keep living life as if we never read this file. Whatever is going to come to pass, is going to pass. There is nothing we can do to stop it."

Tom removed a business card from his wallet. "Dave gave me his card. Tomorrow, well, now it's today, I am going to call Dave and tell him to take this file back to wherever he got it. I don't want it in this house. If Averie was to find it and read it… I don't even want to think about what it would do to her."

"I agree," Sarah said. "For all I care, we should burn the damn thing."

"No, I would not do that," Mike said. "We'll give it back to the scientists. I don't think any of us should play a part in its destruction. It survived this long for a reason. Possibly to warn us."

"Are you talking about a higher being has planned all this out?" Sarah asked Mike.

"I don't know what I am saying anymore."

The squeak of a bed down the hall got their attention. "Averie is waking, hide that damn folder in our room," Tom told Sarah.

Sarah snatched the folder from Jennifer and tore off down the hall.

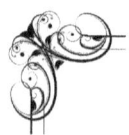
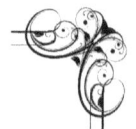

Chapter 61

ou could see the sigh of relief on each of their faces when Pegan led them out of the Shadowed Mountains. No longer did they have to be concerned about bottomless ravines which threatened to devour them, the tall twisted spires which hindered their direction, or deadly boulders which broke loose from somewhere above and crashed down nearby.

Before them, the new obstacle seemed a lot less deadly.

Pegan followed the edge of the quagmire for some distance before arriving at what appeared to be a living door constructed of dangling dense moss and thick, spiky vines.

Raestmond swished aside the vines to get a better look at what lay beyond. An obscuring mist drifted off the still waters while the musty, stagnant smell assaulted his senses. "I'm not going in there," Raestmond said as he backed away allowing the vines to swing closed.

"I have to agree with Raestmond on this one," Filaurel said. "We need to skirt the outside of this forsaken place."

"It's nothing but a swamp," Dinko said.

"We're here to find the dwarves, dwarves live underground, not in the swamp," Filaurel said. "To enter, we are inviting trouble we don't need."

Pegan appeared devilish with glowing silver eyes in the gloomy environment when he looked their direction. "The party can go whichever direction it chooses, my destiny lies this way."

Saress sighed. She knew he could no longer deny the voice which called him.

"Wait," Filaurel said, but it was too late. Pegan slipped through the folds and vanished.

"Our path has been chosen," Dinko said as he pulled his grossly enlarged two-handed sword free and followed Pegan's footprints.

Travel beyond the edge was tedious as they trudged through the soggy terrain which threatened to swallow them with each step. Within seconds of their passing, the saturated ground removed all traces of their existence.

The narrow path led them deeper into the gloom before coming to a raised central area of dry dirt. From this mound no less than ten different trails spread out. Saress looked back the way they had come but was instantly confused by the gaggle of passages and knew she was hopelessly lost.

Pegan placed his hand to the ground and closed his eyes. He was feeling for something. After a few minutes, he chose a path narrower than the one they previously traversed. Following it for some distance, they came to a fork, and he guided them down the left one without hesitation. He seemed to be leading them with an uncanny sense of direction, and they crossed a series of shallow pools, fallen logs, then under a gangly tree with exposed roots that clung to the soggy ground like massive fingers.

Without the stars or sun, time meant nothing and none knew how long they had been inside the belly of the swamp when Pegan arrived at what appeared to be a dead end. Beyond where he stood, the water was impassible.

"Great," Filaurel complained, noting what lie ahead. "We're going to die here."

Pegan closed his eyes and spoke with a Witch's tongue. When he finished, he stepped out onto the water.

Saress gasped as the soles of Pegan's boots never touched the water.

In less than a minute Pegan reached the other side.

"Now what do we do?" Glorandial asked. "The water here is too deep for us to cross."

Pegan looked back at them from the other side, his silver eyes sparkling in the gloom.

Saress sighed. "Were not meant to follow him."

Pegan moved animal-like as he blended in with the gangly terrain and was gone.

"Fantastic, he abandoned us here to die," Filaurel complained.

"We'll get across," Ameria told them. "Reptiles are excellent swimmers. We'll carry everything across then aid you humans."

It took hours, and they were each exhausted by the time they stood on the other side. It was much further than it first appeared, and an undercurrent continually threatened to suck them down.

Following what they believed was Pegan's purposely left trail of broken branches and twisted twigs, they found Pegan. He stood on the crest of a sizable soggy knoll amidst what appeared to be a toppled watchtower. Both his arms were spread wide, his head was tilted back, both eyes focused on the darkened sky, and he was calling out to something.

"What is he doing?" Ameria whispered to Saress.

"I don't know," she quietly answered.

Behind those who watched Pegan, a beast of pure horror rose up out of the muddy, stagnant waters. It wasn't invisible but blended in so well with its environment it may as well have been.

Raestmond plugged his nose as the foul funk of rotten sewage and decaying flesh assaulted his senses.

Saress spun searching for the source of the stench and nearly tripped over Raestmond backing away. A semi-translucent bloated body entangled in a mass of armor-plated tentacles that dripped toxic resin flooded her vision.

Looking down over the knoll, it released a hideous howl which sounded more like a sinister laugh, then focused solely on Pegan. "WWWAAARRR-LLLOOOCCCKKK," it spoke in a deep, lazy voice from an unseen mouth.

Averie walked into the barn and knocked on the open door that was once

her room. Anywhere else she could go, but not here unless accompanied by Tom or Mike and she followed the rule to the letter.

Sitting at the table, Tom was working a strange device while Mike was taking a stinky black powder out of a canister and measuring it. Tom glanced up at her. "If we're here you can come in," he said. "We don't want you in here alone because there are things in here which can seriously hurt you."

Averie cautiously entered. "Hurt me?" she asked.

"This black powder is extremely explosive. One spark and kablooey, kiss the barn goodbye," Mike said.

Tom's face looked like he licked a lemon when he looked at Mike, "Kablooey?"

"I'm simplifying it for her."

"Kablooey?" She cocked her head in confusion. "Anyway, Sarah sent me to get you because there is a man outside to fix the van."

"About time," Tom complained.

The trio met the man by the van who held the shredded wiring harness in his left hand. "Whoever worked on this sure did a number."

"You can fix it though, right?" Tom asked.

"Well, anything can be fixed. It all depends on how much money you want to throw at it. The problem isn't the window. I can fix that in an hour. Whoever did this was pulling on the wires and tore a bunch out of the ECU under the dash. You're going to have to replace the entire wiring harness to make the vehicle reliable. That won't be cheap as the dash has to come out. I bet you're looking at four to five grand and that doesn't include the wiring harness."

"Holy Jesus," Tom said.

"Honestly, if it were mine I would get rid of it for whatever you could and buy something new. The vehicles not worth the cost."

Averie never spoke as she walked away and entered the house then went straight to her room.

Sarah knew something was wrong by Averie's odd behavior and went to investigate. Outside, she joined up with Tom and Mike, who were still discussing options with the mechanic. "What the hell happened?" She interrupted the conversation.

Tom shrugged his shoulders. "What are you talking about?"

"Averie walked in and went straight to her room and closed the door. Something has her upset."

"I'm sorry, but I'm going to have to worry about this later," Tom told the guy. "What do I owe you for coming out?"

"Seventy-five for the service call and drive out."

Tom handed him eighty. "Keep the change for being honest with me."

The hideous beast ignored the mortals for he knew where the threat lie. It would be upon the soggy knoll that these two creations would battle, and only one would be the victor.

Pegan's weapons sprang to life, but then he dropped them.

The beast uprooted trees searching for leverage as it rounded the knoll.

"This is what Pegan has been searching for… this is what has been calling to him," Saress said.

Filaurel raised his bow and fired, but the projectile passed straight through, then vanished in the gloom.

"I don't think we're meant to fight this," Saress said, shaking her head. "I don't think any mortal is." If you listened close, you could hear her voice crack.

"Now we know why Pegan took us the way he did. He didn't want us here; he didn't want us to see this abomination," Ameria said.

Pegan remained expressionless, his eyes trained on his mortal enemy.

They both appeared to be evaluating the other, searching for a weakness, or an advantage.

"HHHEEELLLLLLLSSSHHHAAADDDEEE," Pegan hissed back, exposing his teeth. Both of his silver eyes pulsating with energy. The voice was no longer his, but something far beyond their realm.

Rising and growing in size, its tentacles whipped and thrashed thirsty for action. Deciding now was the time to destroy its natural enemy. The beast became a blur of burnt oranges, yellow pus, and moldy greens as it lunged at Pegan.

Pegan proved the faster and rolled clear of the tangled mass of thrashing tentacles and returned to his feet unscathed.

The Hellshade crashed into the ground launching stones as it rolled partway into the water.

Saress threw herself out of the way narrowly avoiding a wagon-sized chunk of granite as it crashed down behind her creating a splash which sent water into the atmosphere.

Throwing trees like twigs as it righted itself, steam drifted off its pulsating blubbery skin as it concentrated on Pegan.

Pegan darted across the clearing slipping and sliding in the mud drawing the Hellshade away from his companions. He knew it would harm them to get at him.

Climbing the twisted trees, the Hellshade looked more like a spider on its web as it circled the knoll deciding its next move.

Turning as it moved, Pegan never took his eyes off his enemy.

His companions too moved as the Hellshade moved ready to run if needed.

Fading out of existence, they could only detect its location by the bending trees and wake created as it passed. Even its smell dissipated, making it untraceable.

"Where is it," Glorandial screamed, turning in circles as she lost track of the thing.

There was a deathly stillness in the air, and the only sound was the gentle lapping of the waves against the shore.

Sarah knocked on Averie's door, behind her, Tom patiently waited. "Can we come in?"

Averie slowly opened the door. It was she who destroyed the van and was not sure what her punishment would entail.

"Is everything okay?" Sarah asked.

Averie never answered; her vision remained on the floor.

"It's what you heard about the van, isn't it?" Tom asked.

Averie nodded, yes.

"I'm not mad at you, and you're not in trouble," Tom explained. "Your heart was in the right place, and your intentions were good. All you can do is learn from your mistakes and move on."

"What I am upset about is that you didn't say a word. You have to talk to us if something is bothering you," Sarah said. "We're not mind readers."

Pegan continued to turn slowly. His companions might not be able to see it, but to him, it glowed like a torch in utter darkness. He could see its two beady black eyes sunk back in the folds of rotten flesh as they bore down on him.

The Hellshade readied its attack building up a tremendous amount of energy in its tentacles, then sprung at Pegan materializing seconds before impact.

Saress cried out as she lost sight of Pegan.

Pegan exploded in an array of silver and blue sparks, only to reemerge on the other side of the knoll.

The Hellshade hissed and screamed as the sparks seared its unworldly transparent flesh.

Pegan screamed something and his hands instantly glowed green and a blue ball of pure energy formed in the air. Throwing it at the beast, the sphere left behind a trail of golden sparks and swirling smoke. Upon impact, it exploded launching the Hellshade clear of the knoll out into the murky water where it sank.

Ameria cheered, Pegan had killed the beast from hell.

Climbing clear of the water onto the knoll, the creature shook off the moss and water like a dog drying itself.

"How can you kill something like this?" Glorandial mumbled.

"If there's a way, Pegan will find it," Saress said.

The Hellshade came at Pegan again darting side to side like a cobra avoiding a deadly barrage of magical missiles.

Pegan darted at an angle repositioning himself to better his angle when an unseen tentacle caught him across the chest launching him into the bog where he vanished below the surface.

Glorandial covered her mouth. She knew from the horrendous splat, Pegan was destroyed.

Pegan scrambled from the depths looking like a bog monster covered in long stringy moss and leeches. Water poured from his open mouth and his leather armor was torn loose and hung like dying skin. His eyes were still bright silver though and he appeared uninjured from the attack.

Sensing Pegan's return, the Hellshade faced its mortal enemy and parted its tentacles revealing a mouth lined with twisted teeth. "DDDIIIEEE," it snarled in a barely discernible tone.

Cautiously, the two equally opposing foes circled the other. Pegan revealed no trace of injury, yet on the ground he left a trail of glistening bright red blood from an unseen wound.

Again, the Hellshade was the aggressor and viciously attacked. Its speed was blinding and before Pegan could react the beast had him tangled in a gaggle of tentacles.

Pegan mentally fought off a psychic attack designed to turn his brain to mush.

Surging back and forth across the knoll, the pair destroyed everything they crossed in a battle for life and death.

Pegan gained the upper hand and ripped a tentacle free from the Hellshade and threw it across the knoll where it dissolved into the ground.

The Hellshade returned the pleasure and caught Pegan across the jaw with a tentacle that sent him doing cartwheels across the knoll. Instantly, the Hellshade set to chase not wanting to give his foe a chance to recover.

Pegan recovered before the beast could do further harm and he latched onto a tentacle and swung the creature in the air and launched it into a row of trees in the distance. Remaining on his knees, he fired both arms straight out facing both palms at the beast. Screaming words in an ancient language, the Hellshade began withering and screaming in intense pain. For now, Pegan seemed to be winning the struggle.

Tentacles threw acid and hurled stones at Pegan searching for a way to break the Warlocks concentration.

Pegan was relentless with the attack forcing the beast to shriek out in pain.

Saress cheered. For the moment it appeared Pegan was about to send the creature back to hell where it was born.

Hissing and screaming, the Hellshade placed all its energy into its tentacles and thrust itself out of the muck landing on Pegan where the pair squirmed on the ground, before rolling into the water and vanishing.

"No," Dinko screamed as he bolted across the knoll and leaped into the water in an attempt to save Pegan from drowning.

Thrusting from the water, a tentacle caught Dinko across the chest and launched him the length of the knoll. Landing hard, Dinko bounced a few times then rolled partly into the water. Across his chest was a huge gash where the scales were ripped free exposing the pink, unprotected flesh. Around the edge of the wound, steam rose as acid began dissolving everything it touched.

Climbing onto the shore, the Hellshade looked for Dinko and upon spotting him, quickly came.

Pegan rose from the water and sprinted across the murky surface. He could not allow the Hellshade to reach Dinko, for the lizard had no defense against this immortal beast.

"No," Ameria screamed in hysteria and fell to her knees. She knew nothing could prevent Dinko's death.

Pegan was upon the beast in a flash pummeling the beast with closed fist.

On the ground the two rolled until Pegan snatched its bulbous body and threw it out into the water.

Clawing its way out of the muck, the Hellshade was more determined than before to destroy Pegan. Snarling and hissing it spit acid at Pegan as it circled.

Averie volunteered to cook dinner that night, so Tom and Sarah could relax and watch television. Joining them, Jennifer sat beside Sarah, her eyes glistening wet and cheeks puffy red while Mike relaxed in the recliner.

"I'm so sorry," Sarah said. "If I would have known she was going to pass away, I would have went with you. It's not good to be alone at a time like this."

Jennifer shook her head in dismay. "The doctors at the hospital said they never seen the Bubonic Plague manifest so rapidly. When Debra was there earlier, all she had was a slight fever and chills. By the time she returned, she had to be put on a ventilator and died within minutes."

"It's happening to us as well," Sarah said.

"What is?" Jennifer whispered back wiping her eyes.

"Exactly like that folder read. The family who took care of Avicia experienced hardships the entire time she was with them. The guy was out to fix the van today said it can't be fixed. Not without a great deal of money. I fear this is only going to be the first of many encounters."

"Tomorrow were going to go down and buy a new van," Tom said to Sarah's shock, then approval. "Doug at the dealership owes us a favor for the beef we gave him at a huge discount because sales were slow last year. Time for him to repay the favor. I'm getting the full bumper to bumper, every nut, bolt, screw, and Averie proof extended warranty available."

Jennifer cracked a smile. She needed something to raise her spirits, and the Averie proof did the trick.

"Before we do that, perhaps we should go talk with Dave and Sandy in person. They probably know more than what's in that folder. Perhaps they can inform us what to expect," Sarah said.

"That's fine, but were not discussing the experiments or Karayan," Tom explained.

A loud crash in the kitchen forced them all to come running.

Averie lay on the floor twitching, her necklace glowing bright and rapidly pulsating.

Concentrating on the Hellshade that slowly skirted the knoll, Pegan no longer focused on the shard allowing his anger to flood into the stone.

Charging directly at each other, they collided with such force shockwaves flattened all members of the party leaving them stunned.

One minute the creature seemed to have the upper hand having Pegan pinned to the ground and pummeling him with iron-like tentacles. Seconds later, the roles were reversed and Pegan now rode the giant octopus-like beast beating the monster with its own tentacles.

The struggle continued growing more violent when Pegan took a blow to the back of the head which left him dazed. Stumbling backward his legs became weak, and he collapsed face down in the mud.

The Hellshade took to flight circling in the air then crashed down upon Pegan entrapping him in a cage constructed of thorn infested tentacles. The fight appeared to be coming to an end and the Hellshade would be the victor. Releasing a cackling laugh, the beast moved in to devour his prey.

Averie thrashed violently sending Tom sailing into the wall leaving him lying like a rag doll. Mike tried to hold her down but was no match for her sudden and unexplained strength and ended up landing on the kitchen counter destroying the faucet.

Water shot straight up in the air hitting the ceiling.

Sarah moved moments before a fist crossed her path which would have probably killed her had it connected.

"Kill it... kill it now," Averie screamed.

Jennifer was the wise one of the bunch and stepped back knowing it was useless to intervene. All she could do is wait for it to end then provide medical attention if needed.

Averie gripped the kitchen table leg and jerked it free of the table leaving twisted screws poking out like deadly spikes. Slamming it violently against anything nearby, tile shards filled the air as the floor was dismantled. "Kill the damn thing," Averie screamed again.

Mike rolled off the counter holding his back. He could already feel the large bump forming and it hurt to breathe. On his knees he pried open the door and crawled under the cabinet turning off the water.

From the living room, a cry from Robyn filled the air.

Jennifer glanced at Averie and knew there was nothing she could do. Whatever Averie was experiencing was happening on Icearaus, and she alone had to fight this battle. There was no reason for Robyn to suffer, so she ran to comfort the child.

Sarah ran to Tom, who appeared quite dead crumpled in the corner of the kitchen. Against the wall was the impression of a full-sized man in the sheetrock.

Billy stood there with his mouth agape. He had never seen such carnage, not even in the movies.

Tom came to and released a hellish, pain-induced scream. He would have sworn every bone in his body was shattered. With the aid of Sarah, he managed to escape the kitchen into the living room where he collapsed.

Pegan looked at his companions as if to say everything was going to be okay.

"He's going to sacrifice himself to save us," Saress said.

"Let's run while we have the chance," Filaurel screamed. "If he can't kill this thing, then none of us can."

"What about Dinko? I'm not leaving him," Ameria hissed at Filaurel.

"He can be desert," Filaurel screamed, he was already halfway across the knoll and still running at a full sprint.

Saress drew her sword. "I won't leave him, or anyone behind. If Pegan dies, then I die right here beside him." Drawing a deep breath, she raised the weapon, then charged at the beast.

Ameria snapped her staff extending it to full length. Yelling a cheer in reptilian, she passed by Saress on her way to make the beast pay for harming her brother.

Glorandial drew both her swords as well. She would not abandon those who fought beside her. Not even when she knew the only possible outcome was her death.

"Damn, we're all going to die," Filaurel mumbled as he reached the water's edge realizing he was the only one fleeing.

Nearing the beast, they slammed into an invisible barrier placed there either by the Hellshade, to prevent interference, or by Pegan telling them to flee.

To their horror, in the center of the beast between a gaggle of tentacles a large mouth full of crooked teeth opened then it slowly closed around Pegan.

Saress felt like she was dying as Pegan's body faded from view, lost in the fold of an angry mouth. Dropping her sword, she walked away with her head down and tears in her eyes. No longer did she have the desire to fight, live, or exist.

Ameria tried to comfort Saress but the words fell on deaf ears.

Saress was lost in a state of confusion. She and Pegan had been through so much together, and now she would be left alone to face the horrors which were still to come. Eventually, evil would prevail and she, like all those around her, would die.

Ameria faced the elves. "You two continue the search for the dwarves. I'm taking my brother home for a proper burial. I won't allow that beast to feed upon his corpse after it digests Pegan."

The beast began to fade in and out of existence, then solidified.

Saress picked up her sword, not sure if the monster was ready for a nap or another meal.

"Look, something's wrong with it. It seems to be in distress," Raestmond said, pointing his small dagger towards the thing.

Twitching and jerking violently, the creature appeared to be trying to open its maw, yet something was preventing it.

"I hope Pegan gave it heartburn," Glorandial yelled.

What was barely discernible at first grew into an intense light which left the creature glowing like a lamp shade. Through its slimy membrane, they could see Pegan standing with his arms across his chest, head lowered, and he appeared to be speaking.

Two beady little black eyes darted left and right as if pleading for those around it for help.

"Die you heathen," Glorandial screamed and threw a rock at it, but the stone harmlessly bounced off the shield.

"I love you Averie," Pegan screamed, and focusing all his energy outward, then faded into unconsciousness.

In a single flash which lit up the entire quagmire, the creature exploded outward leaving slimy goo, pus, blood, acid, and blubber sliding down the interior wall of the shield. Smoke slowly filled the bubble obscuring the man inside.

"Pegan did this to protect us, he knew what he was doing all along," Saress whispered.

—⁓◦⁓◦⁓ ◆ ⁓◦⁓◦⁓—

Averie woke drenched in water; still clutching the table leg. "He did it," she whispered as the table leg suddenly felt like a tank and fell from her weakening grasp. "He destroyed the indestructible. He killed the Hellshade."

"The what?" Jennifer asked as she knelt beside Averie.

"The Hellshade, a creature from another plane of existence."

Sarah helped Averie sit up. The girl was exhausted, unable to rise. "I think you need to rest. Whatever you experienced has drained you."

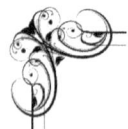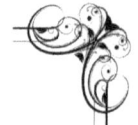

Chapter 62

etective Weaver was so hot you could fry an egg on his forehead. What was supposed to be that afternoon turned into days as Judge Burger had to leave the courthouse immediately before she could begin the process due to a family emergency. It was not until days later when a folder arrived at his desk with an apology did he understand. Judge Burger's daughter was giving birth to her third child, and there was a sudden, unexpected complication. Suddenly, the case didn't seem all that important. Still, she came through and in his hot little hands, he held two arrest warrants. One for Tiny Lunquest and another for Savannah Henderson. What he didn't like though was the note which read to deliver these warrants to Danny Weinstadt, head of the Special Weapons Attack Team to carry out the arrest. Guess she felt the pair were too dangerous for him to take into custody.

The walk to the SWAT office seemed to take forever as he navigated a maze of narrow corridors and dangerously steep stairs. It made no sense why they put the SWAT offices three floors underground. With the lit-up hallways and fresh air, you would have never known you were even underground, except for the lack of windows.

Knocking on the safety glass window inlaid in the wooden door, he caught the attention of Danny sitting behind the polished oak desk.

Danny Weinstadt was a military man who joined the SWAT team after twenty-five years of service. Even though he never spoke of his past career, you could see it in his eyes, and the long scar that stretched from his left temple down to the protruding jawbone he had seen enough combat to author more than one book—had he chosen.

Danny stood as he waved for the guest to enter. "Detective Weaver, what can I do you out of?" he said in a deep, husky tone.

"I have a couple arrest warrants for you to serve. I originally planned to do it, but I think Judge Burger believes these two may be more dangerous than first believed."

"Have a seat and let's see who we need to bring in," Danny said, pointing at an uncomfortable-looking plastic chair.

Detective Weaver laid the papers on the desk. "Think I'll stand."

"Suit yourself," Danny said as he leaned back in his black leather chair and examined the warrants.

"We need to get these two off the streets immediately," Detective Weaver said. "We know without a doubt their responsible for a robbery/home invasion in Willowdale, and possibly involved with the murder that occurred at the DMV."

Danny dropped the papers on the desk and looked at his watch. "Fantastic, I'll assemble my team and see what we can do. I'll call you when we have them in custody."

"Excellent," Detective Weaver said as he walked out. In all actuality, he was relieved the pressure was now off him and placed in a much more experienced man's hands.

Right after lunch, Danny requested a special meeting with his team and told them of the meeting with the detective. After handing out copies of the warrants to each member, he took his place at the head of the table. Behind him was a large drawing board. "We need to get these two off the streets ASAP."

"What do you know about them?" a member asked.

"The female, Savannah Henderson, is clean as a whistle and comes from a well-to-do family. I think she fell in love with the bad boy image and now has no way out. I don't see her being an issue. The male, Timothy Lunquest, on the other hand, is going to be a handful. Extensive criminal record with two ventures in San Quentin. He's been involved with everything from drug smuggling to kidnapping and extortion. They tried to get him on murder with a chainsaw which would have put him away for life, but he weaseled his way out on a technicality. After reading the report on the home invasion, it appears he stole a custom-made high-powered AR-15."

"How did he end up here in Kentucky?" a second member asked. "San Quintin is in California."

"Good Call," Danny said. "I called his last known probation officer, and it appears he was not allowed to leave the state, yet he did anyway. There is an arrest warrant for him in California for failure to comply with his probation obligation, which makes him all the much more dangerous. I don't think this man intends on going back to prison."

"Do we know their current location?"

"Yes," Danny answered. "A confidential informant told me they're at the *Flying High Pawnshop*. Savannah Henderson owns it, but it appears Mr. Lunquest has been doing business out of the back."

"Explains how he's been able to avoid detection for his arrest warrant. All business falls under Savannah's name," a man wearing body armor suggested.

"Precisely," Danny agreed.

"I know that building," a member said. "The entire front is glass. There is no way we can get in unnoticed."

Danny sketched out a map of the area. "What we're going to try will be a first of its kind. Agent Grover has agreed to be the bait. She's going to enter the pawnshop attempting to sell her wedding ring. Inside her purse, we placed a flash-bang grenade fastened to the pin of a green smoke grenade. A few blocks away the Bearcat Armored Vehicle operator will detonate the charge by remote. When the building is clear except for the two suspects, she'll place her purse on the counter then drop her ring by accident. When she ducks to find the ring, that is the signal for the operator to detonate the charge."

"I take it Agent Grover is going to be wearing a camera?" someone asked.

"Yes, multiple," Danny answered, "as well as body armor under her clothing. After the flash-bang detonates, the smoke should saturate the area obscuring their vision. Immediately after the flash-bang, the second team is going to shatter the glass windows with beanbag rounds adding to the shock and awe. A third team will then enter wearing night-vision goggles which will allow them to see through the smoke and immediately take both suspects into custody without incident."

"What about Agent Grover?"

"She is instructed to lie flat on the ground until the all-clear signal is given," Danny explained before continuing. "Across the street on the rooftop of a nearby building, we'll have two snipers ready. Gentlemen. I shouldn't have to tell you this. If anything goes wrong, our number one goal is to get Agent Grover out of there at all costs. We cannot allow this to turn into a hostage situation."

Minutes before closing Agent Grover entered the *Flying High Pawnshop*. At the counter, Savannah was arguing with a customer, so she made her way to the electronics where she examined the televisions and car stereos. From there Grover toured the movies before moving onto the musical instruments then onto the counter to look at the jewelry. To her surprise, the customer and Savannah were still in a heated argument.

"Can I help you?" Tiny asked as he came from the back.

Agent Grover recognized him immediately as Tiny Lunquest. "Um, yes," she said in a confident tone. "I've recently divorced, and I think it's time I sell off my wedding band and ring. Before I do though I have a few questions. I like wearing jewelry, so, would I get more for my ring if I traded it for a few items in your display case, perhaps something for my daughter and me, or sell the ring outright?"

"Before I can make that decision, I have to see the ring you're talking about," Tiny answered her.

Agent Grover held out her hand revealing a ring with a large diamond and a band littered with tiny diamonds.

"From what I can tell, I think we could arrange for a nice pair of rings for you and your daughter in trade."

"Fantastic," Agent Grover said as she set her purse down on the counter. "That man doesn't sound pleased at all," she whispered to Tiny.

"No, he is—"

"*BOOM,*" the explosion was horrendous.

Agent Grover was thrown back against a rack of Cd's spilling the contents then crumbled to the floor unconscious.

Dense green smoke bellowed from the shredded handbag flooding the lobby.

The customer staggered away, bewildered by the sudden concussion of the blast.

Sheba staggered sideways then fell to her knees. Both hands found her ears in an attempt to squelch the ringing as her world came crashing down in mind-numbing blindness.

Tiny stumbled back dazed as glass from the display case tore through his arm.

The sound of glass shattering filled the air as every street-front window exploded at once.

Tiny fumbled in his pockets recovering his pistol and began shooting into the blinding smoke. *Bang, bang, bang, bang, bang,* he repeatedly fired.

Lost in the smoke, the customer somehow got turned around and took a bullet to the chest sending him to the ground screaming.

Bang, bang, bang, bang, bang... Tiny continued to pull the trigger until the slide locked back signifying the magazine was empty.

Ratt, tat, tat... Swat returned fire, but Tiny fled through the opening into the backroom followed by Sheba.

Agent Grover screamed hysterically when she woke. Her head pounded, and she could feel the warm blood running down her face. Patting herself down, she tried to find her pistol, but couldn't. It must have come loose during the explosion and lay somewhere obscured by the smoke.

"AHHH," the man screamed as he rolled around in the broken glass gripping the hole in his chest. Each time he coughed frothy blood spewed from his mouth.

Danny was not supposed to enter the building, yet he didn't care. His close friend was in trouble, so he charged in through the shattered window frame and vanished in the swirling smoke. "Get him out of here," he yelled to the two members who followed.

Bang, bang, bang... Tiny returned fire from the small doorway.

Danny could hear the bullets whizzing past. The high-pitched zing of one deflecting off something steel filled his ears. "Grover," he yelled, fumbling his way through the smoke.

Smoke billowed out of the windows as if the place was engulfed in green flames.

She heard the voice and tried to call out, but in her daze, no words came as she clung to a steel rack and tried to pull herself up. The damaged stand was unable to support her weight, and they both came crashing down.

Ratt, tat, tat... Danny fired into the ceiling hoping it would keep the enemies pinned down as he didn't know their location. In the smoke, he was blind as they were. "Grover," he called out again.

Agent Grover felt intoxicated as she tried to stand and fell back down swimming in a sea of slick CD's. "Help me," she finally managed to scream.

"She's over there," a SWAT member wearing goggles yelled out. To him, the smoke was more of a nuisance than a hindrance. *Boom, boom, boom, boom...* The SWAT member released a barrage of bullets at the door keeping Tiny pinned down in the room.

Danny never heard the SWAT member yell. Instead, he pinpointed Grover's location from her screams. *Ratt, tat, tat...* he fired again, but this time towards the wall knowing she was not in his line of fire. He wanted to make sure the suspects didn't hear her cry and decide to shoot in that general direction.

"Help me," she screamed louder.

Danny was there in seconds grabbing Grover by her shoulders.

"Get her out of here," a SWAT member screamed as he emptied his thirty-round magazine providing cover fire. Slamming in a new magazine, he continued to fire as they vacated the building.

Exiting the doorway, Danny sprinted carrying Agent Grover towards a waiting ambulance. From her ear, he could see a thick trail of blood.

Words could not describe the anger flowing through Danny as he nearly ripped the door off the Bearcat. "You son of a bitch, I oughta shot you in your goddamn face," Danny screamed as he fumbled with his colt 1911.

The Bearcat operator came to his feet in a flash and grabbed Danny by his flak jacket and slammed him against the wall. "I never dumped the charge... damn you... I never triggered it. It went off on its own." There were tears in his eyes as he yelled.

Danny glanced down at the switch and saw it was still charged.

The man's face was beet red and glistening beads of sweat ran down his face. His fingers held an iron grip on Danny's flak jacket. "I loved that woman as much as anyone.".

"I'm sorry, I thought..."

The man released Danny and sat back down. "How is she?"

"I don't know," Danny admitted. "When I carried her to the ambulance, there was a thick trail of blood coming from her ear, and she was mumbling incoherently. At a minimum, I think she has a severe concussion."

The Bearcat operators face turned red. "At least we know the buildings empty, let's get in there and get that son of a bitch."

Tiny slammed a new magazine into the .45. "I'm not going back to prison."

"What are you doing?" Sheba cried out.

The smoke dissipated enough he could see the cop cars lined up and blue and red lights flashing. Stepping into the doorway, Tiny emptied all seventeen rounds into two cop cars shattering windows, blowing out tires, and causing one set of lights to explode.

Cops ran for cover as stray bullets zinged in all directions.

The Bearcat with its enormous diesel engine easily pushed the disabled cars out of the way and offered much better protection with its inch-thick steel sides.

Danny took the mic which was attached to the protected speaker on the Bearcat. "Mr. Lunquest. There have already been two people injured. There is no need for more. We have the building surrounded. Please come out with your hands up. Don't make this difficult."

Tiny emptied the magazine into the side of the Bearcat, but the bullets bounced harmlessly away.

"Well, I guess he answered my next question," Danny said to the operator. "I don't think this is going to end well."

Tiny tossed down the useless pistol and snatched the AR15 off the table. Searching through the magazines he quickly located one he had preloaded with armor-piercing rounds and slammed it in. "This should do the trick. When I go out the front, you sneak out the back and run like hell."

"They're going to kill you if you go out there," Sheba pleaded.

"I'll die before I go back to prison."

"Mr. Lunquest," Danny called out. "There is no need for more bloodshed. Surrender now and let's work something out. It will look better before the judge if you come out peacefully."

Tiny tore open a bag of Cocaine and buried his face in the fluffy white powder. Snorting as much as possible, he wiped away what remained with his hand and licked his fingers. Higher than the Empire State Building he grabbed the rifle and pulled back the charging handle, waited for a second, then released it allowing the bolt to slam forward driving a round into the chamber.

"This is ludicrous," Sheba screamed. "All they have us on is robbery. We'll spend a few years in prison and get out."

"You, maybe. Me, if I go away now, I go away for life. Three strikes and I'm out for good."

"Please don't do this," she cried.

Tiny never said another word; he didn't have to. His stiff jaw, powdered nose, and blood-shot eyes did all the talking.

The movement inside the building forced every cop to jockey for a position behind the Bearcat.

Tiny ducked behind a toppled shelf and slid the needle into his arm. The Liquid Crystal Meth would provide the instant energy required to continue fighting while the Cocaine would dull any pain from being shot. Pushing in the translucent liquid, he tossed the spent needle across the room.

"Come out with your hands up," Danny screamed through the mic.

Tiny howled at the ceiling like a baying wolf when the juice hit him.

"What in the hell was that?" Danny asked the operator.

Tiny charged the front door, then darted to the left. Raising the AR15, he knew this would be his final stand. *CLICK.* The rifle malfunctioned.

Boom, boom, boom, boom...

Ratt, tat, tat.

Pop... pop, pop, pop...

Multiple calibers all fired at once.

Bullets whizzed and zinged in every direction. Televisions exploded from stray bullets, instruments made strange sounds as strings were cut, glass erupted from what few display cases remained, and the clash of a symbol filled the air as a bullet ricochet off the copper top.

Sheba tried to crawl under the floor as bullets tore past inches above her head. On the desk, the coffee pot exploded speckling her with razor-sharp shards, and hot coffee ran down scalding her hand. On the wall, the clock exploded like a time bomb sending springs and gears sailing.

Tiny hit the ground like a safe but bounced right back up to his feet. Blood ran from a dozen or more holes. Releasing a dying howl, he charged directly at the Bearcat.

Every officer fired again.

Sheba climbed to her feet to surrender when a bullet tore through her calf shattering the bone. Clutching the wound, she let out a blood-curdling scream and collapsed.

When the smoke cleared, Tiny lay partly on the curb, partly in the gutter, but still as only a corpse could be.

Danny climbed from the Bearcat and was greeted with an eerie silence and the heavy smell of gunpowder. He didn't want it to go down this way, both sides had taken losses, and he contemplated retirement right there on the spot.

Sheba screamed out as if she was giving birth to twins. She could feel the blood pumping from the wound, and her foot flopped like a boneless chicken wing.

"Clear," a SWAT member yelled as he finished his cursory search of the lobby.

They all knew from the scream coming through the mangled door the back room was still hot.

More concerned with their safety than her care. The men cautiously entered, weapons drawn, ready to fire in a moment's notice.

Danny entered and knelt beside Savannah, who was hysterical. "Easy now, an ambulance is on the way." Even though she was the suspect of a horrendous crime, she was still human and would be afforded the proper medical care.

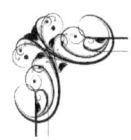

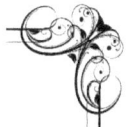

Chapter 63

vening arrived in glorious fashion filling the sky with rays of liquid gold and silver.

Lady Alenia gazed up from her perch in wonder. In all her years of living, she had never seen anything quite like it. "It's beautiful," she whispered.

Elwrick's mouth curled upward at the ends. A significant event had occurred somewhere, and he wondered if it had to do with the Pegan and the others. The heavens were more than just stars and moons, but a way for the Creator to communicate with mortals when he was pleased or angry. Judging from the view He offered, the Creator was highly delighted.

Since the stranger's arrival, Elwrick employed many tactics keeping Lady Alenia's mind preoccupied so she wouldn't think about the woman who lay up in the medical ward. He was curious, too, but Lady Alenia was the most important person in his life, and her mental state was his priority.

The large log extended out over the slow flowing waters of the Tlumn river where Lady Alenia dangled her toes in the cold water. Giggling delightfully, she watched a small fish come to investigate what was intruding upon its watery world. Sitting beside her, Elwrick explained about the Realm of Light and how it was similar to the Mortal Realm. So similar in fact, he was often confused about his location.

A commotion near the tree line caught their attention, and Elwrick stood. They should have been safe here, but Karayan was both cunning and desperate and would stop at nothing to see the elves destruction.

Busting through the trees an elf ran at full sprint.

"Remain here," Elwrick said, then swiftly navigated the thick log to meet the elf on the bank.

The elf hunched at the waist as he handed Elwrick a note folded in half and sealed with a wax stamp symbolizing the Rod of Asclepius. "I was told to deliver this to Lady Alenia or you immediately."

Elwrick looked down at the note before accepting it. He could sense no evil taint on the page. "Thank you."

"Will you read it to me, please?" Lady Alenia asked.

Elwrick knew why she asked. Along with her mind, her vision was fading as well. Reading it out loud, he smiled. "Well, it appears our guest is awake and nearly healed. It seems Ellusia didn't use all the Angel-Wing Powder to save Pegan that day on the boat."

The walk back to Rhunsiire was slow, but not because of the pace. Along the way, elven soldiers emerged from the shadows to pay their respects to the passing Queen. It was in her nature to greet each one with a hug, kiss on the cheek, and many other elven rituals which delayed their arrival substantially. Elwrick was happy though observing the smile it brought to her face. She didn't have much time left, so why rush what time she did have.

Ellusia greeted them at the door and escorted them back.

Beside the woman, Gleia sat on a three-legged stool rubbing yellow cream on the woman's gums. "This will ease the pain as your new teeth punch through the skin," Gleia told her.

"Thank you," the woman whispered.

Lady Alenia sat on the foot of the bed, needing to rest. The walk back and the stairs left her exhausted.

Elwrick was shocked, nearly tripping over his feet. No longer was she a battered mess of bruised skin and broken bones, but a healthy-looking young lady he recognized immediately. "Never dreamed I would see you on this side of the Tlumn River."

"You know her?" Gleia asked Elwrick as she raised one eyebrow.

"We all know her, but it appears I'm the only one who recognizes her. Perhaps because I've had more encounters with her in the past." Elwrick crossed his arms and eyed her suspiciously. "She goes by the name of Lilith."

Lady Alenia leaped to her feet. "Kill her," she screamed. "Kill her now."

Lilith closed her eyes, expecting a sword to pierce her heart at any moment.

A guard rushed in with a glistening scimitar in each hand.

Gleia jolted to her feet and stood between the guard and Lilith. "Since when is a servant responsible for her master's crime? Leave us now," she demanded of the soldier and pointed to the door.

The soldier looked at Lady Alenia, then to Gleia not sure whose orders to follow.

Lady Alenia hesitated to dismiss the guard. After all, the name Lilith was known far and wide as being synonymous with Karayan. If she was around, Karayan was not that far behind. "Wait outside, but remain close," she told the guard.

Elwrick paced the length of the room while tapping his chin with his finger. "Where's Karayan?" he asked, then made his way to the window and suspiciously looked out. Afterward, he closed the shutters obscuring the view of any who may be watching.

Inside, a lantern magically lit which emitted a warm glow that brightened the room.

"I don't know," Lilith whispered. "I've not seen Karayan since the Bearer reached the portal."

"If not Karayan, then who tortured you?" Gleia asked.

"And why did you choose to come here?" Lady Alenia added.

"Who cast the spell which brought you here?" Elwrick threw his question into the mix.

Lilith looked confused by the sudden barrage of repeated questions.

"Quiet," Ellusia yelled. "Can't you see you're confusing her with the onslaught of a thousand questions. Besides, she's told me quite a bit of her ordeal, and it's because she trusts me. If you give her a chance, she's quite the chatterbox."

Elwrick looked at Ellusia and realized he was letting the situation grow out of hand. He wanted answers also, but he may be forcing the situation before the time was right.

Ellusia sat beside Lilith. "One thing I do know, something has this woman frightened to death which she refuses to discuss."

Elwrick sat on the stool Gleia vacated and looked to Ellusia for answers. "And what did Lilith tell you? Perhaps I can make some sense of it."

Ellusia wiped the sweat from her face as the weight from the gaze of all fell on her. "She was captured by Vexacion—"

"Vexacion Le Torneau?" Elwrick Interrupted.

"What does it matter?" Ellusia hissed, obviously upset about being interrupted. "What matters is the fact she was taken against her will from East Haven to the Lost Sanctuary to be sacrificed to the Dark Master. It was there she was placed inside a device she called the feeding rack. Using her description, I sketched the strange device in an attempt to get a visual of what she was experiencing. Perhaps it would help you?"

Elwrick rubbed his chin. "If it's the same man I believe, it does matter. Vexacion Le Torneau is a ruthless maniac who prides himself on tormenting women and those beneath him. He would have never wasted time taking her back to the Lost Sanctuary. He would have indulged in her company immediately, then disposed of her in the most inhumane and humiliating fashion. If what she says is true, Vexacion is following the orders of someone higher in the hierarchy."

Ellusia grabbed the parchment off the nightstand and handed it to Elwrick. "Here is the device she described."

Elwrick looked at the picture, then up at Ellusia. "You're quite an artist," he said, noting the extreme detail while shaking his head in disgust.

"Thank you," Ellusia said as she blushed. She had never received a compliment on her artistic ability.

"I can tell you though this has nothing to do with torture—it's a gateway to the underworld. Vexacion would never employ a device like this; it's impossible. Whoever created this has ties to Hades." Elwrick looked at Lilith. "Who put you in this device?"

Ellusia patted Lilith on her leg. "I know your frightened and scared, but you have to trust him. Had it not been for Elwrick, Gleia, and Lady Alenia who helped me after Arlin Brack tortured me, I would be dead right now."

Lilith looked at Elwrick but remained tight-lipped. She thought back to the lessons Karayan drilled into her mind about the Spiritual Healer, and how he was a demonic beast in disguise.

Elwrick knelt before the woman and appeared to be pleading. "You came here for a reason, and I assume it's because you want help. If you don't tell me, then I can't help you. I need to know who put you in this device?"

"The woman is frightened of something," Gleia said.

Lilith thought for a moment about what her mother said. She would have never lied to her, unlike Karayan, who always spoke with a forked tongue. "Malvo—" she started to whisper.

"Necrosyse," Elwrick finished the sentence.

"You know him?" Lilith quietly asked.

"Not personally, but I've learned much about Malvo over the last few days. It seems the man has his fingers farther in the pie than we first realized."

"What do you mean?" Gleia asked Elwrick.

"From what I believe Malvo may be related to the Dark Master, possibly his offspring or a Dark Disciple."

Gleia gasped and stepped back. The Dark Master was the Creator of evil, the Caretaker of nightmares, and the Father of suffering. There was no greater evil than him, and all corruption flourished in his presence.

Lilith licked her lips. "Malvo is a Dark Prince."

"A Dark Prince is…?" Ellusia asked.

Elwrick's eyes opened wide. "The son of a Dark King. The Dark Master considers himself a King—*albeit* an unappointed one."

"After I was in the device, that was when Malvo told me. He planned to torture me for a lifetime, but the Dark Master demanded I be placed in the feeding rack. He was adamant my soul be taken immediately to hell, where I could be properly controlled as he stated—I am too powerful to remain in the Mortal Realm."

Elwrick cocked his head sideways. "What do you mean… to powerful? You're a mere mortal woman, what does Malvo have to fear? Karayan no longer has the gift of immortality, and it's only a matter of time before he takes his journey to pay for his crimes."

"He said I am more dangerous than a Witch because I am a Witchling—"

Elwrick nearly hit the ceiling, forcing her to stop talking. "A Witchling," he finally said. "I believe Malvo is sorely mistaken. You can't be a Witchling."

"My mother said I was also," Lilith explained.

"Your mother?" Elwrick stuttered and stepped back.

"Yes, my mother." Lilith closed her eyes deep in thought, then relayed the entire conversation that night.

"And that's how you escaped?" Ellusia asked.

"Yes," she answered.

Elwrick fumbled his way to the window and flung open the shutters fighting to get fresh air. He had to be lost in a dream because what he was hearing wasn't happening.

"What is a Witchling?" Gleia asked Elwrick.

Elwrick had a baffled look on his face when he turned. "A Witchling is a young Witch or Warlock whose yet to learn their innate magical abilities. They are wild, volatile creatures as they don't understand how to control their abilities."

"Why is that so hard to believe?" Gleia asked. "You have magic; Lady Alenia has magic—"

"Because Witches and Warlocks have been extinct for at least a century," Elwrick whispered.

Gleia looked at Lilith, then to Elwrick. "Are you saying Lilith has imagined all this?"

Elwrick looked out the window expecting an attack. "All I know is she has close ties to Karayan, and Karayan will stop at nothing—"

"I am a Witchling," Lilith screamed. "My mother would never lie to me."

Elwrick tapped his chin deep in thought, *if what she says is correct, there can only be one.*

Lady Alenia eyed Lilith suspiciously still not believing what the woman said. "If what you say is true, then why can neither I nor Elwrick, detect your magic?"

Lilith shrugged her shoulders.

Elwrick paced the room deep in thought, then came to a stop at the foot of the bed and waved his finger at her. "Who was your mother?"

"What does it matter?" Lady Alenia asked.

Elwrick ignored Lady Alenia for the time being. "If you wish for me to believe your story, I must know the name of your mother."

Lilith eyed Elwrick… "My mother's name is Arabella—"

"Then your father is Draigh?"

"Yes," Lilith answered. "How do you know my father?"

"Because I was there the night your family perished. Lilith isn't your real name, is it?"

"No," she whispered.

"And your real name is…?" Elwrick asked her.

Lilith closed her eyes. "Lucinda."

"Lucinda Krauss," Elwrick whispered. "That is a name I have not heard in a very, very, long time. I searched for decades after the mob destroyed your home to find you, but you were gone. In time, I assumed you perished."

"This woman is a Witchling then?" Lady Alenia asked.

"It appears so," Elwrick said.

"Why is her magic undetectable?" Lady Alenia asked again.

"What I am about to tell you, you will think I've lost my mind. A Witch's magic cannot be detected because there is no magic—"

"You said," Lady Alenia interrupted.

Elwrick raised his hand. "Please allow me to finish. They have no magic because they do not use magic as you and I do. They use incantations that derives directly from their soul. From the minute they take their first breath at birth, to their last breath at death, they are equally powerful." Elwrick walked over and gripped Lady Alenia's hand. "Mortals like you, the magic is contained within the mind and must be learned. As the mind falters, so does the magic as you recently learned which almost cost you your life."

Lady Alenia sighed as she remembered falling as the spell fizzled.

"It is the magic in the mind which leaves a trace which we can detect. Their magic is in their soul; they are the magic. Neither can exist without the other. It is a natural defense against the Dark Master which allowed the Witch to survive undetected."

Lady Alenia wiped the sweat from her upper lip. "Okay… okay," she said as she rose and wobbled her way to the window and looked out as the fresh air washed over her. "I believe you, you would never lie to me. What do we do now?"

"I think it's time for Lilith to explain everything which has transpired since she fled the angry mob," Elwrick explained.

Lilith's mind drifted back to a time long ago, and she spoke of living in the cave at the base of the Shadowed Mountains with her parents, and how life was good and she was in the early stages of learning her powers. She spoke of the night the angry mob came and attacked them in their sleep. As tears fell from her eyes she spoke of her mother telling her to flee into the Wilds and how she observed their lifeless bodies hanging from a nearby tree.

Elwrick leaned back in the chair and crossed his arms.

Lilith continued reliving her life for them to see. "In the Wilds, I survived by eating things not fit for human consumption. Eventually, I returned seeking the company of others and went to work at a tavern in East Haven. It was there Malvo snatched me, and I was forced to carry his child. Before the child could be born, I escaped to Minx where I gave birth to a baby boy.

Malvo tracked me down though, and I knew if the child were with me, he would forever be in danger, so I abandoned him on a dark rainy night in an alley to perish. It would be better for him to die like that, than by whatever Malvo had planned. Afterward, I fled to the Majestic Forest. It was there Karayan found me, and I was taken to the palace and forced to be his servant and bed maiden."

Elwrick rubbed his fingers through his straggly beard deep in thought.

Lady Alenia sat up. She, too, had grown more interested in what Lilith was saying.

Lilith continued with her life. "That was when I had a vision. A vision of the world falling into chaos and the only way I could survive was to take the Bearers place and flee Icearaus—"

"You had a vision of the *Prophecy of Damnation*," Elwrick whispered.

"I had to find a way out and believed I discovered it in a book buried in Karayan's library. It spoke of a process where I could switch my yellow blood with the Bearers and enter the portal."

"*The Book of Stolen Souls*," Elwrick whispered again.

"How did you know?" Lilith asked Elwrick.

"Please continue," Elwrick said. "I will explain when you finish."

"It was then I set out on my journey searching for the Bearer," she said as she continued with her history. "It was then I woke an ancient demon to aid Arlin who in turn offered me his blood. I used that blood to make a pact with a Lich Lord to acquire the Bearers yellow blood."

"It was you who summoned the demon in the graveyard?" Lady Alenia asked.

"Yes," Lilith answered.

"And the Lich Lord—"

"Yes... yes, it was all me," she cried out. "I did all this."

Ellusia was furious. "Because of you, I was tortured and humiliated by Arlin Brack. Because of you, my good friend Rufus lost his life... Because of you—"

"Ellusia, calm down," Gleia said. "Has this woman not suffered as well?"

Ellusia stormed from the room, stomping her feet.

Elwrick watched Ellusia go. "I will talk to her later. Until then, are you ready for the good news?"

Lilith nodded, yes.

"Your son lives."

Lilith's eyes lit up.

"Yes, he lives, and I know him quite well, but I didn't know he was a Warlock which now explains much."

"What does?" Lady Alenia asked.

"Why Pegan has these strange magical abilities none of us can explain. Pegan, who went by the name of Demetrius for many years, is your son."

Lilith fainted hearing the words.

Lady Alenia's mouth fell open. She too gasped not sure what to say.

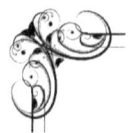
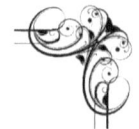

Chapter 64

ony tried to return home on multiple occasions, and each time Donna cursed his name in the nastiest of ways and threw things at him that started with a handle and ended with a sharp-pointed blade. Luckily, her aim was off, or it was highly likely she would be serving twenty-five to life. The last time he tried, he never made it to the door as everything he owned was in the front yard engulfed in flames.

With no were left to go, he turned to the woman he felt started the whole ordeal.

Why did I let sex get the best of me, he thought as he walked down the driveway. Fantastic job, good wife, dignity, pride, respect, reputation, everything right down the toilet, he grumbled. Fumbling through his pocket, he located the pink, heart-shaped key and slid it in the lock. To his surprise, it turned. In less than a week, he had gone from being one of the most respected men in Willowdale, to the most loathed. It was evident by the posters on every corner asking for a recall election.

"Samantha," he whispered as the door opened. "It's me, Tony."

"What the hell are you doing?" Samantha yelled from down the hall. In her hand, she held a shotgun with an illegally short barrel. "Jesus Christ, all I saw was a shadow cross the bedroom window. I thought you were a burglar. You almost got blown away. I told you to always call me first in case I have company or wish to be alone."

"I have nowhere else to go?" Tony explained. "Donna kicked me out and then burned everything I owned."

"What do you mean you have nowhere to go, what the hell are you talking about?"

"Exactly what I just said, I have nowhere to go," Tony explained again, looking at her like she turned stupid.

Samantha placed the shotgun in the corner and flopped down on the pleather couch and looked outside. "What happened?" she asked, then flipped on the lamp flooding the room with a warm glow.

Tony eased back in the worn-out recliner, kicked his feet up, flipped off his shoes, then spilled his guts about the incident at the theatre. "Well, when she got home she found everything."

"Everything?" Samantha surprisingly asked.

"Everything," Tony repeated. "The movies, pictures, toys, even a pair of your underwear I was saving."

"Holy Jesus," she drug it out. "I told you to never keep any evidence where your wife could find it. My God, when are you men going to start listening."

"Probably never," Tony chuckled.

Samantha looked through the contacts on her phone hoping to find someone who might be able to help. "I know, how about your brother?"

"I stayed there a few days until he kicked me out. Well, he had no choice. His wife threatened to leave him if he allowed that no good, two-timing, worthless scumbag to remain living in his house."

"I'm assuming you're the two-timing scumbag?"

"Bingo."

"Well you can't stay here," Samantha said as she looked on the internet for a hotel nearby. "I'm expecting company."

"At this hour?" Tony said as he looked at his watch.

"He works swing shift and won't be off until midnight, then he's coming straight over."

"You're going to have to tell him your busy. Remember, you're partly responsible for this as well."

"Me?" Samantha gasped from the accusation.

"Yes, you. You're the one who wanted Mike fired and the clinic shut down. Had it not been for your little stunt, I would still have my job, and my marriage."

Samantha sighed, she knew Tony was partly right. "Fine. I'll text him and tell him not to stop by. You can stay here for a few days to figure out what you're going to do, but then you have to go."

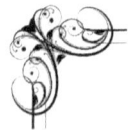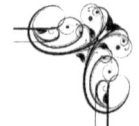

Chapter 65

ot one troll could tell how many days had passed since the Jester incident because they had yet to leave the caves. Underground, there was no changing of the days or the seasons; all there was, was darkness and warm, stagnant air. To the trolls though, the caverns were beautiful from the tall ceilings littered with stalactites, to the deepest regions where an unground river flowed.

Chieftain Ulgra sat on his makeshift throne located in a central meeting chamber and watched each council member arrive. The council was more of a formality as their opinion mattered little to him. As Chieftain and the highest-ranking member of the Clan, he had the final say regardless of the councils ruling.

Chieftain Ulgra walked amongst those who gathered greeting each troll by name and exchanging handshakes. As the last council member entered, he rolled a large round boulder in front of the doorway sealing off the passage. Afterward, he took his position back at his throne. "I've called this meeting with the ruling council to discuss the future of Clan Cave Bane."

Whispers rose among the members—*he didn't call them to discuss plans, he called them to tell them what he had planned.*

Chieftain Ulgra scratched a large ugly hairy wart on his chin as he looked around the cavern. "The decision I am about to make does not come lightly, or without reservation." He sounded more like an educated man rallying the troops instead of an uneducated troll who could not spell his name. "The troll I sent out to investigate the happenings of the world has returned, and it appears we are destined for war. Karayan is gathering an army which appears to be made of every man, woman, and child who walks the surface. I fear we have no other choice but to leave the ravine and seek refuge at the Whispering Woods."

A monster of a troll stood and grunted towards the Chieftain. "Do you know what you're saying?"

"Karayan's wickedness grows out of control," the Chieftain snarled back. "He will come to the ravine and destroy us."

"We can fight Karayan," a different troll grumbled. "I don't think we should abandon our home so easily."

"How?" the Chieftain asked. "All Karayan has to do is wait outside our door. Eventually, we will have to emerge for food or die of starvation. There is more which has not reached your ears. I have heard rumors the Rock Giants have sworn allegiance to Karayan. They outnumber us seven to one and can see equally as well in the dark. If we stay here, this cave will become our tomb."

"You must remember," a female troll said who was rather large around the belly said. "Many of us have babies in our bellies. The walk to the Whispering Woods is far, much farther than I think you realize."

"In the open, we will be exposed. The darkness and the caves have always been our greatest ally." A male troll added to the pregnant troll's comment.

"No," the Chieftain argued. "Our greatest ally has always been the elves. Even now, as we speak, we only survive because of the provisions they provide."

One long sigh could be heard.

Chieftain Ulgra looked over those who gathered. "Do not think for one minute I wish to abandon the ravine. I was born and raised here; this is my home. I must do though what is best for Clan Cave Bane and if that means fleeing to the Whispering Woods, then so be it."

The trolls knew the decision had been made and as Chieftain, his words were final. "When do we leave?" a troll asked in a defeated tone.

"We leave as the sun sets tonight," Chieftain Ulgra informed them. "We will take only what we can carry and nothing more. We must travel light and quick for our passing on the surface will not go unnoticed. We must reach the Whispering Woods before word reaches Karayan of our flight."

The mood was somber as the Chieftain rolled the massive stone out of the way. Outside a line of trolls waited. They all knew a war was brewing.

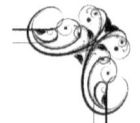

Chapter 66

kylar Nightshade crept through the sewers deep beneath the Lost Sanctuary blending in so well with his environment, a surface dweller would have passed by within feet and not known he was being watched. Waiting briefly to make sure he wasn't followed, he skirted around a puddle then vanished into the gloomy darkness. Behind him, only the drip of water was a witness to his passing.

The narrow corridor traveled straight for some distance then made a quick twist before descending rapidly. Skylar skated down the slippery slope where he arrived at a four-way split and paused. Cautiously stepping over selected stones, he moved to the northern tunnel and hoped over a string no thicker than a hair. Looking back, he waited again before continuing.

The tunnel continued with a faint slope for a good distance then took one last sharp bend where he ran into iron bars embedded deep into the stone walls hindering his progress. Skylar remained silent listening for the subtle sounds of someone approaching. Hearing none, he placed both hands against the wall feeling for vibrations. Time slowed as he waited. Satisfied once more he had not been followed, he climbed the grating and pressed on a flat stone which sunk into the ceiling.

Silently beside the button a door swung down from the ceiling.

Climbing inside, he reached down and grabbed the door by the handle and gently pulled it closed. From below, the door faded into the stone and was gone.

Inside the small room, thirteen men eagerly awaited his arrival.

Skylar struck his flint, igniting the lone candle which released an eerie glow and cast ominous shadows on all their faces. He didn't need the candle as he could see perfectly in the darkness, but it made him feel more human having it there.

"We're all here, what is the sudden urgency for this meeting?" An assassin whispered. Even in this sealed room, voices would carry in the silent, underground world.

"Shhh," Skylar raised his fingers to his lips, then examined each one looking for any signs of deceit or corruption. Finding none, he relaxed and made a quick gesture with his hands informing them to speak only in the assassin's secret hand code. *"Malvo has eyes and ears everywhere. He won't understand the code created long before his arrival,"* he signaled.

They each nodded they understood Skylar's request.

"I'm leaving," Skylar signed. At first, the robes felt silky smooth, but now it's more like a thousand fleas all biting him at once.

Birthright

"How long will you be gone?" Miramar Darkblade, his most trusted and closest ally signaled back as his face held a sour look. The pair had grown up together earning each other's trust, which was uncommon among the brotherhood as each member was always looking for a way to advance.

Skylar scratched his back against a stone corner, then made a subtle, almost nonexistent gesture. *"I don't plan on returning, ever."*

"What?" Darkblade let the words slip out. Recovering a long stick from the wall he began violently scratching his back.

"Shhh," Skylar reminded Darkblade as he scratched his back again against the corner.

Skylar made a quick swishing motion with his finger, a signal for them all to watch his hand movements. *"I never trusted Malvo from the day he arrived. And now, I feel we've been conned into putting these robes on. Something sinister is happening to us. I can feel it in my body. Something is changing."* Clawing at his cheeks, he tore the skin in a futile attempt to alleviate the never-ending itching sensation on his face.

An assassin looked down at his hands before making his gesture to the group. Over the last few hours his fingernails were already turning black. *"I fear too we have been tricked. I tried to remove mine and couldn't. It appears to have grown on us like bark to a tree. As I pulled, it felt as if I were being skinned alive. Only Malvo knows what is to become of us. I fear our future is bleak at best."*

"If we flee, where are we to go?" Darkblade indicated.

"We," Skylar signed back.

"If you go, I'm going with you," Darkblade whispered. "I don't care if Malvo hears me. That scum can kiss a demon for all I care."

Skylar made a laughing motion and gripped his belly.

"I won't stay here without you and will forever remain loyal to you," Darkblade signaled.

"You may wish to reconsider after you hear my plan," Skylar signed, then shrugged his shoulders.

"I don't believe so," Darkblade's signal was mixed as he scratched and signed simultaneously.

An assassin paced the length of the small secret room. *"Are you going to tell us about your plans?"* he motioned.

Skylar scratched his back again on the corner, then weaved his hands in a mesmerizing display of craftsmanship. *"Before I came here I spent hours searching the old tomes in the library but could find nothing about these Robes. Nothing about their creation or where they derived from. Now I fear they're evil by design and come from the bowels of Hell, which means only one man can remove them."*

There was no word in the assassins hand code for Elwrick, so Darkblade mimicked an old man while signing a scraggily gray beard and long flowing white robe with golden rune writing along the edges.

"Which means you plan to go to the Whispering Woods?" An assassin pointed his spread fingers skyward and began a subtle dance.

To someone who may have been watching that didn't know the code, they would have been justified in believing the man lost his mind. But to the assassins, they knew he meant the elves by the dance and his fingers represented the trees.

"You'll be slaughtered long before you see the entrance to Rhunsiire," Darkblade ran a finger across his throat then formed his hands into the shape of a house. Afterward, he scratched his groin. *"By now I'm sure they're aware of the pending war and fortified their borders."* He continued by stacking his fists like bricks.

"I'm counting on it," Skylar gestured. *"That's how I plan to enter. By walking right across the Tlumn River and surrendering."* He placed his hands behind his back and lowered his head in submission.

"And you don't think they will kill you on the spot?" Darkblade quickly swung his hands in all directions.

"They may," Skylar signed, then allowed his shoulders to slump. *"Will that not be better than whatever we are currently becoming? Also. Why would they kill me? If they remove the Robe, am I not an excellent source of information into the inner workings of Malvo?"*

"You're talking about defecting and working with the filthy elves?" an assassin grumbled.

"Shhh." Skylar turned to the assassin who remained quiet in the corner this entire time and placed his finger to his lips.

The assassin covered his mouth.

Skylar continued with his hand motions. *"For the time being, yes. Once the war ends, the brotherhood will be fractured, leaderless. What better way to claim ownership."*

"I think you're optimistic at best," Darkblade signed to Skylar. *"If you do aid the elves. I don't think they're going to allow you to walk away and go back to living the life of an assassin. You'll be forced to live the life of an honored citizen. Is that really what you want? Rules and laws governing the way you live?"* His fingers moved so fast those in the room barely had the opportunity to catch what he was saying.

Skylar thought for a minute. *"It's better than what I am becoming now,"* he quickly answered with a gesture.

"When do we leave?" Darkblade asked by placing his palm skyward and using his two fingers to represent legs walking.

"Now?" Skylar motioned. "Before word spreads of our plight and Malvo can react."

"Which way do you plan to go?" the assassin in the corner asked Skylar.

"I plan," Skylar paused in the middle of his gesture becoming suspicious, then whispered. "If you wish to go, you'll have to follow me. I won't divulge any more."

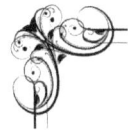

Chapter 67

he crack of thunder woke Tom from his already troubled sleep.

The night sky flashed with lightning, and rain dotted the window.

Beside him, Sarah sat with a book light burning as she read the file on Avicia. There had to be something they missed. Something which explained how Averie had the strength to throw two grown men like they were made from Paper Mache, yet she found nothing. "Jennifer wanted me to give you these when you woke," she whispered. From the nightstand, she collected two large white pills and a glass of water.

"What are they?" Tom whispered, only opening one eye.

"There muscle relaxers," Sarah explained. "Jennifer looked you over and believes nothing is broke but says you're going to be sore for a few days."

Tom groaned as he sat up, his face twisting with pain. "I see you're reading Avicia's file. I thought you wanted it burned?" he whispered.

Outside, the slow rolling thunder sounded like a freight train was about to shred the house.

"It's coming down out there," Tom mumbled as he peered through the slit between the curtains.

"I did," Sarah answered. "But now I'm glad we didn't."

Tom gulped down the pills and closed his eyes. "I hope these kick in quick," he whispered.

Sarah flipped the folder closed then slid it back in the envelope. "This is the most disgusting, foulest, garbage I've ever read. Still, I had to force myself through it in hopes of understanding our situation."

"What situation is that?" Tom slowly asked.

Sarah rested her head against the headboard and waited a few seconds to gather her thoughts. She knew Tom was going to fly off the handle when she told him. "If Averie is to remain living with us. We have to learn how to deal with these sudden outbursts. At first, they were acceptable, but now, she's getting violent. You didn't see it because you were unconscious, but she swung at me with a closed fist. I think if she had landed the punch, it would have killed me."

To her surprise, Tom wasn't angry when he spoke. Perhaps the muscle relaxers had already kick in. "I would be hard-pressed to say it was intentional," Tom explained. "I bet if we ask her in the morning, she'll have no recollection of the incident. Unlike me. I will never forget it, neither will the wall."

"I can't put my finger on it though." Sarah held up the folder. "This Loren man said Avicia was the most docile, non-violent, easy-going woman he ever met, and never once committed a violent act against the staff, even when she was facing experimentation. Why is Averie so different?"

"I don't think she is," Tom said without opening his eyes. "When have you ever seen Averie get violent besides when that necklace is flashing like a disco light? You won't, and you can't," he continued.

"This time it was bad," Sarah admitted. "When she came to, she said something about a Hellshade, a creature from another plane or world. I guess Pegan was fighting it and eventually killed it."

Sarah placed the folder on the nightstand then turned off the light, "Let's get some sleep," she whispered and kissed Tom's cheek.

With the kitchen inoperable, Tom advised they go out for breakfast before going to look at a new vehicle.

Sarah agreed with Tom's idea.

Billy agreed, expressing his desire to eat decent pancakes for a change. The good fluffy kind you can only find at a restaurant made on a skittle, not from home in a frying pan where they were paper thin and tasted like cardboard.

"Keep it up and you'll be eating cold cereal here alone," Sarah grumbled.

Averie neither agreed, nor disagreed as she slowly moved through the kitchen which resembled a battlefield. "What happened?" she surprisingly asked with her eyes wide.

Jennifer helped Mike down the stairs one step at a time. "He's having trouble lifting his right leg. Think I better take him in for X-rays."

Averie looked at Mike, then to the kitchen, and ended at Tom, who didn't look too well himself, and her head lowered. She knew she was involved somehow with this disaster. "What happened?" Averie asked again.

"You're what happened," Mike grumbled as he hobbled past with Jennifer's help. He swore never to get angry with Averie, but the pain racing through his body did the talking.

"I did all this?" Averie whispered.

"Let me fill you in," Sarah said, then relayed the night's events to her.

Averie sat on the couch, but her vision remained on the floor. "What is wrong with me?" she cried out. "I told you my father was right. I'm nothing but a heathen, a burden on society. A disease that needs to be eradicated."

"No, you're not," Sarah assured her. "These events are taking place because of a reason none of us can control, and it has nothing to do with you. I want to show you something," Sarah said, then retrieved the folder. "We got this a few days ago from a scientist from Florida who knows you're living with us."

"Scientist?" Averie asked.

"Please allow me to finish," Sarah begged, then she read the file keeping out the parts with the experiments and Karayan.

"She's beautiful?" Averie said as she looked down at the picture.

"Did you know her?" Sarah asked.

Averie shook her head, no.

"It doesn't matter," Sarah said. "Don't you see it, there's a reason these things are happening, but we don't know why. It has nothing to do with you or anybody else. If it were another woman here, we would be experiencing the same thing," Sarah told her. "But I'm happy it's you."

"Can we go now, I'm starving," Billy groaned.

The look Sarah flashed Billy had him peddling backward.

"I think it has to do with the necklace," Tom suggested.

"Then it needs to be destroyed, it's evil," Averie said as she lifted it from around her head. "Let me find a stone, and I will crush it to powder."

"No, don't," Mike screamed from the front porch, then hobbled back inside and sat down beside Averie. Taking the necklace from her trembling hands, he carefully lowered the golden chain around her head then tucked the faint pulsating diamond under her sweatshirt for protection. "That necklace is your life. It is what makes you, you. It's what makes you the woman we've come to adore. Something tells me you were meant to wear it for a reason. If you destroy it, I fear the consequences are going to be fatal, for all of us."

"But—"

"There's no buts about it. We'll deal with whatever trouble comes our way. Besides, I don't think it has anything to do with the necklace, Tom is wrong. I think it has to do with fate."

"Are you saying this is divine intervention?" Jennifer asked.

"No, well, kind of, I don't know," Mike finally admitted. "Jennifer's read the file, I've read the file, Tom has and now Sarah. Each time I hear it, it gets clearer like a flowing river full of sediment. The first time you look at it, the water is murky. As time passes, the sediment settles, and you begin to see things that were once obscured. Perhaps it has to do with my years of performing investigations; I don't know. What I do know is each time I hear it, I am starting to see a pattern and a gruesome picture is forming." Mike stretched until his back made a loud pop, and he instantly felt better. "There we go, something was out of place, that's all."

"A picture, what picture?" Jennifer asked, ignoring the comment about his back.

Mike spoke as if he were a clergy of a church. "I think we're being tested; there can be no other reasoning for what is occurring."

Jennifer busted out laughing. "You've said in the past, and I quote, '*how can there be a God when atrocities like this are allowed to occur daily*' end quote."

"I was wrong, okay," Mike said as he rose and stretched again. "Actually, I feel pretty dang good right now," he said before continuing. "I'm human, can't I make a mistake?"

"Sure, you can make mistakes," Jennifer said. "But to hear you admit to one, now that's a rarity."

"To help us," Tom said to Averie as he carefully made his way to the recliner and slowly lowered himself down. "Will you please tell us everything you saw, or what occurred inside your mind last night? Perhaps next time we'll be more prepared."

Averie closed her eyes and thought back. "I was inside Pegan," she paused. "It's hard to explain, but it was like we were two beings but with a single soul. I could see what he saw, hear what he heard. The smell, it was like rotting chicken hung out in a bog. Then a strange event occurred. I felt something flow into me, a strange sensation filled every fiber of my being, and I saw things that weren't there; colors that shouldn't exist. There was this beast there as well. A hideous monster which was immune to mortal weapons. I watched as the folds of its mouth surrounded Pegan, surrounded me, and my heart fluttered with fear. Inside the mouth was glistening twisted teeth pointing in all directions. Slowly the mouth closed as if the beast was relishing in the moment of its victory." Tears started streaming down Averie's face. "I was so scared I didn't know what to do. I felt myself dying, I felt Pegan dying," Averie looked around the room. "We were both dying; you have to believe me,"

"I do," Sarah whispered.

"I screamed for Pegan to kill it. We were both going to die. Pegan suddenly relaxed, and he focused every ounce of energy directly at the beast. I focused every ounce of energy, as well. Then he told me he loved me. I could hear him as clearly as you're talking to me now. I released all my stored-up energy, all my hate for the beast, all my anger, and all my fear into the beast. Pegan did the same. To my horror, the beast, this monster he called a Hellshade, exploded staining the invisible walls Pegan created."

Sarah hugged Averie, who was still sobbing. "It's going to be okay," she whispered.

"Can I still live here? I have nowhere else to go?" Averie asked in between the sobs.

"What kind of question is that?" Tom asked. "We're here for the long haul, good or bad, right or wrong, we'll be at your side."

Hours later they walked down the aisle looking at all the new shiny cars, trucks, vans, sports cars, and daily commuters.

"Can I help you?" a salesman asked as he stepped out from the office.

Tom was in no mood to deal with a salesman. "Is Doug here?"

"Normally Doug doesn't deal with the customers. As the owner—"

"Listen," Tom interrupted. "Doug and I go way back. He told me if I was in the market for a new car to come to see him personally."

"Okay, sorry," the salesman grumbled and quickly departed.

Minutes later, Doug stepped out and jogged across the lot. "Tom, you old goat," he said with a laugh, then looked down at the child carrier. "I didn't know you and Sarah—"

"We didn't have another baby, this little cutie belongs to her," Tom pointed at Averie, who was being led by the hand towards a Corvette by Billy.

"Now this is what we should get, right here," Billy said to Averie. The screaming yellow sports car had a sticker in the window of a hundred and nine thousand dollars.

"Billy, you get away from that, we can't afford the paint job on it."

"That's the new Corvette ZR1 roadster. It's a beauty that's for sure. I can't afford it either. I only have it here on loan from GM to draw in customers. Sold three C8 Corvettes because of it though."

"I'll be upfront with you," Tom said as he rested his hand on Doug's shoulder. "We need a new van, one that can hold eight comfortably, reliable, and safe with a bumper to bumper warranty. We're on a budget though so I was hoping you could work with us on the price."

Doug smiled. "I have just the thing for you, came in last week on special delivery. It's a bit spendy, but I'll give it to you at a smoking deal. Follow me, it's in the back getting prepped."

Doug easily lifted the bay door with a single hand then allowed the springs to drag it the rest of the way up. Sitting on the lift was a van with the doors open and two young men preparing it for delivery.

Sarah gripped her chest and nearly fainted. The van looked like something from the presidential motorcade with its triple-black metal-flake mirror-like paint, chrome wheels and matching chrome trim. The windows were so dark you could fly it by the sun and not get burnt. "I don't think we can afford this."

"Watch this," Doug said as he took the key fob off the mechanics toolbox. Pressing a button both sliding back doors opened revealing plush camel tan leather interior. Pressing another button, the engine roared to life. "This winter you can start it from the house and let it warm up so you won't be cold when you get in. Also, it has third-row seating, TV's in the headrests; a built-in car seat holder do-dad thingy to keep the baby safe and get this, it has seventeen air bags. Here's the build sheet." Doug handed Tom the paper.

Tom looked it over. "Jesus, this thing will do everything including make me a sandwich."

"It will make food?" Averie asked, both eyebrows crawled up her forehead like frightened caterpillars.

"No," Sarah told Averie. "Tom's exaggerating. Doug, I don't think we can afford this."

Doug dug through the envelope which came with it and pulled out the invoice. "I'll give it to you for twenty-two, five. That's the price I would have paid, excluding delivery and setup, but don't worry about that. You helped me out big time last year. I honestly thought my family was going to starve."

Tom looked at the invoice price, then at Doug. "Twenty-two five, that's thirty K' below the invoice price, you can't afford that kind of loss."

"How much I can afford to cut or not cut isn't your worry. Let's go inside where it's warm and do the paperwork."

Tom decided to see what he could get for the van in trade as well. "What can we get for our van on trade? It has major electrical issues and died three times on the way here."

"Don't worry about it," Doug reassured Tom. "We'll find a way to get you into this van, even if I have to cosign the loan."

As they drove away Tom glanced over at Sarah. "Somethings wrong?"

"Already, we just bought it," Sarah replied with a troubled look on her face.

"Not with the van, the price. This is a fifty-five-thousand-dollar rig, we got it for seventeen out the door."

"I see your point," Sarah said.

Later that evening, they met the scientists for dinner at Averie's favorite place, the Spaghetti Bucket.

"Welcome," Dave said as he met them at the door. "I got here early not wanting to take a chance on missing you."

Sandy extended her hand, offering Averie a warm gesture. "You must be Averie?" she asked, noting the piercing eyes.

Averie reluctantly took Sandy's hand. The incident with Frank still hot on her mind.

"Let's go inside," Dave said as he held the door open. "I picked a table near the back by the large picture window. It has an awesome view of Willowdale."

With introductions complete, they ordered.

"I must say," Mike said. "You both appear much more professional than Frank."

"Frank is a piece of work," Sandy said.

"You mean a pig," Sarah corrected her.

"Frank's tried to make the moves on Averie on multiple occasions, even calling her when he knows she's not interested," Jennifer enlightened Sandy.

"Allow me to fill you in," Dave said as he watched the waitress lower his plate of spaghetti. "Frank isn't interested in a relationship with Averie; he's motivated by greed, nothing more. He knows Averie is from another world and wants what she has to pad his bank account."

"What do you mean?" Mike asked as he twirled the spaghetti on his fork.

"It'll make sense if I start at the beginning," Dave said, then laid everything out on the table.

When Dave finished, they all sat there with eyes wide open. It was Sarah who spoke first. "Now he's even more of a pig for wanting to use Averie for his own financial gain, even if it means harming her."

"Okay, okay," Tom repeated. "We can deal with this. Now that we know we'll simply tell Frank were on to his game. If he keeps it up, we're going to sue for harassment and drain his damn bank account, see how he likes that."

"Be careful," Dave said. "Frank is a very wealthy man who I believe isn't used to hearing no for an answer."

"I have to ask you," Sarah said to Dave, changing the subject, "Did Avicia have a pulsating necklace like Averie does?"

Dave sighed. "Honestly, I don't know. It all happened before my time working there, and the only information I have was from Loren before he died."

"Loren who…" Mike slowly changed where he was going with this, not wanting to mention the experiments. "Who worked there."

"Yes," Dave answered.

Sarah poked at her salad searching for a tomato. "What happened to the family who had Avicia, there is no mention of them after they were arrested? They seemed to have vanished."

Dave leaned back in his chair. "I had to do a bit of research on my own. It appears they lost everything. Their home, car, savings account, everything was seized. When they were released, the woman had two dollars and used the money to buy a lottery ticket. Go figure; she won four hundred and twenty-five million. As far as I know, they remained in California living the good life until they both passed away from old age."

"So they came out smelling like a rose?" Mike asked.

"Yes, but they had to swim through the fertilizer first," Dave said.

Averie pushed her empty plate away and rubbed her eyes. "I'm sorry. I'm still exhausted," she said.

Dave looked at his watch. "It's getting late. If you don't mind, I would like to meet all of you again and learn more about Averie."

Mike eyed Dave suspiciously having read the barbaric experiments performed on Avicia.

Dave raised his hands to surrender. "Not in the way you're thinking, believe me. We want to talk to her about Icearaus. What life is like there? How did she get here? I'm sure there is a lot we can learn from one another, without the use of a knife."

"I don't see a problem," Tom said. "Stop by the farm in a few days to give us a chance to think about what we've learned."

"Sounds good. Don't worry about the tab, the state of Florida is picking it up," Dave told them as he broke out the state credit card.

"I knew it, I knew it, I knew it," Mike kept repeating.

"Knew what?" Jennifer asked.

"This is making more sense each time we talk about Avicia. The family that helped her went through hell but came out golden. Doug was damn near out of business last year. Tom helped him out with beef, in exchange and he gets this smoking deal on a van. The dealerships business is booming. This was all planned long ago. Doug was tested then as were being tested now."

"Well, if what Dave told us is true about all those who crossed Avicia experienced some form of trauma in their life, Frank better start walking a fine line and saying twenty-five Hail Mary's a day."

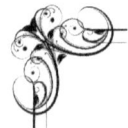
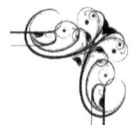

Chapter 68

Ameria heaved and grunted as she attempted to lift **Dinko**. Had it not been for the aid of Saress, she would have failed.

Raestmond looked in different directions. "Which way do we go from here?"

Saress spun in a circle. She had no idea which direction they had come, or which way they should go. To go the wrong route could cost them days, possibly their lives if they wandered aimlessly in circles.

Glorandial shimmied up a slick tree nearly falling a dozen times before she was high enough to look out over the vast quagmire. To the far north, there appeared to be a broad clearing. To the south, more swamp. "That way," she pointed towards the north. "There's a large clearing less than a day from here." She told them after she successfully climbed down without breaking her neck.

Throwing caution to the wind, Ameria had her staff glowing brightly as she led the way.

Saress supported Dinko while Filaurel and Raestmond carried Pegan on a makeshift gurney constructed from woven branches tied together with leathery vines.

Hindered by deep pools, thorn infested trees, and soggy ground, the terrain grew worse before it got better. Along the way, Glorandial continued to climb trees whenever possible alerting the others when they strayed off course. On the ground, it was impossible to tell which direction they traveled as everything appeared identical.

"We need to keep moving," Glorandial said as night fell on the quagmire.

"You said we would be out of here before nightfall," Filaurel argued.

Glorandial's eyes narrowed. "I didn't account for all the time we had to backtrack and search for other routes, or the abysmal pace we had to keep."

The night brought on a new feeling as darkness covered them like a wet blanket. Even with Ameria's staff glowing brightly, they could see no more than a dozen yards.

Saress drew her sword as a splash warned they were not alone.

"We're not far now, maybe another hour," Glorandial hesitantly said. She was not positive as the gloomy darkness had a way of playing tricks with her mind.

"We need to rest again," Raestmond said, he'd lost feeling in his fingers hours earlier, and fear of the unknown was the only fuel keeping him going.

Saress lowered Dinko down then stretched. She too was beginning to feel the burden of the big lizard. "We're going to rest here for the night. For all we know we're wandering deeper into the quagmire."

Ameria jabbed her staff into the ground, lighting the area.

Raestmond went to work on Dinko repacking the wound with new moss which slowed the acid, but the injury was beginning to rot from the infection. Pegan remained still as a corpse, his chest barely moving as he breathed.

They kept watch in shifts, but none truly slept. Gnats and other flying bugs pestered them continually, and the warm, stagnant air made sleeping intolerable.

Glorandial climbed the closest tree as the sky lightened, then quickly returned. "Had we gone another thirty yards we would have been free of this place."

The elf's words were a godsend, and their pace quickened. Less than twenty yards away the ground dried and within minutes they broke through a tangled mass of vines out into an enormous valley. Far and wide, tall lime-green and rusty brown grasses peppered with blue and yellow flowers danced on the faint breeze. To the east was an extensive mountain range while to the north, an ancient forest waited. "We should head east," Filaurel said, propping his foot on a good-sized boulder.

Saress looked around, *what would Pegan do,* she thought.

"Speedwell," Raestmond cheered, then sprinted to a patch of large leafy bushes not far from their location. "I've never seen it grow in such abundance."

Saress began barking orders. "Glorandial, Filaurel, help Raestmond gather as many of those plants as possible." She knew it was that plant which saved her life when the barbarians poisoned her.

"Who are you to tell me what to do?" Filaurel grumbled. "I agreed to follow Pegan, not a cold-blooded, beady-eyed, forked tongue reptile."

Glorandial fired Filaurel an evil glance.

Raestmond returned with a handful of Speedwell. "We need a fire so I can turn these into a paste and a drink. If it works, this should neutralize the acid and stem the infection until we can locate the dwarves, hopefully."

"We're going to remain here for now," Saress said. "We can all use the rest, and we seem to be in no danger."

Filaurel complained once more, but the party had decided, and he had no choice but to concede.

The next morning Saress woke them before the sun rose and told them they were heading north.

"Why north," Filaurel complained.

"Unbeknownst to you on my watch, I scouted the area and discovered this." She tossed down an axe head clinging to a rotten splintered shaft. "It was partially buried but not in a way as if it had fallen from a dying man's grasp. It was placed as if it were a directional marker to guide someone home who lost their way."

"Where did you find it?" Glorandial asked.

"Near the edge of the forest."

"You abandoned us for that long?" Filaurel was furious. "We could have had our throats slit before you returned."

"I was awake," Ameria hissed. "We were never in danger."

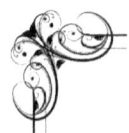
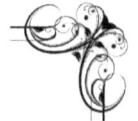

Chapter 69

 ony stumbled down the hall rubbing his pounding temples. "How much did I drink last night?" he asked Samantha who stood wrapped in a robe at the stove cooking bacon.

"After your eighth shot of Tequila, I figured you'd stop, but you just kept slamming them down." Samantha laid in a fresh row of bacon on the skillet.

Tony flopped down at the kitchen table, nearly falling from the chair. "Do you have any aspirin?" he asked, then looked at the ceiling. "Please let me live, and I swear I'll never drink again," he promised.

Samantha arrived with a glass of milk and a few Advil. "This should help."

Tony sat there with his head laying on the table, and both eyes closed.

"I think you should go home today and throw yourself at your wife's mercy. She's had a chance to cool down, took out her anger on your belongings… I bet she'll be more reasonable now."

"I don't know," Tony said. "She was mad as a mosquito in a mannequin factory."

"If not there, then you're going to be homeless. You can't mope around here anymore." Samantha placed his breakfast on the table. "You don't understand, I like being promiscuous and don't give a rip what people think. I don't want to be cooking breakfast for a man or sharing my couch with him while he watches football. Truth be told, I don't even want a man in my bed or my house after we get done with our extracurricular activities."

Tony picked at the eggs with his fork. "So I can't stay here tonight?"

"No, not tonight, tomorrow night, or the next. It's time for you to go." Samantha looked through her phone at the many upset messages about how she was putting them off to help that scumbag.

Tony finished eating all he could stomach then slid the plate on the counter. "Damn it," he grumbled.

Samantha flipped her eggs. "What?"

I knocked your damn ring in the disposal with my plate."

"Don't worry, I'll get a plumber out here to retrieve it."

"No, we don't need a plumber for this." Tony used a butter knife to press down the rubber cover to better view inside. "I can see it." Against the stainless-steel edge wedged between teeth designed to devour anything placed inside, the ring mocked him.

Shoving his hand into the hole, he wiggled his fingers, pushing the ring around like a hockey puck, but the small band evaded his grasp. "Damn it," he snarled again.

"I told you not to worry about it; I have a good friend who's a plumber. Trust me. He'll take it apart and get my ring back for free."

"No," Tony became angry. "I've screwed up enough. At least allow me to fix this."

"Fine," Samantha said as she went back to cooking.

Tony attacked the disposal from a different angle, believing he could grasp the ring, but the ring had other plans and seemed to have a mind of its own avoiding his grasp.

Using his other hand, Tony pushed the ring harder, wedging it between the teeth. "Now I got it," he said, placing his other hand on the wall for support, he shoved his hand back into the hole at a painful-looking angle. Closing his eyes, he concentrated on nothing but the ring, and his hand slipped from the wall catching the very tip of what he thought was a light switch.

CLICK—

Samantha froze, the sound reminded her more of a jet engine starting up than the garbage disposal.

Tony never screamed but went instantly pale as the device began devouring his hand.

Samantha screamed and backed away.

Tony tried to jerk his hand free, but the angle he employed effectively locked his hand inside the device.

Gurgling and snarling, the device was relentless in its attack stripping the bone of meat and spitting it back up through the opening in stew-sized chunks. Blood sprayed like an oil geyser hitting the ceiling, then hung in long strands. The beast wasn't done yet though and latched on harder ripping fingers free and expelled bone back out, leaving them to bounce like dropped dice.

Samantha screamed like a scalded cat as a knuckle bounced off the window smacking her in the face then getting tangled in her hair.

With nothing remaining below the wrist, Tony was finally able to free his arm from the demonic device. Fading in and out of consciousness, he slid down the cabinet holding what remained of his limb against his chest.

Samantha nearly fainted looking at the carnage. From Tony's wrist, nothing but shredded meat dangled.

Tony inspected the damage in a pain-induced delirium, then screamed. It had a raw quality, like someone consumed by pain that saw no end, or limits. Afterward, he sat there staring into oblivion.

Samantha tried to lift him but slipped in the blood and fell backward smacking her head against the stove. Crying out in pain, she tried again and was successful as she guided him to her car. Her foot pressed the pedal to the floor as the shifter found drive forcing the tires to scream as the car lurched forward. In minutes, she would arrive at the Live Well Clinic and someone with more experience could take him.

Tony remained silent except for an occasional whimper.

"What the…" Samantha screamed as she pulled into the vacant parking lot. It was after nine; the clinic should have been open, then she remembered and her heart sank. If he died, his death would be on her hands. "Damn." Backing out of the parking lot, she had no choice but to go to the hospital in the next town, forty miles away.

Tony never responded as he watched out the window, his face growing whiter by the second and his eyes held a doll-like quality.

Samantha passed cars at every possible opportunity as the dial on the speedometer topped one-ten. "Hang on," she whispered. "We're almost there."

Skidding sideways into the emergency parking lot, she leaped from the car and sprinted inside screaming for help.

Doctors, nurses, janitors, and visitors all ran towards her believing she was the victim from the amount of blood.

With everything sorted out, the last thing she remembered was Tony being wheeled back on a gurney with nurses inserting IV's into each arm as they rolled him through the swinging doors. A look of defeat on his expressionless face.

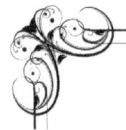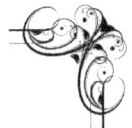

Chapter 70

hieftain Ulgra stood on the rim and looked down into the ravine he once called home, then vowed to someday return. At first, they made good time covering vast distances. Now, the pregnant women were exhausted, and the bottoms of their feet bore ugly festering blisters. The children fared no better, forcing the mass movement to stop and wait on multiple occasion. Leaving with nothing more than what they could carry, their supplies quickly dwindled. Add in the fact Chieftain Ulgra had grossly miscalculated the distance, there was a good possibility few, if any, would reach the Plains. Their biggest threat came not from a sword or spear, but the weather. The unseasonably warm temperature left them all on the verge of dehydration.

"The women need to rest," Envaile said. "We can't keep this pace; they're on the verge of losing their babies." She wiped the sweat from her blistered red face.

"We must find water, and food," another troll angrily said as he lifted an enormous rock searching for nourishment.

Skylar raised his hand in the air motioning for his followers to stop.

Darkblade crept up to Skylar, "What is it?"

"I'm not sure," Skylar whispered to Darkblade. "It's highly unusual for a single Cave Troll to be this far south, let alone the entire Clan. It's common knowledge they rarely leave the ravine, and that's only when hunting for food."

"Perhaps they've joined with Karayan?" Darkblade asked.

Skylar watched the trolls for a few more minutes. "Doubtful. If they had, Karayan would have men here escorting them. The trolls would never make it to Lynn Brook alone. They travel to slow and require a substantial amount of food. Anything with legs could easily outrun them. Their only hope is to throw boulders at wild animals in hopes of killing them. Even then they won't get enough to support the entire Clan."

"Then where else would they be going?" Darkblade asked.

"If they keep their current direction, to their deaths," Skylar said. "I don't think the Chieftain realizes he's leading them into the Cursed Desert. If they enter that inhospitable terrain, they will die within hours. Their leathery skin will retain the intense heat cooking them internally."

Chieftain Ulgra pointed towards a clump of trees farther down the moun-tain. "We will go there and wait until nightfall. Perhaps we can find a spring."

The council spread the Chieftains words then they set out lumbering down the mountain. Even though it appeared close, hours would pass before their arrival.

The temperature here was substantially less than when exposed to the elements offering some relief.

"We must set traps and remain here until we eat," a troll said.

"Because of the heat, the women with babies have run dry of milk," Envaile said. "It won't be long until Ukiah dies as well," she sobbed.

Chieftain Ulgra wiped away a lone tear. Ukiah was his only son, if he perished, his bloodline would end and a new Chieftain would be selected from those who survived. "We will find water," he groaned. Flipping over stones and logs, he dug at the soft ground, searching for water and food.

The assassins followed always remaining just out of sight, which wasn't hard giving the trolls terrible daylight vision.

"Darkblade," Skylar called out. "I need you to enter their camp and discover their plans."

Without answering, Darkblade blended in with his environment and crept into the trees.

A troll returned with a water skin dripping with water. "There is a mossy pond not far from here," he grunted, then handed the skin to a female who looked on the verge of collapse. "Perhaps we catch a fish?"

"One fish won't feed all of us," the Chieftain said.

The troll collected what dry skins they had and left to get more water.

"We need meat," another troll said. He was in the process of bending a branch trying to figure out how to make it into a trap. "We will die long before we reach the elves."

"And what if the elves reject us, cast us from their realm," another troll grumbled.

"The elves have always been our allies," Chieftain Ulgra snarled back. "They will accept us."

There could only be one reason the trolls where heading to Rhunsiire, Karayan had threatened them as well, he thought. There was only one way to discover the truth, so he revealed himself.

Each troll drew man-sized clubs when Darkblade materialized in the center of their makeshift camp. On him, they could see a gaggle of weapons, each one having seen more than its fair share of combat.

Darkblade never drew his weapons, but instead, placed his hands in the air as if surrendering. "If you're heading to the elves, you're going in the wrong direction. Your current path leads you towards the Cursed Desert."

"Why would you concern yourself with our direction?" Chieftain Ulgra asked.

"A friend of the elves is a friend of mine," Darkblade answered.

The Chieftain never lowered his weapon. "Why would an assassin be going to the elves? They are no friends of yours."

"I would ask you the same question?" Darkblade fired back.

Chieftain Ulgra thought for a minute as more trolls gathered, waiting for a decision to be made.

Skylar raised his hands again. "I am no threat to you and have not reached once for my weapons." *It was apparent the trolls were not associated with Karayan or Malvo.* "Lord Malvo has taken the brotherhood in a direction I, and a few of my companions do not agree with. Therefore, we decided we would rather coincide with the elves than live under Lord Malvo's dictatorship. I have told you why I travel, now you?"

Chieftain Ulgra considered the assassins words. "War is coming to Icearaus, and I refuse to kneel at Karayan's feet. Therefore, I'm putting Clan Cave Bane in great danger. I seek the elves for refuge."

"Then it appears we are both going there for the same reasons. I recommend we band together and join forces. There is safety in numbers, and I have witnessed some strange events in these mountains."

Chieftain Ulgra didn't want to reveal their dire predicament and appear weak. "If my path is wrong and leads us astray, then why are you here?"

"Because our paths crossed some time ago and we've been following you to learn of your intentions. We have watched you scrounge for food and know your Clan is starving. You will not reach Rhunsiire without aid. I believe your intentions are true, but you have miscalculated the harshness and distances on the surface world."

"I think you should listen to him," Envaile growled, "or we'll have to stop in a few days to bury our child. Not all humans are evil."

Chieftain Ulgra extended his hand. "We have an agreement."

Darkblade refused the hand. "I must first talk with my superior, but I don't believe it will be an issue."

Chieftain Ulgra pulled his hand back.

"I shall return with the others," Darkblade said, then quickly left.

You could taste the tension in the air as the trolls waited.

Within minutes Skylar strolled into camp. "I am Skylar Nightshade, and humbly accept our strange alliance. My companions have already been informed to spread out and gather food. Tonight, your women can rest peacefully as they are in no danger. My men will stand guard."

That night as they sat around the campfire eating fresh meat and drinking cold water. Chieftain Ulgra told them of their encounter with Jester and the outcome.

Skylar returned the favor and told them of the Chieftains miscalculations and what direction they would need to go to avoid the desert.

As the sun rose, Skylar woke Darkblade. "I need you to run ahead and inform the elves of our flight. Even with our aid, the journey is going to be long and hard for the trolls."

Darkblade grabbed his pack and fastened it tightly to his back. Ever since dawning the robes, they somehow avoided the effects of exhaustion.

"Alone you can be there in days. Run like the wind and may faith follow you and guide your footfalls," Skylar said.

After clasping hands, then a hug, Darkblade swiftly departed.

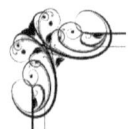
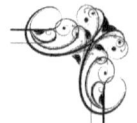

Chapter 71

rank arrived at the parking lot of the Grandiose Maple Resort and Spa thirty minutes before his scheduled meeting. It was an attribute he acquired as a child, and it always worked well for him. Easing the Corvette to a stop at the valet booth he climbed out and handed the keys to the attendant—a young man who's eyes lit up, only now realizing what he was going to get to drive. If even for the short duration of parking it in the back.

"Make sure to leave enough space around it that it doesn't get scratched. I don't think your parents could afford it."

"Sir, if that were to occur the Resort's insurance policy would cover it," the kid informed him in a meek, broken voice.

The twin double doors made of tinted glass were taller than they were wide and automatically slid open as he reached them. His pace never slowed as he followed the red-carpet runner with an elegant amount of black swished across the surface in a contemporary design. The walls were tastefully done in paper then covered by large paintings by well-known artists such as Rembrandt and Van Gogh. At the end of the hallway was a large seating area with plush leather chairs and soft music played through a hidden speaker somewhere in the ceiling. Just beyond the seating area, a man wearing an Emporio Armani suit waited at the decorative, hand-carved, podium.

"Can I help you?" the *maitre d'* asked in a snobby tone.

Frank checked his watch before answering. "I have a reservation at eight."

"And you are?"

"Middleton, Frank Middleton, Professor of Metallurgy at the University of Frankfort."

The *maitre d'* looked at Frank with elevator eyes. "So you are," he said as he carefully looked through a log. "Ah, there you are, right where you should be. Follow me, sir."

Beyond the podium, the environment was surreal with the dimmed lights and warm glow from candles reflecting off the hand-rubbed wooden tables. Near the back on a raised platform, a lady in a white dress strummed a majestic harp. Conversations were kept hushed to hear the sweet music flowing from the strings.

"Here we are sir," the *maitre d'* said when they arrived at a secluded table near the back which afforded a priceless view of Frankfort. "When your guest arrives, I will promptly escort him back as you have requested."

"Thank you," Frank said, then sat watching the lights of Frankfort twinkle. Out their either in jail or the hospital, his ticket to financial freedom waited.

"Would you like to see what we have to drink?" the waitress asked.

Frank diverted his gaze from the window to the waitress. She was an older woman who would have complimented the cover of Cosmopolitan magazine had the right opportunity presented itself. "No, thank you," he answered. "I already know what I want. Bring me a glass of your very best Chardonnay and leave the bottle."

The lady nodded she understood, then quickly departed.

Franks gaze fell back on the window. For days now he had been trying to get ahold of Averie, and each time the skank she lived with told him Averie was either busy or didn't want to talk. He would have no choice now but to do something which would send the public into an outrage, but he didn't care.

Frank glanced down at his watch and became nervous. Eight 0' three. Damn, I hope he got the message. His fears were put aside when he saw a tall drink of a handsome man being escorted his way, and he stood to greet his guest. "Glad to see you could make it," Frank said with a smile.

"I was in the middle of a case when you called."

"Did you win or lose?"

"Is that even a question," Jacque answered, then ordered a rum and coke as the waitress returned with the Chardonnay. "My clients almost always walk without prison time, most end up with parole, but at least they get their freedom. All except for two cases which I knew were a lost cause, but what they offered I couldn't pass up. They both should have received life. One got three years and the other five. They both considered it money well spent."

Frank took a sip from his funnel-shaped wine glass. "I have a significant case for you, and, money is no object. I need this woman released ASAP." From his pocket, he removed a folded sheet of paper and slid it across the table.

Jacque carefully unfolded the paper and read it over. "She was involved with the murder of a security guard?"

"No," Frank said. "She didn't kill the guard. From my understanding, Tiny, her boyfriend did—"

"I read the paper," Jacque interrupted. "This woman is an accomplice to a murder which reached national headlines. People were talking about it in New York City. DMV policies around the United States are being changed because of this incident. Let me ask you. Why in God's name would you want this woman out?"

"I need her out for personal reasons. She has something I want."

"Are you ready to order?" the waitress asked.

"Nothing for me," Frank said.

The lady looked upset from the lack of tip she would be receiving. Most people knew waitresses received most of their pay from the generosity of others.

Jacque glanced at the hors d'oeuvres section. "Give me a plate of your Easy Tomato Bruschetta with Balsamic sauce." Along with the menu, he handed her a fifty. "You're doing a hell of a job."

Frank watched the waitress depart. "If you think you can't get her off—"

"Wait a damn minute; I didn't say that," Jacque mumbled. "What I said is, why would you want a woman like this back on the streets?" Jacque took a sip, then stirred the glass with the straw. "Frank, this isn't like you. I've known you for a while. You've always been on the up and up, very professional. This woman is trouble you don't need."

"She has something I want, and as long as she remains in jail, I can't get it," Frank answered.

Jacque's mouth formed into a smile. "Really, you want to get her out so you can—"

Frank swished around his glass of wine before interrupting the lawyer. "I don't want her out to get laid, that's the last thing on my mind. I care little for the druggie, but she has something in her pawnshop. A very rare set of coins I'm after."

Jacque leaned back in the chair and reread the paper. "And you can't buy them somewhere else?"

Frank emptied his glass, then waved for the waitress to refill it, even though the bottle was within reach. Waiting for the waitress to depart, he rested his elbows on the table then told Jacque everything.

Jacque ordered another rum and coke, then gave the waitress an extra ten spot for her prompt service. "You're out of your goddamn mind. Why would you even get involved with something like this? And that's even if it's true."

"I know it's true. I held the damn coins in my hand."

"What about…" Jacque let his thoughts fade away. "Wait, I don't even want to know. If it's that important to you, then I will draw up the papers tonight and submit the offer tomorrow to Judge Burger, and the DA's office. It may take a few days, possibly a week to get her out, and it won't be cheap. This case has touched the lives of so many people, and the public wants to see all those involved hung."

"The money I spend now is a drop in the bucket compared to what I will receive in return."

"Well, I need to run," Jacque said after he drained the glass of its contents. "I will get the papers drawn up tonight and submitted first thing in the morning."

Frank watched Jacque walk away. Perhaps his luck was about to change. Maybe this shooting was a blessing in disguise.

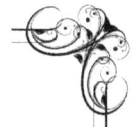

Chapter 72

he clock had yet to strike seven when the phone rang, waking Tom from a dead sleep. Knocking over the lamp as he felt around, he eventually located the obnoxious device and placed it to his ear. "Hello," he grumbled. Beside him, Sarah—who usually slept light as a feather—was out cold.

"Tom Fischer?" Detective Weaver asked.

"What?" Tom groaned. "Do you know what time it is?"

"Sorry. I know it's early but I wanted to inform you we have Savannah Henderson in custody for the robbery. Her boyfriend chose not to surrender and charged at the police with his firearm at the ready. The police had no choice but to shoot, he was declared deceased at the scene. The good news is we recovered the items stolen from your residence. The bad news is we can't release said items until after the trial. We have to keep them as evidence for the jury."

"That's fine," Tom said. "Keep the items as long as you need them."

"Who's on the phone, honey?" Sarah groaned.

Tom covered the receiver. "It's Detective Weaver."

"Anyway," the detective continued. "Ms. Henderson is going to have her first hearing in a few days if you want to go, or I can give you regular updates?"

"I'm not going to drive five hours to watch her trial."

"Sounds good to me," the detective said. "I'll keep you updated and let you know when you can come recover your items."

"Thanks for calling," Tom said as he hung up the phone.

Sarah sat up in bed and yawned until her jaw popped.

"It sounds like Savannah surrendered, but Tiny went down in a hail of gunfire."

"He died?"

Tom blinked a few times confused why she would even ask the question. "If my understanding of the word deceased is correct, then yes."

"Let's roll," Tom told Mike as he pushed the plate away. "The cows will be here later today. We have one more string of fence to run on that back forty."

"How many cows do we have coming again?" Sarah asked.

"Two hundred head and a dozen sheep."

"Can I drive the tractor?" Billy asked.

Time took the keys off the table. "Once we get down there, sure."

Sarah found the van keys on the counter. "I'm going to run into town for a bit, there are a few things I want to do."

Tom squinted his eyes at her.

"I want to pick up a few things, that's all."

"Want me to go with you?" Jennifer asked.

"Nah, will you stay here with Averie?"

"Sure," Jennifer responded.

Sarah pulled into the parking lot and lowered her head against the stee-ring wheel. She wasn't sure why she came here. What was she going to say? What was she going to do? She didn't know why and considered driving away. Instead, her hand located the handle, and the door swung open.

Sarah was rigid, and each leg resisted the will to move as she wobbled towards the door numbered nineteen. Maybe she would get lucky and they wouldn't be here. If she got really lucky, perhaps they already left back to Florida, but she knew better. These two scientists were here for the duration.

Sandy opened the door moments before Sarah knocked. "Come on in."

Sarah hesitated at the door, then cautiously entered.

Sandy looked outside. "Did you come alone?"

Sarah nodded. "I wanted to talk to you. Well, both of you."

"Have a seat at the table," Sandy said. "Dave's still in the shower but should be out soon. Until then, you seem to have something on your mind. Do you want to talk to me until then?"

"No, I can wait," Sarah said.

Sandy departed to the bathroom and pounded her fist against the door. "Hurry up; we have company."

"I'm sorry, did I interrupt..." Sarah blushed as she looked away.

"No," Sandy laughed. "It's not what it looks like. We're not dating."

Sarah cocked her head sideways, not believing her.

"Who is it?" Dave walked out with a towel over his head.

"Sarah is here to see us?"

Dave dried his face, then sat on the bed. "We didn't cause any problems at dinner, did we?"

"No, no," Sarah said. "In fact, Averie has been talking about wanting to meet you guys again to learn more about Avicia. I think she likes Sandy. The reason I'm here is I want to talk about the file."

"Oh," Dave said. "It's quite interesting, that's for sure."

"It's disgusting," Sarah corrected Dave. "I'm here because there's now been a second death associated with us," she solemnly said.

"A second death?" Dave asked.

"What are you talking about?" Sandy asked.

"Tiny, the man who killed the security guard to get our information, was killed recently. From my understanding, it ended quite ugly."

Dave's face drained of color. "It's beginning again."

Sandy sighed. "And this time we're involved."

Sarah's eyes glossed over like frozen puddles. "Why is this happening?"

Sandy shook her head. "I don't know, none of us do."

"This is why we're here," Dave said. "None of us were around when the Avicia incident occurred. All we have are the records to go by."

"And we don't want to see a bunch of innocent people get killed or hurt," Sandy continued.

"I don't consider the people who did that to Avicia innocent," Sarah screamed and got up and turned away.

Dave could tell Sarah was crying.

"Why are you really here?" Sandy asked.

Sarah turned around and faced them. Her eyes were red, and mascara stained her cheeks. "Because I don't want my family to die some gruesome tragic death like those described in that goddamn file. I want you to tell me how to stop it."

Sandy hugged Sarah. "We don't know how to stop it, or if it can be stopped. After Avicia died, people continued to die in strange ways; janitors, receptionist, delivery drivers… Loren was the last one on the list to perish."

Sarah buried her face in Sandy's shoulder. "What am I going to do?"

"First thing you're going to do is wash your face, you look terrible," Sandy said.

Sarah slid from Sandy's grasp and collapsed to the floor, covering her face she sobbed. "You both lived and you won't help me," she cried out while pounding her fist against the floor. Gasping for air in between sobs, her breathing became heavy, and her vision faded.

"She's going to hyperventilate," Sandy said as she knelt beside Sarah.

Dave grabbed his cell phone. "I'm going to call your husband. I think you need him right now."

"Why won't you help me?" Sarah cried out again as she wiped the snot from her face using her sleeve. Her entire body trembled, and her heart felt as if it was going to burst from her chest.

Tom didn't recognize the number but answered the phone anyway. "Hello?"

"This is Dave, the scientist," a deep voice blurted into Tom's ear. "Sarah is here at the hotel having a nervous breakdown. You may want to get over here."

"What the hell is she doing over there?" Tom asked.

"She came here to talk to us because she is worried, get over here ASAP."

Mike chose to drive as Tom didn't seem fit to be behind the wheel.

The screech of tires outside brought Sandy to the door, where she quickly ushered Tom and Mike inside.

Sarah sat on the floor with a blanket lying across her lap. Both hands were shaking, and she swayed side to side. In one hand she gripped tightly to a picture of Tom and Billy.

"What the hell happened?" Mike demanded of Dave. "Sarah's my sister and I've never seen her break down like this."

"Calm down," Dave said. "Sarah believes her entire family is going to die in some gruesome manner. She came here to ask us how to stop it."

Tom lifted Sarah and placed her on the bed.

Sarah looked like a raccoon with her makeup smeared across her face.

Dave sat at the end of the bed and looked at Sarah. "Sarah, the reason Sandy and I were not affected by Avicia is because we were both young at the time. The last thing on my mind was working for this agency. Hell, in my mind I wanted to be a firefighter."

"And I a cheerleader for a pro football team. As it turns out, Dave's too fat and out of shape, and I'm too ugly and short."

Sarah flashed Sandy a half-smile, then gripped both Mike's and Tom's hand. "Mike believes this is done by divine intervention, written in the stars. You know, controlled by a higher being. I'm not a religious woman; none of us are. We don't go to church or read the bible. All I know is how it starts… In the beginning, that's it."

"Neither was the family Avicia settled down with," Dave said. "I don't think it has to do with how much you believe, or if you believe. I think it has to do with your heart and intentions. You and your family appear to be genuinely good people, that's what matters. You would throw yourself in front of a train to save Averie or catch a grenade for her. Even coming here and confessing your fears takes a great deal of courage most wouldn't have."

"There's more," Sarah continued. "Mike thinks we are being tested. If we are, what are we being tested for?"

Dave shook his head, then looked at Mike. "I don't know, but Mike seems like a brilliant man. A man who can pick out the finer details most people would overlook. If he suspects something, I wouldn't brush it off so easy."

"I was a sheriff for fifteen years until I was fired because of a lie," Mike said.

"What was the lie?" Sandy asked. "That is if you don't mind me asking?"

"Let me start at the beginning?" Mike said, then told them everything which has occurred since Averie's arrival.

Dave scrubbed his chin, not sure what to say. "Here is what I do know. My mother was very religious and she always told me that God tests us in various ways but would never give us a test we couldn't pass, or something along those lines. Hell, I never listened to her and thought she was a nut case. As it appears now, she may have been on to something. If she were still alive, I would ask her, except cancer took her from me a few years back. The best advice I can give all of you is stay true to what you believe, right or wrong, good or bad, regardless of what those around you say."

"We already planned to do that," Tom said.

"You mind if Sarah takes a quick shower, I don't want Averie seeing her like this. Averie believes she's the root of all evil. If she discovers Sarah broke down, she's going to blame herself, and I don't want that."

"Not a problem," Dave said.

Sandy pulled Tom outside by the sleeve when Sarah was in the shower. "Don't be upset with her. She really loves you, all of you including Averie and is generally worried bad things are going to happen."

"I'm not upset with her and to be honest, I'm worried too. All we can do is keep a stiff upper lip and go down swinging if we have to."

Mike called Jennifer and told her what happened and to keep Averie preoccupied. They would find something to do afterward to give Sarah a reason for coming into town.

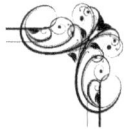

Chapter 73

he forest was like nothing they had ever encountered and seemed to exist for no other reason than to hinder there progress. The sponge-like ground was made up of trees that had fallen over a period of centuries and were in various stages of decomposition. Inches above the tangled mass of limbs, twigs, branches, leaves, and logs, an obscuring haze floated.

Saress took a deep breath and released a grunt as she helped Dinko stand.

Dinko released a groan as his weak legs somehow managed to support his weight, but only with Saress's assistance.

Never once complaining about the extra burden, Saress placed one arm around Dinko to keep him from falling and in her other she held her sword as she led them onward into the shadowed world that waited.

At first, the trees were thin and sparsely spaced making travel easy. The deeper they traveled though, the forest became an opposing foe with towering clumps of dense vegetation which clogged every possible path. Sprouting up through the vegetation were mile high millennial-old trees whose branches created a latticework of green, yellow, and brown leaves which blotted all but the hardiest of light beams.

Glorandial was left with no choice but to use her dual swords in a whirlwind of flurry hacking through the foliage creating tunnels. Sweat dripped from her body and both arms were nearing dislocation when she broke through the foliage into a large clearing edged by a slow-flowing crystal-clear river.

Filaurel and Raestmond were both dripping in sweat and numb from the shoulders down when they lowered Pegan to the ground. The unconscious man must have put on a hundred pounds since leaving the quagmire.

Saress positioned Dinko to where his back rested against a tree. "Hang on old buddy, were doing all we can," she whispered into his ear.

Raestmond used his hat to hold water and began cleaning Dinko's wound. The high humidity of the forest made conditions ripe and the wound festered out of control.

Filaurel wobbled his way to the water's edge on shaking legs, then dropped to his knees and splashed the cool water against his hot skin. The sudden shock forced an uncontrollable shiver to transcend his spine.

Glorandial located a large tree with thick branches and started to climb. She understood the importance of knowing their direction.

Ameria leaped over Filaurel, performed a flip, then belly-flopped in the water drenching Filaurel, who in turn came unglued calling the reptile all sorts of filthy names.

Ameria emerged with a fishtail hanging from her mouth.

Noise near the clearing's edge caught their attention as Pegan fought with the gurney and the vines used to secure him. Scampering to his feet, he appeared to have grown tentacles as the vines hung loosely off his body. Jerking his weapons free, he slashed at the haphazardly constructed device until it lay in a pile of rubble.

Saress watched with open eyes, not daring to intervene as the man seemed to have gone mad.

"Guess Pegan's awake," the soaked elf said in between continuing to curse the reptile.

Glorandial was partway up a nearby tree, but quickly descended.

Pegan looked around studying the strange environment, then rubbed his eyes. "Where are we?"

"Deep in a strange forest," Saress said, then suddenly remembered Pegan was unconscious during their flight from the quagmire. "Much has occurred since the incident."

Pegan looked baffled. "What incident?".

"You, you don't remember anything?" Glorandial asked.

Pegan's eyes widened. "No. The last thing I remember was leaving the cave."

Perhaps you should sit while I tell you everything you missed.

Hours later, Pegan's mouth hung open. "What the hell is a Hellshade?"

"I don't know," Saress said. "But it was immune to physical attacks and you killed it. It called you a Warlock, and you called it a Hellshade, and the battle was on."

"Why would the Hellshade call me a Warlock?" Pegan asked.

"I don't know," Saress answered. "Perhaps Elwrick can explain more once we return to Rhunsiire."

"If we ever return?" Filaurel grumbled. "We still don't know where we're at and are no closer to finding the dwarves."

"I hate to interrupt," Raestmond said. "But Dinko is growing worse by the minute. We need to do something."

Pegan examined the damage. "Is this the wound from the Hellshade?"

"Yes," Ameria said. "The Hellshade hit him with a tentacle and launched him across the knoll. Immediately afterward, the Hellshade came to devour him but you attacked the Hellshade and threw it out into the water."

Pegan lifted Dinko's massive clawed hand and gripped it tightly, then looked into the big yellow eyes that lacked life. "Hold on my friend. We're going to get you help. Raestmond," Pegan called out. "What do we need to cure this?"

"I'm doing everything I can, but the wound isn't from this world. The Speedwell has bought us some time, but that's about all. In time, Dinko is going to die."

Ameria turned away hearing the news.

"Damn," Pegan grumbled. "How long do we have?"

"Four days, maybe five. The acid is devouring the flesh at an alarming rate. Once it reaches the heart, it will only be a matter of minutes."

"He grows weaker by the hour as well," Saress said. "To get here I had to all but carry him."

Pegan spun in all directions taking in the foreign terrain. "Saress, you said the axe head pointed in this direction, as if it were placed there as a marker?"

Saress thought back to how it sat in the ground. "Yes."

Pegan thought for a second. "It's common for the dwarves to mark their route of travel. They probably did it without even realizing it would be a clue revealing their location. I believe we are heading in the right direction."

"Do you think the dwarves are close?" Raestmond asked.

Pegan rubbed his stubble-infested chin. "Glorandial, you're an elf who's lived her entire life in the trees. Pick the tallest one you can find and scurry to the top. It's imperative that we know which direction we're going. We can't waste time going in circles, or the wrong direction. We need to know what lies beyond this forest."

Glorandial did as instructed and quickly departed.

Pegan began barking orders faster than his companions could comply. "Ameria, get back in that water and catch your brother a fish. Saress, scout the area and return with what you discover. Raestmond, repack the wound, we need to buy as much time as possible."

"What should I do?" Filaurel asked.

Pegan considered what remained. "Get a fire burning. Before we depart a hot meal will raise our spirits."

Twenty-minutes later Glorandial returned with a smile from ear to ear. "To the north is a stone bridge. It's a good distance away but I don't believe it's natural, someone made it."

"Is there a town or village nearby?" Pegan asked. "You might not be able to see it due to the trees. Look for smoke from chimneys."

"I thought the same thing, but we are alone out here."

Ameria emerged from the water with a handful of fish. "I gathered enough for all of us."

"What are we waiting for? We can eat later," Filaurel excitedly said. "Let's get to the bridge and discover what waits beyond this forest."

"No," Pegan said. "We need to eat. We need our energy for whatever awaits us."

With the fish cleaned the smell of trout filled the clearing and not one bone contained meat when they finished. Pegan only ate part of his, offering half to Dinko who greedily accepted it. Ameria made a few more trips into the water coming back with shellfish, and other crustaceans which were quickly cooked and devoured.

Evening fell on the forest and the sky twinkled with stars when Dinko requested to be moved into the water, which they obliged. Raestmond agreed it was a good idea as well. The cool waters would slow the rate of infection and lower the fever.

Saress finally returned dropping a gaggle of unusually large hares on the ground. "To the north is an enormous bridge unlike anything I have ever seen."

"I know, I saw it from the trees," Glorandial said.

"But you didn't see it up close. I brought back a chunk of stone. Look at this?" She handed the chunk to Pegan.

Pegan examined the small chunk in the dim light. One side was perfectly smooth. "This cut was made with a tool, a dwarven tool. I've seen it before in the Dügab Caverns."

As the sun rose they set out. Pegan had the uncanny ability to find paths when none existed and they made good time never diverting from their northern direction, regardless of the obstacles they crossed. Along the way Pegan brought them to a rest whenever they encountered water so Dinko could cool his body and afford Saress a much-needed rest, who also indulged in the cool water.

Ameria proved to be the best fisherman and always provided fish whenever the opportunity presented itself.

The sky was glowing red as the last rays of the sun blessed their presence when they reached the bridge which stretched across a great chasm. Pegan stood on the edge and looked down, then cringed. Any who survived the fall would be crushed against the jagged stone walls by the turbulent waves, then swept out to see to be devoured by whatever lived out there.

Raestmond reached out and ran his hand along the stone. The structure was not only a thing of beauty, but an engineering marvel. Each stone was expertly cut then precisely placed until they mated perfectly together. The arch had been precisely calculated to provide both maximum strength and longevity. Along each edge was a balustrade with perfectly spaced spires designed to hold a torch on all four sides. Had it been in operation, the entire structure would have glowed brighter than the sun. "This is a magnificent structure well beyond anything I could hope to achieve," Raestmond said with a tear in his eye. "What I wouldn't give to work under this man, to learn his skills..." Raestmond allowed his words to fade away as he ran his hand along the Balustrade examining the elaborate detail carved into each individual stone.

"If we survive this ordeal, you may be given the opportunity," Pegan said.

Filaurel folded his arms across his chest. "Nothing from this world could build something like this."

Pegan shook his head in disagreement. "There is one man and someday Averie is going to wake him from his slumber."

"And who might that be?" Filaurel asked.

Raestmond's eyes opened wide waiting to hear the answer.

"Nümribelyn," Pegan said as he walked away lost in thought. "With the sun setting I recommend we remain here for the night and set out at first light. None of us know what waits in the darkness beyond this chasm."

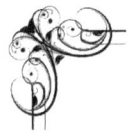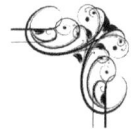

Chapter 74

he house held an abnormal chill when Tatum woke. Usually, she was awake, dressed, and out the door long before her mother stirred. Today, this was not the case, and she had to be woken multiple times before stumbling from her rack. Wrapped in a thick wool blanket pulled up to her neck, she made her way to the small kitchen.

"I already packed your breakfast," Tuzebelle said while handing Tatum a bloated satchel. "Hurry now before you're late."

"Why do I have to go today?" Tatum complained as she sat on the wooden bench near the door and fought with her boots. "It's always the same thing day after day. I stand up there from sunup until sundown and never see anything. Can't I take one day off and enjoy some time with my friends? Go down to the dock and do some fishing, or swim in the water?"

"I wish we all could take a day off and enjoy ourselves," Tuzebelle said. "But right now we have other responsibilities. You must work the look-out, while I run the tailor shop. Winter will be here soon, and our clothes are worn and ragged. Other dwarves count on us to do our jobs while they do theirs."

"That's different," Tatum complained. "You get to see the fruits of your labor, what do I get?"

"Tatum," Tuzebelle sternly said. "Your job is more important than all the others. We cannot allow our guard to fall."

Tatum knew her mother was referring to the incident when the monsters ambushed them in the homeland. None of them expected it, nor were prepared and it nearly drove the dwarven race into extinction. Snatching the satchel, she stormed off grumbling and moaning.

Tuzebelle watched her go, and when she was gone, she cried. Her daughter was right. It was not fair that Tatum already forfeited her childhood and was now forced to live a lifestyle she had no part creating. Perhaps it was time for someone to take Tatum's watch on the outlook. Later she would talk with King Fomour about getting Tatum reassigned.

It was pre-dawn when Tatum arrived placing her satchel on the cold stone bench, exactly how she had done it for as long as she could remember.

"I thought you were going to be late today," Jasmine said.

"I didn't want to come at all," Tatum offered an honest answer. "It's the same thing every day, and nothing changes. I spend hours looking through this dumb glass, and all I see are birds and woodland creatures."

"Your job is very important," Jasmine reminded her. "Don't get discouraged.

You still have your whole life to live. You're young, you won't spend all of it up here on this stone."

"I guess you're right," Tatum grumbled as Jasmine quickly departed down the trail. Digging through her satchel Tatum located a thick slice of buttered bread and a small bag of nuts and berries. She was always fond of her mother's bread and didn't get it often, as the time to make it took most of the day. Time her mother didn't have running the tailor shop, yet somehow, she always managed to put something special in her lunch. Enjoying each bite, she licked the butter from her fingers then popped a few berries in her mouth. *Guess I better begin,* she thought, and carefully removed the glass from the leather pouch and placed it against her eye.

Beginning from the north, she slowly turned to the south stopping when she reached the bridge. "Nothing," she grumbled. "Exactly like yesterday, and the day before that. There's never anything," she groaned. *I don't believe there is anybody else, and the stories about other races are all lies.*

Eventually, the sun crested the horizon filling the sky with rays of hope and brought with it a warmth no campfire could replicate. Stretching wide, she allowed the heat to soak into her bones and she suddenly felt better. Unlike her friends and mother who enjoyed the shadowy underground world, she preferred the outdoors.

Waiting the allotted time, Tatum put the glass back to her eye and started back at the north. Scanning once more through the valley, she observed all the familiar places then focused on the bridge and nearly dropped the eyepiece. On the structure, seven figures were midway across. Rubbing her eyes, she knew it had to be a mistake, spots on the lenses, shadow of a bird, heard of small animals. There were no hunting parties or gatherers scheduled, and besides, these people where huge, giants in her eyes. Putting the glass back to her eye, she watched them for some distance describing each on a parchment. At their current rate of travel, they would be knocking at their door by nightfall. Returning the eyepiece to the protective bag, Tatum sprinted for the caves. The elders would need to be informed immediately.

Opposite the bridge they discovered travel to be quite easy and they made excellent time. Winding their way through the trees and lose brush Pegan easily followed the dwarven tracks. Breaking over a ridge, Pegan brought them to a halt at a wide, easily navigated section of the trail. To the untrained eye, they would have missed the split and spend days, if not weeks walking in circles as they navigated the island. Pegan though was a master at following those who wished not to be tracked and quickly spotted the deception. "We need to go that way." Pegan pointed up a steep slope littered with flat stones. "We must be getting close."

Ameria lowered Dinko to the ground searching for a much-needed rest. Looking back the way they had come, she looked forward, her eyes following the wide trail. "The path continues that direction," Ameria pointed.

"My young lizard friend," Pegan said. "If we continue that way, we will be lost for days. The designer of the trail is a master craftsman who has taken great

strides to lead unwelcomed guests astray."

Saress cocked her head sideways.

Pegan could see Saress wanted a better explanation. "It's hard to explain, and only with decades of dedicated study am I able to decipher what I see. The flat rocks which look to have fallen naturally from above, are strategically placed to provide footing for people to pass undetected. If you look closely, you will notice they are anchored to the ground and extremely well disguised."

Glorandial brushed some of the muck aside and could see a camouflaged rod perfectly hidden.

"Most trackers, even elves would have never discovered the trickery," Pegan said as he looked at Filaurel.

"Told you he was amazing," Saress said to Ameria.

Steeper than it first appeared, it took both Saress and Ameria to get Dinko up the slope, and by the time they crested the ridge, most of the stones were either knocked free, broken in half, or pressed so far into the ground they were no longer visible.

King Fomour almost fainted. Had it not been for Gruvulir's quick reaction, he would have landed hard on the ground.

"And you're positive what you saw?" Gruvulir asked.

"Yes," Tatum excitedly answered.

Fomour rubbed his bushy eyebrows then scratched his beardless, wrinkle infested chin. "You didn't perchance doze off and dream this? Sometimes boredom can overtake us, and we imagine things. Your mother talked to me about having you moved inside to work in the tailor shop. Perhaps you have spent too much time up there and now is a good time for a new job."

"Are you calling my daughter a liar?" Tuzebelle snarled, and then curled her short stubby fingers transforming both her hands into fists.

"No, no, calm down, Tuzebelle," Fomour said. "I believe she saw something, maybe a pack of animals or perhaps a flock of birds on the bridge resembling the other races."

"What I saw was no pack of animals or birds," Tatum screamed. "I watched them for some distance. They were guided by a man who deciphered our trails as if he was here the day we made them."

Gruvulir reread the parchment going over every detail, then spoke clearly. His deep voice carried through the cavern. "Two of them are elves; that description is obvious with their pointed ears and slim bodies. Three are reptiles, which you state one appears critically injured and having to be supported. One is a man, older in appearance but not much bigger than a dwarf. The last one though has me concerned. A man dressed all in black and moved like a phantom fading in and out of existence. I only know of one who fits that description, and he isn't welcome here."

"Who might that be?" Tuzebelle asked.

Fomour's eyes narrowed. "Karayan."

Gruvulir shook his head in disgust. "Why would Karayan work with the elves?"

King Fomour shook his head in disgust. "I don't know."

"Regardless, it appears they are on a mission to find us," Gruvulir said.

"Nobody knows we went this direction, except Nümribelyn," Tuzebelle said.

"There is one other who I believe may have documented our travels. A man by the name of Malvo Necrosyse," Gruvulir said. "If the man you describe in black is indeed Karayan, you can bet Malvo has sent him to finish what he started so long ago."

Fomour reached towards Tatum. "Let me have the glass. Gruvulir and I will have a look. If we are to be attacked, I wish to see who we face with my own eyes."

Gruvulir handed a parchment to Tuzebelle. "Deliver this to Horback immediately, and make sure he understands the urgency of my request."

Beyond the slope was another ridge where Pegan brought them to a halt. His vision followed the wide trail as it wound its way through a graveyard of trees, past an outcropping of boulders, past some dense brush before vanishing over the hill. He knelt to examine the ground. "People have come this way, and recently." He used his finger to trace the outline of subtle boot prints on the ground. "Either their small and light, hence the faint impression, or all females."

"Wait here," Glorandial said. "Let me scout ahead, with my keen elven vision I should be able to spot anybody or anything hiding."

"We already have one wrapped in the thralls of death. We can't afford to lose anymore," Filaurel complained.

"Glorandial is right. We have to know what lies ahead. Don't go too far to where if you encounter trouble we won't have the time to intervene," Pegan told her.

Pegan helped Saress lower Dinko to the ground. "He looks bad, I wish there were something I could do," he whispered to Saress.

"We're doing all we can," Raestmond said, he went to work again on the reptile packing the wound with more Speedwell, but the festering hole had grown encompassing half the lizard's chest.

Filaurel wiped the sweat from his face. "I hope these dwarves welcome us with open arms. By the time we arrive we're going to be exhausted."

"Speak for yourself," Pegan said as he helped Raestmond. Slicing off part of his cloak he created a bandage that would hold the paste in place.

Glorandial was gone longer than expected but returned with valuable news. "I didn't discover the dwarves location, but the farther I went, the more traces I found of civilization. I feel we're now knocking on their door."

Fomour held the glass to his eye and quickly spotted the intruders. They were less than an hour away and coming at them with relentless pursuit. "With them this close, I can now see the leader is neither Karayan nor Malvo."

Gruvulir could hear the relief in King Fomour's voice. "Let me have a look." Gruvulir took the glass and held it up to his eye. "Do you think there a forward scouting party for an advancing army?"

"No," Fomour answered. "They're too well-armed. Scouts would be lightly armed not expecting to encounter any fighting."

Gruvulir watched them for some time. "I don't think we should welcome them with open arms, not at least until we know their intentions."

"I couldn't agree more," Fomour said.

Horback suddenly appeared as if he'd been dropped from the heavens. "The elderly and children have all moved to the farthest caverns, and any able body, male or female, has been ordered to arm themselves with whatever they can find."

"Thank you for doing such a fine job on such short notice," King Fomour said as he patted his longtime companion on the shoulder.

"Rumors have begun to circulate this will be our final stand, that our story will end right here in the depths of this cold mountain," Horback said.

"If this is to be our end, let's make sure it's one worthy of song," Gruvulir roared proudly.

"Our warriors are ready. Here soon, the advancing party will be within our sights," Horback spoke of the battle plan.

"Remember, the surprise is on our side. They have no idea of our numbers, our location, or our weaponry," King Fomour said.

Saress knelt and raised her fist in the air. This was the signal they were waiting for; the signal life had been detected. The trail which was once quite broad and allowed them to walk abreast narrowed to the point they were forced to walk in a single file. To either side, enormous granite mountains rose almost perpendicular and were speckled with dense patches of leafy bushes. From somewhere unseen, the sound of angry, turbulent water echoed. "These hills are littered with tiny people," she whispered to Pegan.

"Well, it seems our arrival has not gone unnoticed," Pegan said.

Ameria wiped away the blood that ran from Dinko's mouth. It was evident from the pain on her face, the burden of having to support Dinko's weight was taking its toll.

"Saress," Pegan whispered. "Relieve Ameria of her burden; she looks exhausted."

Ameria gladly accepted the help.

"How should we approach this?" Filaurel asked. "You're the assassin, sneak up on them and determine their numbers."

Pegan studied the cliffs. They were perfectly chiseled to create a choke point making intruders easy targets and prevent the dwarves from being overrun. "My plan is simple. I'm going to walk out, alone, and greet them with open arms."

"Are you crazy," Filaurel said. "You don't know if it's the dwarves out there. You could be dead before you have a chance to speak."

"And that's a chance I'm willing to take."

"And the rest of us?" Raestmond asked.

"Everyone else stays back. If they kill me, prepare for battle."

Saress wrapped Pegan in a hug lifting him from the ground. "Don't believe you have to do this alone. All you have to do is ask, and I'm right there beside you until the bloody end."

Pegan gazed into her big yellow crescent-shaped pupils. "I know you would, but I'm not doing it alone; I have Averie right beside me." He held up the pulsating shard.

"Still, if you need help," Glorandial whispered, she slid her swords free.

Filaurel nocked an arrow.

Pegan never reached for his weapons as he walked out into the open. Arms raised, he studied his surroundings. Holding his breath and expecting the unexpected, a sudden stillness fell over the land, and for a moment, life stopped. "I come in peace," Pegan yelled. The echo of his voice sounded like thunder as it bounced off the sheer walls of the surrounding terrain.

"Halt, or you die where you stand," snarled a dwarf who stepped out from behind a large stone. He was a short man, maybe three feet tall but covered from head to toe in shiny plate armor. He carried a large, but worn battle-axe with both hands and over his shoulder was slung a small, one-handed crossbow.

"I come in peace," Pegan said. "I have an injured friend who teeters on the verge of death." He thought for a minute longer. "I would also wish a meeting with the dwarven council, to earn their allegiance and welcome them back to the world of man."

All around him, dwarves leaped from unseen cracks in the mountain to ambush the intruder. Most held small rusty broken daggers or rotten, twisted staves and wore little to nothing for armor.

Pegan turned to view the masses which arrived. They were a ragtag bunch of mostly untrained female warriors who offered little in the way of threat. Had they attacked, he could have destroyed the entire bunch single-handedly. Still, he could see their pride and courage as they tried to fight with whatever means available.

The heavily armored dwarf raised his right hand high in the air then closed it creating a fist. Afterward, he pounded it against his chest. The rest of the dwarves seemed to relax. A few even released a sigh of relief.

Pegan could tell none wished to fight, and most were probably more experienced at fleeing.

"I have informed my troops to stand down; we will hear what you have to say."

"I have a severely injured companion. We are at your mercy for aid," Pegan said, then waved for the others to join him.

OOOH's filled the air when the dwarves saw the reptiles for the first time. Many were less than waist-high to Saress.

"Follow me," the armored dwarf directed the strangers.

They walked for a good while up a narrow trail then entered a shallow cave. Inside, two dwarves stood behind a stone table.

Pegan bowed lowering to one knee. "Good day my stone loving friends, and at one-time faithful allies. I am Pegan Rhoe, and I come here to re-forge a century-old alliance between the realms of elves and dwarves."

The two dwarves looked to each other then back to Pegan. "I am King Fomour, and this is Gruvulir, second in command. If what you speak is true, then Nümribelyn has returned. Why has he not come with you? It would make your story much more believable."

"Nümribelyn has not returned. I was sent here, along with my companions, to find you and rekindle our allegiance. War is coming to Icearaus, and none will be spared."

Once again, the two dwarves looked at each other and spoke in an ancient language. After a few minutes, Fomour addressed Pegan. "If not Nümribelyn, then who sent you?"

Usually, Pegan was reserved about revealing names, but these dwarves were old and would know exactly who he was referring to. "Elwrick, Order of the First Flame, Spiritual Guide to Icearaus, and Lady Alenia, Queen of the elves, Ruler of Rhunsiire," Pegan proudly answered.

The two dwarves spoke again, and then they relaxed. It was apparent the names were highly respected amongst them. "We welcome you to the Island of *Huelgrawt*," Fomour said, reaching out with a grizzly paw of a hand. "You and your friends are welcome here, and you can remain as long as you wish. Food and bedding will be provided along with aid for your wounded companion."

"Thank you," Pegan said. "We are forever in your debt."

"May I ask what injured your companion?" Fomour asked. "It may be instrumental for his treatment."

"I honestly don't know," Pegan answered.

"I was there," Saress said. "And the horror of that incident will be forever scarred within my mind."

Gruvulir's eyes narrowed; he knew of only one such beast which could create such fear.

Saress seemed lost in the past as she told them of the encounter with the Hellshade, and how Pegan allowed himself to be swallowed to destroy the beast. When she finished, all eyes fell on the assassin.

"Impossible," Fomour whispered in disbelief. "That creature is indestructible, immune to any device we possess."

"I saw it with my own eyes," Glorandial told them as well.

"If what you say is true, then this is a glorious day as that beast is the father of all nightmares."

"I can assure you it is quite dead," Saress explained.

"Shall we go inside, I'm sure your party would like a hot meal and a good night's rest," Gruvulir said.

Fomour led them from the cave and down another trail to an enormous steel door built into the side of the mountain. Using his dagger, the King tapped a secret code then waited for a small window to slid opened. After a few hushed words were exchanged, the door swung wide revealing a massive cave and vacant city.

"Send out the all-clear signal," King Fomour told the guard. "No reason for our people to remain in hiding any longer."

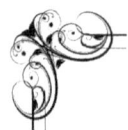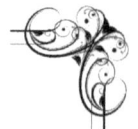

Chapter 75

acque Beau arrived at the records office an hour before eight. Waiting there was a young lady with a large key in her hand.

"Normally records don't open until eight," she told him as she unlocked the door.

"I understand," Jacque said as he held the door open as she removed the key from the lock. "Normally I wouldn't ask such an unusual request, but at eight I have an extremely important hearing and won't have time to get the information to represent my client effectively."

The lady knew she was breaking the rules, but everybody should be allowed legal representation. "I only ask that you don't tell a soul. I don't want to get in trouble."

"You're not breaking any rules," Jacque said to ease her tensions. "It's not like you're giving up classified information. I would have gotten exactly what I'm getting now, only an hour later. If they do harass you, come see me." The real reason he needed the file was he had a scheduled appointment with Judge Burger and wanted to know precisely what evidence the DA had against Savannah Henderson.

Jacque thumbed through the file and stopped on the prosecutor's page and looked it over, then released a hearty laugh which echoed down the vacant hall when he saw the name printed in the box labeled Prosecuting Attorney—Nancy Ackerman. She was not a bad prosecutor, she was just new… er. Given enough time, he could see her becoming a thorn in his side forcing him to work for his money. Today though would not be that day as he looked over the evidence and chuckled again. "I love the smell of easy money in the morning."

At eight sharp, Judge Burger looked at Defense Attorney Jacque Beau with disgust in her eyes. "Why would a man of your reputation represent such a low-life thug?"

Jacque Beau was no rookie at the game and knew how to play hardball when needed. Removing a pen from his breast pocket he wrote down the date and time, then—Judge Diana Burger referred to my client as a low-life thug. "That alone could be grounds for a mistrial due to extreme prejudice."

"Oh, come on now," the Judge grumbled.

Jacque removed a file from his briefcase and laid it on the desk. "I'll be upfront with you, it makes it easier that way. No beating around the bush or sugar-coating the candy," he said as he flipped open a thick manila folder. "As you probably already figured out, I was hired to represent Savannah Henderson—"

"Who hired you?" Judge Burger asked. "I know she doesn't have the kind of money you demand."

Between the pair, an awkward silence formed like two alpha male wolves jockeying for control of the pack.

"My client wishes to remain anonymous, which is their legal right," Jacque finally said.

"Hmm," the Judge sneered.

Jacque Beau flipped through a few pages of the folder. "After discussing available options with my client—*He had never talked with Savannah Henderson and was making this up as what he believed would be in her best interest*—we have come to what we believe is a fair plea deal which is a win-win for all parties involved."

"And what is this deal?" Judge Burger had to ask as Nancy was shaking in her high heel shoes.

Nancy knew the reputation of Jacque Beau as a bloodthirsty DA who would stop at nothing to see his client walk, even if it required destroying the prosecutor's career. She had recently married and only days prior to this meeting discovered she was pregnant. To lose her job now would be devastating.

"My client isn't disputing the fact she was involved with the Fischer Farm robbery in Frankfort. What she is disputing is her involvement involving the murder of Mr. Shriver explaining she had no part in its design or execution. To explain how we arrived at the murder, we have to go back about five years."

"Is any of this relevant or are you wasting my time?" Judge Burger asked.

"This is extremely relevant as I prove that Mr. Lunquest took an upstanding member of the community and molded her to his will with threats of serious bodily injury and the influence of drugs leaving her nothing more than the broken shell of the woman we see today sitting in a cold cell."

"This sounds more like the opening statement at a trial than a simple explanation," Judge Burger said.

"You want the whole scenario or just the facts?" Jacque asked.

"We're not in court so the facts will suffice," the Judge answered.

Jacque began with how his client was a model citizen with a master's degree, owned her own business, paid her taxes, and supported the community even attending the city parade and donating her time at the homeless shelter. Everything went bad though after her divorce and she met Mr. Lunquest who preyed on her vulnerability and saw the opportunity to run his illegal syndicate out of the back of her pawnshop. After getting her hooked on illicit drugs, he knew then there was no way for her to get out without doing a lot of time, so he twisted the screws tighter turning the pawnshop into a full-blown illegal drug trade center where drugs were trafficked from all fifty states. It was not until Mr. Lunquest's greed got the better of him over a few rare coins he received and needed the address of the coin owners. The only way to acquire the Fischer's address was to use the DMV database, which he knew Savannah's sister, Debbie Sniperton worked. To get the alarm code for the DMV, Mr. Lunquest killed a homeless man with a chainsaw and forced Savannah to help clean it up reinforcing what he would do if she didn't cooperate. Fearing for her life, she talked Debbie into providing the DMV alarm code… "From that point on, we know the facts. As you can see, my client is as much a victim as the Fischer's."

Judge Burger knew his synopsis was nothing but hogwash, but a jury would soak it up quicker than a dry biscuit dropped in a bowl of warm soup. "What are you proposing for a plea deal?" Judge Burger asked.

"My client has agreed to forty-eight months of supervised probation, one-hundred hours community service, full restitution to the Fischer family for damages accrued to their property, and for the state to provide drug treatment as she has lost everything and has not one red cent to her name. In exchange, she has agreed to drop the lawsuit against the city for pain and suffering endured during the incident." Jacque wanted to make sure it appeared his client was an innocent bystander who was victimized by the brutality of the SWAT members aggressive, and unnecessary behavior. Fudging the truth slightly wouldn't hurt the situation one bit. "You must remember Ms. Henderson was unarmed, AND, on the ground doing as ordered when an officer shot her for no better reason than to hear her scream."

Judge Burger considered the attorney's plea. Savannah did have a case of neglect on their part. The report clearly stated over one thousand rounds were spent in a matter of minutes to clear the scene. Especially since she was unarmed, and the report from the medical examiner revealed no gun powder residue on her hands.

Jacque slid the chair out and sat down. "Think about it. Ms. Savannah Henderson isn't a threat to society. Why do you want to waste the taxpayer's money driving a case you can't win? Look, we all know who killed the security guard, and he's dead. I recommend you accept her plea and let your prosecutor get a victory instead of a career-ending beatdown that'll be strung through every paper from here to California."

"What do you think?" Judge Burger asked Nancy.

"I'm good with that as well," Nancy answered. "There's no need to drag this through the papers making the family members relive their tragic loss. This way they can get closure."

Judge Burger squinted at Jacque. She knew the man was up to something but he had them both over a barrel. "I'll start the paperwork for her parole and drug treatment," Judge burger said. "You make sure Savannah Henderson understands she steps even one toe out of line and her butt will be back in jail so fast it will make her head spin."

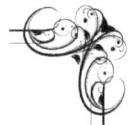

Chapter 76

lwrick believed enough time had passed for Ellusia to recover from her childish tantrum, but he was wrong.

"Go away," Ellusia screamed, then threw a glass bowl at Elwrick. "If you ever cared for me, cared for the elves, you will ask her to leave."

Elwrick didn't have to move, duck, or run for cover. Ellusia's aim was terrible, and the glass bowl sailed right out the window. "We didn't need that anyway," he said with a slight chuckle.

"I said get out!" she screamed and reached for a plate.

Elwrick's movement was mind-numbing quick as he covered the small room and pinned her to the bed. "You need to listen to me."

Ellusia wiggled and wormed as she fought to break free from Elwrick's incredible strength.

"Don't you even consider hurting her," Lady Alenia yelled as she entered.

Elwrick looked at Lady Alenia. "You should know me better than that by now."

The clack of Lady Alenia's cane was the only sound as she neared. "Ellusia, you need to listen to Elwrick," she softly said, then stroked Ellusia's tangled mess of hair. "There's more to Lilith than what we first believed."

"I don't wish to be dodging plates the entire time I'm talking," Elwrick said. Waiting a few seconds, he released her.

Ellusia crossed her arms and looked away.

"Did you want this back?" an elf asked as he peered into the room holding the bowl.

"Keep it," Ellusia said, partly with a laugh.

Elwrick slid a chair over and sat beside the bed. "Lilith's actions have set in motion some horrible deeds. Things which can never be undone." Lifting up his robe, he revealed to her the burn marks from his encounter with the Lich Lord. "Things which will never be forgotten. She did them because she saw a vision of the future and knows what's coming. Knows the horrors we're all bound to face. Horrors beyond anything you could ever imagine. Things which would make you wish you were Arlin's slave again."

Ellusia's eyes opened wide.

"Here is what you don't understand. Lilith may look like an adult, but she has the mind of a child. Right now she thinks irrationally and only of herself. In time and with the proper training, she is going to become a valuable asset to the elves."

"How is that possible?" Ellusia asked.

"Because she is a full-blooded Witch, and not to mention Pegan's mother."

"Pegan is a Warlock?"

"No," Elwrick informed her. "Pegan is something entirely different."

An elven soldier bolted into the room skidding to a stop inches before slamming into Elwrick. His face was fiery red and drenched in sweat. "Something awful comes this way!"

Elwrick came to his feet in a flash. "Define awful?"

The elf thought back for a moment to what he saw. "I can't," he admitted. "It's bi-pedal, like a man, but moves like the wind and fades in and out of existence. When it could be observed, it was black as death. I have seen nothing like it in my time in this world."

Lady Alenia's eyes welled up with tears.

Elwrick kissed Lady Alenia's forehead. "You stay in the center of Rhunsiire where you're most protected. I will deal with this entity which so boldly approaches our borders."

"It will arrive long before we can assemble a force," the elf told Elwrick.

"Where do you believe it plans to enter?" Elwrick asked in a rushed tone.

"It's coming towards the location where the old Oakenwood Bridge once expanded the river."

Elwrick thought for a second. "I want a squadron of soldiers stationed around Lady Alenia. NOTHING goes near her without my knowledge. Inform Ryul to assemble a small force and meet me at the river. This very well may be a test of our defenses. We cannot allow it to enter Rhunsiire. Set out the alarm, I want every soldier at the ready."

"I will see it done," the soldier said, then quickly departed.

"What are we going to do?" Ellusia asked.

"You're going to return to the Medical Ward. If war does come this day to our borders we're going to need your skills. Put aside your anger; now isn't the time."

Ellusia took a deep breath; she knew Elwrick was right.

Elwrick kissed Lady Alenia again. "Don't reveal yourself until I return. This may be an attack aimed directly towards you. With your magic failing, I would hate to think what Malvo—" He turned away without finishing. "I would hate to think what Malvo would do to you if he had the chance." Elwrick choked on the words.

She kissed and hugged him. "Don't go," she whispered.

Right outside the door, Midnight Materialized. "I have to, this thing might be something created in Malvo's twisted mind and brought here to destroy us. Something only I can fight." He kissed her again. "I ride for the river." Then he was out the door and on Midnight's back in a single bound.

The man-thing never slowed as it ran across the surface of the water.

Unlike the elves, Elwrick could see him. It was indeed a man but cloaked in something which altered his appearance and afforded him abilities not naturally acquired. Casting an invisibility spell, he waited. "And where might you be heading?" Elwrick said.

Darkblade halted, then looked directly where the voice originated. He could not see the speaker, only the faint outline of an elderly man. "Reveal yourself. I don't have time for games with a phantom."

Elwrick materialized not five feet from the intruder. "Thought you could sneak into Rhunsiire?" Elwrick asked.

The man didn't move towards his weapons, for which he had plenty. "If that were my intentions, I would already be inside walking among the elves. I came here intending to be discovered under the direct orders of Skylar Nightshade, leader of the Resistance. I have crucial information which must be relayed immediately to Lady Alenia."

Elwrick didn't recognize this man but knew the name Skylar immediately as an upstanding member of the brotherhood, who once trained beside Pegan. Elwrick crossed his arms and took a long, hard look at the stranger hoping to validate his identity. Beyond the cowl, he could see a pair of remorseless green eyes that held a primal rage, but nothing more. He sensed though this man was no rookie to battle and his weapons had seen their fair share of combat. "Who are you?" Elwrick asked.

"I am Miramar Darkblade, high ranking member of the resistance."

Elwrick thought for a second trying to determine what he meant by the resistance. "Well, Mr. Darkblade. The Elf Queen isn't taking visitors at the moment, if you have something to say, I am your only option."

"My message is for the Elf Queen, and none other," Darkblade said.

"Then our time here has come to an end," Elwrick said. "I am a merciful man and will allow you this one opportunity to return from the direction you came and tell Skylar Nightshade of your failed attempt to speak with the Queen. Most would not afford you this opportunity, so do not waste it. Entering the Whispering Woods during a time of war is punishable by death."

"Yes, war is coming to Icearaus," Darkblade said. "And the information I hold will reveal much about the true enemy you face."

Many elves emerged from the tree line and circled the stranger. Most held swords, yet a few remained at a distance with arrows nocked.

Elwrick watched as the man became translucent before fading back into existence.

Not far from them a silver portal opened, and Lady Alenia stepped out. Using her cane for support, she slowly approached Elwrick then took his hand in hers. Beside her, Ryul slid his second sword free.

Unbeknownst to Lady Alenia, Elwrick murmured a spell of protection on her the moment she arrived.

Lady Alenia studied the strange man.

"You should be at home resting," Elwrick whispered to Lady Alenia. "This matter does not concern you."

"Whether I am at home resting or stand here and see who intrudes upon my Realm. I am still Queen of the elves, and it is my responsibility to protect them."

Observing the Queen, Darkblade instinctively bowed coming to one knee. Even though she was older, she still held an awe-inspiring presence. "My Lady, I humble myself at your feet."

"Why have you come here?" Lady Alenia nervously asked.

"I have come here for multiple reasons," Darkblade answered. "First and foremost, I am not alone."

You could hear the elves ready themselves for battle, expecting more enemies to materialize at any moment.

Lady Alenia stepped back placing some distance between her and the intruder. Elwrick's hands held a faint aura, ready to fight if needed.

Darkblade suddenly realized he used a poor choice of words to begin the conversation with the Queen. "The others have not arrived yet and are still venturing through the Ash Mountains. As I speak, they are escorting the Clan of Cave Trolls to Rhunsiire."

"Cave trolls?" Lady Alenia whispered.

"We encountered them far from their homeland heading towards the Cursed Desert. Chieftain Ulgra believed he was leading them here, but in reality, was leading them to their deaths."

"How many more are there?" Elwrick suspiciously asked.

"Thirteen," Darkblade answered.

"You did not come here to inform us of the trolls, you have more on your plate," Ryul demanded.

Darkblade eyed Ryul. "You're correct," he said, followed by a long, painful pause. "There are a few of us who do not agree with Lord Malvo or his radical ideologies. At first, he seemed knowledgeable, respectable, and had brilliant ideas where he planned to take the brotherhood. In time those plans changed, and we clearly understood the errors of our ways. In the furthest reaches of the darkest sewers, Skylar Nightshade held a meeting, and a decision was made. Our only chance of survival was to seek refuge in Rhunsiire."

"This is trickery," Ryul said as the man faded in and out of existence. "This man has evil intentions and while we remain here, we may be getting attacked elsewhere."

"Why would we attack you elsewhere?" Darkblade asked. "Had I chosen, I could have easily destroyed all who stand here now."

"And you would have died before your first stroke fell," an elven archer said.

Darkblade laughed but never reached for his weapons. "Shall we test your hypothesis?"

Ryul licked his dry lips. He knew this man was no stranger to battle by the way he carried himself.

"Lucky for the elves, I came here seeking refuge, not war."

Elwrick could feel Lady Alenia's hand trembling. "I wish Pegan were here," she whispered. For some reason, she believed Darkblade's words to be true.

Elwrick pried his hand from Lady Alenia's grasp, then moved closer to the stranger. "If what you say is true, then why do you remain hidden behind the folds of that robe?"

"Because it cannot be removed."

Elwrick reached out to touch it but quickly jerked his hand away. Pulsating off the robe, he could feel dark, vile magic flowing through the threads.

"It's a lie," Ryul hissed.

"No," Elwrick cautiously said. "I don't believe it is. This man does not understand the repercussions of his actions by wearing this robe."

"What are you saying?" Lady Alenia asked Elwrick.

"This man wears a Demon-Hyde Robe, but I don't understand how it came to be in his possession."

"It is a requirement for all members of the Brotherhood of the Dark Prince to wear this garment," Darkblade said.

Brotherhood of the Dark Prince, Elwrick thought. This was the second time now he heard that name.

Lady Alenia looked concerned. "What's a Demon-Hyde Robe?"

Elwrick rubbed his chin deep in thought. "A Demon Hyde Robe is constructed from the skin of condemned souls. After its careful removal, much to the distress of the condemned, the skin is soaked in a mixture of demon and mortal blood until it turns black as burnt flesh. What the Robe truly does is still up for much debate as only one has ever been recovered intact. It is believed though that it defiles the mind and bends the wearer to the will of the Dark Master. There are a few requirements, though. One, it must be placed on willingly, and two, an oath to the Dark Master must be spoken freely with their tongue. After the inauguration is complete and the robe is gifted. It grows to the bearer and cannot be removed without the host being destroyed, and his skin offered to the Dark Master to create the next robe. Unbeknownst to all involved, there is a darker side to the robe. Given enough time, the wearer of this robe will mutate into a lesser demon whose only desire is to please the Dark Master."

"This sounds—troubling," Lady Alenia said.

"Very much so," Elwrick agreed.

"And what did you hope to gain from coming here?" Lady Alenia asked.

"Doing research, it is believed that one man has the abilities to remove this robe and save our souls, and that man is Elwrick."

Elwrick observed the assassin's actions. "And why would I help you when it is only now, in your darkest hour, you seek to change your ways. When you were in your prime, killing and plundering, you would have cut my throat given the opportunity."

"My fellow companions and I are not evil people. Yes, we have sinned, but are our sins so great that it does not warrant the opportunity to repent?"

Lady Alenia listened to his words carefully, not sure if he was lying or telling the truth.

Elwrick cringed internally from what he heard. Being a creation of the Creator, he knew every man was allowed to repent for their sins. To allow them a chance to change their evil ways and start living a life based on moral decisions. If he did not offer these men that opportunity, he was no better off than them.

"Time is of the essence," Darkblade said. "The others will need help with the trolls as they cross the Plains of Gedeon."

Elwrick sent a mental message to Lady Alenia. *I have to help them; I have no other choice. As a Spiritual Guide, it is my job, my obligation to guide those lost in darkness to the light.*

Lady Alenia adjusted her stance to one side and gripped Elwrick's hand for support. "If Elwrick agrees to remove the robes, I will grant you asylum, but there will be requirements. Before you're allowed to enter Rhunsiire, you must agree to a mind trace to reveal you're true intentions and must swear an oath on your lives to uphold the elven laws."

"My help does not come unconditionally," Elwrick said. "I also have requirements beyond those set forth by Lady Alenia. Upon removal of the robes, you must swear your faith to the Creator on bended knee. This means you will have to put away your assassins views and uphold a moral standing within the communities you serve."

"I will swear my oath now if that is what is required," Darkblade said.

Elwrick looked at the assassin. "You cannot swear it now. As long as you wear the Demon-Hyde Robe, the Creator will not accept your plea for forgiveness—"

"And I will not accept your oath," Lady Alenia added.

"What shall we do with him until the robe can be removed?" Ryul asked Elwrick.

Elwrick thought for a moment. "He is to be stripped of all weapons and remain under constant surveillance until my return."

"Until your return?" Lady Alenia mumbled.

"Yes, we cannot abandon the trolls. If they are caught in the open, they will be easily destroyed by Karayan's forces."

Darkblade unclasped his weapons belt and handed it to Ryul. Afterward, he removed no less than ten more weapons from hidden pouches and pockets. "I have nothing to hide."

Once Elwrick was satisfied Darkblade had no more weapons, he mounted Midnight and rode off into the distance, leaving the protection spell he placed on Lady Alenia activated.

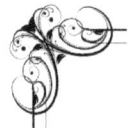
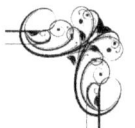

Chapter 77

 verie woke shivering. The house felt cold as a crypt, and she could hear the wind whipping past the window. Pulling on the thick fleece housecoat Jennifer bought her, she slipped her feet into the warm furry slippers she mischievously acquired from Sarah, then crossed the room to check on Robyn.

Averie smiled as she watched Robyn. She was beyond beautiful and her heart sank at the thought of her someday being jerked back to Icearaus. Unfolding the cotton blanket that hung on the side of the crib, she draped it over Robyn and gently tucked it in then kissed her buttery-smooth cheek.

Averie left her room, tip-toeing down the hall towards the living room. Exactly as she suspected, the fireplace was ice-box cold as the fire she started earlier was nothing more than fine ash. Pulling back the drapes, Averie looked out the window. The dim glow of the porch light highlighted the billowing snow. Not too far away, the silhouette of the barn mocked her. She should have retrieved more wood before nightfall, but she wanted to spend as much time as possible learning about Avicia. Dave and Sandy had been coming over each evening, and she enjoyed their visits. Now, she had no choice, the wood rack on the porch was empty, she would have to make the trek to the barn. Locating Tom's big winter coat hanging on the coat rack, she slid it on over her housecoat and made for the door.

"Where are you going, young lady?" Tom mumbled as he stumbled down the hall, one eye had yet to open.

Averie froze with her hand on the knob. *It was her job to keep the fire going, and she failed.* "I have to go out to the barn to get more wood for the fire. I'm sorry, I forgot—" she began apologizing.

"The hell you are," Tom interrupted. "If Sarah found out I sent you out in these conditions to get wood, she would skin me alive."

"But it's my fault, I should have gotten more," Averie explained.

"No, it's not your fault. I should have gathered some while you were visiting, but I was just as interested as you were with what Dave and Sandy had to say," Tom confessed. "All of us are guilty."

Averie relaxed knowing she was not in trouble. Not that Tom would have done anything to her anyway. Since her arrival, she had learned to trust Tom like the father she should have had on Icearaus.

"Fire up the kindling," Tom said. "I'll be back in a jiffy with some red fur logs."

"I'll help you," Mike groaned. "I wasn't sleeping all that well anyway and heard voices, figured I better come investigate."

Tom sat on the couch and began lacing up his boots as he glanced out the window. Even though they were triple pane Penguin Brand, he could still feel the cold creeping through numbing his cheeks. "This storm doesn't make any sense. We never get snow this early, yet here we are in the midst of a full-blown blizzard."

Mike opened the door only to get slapped directly in the face with a blast of icy air. "Jesus all mighty," he exclaimed. "We're going to need something to cover our faces."

Tom retrieved two scarves from the closet and handed one to Mike. "Here we go, this will work for the short duration we're out there."

Averie watched the pair until they vanished into the blustering snow and darkness. It was now she thanked the Creator for providing her with such a loving family. Had she been alone out there with Robyn, they both surely would have perished by now.

Averie did as asked and stacked the kindling in a crisscross pattern over the crumpled paper. Finding the box of matches, she lit the paper in a few places then tossed the burning matchstick directly in the center.

Tom and Mike returned to the porch, covered in snow, each holding an armful of wood. Catching their breath, they ventured back to the barn repeating the process until the wood-rack was loaded. Knocking off the snow before entering, they both came in shivering, red-nosed, and sniffling.

"My God, it's freezing out there," Mike complained as he removed his coat. "I'm going back upstairs and slip under the covers. Don't expect to see me until noon," he said as he yawned.

Tom curled up with a blanket on the couch while waiting for the wood to ignite. It didn't take long until the room warmed, and his eyes grew heavy, and he dozed off.

As dawn broke, Jennifer stumbled down the stairs dragging her tongue. Mike followed glistening like a wet slug.

Averie stirred the pulsating red coals then carefully situated three more logs on the fire at an angle to promote optimal combustion. She had remained awake, continually stocking the fire. Never again on her watch would she allow it to burn out and leave them cold.

Sarah tossed and turned, kicking the blanket to the floor. *The meteor grew brighter and bigger until it blotted out the sun. Every news station sent out warnings to seek shelter, but it would do no good as the meteor was moon-sized and hurtling straight at them. Screams filled the air; cars crashed into each other, and panic flowed rampant as people searched for an escape route.* Throwing her pillow to divert the meteor was useless as the cloth material vaporized instantly in the dreaded heat. *The impact was horrendous, and the entire planet shook violently as the smoldering rock clipped the edge of the earth, knocking it free of its orbit and sending it spiraling out of control straight for the sun.* Sarah woke in a fit of rage. Drenched to the bone in sweat, she no longer believed it was a dream, but reality as it hurt to breathe and her throat was dry as a desert bone.

Tom wished for a moment he had a three-foot tongue so he could lick the sweat off his eyeballs, as it was the only moisture on his body. The rest had evaporated sometime after he fell asleep.

Sarah stumbled down the hall wanting to scream, but she couldn't. Her throat was nearly clenched shut.

Tom rolled free of the couch, behind him remained a perfect wet impression. "Why? How?" he confusingly asked while spinning in a heat-induced delirium.

Mike ran his sweaty hand down his face. He needed an excuse, any excuse to vacate the premises, and didn't care how ridicules it sounded. "I'm going to step out and get the paper."

"Have you looked outside," Tom said. "Do you think the paper got delivered?"

"Well, I better check, you never know. Perhaps the delivery boy is highly dedicated and extremely motivated to do his job," Mike said as he fought with the lock on the door nearly blistering his fingers. Once outside, Mike leaned on the railing looking out over the new-fallen snow and basked in the frigid air.

"I better go with him, don't want him getting lost," Jennifer said as she slipped out the door.

"Me too," Sarah agreed, but heard the squeal of Robyn waking and ventured back into the inferno. Before long, they all gathered on the porch with the door swung wide open. Inside, the fireplace pulsated on the verge of a nuclear thermal melt-down.

"Why don't we all go back inside, take a cool shower, then go out for breakfast. It's going to take a week for the house to cool down," Sarah suggested.

"And they'll have the paper as well," Jennifer said. Very rarely did Mike go a day without reading the news.

Tom scooped up a handful of snow off the railing and rubbed some on his face. "And I can explain to Averie about insulation and why we don't need a huge fire."

On the advice of Sarah, Averie paid Tom no mind about the fiberglass insulation as her only focus was the enormous stack of pancakes the waitress brought.

Sarah finished first and pushed her plate aside. "Since we can't go home unless we put on sunblock nine-thousand, why don't we hit the flea market?"

Mike peeked over the paper and gave his sister a nasty look. "Can I finish reading this first?" he asked, then took a drink of his coffee. "I like to stay up to date on current events; you should try it sometime."

Jennifer smiled at Sarah. "Watch this," then flicked the backside of the paper, making it wobble like spread-out jello.

"Really," Mike snarled at Jennifer.

"I'll buy you a paper on the way out if it makes you feel better," Jennifer said. "We have things to do today?"

"Like what?" Mike asked as he slowly turned the page.

"Like go to the flea market," Jennifer grumbled.

Mike flipped the page again. "Whoa, hold on a minute, listen to this." Mike suddenly became dead serious. "A few days ago, the Mayor, Tony Pinkerton, was emitted to the Lane County Hospital after having his hand amputated by a garbage disposal. After several operations, doctors believed they had Mr. Pinkerton stabilized, but he died days later when a blood clot from the surgery broke free and entered his heart sending him into cardiac arrest, where he was pronounced dead a short while later."

Sarah covered her mouth. "The Mayor's dead?" The muffled words squeezed out through the cracks between her fingers.

Tom knew Sarah was on the verge of another melt-down and needed to do something quickly. "C'mon, enough of the news. Let's get to the flea market. We have sights to see and things to buy."

Mike tossed the paper on the table. "Couldn't have happened to a nicer guy."

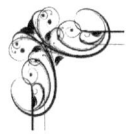
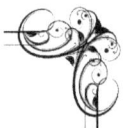

Chapter 78

kylar Nightshade altered their direction, causing concern amongst the trolls. By the next day, though, those concerns no longer existed as they were almost halfway down the mountain on a wide, easily traveled trail. Along the way, they traveled through lush meadows, encountered fresh springs, and the assassins kept their bellies full.

By noon the following day, the Ash Mountains were at their backs, and they remained hidden behind a landslide of boulders. The lead assassin stood atop a large stone and raised his fist in the air, signaling for them all to stay hidden. Swishing his fingers, he signed a large group of men approached on horseback.

Skylar crept to the edge where he could see, yet remained in the shadows. Coming their way, a group of twenty-five men on horseback was riding hard. Never slowing or showing concern, they continued on their path south towards the Cursed Desert.

"Why would they be heading that direction?" an assassin asked Skylar.

Skylar shrugged his shoulders. "I don't know, but Karayan is no fool and has put his evil intentions into play. That many men moving with a single purpose is no random act. We need to hurry before more come."

Chieftain Ulgra cringed at the thought of entering the Plaines of Gedeon. The cave trolls were more adept at fighting in the dark, in the mountains, or deep underground. In the open, their large, cumbersome bodies made them easy targets for ranged weapons.

Skylar moved silently as a shadow to stand beside the Chieftain. "Out here, we will be exposed to every eye. Karayan has allies everywhere, and they are watching everything that moves. We will have no choice but to move like the wind and be just as invisible."

"This we cannot do," the Chieftain said. "We have women with babies who cannot run, and our size is impossible to hide."

Skylar looked to the sky. "It will be dusk in a few hours. We will remain here in the shadows until then. Afterward, we must make hast across the Plains. I know an area about half-way there where we can take shelter from prying eyes, but we must make it there before dawn."

The assassin waved his hand again, signaling a lone rider on a black horse was heading their way.

Skylar slid his blades free. "We may have been detected by that passing group. This man may be coming to investigate. I will deal with him promptly."

As the rider neared, they could hear the thump of the beast's powerful hooves.

Skylar remained in the shadows.

The rider sniffed the air, then dismounted, leading his horse directly towards them by the reins.

Skylar came at him, forming from the darkness with both blades ready to slice the stranger's throat. Slashing outward, sparks flew as the steel hit an invisible shield.

"Skylar Nightshade," Elwrick said, he could see the assassin wore the same Demon-Hyde Robe. "I wondered when I might see you again."

Skylar stepped back as the stranger lowered his hood revealing his identity. "Elwrick," Skylar whispered. "I take it Darkblade has reached Rhunsiire?"

"To say Darkblade had Rhunsiire in a panic would be an understatement."

Skylar sheathed his weapons. "We currently have no means to cross the plains undetected. Rumor is Karayan has eyes and ears everywhere."

Elwrick reached out for Chieftain Ulgra's hand and grasped it firmly. "Good to see you again."

Chieftain Ulgra agreed with a nod.

Elwrick turned back to Skylar. "I thank you for looking out for the trolls. They are a good race, a peaceful race. Yet they are demonized because of their appearance."

Skylar agreed. "I have never heard of a troll attacking a single person unless provoked. Unlike the Rock Giants that attack anything without cause."

Elwrick looked out onto the plains deciding on the best course of action.

Skylar looked as well, but more towards the south. "A group of riders wearing the colors of Karayan, twenty-five strong, headed south towards the Cursed Desert not long before your arrival."

"Interesting," Elwrick whispered. "Immediately upon our return, I will dispatch a small group of elves to track them down and discover their plans. As of now, we must get the trolls to Rhunsiire. There is only one way to accomplish such a mass movement, and that is to get started. I will remain with you throughout the journey, offering protection from the enemies we may encounter. I have no doubt we will be spotted but less likely to be attacked with me leading the parade."

"What about Karayan? Do you wish for him to know the trolls have come this way?"

Elwrick thought for a moment. "He will discover the truth eventually, and knowing the trolls are in Rhunsiire may buy the elves some more time to prepare. Karayan is a wicked man, but even he understands how deadly the trolls can become when their offspring are threatened."

Skylar flashed the hand signal to his men to prepare to move out. "We will remain on the perimeter of the parade keeping the trolls engulfed in protection."

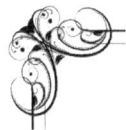

Chapter 79

rank had driven by this building a thousand times and never once considered stopping. The towering medieval gray stone walls rose up out of early morning fog like an evil monster from some Stephen King novel. The only thing keeping it from devouring the city was three rows of chain link fence, each topped with a crown of coiled razor wire.

Taking the sharp left-hand turn, he pulled into the empty, but well-lit parking lot and drove to a spot directly in front of the double doors. Printed on the tinted glass were the words—FRANKFORT CITY JAIL—in big, bold white letters. Inches below the name the writing continued—Visitors Entrance.

Shuffling through his briefcase, he located the approval letter from Captain Dunn, neatly folded the paper and slid it in his breast pocket, snapped the briefcase closed, then exited the vehicle.

The entrance hall was elegantly designed with white tile floors inlaid with an Inca design that flowed the distance to the receptionist. The walls were beige in color and thick with modern art décor. Stone sconces created a warm atmosphere, and glistening ceramic vases grew up in sporadic patches and were overflowing with stark blue flowers, which released a lavender scent.

Above a wide doorway was a wooden placard with the words WAITING AREA neatly engraved into the surface. Inside were multiple rows of gray plastic chairs, vending machines, a bank of telephones separated by a black plastic divider, and a giant ATM. A man in a yellow jumpsuit labeled—TRUSTEE—written on the back mopped the floor while humming a tune.

At the far end of the foyer was an octagon area where an older woman sat at a steel desk wearing an olive drab uniform. Her ashen gray hair was pulled back in a tight bun, and her attention remained focused on the overly large monitor. Unsure where to go from here, Frank approached the desk.

"Can I help you?" the officer asked without looking away from the monitor.

"Hopefully," Frank uncomfortably said. "I have a visit today."

The officer looked at Frank like he was an imbecile. "Visiting's closed on Mondays and Tuesdays." Slapping a few keys on the keyboard, the monitor went black.

"I don't understand," Frank said as he removed the letter from his pocket. "I have a letter from Captain Dunn telling me to be here today, and at this time."

The officer took the note and quickly read it, then searched the computer riffling through multiple screens. "You have a special visit scheduled; there's a difference. I wish they would tell me these things in advance; it would make it go much smoother in the long run."

After being searched twice, then walked through a metal detector, Frank was escorted back to the visiting area by a very polite young lady who appeared to nice to be working behind bars.

The visiting room was large and split into two sections. One section was where the visiting took place and held a hundred tables. Frank knew that because on each table was a large white placard with a black number. Large tinted windows spiderwebbed with white bars looked out over the city, and from here, he could see the University. The other side was split into two different sections. One section was a children's play area with a plush rug, cubicles for toys and games, and a giant rubber turtle with its trail molded into a slide. The other side contained a row of vending machines and a separate door labeled visitor's bathroom. Above this area was a large sign which read—NO INMATES allowed in this area.

"This way, sir," the officer said as she led him to table numbered twenty-seven.

Frank watched as a door in between the two sections opened, and Savannah hobbled out with a disheveled look on her face. She was wearing a bright orange jumpsuit with the words—INMATE— written across her chest, and her hair hung loose and uncombed. She moved slow, working the crutches as her right leg was in a knee-high cast.

Frank waited until she neared then slid out the blue plastic chair.

Leaning the crutches against the table, Savannah haphazardly sat, releasing an exhausting groan.

Frank leaned against the table. "Glad to see you accepted my visit."

"Excuse me, sir," the officer said from the desk. "All visitors are required to be seated while talking with inmates."

"Oh, sorry, I didn't know," Frank said as he quickly sat.

The officer pointed to the big sign on the wall that said the very thing she told him.

Savannah waited until the officer went back to doing paperwork before speaking. "I almost refused to see you as you're the one who turned me in."

"Yes, and no," Frank explained. "I turned in Tiny. A man lost his life for God's sake. Shriver was a good man who used to work for me. It broke my heart when I heard the news. It was the Fischer family who turned you in for the robbery. They had you on surveillance breaking into their home."

Savannah cocked her head sideways. "Why are you here?"

Frank rested his elbows on the table. "I'm here to help you."

"Help me," Savannah said. "The prosecutor already informed me I'm looking at twenty plus years."

Frank smiled. "The prosecutor is wrong." Removing a file from his briefcase, he slid it across the table. "Here is the plea deal my attorney has arranged."

Savannah read the file.

"All you have to do is sign your name on the dotted line at the bottom and you'll walk out of here before they serve dinner. You won't serve any prison time, or jail time beyond what you already have."

"And what do you want from me, a live-in whore?"

"No," Frank said with a gleam in his eyes.

Savannah sank back in the chair as his gaze hit her like a sledgehammer.

"I want the coins you stole," Frank said.

Savannah slid the document back to Frank. "I can't. The prosecutor told me the police took the coins for evidence."

Frank slid the document back to Savannah. "Okay," Frank said. "Then give me the two coins you legally obtained."

Savannah looked down at the paper again. Truth be told, she didn't want the damn coins anyway. Since taking them her life had spiraled out of control.

"Twenty plus years is a long time to sit behind bars," Frank reminded her.

Savannah took Frank's pen and signed on the dotted line.

Frank smiled as he watched the ink flow onto the page. "Excellent. This really is for the better. With Tiny gone you can start rebuilding your life."

"I hope so," she whispered.

Frank tossed the court document back in the briefcase and softly closed the lid. "I need to get this turned into the release department ASAP. I was told by Captain Dunn it should only take a few hours after the document was signed by all parties to get you the hell out of here." Frank looked at his watch. "I'll be seeing you shortly."

Three hours later, Frank waited outside the release door for his cash-cow to arrive.

Savannah hobbled out wearing gray sweats, and matching sweatshirt. Looking in all directions she released an astounding stretch. For some reason the air smelt cleaner on this side of the fence.

Frank met her halfway across the parking lot and helped her to the car. "I took the liberty to get a handicap parking permit as well. It should make things easier."

"Thank you," Savannah said to Frank as he helped her climb inside. With the car this low to the ground, she was having a hell of a time climbing in with her foot in a cast.

Savannah felt like crying when she saw her pawnshop. Every window was boarded up and covered in graffiti. On the sidewalk glass sparkled like diamonds and a big brown stain marred the sidewalk and gutter where Tiny made his final charge.

Turning down the alley Frank came up to the rear of the pawnshop and eased to a stop beside a large steel man door. Strung across it in multiple angles was yellow banding covered in writing which read—Caution-Police Barrier-Do Not Cross.

Savannah climbed from the car with the aid of Frank and hobbled to the door. Digging through her purse she located the key while Frank ripped down the Barrier tape and tossed it aside. The mechanism released a heavy *click* as she turned the key. Turning the knob the door released a resistant squeal as it swung inward. Reaching inside she flipped the light switch, then flipped it multiple times but the lights failed to turn on.

"The police probably have the power shut off," Frank explained. From his pocket he removed his cell phone and turned on the flashlight app and shined it inside.

Savannah covered her mouth. This was the first time she had the opportunity to view the damage. The wall between the office and the floor looked like Swiss cheese and debris littered the floor. The door to the sales floor hung by a single twisted hinge. Near the door was a large brown stain marking the location where she was shot.

Frank walked in first and made his way to the mangled door and looked into the other room making sure they were alone. Every shelf lay toppled and graffiti marred the walls. In one area sectioned off by the racks was a large pile of blankets, a stack of pornographic magazines, a small hibachi grill, numerous empty bottles of liquor and wine, and a rusty bucket half filled with what he believed was urine from the rancid smell. "I think a homeless man has moved in," Frank said. "Luckily we're alone now, but no telling when he, or they will be back."

"We need to go this way," she told Frank who pointed his light towards a rickety desk which now lay cockeyed. Every drawer had been removed and tossed aside and anything worth value was gone. "They we're in the top drawer, but not now." She pushed the broken drawer with her crutch flipping it over in case they lay beneath it.

Frank tipped over the desk and searched around on the floor kicking the debris out of the way. "Whoever is living here now probably has them."

Frank went to the other room and searched through the rubbish but found nothing. Returning, he had a depressed look on his face, but suddenly smiled. "I bet when they took the coins for evidence, they also collected the two you legally bought thinking they were stolen as well."

"They were all stored together, so it's possible." Savannah agreed.

"Guess we're taking a trip to Willowdale," Frank said. "Let's get out of here. The stink is making me nauseous."

"I did my end of the bargain. I brought you here," Savannah pleaded.

"No, not yet," Frank said. "You agreed to give me the coins you bought. We're going to the Fischer residence and you're going to demand your two coins, or we're going to file theft charges against them."

"I have no proof I bought them. We didn't do any paperwork," Savannah explained. "In the eyes of the law, I never legally had possession of those coins."

Frank helped Savannah back into the car leaving the steel door wide open. "We'll figure something out along the way."

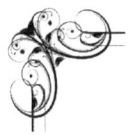
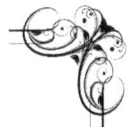

Chapter 80

hree days had come and gone since their arrival, and **Pegan** wondered if the dwarven council was ever going to reach a decision. In the meantime, he must have told a thousand stories. The dwarves were a curious bunch wanting to know what had transpired since their departure from the mainland. More importantly, though, the elders who still remembered Nendorühl wanted to know if their city remained.

On the morning of the fourth day, before the sun rose, Pegan was summoned to a meeting with King Fomour.

"What about my companions?" Pegan asked Horback.

"He only requested you."

Pegan followed Horback down a windy tunnel to a twisted stairwell that spiraled downward into the darkness.

Knowing Pegan's inability to see in the dark, Horback removed a lantern form a rusty hook, lit it, then handed it to the surface dweller. "You'll need this," he whispered.

Pegan held the lantern at arm's length chasing away the darkness. The stairs were narrow, uneven, and one side was open to a deep gorge. Now he understood why the lamp was offered, one slip, and the results would be fatal.

The stairs traced the face of the cliff for some distance before reentering the mountain through an arched-shaped tunnel. They walked for a time in silence before arriving at a large central chamber with massive pillars reaching the ceiling. From here, numerous openings where cut into the surrounding stone walls. Horback directed Pegan down a wide, tall tunnel with an intricately carved arched ceiling. Along each wall, statues of dwarves posed in positions of victory. The hallway traveled straight for some distance before climbing a simple set of stairs that spiraled up and to the right. From there the hallway continued straight but at a slight incline before arriving at a massive doorway. Inside, King Fomour and Gruvulir waited at a stone table that had been chiseled perfectly smooth.

"Welcome," King Fomour said.

Pegan entered, then paused. On each wall hung enormous maps and diagrams of places he never knew existed. "What is all this?

"We don't know?" King Fomour admitted. "We're hoping you could tell us?"

Pegan appeared baffled by the question.

"Let me explain," Gruvulir said. "It's only recently we've been able to enter here. When we first arrived, the door was sealed tight. Everything we tried failed. One night as the moon was setting, it silently opened. As you see it today, it is exactly how we found it. What has us concerned the most is from the stories you've told. It opened the very day the bearer entered the portal. You probably can't read the writing, but above the door, those marks translate into—The War Room—in your language."

Pegan walked around the room, holding the lantern high, examining all the maps. He recognized the mainland instantly as he explored most of it. There was also a map of what he knew to be called the Wilds. To the south of the Wilds was an enormous landmass named Eoforiun. To the north above the Barren Tusk was another map titled Iazira. It was only now Pegan realized what he thought was the world, was only a small fraction of what existed.

"Why did you bring me down here?" Pegan asked. "What bearing does this have with the task I've been given?"

"I didn't want to say anything because I believe your love for the Bearer is strong," King Fomour whispered. "But we believe she has set in motion a series of events that cannot be stopped."

Pegan became serious. "What do you mean, events?"

Fomour slid out a wooden chair and sat with his arms resting on the table. "There is an ancient prophecy which clearly states, when four golden eyes return to Icearaus, the world is going to experience a great tribulation that will challenge the very core of its existence."

Pegan closed his eyes and rubbed his temples. "Are you telling me Averie and Robyn are going to return and be responsible for the destruction of the world?"

The color drained from Gruvulir's face. "I told you it was true, she is the one."

Pegan's hands instantly fell to his daggers. "What are you talking about? What do you mean the one?"

"We still don't know for sure," King Fomour said. "The prophecy is long and very complex. Many things have to take place for the truth to be known—"

"I think you're wrong," Pegan was seething when he interrupted King Fomour. *To speak bad of Averie…* He let the thought trail off before someone died. "Averie is the kindest, gentlest, most loving woman I know. She would never do anything which would hurt another living soul, EVER! This talk of her causing something which is going to cause cataclysmic events to occur is a complete fabrication constructed in your demented mind. Perhaps it's time for you to leave these caves and come back to the world of men?"

"I am sorry," King Fomour said. "We must stay true to the prophecy. We will not be joining you on the trip home."

"Then my time here has come to an end. We will leave tomorrow at first light after I gather some supplies." Walking from the room, Pegan never looked back.

The dwarven guard had the door open by the time Pegan arrived.

Not far behind him, Tatum followed. She sensed something had gone wrong in his meeting with the King. "The dwarves are staying, aren't they?" she asked.

Pegan nodded, yes.

Tatum sighed. "I'm going with you?"

"No, you're not. The world beyond these caves is dangerous. How could I look your mother in the face and tell her I failed to protect you?"

Tatum looked around and splayed her arms. "This isn't for me. I'm not like the other dwarves. I need to feel the sun on my face, feel the wind in my hair."

Pegan looked up to the sky and watched a flock of birds fly west until they blended in with the clouds. "What is that way over there?" he pointed off towards something.

"What? Where?" Tatum asked.

"Way over there." Pegan tried to explain as he pointed.

Tatum's vision followed to where Pegan pointed. "Oh, that's a dock."

"A dock," Pegan said. "Who would build a dock here?"

Tatum shrugged her shoulders. "I don't know. I was born on the island, and it's been here as long as I can remember."

"Do boats ever come here?"

"I've never seen one," she said after thinking about it for a minute. "But I've caught enough fish from it to keep my mother and I from ever going hungry."

"Could you take me to it, please?" Pegan asked.

Tatum's pace quicken to a jog to keep up with Pegan's long strides once the dock came into view.

Pegan arrived at the dock and fell to his knees. Running his hands along the smooth stone, he knew without question, Nümribelyn also constructed this structure. "How could he have done all this?" Pegan screamed the question to the sky. "How could he have known?" Tears streamed down his face, and his hands gripped the stone.

Tatum took a step back. She could see his daggers glinting in the sun and wanted to keep her distance.

"He won't hurt you," Saress said.

"Saress, when did you arrive here?" Tatum asked.

"I followed you down from the caves," Saress said. "Reptiles have a keen sense much stronger than that of man. I know when Pegan is stressed, and something right now weighs heavy on his mind."

"Perhaps the woman he loves?" Tatum asked.

"I believe that is part of it, but there's something more."

Tatum sat on the edge of the dock letting her feet hangover

Saress knelt beside Pegan. "Pegan," she caught his attention. "Why did you come here?"

Pegan looked up, then around. "Because I was hoping to discover a boat to take us home. I knew there would be a boat here; there had to be. As you can see, it was nothing but a dream."

"No boat is going to come here; nobody knows we're here," Saress said.

"You're wrong," Pegan grumbled as he stood. "Nümribelyn built this dock for a reason."

"You don't know who built it," Saress argued back.

"I do," Pegan said. "What I don't know is why, when, or what for."

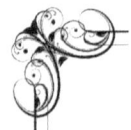
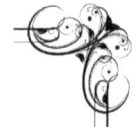

Chapter 81

he sudden ring of the phone startled Sarah forcing her to nearly dropped the eggs she carried. No one had to tell her; she knew each time it rang; bad news was on the way. Tom and Mike had already left to make sure the cows were surviving in this extended cold spell, and Jennifer was in the shower.

The phone rang again.

Sarah stood there, frozen, looking at the device like it was her mortal enemy. Setting the eggs down, she slowly picked up the phone and held it to her ear. "Hello," she whispered.

"Sarah, Sarah Fischer?" a deep voice asked.

"Yes," she cautiously answered.

"This is Detective Weaver, is Tom Available?"

Sarah relaxed, but only for a moment. *Why would the detective be calling them? It was too soon for Savannah's trial. What else could have gone wrong now?* She wondered. "He's checking on the livestock; can I take a message?"

"No worries, I can tell you," he said. "I wanted to inform you Ms. Henderson was offered a plea deal, and she accepted it. I won't be needing the coins or rifle anymore, so yesterday I packaged them up and you should be receiving them today. With the weather as bad as it is, I saw no need for you guys to risk your necks driving here to get them. You or Tom will need to be there to sign for the certified package."

"WHAT?" Sarah howled into the phone. "HOW?"

"She hired a well-known attorney named Jacque Beau who's known for eating prosecutors alive. He called a meeting with the judge to review the case and…" Detective Weaver changed the subject. "Regardless, there's nothing that can be done now. The good news is I don't think you'll have to worry about her. Part of her probation was that she couldn't have any contact with the victims."

"Who paid for this well-known attorney?" Sarah asked. "From my understanding she had no money."

Detective Weaver released a heartfelt sigh. "Frank Middleton hired Jacque."

Sarah covered her mouth. For a minute, she felt like vomiting. "How? Why would he do something like that?"

"Nobody knows what was going through his mind when he called Jacque. Remember though, it does no good second-guessing his motives, what's done is done. I highly recommend you guys put this ugly event behind you and move on with your life, or it's going to drive you crazy, trust me."

"Thank you for the information," Sarah robotically said. Her legs felt weak and she leaned against the wall for support. The bleating sound of the disconnected tone screaming like an alarm.

Billy sprinted into the kitchen to get a soda and skidded to a halt. He could see in his mother's eyes as she stared into space, something was terribly wrong. Flipping a U-turn, he tore up the stairs to get Jennifer.

Jennifer appeared homeless as she traveled the stairs two at a time en route to the kitchen. Sarah still leaned against the wall, her hand clinging to the phone.

"Mom," Billy screamed.

Sarah looked at Billy, then to Jennifer. "She was released."

"Who was released?" Jennifer asked, then pried Sarah's hand off the phone and hung it up.

"Savannah, she was released."

"What?" Jennifer said. "Are you positive?"

Sarah nodded. "Yes."

"Billy, get on the phone and get Tom and Mike up here."

The roar of the farm truck sounded like an angry, prehistoric monster as it chugged across the icy ground. Popping the beast in neutral, Tom killed the engine while the truck was still rolling. The moment it stopped, he leaped out nearly falling on his butt when his feet hit the ground. Gripping the door for dear life, he gathered his footing, then followed Mike inside.

"Is something wrong with Robyn?" Tom asked Jennifer, who sat beside Sarah, who sat beside Averie, who held Robyn, who was testing out her vocal cords.

"No," Jennifer said. "Robyn is, well, being Robyn. Sarah heard from Detective Weaver—"

Tom could see Sarah was flush of color. "What happened now?"

Sarah relayed the phone conversation.

"What kind of bone-headed, pea-brained prosecutor would agree to that. We had her dead to rights with the video, and it was obvious she was involved with the security guards murder," Mike grumbled.

"Detective Weaver said this Jacque guy had a reputation—"

Mike interrupted Sarah. "I know Jacque Beau. When I started my career in Frankfort, he was around then too strutting his crap like a rooster through the hen house. He's known for exaggerating the truth when it comes to why his client should be released."

"Why would Frank pay for her attorney?" Tom asked.

"Probably because he's a perverted old man and couldn't get what he wanted from Averie, so he moved on to her," Jennifer said.

Mike paced the living room deep in thought.

"I don't believe that's it," Tom said, shaking his head in confusion. "With the kind of money he has, he could get any college bimbo he wanted."

Mike stopped, then glanced out the window as faint flakes of snow fell. "I think the detective is right. Let's put this behind us. We're worrying about nothing."

"I'm not worried about her. I'm worried about Frank," Tom said.

"What do you mean?" Mike asked.

"I'm worried why Frank would have paid the kind of money he did to get a druggie out of jail. He did this for a reason. A reason we won't know until it may be too late."

Mike scrubbed his chin. "When the package arrives were taking it straight into town and putting it in a safety deposit box. Averie can keep a few coins as a keepsake. Other than that, nobody except Averie is going to have access to them. Afterward, we can hit the mall. I think Sarah needs something to take her mind off the phone call, and shopping usually does the trick."

Averie clutched the key like it was the only thing keeping her from falling off the planet.

"Relax," Mike told Averie. "I told you not to give that key to anyone, not squeeze it until it punctures your skin."

Averie looked back as they drove away from the Willowdale Bank. "And they will be safe here?"

"Yup, nobody. Not I, not Tom, Sarah nor Jennifer, not even the government has access to them," Mike reassured Averie.

Averie fastened the key to her necklace. "And this is where the key will remain."

The mall was unusually crowded, considering it was the middle of the week, and the weather was god awful. Meandering through the crowd, Averie explored multiple stores before deciding to buy a thick coat with a fur hood, knee-high boots, gloves, and a scarf. Sarah picked out a few things she'd been wanting, and Jennifer did the same. Tom and Mike were long gone off to the gun store getting who knows what, but Sarah was sure it wouldn't be cheap.

"What is a fire sale?" Averie asked Sarah.

"A fire sale is the sale of goods at extremely discounted prices," Sarah answered. "Why do you ask?"

Averie pointed to the Perfume Emporium. "It says fire sale, everything goes."

"That's strange," Jennifer said as she looked through the glass window. "Why would she have a fire sale? This store always had a crowd."

"Can we go in?" Averie asked.

"I'd rather not," Sarah complained, noting her sinuses, and distaste for the woman who owned it.

"I'll take her inside," Jennifer offered. "I'll make sure we don't have an experience like the last."

Inside, Jennifer and Averie were greeted by an older, dark-haired man casually dressed handing out flyers. Everything is fifty percent off or higher, he said.

"Why the sale?" Jennifer confusingly asked.

"Because Samantha stiffed me. I'm here trying to recover what I can."

"You're not the only one," a customer said. "The bank is mad as a wet cat right now."

"Am I living in the dark ages?" Jennifer asked. "What in the world are you all talking about?"

"Have you been living under a rock or something?" the customer asked Jennifer. "Right after Tony's death, Samantha's house burned to the ground. The fire department said she left the stove burning."

"Something like that," the dark-haired man agreed.

"Anyway," the customer continued. "I guess Tony was supposed to be paying her mortgage in exchange for a little slap and tickle. As it turns out, he had struck a deal deferring the payments for twelve-months. The bank reluctantly agreed since Tony was the mayor. Well, it appears the time has ended, and the bank wants their money, or the house. "Well, she skipped town so there not getting a nickel out of her, and the house is nothing more than a pile of ash and charred concrete."

"What about insurance?" Jennifer asked.

"It lapsed a few months ago," the customer said.

"And you know this, how?" Jennifer questioned the man. She had a feeling there was more to this story.

"Because I work at the bank and am responsible for serving the foreclosure papers."

Jennifer knew the man was lying. David Reinhardt was the foreclosure specialist at the bank, not this greasy haired little creep. More than likely he was the insurance agent and was receiving his payments in satisfaction, and not keeping the tab up to date.

"And that's why I'm having this fire sale," the dark-haired individual spoke up. "I'm trying to sell off what I can before her creditors come looking for any merchandise they can seize to reduce their losses."

Averie looked around in horror as people fought to get their hands on anything available. "I don't want to sound dumb," she whispered to Jennifer. "But what does all that mean?"

"It means you're going to get a hell of a deal on some perfume."

Averie nearly had to drag the bag from the store as they met Sarah waiting outside, who was eating a pretzel.

"My God, how much did you allow her to spend?" Sarah asked, noting the full-sized grocery bag full of perfume boxes.

"Thirty-five dollars," Jennifer proudly said.

"What'd you do, rob them blind when they weren't looking?"

"Nope," Jennifer said, then burst out laughing.

"What so funny?" Tom asked as he and Mike neared.

Jennifer relayed the story the owner told them.

Sarah stood there with her mouth open.

Averie dug through her bag and pulled out the large bottle of Versace Bright Crystal perfume. "This time, I purchased the big bottle," she proudly said.

"And tell them the best part," Jennifer told Averie.

"I negotiated the price down to four dollars and fifty cents."

"That's like a sixty-dollar bottle," Sarah surprisingly said.

"Averie was brutal in there. Damn near talked the poor guy out of his shirt," Jennifer told them.

"Well, Miss Averie SnowBriar, entrepreneur and perfume tycoon, I think you should see what kind of deal you can get us for dinner," Tom said.

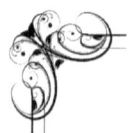
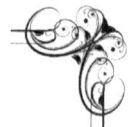

Chapter 82

he clash of thunder could be heard far below the mountain, reaching the ears of Saress.

"Perhaps you should check on Pegan?" Raestmond asked Saress, who continually paced the length of the room. "You know him better than all of us."

Saress shook her head, no. "Pegan asked to be alone, and I am going to afford him that request."

"What if he leaves without us?" Filaurel asked. "If we encounter another beast like that Hellshade, we're going to need him."

Ameria entered; her yellow eyes showed a tinge of red.

"Is everything okay with your brother?" Saress asked her.

"The dwarven healer believes he is going to survive, but recommends Dinko remain here. He thinks if Dinko leaves, he will die. Telling him to stay was the hardest thing I've ever done."

Saress hugged Ameria.

America lowered her head. "He's always been there for me, and now, I abandon him."

"I give you my oath. After we return with the information about the dwarves, we'll return to get Dinko," Saress said.

Ameria smiled. "You can't speak for Pegan."

"I know Pegan, and I know his thoughts. He won't abandon Dinko. That man will crawl here using only his lips if he has to, to bring Dinko home."

Raestmond burst out laughing, then slapped his knee. "Using only his lips." He continued to laugh.

The boom of thunder knocked dust free from the ceiling.

Pegan stood on the dock resisting the gale-force winds, which threatened to blow him into oblivion. All around him, the turbulent sea lashed at the stone structure, yet its stout construction resisted failure.

Angry, gnarly waves crested the platform threatening to accomplish what the wind couldn't. Pegan's eyes slammed shut, and he concentrated on the dock and wondered why someone would build it.

His mind quickly drifted to Averie, though, and he could see her face. See her clear as if she was there with him. Her beautiful smile, the way the sun danced off her hair. His mind drifted back to the day they exited the caves and the joy on her face as she spun like a ballerina. When he opened his eyes, they were no longer bleak pools of sorrow, but radiant orbs of mercury.

"Close your mouth," Sandy told Dave.

Dave blinked twice, his mouth still stuck open. "The letters left the page and floated in the air surrounding you as Elwrick initiated the spell?"

"Yes," Averie answered. "It was not only Elwrick, though. He had three disciples who placed their hands on the book as well."

Sarah intently listened as well. Each time Dave and Sandy came over, she learned more and more about the world of Icearaus.

"And when you arrived at the portal, that was when this demon thing came up out of the ground to stop you?"

"Yes," she answered again. "It was a hideous beast with a flaming sword that spewed lava. It was Ellusia who threw me through the portal the very moment it closed. Otherwise, I would have remained there, and Robyn would've died."

"Why would Robyn die?" Jennifer asked. "She, too, was becoming more interested in the story.

"I don't fully understand it either," Averie said. "All I know is if the child is born on Icearaus and is allowed to live, then another woman cannot become with child from the Creator and there will be no more bearers. Because of this if the child is born there, they must be sacrificed for the good of all."

"WOW," Sandy said. "That sounds barbaric, almost criminal."

Pegan pressed the stone tightly against his chest and called to Averie. *"I need you, Averie,"* he sent out the message in his mind. *"More than words can say I need you now. Without you, I am lost in a sea of perpetual darkness only you can chase away."* Pegan fell to his knees, gripping the stone until his hand went numb. *"I don't know what to do?"* he cried as if he was losing his mind.

"My world is hazardous, though. There are…" Averie's eyes slowly closed as she swayed to the side, falling against Dave. For all intended purposes, she looked dead.

"What in the world?" Dave screamed.

"No need to panic," Jennifer calmly explained. "She's having another incident, that's all."

"Let's move her to the floor where she won't hurt herself or anybody else," Sarah recommended.

The red necklace pulsated with the intensity of the sun.

"Sometimes, she can talk with those on her world, and each time she goes into a state like this," Jennifer explained to Dave and Sandy.

"The last time she became extremely violent exhibiting inhuman strength," Mike told them. "I recommend we all stay back until it passes."

This incident was different though, she didn't kick, scream, or fight. She laid there unresponsive, like a doll.

Pegan looked back when he heard something strange. It was an odd buzzing or crackling as if something of pure energy arrived.

Averie's lips had a faint smile, like that of a child fighting back the tears of joy. Pegan was more handsome than she ever remembered. His raven black hair held a few streaks of gray, but his muscles were every bit as ripe, and tense with energy.

Pegan slowly stood, who was this apparition that mocked him?

"Pegan," she screamed out and extended her arms.

A tear found Pegan's cheek. There could be no other. No apparition, no heathen, no creature of darkness could replicate the way her voice entered his soul and drove a shiver up his spine.

Averie ran to him, and him to her. Nothing, no angel from heaven or demon from hell, would dare stand between them.

The two met in the middle, falling into each other's arms and tumbling to the dock.

Lightning flashed across the sky, and the rain fell in almond-sized drops.

His eyes were fierce flames of silver: Hers, radiant pools of gold.

"Elwrick told me you only find true love once," Pegan whispered. "But that's a lie. Each time I think of you, I fall in love all over again."

Averie's heart fluttered at the sound of his voice, and she clasped her hands on either side of his face. Never has her name sounded so good, especially filtered through his lips. Closing her eyes, she moved her head towards his and slightly tilted her head.

When they kissed, the world faded from existence, and they were left wandering in a sea of passion.

It took every ounce of stamina Averie had, if only to pull away for a brief second to gasp for a breath of air.

Pegan's hand trembled as it rested against her fragile neck, and he caressed her perfectly smooth cheek with his thumb.

In return, she ran her hand down his back and forced his body against hers.

His breathing quickened as did hers.

Softly kissing her neck, Averie released a faint whimper of submissiveness, giving herself to him entirely and willingly.

Pegan tried to speak when they separated, but she playfully bit his lip driving him wild.

Pegan licked his lips tasting her, then put his finger against her lips. "Averie, my love," he whispered. "In this world, there are many evils I have crossed, and many more I have yet to meet. I make my oath to you this very day. If the time ever arises where I have to choose to protect me, or you, I choose you. I will always choose you until nothing remains of my mind or body; whichever comes first. I offer this vow to you now, and it shall remain that way until the last breath of life escapes my body."

Using the back of her hand, she slowly caressed the side of his face. "I accept your oath, Pegan Rhoe, and I promise you this very day none other will take your place at my side by love, torture, or death."

"Never again will I let you go," Pegan said after he kissed her again, and ran his fingers through her wild hair. "From this day forward, you will remain not at my side, but before me as a guide, showing me the path which I must follow."

Averie massaged Pegan's back. "I will not be a guide, but your partner as we explore all the world has to offer."

"I love you, Averie," Pegan whispered again and kissed her one more time.

Averie looked towards the sky, then to Pegan. "I can't stay," she whispered then softly kissed his lips. "The Creator is sending me back."

Pegan's face lost all color. "It can't be, tell him you won't go."

"I have to. It's for the best, trust me," Averie said as she glanced towards the sky again.

"I can't do this again," Pegan wept. "I can't watch you be stolen from me again."

"I can't stay, I have to go," she kissed him again. "Remember, I will never stop loving you, and someday we will be together again, forever and ever," she whispered.

"If you ever loved me, you won't go," Pegan cried.

"I love you more than you will ever know. That's why I must go," Averie whispered, then ran her hand down his face wiping away the tears.

The subtle thunk of wood hitting stone caught their attention. Alongside the dock, the *Albatross* waited. Captain Royston was half-way down the plank with his hand extended when Averie pulled herself away from Pegan's arms.

Averie walked up the plank and took Captain Royston's hand.

Pegan tried to follow, but he found his feet fixed to the stone.

"Please, no," Pegan pleaded to Captain Royston. "Don't take her," he begged.

"I do what I must," Captain Royston told Pegan. "I have no other choice."

Pegan remained there, screaming at the heavens, cursing the Creator as the boat faded from view.

***

Averie woke, her body slick with sweat.

Sarah was on her knees, screaming hysterically.

Tom was there beside Sarah doing what he could to comfort her.

Dave and Sandy stood back as Jennifer began CPR.

Averie screamed as the sudden pressure on her chest forced the air from her lungs, and each rib buckled.

Observing her gasp for air, Billy threw himself on Averie.

"Give her some room," Jennifer said as she pried Billy free.

Sarah saw the opening and wrapped Averie in a hug. Crocodile-sized tears ran down her cheeks and dripped on Averie's face.

Moments later, Jennifer pulled Sarah free.

Averie looked around the living room as if she'd never been there before. "What happened?".

"You died," Billy said in between sniffles.

Averie raised her eyebrows. "I wasn't dead. I was with Pegan."

Sarah could barely breathe, and her chest felt like it was on fire. "You stopped breathing, and your face turned blue." Sarah turned away and wiped away the fresh tears. "The necklace dulled… Jennifer couldn't find a heartbeat…" Sarah rubbed her eyes.

Averie looked confused by all the commotion. "I wasn't dead. I was with Pegan, and we were on a dock. I know now, without a doubt, he loves me. I wanted to stay—I wanted to stay in his arms forever. The Creator told me he had to send me back, or we would both surely die as I was not supposed to be there."

Sarah sat with her back against the couch. "You were physically on Icearaus?"

Averie thought for a moment. "Yes, in Pegan's arms on a dock. We danced, we kissed…" Averie smiled remembering what happened.

"Do you want to talk about it?" Jennifer asked.

Averie thought for a moment. "If I talk about it, then it will no longer be special. I want it to remain our special memory."

"Sure," Jennifer said. "I'm sorry that you were stolen from Pegan, but we're ecstatic you're back in our lives."

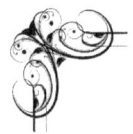
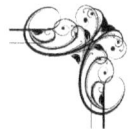

Chapter 83

egan's momentum never waned as he neared the iron door to the caves.

The two guards stationed there panicked. They had never seen anything, living or dead, which looked quite like Pegan at this moment. "Should we open the door?" one guard asked the other.

"Why are you asking me? You're higher ranking."

All the while, Pegan's mind remained focused on something other than the obstacle blocking his path.

"He looks inflicted with something…" The guard began to say, but allowed his words to drift off as the wheel located near the door started to crank on its own.

Behind Pegan, lightning flashed giving his body an unnatural aura.

The wheel continued to crank until the door creaked open wide enough for Pegan to pass unimpeded.

Both guards stepped aside, neither choosing to challenge the deranged-looking man.

Pegan followed the wide road down the center of the large cavern, then took a sharp turn down a narrow pathway that traveled between two buildings. Climbing the ramp for some distance, it eventually leveled off then snaked its way, tracing the wall high above the central area. Going through a tunnel, he emerged out the other side into what appeared to be a large housing community. Meandering his way through the streets, he arrived at a large two-story building with a man-sized door barely big enough for the reptiles to squeeze through. After entering, he lit a lantern and woke the others. "We need to go NOW!" Pegan demanded.

Filaurel yawned as he looked out the window. Across the cavern, large openings were chiseled into the stone ceiling allowing natural light to grace the underground world. "It's still dark. You said we were leaving at daybreak."

"I'm leaving now. If you wish to remain until daylight, that choice is yours."

"We need to gather our supplies," Ameria said as she climbed from her thick hay bed.

"We won't need any," Pegan said as something short caught his attention as it darted past the window. "Our transportation has already been arranged."

Filaurel looked out the window, trying to identify what captured Pegan's interest, but it was already gone.

"I don't know what's rattling around inside his mind," Saress told the others as she buckled on her array of weaponry. "But, I highly recommend we start a fire under our feet and get moving."

Quickly gathering their weapons and satchels, Pegan led them out of the cave and into a storm of epic proportions.

"Feels like a good night to be out," Filaurel complained as they sloshed through the mud and muck traveling down an unexplored trail.

Near the base of the mountain, Pegan altered their direction heading due west, not south, much to the party's surprise.

"The bridge is that way." Filaurel pointed towards the south.

Pegan paused and looked south, then turned to Filaurel, his silver eyes almost spit sparks at the elf. "Then go south. My destination lies this direction."

"What's this direction?" Filaurel asked Pegan, but the assassin was already out of earshot.

Saress knew it was the dock, and her heart melted. He wanted a boat to come here so bad he was willing to lead them all to their death to make it come true. "There is a boat dock this way. Pegan believes a boat will come here to pick us up and take us home," Saress explained to the others.

Pegan's pace quickened as he sloshed through the mud. Not much further now, he would be back at the dock.

Behind him, his companions tried to keep pace but were falling steadily behind.

As the dirt path turned to sand, Pegan's quick pace turned into a full sprint across the beach to the stone steps which led up to the dock's surface.

Saress ran on all four legs to catch up with Pegan.

Pegan scaled the stairs, and at the top, his heart sank. No boat waited for them, nor could one be seen on the horizon.

Saress cautiously approached as Pegan slumped to the dock's smooth surface. "I know you wanted a boat to be here waiting, but I don't believe anyone knows we're here," she softly whispered.

Pegan looked up at Saress; his eyes were a turbulent sea of mercury and water. "No," Pegan whispered. "I came here to fulfill a promise I failed to keep. Last night, I sat here for hours, and Averie came to me. We danced, we hugged, we kissed. I swore I would never let her go, and I broke that promise. Captain Royston arrived, and he took her from me. I pleaded for him to bring her back or take me with her, but he didn't. As they drifted away, I begged him to return. I can still see her on the deck of the boat. Her face was getting smaller and smaller until she faded from view. Eventually, the boat too drifted out of sight. Don't you understand, I have to be here so Captain Royston can take me to her."

Filaurel rested his hands on his hips. "No boat is going to—"

"I'm telling you she was here," Pegan violently lashed out forcing Filaurel to take a step back, and nearly falling off the dock. "Captain Royston stole her from me. He is the reason I broke my promise. He will be the reason I keep it. I commanded him to return."

"I believe you," Glorandial said.

Filaurel looked at his wife like she lost her mind.

Saress paced the length of the dock, then returned. She was looking for any sign of a boat having been there, but the violent storm destroyed any evidence.

Filaurel approached Glorandial. "We need to go. Each hour we sit here is an hour the elves could be fighting for their lives. Does our race mean nothing to you anymore?"

"What kind of question is that?" Glorandial hissed at Filaurel. "I value the race of elves over all others, but I also believe in the race of man, reptiles, and dwarves. Should we forget them and worry only about ourselves.?"

"No, of course not," Filaurel grumbled back. "I don't understand why we sit here and waste our time when we all know Pegan had nothing more than a dream."

Pegan could still taste Averie's kiss. "It was no dream. Averie was here in my arms."

"It is true, I saw it myself," Tatum said as she climbed the stairs. Dangling from the string of her fishing pole, a small fish fought to escape. "I was on the other side of those bushes fishing when I heard talking, so I snuck up the stairs and Pegan was lying on the dock, wrapped in his arms was the happiest woman in the world. When I looked at her face, I couldn't turn away. She was beautiful, but it was her eyes that captured my heart. They were the most beautiful golden nuggets I ever saw."

Ameria never heard a word the dwarf said. Instead, her vision followed the fish. "Are you going to eat that?" She licked her lips.

"This," Tatum pointed at the fish. "Why would I eat the bait?" Walking past, she cast it out into the water then sat down.

"You saw Averie?" Saress asked Tatum.

"Yes?" she answered. "And the boat as well. It was big as a city and had three levels with three large white sails, one had a huge *albatross* painted across the material in black. It closely resembles the one on the horizon..." She let her words fade away. "I bet it's the same one."

They all diverted their gaze form Tatum to the horizon. On the thin line that separated the water from sky, a small dot with three sails was visible."

"Got one," Tatum screamed as she fought with the pole. Minutes later, she landed a twenty pounder, which she offered to Ameria.

Ameria bit off the head, chewed twice, then swallowed. Afterward, she handed the body to Saress who eagerly accepted the meal.

"Can I go with you?" Tatum asked Pegan.

Pegan knelt before Tatum. "I need you to do something for me, something very important. You must remain here with Dinko. He needs to know we haven't abandoned him. When he gets better can you tell him that? When we return, I will take you wherever you want to go. But right now, I need you to stay here with Dinko, and your mother. She's not ready for you to move on." Pegan removed a small knife from his boot and placed it in Tatum's hand. "This is my favorite knife; I call it the Goblin Slayer. To me it is more valuable than all the others I have. This weapon is proof to you I will return, and when I do, you can have it as a reward for being brave in the face of adversity."

Saress could almost hear Averie speaking through Pegan.

A tear fell from Tatum's cheek. She wanted to go so bad she could taste it. To get away from the island and explore the world. "Will you take me to the city under the mountain?"

"I will take you there, and to places you can only imagine," Pegan said with a smile.

Tatum looked at the knife and her reflection in the tiny silver blade. "Don't forget me," she whispered.

"I'll make sure he doesn't," Saress said.

The rain wasn't much more than a drizzle by the time the boat reached the dock. "Ahoy mateys," Captain Royston called out from the upper tier. Afterward, he danced down the stairs and waited by a doorway in the bulwark.

Saress cheerfully waved.

The plank landing sounded like wood splitting as it hit the dock.

Captain Royston cupped his hands around his mouth to amplify the sound. "Hurry now. We must reach the open sea before nightfall. The bay here is a treacherous place in the dark. Landmasses rise out of nowhere and inches under the water lay razor-sharp reefs."

Saress hurried up the ramp first and gave the man an emotional hug. "How did you know we were here?"

Captain Royston looked at her like she had a purple tongue. "What do you mean how did I know, Pegan ordered me to come here."

They each spun in unison and looked at Pegan.

Pegan said nothing as he passed.

Saress waited until Pegan vanished below deck and out of earshot. "He has much on his mind this day," Saress told the Captain.

"More than you or I could ever imagine," Captain Royston said.

Saress suddenly halted, then spun back to the Captain. "The way you spoke, you make it sound more troubling than it first appears."

Captain Royston removed his hat and ran his fingers through his thinning hair. "Inside Pegan is a war, a war none of us can imagine. A war between heaven and hell, right and wrong, good and evil—and the spoils of his soul belong to the victor."

Saress didn't know what to say, so she said the first thing which came to mind. "Can he win?"

Captain Royston looked out over the bay. "If he doesn't, may the Creator have mercy on all of us."

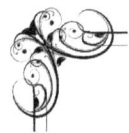
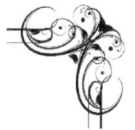

Chapter 84

he subtle knock at the door alerted Lady Alenia that someone sought her attention. Since Elwrick's departure, she chose to remain at her home, rarely coming out. Whoever it was must have had vital information as her two guards, one of which was Ryul, would not have allowed anyone to disturb her rest otherwise.

Lady Alenia opened the door only wide enough to see who waited.

Outside, in the shadows of the extended roof eave an elf waited flanked by her two guards. "Lady Alenia," the elf whispered, knowing his voice would carry in the still of the night. "Elwrick was spotted nearing Bullwhip Gully."

Lady Alenia scratched her chin. Bullwhip Gully was nothing more than a dried-up river channel that branched out like the roots of a dead tree. More importantly, though, it was only a few hours north of their border. If they had made it that far without altercation, there was a good chance they would make it the rest of the way. "And the others?" she asked in between shivers.

"I don't know the actual numbers, but from my understanding, it is quite the caravan."

Lady Alenia pulled her robe tightly about herself as the cold night air brought tiny bumps to her flesh. "Thank you," she whispered, "That is all, you may return to your watch."

The elf graciously bowed, then quickly departed.

Lady Alenia waited until she knew the messenger was gone, then looked at Ryul. "You remember the plans we discussed."

Ryul nodded. "I will see its completion."

Lady Alenia softly closed the door. She wanted to be there when Elwrick crossed the river, but it was not feasible. Coughing a few times, she laid back down and pulled the dense, heavy blankets up to her neck. Perhaps in the morning, once the sun warmed the forest, she would feel more apt to venturing out.

A sigh of relief escaped Elwrick's lips as the towering trees of the Whispering Woods came into view. Somehow, they managed to avoid an attack, but he knew their passing hadn't gone unnoticed. Before this day ended, Karayan would know of the troll's flight from the ravine.

Waiting across the watery border, Ryul waved to the approaching caravan and directed them in his direction.

Elwrick crossed first riding Midnight. The assassins came next—their Demon-Hyde Robes allowing them to walk upon the watery surface. The trolls were the real surprise. Upon entering the water, they revealed to all that despite their clumsiness, they were incredible swimmers and easily navigated the river.

Ryul raised his hand, signaling for the convoy to stop as the last troll climbed the muddy bank. From his pocket, he retrieved a rolled-up parchment. "I've been sent here as an official representative of Lady Alenia. The words I read from this parchment are not mine, but hers, and written by her official scribe." Ryul unrolled the parchment and held it out to read—*Hello, and welcome to the Whispering Woods. To Skylar Nightshade*—Ryul looked directly at Skylar—*I apologize for any inconvenience or miscommunication, but the assassins cannot enter Rhunsiire. Accommodations are set forth for you, and those with you, to be housed near the Freihn Sea until such time Elwrick removes the robes.*

"I understand," Skylar said. "Please relay the message to the Queen she has already done more than I expected and we will be forever within her debt."

Ryul nodded he would, then continued to read—*Chieftain Ulgra, we may not have always agreed on everything, but we remain faithful allies putting our differences aside when needed, even during the Great War, when madness ran rampant. You are more than welcome here, and the elves greet you with open arms. To the south of Rhunsiire are a series of caves we have vacated to allow you to inhabit.*

Chieftain Ulgra bowed out of respect. "Your help is much appreciated," he said in a deep booming voice.

Ryul rolled the parchment and returned it to his pocket. "As for you, Elwrick, Lady Alenia wishes an audience with you immediately."

"Follow me," an elf said to Skylar. "I'll take you to your new homes."

Elwrick watched the assassin's depart in one direction while the trolls went another. "How is she doing?" Elwrick asked Ryul.

"Every day, she grows worse. Since your departure, she has remained in her home wrapped in blankets."

Elwrick wiped away a tear. He knew her time was expiring, but it seemed to be advancing at an alarming rate. "I will see her at once."

Elwrick sat beside Lady Alenia—who remained wrapped in her robe and a thick blanket—on the balcony of her home well past noon. Far below, elves went about their business working, weapons training, or allowed to play depending upon their age.

Snuggling up closer, she rested her head against Elwrick's shoulder. "Ellusia came to me earlier," she finally said.

"I knew you wanted to tell me something, but I felt no desire to press the issue."

"She relayed to me the message Lilith wants to begin her training. I think it's too soon, what do you believe?"

Elwrick rose from the bench, much to Lady Alenia's dislike, then paced the length of the balcony. When he turned, both eyes were closed, and his fingers were interlaced. "I've been waiting to hear those words ever since I started my search for her."

"You don't believe it's too soon?"

"Not at all," Elwrick said. "Once she begins her training, she will grow substantially both in power and health until she is well beyond our control."

"Is that not dangerous?"

"No," Elwrick said. "Right now, she's dangerous, wild, and out of control. To have a full blooded Witch amongst our ranks will make even the most determined foe reconsider their actions. It may prevent this frivolous war, or at least buy us many more days to prepare."

"Then I will send word you have agreed to begin her training immediately," Lady Alenia told Elwrick.

"Have her brought here at midnight," Elwrick told Lady Alenia.

Lady Alenia made a funny face as if she licked a lemon. "Midnight?"

"Yes," he softly spoke. "Witches have a special ability called the Mind's Eye. It allows them to vacate their bodies and travel in spirit form."

"Like a specter?" Lady Alenia asked.

"No, a specter is a spirit trapped in our realm because both heaven and hell have rejected them."

"Hell can reject people?" Lady Alenia sounded startled.

"Yes, even hell has requirements to enter. Lilith, though, isn't a specter. She can return to her physical form at any time. After she learns to use her Mind's Eye, all future incantations are learned in the Holy Realm. The Dark Master cannot enter this realm by mind, body, or soul, thus protecting the Witch. Learning an incantation drains a Witches' power leaving them susceptible to both physical and mental attacks. It is at this point the Dark Master would attempt to strike them down."

"And you can do this?" Lady Alenia asked.

"No, not all of it. I can teach Lilith to use her Mind's Eye and a few minor incantations. But soon, her powers will grow beyond my capabilities. Perhaps she can summon her parents again who can take her further, but in time she will have to seek guidance elsewhere, perhaps from the Creator himself." Elwrick looked baffled. "Honestly, I don't know."

Lady Alenia sat in silence for a long time. "She's a smart woman; she'll figure it out."

Elwrick ran his fingers through his beard. "For all our sake, I hope so."

An hour before the ritual was to begin, Elwrick departed to the solitude of a separate room to prepare for tonight's ritual. He had not performed the Mind's Eye ceremony in centuries. Usually, it was performed by the mother and father when the child was shy of their fifth birthday, but for some unexplained reason, they chose to wait with Lilith.

With Rhunsiire cast in darkness, Ryul escorted Lilith in secrecy to Lady Alenia's residence. Along with them came Gleia and Ellusia.

Elwrick walked from the room unrecognizable. His robe was blood red with black trim and elongated sleeves that extended well past his hands. His face was clean-shaven, and upon the skin were rune words and diagrams scribed with ash and soot. Elwrick calculated his movements precisely, and his piercing green eyes remained focused on Lilith the entire time.

Lady Alenia hobbled out of Elwrick's way. Something about him frightened her down to her soul.

Elwrick reached Lilith, then snatched her trembling right hand and turned it upward to view the palm. Running his finger down a thick crease in the palm, he let it go, then performed the same action on the left. "Ryul," he said in a deep penetrating voice, but never looking at the elf, his eyes always remaining on the Witchling. "After we begin the ritual, there can be no interruption."

"I understand," Ryul said, but he doubt Elwrick heard.

"Gleia," Elwrick called out next.

Gleia felt naked when Elwrick's gaze fell upon her to the point she looked down at her clothes to verify she wasn't.

"After the ritual, the Witchling is going to need great care. She is about to experience great trauma, unlike anything any of us can imagine."

Gleia nodded; she understood.

"Lilith, are you willing to accept the incantations afforded to you upon this ritual, and not to use them for personal gain? To uphold the laws of the righteous, and protect the meek? To banish your enemies without prejudice, and protect those under you without reward?"

Lilith hesitated. She had no idea the process was going to be so complicated.

"Without a verbal yes from your tongue, your mind, and your soul, the Mind's Eye Ritual will falter."

Lilith closed her eyes; anything would be better than her past experiences. "YES," she wept as she cried out.

Lady Alenia watched intently.

"Then we shall begin the Ritual of the Mind's eye."

Elwrick walked Lilith to the balcony and held both her hands in his for a length of time while he quietly spoke in a foreign tongue. Afterward, he lowered both her hands onto the railing.

Lilith appeared trancelike as she stood there unblinking.

Elwrick skillfully used his finger to scribe a design on Lilith's face. One translucent green line connected the eyes, while a second translucent blue line started at her forehead then ran down the center of her nose, crossed her lips, and ended at the base of her chin. From the folds in his robe, he removed a purple pouch and poured a thin line of pure white sand around her body.

"This almost looks demonic," Ellusia whispered to Gleia.

"I read about this procedure in an old tome when I heard what he planned to do. The lines connect the body, mind, and soul while the Holy Sand allows separation between our realm and the Holy Realm. It is quite fascinating."

Elwrick waved his hand and on the air in the darkness silver writing came to life. Crackling and hissing each letter spit sparks setting the night aglow. Within minutes the words faded and the sky appeared dark as death. "Tell me what you see?" Elwrick demanded of Lilith.

"Nothing, it's too dark."

"Don't use your eyes; use your mind. Tell me what you see?"

"I can't see anything—"

You concentrate on the darkness, not the light," Elwrick said with a shout. "Free your mind, and your vision will clear. Tell me what you see?"

"I see nothing," Lilith screamed, her hands clutching the railing.

"You see nothing because you focus on the darkness and it clouds your mind. Don't look at the darkness; look through the darkness."

Her eyes sparkled silver for a faint second. "I can't; they hurt." Lilith cried out as if searing needles were jabbed into each eye, then twisted.

"You're fighting with your mind," Elwrick screamed at her. "I can see it on your face. Forget everything you have ever seen with your eyes, for they no longer exist. Clear your mind, and your true vision will follow. Tell me what you see?"

Elwrick put his hands on her shoulders and screamed out words in an ancient tongue, and Lilith's knees buckled.

Lilith's fingernails bore into the wood, ripping them free of her fingers and leaving them to flutter into the darkness like tiny butterfly wings. "I can't do it," she screamed, "My eyes they burn…" Tears streamed down her face dotting the wooden deck.

"They burn because you've never truly used them. Open your mind, allow the pain to flow from you." Elwrick hated doing this to her. It was always easier for children because their eyes had not seen the world. Elwrick was asking Lilith to forget everything she knew to be accurate and accept the impossible, the intangible, the unimaginable. Elwrick squeezed Lilith's shoulder's and released another stream of magic flowing through her designed to separate her mind from her body. Lilith's scream came in broken gasps, sometimes loud, sometimes dull, but none the less distressing and intense.

"Stop it," Ellusia screamed as she lunged at Elwrick.

Ryul was the quicker and grabbed her before contact, pulling her away.

Ellusia raked at Ryul's face drawing blood with her nails. "Let me go, he's killing her," she screamed at him. All her fears, all her trauma came raging back in a vision of vivid, yet torturous memories.

Ryul pulled Ellusia tight against him and hugged her with both arms. "He's not hurting her, he's helping her," Ryul explained, ignoring the blood on his cheek.

"My eyes, they burn," Lilith wept. All the pain she had ever experienced at the hands of Malvo or Karayan couldn't compare to how she felt at this very moment. "I'm blind…" she sputtered and choked on the words.

"You're not going blind, your resisting. Inside you are incantations fighting to be released. Stop resisting and let the essence of life flow through you. Release your fears, release your mind." Elwrick sent another wave of energy coursing through her.

Blood dripped from Lilith's eyes as they briefly sparkled silver.

"Stop it, you're hurting her," Ellusia sobbed as she buried her face in Ryul's shoulder.

"She's going to be fine," Ryul reassured her.

She should have already separated, but she was resisting to the point Elwrick may have to stop the ritual or risk her dying. She may have spent too many years living amongst mortals, too unwilling to make the change. He would try once more. If this failed, she might be beyond the age to make the change. "Do not use your eyes, use your mind, look through the darkness searching your soul, come out of your shell, and become the Witch you're meant to be. Make your parents proud," Elwrick whispered into her ear. At the very moment, he released another shockwave through her, he accepted her pain onto himself, and it felt as if his mind was going to dissolve into mush. Stumbling backward, he fell against the wall, then crumbled beneath his robe.

Lilith relaxed, her shoulders slumped, and she swayed side to side as if she might fall. The searing, unimaginable pain behind her eyes faded until she felt nothing. Fading in and out of consciousness, she no longer felt the cool railing against her hands. She was free, and nothing could hold her down. Leaping from the guardrail, she soared over the forest, which was bright as a spring morning. On the ground, she could see every elf, every animal, every bug. Flapping her arms like a bird, she caught a wind current and sailed higher and higher before looking back. On the balcony, she could see Gleia tending to Elwrick, who lie there unconscious, Ellusia wrapped in Ryul's arms, and Lady Alenia on her knees sobbing holding Elwrick's hand.

Elwrick woke, then scrambled to his feet and nearly fell over the railing. Had it not been for Ryul grabbing him by the robe, he would have.

Lady Alenia ignored the pain running through her leg and threw herself at Elwrick. "I knew you were dead; I just knew it."

Elwrick caught Lady Alenia. "I had to take her pain; it was the only way."

Gleia touched Lilith's dead, cold, eyeless face.

"She's not at home," Elwrick said.

"Where is she?" Ellusia asked in between the sobs.

Elwrick looked to the darkened sky. "She's out there somewhere soaring free tonight."

Lilith sailed over the Whispering Woods then out across the Freihn sea. Diving down, she ran her fingers through the salty water, felt the cool mist against her face. With a simple thought, she sailed higher then ventured out over the Plaines of Gedeon to Lynn brook. The town where she spent so many years of her life. She saw clearly through the smoke and haze erupting from the chimneys far below.

Moments before turning back, something to the west caught her attention. Soaring in that direction, she was fraught with horror. Karayan was there, and he had men destroying trees and turning them into massive machine's. The elves needed to know; they had to stop them before these things could be completed. Quicker than thought, she was back in her body.

Elwrick caught her moments before she tumbled over the edge. "You need to rest now."

Lilith looked around, startled. Her once vibrant blue eyes were now piercing silver. "I can't," she mumbled. "I saw something; Lady Alenia must be notified."

"You need to rest first," Elwrick told her.

"No," she hissed. "There is no time. The elves must be warned."

"What did you see?" Elwrick whispered.

"To the north, and west past Fairdenn, Karayan is there, and he has men building these machines. I have never seen such wicked devices with only one purpose, to destroy an entire race. They must be stopped."

"You need to rest now," Elwrick said as he brushed back her hair. "You have experienced much tonight."

"Put her in my bed," Lady Alenia recommended.

Elwrick faced Ryul. "We need this house surrounded by your most trusted guards. Right now, Lilith is at her most vulnerable. If Malvo has any spies among us, their main objective will be to strike out at her now."

"Consider it done.".

"What about these strange machines?" Lady Alenia asked.

Elwrick deviously smiled. "I believe it's time to test Skylar's loyalty."

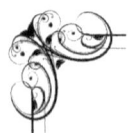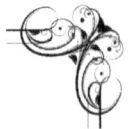

Chapter 85

rank lay on the bed, staring up at the white-washed ceiling of the hotel room. They had been here for days debating how to acquire the coins.

Savannah sat at the desk still in her pajamas, looking at the internet on her laptop.

Frank sat up as if he had a sudden revelation. "How good are your acting skills?" Frank asked.

Savannah typed in a new country on the internet. "I've never acted."

"You know, Averie's so stupid that if you looked the part, I bet you could talk her into giving you those coins."

Savannah scrolled through a few more pictures of Morocco, then closed the internet browser. "How so?".

"Get dressed, I'll explain on the way to Frankfort. We need to buy a costume."

Dave sat in the chair next to the large picture window looking out over the hotel parking lot, watching the faint flakes flutter to the ground. "I'm going to call in today and give my official resignation. The time we have scheduled off is coming to an end. If you want to go back, I'll drive you to the airport today and pay for your ticket. I'm going to hang here for a bit longer. Hell, maybe I'll relocate here. It seems like a nice little town away from all the hustle and bustle of the city."

Sandy came from the bathroom wrapped in a robe, and a towel slung over her head. Violently thrashing the towel, she worked to dry her hair. "How are you going to make ends meet? You still have an apartment in Florida with a lease, a car payment on a car that's sitting there doing nothing."

Dave yawned, then smacked his gums. "I've been pondering that as well over the last few days. Right now, I have investments in stocks and bonds that are valued right around Two-Hundred K'. If I cashed those in and was careful with the money, I could live for two, maybe three years before I had to find a job."

Sandy tossed the towel on the back of a chair and looked at herself in the mirror. "You know, if we combined our money, that would give us about three hundred and Fifty K'."

"You've been thinking about leaving as well?"

Sandy flopped down on the bed and turned on the TV. "I didn't want to say anything, but I've been thinking about leaving long before this even started. We've been partners so long I wasn't sure how to tell you, or how you'd take it. My kids are grown and gone, divorced, tired of the city life…" she continued to complain.

"Sounds like you made your mind up," Dave said.

"You as well," she fired back.

"I'll write up a few resignation letters and get them faxed off. I'm sure the hotel has a machine."

Sandy began dragging a brush through her hair. "We're going to have to find a house to rent. I'm not staying in this hotel much longer. As a woman, I would like to have some privacy, and my own bathroom."

"Whoa," Dave mumbled. "Hurry, come see this."

Sandy peered out the window. "That's Frank, but who is that scrawny looking wreck of a thing with him?"

"I have no idea," Dave said. "I think we should inform Averie. Especially after the bad experience she's already had with the creep."

"Well, let me put my face on. I don't want to traumatize them with my looks."

Dave and Sandy spent the better part of the morning driving around Willowdale looking at houses for rent, before heading out of town to the Fischer's residence. By the time they arrived they were nearly in white-out conditions as the wind swirled the snow.

"Have you both lost your mind?" Tom asked as he met them in the driveway. "You shouldn't be out on a day like this. The weatherman says we're looking at a good foot or two of snow, and that's not counting the drifts. You'll be lucky to make it back to the hotel, unless you don't mind sleeping on an air mattress here tonight? Hurry, up let's get inside before we freeze to death."

Dave shook off the last bit of snow on the porch before stepping inside and closing the door. "Well, we weren't planning on coming out, but we saw something strange at the hotel, and thought Averie might want to know."

As if on cue, Averie came from her bedroom carrying Robyn on her hip, and a diaper extended as far as possible away from her nose.

"She should be proud of that one," Mike said as he almost gagged.

Averie walked up, handed Robyn to Sarah, then went out the front door to where a garbage can waited on the porch, safely out of nose range.

"What's going on?" Sarah asked, as she held the door waiting for Averie's return.

Jennifer came from the kitchen carrying two cups of coffee. "This should warm you both up."

"Thank you," they both said in unison accepting the cups.

Dave took a sip. "Dang, now that's some good coffee."

Jennifer blushed. "It's my own special Amrita Mocha Lotta Double Drip…"

Sarah rolled her eyes. "She gets it from the Dunkin Doughnuts bag."

Sandy busted out laughing.

"Anyway," Dave said after another sip. "At the hotel while we were getting ready, we observed Frank leaving room one-twenty-seven, and he had this woman covered in tattoos with him."

"Trust me, he uses the term woman loosely in this situation," Sandy explained. "I would never say this about anybody, but this woman was ugly."

Averie returned complaining about the abysmal conditions, said hello to Dave and Sandy, then entered the kitchen searching for a soda.

Mike ran his hands down his face, then began describing Savannah.

"You nailed her to a T," Dave said.

"That's Savannah, the woman who owns the pawnshop. We recently discovered Frank is the reason she's out of jail."

"But why would he bring her here? What does he hope to accomplish?" Sarah asked.

"That's a damn good question," Tom said. "Averie," Tom called into the kitchen. "It seems Frank is lurking around Willowdale, and I wouldn't put kidnapping past him at this point. Until we know what's going on, the doors are to remain locked at all times. Don't open them for anybody without us here."

Averie looked at Tom funny.

"I'm dead serious." Tom had an angry sternness to his voice. "It's for your own protection."

Averie cracked open the soda can. "Okay."

"I'll kill the SOB, and proudly smile for my mug shot if he tries to come in here and take her—" Mike started to say.

"You'll only kill him after you pry me off his cold mangled corpse," Sarah interrupted.

It was nearing evening when the lights of Frankfort came into view.

Savannah turned the radio down. "You still haven't told me yet of the plan."

"It's simple, we are going to acquire a mid-century costume, and you're going to pretend to be from her world and tell her Pegan—the man she loves—needs the coins back right away or bad things are going to happen to him. She will believe you, trust me."

"And if she doesn't?"

"We'll cross that bridge when we get there," Frank groaned.

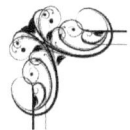
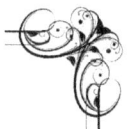

Chapter 86

yul arrived at the make-shift encampment to notify the assassins, Elwrick would begin the process to remove the robes. "I have been sent here under his command to escort—the resistance—as the location is only known to a select few.".

"This is much quicker than we anticipated," Skylar said. "But I don't believe you will find any complaints." Skylar looked around, then spoke with a hushed voice. "None of us will admit it, but we're terrified of the outcome. We've all heard the rumors that our souls will be delivered straight to the Dark Master upon the removal of the robes."

Ryul scrubbed his chin. "I believe if your heart is true, this will not be the case. Elwrick is a good man. If he says he can remove them and prevent your souls from going to hell, then I would bet my life on his word."

Skylar looked at the assassins who gathered nearby, then to Ryul. "We are… we are betting our souls."

"When do we leave?" Darkblade asked Ryul.

"Now."

Elwrick looked at lady Alenia who sat in a plush chair near the back of the large chamber. Across from her, Rhimdruzial floated flexing his tentacles. The mind-reading creature was aware of the task at hand. "Are you ready?" Elwrick asked Lady Alenia. "Ryul should have arrived by now with the assassins."

Lady Alenia glanced at Rhimdruzial, then to Elwrick before hobbling her way to the large tub and dipping her finger into the gel-like substance. "What is this again, and how does it work?".

Elwrick knew Lady Alenia would have questions as she recently arrived here herself. He had prepared the room in solitude, allowing Lady Alenia to relax in the comfort of her bed. With the preparation of the room complete, a hundred of the best archers arrived and were concealed high above the central chamber. It was only then Lady Alenia arrived under heavy escort. "It is Terrestrial Cerebral Fluid," he told her. "It acts as a buffer between the robe and its host interrupting the Cerebral Link to the Dark Master. Once the assassin is submerged in the fluid, the Dark Master will be none the wiser of the removal of the robe. If the Dark Master were aware of the situation at hand, he would recall the spinal link, which in turn would sever the life cord, thus killing the host instantly and taking the soul back down into hell with it."

Lady Alenia examined the slimy fluid by rubbing her fingers together.

Elwrick could see the worry in her eyes, sense the fear flowing through her veins. "You're in no danger," Elwrick comforted her. "Your presence will only be known once the robes are removed, and the mind trace is complete. This way, if anything is to go astray, none will be the wiser."

"Should we perform the mind trace first? Why waste time removing the robes if they show deceitfulness?"

"No," Elwrick whispered. "Rhimdruzial will be unable to get a true understanding of the assassin's mind as the Dark Master is the Father of Lies. While wearing these robes, their minds are his play toy, and he could have them truly believing anything he wants, thus fooling Rhimdruzial."

"This could be a trap by the Dark Master wanting me to receive false information, thus causing serious harm, even destruction to the elven race."

"Yes." Elwrick agreed "To make you believe in something which isn't true is one of his greatest deceptions. With the removal of the robes, there will be nothing preventing Rhimdruzial from discovering their true intentions, and those who reveal deception can be dealt with appropriately."

"How so?"

"Those who you tell me are true; I will place a blue aura around. Those who are not will wear red. When the process is over, all those in red must be executed. It is the only way."

Lady Alenia wept at the thought of the senseless killings, but she understood. "Thank you," she whispered, then kissed his cheek. "Thank you for doing much more than you have to."

Elwrick smiled her direction, then weaved a spell, and her form faded from view.

Heavy clouds shrouded the moon casting the grove into a perpetual state of darkness when the assassins arrived under Ryul's guidance. Near the center was a large tree with an arched door built into it. Around the door was a faint blue aura. To either side of the door, rustic lanterns hung by golden chains fastened to thick branches. "We are directed to wait here in complete silence until Elwrick's arrival."

The door opened with a resistant groan, and Elwrick stepped out. Behind him, it closed without being touched. Using his finger, he counted each member making sure all were present. "Good to see each one of you has found your way here," Elwrick said. "Before we enter the Chamber of Verisimilitude, I believe it's best to inform you what you're about to experience."

An assassin in the back eyed Elwrick suspiciously.

"After the robe's removal, you will encounter a telepathic creature who will explore your mind and discover your deepest thoughts. Before Lady Alenia allows you to enter Rhunsiire, she must know you hold no ill intent against the elves."

A few assassins voiced their displeasure about this procedure.

"This is the only way. Otherwise, you will be escorted from the Whispering Woods, and your weapons returned once you cross the river," Elwrick informed them.

"I have nothing to fear as my thoughts are true," Skylar said.

Darkblade agreed with a nod. "As are mine. I have nothing hidden that will tarnish my name."

A few assassins grumbled, but none walked away.

"If no one wishes to leave, then we shall begin." Elwrick faced the door which opened on its own.

Directly beyond the door, a broad set of stairs angled downward.

Elwrick followed them for some time before they leveled out and became a long corridor with an arched ceiling. Along the way, bronze-colored lanterns illuminated the path. Eventually, they arrived at a pair of plain double doors at the bottom of the second flight of stairs.

Elwrick motioned with both hands as if he was opening the doors, and they swung wide without being touched.

The room was daylight bright from magical lamps chained to polished brass hooks fastened to the alabaster colored walls. The shadowed ceiling lacked solidity, but the floor was pure marble, the color of a clamshell, and infused with golden veins that spread out like spider webs. At one end, a polished oak dais with matching podium rose up from the stone, and before it, fourteen chairs sat unoccupied. At the other end was a large Porcelain tub filled with a sparkling blue substance the consistency of warm, maple syrup.

Elwrick motioned for each man to sit, which they did except for Skylar.

Skylar moved to the front and knelt before Elwrick. "As I speak now, I believe I speak for all of us here today. You're right, and I understand the Elf Queen's fears to allow us entry into Rhunsiire. We have tortured, raped, kidnapped, extorted, and only the Creator knows what else. Beyond our words, how can we prove our sincerity that we wish a life of change?"

Elwrick listened to Skylar's words carefully. "That's why we are here today. For those seeking redemption, I offer that to you now."

Skylar rose from his kneeling position. "My words are only words, but my heart has truly changed. I don't understand the process, nor do I wish to learn it. As the leader of the resistance, I will experience the process first as an example to those who follow me. Whatever you need to do, whatever pain I must endure, I will accept for the hardships I have caused, and the punishment will be justified."

Elwrick guided Skylar to the steps at the back of the tub and directed him to enter. Knee-deep in the slime, Elwrick handed Skylar a breathing tube and told him to place the device in his mouth. "You must be submerged for a length of time well beyond your capabilities to hold your breath. Upon your removal from the fluid, you will be in a state of delirium as your mind reorients itself to the real world."

Skylar nodded he was ready, but Elwrick could see the fear in the assassin's eyes.

When the assassin was submerged entirely, gurgling screams could be heard filtering up through the fluid. Elwrick spoke in an outmoded language, and the robe slowly began to peel away like a snake shedding its skin. Reaching in with a large hook, Elwrick removed each piece and dumped it beside the tub in a large ceramic bin filled with Holy Water. Upon contact, the robe dissolved, and a faint wisp of smoke could be seen drifting off the mirrored surface.

In time, the robe separated from the body and floated to the surface leaving Skylar's nude body suspended in the bath. With the process complete, Skylar was relocated to a stone chair and fastened at the neck, wrists, and ankles.

"Do not resist Rhimdruzial as he probes your mind. If you do, it will feel like molten gold being poured in your eyes," Elwrick advised Skylar.

First, Rhimdruzial used his tentacles to search the exterior. Next, he guided a tentacle into each ear, and they slowly fused with the frontal lobes where the subconscious history of the assassin was stored.

Skylar's body convulsed, and his eyes fired backward. His fingers tightened and clutched at the stone armrests, and both legs quivered. More than an hour passed since the process started when Skylar was removed from the chair, wiped clean with a soft cloth towel, then clothed in a brown robe. His steps were slow, and his bare feet scraped the floor as he moved like a zombie. It took minutes for Skylar to reach the chair where he sat, hunched over, held his stomach, and wept.

Rhimdruzial relayed the discovered information to Lady Alenia, who, in turn, sent it to Elwrick. Elwrick nodded his approval, and a faint blue, undetectable aura surrounded Skylar.

With Skylar complete, the process started again as Darkblade voluntarily stood and walked to the back of the room.

It was well into the next day when the last assassin climbed from the chair and made his way to the remaining empty chair. Eight assassins glowed red, while six were blue.

Death came from above, and one hundred arrows took to flight. Eight assassins dropped dead never making a sound, their blood flowing like little rivers.

Nightshade's mouth fell open as he struggled to breathe, having observed more than half his companions die.

Darkblade fell to his knees, then lifted a chair above his head, searching for protection.

Elwrick made his way to the dais and stood at the podium. "Kneel," he directed those who lived. "Those who have fallen were deceitful, with evil thoughts and dastardly intentions," Elwrick said. "It is now you must take your oath to Lady Alenia."

Each assassin knelt, a few still wept.

Elwrick released the invisibility spell.

The lone clack of a cane against wood was the only proof Lady Alenia approached.

Skylar looked up at Lady Alenia, who now stood beside Elwrick. "What must I say?" he whispered.

"Repeat after me," she softly spoke as she quoted the elven oath which included such things as protecting the innocent, act in an honorable manner always, never lie, even when the outcome will mean your death and a hundred other commands none of them would remember. It ended with them knowing if they broke these laws, their life would be forfeited by having their heads removed.

All six assassins spoke in unison.

Elwrick whispered to Lady Alenia. "Would it not be quicker to ask them to all live a moral and honest life?"

"Yes," she whispered back. "But I want to make sure they each understand the expectations."

Elwrick smiled and rubbed her shoulder.

"With that said, I now welcome you into Rhunsiire, where you will be afforded everything as if you were born within these borders," Lady Alenia said.

"What about the oath to the Creator?" Skylar asked, looking up from his knees.

Elwrick rested his elbows on the podium. "You already have. The bath not only separated you from the robes, but it also washed away your sins. You must now walk a Holy life, an honest life. For those of you who fail." He directed them to look back at the eight corpses. "Only pain and suffering will be your reward."

Skylar climbed to his feet and gripped Darkblade's hand. "We did it; we're free of those horrid things."

"Don't be so quick to relax. We hastened the removal of the robes because we require your services immediately."

Skylar adjusted his position and stretched. "Name the task."

Elwrick went on to explain the situation with the strange war machines Lilith spotted and their general location. "We need to know everything possible about them. Being a human you will easily slip through their watchmen and have no problem discovering Karayan's intentions."

"Consider it done," Skylar said. "When shall I leave?"

Elwrick thought for a moment. "Removing the robe has taken a great toll on your body. Get some rest tonight then leave at first light."

"Shall I go with him?" Darkblade asked.

Elwrick thought for a moment. "No. I can't explain it, but I have a feeling your services are going to be required elsewhere."

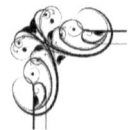
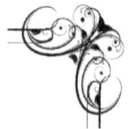

Chapter 87

 hree more days would pass before the *Albatross* made landfall at a rickety dock not fit for use.

"We are forever in your debt," Saress said to Captain Royston, who waited at the plank.

"Make no mistake," Captain Royston whispered. His eyes held a glossy haze, and his vision focused on something in the distance. "It is I who am forever in yours."

Filaurel neared, then stopped. "We need to hurry.".

Saress started to walk away when Captain Royston stopped her. "The evil entity in Pegan must be destroyed before its Master awakes it. I fear his mother cannot keep it hidden much longer. The time is shorter than you think."

"What do you mean? What are you saying?" Saress sputtered.

Captain Royston's vision cleared. "What are you talking about?" he asked. "I recommend you get going before your party abandons you." He pointed to the land.

Saress saw Pegan was leading them off the dock and into the forested hills.

They walked the remainder of that day and well into the next traveling through densely forested hills, and rich grasslands. In one area, they followed the bank of a swift-flowing stream before turning south and entering a heavily wooded area clogged with thick underbrush. Partway in, Pegan brought them to rest at a small meadow where a circular fire pit made of stone sat cold. "We'll rest here.".

Filaurel looked around. "You've been here before," he said. Not so much as a question, but a statement.

Pegan waited a few minutes before answering. "Once or twice, perhaps."

Raestmond gathered sticks and soon had a grand fire roaring. It would feel good to stretch out and relax for a bit.

Filaurel watched Raestmond work. "I recommend we avoid every town. Our odd party will not go unnoticed."

Glorandial tossed a few sticks into the blaze. "I agree.".

Pegan sat there in silence, watching the smoke curl up and float away.

"Something ways heavy on his mind, on his soul," she softly spoke, then thought back to what Captain Royston told her.

The morning arrived with dark clouds rolling in from the west. Lightning was in the area, and thunder boomed in the distance. Soon, the first drops of rain pelted the ground, and blustering winds whipped at their backs. Fueled by the desire to be home, to have Averie in his arms once more, Pegan's gait quickened as he led them through the onslaught.

Day faded into night, yet Pegan kept the blistering pace, and by sunrise, they started down the backside of the mountains to the narrow opening, which led to the Wilds. From here, they could see the very location they began their life-altering journey.

"We have to hurry," Filaurel said. "To get caught in the open would not bode well for our health."

Raestmond scrubbed his chin, which now bore a faint beard. "Perhaps we should wait until darkness to cross."

"In this rain and fog, none will notice our passing," Pegan said as he stepped into the open.

Crossing the distance at a pace slightly quicker than a jog, it took three hours to cross, yet they saw no other forms of life.

"Would the flatlands be quicker?" Filaurel asked Pegan, who methodically picked his way through the broken, and inhospitable landmass guiding their direction.

"Yes, but would also make our presence that much more easily known. We will remain in the mountains until we reach the Nymph Pass before coming down. From that point, we will follow the coastline of the Freihn Sea before entering the Whispering Woods. If we're not delayed, we should be home within a week."

Two more uneventful days would pass as they traveled across the mountain's gnarled face. Saress spent most of her time scouting ahead and reporting back anything unusual. This time upon her return, she arrived with dreadful news. "Near the Nymph Pass lies an army of men. There is no way to pass undetected. We must turn back and find a more suitable route."

"An army," Pegan whispered. "What army?"

Saress pointed to the south at a high ridge. "Once we pass there, you can see them."

"We've come too far to turn back now," Pegan said. "Let's have a look and weigh all our options."

Two hours later, Pegan peered over the ridge. Between East Haven and the Nymph Pass was a sea of blackness. Like a storm cloud that was too heavy to float, and this was where it settled. Pegan studied the darkness for a length of time. From here, his human eyes could not decipher what he viewed. "Are you sure it's an army?" he asked Saress. "Not a fog thick with ash and smoke."

Glorandial peered at the mass with her elven eyes. "Saress is correct. It is an army, but whose I don't know."

"Follow me," Pegan said. Carefully picking his path, he led them to an area much closer but still protected them from detection.

From this vantage point, Glorandial could view the camp in excruciating detail. "It is the barbarian army."

Pegan leaned against a towering stone spire and watched the men—who were not much larger than ants—go about their business. "Why would the barbarian army be gathering here?" he asked no one in particular. "It makes no sense and defies all logical reasoning."

"They gather here to strike at Rhunsiire, to destroy the elves," Filaurel said.

Pegan thought about what Filaurel suggested. "Possibly, but doubtful. There are much quicker routes to Rhunsiire. Besides, the barbarians are not enemies with the elves and have traded wares in the past."

Glorandial moved slightly closer. "They appear to be in limbo. Hundreds of tents are erected in the center while smaller groupings line the outskirts. To the north is a large archery area where straw dummies constructed into the shape of surrendering reptiles stand, and each is plumb full of bolts and arrows where vital organs are located. Near there is a large fenced area holding cows, oxen, chickens, pigs, and other animals. My guess is they wait to be butchered to feed the army. If I had to guess, I would say the entire town of Timber Hall has relocated here."

Raestmond rubbed his eyes. "They would never do that willingly. Something in the Frozen Tundra has gone awry."

"Something or someone," Pegan said. "Karayan's hatred for the reptiles is well-known and he would do anything to eradicate them." Pegan faced Glorandial. "And now you say they are using targets shaped as reptiles with vital organs marked. This news does not bode well for King Hulradeeh and the reptiles. We must capture one and discover the Emperor's intent."

Raestmond watched the ants move about their business. "Impossible. The camp's design prevents this very thing from occurring."

"It doesn't matter," Filaurel groaned. "The camp's location prevents our passing. We're going to have to backtrack adding weeks to our journey."

America nervously looked around. "There is a way, but we'll have to navigate the treacherous Nymph Pass. Once we enter the 'Anor, we would have all the help we need from the reptiles."

Glorandial tapped her finger against her chin. "What if we could lure one away, get him away from the rest using the darkness of night as cover?" Glorandial asked Raestmond.

Filaurel nearly vomited from his wife's suggestion. "No, I forbid this from happening."

Raestmond understood as well. "That would be extremely risky. If Glorandial gets captured, she'll become the property of the Emperor, to do with as he sees fit. The results will not bode well for her well-being, to say the least."

"If we must capture one, allow me to lure him out," Filaurel suggested.

"Won't work," Raestmond solemnly said. "You'll be perceived as a threat and the alarm sounded. We'll have the entire barbarian camp breathing down our necks. With Glorandial, we'll have a chance as the barbarians may chase her wanting first dibs before she's handed over."

"Then I demand we pass on the idea," Filaurel said. "I will not subject her to the possibility of capture."

"The rest of you move on without me through the Nymph. After you're gone, I will capture one. Their plans must be discovered, and King Hulradeeh warned."

"I'll stay with you," Saress told Pegan.

Glorandial stripped off her armor, undid her hair, and made herself much more appealing to the eye by ripping her shirt exposing much more cleavage than Filaurel desired.

Filaurel began to argue. "Glorandial, I forbid this—"

"You're my husband," she interrupted, "but you don't own me. If this is for the best, then it must be done."

Filaurel pointed his finger at Pegan. "If something goes awry, I'm holding you responsible, and you WILL face an elven council for the crime."

"Pegan has nothing to do with this," Glorandial hissed. "I am doing it on my own free will, and I have all those who stand here with me as a witness who will testify on his behalf."

"Nothing will happen," Pegan said. "If something does goes awry, I plan to charge in and challenge the entire barbarian army if needed."

"I as well," Saress said. "Either we all leave here—"

"Or none of us," Ameria finished the sentence.

Filaurel wiped the sweat from his face. "Okay Raestmond, you know the barbarians better than all of us. What is the plan?"

Raestmond thought for a minute. "After you get their attention, pretend you have another woman with you who is injured. This will make them want to come to collect both as trophies. One of them will have a horn around his neck as an alarm. He must be killed first before the alarm can be sounded."

"What a disgusting race," Glorandial hissed.

Raestmond sighed. "The barbarians were not always like this. At one time, they were a proud, honorable race. Ever since Emperor Tak-Thukmand was appointed..." he let his words fade away. "They are nothing more than savages. Disgusting creatures I don't even consider human."

"I'm sorry," Pegan said. "It must hurt knowing the people you came from degenerated to this point."

"You're no exception," Raestmond said to Pegan. "You came from a group of murderers and rapists."

Pegan nodded his head. "And some of the things I've seen still haunt my dreams."

The shadowed moon and blotted-out stars were both a blessing and a curse.

Pegan guided them strictly by feel as any light would have easily allowed their detection. Moving at a pace not much faster than a snail, he skillfully guided them down the haphazard trail of broken razor-sharp stones and deathly-steep drop-offs.

It was well beyond midnight before reaching the bottom. Luckily, the fire's roar and whoosh as it consumed all oxygen nearby, combined with the obnoxiously loud conversation of drunken men arguing or bragging muffled any sound they made.

Glorandial took a deep breath. "May the Creator bless me this night and guide my actions," she whispered a quick prayer.

Filaurel mumbled something and looked away.

"Ready yourselves," Pegan whispered as he slid his daggers free. "A delay now could be fatal for Glorandial."

Saress snatched a handful of arrows from Filaurel. To use a magical arrow would reveal their location. She didn't want to admit it, not to Filaurel, or herself, but it felt good hearing the nock snap onto the string and watching the arrow slide into place.

"Saress," Pegan whispered. "It falls on you to locate the one with the horn."

"I can't right now," she whispered. "In this darkness, they will spot my eyes. I have to wait until the barbarians get closer."

Glorandial crept to where she was inches from the light, but still out of view then took a minute to gather her composure. In her eyes, even the smallest of the five men sitting near the fire drinking and talking were huge, and now she wondered if this may have been a mistake. Luckily, all the men were on the near side of the fire. The wind shifted coating her in black oily smoke, thus concealing her presence even more. Turning slightly away to keep her eyes from burning, she waited until the wind changed again then stepped within view. "Can one of you help me, my daughter has fallen, and I think she broke her leg," Glorandial said.

Caught by surprise and utter embarrassment, the five men jumped to their feet and reached for their weapons. One man glowed like an eclipse as his body blocked all light from the fire. Lost in a drunken, lust-filled rage, his night of complaining suddenly took a turn for the better. "She's mine," he snarled to the others, then slid a massive steel-headed mace free from his belt loop.

"The wounded one is mine then." A second barbarian staked his claim to the prize.

"Take us to her," the mountain of a man thick with furs said in a pleasant voice. "Outside our encampment, it's too dangerous for women to be alone."

Glorandial backed away then broke into a jog. She could have easily outrun them, but she slowed her pace remaining at the very edge of their view. She knew the chase was part of the game, and her capture would make the reward all that much sweeter.

Saress allowed her eyes to blink into the thermal spectrum. "Here they come, she has five barbarians chasing her."

Filaurel drew back his bowstring.

"Not yet," Pegan whispered. "Wait until my word."

The barbarian sensed his error and cranked back the lever on his crossbow and fired at what he believed was the woman. The shot was inaccurate at best, and the bolt ricocheted off nearby stones sending sparks sailing.

Glorandial could hear the pounding of feet getting closer. Before her, the outline of her companions waited. *I'm going to make it*, she thought, then a piercing pain in her calf stifled her progress. Gripping her leg, she tumbled to the ground slamming her face into a jagged stone tearing the skin from her cheek. She wanted to scream, to cry out for help, but to do so would reveal them to the nearby sentries. Gripping at the bolt to rip it free, she bit her tongue as the shaft did more damage each time she tugged.

"She's down, she's down," Saress mumbled in a rush.

Pegan flew in action, leaping over a horse-sized stone and bolted towards the barbarians at a full sprint.

Saress located the barbarian with the horn and fired. The arrow flew true, and it severed both arteries and destroyed the voice box.

Gripping his throat, the barbarian tried to scream but only the slightest gurgling sounds were made.

Glorandial tried to crawl, but the bolt wedged itself between two stones trapping her leg. Above her, she could sense the largest of the group arrive. See his yellow teeth as he smiled. Hear the sound of the weapon dropping to the ground as he began to unbuckle his pants.

Filaurel waited for a few seconds to ready his aim. He was not gifted like Saress, so he had to be proof positive of his target before letting the arrow fly.

The twang of the bowstring cut through the air as the arrow sped away.

The lust-filled barbarians were oblivious of their dead companion, or Pegan quickly approaching.

Glorandial's nightmares were all coming true when she heard the barbarian's weapons belt hit the ground.

"I'm going to make you my—"

The barbarian suddenly went rigid, and his fingers curled into fists before he fell forward. His sheer weight snapped the bone inches above her knee as he landed across her. Black blood pumped from the hole through his face staining her hair and clothes. Trying to move, she could feel his blood surround her.

A third barbarian died instantly as the arrow Saress fired broke out what few teeth the brute had and blew out the back of his neck, severing the spine.

Filaurel nocked another arrow, but in the darkness was having a hard time focusing as Pegan's cat-like reflexes made him appear to be everywhere.

Fear and panic raced into the remaining barbarians, and they tried to retreat when Pegan materialized from the darkness.

Pegan tore past with both blades slashing in a flurry fueled by hatred. Now was not the time for intricate movements designed to baffle his opponent, or show his skill with a blade. Now was the time for killing. The barbarian continued to run for a good number of paces before the body realized the head was gone, then collapsed.

Filaurel aimed at the last one.

The barbarian spun in circles, confused which way to flee as there was movement all around him.

Pegan came in from behind with the pommel of his dagger towards the enemy to render the barbarian unconscious.

Filaurel fired low with a shot designed to cripple the barbarian.

The barbarian leaped out of the way sensing the shot.

Pegan sprung towards the barbarian when an intense pain drove him to both knees. Looking down, he could see the gaping hole through the palm, the tendons hanging, and bone chunks falling.

Ameria entered the fray twirling her staff like a propeller.

The barbarian raised his giant sword, the nicks in the blade evidence of its recent use.

Ameria was the quicker taking the feet out from under the barbarian, then spun back, twisted at an angle, then landed hard with the blunt end of her staff connecting with the barbarians forehead leaving him dazed. The second blow from the staff rendered the large man unconscious.

Pegan climbed back to his feet, his head swooned, and his balance faltered. Crashing back to his knees, he tried to grab the weapon, but his fingers failed to function.

Glorandial trembled, and her face was ghost-white pale.

Saress quickly bound the unconscious barbarian.

"Easy now," Filaurel whispered to Glorandial. "Bite down hard on this," he said as he placed a chunk of wood in her mouth. Waiting for a few seconds, he snapped the bolt then pulled the shaft free.

Glorandial fainted from the pain.

Ameria scooped up Pegan, who mumbled in a pain-filled state of delirium.

Raestmond collected Glorandial's armor and Pegan's dagger.

Ameria knew the area and led the party into the darkness towards the Nymph Pass. The capture was a success, but at a substantial cost.

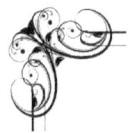
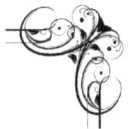

Chapter 88

he rim of the Nymph Pass arrived like the edge of a sharp knife. One moment there was upturned ground heavy with broken stones and littered debris, then there was nothing as if that piece of the world broke away and fell off the planet. Ameria followed the rim for a time until arriving at a sloped path, which traced the edge of a sheer face wall. "This is the only way in or out."

Filaurel lowered Glorandial to the ground, then stretch his aching back.

Raestmond examined the wound, then tore away a piece of his shirt and covered the wound. "It's not the best but will suffice for now. Luckily, it appears to have missed the major artery running through the leg. It's painful, but not terminal, as long as it doesn't become infected."

Pegan mumbled incoherently, and his eyes were nothing more than dark pools of shock.

Raestmond examined Pegan next, and his face turned grim. "Pegan isn't so lucky. The deep artery which feeds his fingers is severed." Using a piece of twine, he tied a tourniquet partway up the arm. "We'll have to release this every so often or he'll lose his hand, possibly his life."

Saress grabbed the prisoner by his neck and lifted him off the ground. "If he dies because of you, words cannot describe the amount of suffering I am going to put you through."

The barbarian attempted to chew through the gag.

Filaurel looked away. He knew it was his arrow that did the damage, not something caused by the barbarian.

Resting a bit longer, they waited until the sky revealed the first signs of life before venturing into the Nymph Pass.

It was only now they understood the severity of the situation. The Nymph Pass was comprised of sheer granite ledges and covered in a fine powder, which made each step more treacherous than the last. Partway down, Ameria ordered them to stop on a broad shelf where the single path split off in many directions. "We need to rest," she groaned, then lowered Pegan to the stone floor.

Filaurel positioned Glorandial to where her back rested against the smooth stone face then wiped the sweat from her face.

Glorandial woke up screaming as if she'd been set on fire and tried to stand.

"We must keep moving," Raestmond pleaded. There was a sense of urgency in his voice that caught their attention. "I'm positive the barbarians have discovered the bodies by now and are organizing a search party to find those responsible."

Filaurel worked diligently to calm Glorandial, reassuring her it wasn't as bad as it felt, but he knew otherwise.

Saress moved away and glanced up at the rim. "Where we currently sit, the ledge conceals our location," Saress said. "Besides, I don't believe they would expect anyone to enter the Nymph Pass."

"Barbarians don't hunt as we do, they hunt by scent—"

"They use dogs," Saress said. She remembered her first encounter with the barbarians, and the scar from that encounter remained on her leg.

"They'll track us to the edge of Rhunsiire if needed to avenge the death of their brothers," Raestmond informed them.

Pegan tried to stand, but his vision blurred, and he collapsed to his knees, dropping Fel-Strike.

"What are you trying to do?" Raestmond asked Pegan. "You're in no condition to stand."

Pegan swayed side to side as he repeatedly tried to pick up Fel-Strike, yet the weapon avoided his grasp. "We must fight them.".

"You're not fighting anybody," Raestmond told Pegan. "You've lost enough blood as it is. Any more, and you won't survive to see the bottom."

Saress stepped out but quickly jumped back as a bolt whizzed past. "Well, they know where here."

"How far is it to the bottom?" Filaurel asked Ameria.

America looked down at the 'Anor. "I could do it in a few hours, but with two wounded and a prisoner refusing to walk. A good day, perhaps longer."

Thwack! A bolt bounced off a nearby stone.

Saress glanced out, then readied her bow. Where the arrow should have been, a blue shaft of pure energy formed. Locating the one who fired, she aimed, then released the string. The electric blue arrow screamed towards the enemy. Seconds later, they watched a barbarian bounce by with a fist-sized hole through his chest. Behind him, a broken crossbow followed.

"We can't stay here forever, we have to go," Filaurel said as he watched Saress release another arrow. Moments later, a barbarian tumbled past. The loose skin which once formed his neck flopped like a flag in the breeze as the headless body faded in the distance.

"If we step out, we'll be easy targets. The only thing keeping them back now is Saress. Eventually, they will come in troves and overwhelm us," Raestmond explained.

Filaurel pointed to an unobstructed path not much farther down the Pass. "If we can get to that location, we'll be out of their range."

"I wouldn't go—" Ameria started to explain.

"Then you can wait here and get turned into a pair of boots. I have no desire to get captured and skinned alive." Picking up Glorandial, he made his way towards the path.

"Why don't you listen to her, she knows the Nymph better than all of us," Saress yelled to Filaurel.

"Listen here, bug breath," Filaurel hissed. "If you want to stay, you can. Glorandial and I are getting off this forsaken rock."

Saress released a long-winded breath then sniffed the air. "I haven't eaten a bug since I was a hatchling." Eventually, she turned to Ameria and asked, "do I have bug breath?"

Ameria sighed, then allowed her shoulders to slump.

"Get Pegan ready to move," Saress told Ameria, then lifted the barbarian to his feet using his scraggly hair.

Filaurel led them down the path, which soon turned deathly narrow and dangerously sloped away from the smooth mountain wall as it rounded the bend. Each step should have been their last, yet somehow, they survived. Beyond the curve, the trail leveled off, and they made decent time until encountering a sheer drop.

Filaurel peered over the edge. "I can see the bottom. It's maybe twenty feet down."

Higher up the pass, they heard the faint echo of dogs barking.

"We need to keep going," Filaurel demanded. "It sounds like they may be gaining on our location."

"I wouldn't—"

"Shut up," Filaurel screamed at Ameria. "Had Pegan listened, we wouldn't be in this predicament."

Filaurel lowered Glorandial to the ground. "Once I reach the bottom, lower her down."

Ameria looked at Saress for help. "Why won't he listen to me?"

Saress shook her head. "I don't know, but we have to stick together."

Filaurel hung from the edge, then dropped. Almost instantly, a loud thump echoed off the stone walls. "Okay, lower her down."

It took a bit, but soon, they all stood at the bottom, looking back at the sheer wall.

"If they follow us now, they'll become easy targets," Filaurel said.

The path continued at a downward angle for some distance then abruptly began to climb and snake its way back up the side of the Nymph Pass. Soon, they arrived at a sheer drop whose bottom was nothing more than a swirling mist. It was now Filaurel realized why Ameria warned him not to go this way. "We're trapped," Filaurel angrily snarled.

Ameria opened her mouth to speak, then slowly closed her maw. To say she told him so would not help their situation.

"How many barbarians are there?" Pegan fought with each word.

"Too many to fight," Raestmond said.

Filaurel closed his eyes and shook his head. "If you only would have listened to me."

"I don't think they know we took this route, so we have some time," Saress said.

"It's only a matter of time before they find us," Raestmond said.

Saress had a sudden revelation and placed her hands on Ameria's shoulders. "Ameria, can you get down from here?"

"Yes," she answered.

Saress hugged Ameria. "You're our only hope. You need to get to the 'Anor and find help. The reptiles need to know we're trapped up here and fighting for our lives. You have to do this; failure isn't an option. Run like the Bunyip chases you."

"What's a Bunyip?" Raestmond asked after Ameria was gone.

"It is a mythical beast said to roam the swamp. It looks like a giant hairless rat with an enlarged head and giant fangs."

Filaurel knelt beside Glorandial and adjusted her position, trying to relieve the growing pain.

Pegan offered Glorandial a smile. "None of us ever expected it to end this way," he coughed as he laughed.

"Ameria won't abandon us. She is an honorable reptile and will do as asked."

The sun was setting when Ameria reached the 'Anor. Lighting her staff, she purposely splashed through the mud and the muck making as much noise as possible. Every so often, she would stop and release a series of high-pitched squeaks and squeals.

Saress looked back up the Nymph. "I still don't see any movement. Perhaps they've given up and returned to camp."

WHAM! A bruised and battered body landed on the ledge, not ten feet from where she stood. Drawing a sword, she severed the head to make sure he was dead, then kicked the corpse over the ledge. Not long after, they heard a splat as the body exploded against something hard.

"Guess you were wrong," Filaurel said.

"They will never give up," Raestmond whispered. "To allow our escape is a direct slap to the Emperor's face. Something he will not take lightly."

Airriossalth, Ameria heard her birth named called. Altering her course, she ran at break-neck speed towards the voice. Not far away, she encountered a scouting party.

"Airriossalth," the reptile said again. "Why are you here?" he asked, slightly confused. "It was my understanding you and—"

"You have to help them; they're going to die," Ameria cried out.

"Who?" the reptile hissed. "Who do we need to help?"

Ameria was exhausted to the point she had a hard time remembering names. "The others, you have to help them."

"Take us there," the scout leader ordered Ameria.

Filaurel looked up at the ashen black sky. "She's been gone a long time. I don't believe she's going to return."

"We're staying right here until Ameria returns," Saress said, then looked directly at Filaurel. "You got us into this, she'll get us out."

Raestmond stood and stretched, then checked Pegan's hand. The fingertips were turning the color of soot, so he loosened the tourniquet allowing blood to reach the fingers. "I hope your right. Barbarians are skilled climbers and are no doubt affixing ropes to lower themselves down at first light to collect us."

"Look, down there," Filaurel pointed. In the darkness, a faint light bobbed and weaved.

"Does she have help?" Raestmond asked.

"I don't know," Saress confessed. "Reptiles are cold-blooded; they don't glow like warm-blooded creatures in my thermal vision."

The scout leader pointed half-way up the Nymph Pass. "Is that them, huddled at *Pasithelle Plummet?"*

"Yes," she quickly said. "I told them not to go, but the elf wouldn't listen to me. You have to help them."

"We'll get them down, you return to the nest and let the healer know we'll need her services immediately upon our return."

"Thank you," she said, then hugged the reptile.

Raestmond's heart sank as the light faded from view. "It wasn't her, and soon it will be light enough for the barbarians to begin their descent. All of us are going to catch hell at the hands of the barbarians. Glorandial will get the worst."

"We must remain positive, and besides, I don't plan on surrendering. I'm sure all of us intend to fight to the death if needed." From her weapons belt, Saress removed a spare dagger and handed it to Raestmond. "I know fighting isn't your chosen lifestyle, but as of now, I see no other alternative."

Near the top of the Pass, orange fires glowed brightly.

Raestmond shook his head knowing the future was bleak.

CLLLKKKKKK... CLK. CLK. CLK. CLLLKKKKKK...

Saress froze, then raised her snout in the air.

"What kind of strange noise was that?" Raestmond asked.

CLLLLKKKKKK... CLK. CLK. CLK. CLLLLKKKKKK... The noise came again.

Saress partly opened her mouth and made a similar sound.

"What is that clicking?" Filaurel asked.

"The scout leader told us to hang on. Help is on the way."

Raestmond clenched his fist and cheered. "She did it. Remind me to give that lizard a big wet sloppy kiss right on the lips when I see her."

"That's disgusting," Saress said.

Saress was good with her word, and within minutes, twelve giant, heavily armed reptiles appeared. "We're here to help," he said with a heavy hiss. "Good to see you again, Augeessareth."

Saress embraced the reptile with a hug, and then the two licked each other's cheeks.

"What are they going to do, eat each other?" Filaurel mumbled

Saress looked at Filaurel and squinted her eyes. "It's our way of greeting the other."

Raestmond hugged the lizard's enormous leg. "You have no idea how glad I am to see you."

The scout leader looked down at Raestmond, then back to Saress. "Airrio-ssalth told me you have two critically injured?"

"Yes, and a prisoner who is refusing to walk and resisting the entire way hindering our progress."

The reptile looked to the bound barbarian. "We'll let's see if we can't change his mind. You all appear exhausted from your travels. We'll take it from here."

The barbarian released a groan. He knew his days were now numbered, and not in a good way.

"You're more than welcome to take charge," Saress said.

"I've sent another group further up the Pass to deal with those who have already started down," the reptile informed them.

"Kill every one of those filthy bastards," Filaurel snarled, then watched a reptile carefully lift Glorandial while supporting her broken leg.

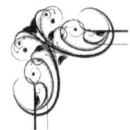
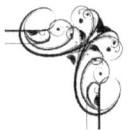

Chapter 89

wo weeks had passed since Frank and Savannah returned from Frankfort with the costume. Occasionally, Frank encountered the Fischer family when he was out and about, but he never said a word and always kept his distance. He could not allow them to think he was up to something. With the cast now removed from Savannah's leg, it was time to set his plan in motion.

Savannah turned left, then right as she admired herself in the custom-tailored eighteenth-century medieval dress. It was baby blue with ruffled shoulders, long silk translucent sleeves, and a square-cut neck. Down the front was a broad white satin strip with black strings running crisscross. The costume, though, would not be complete without the authentic replica footwear—brown leather boots with rawhide strips for laces that covered her ankles.

"You remember the plan?".

Savannah spun viewing herself in the mirror. "Yes."

"Remember, the man's name is Pegan Rhoe. It's crucial not to screw this up."

Savannah looked at Frank's image in the mirror. "I already told you I got this, now give me the keys to the car."

Averie woke to Robyn fussing. "You must be hungry?"

The clock on the dresser flashed red numbers. She had never seen them blink before, so she glanced out the window to tell the time. On the horizon, there was a faint silver glow, and snow fell in thick flakes. "No wonder you're hungry," she said, lifting Robyn out of the crib, "You've slept the entire night." Laying Robyn on the bed for a quick diaper change, she slipped into her robe, tied the cloth belt around her waist, then ventured out in search of sustenance.

"How about some blueberry puree for breakfast?" she asked, removing the tiny jar from the cupboard.

"That sounds awful," Sarah complained.

Averie nearly dropped the jar when she heard a voice answer.

"You could start some coffee, though," Sarah continued.

Averie's racing heart slowed. "I'm glad that was you, I thought for a minute Robyn answered me."

"She's much too young to be talking," Sarah said with a laugh as she retrieved the coffee can from the pantry.

"I'm sorry if I woke you," Averie said as she placed Robyn in the high chair.

"You didn't wake me. I came out to get some coffee started. Tom and Mike have to check on the animals here soon. We lost power last night, and they have to make sure their water isn't frozen. I know they're each going to want a thermos to go."

Averie slid the spoon into Robyn's mouth as she looked back at Sarah. "If you want, I can make it so you can get some sleep?"

Sarah dumped two scoops into the maker. "Na, I got it. It won't take me but a few minutes to get it going, then I plan on laying back down."

Averie fed Robyn a few more bites, then left to the living room and put another log on the fire and opened the vent slightly to allow more air to enter so it would catch faster."

"Coffee's going," Sarah mumbled as she stumbled by yawning. "I'm going to lay down for a bit. You going to be okay out here?"

"Yes. I'm going to finish feeding Robyn, then turn on some cartoons."

"Television is the best babysitter in the world," Sarah said from down the hall.

Averie fed Robyn a few more bites when a faint rapping on the door caught her attention. "Did you hear that?" she asked Robyn, who offered no response.

Seconds later, the rapping came again.

Averie glanced out the window and could see the outline of a car in the driveway and the fresh tracks behind it. *Who would be out on a morning like this*, she wondered. Perhaps it's Dave and Sandy, but they have never come over this early, except for the few times they stayed the night, of course.

The rapping came for the third time.

Averie peered through the peephole and could see a woman on the front porch shivering. Perhaps she got lost and needed help. Her hand reached for the lock, then she jerked it away as the words Tom told her resonated inside her mind—*never unlock or open the door for anybody*. "Give me one minute," Averie told the woman, then quickly went to wake Tom.

Tom grumbled as he sat up. "Who would be here at this hour?"

"I don't know, but she looks cold, probably hungry too," Averie said.

"If she needs help, we'll help her, but not before we find out who she is," Tom said as he staggered down the hall. Looking through the peephole, he could see the woman standing there looking lost. Flipping one lock, then the deadbolt, Tom swung the door open. "Can I help you?"

Sarah stood back out of the way.

Savannah's eyes widened. He was the last person she wanted to see, but it was too late now. She would have no choice but to put on her best charade. "This is going to sound a bit strange, perhaps even unbelievable." Savannah looked around to make sure nobody else was within earshot. "I was sent here by Pegan Rhoe to locate his lover, a woman named Averie."

Tom's eyes widened, as did Sarah's.

"Averie does live here, correct?".

Averie shoved Tom out of the way, nearly knocking him over. "Pegan sent you from Icearaus? When can I see him? Am I going home?"

"You must be Averie," Savannah said. "Pegan was sorely mistaken when he said you were beautiful, your gorgeous. I see now why his heart flutters for you." Savannah laid it on thick.

"Come in out of the cold," Averie said as she led the woman inside.

Tom closed the door and viewed the woman from every angle. She was not from around these parts, judging from her attire.

"Have you seen Saress?" Averie asked. "Is she doing good?"

"I can't answer those questions because I don't know," Savannah explained. "Pegan sent me here because he needs the coins back he gave you. He's landed himself in an awful position, and without them, he may not be around when you do return home."

"I don't have all of them, only a few. The rest are in safekeeping."

Sarah started to say something then stopped, realizing she didn't know exactly how to respond.

"A few will work for now. In time though, I'm sure Pegan is going to need the rest." Savannah continued playing the part to perfection.

Mike lumbered down the stairs and walked past, scratching his butt and yawning. "What is all the ruckus? Do you know what time it is? The rooster hasn't even cleared his throat yet."

Tom stopped Mike. "This woman knows Pegan and is here to retrieve the coins."

"That's nice," Mike said in between yawns, then started to walk into the kitchen before abruptly stopping and spinning around. "What the hell did you say?"

"This lady knows Pegan—" Tom started to say.

"Oh! I have got to see this. Are you telling me we have another alien here?"

"Let me get you the coins," Averie said as she walked away.

God, she is stupid, Savannah thought. "Thank you. I'm sure Pegan will appreciate it."

Mike snatched Averie around the waist, stopping her progress. "Not so fast, young lady."

"Time is of the essence," Savannah told Averie.

Averie wiggled and squirmed, trying to break free of Mike's grasp.

"I think we need a little bit more information before we hand over the coins, don't you think?" Mike asked Averie.

"Pegan needs the coins, that's all that matters," Averie said as she fought to free herself.

"And that's fine. When Pegan shows up, I'll drive you there to get them. This lady needs better credentials than a name," Mike said.

"If Pegan doesn't get those coins back, he is going to be highly upset with you," Savannah told Averie.

Averie eventually broke free, or Mike let her go, she wasn't sure.

"Don't go anywhere," Mike told Averie, then focused on the woman. "Answer me a few questions to prove you're from her world. What's the name of the world she's from?"

Savannah considered the question, then blurted out, "Icearaus."

Tom could sense the hesitation in her voice. "You only know this because Averie said it earlier."

"Who is the man Averie fears most on Icearaus?"

Savannah blinked her eyes, looking suddenly stupid.

"Who was Averie's protector? What is the Elf's Queen's name? What town is

Averie from?" Mike fired off the questions.

"Pegan told me I would have trouble with you and to only deal with Averie," Savannah tried to regain the upper hand.

"How did Pegan send you here?" Averie asked. "Only one man can activate the portal."

"I know what his name is," Mike said to Savannah. "Do you?"

Savannah backed away to the door.

"You can't answer any of these questions because you're a fake, a fraud sent here by Frank, aren't you?" Mike was furious as he screamed at Savannah.

Savannah ran from the house to the car and sped away, nearly crashing into the fence.

Averie barely made it to the couch before she collapsed and started to cry.

Sarah sat beside Averie, holding her tight. "I'm so sorry she did this to you."

Jennifer stopped halfway down the stairs. "What did I miss?"

"Frank being a jerk," Sarah told her.

"How did you know she was a fraud?" Tom asked Mike.

"Are you telling me you didn't recognize her under all that phony makeup, or see the tag on the dress which read Dicks Medieval Costumes, Frankfort KY."

Tom still looked confused.

"That was the lady from the pawnshop, Savannah Henderson," Mike said.

"Now we know why Frank spent the money to bail her out, boy is he going to be disappointed," Tom said.

"Regardless, enough is enough." Mike was seething mad as he snatched his coat from the rack. "I'm going to go have a chat with Frank. This crap is stopping today."

"I'm going with you," Tom said, snatching his coat as well.

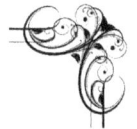

Chapter 90

om glanced at Sarah using the rearview mirror. "I wish you would have stayed at home."

"No way in hell," she answered. "What she did was beyond mean, it was downright cruel. She needs to apologize to Averie, or you might be sleeping alone tonight as I'm going to prison."

"Nobody's going to prison," Mike said. "We're going to go over there and act like adults and discover what his problem is. We know he doesn't need the money. It must be something else."

"He's a freaking creep," Jennifer complained from the back seat. "That's all there is to it."

"We're almost there," Tom said as he turned down River Road. In the distance, the glowing sign ahead read Double River Hotel, which derived its name from the rivers which ran down either side, placing it on an island near the center of town. Crossing the narrow, two-lane bridge, Tom guided the vehicle into the crowded parking lot.

Savannah knew there was going to be trouble when she observed the glistening black van come to a stop near their hotel door. Through the windshield, she could see Tom, both his hands clutched the steering wheel and his narrowed eyes focusing on nothing but their door. Any doubt that remained quickly drained away in sweat as she observed the Fischer family climb from the van. There was going to be trouble, she had no doubt.

"Let me handle this," Mike said. Then knocked on the bright red door.

Lined up behind Mike like a vigilante force were Tom, Sarah, Jennifer, Averie, who held Robyn, and Billy. The only thing missing were the pitchforks and torches.

Savannah tapped on the bathroom door. "Frank, you have company."

"Who would come here?" Frank asked as he walked out of the bathroom with half his face covered in shaving cream. "Nobody knows I rented this room. Did you tell anyone?".

Savannah stepped back to watch the sparks fly. "Nope."

Frank opened the door. "Good morning gent—"

Tom never allowed Frank to finish as he stepped around Mike and pointed his finger inches from Frank's face. "What in the hell is your major malfunction?"

"Whoa," Frank sneered, slapping away the hand. "Where do you get off coming at me like that?"

"Ever since you—" Tom started to say.

"Calm down," Mike interrupted. "Look, we came here for a peaceful resolution."

"And for that floozy to apologize to Averie," Sarah yelled at Frank.

Mike turned around and located his sister. "Will you shut up for a minute."

"I see," Frank said. "I'm still not sure what I did wrong."

Mike scratched his forehead. "Not sure what you did wrong? How about having Savannah portraying someone she's not in an attempt to illegally acquire Averie's coins. In Kentucky, that falls under the crime of false pretense, which is punishable by up to six months in prison. I know Savannah is on probation, and another crime would slap her right back in jail. Knowing this, I'm sure in court she would be more than happy to testify you put her up to it."

Frank's face was slowly turning red. "Are you accusing me of committing a crime?"

"I don't need to accuse you. We have it all on video," Mike lied. "Look, I don't want it to end this way, that's why we're here. Let's come to a resolution and put this behind us, and we can all get on with our lives."

"Your right," Frank mumbled. "You know your right. I'm going to cut it right to the bone. How much do you want for the coins?" From the desk drawer, he grabbed his checkbook.

"You have to ask Averie," Mike said.

Frank looked at Averie, then asked the questions again.

Averie thought for a moment. "They're not for sale."

"How about one million dollars? Everything has a price."

"Why are these coins so important to you?" Tom asked.

"Let's say it's personal," Frank grumbled.

"Frank," Mike sighed as he spoke. "We know it was an item you got from Loren which made you a very wealthy man. It seems to me you only want these coins to thicken your bank account."

"That isn't true. I also used that information to better humanity."

"And what have you given back to the community without charge?" Sarah asked.

"It's complicated—" Frank started to say.

Averie shook her head. "No. I won't sell them for any price."

"Think about what that would mean to your family, to your daughter. The things you could buy her, the life you could give her. You could move away from this rat hole of a farm and buy a lovely house. Anything YOU desire could be yours."

"No, there not for sale for any price," Averie said. "I'm happy where I live, and my family loves me for who I am, not what I have."

Sarah squeezed Averie's hand and smiled at her. "Thank you," she whispered.

"There," Mike said. "You've heard it straight from Averie. The coins are not for sale for any price. If you keep harassing her, you're going to force my hand into filing a stalking complaint. I recommend we don't go there and we move on with our lives and let bygones be bygones. No harm or fouls committed."

Frank's neck was the color of a ripe radish. "As far as I see it, you stole two coins that Savannah legally bought. I want them returned today, or I'm calling the police, and Averie will go to jail, and her child taken away."

Averie's face drained of color. The one price she would pay for the coins was not to have her child taken away. "Should I give him the coins?" Averie asked. "I don't want Robyn taken away."

"No." Sarah smelled the bluff like a dirty diaper left in the back seat of a hot car. "The coins are yours, not his. He has no rights to them, and he's only trying to scare you."

Tom was foaming at the mouth. "Savannah bought them, not you. As far as I see it, the coins are payment for damages she caused."

"I'm not trying to scare anyone," Frank explained as he dramatically swung his arms. "The fact is, Averie is now in possession of the stolen property."

Tom lunged at Frank, rearing back with his fist closed. "I'll show you stolen property."

Outside, the sounds of doors opening echoed as people came to watch the show.

Mike grabbed Tom before the attack could occur.

"You come near me, my family, or anyone I know and—" Tom snarled.

"And what?" Frank asked.

"Let me leave it at this. I have a lot of property, pigs, a backhoe, and an alibi. I'll be long gone before they ever find your bones."

"Are you threatening me?" Frank asked.

"Nobody is threatening anyone." Mike tried to calm the situation, which was steadily growing out of hand. "Frank, all we want is to be left alone?"

Steam was spraying from Frank's ears. "I want you out of my hotel room, NOW!" he screamed and pointed to the parking lot.

"You don't have to ask me twice," Tom said. He was the last one out and slammed the door behind him.

Outside, a crowd gathered, whispering amongst themselves.

"I'm sorry," Tom pleaded for mercy from Mike—who he knew wanted to beat him senseless for his sudden outburst. "He makes me so damn mad. Why can't he leave us alone?"

"Maybe he'll get the message now," Sarah said. "You were pretty upfront about your intentions."

Mike shook his head, "Doubtful. He's hell-bent on getting Averie's coins, I wouldn't let our guard down for a second."

Savannah waited for the situation to simmer down before speaking. "I don't think she's going to surrender them willingly. I see no other choice but to go back to Frankfort and forget the whole thing."

Frank thought for a moment and then slammed his hand against the desk. "No," Frank hissed. "There's more than one way to fry a frog. Let me contact Jacque and see what he can do."

"Do you think he can make her give up the coins?"

"I don't know," he answered. "I know Jacque has close ties to CPS, perhaps a letter directly from them informing Averie of an investigation may be enough to sway her to cough up the coins."

"What if she goes to the police?"

"She won't… hey, wait a damn minute here," Frank suddenly was hit with an idea. "Half the hotel heard Tom threaten to kill me. Perhaps I can use that very threat against him."

"It's possible," she said, smiling devilishly.

Later that evening, with revenge still festering on her mind and how to successfully pull it off, the answer came from Frank earlier—*half the hotel heard Tom threaten to kill me.* She would have to act quickly while the argument was still fresh in the witness's minds. All her nights spent searching airline tickets, which countries offered asylum over extradition, foreign currencies, how to withdraw large sums of money without drawing attention, home remedies for tattoo removal, and most importantly, the proper application of Rohypnol—a drug that can incapacitate a person to the point they lie paralyzed, yet fully conscious—was about to pay dividends.

Savannah needed a way to get the Rohypnol into Frank's system without drawing suspicion, and what better way than Chinese. "I'm starving," she complained. "I haven't eaten a thing all day. Give me some money so I can go across the street to grab dinner."

Frank pulled a fifty from his wallet and handed it to her.

"What do you want?"

"Get me a bowl of Lo Mein," Frank said as he turned on the game. "And a couple of egg rolls."

"Anything else?"

"See if they have a bottle of Chardonnay?"

"Okay," Savannah said as she walked out.

Savannah waited at the counter, searching through the menu.

"Need a bit more time?" The wiry thin waitress politely asked.

Savannah looked up from the menu. "No, I'm good. Give me one order of number three, and a large bowl of Lo Mein, and two egg rolls. If you have any Chardonnay, I'll take that as well."

The lady tapped on the register like a pro. "To go?"

"Um. yes," Savannah replied.

Savannah went to the lady's room and locked the door. Dumping out five large white pills on the counter, she was extremely cautious not to get any residue on her hands as the chemical would absorb through the skin. Covering the pills with a brown paper towel, she employed a butter knife to crush the pills into a fine powder. Satisfied with her work, she scraped the powder into a folded sheet of paper and tucked it into her purse, then cleaned up the mess.

With the first part complete, she moved on to the next. From a separate pouch in her purse she removed a small syringe, spoon, lighter, and tiny white rock of cocaine. Placing the rock in the spoon she heated the bottom until the rock dissolved into a puddle then slurped it up with the syringe. Wrapping her belt around her arm she pulled it tight then inserted the needle into the bulging vein and pushed in the cocaine. Almost immediately she felt suddenly alert, energetic, and ready to handle business.

Leaving the bathroom, Savannah paced the waiting area.

"Here's your order, ma'am," the waitress said.

With the order in hand, Savannah went outside and dug through the bag locating the Lo Mein. Carefully opening the lid, she dumped the powder in and stirred the contents until the white powder was dissolved before venturing back to the hotel.

"Here you go." Savannah handed Frank the carton and a small bottle of wine. "They didn't have any Chardonnay, so I bought a bottle of Riesling. The waitress highly recommended it."

Frank looked at her suspiciously. "Why are you acting so weird?"

"It's been a while for me but when I was over there I smoked a blunt, okay, its legal in this state."

Frank watched her for a few more minutes, then held the bottle up to the light and examined the color.

"Who's playing tonight?" Savannah asked as she flopped down in the chair on the opposite side of the bed.

Frank opened the box and stirred the contents. "The Bears and Eagles, it should be a good game."

Savannah closely watched as he took the first bite. According to the internet, there should be no taste or aftertaste.

Frank swallowed, took a drink, stirred the contents, then continued eating.

Savannah ate hers as she watched the game. Near half-time, she glanced over at Frank, who still cheered on the Bears.

C'mon, c'mon, c'mon she thought, *the drugs should have taken effect by now.*

As the buzzer rang and the third quarter came to an end, Frank lay in the recliner staring at the ceiling still as a corpse, yet very much alive.

Savannah snapped her fingers in front of his face, and he never moved. To be proof positive he wasn't sleeping, she slapped his cheek a few times gaining no results. The pills worked precisely as described, and the best part was he would feel everything she did and couldn't do anything about it.

Working in a precise order she first closed the blinds, then placed the air conditioning on max cool. She learned from Tiny, the colder the room, the longer it would take for the crime scene to be detected, thus giving her more time to flee as it would take the body much longer to start stinking.

Stripping down naked, she neatly folded her clothes and placed them on the back of the toilet then stripped off all Frank's jewelry, acquired his credit cards and cash, cell phone, car keys, and the gold caps off three of his teeth, then went to the kitchen. Searching through the drawers, she located a paring knife. "This should do the trick," she mumbled, then held the knife before Frank's face so he could see it.

Giggling with excitement, she started at Frank's right ear slowly inserted the knife into the squishy part of his neck. A stream of sticky blood coated her hand, making the black plastic handle slippery. Jerking hard to get the blade moving, she followed the jawbone with a sawing motion stopping under the chin. Switching hands, she traced the bone back up, ending at the left ear. At first, blood sprayed like a broken sprinkler leaving her pale white body streaked and splattered.

In the air she could almost taste the metallic scent.

As the pressure faded, it gurgled and chugged, filling up the recliner faster than the cloth material could drink it up. Once saturated, it dripped through the bottom and flowed from beneath the chair in twisted streams staining the twill carpet. Afterward, she plunged the knife clear to the handle directly in his heart. "That's for Tiny, you son-of-a-bitch," she snarled while looking into his cold dead eyes. Removing the knife, she stabbed him twenty-seven more times, one for each bullet. There should have been more, but the blade snapped partway imbedded into the breastbone.

Tossing the handle, the bottle of Rohypnol, and a few carpet fibers tainted with blood into the brown bag their dinner came in, she decided it was time to wash away the evidence.

After she was washed, dressed, and had all her materials loaded into the car, Savannah realized she had no desire to remain in this makeshift morgue, but it was too early to finish her plans, so she headed to the mall. At the sports store, she bought a black raincoat, a tan hat, and dark glasses. Afterward, she hit every bank in town withdrawing cash advances on Frank's credit cards, knowing there was no limit. With the banks drained of cash she went to eat, then spent the next five hours driving around town watching all the lights twinkle off the snow-covered ground. It almost looked like a Thomas Kinkade winter wonderland picture. Too bad it had to end this way, she could almost see herself living here.

At one-thirty in the morning and with well over a hundred thousand in cash, it was time to make her get-a-way, but not before one final stop to visit the Fischer's. Not wanting to be noticed she eased the car to the side of the road next to the drive-way, then rested her head against the steering wheel and collected her wits. This would be the final step to ensure her escape went unhindered. Slowing lifting the handle the door swung silently open and she stepped out.

The crunch of snow under her feet made her hesitate.

She didn't have a choice, she had to go through with the plans. Walking in the tracks of the van to conceal her arrival, she neared the van with cat-like precision. Checking each door she was not surprised to find the van locked, but locks were a mere inconvenience and she broke out a Slim-Jim and quickly allowed herself free entry.

In the rear cargo area, she partially hid the broken handle, the bottle of drugs, and the few fibers. In the back seat, she tossed the raincoat, hat, and glasses. Closing the door softly as a sweet kiss, she crept back down the drive way to her waiting vehicle.

By the time police discovered the body, talked with witnesses, and linked the murder to Tom, she would be in Morocco drinking fruity drinks on the beach living the good life—a free life.

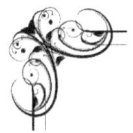
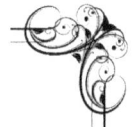

Chapter 91

egan woke on a bed of hay covered with a thick hide blanket. His body ached, his hand throbbed, and his head pounded. Sitting up, he waited for the fogginess to clear so he could take in his environment. The room was large, and well-lit from Ameria's staff which was jabbed in the sandy ground directly in the room's center. The walls were made of grossly misshapen mud bricks wedged between twisted roots, and the stagnant air held a dense, warm, swamp-smelling scent.

Twisting his head left to right, he took in all the occupants. Glorandial lay beside him in a similar bed. Her calf was wrapped in a dirty cloth while a wooden splint held her leg immobile. Near a cloth flap concealing a doorway, Saress lay sprawled out like a giant rug and beside her Ameria slept, using Saress as a pillow.

Pegan tried to flex his fingers, but a searing, burning pain shot up his arm, forcing his eyes to slam shut. Waiting for the pain to subside, he slowly opened his eyes and examined the covered wound. The nasty hole was filthy with infection, and ugly red lines grew from the injury, reaching clear to his elbow.

A moss-colored reptile with crooked teeth wearing a flowery headdress pushed the flap aside and entered. Around her neck, a long necklace fitted with different colored beads swung with each step. "I wondered when you were going to wake."

Pegan could barely understand her words as they held a predominate hiss.

"Eat this," she said, then handed Pegan a rolled-up leaf filled with thick yellow cream.

Pegan accepted the item but looked it over first.

"It should slow the infection and ease the pain. Our methods are rudimentary, but it should keep you alive long enough to get you to the elves."

Pegan took a small bite and found it quite tasty. "Not bad, what is it?" he mumbled, then took a second bite.

"The pulverized warts off a swamp toads back."

Pegan nearly threw up as he lowered the roll to the mat.

"Eat," she said again. "You must eat it all to get the full effect of the medicine."

Pegan looked down at the item and found it suddenly repulsive. "Death might be better," he mumbled.

Saress woke first and rolled over, leaving Ameria's head to smack against the ground.

Snarling and grumbling, Ameria complained about Saress's insensitivity as she climbed to her feet.

"How's he doing?" Saress asked the shaman.

"The infection grows worse. If Pegan doesn't eat the rest of the medicine roll, he may not survive."

Pegan looked down as the medicine roll for the third time.

"Eat it now," Saress hissed. "Or I will feed it to you myself."

Pegan grumbled as he took a small bite. "How long have I been asleep?"

"Two days," Saress answered.

"Two days," Pegan screamed. He tried to get up, but his head swooned, and he collapsed back to the mat.

"You're in no condition to be walking," the shaman told him.

"I have to," Pegan explained.

"What you have to do is finish eating that medicine roll," Saress snarled.

Pegan looked down at the roll for the fourth time. "We have to get the prisoner to the elves for questioning."

"For your information, we spent hours questioning the barbarian but got nothing out of him. Therefore, yesterday, in the dark of night, a squad left for Rhunsiire with the prisoner. My guess is they should be at the Ghu'lane stairs by now."

"What if he escapes, I should have been there," Pegan complained.

"Eat," Saress said and pointed to the medicine roll.

Pegan took another bite.

"The prisoner will not escape. Remember, it was us who saved you from the barbarians," the shaman said.

Filaurel entered chewing on something that looked like a long-twisted root sprouting little gray hairs. "How much longer is she going to be asleep?"

"Her body has experienced a great deal of trauma and is now recovering. She will wake when her mind believes the time is right."

"We need to get her to the elves where proper medical treatment can be provided," Filaurel told the shaman.

"I agree," the shaman said. "Right now, the most important thing is for her to rest."

"If she dies, I'm holding every reptile responsible," Filaurel hissed.

Saress stood to full height towering over Filaurel. "I've grown tired of you threatening all those who try and help. If you wish to leave, go, I'll show you the way out. You're not taking Glorandial, though. She will remain here until such time the shaman believes it is okay for her to travel."

Located on the other side of the 'Anor, the eldest reptile effortlessly scaled the Ghu'lane unhindered by the dark of night. The clear night sky offered a view of a thousand stars, and the moon glistened brightly in the sea of black velvet. When his vision broke the edge where stone met dirt, he paused and lowered himself to one knee. Not far from the entrance to the Ghu'lane, an encampment of soldiers grew up out of the ground. In the center was a large bonfire spewing thick, oily smoke, and to one side was a row of hastily constructed dung-colored tents. Not far from there, horses were fastened to a post driven into the ground. Men walked about, showing little care or worry.

Retreating to the midpoint, the elder informed the rest of the situation.

"And you're sure they're not barbarians?" a reptile wielding a long sword asked.

"Positive, these men are human and flying Karayan's purple elite colors."

A small, bright green reptile with a glowing yellow belly paced back and forth, fingering an arrow. "Word must have reached Karayan of the capture, and they were sent here to intercept us."

"Doubtful," the elder schooled the youngster. "If that were true, the men would be hiding. These men meander about as if they're waiting for something or someone to come. They seem to have no care in the world."

The barbarian fought and jerked on the shackles gaining a new sense of urgency, knowing Karayan's men waited at the top. It was only a matter of time now until he would be released and seek his revenge upon the muck dwellers.

"We have no choice but to fight them," the youngster hissed, sliding the bow free of his shoulder.

The elder raised his hand, signaling for him to calm down. "Let's not charge straight into battle. We'll be outnumbered five to one, and our object is to deliver this man to the elves, not begin the war."

"You said it yourself; there is no way to pass without drawing the attention of the soldiers," the youngster hissed back at the elder.

"Perhaps if we wait for a few hours, they will turn in for the night, allowing us to sneak past undetected," the elder suggested.

The elf knelt in the shadows provided by a large stone observing the encampment. His orders were clear. Discover their location and intent but not to engage the enemy. Regardless, he could sense the ill intent of their presence and made the command decision to attack. Why allow them to gain a foothold at their southern borders when they could easily be defeated now.

Directing the archers to circle the encampment they effectively surrounding the enemy. They would have nowhere to run except to the stairs. Motion to the second group of foot soldiers, they each drew their weapons. It would be their job to face the enemy head-on once the archers thinned the ranks.

Five reptiles made their way up the stairs. The sixth, a smaller female, objected as she was ordered by the elder to remain with the prisoner.

Lying belly down on the stairs, they studied the layout of the camp and the location of each man placed on watch. Beyond the encampment, they caught their first glance of the elves hiding in the shadows.

"Why are the elves conspiring with Karayan?" the young lizard asked the elder.

The elder shook his head baffled as well. "I don't know. If they have, then we truly are in troubling times."

The elven leader raised his hand in the air, created a fist, then slammed it down as if chopping something. The signal had been given to engage the enemy.

The solder never made a sound as the arrow tore through his ear hole and exploded out the other side of his head. Blood and bone splattered those nearby as the body spun in a circle then crashed down onto the fire sending embers and debris sailing. Nearby, a tent erupted into flames. The man inside came running out screaming. Both of his legs were on fire. Behind him a trail of smoke twirled like a pigs tail.

Thump-thwack-crack-clang-chink. The sound of arrows hitting flesh, armor, and bone filled the air as men dropped in random places. Those who avoided the death from above broke for the concealment of their tents.

The elven leader signaled the foot soldiers into action. Chanting the elven war song, the soldiers crashed down upon the encampment like locust on a wheat field destroying everything living. The ones who fled inside tents were forced out by fire then immediately cut down. Those who escaped were either chased down and killed by the blade, or dropped by deadly arrows.

The reptiles flattened themselves, becoming one with the stairs as the slaughter played out right before their eyes.

It was over as quick as it began, and the elves walked amongst the battlefield plunging their swords into each lung of every man, regardless rather they were living or dead. In the eyes of a commoner the act would have seemed barbaric, but the elven leader knew if air remained inside the lungs, the soldier still held the ability to tell what happened—depending on the magic used.

The elder looked to the others. "Well I guess there not conspiring with Karayan."

The youngster watched with wide eyes. This was his first time observing real combat. and never would have believed it to be so gruesome.

The elder could see the look of horror on the youngster's face, and his sudden realization, death was real. "Now, you understand why I wanted to wait. War is different than the training ground in the dens. There is no getting up when the sword plunges through your chest. There is no—I made a mistake, can I try again. War is brutal, ugly, and there are no winners even in victory."

"Leave him alone, he is still young," another reptile said.

"I only wished for him to learn," the elder explained.

"I think it's time for us to make our presence known, though," the reptile said to the elder. "We come in the name of Pegan Rhoe. I don't believe they will attack us."

The elder nodded his agreement. "Hold your fire," the elder called out from the Ghu'lane safely hidden below the stairs.

"Reveal yourself," the elven leader called out, ordering the elves into a new fighting position. He was taking no chances since he knew not who the enemy was.

From the stairs, the elder reptile emerged. "Am I glad to see you."

The elven leader looked the reptile over. "What brings a reptile out of the 'Anor?"

From the stairs, four more reptiles emerged.

"We were not sure how we were going to get past. We currently escort a prisoner to Rhunsiire for questioning," the elder advised the elf.

The elf looked about. "Where is this prisoner?"

The elder signaled for the female to bring the barbarian up.

The elf eyed the barbarian.

"Pegan captured him near the Nymph Pass. The barbarian army is gathering there and where not sure why."

"Where is Pegan?" the elf asked the elder.

"He is still at the den and critically injured, along with a she-elf named Glorandial. Saress sent us here telling us not to delay."

The elf looked down at the barbarian who struggled with the shackles, then to a slim elf. "Run ahead and warn Lady Alenia we're bringing back a prisoner directly to the interrogation chamber."

The elf nodded he understood then bolted off into the darkness.

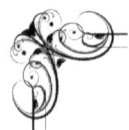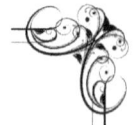

Chapter 92

exacion was furious when he heard the news. "How could you allow them to walk away without repercussion?" he yelled at Malvo. "I never trusted that traitorous Skylar Nightshade, or his companion Miramar Darkblade. You know as well as I do, Skylar is the one responsible for this… this unforgivable act of betrayal against the brotherhood."

Malvo continued to study the parchment.

"Are you not troubled by this?"

Malvo slowly looked up from the parchment, his pale face glowing brightly in the dim candlelight. "Not in the least."

"How can you say that?" Vexacion asked. "Skylar was one of the highest-ranking members. He knows," Vexacion paused. "He knows things about the brotherhood very few do."

"He knows much about the Assassin's Brotherhood, yet very little of the Brotherhood of the Dark Prince. That is unless you've told him of our future direction?" Malvo's eyes narrowed, and he grinned.

"No," Vexacion quickly answered. "I have told not another living soul."

"Good," Malvo said, then went back to reading the parchment. "You've been good to me. I would hate to oversee your untimely death due to a slip of the tongue."

The room suddenly grew bright as a blue portal opened, and an elf stepped out. His flowing green robe rimmed with bright silver and sewn with golden thread fluttered in the breeze created by the magical portal as it slammed shut.

Vexacion instantly recognized the elf as Ruven, a highly respected and prominent member of the elven ruling council. Both daggers leaped to his hands, and he moved in for the kill.

"Ruven, good to see you again," Malvo said, looking up at the elf.

Ruven looked at Malvo, then at Vexacion, who was within striking distance.

"Vexacion, put your weapons away," Malvo hissed at the assassin, then turned back to the elf. "What news do you bring me from Rhunsiire?"

Vexacion slid his daggers back into their sheaths. "This elf is an associate of the brotherhood—"

"And has been since long before you were born." Malvo finished Vexacion's sentence.

"How?" Vexacion asked.

"The Brotherhood of the Dark Prince has eyes and ears everywhere," Malvo said without giving a real answer.

"You're truly amazing," Vexacion said.

Ruven sat down and propped his feet up on the desk as if he owned the establishment. "Much has transpired since our last meeting. The elves are aware of the looming war and are preparing to fight Karayan."

"Excellent," Malvo cheered. "They're doing exactly as I expected. The elves are a proud race and will not flee their homeland, which will be their downfall."

"Something else is going on between Lady Alenia, Elwrick, Gleia, and a strange woman who magically appeared by a portal. They work in secret behind closed doors revealing nothing of their doings."

"So that's where she went to," Malvo said.

"Who?" Vexacion asked.

Malvo fired a wicked glance at Vexacion. "Lilith, that's who."

"I think Lady Alenia suspects something," Ruven said. "She has tightened the circle around her, only allowing a dedicated few to get close, and Elwrick rarely leaves her side."

Malvo tapped his finger against his chin. "Elwrick always has been, and always will be a thorn in my side."

"Perhaps it's time to dispose of him," Vexacion recommended.

Malvo cocked his head as he looked at Vexacion. "And how do you accomplish the impossible?"

"You have Pegan Rhoe to deal with as well," Ruven suggested. "Although he isn't in Rhunsiire as we speak, but out on a mission searching for the dwarves."

"I am aware of that," Malvo said, remembering the punishment his father administered.

"We also have the traitors to deal with who fled to Rhunsiire," Vexacion said.

"I forgot about them," Ruven sighed. "Lady Alenia refused them entry no matter how much I pleaded. They were taken to a secure location, not even I am aware of and had their robes removed. From the fourteen, the rumor is only six live and they swore allegiance to the elves and the Creator."

Malvo reached across the table and snatched Ruven by his robe and lifted the much larger elf off the ground. "You should have told me the minute she refused. Their deaths will severely hamper my plans."

Ruven struggled to breathe. "I believed discovering the identity of this strange woman would be more important."

Malvo slammed Ruven back down to the chair, breaking it. "We have no choice now; my hands are tied. You must KILL Lady Alenia. Afterward, dispose of Lilith as well before she gains knowledge of her powers."

Ruven bowed. "I will see the task completed."

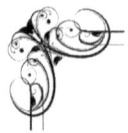
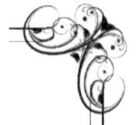

Chapter 93

ater that day, **Elwrick waited on the lower half of the stairs** that lead to the interrogation room. Coming through the enormous arched gateway, he could see the line of elves intermingled with the much larger race of reptiles. In the middle of the caravan, the elder lizard drug the barbarian by his ponytail.

Screaming and flopping, the brute pleaded for mercy as blood ran from his head where his hair was forcefully being ripped free of the scalp.

Elves hid in the shadows that lined the main road watching the spectacle. Most of them had never seen a barbarian besides Thathra, but this man towered over Pegan's once faithful ally and induced fear in even the hardiest of elves.

Within minutes the caravan arrived at the bottom of the stairs. "Walk," the elder hissed as he pointed up the stairs.

The barbarian stood then spit in the elder's face.

The elder licked off the spit with his long bright-pink tongue, then slugged the barbarian in the face with his clawed fist.

The sound of the cartilage collapsing in the barbarian's nose was not for the squeamish, and seconds later, the prisoner collapsed like a house of cards. When he tried to get up, his dark-skinned chest was painted bright red with blood.

"If he refuses to walk, drag him by his face up the stairs," Elwrick snarled.

"My pleasure," the elder said. He had never met Elwrick but knew him instantly by the stories King Hulradeeh told when he was a youngster.

Elwrick waited at the top holding the door open as the entourage entered dragging behind them the guest of honor.

The elven leader paused at the door, then whispered to Elwrick. "I've done a terrible thing. I ordered the attack on those who we were sent to investigate. We killed every last one of them and punctured their lungs to dispose of any words which may linger."

Elwrick sighed, then covered his mouth with his hands.

"Before we attacked, I eavesdropped on their conversation. It seems the men didn't know for sure why they were there, only that they were waiting for a man named Jester, and he would inform them of their future obligations."

Elwrick ran his fingers through his beard. "I can tell you this. Chieftain Ulgra killed Jester after he tried to recruit the trolls into his army."

"I wanted you to know I am the one responsible. The other were only following orders."

"We'll look into the killing later. For all we know, at this point, it may have been justified. Right now, we have to discover what secrets this barbarian holds."

Birthright

Near the interrogation chair, Lady Alenia sat. Her chair, unlike the other, was made from elegant wood with a plush cushion seat and soft supporting arms. Across her lap was the cane Raestmond made, and to either side was a heavily armed guard.

Elwrick oversaw the barbarian placement in the chair where Pegan once sat.

It was only after the barbarian was secure with no chance of escape did Lady Alenia stand with the aid of Elwrick.

The clack of Lady Alenia's cane against the marble floor was the only sound as she approached the barbarian.

The barbarian eyed her suspiciously in return.

"What is your name?" she politely asked. Using her finger, she traced the claw marks and puncture wounds on his face from where the elder showed little care for his well-being during the escort.

The barbarian spat in her face, then laughed as he watched the glob run down her cheek. "It's the job of a woman to cook, clean, and bear children, not question men. Release me now, and I will reconsider making you experience the tents once this war is over."

Ryul took a soft cloth from the desk and wiped the glob from Lady Alenia's cheek.

"I'm sorry," Lady Alenia whispered to the barbarian. "At this time, your release is non-negotiable. Not unless you wish to reveal to me why the barbarian army gathers north of the Nymph Pass."

The barbarian sneered, revealing his crooked yellow teeth, then spit on her again. "The filthy muck dwellers could garner no information from me. You will find the same problem."

Ryul was furious and slugged the barbarian in the jaw knocking a few teeth free.

"Do what you wish with me," the barbarian hissed at Ryul. "You will discover pain is my companion."

Lady Alenia wiped the spit away. "Ryul, is that any way to treat our guest?"

"My apologies," Ryul answered the Queen's question.

Lady Alenia almost fell over as she tried to knell. It was only with Elwrick's help did she succeed. "Normally, I would prefer to lengthen our conversation, but time and circumstances prevent this from occurring. Therefore, I have decided not to waste my time and rely strictly on my pet to recover the information which I desire."

The barbarian spit at her again. Unbeknownst to the savage, and Lady Alenia, Elwrick placed a reflective spell on the Queen, and the spit flew back splattering on his face.

Elwrick could see the somber look on Lady Alenia's face. He knew she didn't want to interrogate the man. It almost seemed as if his pain would become her pain. "Do you wish to return home to rest while I finish this?"

Lady Alenia waited a few minutes. "No," she said. "This is something I must do. Can you please help me stand?" she asked.

"Certainly," he whispered.

Lady Alenia hobbled her way to the small door built into the wall and slid it open. Afterward, she tapped three times on the edge.

"You had your chance," Elwrick informed the barbarian. "Now, what you're about to experience can only be described as life-altering."

The barbarian sank back in the chair as far as possible when Rhimdruzial poured himself through the small opening. "What is that thing?".

Lady Alenia ignored the barbarian's cries for mercy, instead, focusing her attention on the floating blob with six eyes. "Rhimdruzial, I wish to know why the barbarians gather at the Nymph Pass and anything else you feel important. The amount of pain required to gather this information matters little to me."

You could almost see a mouthless smile form on the beast as all six eyes focused on the barbarian as if they were mortal enemies.

"Keep that thing away from me," the barbarian screamed.

Rhimdruzial cautiously approached, bobbing on the slight breeze through the open window. Upon his arrival, he went to work examining every inch of the exterior before sending his slim-covered tentacles through every possible orifice.

The barbarian shrieked in unfettered terror as he swam in a pool of unimaginable pain.

Below the barbarian's skin, you could see ridges form as the tentacles worked their way between the muscle and skin, effectively skinning him alive without spilling a drop of blood. The loud pop of a rib breaking forced Lady Alenia to look away. At one time, she would have watched in delight, but not now. Now, she secretly wiped away a solitary tear that dripped from her eye.

Elwrick sensed Lady Alenia's discomfort. "Rhimdruzial, silence his screams," Elwrick demanded of the creature.

Rhimdruzial reverted to his evil ways when he once roamed the ethereal planes. Guiding a tentacle up through the chest cavity, he tore away the vocal cords and expelled them up through the barbarian's mouth, leaving them to hang like partially-eaten noodles. *Crack*, the sound of a shoulder blade breaking followed by the sound of his spine collapsing, forced Ryul to cringe as he looked away.

"What is that thing doing to him?" the elder reptile asked Elwrick.

"What you're observing here can only be described as horrific, and is often only completed in the solitude of Rhimdruzial's private chamber, as it is purely disgusting. Rhimdruzial has no mouth and eats by dissolving the innards of his victim," Elwrick explained. "Once every muscle is liquified, he sucks up the juices with his tentacles."

"The barbarian is already dead, then?" the elder asked.

Elwrick cringed. "Oh no. The barbarian will remain alive during the entire process until the very end. Normally, he would leave the victim to scream as the screams incite the feeding frenzy, but Lady Alenia was troubled by the incident."

"What about the information?"

"I'm sure by now he's recovered the information, but you never interrupt a Skasus while their feeding. It may turn on us even though he knows who his master is."

A grotesque slurping sound drew their attention the very moment the barbarian's right eye vanished into the skull.

When nothing remained but a shriveled-up dehydrated husk of skin, Rhimdruzial retracted each tentacle then relayed the information gained to Lady Alenia.

The look on Lady Alenia's face was pure horror.

"What have you discovered?" Elwrick asked Lady Alenia.

"The barbarians plan to eradicate the reptiles using a deadly gas to poison them in their den." She turned and looked to Elwrick. "He plans to kill every last reptile. We can't allow this to happen. We have to do something."

Elwrick scrubbed his chin.

Lady Alenia grabbed Elwrick by his robes. "Don't you hear me? We have to do something."

Elwrick pulled Lady Alenia into a hug. "And we will," he whispered into her ear. "I swear to you this day. I will not allow this wanton annihilation to occur."

Lady Alenia appeared petrified. "What do we do?"

"We have no choice but to bring them here," Elwrick said. "I must prepare a few things first before my departure. In a few days, I'll leave for the 'Anor and escort them here."

Outside the window, Ruven knelt on a thick limb concealed behind a gaggle of broad leaves watching everything unfold. Smiling with excitement, this was the exact news he wanted to hear. With Elwrick gone, Lady Alenia and Lilith would be easy targets.

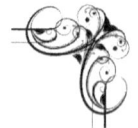

Chapter 94

mperor Haumlell paced the length of his tent, arms tightly folded behind his back, waiting for Karayan's arrival. On his mind was the brutal slaughter he endured on the rim of the Nymph Pass, and how he planned to explain the blunder to his King, whose words still rang heavy in his ears—*Do not reveal yourselves to the reptiles until you're ready to engage them in all-out war. They are cunning beasts and given the opportunity to prepare, will only prove to be a thorn in your side. The surprise is on your side, use it to your fullest advantage.*

Outside the tent, the thunder of hooves and the snarl of angry horses drew his attention to the hide flap covering the door. Emperor Haumlell popped his knuckles, flexed his stiff shoulders, and prepared for the severe beating he knew was to take place for his failure. His only wish was for it to be quick, and not in front of his men.

Karayan entered throwing the flap to the side, then carefully removed his riding gloves one finger at a time, then tossed them on the rickety table. "From how it appears on the way in, the war has already started. How many men did you lose fighting those filthy reptiles?"

Emperor Haumlell licked his dry lips then started to answer when two of Karayan's guards entered. Their glistening wet armor held a blood-red tint from the overloaded brazier. "You're correct, M' Lord," the guard said to Karayan with a heavy western accent, possibly from far away as Talons Peak. "After questioning the gravedigger, the dead were killed by reptiles."

"Don't ever doubt me again," Karayan sneered at the guard.

"Allow me to explain," Emperor Haumlell said.

"Please do." Karayan crossed his arms and waited.

"Pegan Rhoe and a small band of elves captured one of my men and used him as bait to lure us into the Nymph, where a squad of reptiles waited in ambush. We were severely outnumbered, and in the dark, had no chance to win. I didn't realize the severity of the situation until daybreak." Emperor Haumlell lied putting his men at a disadvantage.

"How many did you lose?" Karayan asked.

"Twenty-three, and twice as many injured."

"And how many did you kill?" Karayan asked.

Emperor Haumlell lowered his head, "None."

"Let me see if I understand you correctly. Counting the wounded, you lost nearly seventy men to save one?" Karayan didn't care and was quite delighted with the slaughter. It would be less his men would have to deal with once the reptiles were defeated.

Emperor Haumlell never answered, but instead walked to the doorway and looked out over the encampment. Fires burned brightly as far as he could see, and around each, men gathered. Smoke and ash floated heavy on the wet, night air, and if you took a hard sniff, you could catch the faint scent of cooked meat. When he turned, there was a fit of unmistakable anger on his face and wetness to his eyes. "That one man was my brother. Growing up, we always agreed to look out for each other. Each time I needed him, he was there for me. The one time he needed me, I didn't come through."

Karayan revealed little concern for Haumlell's brother. "Thus are the casualties of war," Karayan explained. "Before this war ends, all of us are bound to loose someone close. Still, I need someone in command who understands what we are trying to accomplish here is for the greater good for all. If you feel you're no longer capable of performing the duties required as Emperor, let me know now, and I will have no problem finding a suitable replacement."

Emperor Haumlell thought for a moment. "Now that the incident is in the past and I have grieved his loss. My heart bleeds for nothing but revenge."

"And you shall have it," Karayan said. "As you have those responsible for your loss hanging by their toes, their shrieks of pain filling your ears. It will make revenge all that much sweeter as you peel away their skins and wear them as boots to cover your feet."

Emperor Haumlell relished in the thought of skinning the reptiles alive. What he liked, even more, was the fact Karayan whole-heartedly swallowed his lie about the man being his brother. "My King, how much longer must we wait before we begin the true assault upon the reptiles?"

"My men will be here in ten days," Karayan informed him.

A third guard entered the tent. His armor was covered in mud, and his face appeared exhausted as if he'd been riding hard. From a pouch designed to keep the contents dry, he removed a rolled-up parchment sealed with a drop of red wax and stamped with the letter—K. "My King, I have strict orders to deliver this to you directly."

"What news do you bring?" Karayan asked.

"My King, I was given strict orders not to speak out loud as the enemy has ears everywhere. Everything is contained upon this parchment for your eyes only."

Karayan snatched the parchment and carefully broke the seal then casually unrolled the item. His piercing blue eyes darted side to side; then, a sinister grin crossed his thin blackened lips. "Well, it appears the construction of the bellows along with the smoldering pot has been completed ahead of schedule. Counting the travel time, they should be here within a week. Your lust for vengeance will be quenched much sooner than expected."

Emperor Haumlell wickedly smiled.

"Will your men be ready for all-out war?" Karayan asked.

"As we speak, my men are ready to rip out their own guts and eat them. What I don't know yet is how this device you created works."

"The device is none of your concern. It is your job to force the reptiles back into their den, then protect my men while they deliver the decisive blow, which will send them all to hell."

"And if your men are killed during the battle, who will work the device?"

"If my men die, I recommend you slip on a mossy rock and fall upon your sword," Karayan said.

Emperor Haumlell was relieved knowing if something went wrong with the contraption, it would be Karayan's men taking the blame, not his.

Karayan unfurled a map and laid it on the desk. "See these spots here designated with a red X; those are the escape tunnels. You will have to place men there to kill all who try and flee. The bright purple X is the main entrance. That is where the contraption will be installed."

"Why not destroy the escape tunnels first?" the Emperor asked.

"Because airflow is required to distribute the chemical agent throughout the network of tunnels. If we destroy the escape tunnels, the air will become stagnant, thus leaving pockets unmolested."

The Emperor held a sadistic grin. "Excellent."

"This will be the first decisive blow against the enemy. The next will come against the elves and Rhunsiire. As we speak, my army gathers to the west of Fairdenn far away from the prying eyes of the elves. They will have no idea what they are bound to encounter until it is too late, and their fate is sealed."

Emperor Haumlell cheered. "I can already smell victory."

"Don't get too excited. Victory has not yet been achieved. You know as well as I do, both the elves and the reptiles are complex enemies and extremely dangerous, especially when they know their extinction is near."

Emperor Haumlell looked out the doorway to his gathering army. "Still, it's hard not to celebrate when victory is so close at hand."

"I am unsure if we will meet again until after the war, so I will tell you now of future events. With the reptile's destruction, travel to God's Perch. I will have a small band of men waiting there for you. The runner will then inform me of the job's completion. You will then wait for my signal, which will be billowing red smoke. You will enter the Whispering Woods from the South. I will come down from the north, and we will meet at Rhunsiire, thus preventing the elves from escaping. Any that slip through and flee west will be swiftly cut down by the rovers."

"Can the rovers be trusted?" the Emperor asked. "They're nomads, criminals, and swear allegiance to none."

"They have sworn allegiance to me," Karayan said with a smile. "Regardless, I must take my leave back to my army. Until we meet again," Karayan said and offered a quick nod.

Emperor Haumlell bowed. "We will drink fine wine from glasses made from the bones of the fallen elven army."

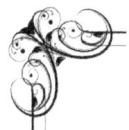

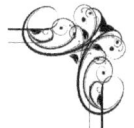

Chapter 95

he next day Lilith sat on a bench in front of the full-length mirror and brushed her tangled hair while admiring her new eye color. Her once anorexic body and emaciated features were nothing but a distant memory while her twisted and bent fingers appeared strong and healthy. The ugly scar's that marred her body were fading, and the bones Malvo broke had mended. The debilitating pain which tortured her mind was nothing but a nuisance she efficiently managed.

Climbing into a pair of drab green pants, she pulled on a dirt-brown shirt that extended past her waist and had sleeves that went clear to her wrists. After tucking in the excess, she wrapped a black belt around her waist and strapped on a small dagger provided by the elves. Cotton socks covered her feet then she slipped on a pair of black boots that went halfway to her knees.

Thump, thump, thump—

Lilith closed her silver eyes and focused on the door. Instantly, the solid object dematerialized. No longer did she see the dense wood, twisted grain, or cut marks. The metal hinges melded into molecules then blinked out of existence. Each nail popped into oblivion. The last part to vanish was the steel handle, which left in a shower of bright sparks. Within seconds she saw who waited outside as if there were no door. "Come in, Elwrick.".

Elwrick located a chair after entering and moved it to where he sat beside Lilith. "I see you discovered the ability to see through solid objects?"

"Yes, it's amazing—"

"Remember," Elwrick scolded her. "The same as you like your privacy, so do those who live around you. Don't use the ability to pry where it doesn't belong."

"Are you going to teach me something new today?"

"Yes. Today we are going to begin the basic concepts of defensive incantations. You must learn to defend yourself before you can fight."

Lilith cocked her head slightly sideways, and her hair fell partly covering her face. "Elwrick, I think there is something you should know."

Elwrick squinted his eyes, and he leaned back in the chair.

"The entire time I was with Karayan, I hated you. Everything wrong with the world, all the disease, all the pain and suffering, all the crime, everything was your fault, your doings. I wanted nothing more but to watch you burn and dance upon your charred bones." Lilith looked down at the brush she held. "Everything Karayan told me was nothing more than lies, and I fell for every word. Every word he said, I swallowed without question. You're nothing like that. You're compassionate, caring, helpful, and more concerned about the well-being of those around you more than yourself. I feel so disgusted with myself, can you ever forgive me?"

Elwrick scratched his chin. "Thank you for the kind words," he whispered, his vision locked on something else. "Karayan is a spiteful man with a corrupted heart. He was once a bearer's child and should have been an inspiration to all; instead, he turned out to be a disease. He allowed greed to take hold of him, and he sold his soul in the process."

Lilith looked at Elwrick. "That is a lie. He isn't a bearer's son. He doesn't have the gold eyes of a bearer."

"He did, at one time long before you knew him. He traded his gold eyes for immortality, and now he has neither."

Lilith hugged Elwrick. "Thank you. Thank you for saving me. Thank you for showing me a better life."

Elwrick kissed her forehead. "Hearing this means more to me than anything in this world. To even save one soul from going to the Dark Master—I have done my job."

"You've saved more than one soul." Lilith reminded him of the assassins who changed their way. "Can we please begin my training before I start to cry?" Lilith asked.

"There is no shame in crying," Elwrick smiled. "It's the body's way of expressing emotion."

Ruven remained in the shadows for a long time wanting to be proof positive Elwrick would not be returning anytime soon as he was the only one who could prevent Lady Alenia's death. Moving with the stealth of a shadow, he crept up the stairs to Lady Alenia's home.

"Halt," the guard said as Ruven approached. "By order of Elwrick, Order of the First Flame, none are to enter."

Ruven stopped near the guard. "It is I Ruven Dorharice, high ranking member of the elven council coming to inform Lady Alenia on the inner workings of Karayan's plans. She must be notified immediately as a delay now could cost the elven race their existence."

"Why was Elwrick not notified?" the guard suspiciously asked.

"Elwrick has not been notified as I have only recently returned. Any delay to track him down could prove costly."

"Hmmm," the guard mumbled. Ruven was one of the highest members of the council and has lived longer than most other elves. If he did refuse Ruven entry, and something drastic happened, he would be the one responsible. "Make it quick," the guard said. "She is currently resting."

"I'll only be a few minutes," Ruven told him.

The guard unlocked the door and quietly swung it open.

Ruven crept inside and closed the door. He understood the process of a mimic spell. In order for it to be successful, the said subject had to be terminated, which would be no problem considering her waning health. Going to her bedchamber, he discovered the door securely locked, which was nothing more than an inconvenience as he waved his hand near the knob, and the lock quickly turned.

Lady Alenia sat up in the bed, having heard the click of the lock. Elwrick was not supposed to be back for hours as he was training Lilith.

The door burst suddenly inward, and Ruven charged in quickly subduing Lady Alenia. The glint of his shiny blade reflected in the faint light filtering through the drawn shades. One quick swipe across her throat, and it would all be over. Before Elwrick returned, he would be lying in her place. Later that evening, he would request to see Lilith, and she would meet the same fate.

Lady Alenia screamed as the blade fell.

The clash of steel rung through the darkened air and sparks momentarily lit the room.

Ruven was punched in the face sending him reeling backward.

Darkblade crouched between Lady Alenia and Ruven. In each hand, a glowing dagger was visible.

Ruven backed away, observing the assassin. "Darkblade," he hissed, then fled from the house.

Darkblade chased him to the door and stopped when he reached the guard. "Sound the alarm. There is a traitor amongst our ranks."

The guard watched in horror as Ruven fled into the darkness. He had done the unthinkable. He allowed the man inside who attempted to kill Lady Alenia.

The screech of the alarm made Elwrick's blood run cold, and then he sprang into action bolting from the room towards the designated gathering location. Upon his arrival, Ryul was already there, each hand holding a deadly sword. "What happened?" Elwrick screamed. Around them, elven soldiers gathered ready for combat.

"You need to come with me, both of you?" the guard said, then led them towards Lady Alenia's home.

With each step, Elwrick's heart sank. He knew without a doubt where they were heading, and something had gone drastically wrong.

Before entering, Elwrick could hear the sobs coming from Lady Alenia. At the door, Darkblade remained at the ready, never replacing his weapons. "What happened here?" Elwrick demanded an answer from Darkblade.

The guard admitted his failure by allowing Ruven to enter.

Darkblade next told his story of how he prevented her death.

Elwrick was furious as he grabbed the guard by his neck. "I told you none were to enter."

The guard pleaded for forgiveness. "I didn't know. He's a high-ranking member..."

"I believe it was an honest mistake, and one he will not be making again anytime soon," Darkblade said.

Elwrick released the elf, then thanked Darkblade for his quick reaction, which saved Lady Alenia.

"I swore my allegiance to the elven Queen, no need to thank me."

"Am I removed of my position?" the guard asked.

Elwrick shook his head no, then walked towards the window and looked out. After a few minutes, he closed the shutters and locked them. "Ruven must be located. We cannot have a rogue elf running wild. Especially one who's intent is murdering the Queen."

"I will begin the search immediately," Ryul said.

"From this time forward, elves are to remain in groups of three or more," Elwrick demanded, "and I will oversee the relocation of Lady Alenia to Lilith's private home in the Medical Ward. It will be easier for me to keep an eye on both if they are in the same location. I will place a protection ward on the residence, and only the ones I designate will be allowed entry. This will prevent another mistake, albeit an honest one, from occurring."

Lady Alenia went to object, then closed her mouth. She knew it was for the best.

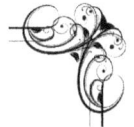

Chapter 96

lwrick remained with Lady Alenia the remainder of the day and into the night. Lilith, along with Gleia and Ellusia, were thrilled to have the company.

"In the morning, I must leave for the 'Anor," Elwrick said as he glanced out the window into the darkness. Out there somewhere, he knew Ruven lurked, waiting to strike again. "I know you ladies are going to object and feel that I am intruding upon your privacy, but I am going to ask Darkblade to remain here on guard."

"At least this time you're warning me," Lady Alenia said. "I had no idea Darkblade was hiding in the shadows of my room."

"I should have told you, but I knew you would have objected," Elwrick said.

Gleia stood by the window, allowing the faint breeze to cool her sweaty neck. "Do you think Ruven will return?"

Elwrick scratched his chin. "Not anytime soon. What I fear, though, is if Ruven has gone to the ways of the Dark Master, how many more have fallen in his footsteps?"

"You think there may be more?" Lady Alenia asked from the comfort of her plush chair.

"I don't know," Elwrick admitted. "Regardless, I am not taking any chances. Darkblade will be stationed inside, and outside at the entrance will be two more assassins along with a few elven guards."

"Are you not putting up the protective ward then?" Ellusia asked Elwrick.

"At first, I planned to," Elwrick told Ellusia, "but have since changed my mind. My power isn't limitless like the Creator. If I over-extend my resources, I will be sent back to the Realm of Light to recover, regardless of how much I resist. To keep such a powerful ward in place, in time, would drain all that I have. Therefore, we have no other option but to use the resources available to us."

Gleia looked at Darkblade for a second before diverting her attention to Elwrick. "You're worried about Ruven returning, yet you're leaving us alone with a man who swore allegiance to the Dark Master?"

"I understand your fears," Elwrick said. "All we can hope for is they remain true to their oaths and the fear of what will become of them if they falter."

"Ladies," Darkblade said. "Had I wanted to harm anyone of you, I could have easily done so when I wore the Demon-Hyde Robe. Rest assured, my actions now are guided by a righteous motive."

Lady Alenia removed a blanket from the back of the chair and covered her legs. "Gleia, you must remember it was Darkblade who saved me in my home."

Lilith abruptly sat up from her chair. "Outside, someone approaches."

"How do you know?" Lady Alenia asked Lilith.

"Witches have a heightened sense of awareness well beyond that of the elves, and myself," Elwrick informed Lady Alenia. Watching through the window, he saw a shadow pass. "With Lilith around, nothing will approach undetected."

Seconds later, there was a faint knocking at the door.

Elwrick turned to Lilith. "Who waits outside?"

Lilith concentrated on the door. "It's Ryul."

"She can see through doors?" Lady Alenia asked.

"Yes, and no," Elwrick explained. "Physically, she cannot see through solid objects, but her Mind's Eye leaves her body and ventures inches beyond the blockage to see what waits. It happens so fast it seems as if she's looking through the door, but in all reality, she isn't." Elwrick opened the door and ushered Ryul inside, then looked in all directions before closing it.

Ryul was nearly out of breath when he spoke. "We've searched all of Rhunsiire and found no trace of Ruven. It seems the man has disappeared."

"Gone into hiding more likely," Elwrick said.

"Could Lilith track him down?" Gleia asked.

"In time, she could track him down and pulverize him," Elwrick explained. "But Lilith is a young Witch, and I would not risk the chance of something going wrong."

Outside, the sky showed the first signs of dawn as the horizon held a faint silver glow.

"Time is short, and I may already be too late." Elwrick rested both hands on Ryul's shoulders. "Gather a small force of elves and in five days, be at God's Perch. If the barbarians attack the reptiles, prepare your elves for war. I will not abandon King Hulradeeh in his time of need."

"Neither will we," Ryul said, then he clasped Elwrick by the forearm. "When you see King Hulradeeh, let him know the elves proudly stand beside him."

Elwrick nodded, then departed.

Lady Alenia watched him ride away on Midnight while a solitary tear traveled down her cheek.

"He loves you," Gleia said.

Lady Alenia sat back in the plush chair. "I know."

Two days would pass before Elwrick arrived at the opening to the reptile's den. Hiding amongst the tangled roots and twisted vines, reptilian soldiers looked to the north and the red glow on the rim of the Pass.

"I must see King Hulradeeh at once," Elwrick informed the reptile, which stepped out of the shadows.

The reptile vividly remembered Elwrick as a great friend to the King. "Certainly," he said, exploiting a deep hiss. "I believe he currently resides in the throne room."

The air grew thick, and the temperature rose the deeper they traveled under the swamp. Each reptile they encountered had a somber look. Nearing a four-way split, they stopped to allow a weaning mother to pass guiding a small group of hatchlings.

"They all look frightened," Elwrick said.

"And why shouldn't they be?" the reptile asked. "They've all heard the rumors. They know the barbarians are here to destroy us."

Elwrick wanted to speak, but he knew the reptile was right.

"Elwrick," the reptile called out. "There is nowhere else for us to go."

"That is why I am here," Elwrick said as he watched a few hatchings sprint past who were lagging. "The elves are welcoming you into Rhunsiire."

"Rhunsiire," the reptile repeated.

"The only issue is we don't know how much time we have until the barbarians attack. We must begin the preparations to flee immediately. If we must, we will fight our way to God's Perch."

"We have seen their numbers. What you speak is impossible. Most of the reptiles have never been out of the den. Of those who have, few have witnessed true combat. We'll get slaughtered in the open."

"The elves gather at God's Perch to lend aid." Elwrick tried to find encouraging words.

Back on the move, they traveled at a steady downward slope for some distance. Intersections came and went, yet they continued deeper following the twisting tunnel. Eventually, they arrived at a doorway covered with a large flap. Pulling back the flap, the reptile directed Elwrick inside.

The mood of the room was dreary. King Hulradeeh sat slightly slumped to one side in a chair carved from a giant mushroom. His partially closed eyes were dull, and from his mouth came raspy wheezing sounds. "My old friend," King Hulradeeh said, struggling with a hoarse cough. "Have you come to join me in my final hour? To watch the last stand of the reptiles?"

Elwrick swiftly approached and knelt before the King. "No. I have come to offer you salvation and guidance in your time of need. I have come to inform you; you don't stand alone in this fight. The elves stand beside you if we can reach God's Perch."

King Hulradeeh had a thousand-league stare. "Elwrick, my old friend…" His words trailed off, and he released a horrendous cough spewing up green blood.

The Shaman wiped away the blood. "King Hulradeeh is very old and extremely sick. His condition deteriorates daily."

King Hulradeeh looked at Elwrick as if he were a stranger. "Elwrick, my old friend…" his mumbled words trailed off.

Elwrick took King Hulradeeh's hand. The once striking green color was now gray, and only two claws remained. "We must prepare to evacuate. The barbarians plan to fill the nest with a poisonous gas that will kill everything which breathes it, including the unhatched hatchlings."

The Shaman covered her mouth.

King Hulradeeh was in a daze. "Prepare the army. We go to war."

Elwrick wanted to weep from hearing those words. Even in his final hour, King Hulradeeh was an honorable reptile, and he would never forget the time they fought side by side in the Great War. "Now is not the time for war. Now is the time to flee. We will fight another day," Elwrick told King Hulradeeh.

King Hulradeeh struggled to raise his fist. "We go to war... Elwrick, my old friend."

Saress barged in, ripping the flap free from the wall. "I'm sorry for the intrusion, but when I heard Elwrick had arrived, I had to find him immediately."

"How is Pegan doing?" the Shaman asked.

"That is why I needed to find Elwrick. The infection grows worse. The ugly black streamers have reached his chest, and he struggles to breathe."

Elwrick took a deep breath. Things were moving way to fast. He needed to take a step back and reevaluate the situation before he made a dire mistake. "Saress," Elwrick called out. "Your father is no longer in his right mind to lead the reptiles. As his only surviving hatchling, it falls on your shoulders to take his place. We need to get the reptiles organized for a mass-movement to Rhunsiire. You need to make that decision."

"What? Rhunsiire. The reptiles place is underground, not in the trees."

"We were able to extract the information from the barbarian and why they gather at the Pass. If you don't flee, these tunnels are going to become your final resting ground," Elwrick hissed.

"What are they planning—" Saress started to ask.

"We don't have time right now. Have the reptiles gather what they'll need for the journey to Rhunsiire, and nothing more. I will see to Pegan's infection."

Hulradeeh suddenly jerked his head upright and released a piercing howl. His hardened jaw was missing all but a few teeth. "My old friend..." he started to mumble then drifted back to sleep.

Saress knew Elwrick was right. Her father was responsible for their flight from the desert. Now it would be her turn to lead them from the swamp.

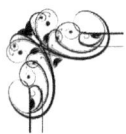
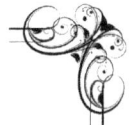

Chapter 97

kylar Nightshade spent the better part of the day meandering through the encampment listening to conversations and learning as much as possible about Karayan's war plans. None questioned his appearance as he wore the uniform of a Royal Guard he acquired by way of the blade. What he learned from those conversations were dreadful to the ear, and made his stomach churn.

The city of Fairdenn now belonged to Karayan, seized under the name of war. Generals moved into the homes while the families were forcefully removed and sent to the encampment for reassignment. Women were made to cook, clean, and tend to the wounded, while the men were directed to the log piles and forced to chop wood into more manageable lengths. Children were not exempt from the labors of war and were forced to wash dishes, sew armor, or any other duties the supervisor deemed necessary. Some families refused and fled, but most were quickly captured and brought back and turned into examples. Men were flogged into unconsciousness while the women were forced to work the tents, raising the morale of the soldiers.

Climbing up a large observation platform, Skylar took in the view.

To the west the Majestic Forest was being devoured, and the logs transferred to the resizing stations. To the east, a long caravan of wagons loaded with coal from the Wruust Mines headed his direction. Before him, men spread out by the thousands in roughly fenced-off training grounds spending hours either practicing with the sword or sending arrow's flying into straw bales. To the north was a row of grizzly-looking machines which resembled catapults, but more massive, and angry looking. These had to be what Lilith saw and a closer look would be required to determine their purpose. Behind the machines was an area where more were in various stages of construction.

Crossing the large mud-covered field, he wound his way through a gaggle of tents before encountering the machines. From their sheer size and deadly construction, it was clear these war machines only had one purpose—the complete and total annihilation of anything on the receiving end of the massive, house-sized steel bucket.

Circling the monstrosity, he located a ladder on the back which led to a platform designed for the commander to oversee the machine's operation. On the platform was a chair and table with three drawers securely fastened to the platform. Searching through the drawers, he located a map showing the location where this machine was to be located. In another drawer was a rolled-up parchment which revealed the plan of attack in excruciating detail. *These are important*, he thought, then tucked both items neatly away in his pocket.

The war machine commander emerged from his tent, yawned, then nearly fainted observing the man standing on his machine. "Hey, what do you think you're doing?"

Men emerged from the nearby tents hearing the commotion.

Skylar looked about surveying the situation. It was too late to silence the man unnoticed.

"What's he doing on your machine?" another commander asked.

Skylar quickly realized the tents were where the commanders resided as more emerged curious to see if their machines were being vandalized. He would need to come up with something quick before a fight ensued. "King Karayan informed me you are relieved of your position, and this machine now belongs to me."

The Commander looked around at those who looked at him as if he'd done something wrong. *What could I have done to cross King Karayan? I have always been loyal to his cause,* he thought. "If what you say is true, then why didn't King Karayan inform me of this change personally?"

Shuffling through the remaining drawers, he found nothing useful. "Don't ask me why he didn't inform you personally. I have learned not to question his motives. Perhaps I've read King Karayan wrong, and your loyalty has paid off and you're up for a promotion."

"Perhaps," the Commander said. "Until I hear the words from his mouth, I want you off my machine."

Skylar pretended to be checking things over as he took note of the Machine's construction. "You mean my machine," Skylar said as he hopped down landing a few feet away from the Commander. "Now you run along like a good dog and find out what King Karayan wants while I make sure this Machine is fit for battle."

The Commander was flush red with anger.

"I'll do no running along or surrender ownership of my machine until King Karayan informs me personally of the change. Until then, your nothing but a liar and a spy." Removing a dagger from his boot, he circled Skyler. "And spy's get cut."

"Slice him good," a commander yelled from somewhere in the back.

Skylar rolled his eyes observing the ineptitude of his foe. A fight was precisely NOT what he needed. If the commander appeared to be losing, there was a chance the others may intervene. He was good with a blade, but not good enough to take on the hundred or more men who now gathered. Regardless, he could not allow the man to slice him as the wound could prove fatal, and to flee was not an option as alarms may be sounded. He would have no choice but to face the enemy.

The Commander came in fast, swinging the blade.

Skylar danced backward, easily avoiding the dagger and latched onto the Commander's blubbery wrist. Twisting his arm, the Commander squealed, then dropped the dagger. Jerking the man in a few different positions, Skylar slapped him more times than he could count. When he released the Commander, the dazed man spun in a circle then fell face first in the mud.

OOOH, the crowd groaned.

Crawling towards his dagger, the Commander hung his head in utter embarrassment.

Skylar planted his foot on the Commander's rump. "Now, I suggest you run along before you get hurt."

The Commander looked back at Skylar with hate in his eyes. "This isn't over yet, not by a long shot," then fled into the crowd.

Skylar watched him leave then headed south.

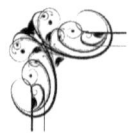 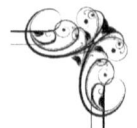

Chapter 98

ason Gilbert—detective for the Federal Bureau of Investigation—stood in the hotel room doorway and covered his mouth. Some cases he investigated took a while to decide if foul play was involved, but not this one, this one was murder without a doubt. In his twenty-six years of working for the department, he had never witnessed such a brutal crime. The body lay in a cocoon of upholstery and coagulated blood like a ghoulish mannequin. A nasty gash stretched from ear to ear, and severed veins and arteries poked up through the bloated purplish skin like corrugated rubber tubes. Only the coroner would be able to tell how many times he was stabbed as the chest appeared to be run over by a riding lawnmower. The only thing worse than the body in the room was the smell… that decaying putrid funk, which could only come from something dead. In this case, it was Frank Middleton.

The flash from the camera lit the room as a cop took a picture of the broken blade protruding from the chest, then snapped a few more he felt may be useful for the crime lab. "What do you think, robbery?" he asked the Detective.

Detective Gilbert grinned, shaking his head.

The cop snapped a few more pictures of the hands where it was apparent jewelry had been removed. "My God, it looks like someone pulled a few caps off his teeth." Using a pencil, he held back the skin that partially covered the mouth and took a picture of the teeth.

The Detective knelt beside the corpse and looked at the hands. Not one broken fingernail, no hair, no wounds… "He appears to have been sleeping or out cold when the crime occurred. I see no evidence of a struggle. We'll need a toxicology report to check for drugs in his system."

"Got it," the cop said as he wrote something down on his note pad.

Joseph Clarence entered the room and covered his nose. "I think I may have found a witness."

Detective Gilbert directed his assistant to follow him outside. "And who might that be?"

"Kaylee Green," Joseph said. "She was staying in the room next door."

"She saw it take place?" Gilbert asked.

"Not exactly. What Ms. Green did see was an altercation between Frank and a man named Mr. Tom Fischer, owner of the Fischer Farms located about five miles south of town."

"Altercation? What kind of altercation?"

The man began to read from his note pad. "About a week ago, give or take a few days, she heard a loud argument erupt next door. Stepping out to see what was happening, she witnessed Tom Fischer yell directly at Frank that he had a lot of property, pigs, a backhoe, an alibi, and that he'd be long gone before they ever found his bones."

"Very interesting," Detective Gilbert said.

"She also gave me a list of names of others who witnessed the altercation as well."

"Excellent. It sounds like we may have our first real lead."

"I guess a woman was staying with him also, but she vanished about a week ago, according to witnesses."

"Hmm," Detective Gilbert groaned. "Another possible suspect, or a second victim."

"Either or," Joseph agreed.

"Regardless, we need to keep this on the low. Whoever murdered this man, didn't want it discovered anytime soon. I know this because its colder than a brass toilet on the shady side of an iceberg, yet they turned the air conditioning on high."

"What do we do in the meantime?" Joseph asked.

"We'll locate the other witnesses and see if their story collaborates with Ms. Green's. By then, we should have something back from the toxicologist."

Two days later, Detective Gilbert met Joseph at a local dinner. "Did you discover anything from the lab?"

Joseph opened his notebook. "Yup, very interesting. It seems the man was doped up on Rohypnol."

"The date-rape drug?" Detective Gilbert surprisingly asked.

"Yup. He had such a high dosage in his blood they found it immediately. The level was enough to render him paralyzed, yet alert enough to experience the pain."

Detective Gilbert scratched his chin. "Explains why the man never put up a fight. The question is, how did he get it into his blood?"

Joseph sipped on his coffee as he watched the snow flutter to the ground. "The toxicologist is not sure. That will take some time, possibly weeks to discover how it was administered."

Gilbert stirred his coffee. "Makes you wonder what's going through someone's mind when they do something like this."

"Do you think this may be the work of a satanic cult or something? I have a hard time believing a successful businessman would throw everything away in an instance."

Detective Gilbert downed the last of his coffee. "I talked with every witness, and they all said the very same thing. Tom Fischer blatantly said he was going to kill Frank. It seems it may not have been in the way he threatened him, but Frank Middleton is dead, and Tom Fischer is our only suspect."

"What about the girl living with him?" Joseph asked.

"Nobody knows her name, who she was, or where she came from. The hotel has no record of a girl staying there. Unless someone comes forward, we have nothing."

The waitress came to the table and filled their coffee cups.

"Thank you," they each said.

Detective Gilbert slowly stirred in the creamer. "Knowing what we know now, I believe we should visit Tom Fischer and see what he has to say."

"Sounds like a plan."

The next morning Averie knelt on the couch and watched out the window as the snow fell. Outside, Billy, Tom, and Mike were bundled up beyond recognition running for cover as snowballs flew in every conceivable direction. Averie greedily smiled; she was thirsty for action.

"You look like you're anxious to throw a few yourself," Sarah said.

"Can I?" Averie asked as she rubbed her paws sadistically.

"Sure, but first you need to get dressed for it."

All decked out in the latest gear, Averie crept from the backdoor unnoticed. Sneaking her way around the house, she arrived at the Jeep. Gathering a handful of snow, she packed it tight, searched for her target, then threw it with surgical precision.

POW! Mike screamed like a frightened school girl and fought to get the freezing snow off his exposed neck before sprinting across the yard.

Tom spun in a circle, searching for the sniper.

Averie was already reloaded and let another fly.

WHAM! Tom took the snowball to the face.

Billy spotted the enemy and circled the barn coming up behind Averie, who was gathering more snow.

POOF! Snow impacted her body, leaving a perfect outline against the Jeep.

Billy busted out laughing, then took off running with Averie in hot pursuit.

Sarah watched the carnage unfold from the safety of the kitchen. "They sure are having a blast out there."

"Did you want to join them?" Jennifer asked. "I'm more than happy to watch Robyn."

"Are you crazy?" Sarah laughed. "Do you know how cold it is out there? It's like… freezing."

Robyn zipped past, bouncing the walker off everything in her path heading towards the living room.

"That little girl sure is on the move. I give her a few weeks, and she won't need that walker," Jennifer said.

"Yeah, it's crazy how fast she learns things. Here soon she's going to start demanding things, like a cell phone," Sarah said.

"And a car," Jennifer added.

From the living room came the sound of shredding paper.

"Oh god," Jennifer groaned. "If Robyn has the paper, Mike's going to kill her. He hasn't read it yet."

"If need be, we can get another," Sarah said as she entered the living room, then took off into a sprint. Robyn had the walker wedged between the couch and the coffee table. All around her were the remains of the TV guide, and she now gripped the much more appealing American Hunter Magazine. "You're as bad as your mother," Sarah said as she pried the magazine from Robyn's grimy little paws. "What do you have to say for yourself?"

Robyn snatched the pencil off the coffee table and began smacking it against the rim of the walker.

"Well, there's your answer," Jennifer said after busting out in laughter.

"Come here, you," Sarah groaned, lifting Robyn from the walker. "Time to end your reign of terror." Grabbing a few toys along the way, she headed for the playpen.

Tom saw the opportunity and broke for the safety of the barn. Ducking under one snowball, he leaped over another before arriving safely at the barn.

Mike circled the house at a full sprint then slid to a sudden halt in the middle of the driveway. Red-faced and exhausted, he raised his hands in a position of surrender, but it was too late. Averie was in mid-throw and pelted him in the leg.

Averie knew something wasn't right when she saw Mike suddenly look down the driveway as if expecting someone. Tom sensed it too and came from the barn. Soon they all three stood looking east.

"Sounds like something is chewing through the snow," Tom said.

Moments later, a glistening black Ford Crown Victorian with black tinted windows, push bar, and blue and red lights behind the grill came into view. Creeping along like a Coast Guard Cutter clearing the way it stopped mere feet from running the trio over.

"Did you invite anyone over?" Sarah asked Jennifer.

"No, why?"

"A car pulled into the driveway. If I'm not mistaken, it looks like an undercover cop car."

Jennifer looked out the window. "The cops around these parts don't drive those, that's an FBI car."

Sarah snatched Robyn from the playpen and bundled her up. "We best go out and see what kind of trouble Frank's starting now."

Tom waited with his arms crossed for the man to climb from the rig. "Can I help you?"

"Mr. Tom Fischer?" the man asked.

"Yeah."

"I'm Detective Jason Gilbert, Federal Bureau of Investigation, and this is my partner Joseph Clarence. We want to ask you a few questions about Mr. Frank Middleton."

Mike eyed the detective suspiciously, there could only be one reason for his appearance.

Detective Gilbert flipped through his notepad. "When was the first time you met him?"

Tom thought back to the first time. "Hmm, let me think a moment." *It was early spring when Averie arrived, it was now November.* "A few months ago, maybe."

"In that time how well did you get to know him?" Detective Gilbert asked.

"Not all that well," Tom explained. "Every time I met him he was a complete jerk, if you want to know the truth."

The Detective scribbled down a few notes.

"What did Frank do now?" Sarah asked.

Detective Gilbert looked up from his notepad. "Nothing, he's dead."

Averie covered her mouth and backed up.

"Dead, how?" Jennifer asked.

"Ma'am, that's why we're out here. I was hoping one of you could tell me?" The Detective didn't want to give away any details as the public had yet to be notified of the murder. If he could get any one of them to slip up. It would place them at the scene of the crime.

"Excuse me," Tom said. "I could be wrong, but this sounds like your accusing one of us of killing him. Should I be talking to a lawyer?"

The Detective had an expressionless look on his face. "Do you think you need one?"

"No," Tom sternly answered. "I've done nothing wrong."

"Did you check on that meth head he had staying there?" Mike asked.

"We heard he had a woman there, but her identity remains a mystery," Detective Gilbert answered Mike.

"Her name is Savannah Henderson, and she is on parole out of Frankfort for the murder of a Security Guard, home invasion, robbery, and dealing narcotics."

"You must be Mike McCullaha, ex-Sheriff?"

"Yes."

"And this must be your lovely wife, Jennifer McCullaha?"

"Yes," he answered again.

"And you both recently lost your jobs?"

"What are you getting at?" Mike hissed.

The Detective sighed. "Listen, we both know how hard life can be when both family members lose their income, and we also know Frank was a very wealthy man—"

"Are you suggesting I killed him?"

"This is ridiculous," Sarah grumbled. "It's freezing out here, I'm taking Robyn inside."

Detective Gilbert watched her leave. "Sometimes, people do things they don't mean to."

"I want you off my property, NOW!" Tom demanded as he pointed down the driveway.

"Not so quick," Joseph said. "You can answer this last question now, or in front of a judge, don't make any difference to me."

"What is that?" Tom was fuming mad.

The assistant read the quote from the witness verbatim. "Did you say that?"

Tom released a ragged breath that hung heavy in the cold air. "I did say it, but I didn't kill him."

The assistant scribbled down a few notes. "You mind if we have a quick look around?"

"Not without a search warrant?" Mike said.

"You asked your questions, now you can leave," Tom growled.

Detective Gilbert looked at his partner, then to Tom. "Thank you for your time. We'll be in contact if we need anything else or if there's something you wish to tell us."

Detective Gilbert pulled the car to a stop at the vacant gas station. "I think they did it."

Joseph ran his fingers through his greasy black hair. "I don't think so. I didn't get that feeling."

Detective Gilbert glanced through his notes. "I think they did, and their heartless murderers, all of them. With Tom admitting he would kill Frank, that's all we need to acquire a search warrant. Then all we must do is locate something tying them to the scene of the crime. One of them will crack under the pressure once I start putting the screws to them… they always do."

Mike was on the phone the minute he entered the house.

"Who are you calling?" Jennifer asked.

"If the murder happened here, there is only one place the body would go for examination. I intend to find out how Frank died," Mike answered Jennifer as the phone started to ring.

"Hello?" A voice came on the line.

"Melvin, it's me, Mike, how you been?"

"Busy, busy, busy," he answered. "What's up?"

"Listen carefully. I need to know how Frank Middleton died."

The phone went silent.

"Melvin, this is important," Mike pleaded.

"I'm under a gag order from the FBI agents not to reveal anything about the murder."

"I've met them, and their accusing Tom and I of killing Frank. You know as well as I do, Tom nor I wouldn't kill anyone."

"Those two guys are top-notch government agents, they really know their stuff. You may be out of your league on this one," Melvin explained.

"Melvin, we go back a long time. An innocent man may go to prison—"

"Okay, okay," Melvin agreed. "But you didn't hear this from me."

"My lips are sealed," Mike said.

Melvin explained everything in exacting detail, which left Mike nauseous.

"Thank you kindly," Mike said as he hung up the phone.

"What did you learn?" Tom asked.

"I learned Savannah is a psychopath," Mike said, then went on to explain what he learned.

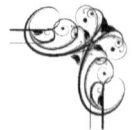

Chapter 99

mperor Haumlell watched the caravan of wagons grow larger with each passing hour. In preparation for the weapon's arrival, thick ropes wound around a pulley system then attached to a team of horses. For the men to descend, rope ladders spanned the distance from top to bottom. Making his way across the muddy compound, Emperor Haumlell climbed the narrow set of stairs built into the back of a large observation deck on the south side of camp. From this location, he could address his army in their entirety.

The barbarians stomped their feet in unison while chanting death to the reptiles when they saw him emerge from the shadows.

Over the last few days, Emperor Haumlell drove the soldiers into a blinding frenzy, and the only thing remaining was a speech to set wheels of war into motion. Looking over the crowd, he raised his fisted hand skyward, a signal for the crowd to silence. In his left hand, he held a device designed to magnify his voice. "Tonight, as the sky darkens, the barbarians are setting in motion an event which will reshape the future of Icearaus," he began.

The stomping of thousands of feet sounded like thunder.

"Since our departure," Emperor Haumlell continued. "Since our departure from Timber Hall, we have experienced hardship, loss, and sorrow, which would shake even the hardiest of souls. I, as your commander, would not have blamed you for turning around and heading for the comforts of home, had I not shared in this exhausting and dangerous march. It may first appear that this war will only benefit those who dwell on the mainland, but that isn't so. The reptiles are a parasite, a sickness, a filthy disease, and, if not eradicated, will spread until we become inflicted with their filth to the far north."

The chanting of the crowd was deafening, so Emperor Haumlell raised his right hand to silence them.

"Some of you will fall from the ravages of war; this cannot be prevented and is a price we each must be willing to pay. You must remember, though. As your physical form dies, your soul still lives—lives on in those who still fight to see this war a success. As long as the barbarians survive, your legacy survives."

The army began clapping and stomping.

Emperor Haumlell looked west. Within the hour, the caravan would be here.

The crowd's chanting never waned.

Emperor Haumlell raised his hand to silence the crowd. "Let us prepare now for what the future holds so that we perform our duties without pause or hesitation. Prepare now so we can set an example for future generations to come. For that generation who will look back at this day and will forever say that this was the finest hour of the barbarian race."

The crowd was ecstatic, and you could taste the electricity in the air as the men stomped their feet, cheered, chanted the Emperor's name, clapped their hands, or banged swords against shields.

Elwrick emerged first into an unnatural eerie darkness that robbed him of his senses and replaced it with a paralyzing fear. It was unlike a typical night where pastel-colored shadows kept the land cloaked in darkness, but the bleakness that fills the heart the very moment you realize death is imminent. To the north, the glow of fires lit the northern rim, and on the warm, stagnant, suffocating air ash fluttered. "So it begins, the second Great War of my time."

"And the first one for me," Saress said. She stood beside Elwrick, looking north.

Elwrick watched as each reptile emerged, carrying what they felt was necessary for the journey. Behind them, they left family heirlooms, trophies, excess weaponry, and their memories.

Eventually, the Shaman emerged with a disheveled look on her face. "I've checked every tunnel and every passage, every room, and each corridor. All reptiles, including the eggs, have been evacuated."

Elwrick thanked her for a job well done.

"We'll survive this," Saress told the Shaman. "Each persecution we face only makes us stronger."

Elwrick looked at the fewer than two-hundred hatchlings and their blinking yellow eyes and sighed. Most had never laid eyes on the night sky, and their first experience would be ash and smoke. How could he tell them they were valued more for their skins than friendship. Looking towards the heavens, he whispered a quick prayer. *What has man become*, he thought, *to drive a race of peaceful creatures to the brink of extinction?*

The scout returned sprinting through the mud and muck. "Elwrick, the barbarians move quicker than expected. They've erected a make-shift camp at the base, and the steel drum is halfway down. I give it less than a day, and they will reach the nest."

"And they will discover their time has been wasted," Elwrick said. "We can no longer delay; we must begin the march of the reptiles immediately."

A giant reptile thick with armor wielding two swords neared. "Go. I will draw them away, buying you a few more hours."

"No," Saress said. "Put your weapons away. Another day will come when we will face the barbarians in open war, but today isn't that day. Elwrick has already devised a plan to hide our movement."

"Who are you to command me?" the reptile hissed.

"I am your Queen," Saress snarled back.

"You're not the Queen yet. King Hulradeeh still has air in his lungs—"

Elwrick stepped between the two. "King Hulradeeh's decisions are no longer sound. The longer we fight amongst ourselves, the closer the enemy comes."

The reptile slammed his weapons into their sheaths, then grumbled as he joined the caravan.

Reptiles spoke in hushed whispers as Saress led them west into the gloom.

Elwrick waited until the last reptile faded from sight before beginning the process. He had no desire to have the reptiles watch the only home they ever knew get wiped from existence. Closing both eyes, he started to chant. Within seconds, both hands glowed faint blue. As the chant continued, the glow moved from his hands until it engulfed his entire body. Screaming out the words, he directed all of his magic in a single beam of light directly down the center of the darkened opening.

Deep below the ground came a rumbling sound that brought the caravan to a stop, and they all turned back to watch. In the gloom, they could see Elwrick glowing like a beacon for those lost at sea. Within minutes, the mournful cry of cracking timbers and roots being ripped free from the ground echoed up through the mouth of the nest. Ghastly moans followed as cracks formed in the mud walls.

"What have you done?" the Shaman solemnly asked.

Elwrick looked at the Shaman. "I had no choice but to remove all trace of your existence. Not only will this baffle the enemy, but it will also allow us to place more distance between them and us before they discover our trail."

Heavy tears rolled down the Shaman's cheeks as the only home she ever knew gurgled and spat up water, torn roots, splintered beams, and liquified mud. "We have nowhere else to go," she whispered.

A gush of wind exploded out the opening sending debris flying and water erupting as the thickest of beams finally broke, and the softening walls collapsed under the weight of the watery ceiling. Where the opening once was, only a bottomless pool remained, which bubbled like boiling water as the last bit of air escaped. In time, the pool calmed to a mirror-like surface.

"The elves will not abandon you," Elwrick said as he wiped away the tears from the Shaman's cheeks. "I make this promise to you. I will never stop searching until I find your race a home where you can thrive and grow strong again. This swamp is not for the living."

The caravan traveled like a giant snake following the narrow muddy trails in silence until the sun crested the horizon. With each step, Elwrick continually looked back, making sure his untraceable spell was working correctly. It would not remain for the entire journey, but long enough to buy them another day. His dry lips formed into a smile as broken limbs, twisted twigs, and torn grasses regrew. Behind them, their trail vanished, leaving no trace of their passing.

Progress was painstakingly slow as they took frequent stops to make sure none of the hatchlings wandered off. The world was new to them, and they seemed more interested in exploring it than staying in line. After all, there were slippery toads and slimy frogs that needed investigating. Even after multiple scolding's and threats of bodily injury, they still had to chase a few who felt a strange creature was more important than their safety.

Near noon of the first day, Elwrick had a concerned look on his face. At their current pace, it would take three more days to reach God's Perch. They would have no choice but to pick up the pace if they planned to reach the Perch without incident. Elwrick knew what the problem was, and it was time to address the situation. If the hatchlings wouldn't listen to reason, they were damn sure going to listen to him.

"They're only hatchlings," Saress said. She could sense the anger boiling in Elwrick's blood.

"And they can still die from the blade or the bolt," Elwrick snarled as he made his way to the area set up for them to play. Upon his arrival, the hatchlings were too engrossed with wrestling around or throwing moss balls at one another to notice the man standing there with his arm's crossed. "STOP!" Elwrick screamed.

They each froze in their current position and looked at Elwrick—their yellow eyes blinking in the dim light.

"Listen up," Elwrick said. "Do you all see that ridge with the glowing red lights?"

The hatchlings looked back, then nodded, they did.

"On the ridge is an army which wishes to see your destruction and will peel the skin from your limp bodies." Elwrick was not lovely with his description.

Saress rolled her eyes. "Sure, frighten them to death before we even reach the stairs."

Elwrick flashed Saress an angry look, then turned back to the hatchlings. "Do you see that little dot to the west?" Elwrick asked the hatchlings. He could see them squinting through the gloom, ash, and smoke. A few nodded yes, but most shook their heads no. "For those of you who do, that is where salvation lies. On it is an army that waits to lend aid. We must reach that ridge within the next few days, or we will all perish in this swamp."

Elwrick could sense the fear he placed in the hearts of each hatchlings.

"Did you have to be so cruel? They're only children," Saress said.

"What's crueler, me telling them what might happen to them, or what will happen to them if the barbarians catch us?"

"Still, it wasn't right," Saress grumbled.

Elwrick looked at the frightened hatchlings. "I understand everything is new to you. There are sights to see, smells to be smelt, and frogs to taste. Right now, we must reach the Ghu'lane. In time, you will have a whole new world to explore. I promise you that."

"Thank you," Saress whispered to Elwrick for softening the tone.

Elwrick flashed Saress a smile. "I better go check on your father."

Emperor Haumlell looked at the map, and then the stagnant pool. "This is no entrance to a nest, but a sloppy, watery mud hole." Spinning in all directions, he looked for any trace of the reptiles, but there was nothing. No footprints, bent branches, or even a scent the dogs could discover.

A barbarian knelt and ran his hand along the ground examining nearby twigs. "Nothing has been here for a long time. If this was an entrance, it's been abandoned for some time now."

"We need to spread out until we find some trace of their passing, which will lead us to the nest," Emperor Haumlell barked.

It didn't take long until the dog picked up the scent from the reptilian scout.

Snarling and barking, the beast was ready to taste lizard blood.

Following the scent for some distance, Emperor Haumlell brought his squad to a halt. "There headed west towards God's Perch."

Graf Hrizlurlund, the highest-ranking general in the barbarian army, examined the broken trail. "We're less than a day behind this one."

"One?" Emperor Haumlell asked.

"Yes," Hrizlurlund explained. "This trail was made by a single reptile, not from a mass movement."

The Emperor sighed. "Perhaps this one was a decoy to lead us astray."

A Barbarian came from the west. "I discovered signs not too far ahead of a large migration."

"Take us there," Emperor Haumlell demanded.

After the sound thrashing, the hatchlings MOSTLY remained in line, allowing the caravan to maintain a steady pace. As darkness fell, Elwrick brought them to a stop and awarded the hatchlings with some playtime. Scouts were sent to check on the barbarian's progress, while others gathered food. The Shaman stabbed the Staff of Life into the muddy ground, and the eggs were stacked nearby in a make-shift nest allowing the warmth to penetrate the thin shells.

"How is my Father doing?" Saress asked.

"King Hulradeeh is doing much better than anticipated. He is a strong reptile, and even now, in his later years, he is proven to be a leader."

"Only because he rides on the back of Midnight," Saress said.

"It isn't uncommon for a King to ride a horse. Besides, Midnight doesn't mind. The two fought alongside one another in the First Great War. It's only fitting they remain together for this one."

Saress looked across the way to where her Father slept. Beside the King, Midnight lay with his ears perked up, ready to stand and fight at a moment's notice. "I never told you this, but thank you for helping my race survive. Without you, we would have all perished," Saress whispered.

"No, it is I who should be thanking you," Elwrick said. "Had it not been for you, the bearer would have never reached the portal, and Karayan would still be in power."

Saress shook her head. "It was not I who accomplished the task. It was Pegan who now lays unconscious. He is the one who always made sure we accomplished the objective. I only hope Gleia can find a cure for his strange infection."

Elwrick looked to Pegan, who lay still as death on a make-shift gurney covered with a fur blanket. "Yes, there is something very odd about his infection. I can't quite place my finger on."

"What do you mean?" Saress asked.

Elwrick picked off a piece of moss from the log where he sat. "The infection appears to stem from the wound on his hand. But I fear a dark and sinister being fuels it."

Saress looked at Elwrick. "What do you mean dark and sinister being?"

"Listen close," Elwrick said. "Pegan's father is the root of all evil, while his mother is the representation of pure good."

Saress nearly fell off the log. Everything was beginning to fall into place. "I forgot," she sadly admitted. "Captain Royston told me inside Pegan is a war, a war for his very soul between good and evil, right and wrong, and to the victor belongs his soul. I don't understand what he means, but Royston said you would."

Elwrick whispered as he scrubbed his chin. "Inside Pegan is a war, and to the victor belongs his soul... Elwrick let the words trail off as every ounce of color drained from his face, and he covered his mouth in shock as he finally understood. "It's not a war for his soul, but a war for his Birthrights. We have to go, NOW!" Elwrick screamed as he jumped up.

Saress looked confused for a moment, then leaped from the log. "What's wrong? What do you mean, Birthrights?"

"Listen to me," Elwrick said as he grabbed Saress by her shoulder's. "When you think of Birthrights, you think of rights, privileges, or possessions which you're entitled upon birth, but that's the mortal meaning. In the spiritual realm though, your Birthright is spiritual consciousness and the unbound joy, happiness, inner peace, and the wonder of enlightenment associated with spiritual awareness and the rights to free will."

Saress looked confused. "I still don't understand," she said.

Elwrick walked away and rubbed his face. "How else can I explain it?"

"You speak in terms only those from the Spiritual Realm would understand. Explain it to me like a child," Saress said.

Elwrick sat back down on the log. "Spiritual awareness is becoming conscious that inside each and every one of us is a soul that has free will, a gift from the Creator. If Malvo's seed wins this spiritual war, the free will Pegan has, will be gone leaving him a slave to perform the Dark Masters biding, yet still retaining all the power of the Warlock. He will become the greatest destructive weapon this world has ever seen. Now I know why Malvo picked Lilith to carry his child."

Saress looked into Elwrick's frightened eyes. "So what must we do?"

"We must call on divine intervention and perform the Ritual of Banishment to expel Malvo's seed from Pegan. The Ritual though is deadlier than Malvo's seed."

Hrizlurlund raised his closed fist signaling for the movement to halt.

"What do you see?" Emperor Haumlell asked Hrizlurlund.

Hrizlurlund looked about raising his torch high. In a large circle, all the foliage was disheveled, and footprints were in abundance. Bits of fish and chewed on frogs lay scattered, and one grassy area appeared to have been a temporary nest. Hrizlurlund plucked a broken stem of grass and examined the breakage. "They were here less than half a day ago." Dropping the stem, he pressed it into the mud with his foot. "From their hasty retreat, I would say they know they're being chased and no longer try and conceal their movements."

Emperor Haumlell looked at the map. "There can be no doubt now. They head for the safety of Rhunsiire and the elves. The prisoner must have revealed our intentions."

"Why would they go there?" a barbarian asked. "The elves care little for the reptiles."

"At one time, the reptiles, elves, and barbarians were trading partners. Ever since Emperor Tak-Thukmand's sudden rise to power, we have become enemies for some unexplained reason," Hrizlurlund explained to the barbarian.

Emperor Haumlell looked at the barbarian. "Regardless of the past, we will be relentless in our pursuit, keeping them on the move until we either slaughter them, or they die from exhaustion. Once the reptiles reach the Ghu'lane, they will be surprised to discover a squad of Karayan's men waiting at the top. By then, we'll be at the bottom. With nowhere to go, we will decimate their ranks. All that will remain is the bartering for their skins."

Understanding this new information, Elwrick kept the reptiles at a blistering pace affording no breaks through the night. As morning arrived, so did the Ghu'lane rising out of the murky waters.

Behind them, they could hear the faint barking of dogs and shouting. The barbarians were hot on their trail, even catching an occasional glimpse of the scouts.

Ryul watched from the rim and knew the reptiles wouldn't survive without help. Setting his men into motion, they scaled the Ghu'lane with cat-like precision and set off at a break-neck speed through the mud and muck.

"Hurry," Elwrick screamed to the reptiles. The barking was nearly on top of them.

Cheers erupted at the front of the convoy when the first wave of elves came into view. Some were heavily armed while others carried nothing—their whole purpose was to relieve the tired and weary of their burdens.

Ryul met Elwrick with a firm handshake. "We could not wait any longer. The barbarians are less than an hour away."

Elwrick pulled Ryul into a hug. "Your help is much appreciated. The hatchlings are on the verge of collapse."

A second wave quickly arrived, and the squad leader approached Ryul. "I know you ordered us to remain at the top, but the enemy is almost within range to rain down arrows. We must go now."

Exhausted hatchlings rode on elven shoulders, while weary females relinquished their eggs. The elderly were urged to continue, and Midnight quickly scaled the stairs to Elwrick's disbelief, bringing the King safely up. Elwrick was the last one out, and when he looked back, he wept. Men, thousands of them were only minutes away from the stairs and destroying everything in their path.

On the rim of God's Perch, Elwrick faced the reptiles which lay sprawled out and breathing heavy. "We made it," he whispered.

"A few barbarians have started up the stairs," an elven archer called out.

Elwrick located Ryul in the gaggle of reptiles and elves. "Have your archers line the rim, and when the barbarians reach the midway point, rain down arrows—"

"Elwrick, we have to get Pegan to Rhunsiire," Saress interrupted.

Elwrick diverted his gaze from Ryul to Pegan. "We don't have a choice. If we don't stop the barbarians here, more will die than one man. You must fight and continue to fight until they retreat."

"You're abandoning Pegan?" Saress surprisingly asked. "After everything he has done."

"I'm sorry," Elwrick said as a glowing white tear came from his right eye.

Ryul ordered his team of fifty archer's to take their place.

Emperor Haumlell looked at the top. The elves appeared as ants looking back down at them. "Charge," he screamed and pointed his axe at the stairs as if it were the enemy.

Surging forward in a massive wave, his men attacked the insurmountable obstacle. Unevenly spaced and deathly slick, a few barbarians were either shoved off or slipped on their own accord and splattered upon the rocks below.

The moment the first wave of barbarians reached the midway point, Elwrick gave the command and a barrage of fifty arrows rained down on the waiting horde.

"Don't stop, don't ever stop firing," Elwrick screamed.

Barbarians fell where they stood and screams filled the air. Attempting to flee, a few lost sight and tumbled over the edge and vanished in the swirling mist below. Those who were wounded or left unscathed, grabbed the fallen to use as human shields.

A fresh group flooded onto the plateau.

Elwrick ran behind the row of elves that lined the rim. "Fire," he screamed again. "Show them no mercy for you shall receive none."

One elf noticed a single climber sneaking up at a different angle. Leaning over to get a shot, he lost his balance and tumbled over instantly vanishing, yet his screams remained until they abruptly ended.

"ꓷ0Ꝫꓕ0ꟻꓕ0ꓷ ꟻꝪꝪ0ꟍ," Saress screamed, and an orange shafted, electrical infused arrow formed on her bow. Upon impact, the missile exploded. Barbarians in the blast radius were pulverized, while those outside the blast radius were launched off the edge.

Those who avoided death fired back, but the great distance and extreme angle forced every bolt to fall short.

Saress readied her bow as a new wave of barbarians broke out onto the plateau, and fresh screams replaced the gurgling cries of the dying.

There seemed to be an endless stream coming as more barbarians waded through the dead.

The next arrow Saress sent burst into flames halfway there and split into three arrows igniting whatever they impacted. Running around and screaming, the tar-infused fire quickly spread to anything it touched.

The smell of charred flesh joined in with the screams creating a hellish nightmare below.

The next wave of barbarians had no choice but to either stand on their companions, or kick them off the edge.

"Fire," Elwrick screamed again.

The barbarians that did manage to get close were easily picked off.

A blood-covered barbarian with an arrow through his shoulder, retreated to the Emperor. "We have no choice but to fall back. The elves are slaughtering us on the stairs. Coming here was nothing more than a death trap."

Cheers of victory came from above as they watched the small dots retreat. From the halfway point to the swirling mist, a river of blood flowed down the stairs like a rippling stream, and the number dead was uncountable as the bodies were piled many deep, burned to ash, or blown into random pieces.

Elwrick went to the stairs and looked down. Beside him, Saress stood. The blue-colored arrow in her bow slowly fizzled from existence. "I want that fallen elf recovered. I will not have his corpse denied a proper burial."

Emperor Haumlell unrolled the map. "There must be another way up," he grumbled.

"You told us an army waited up there to greet us, not cut us down like filthy vermin," a barbarian screamed. Through his leg was the broken shaft of an arrow and another buried in his hip.

From somewhere behind the gathering of wounded, Hrizlurlund slid his axe free of his belt loop.

Emperor Haumlell looked up at the ridge and could see the row of elves still waiting. "Karayan deceived me," he screamed. There could be no other reason for the slaughter. "I only did what Karay—" The Emperor never saw the swing or felt the bite of cold steel as his head slid from his shoulders. It happened so quick, for a moment, his body forgot to bleed. Then all at once, blood fired straight up as the body collapsed.

Satisfied with his work, Hrizlurlund climbed on a rotten stump to where he was visible. "Emperor Haumlell has led us directly into a trap. He has been blinded by his fear of Karayan and his lust for power. As his predecessor, I take my rightful place as Emperor of the barbarians."

"What about the reptiles?" a barbarian asked.

Emperor Hrizlurlund followed the stairs up to the top of God's Perch. "This war isn't our war and I refuse to turn any more women into widows. We are returning to the Nymph, gathering our supplies, then heading home."

Behind him you could hear the cheers, they too had grown weary of the assault.

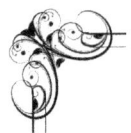
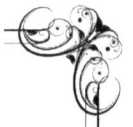

Chapter 100

he runner never touched the ground as he ran himself nearly to exhaustion. He could sense the urgency in both Elwrick's voice, and his trembling hand as Elwrick scribed the note. *You need to get this note to Lady Alenia immediately*—the words still pounding in his brain. Using the trees instead, he navigated the woven branches and thick tree limbs and traveled at a blistering rate. At the door, the runner was hunched over and gasping for air. His long dark stringy hair hung limp and hugged his sweaty face.

The assassin guarding the door took the note and handed it to Darkblade, who, in turn, handed it to Lady Alenia.

Lady Alenia unfolded the note, then handed it to Gleia. "Read this please."

"Gladly," Gleia answered. When she finished, she turned over the note, but nothing was on the backside.

"That's it?" Lady Alenia asked.

Gleia scanned the note again. "Yes," she answered. "All the note says is for me to prepare a room and gives details precisely how to arrange it. Elwrick says he will explain more upon his return."

Lady Alenia took back the note and gently folded it closed. "If he took the time to write this note, and send a runner ahead, it must be important. Make sure you do exactly as the note says." Lady Alenia walked to where she could see out the window and thought. *Usually, Elwrick would have sent her a mental message, but not this time*, and she became worried.

"I will see it done," Gleia said, she could see the worry on Lady Alenia's face.

Gleia recruited the aid of Ellusia, and between the two of them, the room quickly came together. The only thing it needed now was for the occupant to arrive. Nobody had to tell them who it was; they all knew it was for Pegan.

Another day would pass before the caravan traveled under the arched gates of Rhunsiire and ventured down the main road, which separated the town into the southern and northern half.

Lady Alenia watched through the window as Elwrick led the way. She wanted to run out and take Elwrick in her arms and never let go, but she knew better. Elwrick would be furious with her knowing out there somewhere, the rogue elf still lurked.

Beside Elwrick, King Hulradeeh rode on Midnight leaning to one side, but surprisingly alert while at the center of the convoy, four elves carried Pegan's partially covered body on a makeshift gurney. Near the rear, Saress struggled to keep the hatchlings organized as their new world had them enthralled.

"Elwrick is a good man," Gleia said as she joined Lady Alenia at the window. "I know, without a doubt, he loves you with every fiber of his Light Being. Somehow, I feel you two will find a way to be together long after you're gone from this world."

"I don't know how," she whispered. "We are two different species."

"You will find a way," she asserted her opinion, then hugged the Queen. "We should prepare for whatever Elwrick has planned."

Lady Alenia met Elwrick at the door with a lengthy hug and a long kiss. She didn't care if every elf watched, or the world for that matter. Elwrick should have pushed her away, but in secrecy, he longed for that very kiss. The warmth of his body radiated through her, and the aching pain in her knee faded. It was the sound of feet coming up the stairs that finally separated them.

"I wish we could spend more time getting reacquainted, but events are happening, which cannot be ignored."

Lady Alenia pried herself away, but still held onto his hands. "What must we do?"

"Is the room prepared?" he asked.

"Has been for some time," Gleia answered.

"Fantastic," Elwrick whispered. "It sounds like Pegan is on his way up now. He needs to be stationed on the altar precisely as I have described in the letter," Elwrick told Gleia, then he faced Ellusia. "Where is Lilith? I must talk to her now. There can be no delay."

"She's in her room doing her studies. I'll go get her," Ellusia said as she sprinted down the hall.

Elwrick paced the length of the room, mumbling to himself while he waited.

"What is happening?" Lady Alenia asked.

Lilith ran down the hall to the main living area where Elwrick waited. She could sense the urgency in Ellusia's voice.

"Lilith, I need you to sit," Elwrick directed her to a chair.

"What is happening—"

"Listen to me," Elwrick interrupted. "There is someone special here."

Lilith squinted her eyes, and her face became expressionless.

"Don't go searching for what I'm about to tell you," Elwrick snarled. "I want to explain to you what is happening before you see him."

Gleia pulled a chair alongside Lilith waiting with anticipation.

Elwrick knelt before Lilith. "As we speak, your son is being taken to the room Gleia prepared."

Lilith's eyes opened wide. "My son, he's here?"

"Yes."

"When do I get to see him? Take me to him," she pleaded.

"Lilith, listen to me," Elwrick said as he took Lilith's hand. "Your son has fallen into a state of vegetation, and I fear it is self-induced. Pegan understands this war is for his Birthrights, and if he loses, he will become a slave to the Dark Master. What troubles him more is knowing that the woman he loves will meet the same fate. He will not allow that to happen. He will find a way to separate himself from her, then destroy himself."

Lilith lowered her head as the flood gates opened in her eyes.

Elwrick tilted up Lilith's head until their eyes met. "You need to make—"

"Save my son," she pleaded. "Please save my son."

"What I want to perform is a Ritual of Banishment," Elwrick said. "Even then, the results may be devastating."

"What is a Ritual—"

"A Ritual of Banishment will split Pegan into two beings. It is the only way to cast out Malvo."

"How is that possible?" Lilith asked.

Elwrick shook his head. "I don't fully understand it myself. I only know how the Ritual is performed, but have never seen it completed successfully. What we currently face is an evil beyond anything you could ever imagine."

Lilith barely stood as her legs were visibly shaking.

Elwrick supported Lilith but spoke to all in the room. "If successful, Pegan will need to be washed in the Blood of the Creator to prevent Malvo from reentering the void created by his Banishment. Beyond that, I am not sure what will occur as Pegan will be void of his father's traits as if Malvo never had carnal knowledge with Lilith."

The room was dead silent as each wondered what they were about to witness.

The blackened hinge rent an evil shriek as the door closed.

The room was dimly lit by a gold-plated triangle-shaped candelabra which supported seven virgin white candles, each emitting a warm glow.

Elwrick looked at Lady Alenia, Lilith, Saress, Gleia, Ellusia, then Raestmond. "Seven of Pegan's closest family members will be required for this to be successful. I have called you here today because you six are the closest Pegan has to a family, and I stand for the required seventh member. After I consecrate this room, transforming it into a sanctuary, nobody can leave regardless of what you see, or hear. As much as you will want to draw your weapons and fight what we're about to encounter, you will be wasting your time as nothing made of steel, wood, or magic can defeat the enemy we face. The only weapon we have, which can harm this enemy, is the power of prayer."

They each listened intently.

Starting at the door, Elwrick walked clockwise. In his left hand, he carried a white candle that emitted a blue flame. In his right hand, he held a golden censer which secreted faint wisps of gray smoke that smelt of Jasmine. By the time he reached the door creating the circle, a calming smoke had engulfed the room. Hanging the smoking censer on a golden hook fastened on the wall, he faced the door and splayed his arms:

> *By the light, let the darkness flee.*
> *By the fire, which burns within.*
> *By the will, give me the strength.*
> *By my desire, let nothing in.*

"Let it begin," Elwrick said. "Let's relieve Pegan of this evil which resides within his body." Elwrick looked about the room. "And banish this filthy demon back to hell where it belongs."

Each member except Lilith closed their eyes, knelt, tilted their heads back, and prayed. Lilith knelt beside the altar and took Pegan's hand in hers and rested her head against his chest.

Elwrick dipped his fingers in a bowl of Holy Water then flicked the droplets on Pegan's forehead. "Spirit of the Creator, the Angels in Heaven, and all the Saints before me. Descend upon me, purify me, fill me with yourself, and use me. Use me as a channel to aid this troubled soul."

The chanting of the prayers could be heard outside the room, drawing the attention of nearby elves.

Elwrick dipped his fingers in the bowl again and allowed the drops to fall on Pegan's bared chest. "Give me the power to banish all forces of evil from this soul, destroy them, vanish them, so that he can become healthy again and work in Your name."

Pegan's body jerked violently then went suddenly rigid. Both eyes shot open, and black lines spiderwebbed his pale face. "This soul is mine," the cold, scratchy dead voice snarled.

Elwrick dripped more Holy Water on Pegan. "By the power granted to me, I cast you out and banish you back to the fiery pit from once you came. I cast you and every unclean spirit, every satanic power, every evil legion. By the name and power of the Creator, be gone and fly far from this sanctified location never to return. Fly far from not only this soul but all souls made in the Creator's image."

Pegan's teeth began to gnash.

Elwrick placed a drop of Holy Water on Pegan's eyes. "Banish from this soul all evil spells, dark magic, malefice, malediction, and evil intentions. Remove from this soul all diabolic infestations, oppressions, possessions, ailments, and all that is evil."

Lilith was suddenly flung across the room and slammed against the wall. Sliding down until she crumpled against the floor, her robe covered her limp, unconscious body.

Painstakingly slow, the body stood then hovered inches above the slab. The ugly sound of limbs popping free of their joints wreaked havoc on their senses. Pegan's head cranked sideways until his head rested against his shoulder, and both arms contorted into unnatural positions.

Elwrick flicked more Holy Water on Pegan. "Begone from here, Dark Master. Never tempt those created in the light with your dark vanities. What you offer to the living is nothing more than pure evil, and it is not welcome here. Drink the poison yourself!" Elwrick screamed and raised his arms.

The body leaped from the alter and stood on twisted legs. Both pure white orbs for eyes focused on Elwrick as the possessed body swayed side to side.

Saress drew her sword.

"Put it away, you cannot kill it that way," Elwrick screamed. "Only with prayer can we send this demon back to hell."

Dense black smoke filtered up through the cracks in the floor and brought with it the scent of sulfur and the screams of the condemned.

Elwrick threw more Holy Water on Pegan. "In the name of the Creator, I banish you from this location."

Moving at a demonic pace, Pegan ran across the room, joints grinding with each exaggerated step. Reaching the wall, he climbed it like a spider, then moved onto the ceiling. His head swiveled and twisted at a strange angle as he looked down at Elwrick.

Elwrick stepped back, keeping his vision trained on the man who clung to the ceiling. "Oh! You heathen. I know what you attempted, but you have failed. I prevent you now from stealing Pegan's Birthrights to use for your evil intentions and carry out your sick plans against those who remain loyal to the Creator. Begone from him, begone from here. I banish you back to the fiery pits of hell."

Pegan sprung from the ceiling lunging directly at Elwrick.

Elwrick spun out of the way and flicked more Holy Water on Pegan.

Instantly, Pegan sprang off the wall and flew at Elwrick like a specter.

Elwrick rolled out of the way, spilling some of the Holy Water.

Pegan clung to the wall, immune to gravity, blood dripping from each eye.

Elwrick paced the length of the room, his vision locked on Pegan.

"Pegan belongs to me," The demonic voice hissed using the human's vocal cords, then lashed out with a forked tongue.

Elwrick's movement matched that of the demon, and he flicked more Holy Water at him.

The demon reared back and spat acid at Elwrick, then walked along the wall as if it were the floor, then dropped down and hunched over Lilith. "If I lose Pegan, then I take his mother." The demon wrapped his twisted, blackened fingers around the head of Lilith, threatening to rip it free.

"You will not harm Lilith, or her son," Elwrick screamed, then charged directly at the demon flicking more Holy Water forcing it to back away.

The demon crawled half on the floor, half on the wall, his head cocked sideways, blackened lips curled back revealing blackened teeth. "I too can pray to my Creator," Pegan said in a low growl, the muscles in his throat vibrating. The chatter of his hardened fingernails from each contorted movement clashed with the Holy prayers. Screaming something in a sharp tone, Elwrick flew from the floor and slammed against the wall. The bowl of Holy Water flung from his grasp shattering against the far wall. Pegan slithered down from the wall; his jerky, animated movements produced dread in all those in the room."

"Keep praying for the Banishment," Elwrick screamed to his companions. "Pray until your eyes bleed tears."

Pegan swayed side to side, his head jerking and twisting in uncontrolled movements as he neared Elwrick.

"Begone from here," Elwrick demanded of the demon.

"You have no power here," the demon said in a mocking laugh. Jetting his hand straight out at Elwrick, he slowly raised his arm, and as he did, Elwrick slid up the wall until his head smashed against the ceiling, then continued to slide until he was pressed against the ceiling.

Elwrick tried to turn his head but found he couldn't. Instead, he closed his eyes and continued to pray. "Creator, please help me. Send this demon back to the pit from which it was born."

Pegan moved his hands in a twisting-ringing motion, and Elwrick's arms slowly tore free and were left to dangle utterly useless from a few light fibers.

Elwrick screamed was magnified by the unimaginable pain.

"Hear him scream, Father," Pegan hissed in delight.

Elwrick's head cranked to the left, producing a grizzly pop as if the neck bone broke as Pegan jerked his hand sideways.

Elwrick no longer had control of his body. Pegan flipped him over to where his belly smashed against the ceiling. Gurgling something between a scream and a cry, Elwrick's back arched until his feet pressed against the ceiling beside his head. To their horror, the feet started walking dragging Elwrick's torso and face across the coarse stone shredding away layers of skin.

Saress had tears streaming from her eyes, begging for Elwrick's torment to end, but the demon inside Pegan was relentless and continued to torment the Light Being.

Lilith woke and crawled to her knees behind Pegan. "I know your face."

Pegan's head twisted backward to where he looked down upon Lilith, yet his hands continued to manipulate Elwrick into torturous positions, slowly ripping him to shreds, while demoralizing him.

Lilith closed her eyes. "The day I discovered I was with child, I was both excited and frightened. I knew you were something special but also knew your future was troubled. The things I did were not out of hatred, or spite, but out of pure love. I would have rather had you die than experience whatever your father's sick twisted mind could conceive. The day I left you in that dark, cold, wet alley, I held your tiny hand and looked into your beautiful eyes. It destroyed me more than you will ever know, exactly as seeing you now destroys me. My son died in that alley. You are not my son," she hissed.

A flash of light brighter than the sun erupted from the altar, and Pegan collapsed to the floor deathly still.

Elwrick fell from the ceiling, landing partly on the floor, and partly on the altar. His body was a jumbled mess of twisted light fibers, and nothing functioned as it should. "Place him in the tub, NOW!" Elwrick said in between ragged breaths. "Before Malvo can reenter the void," he mumbled incoherently.

Lady Alenia crawled to Elwrick and gathered the torn pieces and held them tight to her chest. Sobbing uncontrollably, she fell to her side and lay there looking at Elwrick's face.

"He's in," Gleia screamed.

Continuing the ceremony from where he lay, tears mixed with Elwrick's words as he spoke. "Father, I deliver this soul to you, bathed in your blood, so that you can look after him, use him for your will, and so he may honor you with his deeds. Protect him as I protect those under me, and guide him as I guide those in your name, Amen."

Chapter 101

lwrick licked his dry lips. "My lovely Lady Alenia." He choked on the whispered words as he looked into her eyes. "It is done. The task now falls on the Witch and Warlock to save the elves."

It's rumored, over time, you become immune to the effects of death, and your heart becomes callous, cold, remorseless. Lady Alenia would have to disagree. She had witnessed death a thousand times, and with each, it got uglier, nastier... heart-wrenching. "No... no, no, no... no..." she wailed uncontrollably while holding Elwrick's deformed body.

Elwrick's arms flopped as Lady Alenia rocked him like a child. What strength he had was rapidly fading. "Malvo poured his malice, his hatred, his vileness into my soul," Elwrick said in-between gasping coughs. "I can feel it choking the life out of me, crushing me under its evil weight."

Lady Alenia brushed aside the gray hair which covered Elwrick's pale face. "Take me with you?" she pleaded. He was her foundation, her reason for living. Without him at her side, she would crumble without a doubt. "I can't do this alone."

Elwrick coughed, his eyes glazed over. "Where I'm going, you cannot follow." His ravaged face revealed the first signs of decay. "How I wish to hold you one last time. To feel your lips pressing against mine, our bodies becoming one..." his last word lingered on the air. There was a sudden dullness to his eyes, the kind you see in an animal the very moment death comes to claim them.

Lady Alenia instinctively relaxed when a warm hand pressed on her shoulder, but nobody was there when she looked back. The warm hand remained, and the sincere, vibrant, compassionate words came only to her. "Remember, through this journey we call life; we must take the bliss with the sorrow while we smile through the tears. Everything happens for a reason, although we may not understand it at the time."

Lady Alenia ran her hand down Elwrick's tired face. "I would rather die in your realm than remain living on this one without you."

Ellusia sat frozen in horror with her back against the wall. Never in her life had she witnessed such evil, such hatred.

Lilith held Pegan's hand. On his clammy skin, she felt a faint heartbeat.

Lady Alenia's world collapsed as Elwrick slowly faded from her grasp. She knew her time with him had ended. Never again would she feel his warm breath against her neck, his loving touch, warm smile, or his reassuring gaze everything was going to be okay. She was now destined to spend the last of her days alone, and she lost the urge to cry or mourn. She sat there unblinking staring into oblivion, her arms still extended as if supporting Elwrick.

Saress never said a word, because, in truth, she didn't know what to say. Crawling across the smoldering floor, she held Lady Alenia. "He did what he needed to do, what he had to do. We all knew the consequences and accepted them without question. What you must understand is Elwrick went home."

Lady Alenia never looked at Saress, but to the floor where Elwrick laid. "It doesn't make it any easier."

Gleia stood on shaking legs using the tub for support. Inside the container, Pegan's body floated in the crystal-clear fluid. He looked to be at peace,. No longer did the demon inside him haunt his thoughts. There was nothing she could do for Elwrick, but she was damn sure going to do everything imaginable to save Pegan. Otherwise, Elwrick's sacrifice meant nothing. Waiting a few minutes to recover her strength, she knelt beside Lilith. "I will do everything I can to help your son."

Lilith looked at Gleia with tears in her eyes. "Thank you.".

Elwrick shimmered into existence near the base of the Altar of Knowledge. His body was nothing more than a tangled mass of fibers ripped and torn, thrashed, and shredded. His arms no longer functioned, each hanging by a single thread. The dense woven fibers which formed his backbone were fractured while the thick cord which constructed his neck was snapped. His vision faded in and out as his optical nerves began to falter.

The real pain manifested deep inside, clear to his soul. It was here he could feel Malvo's malice weaving through him, subjecting him to excruciating pain as if he were a mortal comprised of blood, bone, and tissue. In that darkened moment, he sensed Malvo coiling around every fiber, crushing them as if they were bones. His mind was nothing more than a playground for Malvo as he invaded his most profound thoughts. Inside those thoughts were grotesque images of Lady Alenia, and what was to become of her once forced into Malvo's servitude.

He would need to make it to the Altar if he was to go home. Collecting his strength, Elwrick dragged his head and arms while pushing with his legs like a wounded animal. Moving inches at a time, it took well into the night before he neared his destination. Behind him lay a trail of light fibers that fell from his body. Their glowing color fading to gray.

Looking at the Altar from where his head rested, he closed his eyes for what he believed to be the final time and whispered. "Father, my body is broken; my mind wrecked. I deliver myself now into your hands."

The impossibly old man walked out from behind the Altar. His worn face held a thick scraggly gray beard, and his ghost-white hair hung down past his shoulders. Clothed in a burlap robe, it flowed downward in massive folds that barely touched the tops of his feet, which rested in leather sandals. Lifting Elwrick's head with his finger, he looked at the Spiritual Guide's face. "Look at me," the old man said. "Release your anger." The old man knelt beside Elwrick, then drew something dark and sinister out of Elwrick and cast it away and destroyed it.

Elwrick discovered his body remained nothing more than twisted fibers, but the pain was now a distant memory. Elwrick tried to shake his head, but his broken neck prevented it. "I can't," he whispered. "I can never forgive the Creator for what He's done."

The old man folded his hands neatly behind his back and paced around Elwrick. "You must release your anger, your malice, your hatred. It is the only way to complete the change."

Elwrick could no longer contain his frustration, and his anger came bursting through in shouts and hisses. "All that is wrong in this world is the Creator's fault. He did this, all of it," he screamed as he wept. "All the tomes in existence describe Him as caring, compassionate, forgiving, loyal, and an honorable Being, but He is none of those things. He's a hateful, spiteful Being full of malice and hate who likes to watch those He created suffer, and swim in this cesspool we call life. He's no better than the Dark Master."

"Good," the old man said as he continued to pace around Elwrick. "Let the anger flow out of you. It is the only way you will understand the truth."

"What truth, there is no truth," Elwrick hissed as dirt filled his nostrils. "The truth is the Creator abandoned me, abandoned all of us in our greatest hour of need."

The old man knelt beside Elwrick. "By now, you should be feeling better having released all that poison which clouds your mind."

Elwrick didn't. He remained furious. "Can you please allow me to die in peace? Instead of continuing to torment me."

The old man sat beside Elwrick and calmly spoke. "I cannot do that. I was sent here with a purpose. The purpose of cleansing your mind."

Elwrick saw no hope in the future. The torment would continue.

"Tell me this, Elwrick, Order of the First Flame. What has the Creator done to warrant such hateful accusations? In what ways has he wronged you?"

Elwrick went to speak, but the old man stopped him. "Think hard before you answer the questions."

"Look at me," Elwrick wept. "I preached His word, lived the righteous life, did everything He asked me to and more without question or hesitation. The one time I needed Him. Needed His intervention, He abandoned me, abandoned us."

"Did He?" the old man asked. "Or were you to blind to see Michael inside that room protecting those who prayed for Malvo's banishment?"

"The Creator created Malvo Necrosyse," Elwrick hissed. "Had it not been for him, none of this would have ever come to fruition."

The old man sighed. "So, this anger stems from your belief that He created evil. Therefore He is responsible for all wrongdoings?"

"Yes," Elwrick hissed.

The old man picked up a stone and looked at it, then tossed it aside. "You must remember, Malvo was born in the fires of man's greed. The only way He could have prevented it was to remove the Birthright of Free Will from all mortals. Is that not why you fought the Dark Master? To prevent that very thing from happening to Pegan?"

Elwrick had a sudden revelation, then whispered. "If Archangel Michael was there and he didn't protect me, then there was a reason the Creator allowed this atrocity to occur."

"Yes. Where you're going, a Light Being cannot survive, and the Creator cannot destroy you. Therefore, He had to have someone do it for Him," the old man explained.

"He had this planned long ago—" Elwrick asked.

"No," the old man interrupted. "It took Him totally by surprise as He didn't see this coming, none of us did. Remember, you asked to pick the Bearer, one last opportunity to save mankind to prove faith still existed. When we saw who you picked from the *Book of Life*, we all considered you a fool. The Creator though honored your request and in time a woman became with child, with the soul you picked. Somehow though, you saw something in her none of us could, and I fear that is a mistake we are going to regret for a very long time."

Elwrick tried to think but his mind floundered. "Didn't see what coming? Choose who?" Elwrick confusingly whispered, while lost in concentration.

"Have you already forgotten about Averie?"

The name suddenly hit him harder than Malvo's magic. "No." Elwrick hurriedly answered as the memories of that day hit him. He spent hours flipping through the pages examining possible souls. "Before her conception, I felt something special about her, something different. Something told me she was going to be the one. She is naïve, yes, but a good soul. Please don't speak ill of her."

The old man sighed. "I have never spoken ill of Averie. She has proven more resilient than any of us could ever imagine. She has done something no other could. She has forced the hand of the Creator to do something He never dreamt He would."

"How is that possible?" Elwrick asked. "I believed the Creator to be omnipresence."

"He is everywhere, and nowhere," the old man said. "Not all events are preplanned; thus, is the opportunity of Free Will. Sometimes even He is baffled by the decisions of mortals."

Elwrick closed his eyes for a minute, or an hour, he wasn't sure. "What has she done?"

The old man lifted Elwrick's head so they could see each other. "What she has done, has left Icearaus in turmoil."

Elwrick lay there, breathing in dirt. "I don't understand."

"As you know, the Creator's original intent was to allow the world to fall into disrepair until there was nothing left. Let the mortals have their false Gods and fake idols, unmoral and unholy beliefs. Eventually, He would destroy Icearaus with fire and begin anew. Averie, though, has resisted the temptation of corruption. Because of this, the Creator has no choice but to initiate the *Prophecy of Damnation*, which, He believed, would never come to fruition. She has earned the right to come home, and the Creator is going to honor that right, which is why I'm here."

"She's coming home," Elwrick whispered.

"Yes, and you're going to retrieve her, which is why your destruction was required. The world you're going to isn't like Icearaus, and you would have been destroyed immediately upon arrival."

"Where am I going?" Elwrick worriedly asked.

"Earth, and you won't be going alone. The Creator wishes for you to take Saress. The Creator's not sure why, but for some reason, Averie is fond of that lizard."

I'm not dying; I'm being rebuilt? Elwrick thought.

"Yes," the old man said. "Perhaps now your faith has been restored. The Creator never abandoned you. What happened to you had to be done."

Elwrick closed his eyes. "I never lost my faith in Him. My words were only words, and I was angry. Angry from what I believed was the loss of the woman I love more than life."

"The Creator knows that," the old man assured Elwrick, "which is why he sent me here to explain so your mind would be at ease during the rebuilding process. Sleep now for when you awake; your body will feel different. Upon your awakening, your brain will hold the key to a potent spell to bring them home. You only have one opportunity. Think wise with your decision."

"What do you mean—" Elwrick started to ask as he grew suddenly tired.

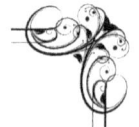

wo weeks to the day after his meeting with the Fischer family, Detective Gilbert received the search warrant. even though he had no physical evidence. The circumstantial evidence he presented from each witness who testified they heard Tom say in no uncertain terms he planned to kill Frank Middleton was sufficient. "We'll see what kind of attitude Tom has when I slap the cuffs on him," Gilbert snarled.

Joseph Clarence shook his head in dismay. "I think we're wasting our time searching the Fischer residence. Whoever did this has been draining his bank accounts and the last time it was accessed, was from a foreign country."

"We both know Mike and Jennifer lost their jobs, is that not motive enough for murder?" Detective Gilbert asked.

"The Rohypnol entered his system from the Chinese food from the restaurant across the street. The owner indicated a woman covered in Tattoos picked up the food, and it was neither Sarah Fischer or Jennifer McCullaha."

Gilbert looked at Joseph dumbfoundedly. "You have to remember this is also a small town. The owner admitted she and Mike were good friends, and she went to school with Jennifer. Do you think she's going to rat on her friends when one outsider comes up dead, and the other one is missing? Hell, in time, we may discover she was part of the plan once we dig deeper."

Joseph paused the ATM video. "Mike's a big man, and Jennifer is no stick. Whoever withdrew that money from the account is a stick."

Detective Gilbert looked at the video. "You saw that spaghetti noddle of a wife Tom has. It fits her perfectly. As I said, I believe the whole family is involved, possibly half the town, for that matter. I think they believe this early winter and mass snowfall is going to hide the shallow grave where they buried Savannah. I'm on to them, though. I have a nose for this kind of thing."

Joseph looked at the video again, then brought up an Ariel view of the Fischer Farms property. "They have a backhoe which can easily dig down ten feet if not more. Why the hell would they dig a shallow grave? If they did do this, which I don't believe they did, Tom is right, we will never find that body, not in a hundred years."

Dave and Sandy arrived earlier than usual and covered with smiles.

"C'mon in," Averie said as she used the door to shield herself from the blustery, ice-cold wind and its instantly numbing bite.

"What brings you two over this early?" Sarah asked, still wrapped in her housecoat and clinging to a cup of steaming coffee.

Sandy picked up Robyn and danced in a circle. "We have fantastic news, and we couldn't wait to tell you."

"Oh?" Sarah excitedly asked.

"We bought a place not far from here. It's only a small little house, but it's something," Dave said.

Tome came from down the hall. "I thought you planned to rent for a while?"

"We did, but this house is perfect for our future endeavor," Dave said.

"And what might that be?" Tom asked.

Dave was all smiles when he spoke. "I'm going to open a community center where people from all walks of life can come learn about the stars. The location is perfect for viewing the night sky, and it's dark enough to avoid the lights of the city from causing problems. Yesterday, I submitted the paperwork for funding from the government to build a high-powered observatory."

"That sounds... well, expensive?" Mike said.

"Not really," Dave admitted. "Because it's education-based, the Federal Commission on Higher Learning (FCHL) is going to step in and fund part of the project."

"You're not going to become another Frank, are you?" Sarah suspiciously asked.

"Absolutely not," Dave said. "It's going to generate very little money. It's going to be more of a donation thing where the money is put back into the center for acquiring better equipment. I'm not going to turn people away because of their financial short-comings. Those who want to learn astronomy can come to learn regardless of their financial situation."

Averie's eyes opened wide. "Can I see my home?"

"I'm sorry, but no. I would kill to get to see your world, but it's too far away. Even using a gazillion-dollar telescope, your galaxy will only be a glowing dot. To see your actual planet will never happen. All we'll be able to see is the Andromeda Galaxy at the beginning unless someone provides a substantial donation, but it's still exciting."

"It sounds like you have something good going on," Tom said.

"We can't start breaking ground on the construction until the spring, but I have an architect who is donating his time to draw up the plans," Dave excitedly said.

"Tell them the best part," Sandy said as she gripped Dave's hand.

"After working with Sandy for over ten years now as partners, we've decided to take it a step further."

Sandy held out her hand, revealing a tiny ring.

"Whoa, that's quick, don't you think," Sarah said. "You never even dated... did you?"

"We might as well have," Sandy admitted. "Dave was there through my ugly divorce, and I was there when his wife passed away from breast cancer. Somehow, we always stuck together, so when he asked me. I had no choice but to say yes."

"When you're ready, let us know. Fischer Farms will make the first sizable donation. Until then, let's celebrate with breakfast, it's on us.," Tom said.

Movement outside the window caught Jennifer's attention. "Great, here we go again."

"What?" Sarah asked.

"Take a look outside," Jennifer said.

Tom looked out the window the very moment the Black Crown Victorian came to a stop. "Oh Jesus, what does the detective want now?"

Dave glanced out the window. "What's going on?"

Sarah gave them a quick overview of their last incident with the detective.

"That's crap, and we all know it," Sandy said. "I would all but guarantee it was that tattoo-covered woman living with him."

Sarah crossed her arms. "Maybe he's here to apologize?"

"Doubtful," Mike said. "As a former member of law enforcement. I can verify if he was wrong, he wouldn't come back to bug us."

Tom opened the door and met Detective Gilbert on the porch. "We're about to leave. Can I help you?"

"You may want to hold off on wherever you're going," Detective Gilbert sneered, then pulled a folded white paper from his breast pocket and handed it to Tom. "Search warrant for the property of Fischer Farms."

"For?" Mike asked. "A search warrant must specify exactly where and what is being searched."

Tom handed the search warrant to Mike for closer examination.

Mike looked it over. "You've must be joking. You're looking for upturned dirt, a broken knife handle, and a bottle of Rohypnol?"

Sarah chuckled. "You must be stupid. There's three feet of snow on the ground, good luck with that."

"I don't find it funny," the detective snarled. "Not in the least."

"Sarah, shut up," Mike scolded his sister. "This is a serious matter."

The assistant looked away in embarrassment. He knew Sarah was right on the upturned dirt part.

"We'll begin our search in the barn and—"

Not without me there, you aren't," Tom interrupted.

"I could have you arrested for impeding the legal process or tampering with evidence," the detective sternly informed Tom.

"Tom, the detective's right. There's nothing we can do but sit tight. Let him do his thing and be gone. We have nothing to hide."

"Excuse me, officer," Dave said. "I can vouch for these people. I've been with them every night and know they didn't kill Frank Middleton. You best go check on that woman that lived with him."

Detective Gilbert pulled out his notepad. "And you are?"

Dave told him without hesitation.

"Good, another possible suspect. The case is growing deeper by the minute," Detective Gilbert said as he wrote down their names.

"Go do your search," Mike said. "You're holding us up."

"I don't trust him, what if he plants evidence?" Sarah asked Mike.

Detective Gilbert looked at Sarah disgustingly.

Mike rested his arm on Sarah's shoulder. "All we can do is hope and pray he's an honest man that's trying to solve a murder. If he does plant something, it will come out in court ruining his career and costing him his pension."

"Well, I guess we'll have breakfast here, what do you all want?" Sarah asked.

Averie looked depressed, then suddenly came to life. "Can we go to the Spaghetti Bucket for dinner then?"

Sarah smiled. "I don't see why not."

Joseph stood in the barn, looking around. "Do you know how hard it's going to be to locate a knife handle and bottle of pills in here?"

"Like finding a needle in a haystack, but that's what separates the great detectives from the good ones."

"I'll start in this room if you want to search that one," Detective Gilbert said.

It was nearly three when the detective emerged carrying a large brown box and placed it in the trunk.

"What the hell did they find?" Tom asked Mike.

"I don't know but I'm about to find out."

Detective Gilbert closed the trunk before Mike could peek inside.

"What did you seize?" Mike asked.

Detective Gilbert looked down at the evidence sheet. "A few suspicious items, that's all."

Mike crossed his arms. "Now who's breaking the law. Everything seized must be documented and categorized to prevent theft. As far as we know, you took fifty thousand dollars' worth of exotic and rare antique guns in that box."

"I have to secure the items first," the detective sneered.

"Well, they're secured in your trunk. You leave here without notification of the items seized, and I'm calling the FBI headquarters and reporting you as a thief. I'm sure I can find something missing."

The sky was growing dark when the detective and his assistant left.

Tom looked down at the receipt. "What are all these items."

"Let's get dinner, I'm starving. We can look the paper over when we get home," Sarah suggested.

"One second," Mike said as he looked at the paper. "Supposedly, they located a bottle of pills, a broken knife handle, a heavy overcoat, a few fibers which appeared to have blood on them, and a few other odds and ends they felt may be needed to prove their case."

"We didn't have any pills or broken knife. The coat could be anything."

Sarah went pale. "Not long ago, I removed a bottle of pills and a broken handle from the back of the van. I figured it had something to do with the animals and never thought twice so I put them in the barn."

"This doesn't make any sense," Tom complained.

Mike scrubbed his chin, then went pale. "These had to be planted by Savannah, it the only plausible reasoning."

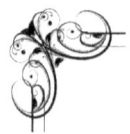
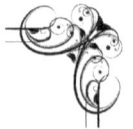

Chapter 103

gainst Vexacion's wishes, Malvo accepted Ruven with open arms. "Tell me my elven friend, is the elven Queen and the Witch dead?"

Ruven paced beside Malvo, explaining the incident with the Queen, and his ultimate failure to complete the task. "Had it not been for Darkblade, the Queen would be dead right now and I in her place."

"This is troubling, troubling indeed," Malvo mumbled. "Still, you have done an excellent job. None of us could have foreseen the extraordinary lengths Elwrick would take to protect Lady Alenia."

"Not only Elwrick," Ruven explained. "Since Elwrick's untimely demise, Ryul has taken command of the Elven Army and has built a literal wall of security around Lady Alenia and the Witch."

"It matters not. Elwrick was the real thorn in my side. The Queen is on her last days and will die soon enough of natural causes. The Witch on the other hand we will need to evaluate further. Depending on how she progresses with her training, we may have to come up with a way to promote her early retirement. What we need now are your eyes back inside Rhunsiire, providing regular updates on the elves, the Witch, and the war."

"Master, my face is known far and wide. I will not make it a foot inside the Whispering Woods before I am struck down."

"In your current appearance, this is true."

"What do you mean—" Ruven started to ask.

Malvo touched Ruven on the hand, and the transformation began.

Ruven tried to scream as excruciating pain coursed through his body, but the squeak was no louder than a whisper. Loud pops and snaps came from deep within his body as bone disconnected from ligaments and repositioned themselves—a few bones reformed bending into unusual shapes. Both eyes shrunk into the skull and became tiny black pinpricks, and then his nose extended and coarse snow-white whiskers burst through the skin. His hands and feet curled into tiny paws with pretty painted black nails. It was only now the fine hair's covering his body morphed into a shiny brown fur coat. From the tailbone grew a thick pink tail then he shrank vanishing in the fold of his forest-green robe.

Malvo reached into the discarded robe and quickly located Ruven and picked him up by the tail. "In this form, you'll be able to go wherever you wish unfettered. Report back to me once you have the information I desire, and not before." Holding Ruven at arm's length, he whispered a spell, and Ruven—the rat—faded from existence.

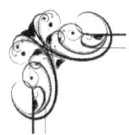
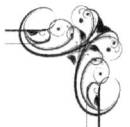

Chapter 104

 he man was as reckless as a wounded elephant pacing back and forth, waiting to discuss the Barbarian's sudden change in plans.

Ghaf Hrizlurlund—newly appointed, self-proclaimed Emperor—stood in the very tent once occupied by the highly unfavorable, and recently deceased Emperor Haumlell. "Show him in," he told the guard who waited at the flap.

The man entered red-faced and foaming at the mouth. "Who do you think you are to go against the wishes of King Karayan. Ready your troops, we're going back into the swamp and completing the mission."

Emperor Hrizlurlund looked down at the desk where the furled map rested. Snatching the map he tossed it at the man. "If you wish to go, go. My men won't stop you."

The man looked at one guard, then the other before stepping up to the Emperor. With his hand curled into a fist except one finger, he poked the Emperor in the center of his broad chest. "You listen to me, and you listen now," the man slowly hissed. "You're going to walk outside this tent, rally the barbarians, then lead them back into the 'Anor."

Emperor Hrizlurlund looked down at the hand, then snatched the man by his neck. Each finger constricted like a boa around its dinner, then he lifted the man free of the ground. "The barbarians are done with this war."

The man gripped at the arm, searching for relief, but the fingers continued to collapse until both eyes bulged, his face shone an ugly purple, both lips swelled, then he jerk violently and went limp.

Emperor Hrizlurlund looked passed the dead man at the soldier.

"Nobody threatens the Emperor in my presence," the barbarian said. The polearm's hefty blade created a seething hiss as it slid free of the stomach spilling the guts.

Emperor Hrizlurlund tossed the body out the door, then faced the guard. "Rally the troops. I feel it's time I made my intentions known."

Hours before dawn Emperor Hrizlurlund stood on the very platform Emperor Haumlell employed to drive the men into a hate-fueled furry. Now, he intended to use it to bring those very men to reason.

Across the expansion, he could see the barbarians spread out like spilled ink in the pre-dawn light. The few fires did little to light the darkness or raise their spirits. None would admit they were glad Emperor Hrizlurlund pulled them from the swamp, but they feared the retribution which would soon follow.

Emperor Hrizlurlund raised his closed fist to silence the chatter. "I can feel the great hatred towards me for the decisions I have made. I can assure you I have nothing but the best interest of the barbarians in mind. No longer will the barbarians cower and hide because of a single man. No longer will we be governed by a man who isn't one of us."

The crackle of the fires amplified the barbarians growing silence.

"Let me ask every last one of you this question. King Karayan has brought us down here from our homeland for what? Because of the threat of war?" Emperor Hrizlurlund paced the length of the platform. "I call that a lie. King Karayan brought us down here because of his war, not ours. His fight is not our fight; his hatred is not our hatred. I look at what we have become, and only one thing comes to mind... pure disgust. It's appalling what we've become. The pride that once flowed through our veins has died, but its rebirth is at hand. Since entering this swamp, how many of our brothers did we left down there to be devoured by the swamp creatures that call it home? How many women sit at Timber Hall waiting for their husbands to come back, that won't? How many children will never see their fathers again?"

The barbarians all looked at each other, pondering the questions the Emperor asked.

"The questions don't stop here," the Emperor continued. "Why do we attack a race that has never once attacked a barbarian. Is this what we have become, blood-thirsty heathens who care of nothing but the taste of flesh. At one time, we were trading partners with the reptiles. They gave us their shed skins, we gave them fur hides, and not one drop of blood flowed by the blade."

"What of the Perch?" A barbarian screamed. "They killed us without remorse—"

"And what would you have done in their situation?" the Emperor shouted. "We chased them from their homes, chased them across the 'Anor, chased them up the Ghu'lane. Would we have not done the same if someone threatened our children and unborn? I don't hold any Ill taste in my mouth for the elves, or the reptiles. It is us who I hold accountable for the death of our brothers, and it is I who will tell each one of the widows of our crime."

It only took one barbarian to raise his weapon and began to chant Ghaf... Ghaf... Ghaf... to get the entire race cheering.

Emperor Hrizlurlund silenced the crowd. "As the sun rises this morning, we head home never again to bow to Karayan or his replacement. Starting now, the barbarians will once again bear the pride we once had."

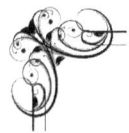
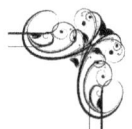

Chapter 105

kylar Nightshade lost track of the days on his return trip to the Whispering Woods. Along the way, he accepted the homeless hiding on the Plains of Gedeon. "We leave none behind," Skylar told them as the pace slowed to allow the malnourished, sick, and elderly to keep pace.

Near the water's edge of the Tlumn River, Skylar encountered a patrol of elves who swiftly drew their weapons. Skylar raised his hands unsure why the sudden hostility towards him. "I took an oath to protect those who cannot protect themselves. These refugee's, have nowhere to go. If we abandon them, they will die. I won't have that on my conscious."

The elves looked through the worn-out and ragged bunch for signs of a spy. With Elwrick's unexpected demise, they took extra caution. "We'll house them with the others," the patrol leader said.

"The others?" Skylar asked.

"Yes, since your departure, we've had random groups come from as far away as Talon's Peak and Millstone. The stories they tell of the current conditions beyond our borders are atrocious."

"I can verify their stories," Skylar said. "The living conditions I've witnessed on my travels are not fit for a pig."

"Karayan has gone insane," an elf mumbled.

"Make no mistake," Skylar told him. "Karayan knows what he is doing. He is making sure once the child returns, they will have nowhere to hide and nowhere to run. By destroying any form of refuge, the child will surely perish, thus restoring his immortality."

"Speaking of Karayan, did you discover his plans?" an elf asked.

Even though Skylar left in secrecy, every man, woman, and child knew of his intent. "I have, and I must meet with Lady Alenia and Elwrick immediately."

"Since your departure, Lady Alenia has relocated to the west wing of the Medical Ward. I must warn you, don't try and enter unannounced. Ryul has given strict orders to all guards to kill any intruder immediately."

"I'm sure my approach will reach their ears long before my feet ever touch the first steps," Skylar said.

Near the stairs, Ryul materialized from the shadows stopping Skylar in his tracks. Near Ryul, no less than five guards formed from the shadows. "Welcome home," Ryul said.

"I must speak with Lady Alenia and Elwrick immediately."

"Lady Alenia is resting, and Elwrick has taken a leave of absence." He didn't have the heart to say Elwrick was deceased. "Because of unplanned circumstances, all correspondence regarding the war has been delegated to me."

Skylar nervously twitched his fingers, wondering if this was a test of loyalty. With the brotherhood, disseminating information to any other than the Lord was considered treason and punishable by death.

"Skylar Nightshade," Darkblade hollered as he danced down the stairs. "I heard you reached the elven border—"

Skylar gave his longtime companion a sturdy handshake. "I must speak with the Queen immediately, and when shall I expect Elwrick's return?"

Darkblade was baffled by the question, then remembered Skylar wasn't here for the Banishment. Kicking at an exposed root while searching for the right way to explain, his face held a somber look. "Elwrick won't be returning. He sacrificed himself to save Pegan. The war now falls on our shoulders."

Ryul lowered his head out of respect for the fallen. "I'm sorry, I should have told you but it stung me to say the words. I honestly believed his death was impossible."

Skylar put his hand on Ryul's shoulder. "We'll survive, it's Lady Alenia who's going to hurt the worst."

"It has affected her greatly," Ryul explained. "Since his death, she's locked herself away and refuses to see anyone, not even Gleia or Ellusia. I fear she has lost the will to live."

Darkblade sighed. "Ryul is right. Lady Alenia needs time to grieve. As for now, the burden falls on him to protect the elven race in whatever way he deems necessary. Anything you've learned is to be passed on to him."

Skylar remained nervous.

Darkblade explained to Ryul the laws of the brotherhood.

"I understand," Ryul said. "Rest assured. There is no retribution for passing on this information."

"I'll hold you to your word." Skylar removed the orders from his breast pocket and handed them to Ryul. "From what I read, the future looks bleak."

"Thank you," Ryul said as he flipped through the pages. "Get some rest. I fear your services will be needed again before this is over."

Lady Alenia roamed through her home like a zombie. Both eyes were bright red, and her cheery cheeks glistened in the dim lamplight. No longer could she sit on the bed and swiftly departed to a nearby chair. The bed didn't feel right being on it without Elwrick. Burying her face in her hands, she wanted to cry, but the tears wouldn't fall. She had spent them all over the last few days. Grabbing a nearby vase, she smashed it against the wall. No longer could she stay here. This wasn't home. It was a torture chamber where she was forced to remember Elwrick, and the reoccurring pain was more than she could stand.

Snatching her cane from the corner, Lady Alenia hobbled her way to the door and exited. Outside, two guards waited.

"Lady Alenia," the guard said as he bowed. "With Ruven still on the loose, we are under direct orders to escort you wherever you decide to go."

"Leave me," she growled, then hobbled down the hallway towards the Medical

Ward. Her home wasn't a detached house, but a room located on a separate wing that branched off the Medical Ward. There were two additional wings, as well. One led to the residence of Lilith while a third belonged to Gleia.

Lady Alenia entered the Medical Ward to find Ryul sitting at the desk where Gleia often studied. On one bed lay Pegan. Beside him, Lilith sat holding Pegan's limp hand. One bed over Glorandial lay steadfast asleep and covered with a cotton blanket. Between the two beds on a nightstand was a large grouping of flowers in a crystal vase that released a faint lavender scent. Tucked neatly into the flowers was a beautifully drawn card that read, 'get well soon.' Across the room, Ellusia dug through a cabinet searching for something.

Ryul looked at Lady Alenia, then around Lady Alenia. Bolting to his feet, he nearly knocked the chair over reaching for his weapons. "Lady Alenia," he called out. "Where are the guards designated to accompany you?"

"I told them to leave me. No longer could I stay in that room. It's not a home. It's a prison cell."

Ryul aided Lady Alenia to a chair near the desk. "My apologies, I only did as you asked by affording you the chance to grieve," he said.

"It's not the solitude which makes it a prison. It's the constant reminder of what I've lost, which turns it into a torture chamber. I will not be returning to that room, ever. Close and seal the door for all eternity."

"As you wish," Ryul said. "Until then, we have important matters which need addressing. I have been able to decipher Karayan's plans, and it doesn't bode well for the elven race."

"What are we facing?" she asked.

Ryul dropped the parchment on the desk. "No longer can we wait for Karayan to attack, we must bring the war to him if we are to have a chance. This evening when the sun dips low and touches the tips of the western trees, I want to assemble a meeting in the celebration clearing. I require every elf, assassin, refugee, reptile, troll, and anyone else who resides within our borders to attend."

Lady Alenia nodded her approval for the unusual meeting. "I wish to be there as well," she said.

"I knew you would, as well as King Hulradeeh. I already have chairs in the making for you two."

Lady Alenia spent the remainder of the day strolling through the forest and running her hand along the branches and caressing the leaves. As if on an evening stroll, she crept down the narrow path taking nothing for granted. Every detail of the forest she soaked in. Stopping along the way, she fed a squirrel and rubbed the forehead of a buck between the antlers.

To the unaware, she appeared alone, an easy target for any who may have evil intentions. If anyone considered it they would have been cut down instantly as Skylar Nightshade, and Miramar Darkblade were nearby watching from the shadows.

Making her way to a small pond, she sat on a stump and dipped her feet in the cold water and allowed her mind drifted back to when she was a child. All the kids she played with then were now deceased. Destroyed either in the Great War or succumbed to the ravages of time. she was the last of her generation.

Skylar formed from the shadows of a nearby tree. "Lady Alenia, we should be going. The time for the meeting is drawing near."

Lady Alenia reached up and touched Skylar's face. He was so young, an infant in her eyes, yet had seen so much. "Why do you kill?"

Skylar pondered the question. He was born into the brotherhood, his mother a slave, his father unknown. He was raised from birth to be a killer, to represent the brotherhood until the end. His good friend Darkblade was the same except a few years younger. "I don't know?" he admitted. "It was the only thing I ever excelled at. Had Malvo never made me wear that robe, we wouldn't be having this conversation."

"Do you ever feel remorseful? Ashamed?"

Skylar started to answer, then stopped. "I don't believe that's what you want to know. You're wondering if the Creator is going to forgive you for your sins? You hope to meet Elwrick in the next life, and you fear that won't happen because of your past?"

Lady Alenia looked at her image in the still water. "Yes."

Skylar turned her head until they gazed at one another. "Even if you don't go to heaven, it won't matter. Elwrick would fly down and escort you through hell. Regardless, I don't see that happening. I think you two are going to hold hands while standing on a mountain watching the sunset somewhere overlooking the celestial plains of the universe."

"Thank you," she whispered, and offered him a slight smile. "I needed that."

"Now, we need to get going before we're late and Ryul grows suspicious of me."

By the time Lady Alenia arrived, the clearing was standing room only. At the far end, Ryul waited on a raised platform with both arms crossed and tapping a rhythm with his foot. Beside him, Hulradeeh sat in a large, custom-made chair with ample room for his tail. To the other side of Ryul was an elegant wooden chair covered with plush purple cushions.

The crowd split, allowing their Queen ample room to pass.

Ryul bowed at the bottom of the stairs. "Good to see you could make it. I was beginning to grow concerned."

"I'm sorry, I was delayed," she said with a smirk.

Ryul eyed Skylar suspiciously.

Skylar stepped back and raised his hands to surrender. "We had a discussion, nothing more. Lady Alenia fears upon her passing she will not be joining Elwrick in the next life."

"I see," Ryul said. "We would have waited all night if needed." Helping her up the stairs and to her seat, he waited for her to get comfortable before whispering. "Hopefully, I am going to make both of you proud. This fight may be our final stand."

Lady Alenia reached over and gripped Hulradeeh's hand. "We're together one last time, let's make it worthy of a song," she whispered.

Ryul took a position at the front of the platform where all could see him.

"Before I begin, there are a few things I must address. Rumors have flourished that Elwrick abandoned us because he knows we cannot win. I stand before you now and inform you it is a lie. Elwrick sacrificed himself to give us the best possible chance to win this war by removing the evil that festered inside Pegan. You must remember, Elwrick is nothing more than a Spiritual Guide. A guide whose sole responsibility was to advise and guide us on a path to righteousness. Not deliver us from our wickedness. Our most magnificent Birthright is the gift of Free Will, to do with our lives as we choose. Some have chosen the way of evil, such as Karayan. Others remain neutral like me, while Lady Alenia and Hulradeeh have adopted the honest approach."

The crowd cheered and stomped their feet.

Ryul had to wave multiple times then blew an ear-drum shattering whistle to get their attention. "There is another rumor which reached my ear and is more treacherous than the last. Rumors whispered in the dark of night that Lady Alenia should step down as she is no longer fit to be Queen. I will tell you now that those words are blasphemous, and any who speak it will be dealt with swiftly. To speak ill of the Queen is to speak ill of me, and I am not one to be trifled with. It makes my blood boil to hear such atrocious accusations."

A tiny, fair-skinned elf with flowing silver hair and tears in her eyes raised her hand to get Ryul's attention. Once she had it, her voice was barely audible. "Ruven told me that Lady Alenia's mind was rubbish and would lead us all to our death. I'm sorry, I told all my friends."

Ryul's face was blistered red by the time she finished. "It's okay," Ryul said. She performed precisely as Ruven knew a child would.

"She's only a child. She didn't mean any harm," the girl's mother pleaded.

Ryul stretched, then took a deep breath to calm himself. It wasn't the child's fault; he kept repeating to himself. "You did an honorable thing by admitting, now the problem can get resolved." Afterward, he told the crowd what the girl told him, then informed them about Ruven's failed attempt to kill Lady Alenia, which drew a horrendous groan. He believed most elves knew, but he was wrong.

"With those issues now cleared up, it is time to address our future. I would typically keep this to the military, but this news affects all of us. After carefully deciphering Karayan's plans, it seems he plans to burn the Whispering Woods to the ground and take Rhunsiire with it. Knowing this, we have no choice but to take the war to Karayan on the open Plains of Gedeon. Over the next few days, the generals and I will decide exactly how to engage Karayan, but it will not be in the Whispering Woods."

The crowd's silence was painful. The elves fighting on the plains would be quickly overrun and destroyed.

Ryul raised his fisted hand. "I will not make a promise to you of victory, as the future has yet to be written. What I will tell you is this. From the tips of my silver hair to the dirt under my toenails, I will fight this scourge known as Karayan until my last breath. If Karayan wants a war, it's a war he shall receive."

Hulradeeh found the strength to stand, then released a roar that shook the heavens.

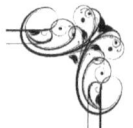

Chapter 106

lwrick gasped for air while an intense burning sensation flooded his lungs. The enemy was upon him. It's dark green body pressing down threatening to crush out his life. Gripping the beast, he flung it away then unleashed a barrage of spells sending the fluttering, flapping demon back to the abyss from which it spawned.

Seraphine watched the ashes rain down and shook her head in disbelief. "That was my favorite blanket."

The damage from the beast remained, and Elwrick clawed at his bare chest. His vision blurred, his sinuses burned. Rolling side to side, he threw himself from the bed onto the wooden floor. Gripping his throat, he could still feel the demon choking the life out of him.

"Breathe," Seraphine screamed. Balling up her hand into a tight fist, she came down hard against his back.

Elwrick gasped, and white bile dripped from his mouth. Fighting to stand, he was hit from behind again. *Breathe*, he heard a woman's voice yell. Then he was struck in the back for the third time.

Seraphine grew concerned. If Elwrick didn't start breathing soon, he would suffocate.

Elwrick stumbled sideways and fell against the wall. His vision was nothing more than dark, inky blotches. *Breathe*, he heard the voice again as he gasped in another long breath. With each breath, the burning sensation faded then quickly returned.

Seraphine chased him down and continued to smack him on the back. "You have to keep breathing. No longer are you immune to our world."

Water flowed from Elwrick's eyes as he looked at Seraphine. He remembered her face but didn't know where. Gasping in another breath, then another the fire in his chest cooled, but the angry pain remained. "I hurt," he mumbled.

"Your chest hurts because breathing is new to you."

Elwrick reached up and touched his sweaty, bile covered chest and felt it expand and contract. "Breathing?" he confusingly asked. He didn't need to breathe, he was a Light Being, and Beings of Light required no air.

"Yes," Seraphine answered Elwrick. "You're as mortal as I am. Without a constant air supply, you will die. There are a few other things you will need, such as food and clothing." She handed him a white robe similar to the one he manifested, then collected a few apples from the table. "Eat," she demanded of him. "You need your energy."

Elwrick looked at his hands. They appeared no different than before he went to the Altar.

"You appear as you did before the change," Seraphine explained. She could see the confusion in his eyes. "As you see from what you did to my favorite blanket, you still retain all your magical abilities, but inside, you're no different than me."

Elwrick poked his stomach with his finger and watched it sink into the skin. "Strange, very strange," he mumbled.

"Only strange to you," she told him, then burst out laughing. "Now, eat your apples."

***

Tom finished tying his boots and waited by the door while Mike zipped up his coat. Tonight, the temperature was expected to drop to record lows reaching negative double digits. The wind bayed like a winter wolf and brought with it a deadly bite. From the window came the faint taps from the first drops of freezing rain.

"You need to hurry," Sarah said as she waited to open the door. "The guy on the radio says there's a good chance this area may lose power. We're going to need a decent stack of wood."

Jennifer held Robyn while looking out the obscured window. "The news said this is the worst winter ever recorded in Willowdale. There have already been multiple deaths reported because of failed furnaces, and one couple tried to walk home when their car stalled. They never made it more than a mile."

"That is so sad," Averie said as she stopped searching through the movies and joined Jennifer at the window. "We've had some ugly winters in Lynn Brook, but nothing like this. To experience this kind of weather, you have to go up north to the Frozen Tundra. Although," she continued to explain as she pulled the sock up on Robyn's foot that dangled by her tiny toe. "When we crossed the Cursed Dessert, I almost froze to death. Had it not been for Thathra…"

"Ready, set, go," Tom screamed as Sarah ripped the door open.

Slipping and sliding the entire way they were lucky to arrive on their feet.

"How much should we get?" Mike asked.

"We need enough so we won't have to come back out. Once night falls, the temperature's going to plummet, and a trek to the barn could be life-threatening."

"Sounds like multiple trips to me." The words came out of Mike in puffs of translucent frost.

"That's what I'm thinking as well," Tom agreed. His lips were blueberry blue, and both cheeks were cherry red.

"What about the animals?" Mike covered his mouth with a glove to keep his tongue from freezing to his lips.

"They'll be fine." Tom started to gather a handful of wood. "I put two heaters in each water tank and doubled-up on their hay so they would bulk up. I suspected this was coming so I took no chances. As long as we don't lose power, there won't be an issue."

"Excellent." Mike loaded his hands with all he could carry.

Twelve trips later and nearly dead, the porch looked like a lumber mill with wood stacked from the floor to ceiling.

"Open wide," Averie said as she held the rubber-coated spoon against Robyn's lips.

Robyn turned away. Whatever Tom was doing at the fireplace was much more enthralling.

"You have to eat your dinner," Averie said, repositioning the spoon against her lips.

"Let me try," Jennifer said as she took the spoon.

"Want me to get that started?" Averie asked Tom.

"Na' I got it," Tom said. "Looks like you have your hand's full feeding the rug thug."

Averie had a lost look, and then it hit her. Tom was referring to Robyn as a thug. "Don't you listen to Tom," she said. "You're no thug."

"Look what I made," Sarah said as she came from the kitchen with a massive bowl of popcorn and a DVD. "I have a good one for tonight. It's called *Destiny's Child*, and before you ask, yes, it's a chick flick."

"Oh' c'mon," Billy complained. "Can't we watch something with some blood and guts?"

Wham, wham, wham, came a desperate pounding at the door.

"Who the hell would be out on an evening like this?" Tom asked while heading for the door. First, he cracked it partway open to keep the cold out, and then flung it all the way. On the porch, Dave and Sandy waited. Both their faces were bright blue, and every hair was frozen white.

"Please help us," Dave mumbled through chattering teeth.

"Oh my god," Tom said, then screamed for Jennifer to come.

Jennifer arrived, then instinctively took charge. "You have to thaw out slowly, or damage can occur to the flesh."

"What in the world are you guys doing out in this weather?" Sarah asked.

Sandy's teeth were chattering so hard she had a hard time talking. "We were going to town, and our car slid off the road. It's nothing but ice out there. I thought we could walk home, but we would have never made it, so we came here."

"You should have called," Sarah said.

"We tried," Dave explained. "The cell phone towers must be down because we had no reception."

"Well, you can't go home tonight, or even tomorrow. This storm is supposed to last a few days. Once it ends, Mike and I will go get your car."

Sandy's teeth still chattered. "Thank you."

Elwrick stood looking out the window at the clouds as they slowly drifted past. He had been to the Isle of Aramoor many, many times. This time it seemed so much different. It seemed real. Running his hand along the wooden windowsill, he felt the textures, real textures. Not that they weren't real before, it just felt more tangible since he had natural skin, actual fingertips, real fingerprints. "Am I going to remain this way?" Elwrick asked Seraphine as he

took another bite of the apple.

She looked down at the ground. "No. Your time as a mortal is limited. You must complete your charge before you revert back to a Light Being. Your transformation occurred on the island as He knew you would need help learning how to breathe."

Elwrick watched a flock of birds take flight, and his mind drifted to Lady Alenia. To kiss her now with lips made of flesh, real flesh made his heart flutter. "I must get to Rhunsiire," Elwrick whispered. "I must see Lady Alenia before I go. To touch her as a mortal—"

"That's not possible," Seraphine interrupted. "You must search for the spell the Creator placed within your subconscious mind. I fear you don't have time to dally."

Elwrick leaned against the wall and felt like vomiting. Now was his chance to hold Lady Alenia as a mortal, and he couldn't. What he could do was bring Averie home. "I already know the spell. I understood it the minute I learned to breathe."

"Let me warn you though," Seraphine said. "Upon your return you will have no recollection of the incident, or this conversation."

"How do you know this?" Elwrick asked.

Seraphine smiled at Elwrick. "Bring her home, she deserves it."

"Yes, she does," Elwrick said.

Averie came from the hall carrying two blankets and wrapped them around Dave and Sandy. "This should help."

"May as well kick back and watch the movie," Tom said. "Not like you can leave anyway."

Billy held up the DVD case. "You might want to reconsider walking home when you hear what it is."

The glance Sarah shot him was colder than the weather.

"I, I, I will gladly watch the movie," Sandy sputtered.

Hours later, as the credit rolled across the screen, Sarah and Jennifer had tears in their eyes and an empty Kleenex box on the table.

"I don't know about you all, but that was a tear-jerker," Sarah cried out.

"It was amazing, sad, but amazing," Jennifer said.

Mike looked at Tom and raised his eyebrows. "I must have either dozed off or missed something."

"Oh shut up," Jennifer barked, then threw a pillow at Mike.

Sarah suddenly perked up like a watchdog and looked out the window. "Did you hear that?"

"Yes," Tom said. "It's the sound of my tears of joy hitting the floor now that the movies over."

Averie stood and glanced out the window, but didn't see anything.

"Tom, I'm serious. It sounds like someone's outside." Sarah's eyes were wide as she scanned the darkness.

Tom looked out the window, then at the clock on the wall. "It's after ten, who would be here now?"

"We know it isn't Frank," Mike said with a chuckle.

Dave looked out the kitchen window. "Perhaps a cop found our vehicle and is looking for the driver by checking local houses."

"The wind is still howling pretty good, probably blew a few chunks of wood off the stack," Tom said. "How about we pick an action movie this time?"

"Sounds good to me," Billy agreed.

Sarah moved to a different angle and caught a glimpse of something black sprinting past. "Damn it," she screamed. "I saw something black, a shadow, or something in the porch light."

Averie panicked. "I'm going to go get Robyn."

Swinging back the battering ram, the monster of a man dressed in white and black camouflage designed for snowy, dark environments let it slam forward directly on the deadbolt. *WHAM*, the door swung in with such force; two hinges were ripped free from the frame. "Police, arrest warrants," the SWAT member screamed as he breached the doorway.

Instinctively, Averie tore down the hall to where Robyn slept.

BOOM, the SWAT membered fired hitting Averie in the back with a less than lethal bean bag round.

Averie collapsed, then flopped like a wounded fish searching for a position trying to relieve the pain.

"Get on the ground, get on the ground," three SWAT members screamed in unison while pointing their rifles at those who watched the shooting with horror.

"On your stomach," a masked man yelled at Averie.

Averie retaliated and raked the man across the face with her nails tearing the mask free.

The SWAT member panicked and punched her in the face splitting her lip and blackening her eye.

Averie's vision blurred, and her hearing became distorted. Unaware precisely what occurred, she found herself forcefully flipped over then quickly restrained.

Spreading out like robbers, the SWAT members searched the house and placed all the occupants in Zip-Tie Restraints.

"We have a child here, better get CPS on the phone," a SWAT member said when he discovered Robyn.

"What in the hell is wrong with you?" Tom screamed when he saw Averie escorted into the living room and forced to sit on the floor. Blood dripped from her chin, and one eye was blackened.

Moments later, another man emerged carrying Robyn, who reached out towards her mother and released a hellish scream.

"You leave my child alone, you heathen," Averie screamed at the man.

Another man entered who appeared different than all the rest. He wore gray sweat pants, black combat boots, and a black hat that read FBI in bold white letters. "Your child is going away for a while until we figure out exactly what is going on here."

Almost immediately they recognized the man as Detective Jason Gilbert.

Averie nearly broke the sound barrier as she came up off the floor and kicked the SWAT member square in the groin lifting him from the floor.

The man howled a devastating cry, dropped Robyn, fell to his knees, ripped off his mask, then barfed.

Robyn ran for her mother, but Detective Gilbert intervened and snatched the child.

Averie squealed as she was jerked backward by her hair and forcefully thrown down. Flailing wildly, it took the man a minute to get both feet restrained. Afterward, a cord was run from her feet up through her hands and cinched tight rendering her immobile. "That little stunt just bought you an assault charge, little lady."

Tom's teeth were chattering as he spoke. "What the hell is wrong with you people. It's freezing outside, and you bust the door open. We're going to freeze to death if you don't do something."

Detective Gilbert knew Tom was right. The temperature inside the house was dropping quick. From his pocket, he removed a small radio. "The house is secure, roll the transport van."

"Affirmative," came the static-filled voice.

One minute Saress was aiming her bow. The next, she was sailing thro-ugh the continuum of space and time that left her spinning like a lone tumbleweed across the desert sands of infinity. Wildly swinging her arms and legs, she tried to grasp anything, but there was nothing, and she soon found herself doing cartwheels screaming like a newborn hatchling. Elwrick remained upright with his arms crossed and hysterically laughing as Saress turned shades of green he never imagined possible. When the portal opened, Elwrick stepped out and wiped the dust off his white robe. Saress was a different story and came in hot and fast, shattering the bed and splintering a nightstand on her way to a smoldering stop partway into the closet. The impact shook the entire house, and the noise was deafening.

"What in the world," Detective Gilbert said as he directed a team member to go investigate. "That sounded like half the roof caved in."

Saress climbed to her feet and ripped off the dress that covered her eyes like a blindfold.

"Remember, we're here to recover Averie and her child," Elwrick told Saress. Saress looked baffled. "It can't be. You' re—you're dead," she repeated.

"I've never been more alive than I am right now," Elwrick said.

"Let me go," Averie screamed from the floor.

Headlights shined through the front door as the transport van neared. Detective Gilbert headed for the door.

"Please don't take my baby." Averie pleaded as only a distraught mother could.

"Keep screaming, and I'm going to gag you. Do I make myself clear?" the masked man told Averie.

Robyn had tears in her eyes and a scream in her lungs.

The scream Averie released could have driven the fleas off a cats back.

Saress growled, hissed, and snarled. The maternity spell Elwrick placed on her so long ago returned, and she could feel the distress flowing through Averie and her eyes filled with hate.

The SWAT member froze when he saw the big green monster standing there whose head nearly touched the ceiling, and then he died without making a sound.

"Averie has nothing to do with this. Let her go you son-of-a-bitch," Tom screamed.

"Please don't take Robyn," Averie pleaded to Detective Gilbert.

Detective Gilbert never looked back as he stepped onto the porch.

No words Saress knew could describe the scream Averie made, and a new wave of anger flooded into her mind. All she felt was hate as if someone was harming her hatchlings, even though she never had any. Lurching forward, she busted through the doorway, splintering the frame. The first thing her vision found was the man carrying a child. She had never seen Averie's child but could tell by Averie's hysterical screams this child was most certainly hers.

The man turned, having heard the crash, then stumbled backward nearly falling off the stairs.

Saress drew back the bowstring until the limbs creaked, and a glistening silver arrow formed. It wasn't an explosive or flaming arrow, but one she knew would fly true and harm only the intended target.

Detective Gilbert fought to get his pistol free, but in his oversight, it rested on the very hip where he supported Robyn.

Saress released the string, and the arrow flew faster than a bullet and plowed directly into the target, striking him in the forehead. Both eyes shot from the skull in different directions, and the back half of his head exploded outward painting the white snow red.

Robyn hit the porch then began crawling inside.

Unholstering his pistol, another member stepped to where he could see down the hall. "What the F—" he started to say when the explosive arrow hit his chest. Both arms shot in different directions, his head fired straight up like a rocket, the torso splattered against the wall and shattered a window while both legs fell like toppled trees.

Mike's jaw hung loose and swung side to side. In all his years of law enforcement, he had never seen such devastation.

Saress released a screech that sounded similar to a dragon's roar.

"Saress, help me," Averie screamed. There was only one creature that destructive with a bow and created such a unique howl.

Saress heard the call of her charge and sprinted down the hall. Pictures were ripped free and tossed like frisbees while the hallway light became a victim to her hardened, scale-covered head. Bursting into the living room, she performed a roll sweeping the feet out from under one man with her tail while raking another across the legs. The human flesh was no match for the dagger-length, razor-sharp claws and was left hanging while both legs snapped like twigs.

"Get on the ground," a SWAT member yelled from the kitchen, pointing his rifle at Godzilla.

Elwrick's white robe flapped in the wind funneled through the open door when he charged into the chaos. Observing the man pointing the strange weapon, he flung his arm as if throwing something, and the man took to flight. The crash was stunning as the wall studs splintered, and sheetrock exploded. Somewhere in the darkness of the front yard, they could hear his dying moans.

Saress pressed her sword into the throat of the man who whimpered with two broken legs ending his suffering.

Gaining his bearings, the one whose feet were swept out from under him crawled for the doorway, but never reached it. Elwrick released a series of glowing red missiles from his fingertips that instantly turned the man into a smoldering charred corpse.

Two others abandoned hope and sprinted for the transport van. One never made it as an arrow entered his back then exploded, making him nothing more than a blood splatter stain on the virgin white snow. The other flailed in the snow as the concussion from the previous arrow left him dazed. "Help me," he cried out while appearing to make snow-angels.

"Are you crazy? I'm not going out there," the man screamed to the stunned man from behind the vehicle. "Did you see that goddamn thing?"

Saress came from the kitchen, holding the head of someone by the bloody hair—the face still frozen in horror. Each step she took sounded like a nail gun firing as each claw dug into the wooden floor. Tossing the table out of the way, she located Averie lying on the floor. On top of Averie, her child clung. Behind Averie, more enemies waited. In one blinding motion, both swords found their sheaths while her bow came alive and a fiery red arrow with three tips formed.

Jennifer could see the hate in the yellow crescent-shaped eyes and fainted landing beside Averie.

Dave was both crying and praying for forgiveness to God, as he could already hear the death knells ringing.

Sandy sat there, expressionless. She never expected death to find her this way.

"They're my family," Averie screamed to Saress. All three arrows blew past, destroying the wall much to the relief of the intended targets.

"We need to get these cut off," Mike screamed, referring to the Zip-Tie Restraints.

Saress looked at Mike and cocked her head sideways, then to the smoldering corpse by the door. Afterward, she tossed the head on the blood-soaked floor.

"I'm losing my damn mind. Now I'm talking to a lizard," Mike mumbled.

"Come out with your hands up, the place is surrounded," an amplified voice sounded.

"We need to get these off," Tom yelled at the man. He had never seen him before but knew it could be none other than Elwrick, the Spiritual Guide.

Elwrick looked at the strange devices, then waved his hand above them, and they slid open.

Tom swiftly freed the others.

Saress looked out the window then her eyes flashed into the thermal spectrum. In the pure darkness, the men glowed like burning torches. Pulling back the bowstring, she whispered ꝑꝋꝗꝚꝋꝗꝚꝋꝗ ꝛꝛꝛꝏꝟ and a lightning blue arrow materialized. Upon release, a trail of glistening sparks followed as the arrow blew through the van unaffected by the steel. On the other side, the bullhorn fell silent.

"Holy crap," they heard someone scream from the darkness.

"Averie, we're here to take you and the child home," Saress said with a growling hiss.

Sarah stumbled sideways. Her mind walked on the razor's edge of insanity, and having heard the reptile speak, pushed her off the edge, and she fainted. Falling face down, she landed hard in a puddle of coagulated blood.

Cutting through the darkness, the faint sound of sirens screamed.

Tom fell to his knees and lifted Sarah from the puddle. Half her face glistened with the red sticky goo, and both eyes were marbled white.

Billy cried as he held tight to Sarah. This fight was nothing like what happened in the video games.

Robyn clung tight to Averie as if trying to re-enter the womb.

Averie looked back at the family that had taken such good care of her. They were in trouble, and once again, it was her fault. The thought to abandon them in their time of need tore at her heart. "I can't leave my family," she whispered. "They're the reason I'm alive today."

"Come out now and make it easy on yourself," someone yelled.

Averie handed Robyn to Elwrick. "Take her home. When she grows up, tell her I love her."

Robyn screamed while reaching for her mother.

"I love you," Averie whispered to Robyn, then began helping Tom wipe away the blood from Sarah's face.

"You're going whether you like it or not," Saress hissed, then snatched Averie around the waist and lifted her from the floor.

Averie wiggled and squirmed until she faced Saress, then began pounding her fist against the reptiles chest until both hands bled. "I am not leaving my family. You take me and I will never forgive you—ever."

Bang…bang…bang. The air sounded like someone let off a brick of firecrackers.

Tom threw himself on Sarah as bullets whizzed past. Luckily, nobody died except the computer, one light, the clock, and the thermostat.

Sirens flooded their ears as a dozen more cars came down the driveway.

Elwrick suddenly remembered the old man's words. *Bring them home-bring them home.* Knowing this, he chose to exploit them to the fullest. "Averie, will you go if I take them with us?"

Outside the house, the sounds of doors slamming echoed.

"Do you want to see my world?" Averie asked.

"What do we have to lose? If we stay here were going to prison for life," Mike yelled.

"You can take them too?" Saress asked Elwrick.

Elwrick shook his head unsure. "I don't know, but I'm going to give it one hell of a try."

Dave glanced out the window. "Oh crap, we have company and they look pissed."

"If we're going to do something, we have to do it now," Tom screamed.

Saress dropped Averie and readied her bow. The first man up the stairs died instantly as the arrow tore through him and planted into the second man. The man behind him tried to alter his route, but Saress was faster and took his head clean off his shoulders.

Boom-tink-tink. A metal canister came through the window and bounced around. Instantly after coming to rest, it spewed a suffocating gas.

"Come out with your hands u—" the man never finished as Saress sent an arrow directly down the tube of the bullhorn blowing out the back of the man's neck.

"Back this way," Tom screamed over the roar of the sirens. Slamming the bedroom door closed, he used a blanket to seal the gap at the bottom. "That gas will kill us."

The remaining members of the SWAT team strapped on their masks and entered the darkened environment. Pointing down the hall, the leader used hand signals for orders.

Elwrick had them all gather in a tight circle, then looked to the ceiling and whispered. "You said to bring them home. Them is an unspecified number. Please accept my request to take them all, for Averie's sake," then initiated the return sequence.

The SWAT leader tested the knob, then leaned back and kicked the door shattering the cheap lock. In the center of the room, the suspects were huddled tightly together.

Elwrick looked at the man at the same time the man looked at him.

Elwrick whispered the last word of the lengthy incantation.

The man raised his rifle, aimed, then pulled the trigger but the bullets only hit sheetrock.

The flash was horrendous and seen in neighboring states while the concussion flattened every wall forcing the roof to collapse down upon the foundation. Cars were blown like plastic toys while bodies littered nearby trees. Within seconds, nothing remained but a mourning moan from an icy wind.

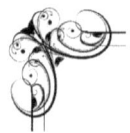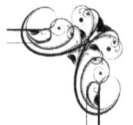

Chapter 107

he main road dividing Rhunsiire was vacant, cold, silent. A soggy, early morning fog rolled off the Freihn Sea obscuring the trees and transforming them into blackened two-dimensional silhouettes. Beyond the trees, it acted as an eraser removing everything tangible. High up in the dense trees invisible from view, sentries stood vigilant. It was believed Ruven fled Rhunsiire after the botched assignation, but Ryul was taking no chances. He tripled the number of sentries while patrols continually roamed in and about Rhunsiire.

The serene beauty and mesmerizing calmness were about to end. In the center of the road, near the Medical Ward, a glistening silver oval-shaped portal spitting golden sparks formed. The *BOOM* created shook the very heart of every soul residing within the Whispering Woods. From the portal emerged a grotesque creature made up of many arms, legs, skin, scales, hair, eyes, and teeth. Wiggling and thrashing, the beast came alive.

The alarm rang out in the still of the night, Rhunsiire was under attack. Each sentry readied their weapons while a runner was sent to warn Ryul. Rhunsiire had been invaded by a creature of ungodly design.

"Kill it quickly," Ryul screamed to the runner through the closed door while searching for his weapon's belt. He always kept it by the door hanging on a hook, but for an unexplained reason, the hook sat empty.

The elves encompassed the beast but remained at a safe distance while waiting for Ryul's arrival when it did something unexpected. It separated into eleven individual beings drawing gasps from those who watched.

Elwrick and Saress were the only members not stricken by the debilitating pain associated with the molecular structure change required to survive on Icearaus. Saress wandered off into the swirling gray mist lost in a daze as if abruptly awakened from a drunken stupor. All around her bells rang, and she shook her head clearing the cobwebs. Elwrick made it no more than ten steps, then stumbled. *SPLAT…* he landed face first in the mud, unconscious. The other members ended up on their knees, violently vomiting from the severe stomach cramps and then blacked out. Robyn was the first one to make a sound as she released a scream that rent the air like a siren. It passed all reason of logical thinking and invoked an emergency response from all, and every elf came running regardless of the danger.

Ryul finally arrived but never drew his weapons. He immediately recognized Averie. Lying on top of Averie was a child, and somehow, the child's leg was trapped under Averie snapping the tiny bone and forcing it up through the skin.

Birthright

The ringing of the bells finally registered inside Saress's mind. It was the alarm bells; they were under attack. Quickly gaining her location, she bolted towards the commotion knocking elves out of the way upon her arrival. "Everybody, get back," she hissed, then her vision landed on Averie and the child.

Gleia arrived shortly after Saress and began barking orders. The Medical Ward was about to get hectic.

Averie woke to a warm, wet cloth covering her face. "Robyn," she hysterically screamed and fought with the hand holding the fabric.

"Easy," Ellusia said as she continued to wipe the blood from Averie's chin from the busted lip. "This cream will make your eye feel better, as well." Using her finger, she dabbed the ointment on the big purple bruise on her cheekbone.

Averie tried to rise, but Ellusia gently held her down. "You need to rest."

"Where's my baby?" Averie screamed.

"Gleia is working on the child's leg. She should have it mended shortly," Ellusia calmly explained.

Lady Alenia looked up from the bed where she lay beside Elwrick.

Tom bolted upright nearly falling from the bed. His head pounded like a war drum, and his vision had yet to stabilize. "How much did I have to drink?"

Near Tom, Sarah tossed and turned searching for a position to ease the pain in her abdomen. Both Ellusia and Gleia checked her multiple times for the source of the blood, but could find no injury, so they assumed it came from someone else.

Mike woke earlier and now sat on a three-legged stool beside Jennifer holding her cold, limp hand while mumbling the words Gleia spoke. "She's fine. She fainted from the ordeal, that's all."

Dave and Sandy both slept soundly.

Billy seemed the least affected and was watching Gleia work on Robyn's leg in a separate room. Even though they weren't blood-related, he looked to Robyn like his younger sister and wanted the best for her. "Is she going to live?"

Gleia placed her hand over the wound and whispered the bone-mending spell. Both ends of the broken bone correctly repositioned themselves then the calcium fibers weaved tightly together. It was not a permanent repair like Elwrick could do, but it would hold the bone in place long enough for it to heal naturally. "She's going to be fine," Gleia reassured the boy while placing a cast on the tiny leg. "Give it a few months, and this will all be a distant memory."

Sarah woke slapping her gums like a grouper fish that swallowed a shark. "What happened?" she mumbled.

Tom looked at her. There was a freshly-waxed gloss look still in his eyes. "I, I'm not sure," Tom confusingly admitted.

Gleia entered carrying Robyn. "Someone wishes to see you."

Averie snatched Robyn and gripped her in a hug. "I'm so sorry," she whispered.

"Welcome home, young lady." Gleia afforded Averie a warm smile. "So that you know, it's not your fault. It's the way you were spat out of the portal. Give it a few months, and she'll be fine," Gleia reassured her. Afterward, she went to check on the others.

Averie propped herself up against the wall and placed Robyn on her lap and looked about the room. Everyone was here except Pegan. "Where's Pegan?" she asked Ellusia. "Does he not want to see me?"

Ellusia lifted Averie's hand and gripped it tightly. "Pegan is very sick right now. If he could, I know he would be here, but he can't."

"I want to see him, NOW!" Averie hollered. She started to rise but grew lightheaded and fell back to a sitting position.

"He is resting," Gleia tried to explain.

Averie heard none of it. "I want to see Pegan. Why won't you let me see Pegan?" She began to sob.

"Okay," Ellusia said, then helped Averie from the bed. "You need to be strong, Pegan won't be the same man you remember." After the explanation, Ellusia guided Averie through a narrow doorway to a darkened room lit by a single candle.

Averie's legs went weak, and she collapsed at the foot of the bed when she saw Pegan lying there still as death. His body was rigid, and his face was sunk in like the surface of rotten fruit.

"He's not dead," Ellusia said. "His heart still beats, and air fills his lungs, but his mind seems lost, stolen from his soul."

Averie touched his hand. It was cold and never acknowledged her presence. Around his neck was the piece of shard taken from hers. "He's so cold," she whispered, then laid her head on his chest.

Ellusia rubbed Averie's back. "We're doing all we can, but I fear this ailment isn't of the body but the mind."

Averie kissed his lips, but they lacked the affection she once knew.

Lady Alenia kissed Elwrick again when she saw one of his eyes crack open. "Welcome home, my love," she whispered into his ear.

Elwrick slowly opened his other eye, then looked about the room. "How did I get here?"

Lady Alenia kissed his cheek. "You came through the portal with Averie and a whole gaggle of people. Saress was with you as well, even though she denies any involvement."

Elwrick rubbed his face. "I went to the Altar of Knowledge to go home. My body was broken. I was dying."

"You may have gone to the Altar of Knowledge, but you returned here through a portal and brought back nine people and a reptile with you."

Saress entered and knelt beside Lady Alenia. "How is he doing?" Saress asked Lady Alenia.

"He's going to be fine," Gleia answered for Lady Alenia.

Gleia patted Elwrick on the leg. "I don't understand it either. How is it possible you left here knowing you were going to die, but return not long after your vanishing and brought back a handful of people, including Saress?"

Saress shook her head, no. "I don't know why people keep saying I was spat out of a strange silver portal. I was practicing with my bow when a strange fog rolled in, and I became disoriented. Moments later, I heard the alarm bells ring, so I gathered my bearings and came running."

Averie returned with tears in her eyes and hugged Saress, then Elwrick. "You saved my family and me. Please save Pegan."

From the look on Elwrick's face, they all knew he was bewildered. Hugging her back, he pulled her in close. "I am thankful you're home, but I don't know what you're referring too. I never saved you. I couldn't save myself."

Averie kissed Elwrick's cheek. "Thank you," she whispered. Afterward, she ventured back to her bed and laid beside Robyn, who was quite interested in the cast.

"I think each of you needs some rest. Tomorrow, perhaps today's events will become clearer," Gleia said, then closed the shutters and dimmed the magical lamps.

Sometime though the night, Averie woke and checked on Robyn, who was sleeping soundly in a crib beside her bed. Hopefully, Robyn wouldn't wake anytime soon, so she planned to spend some time lying with Pegan. Tip-toeing across the Medical Ward, she entered the narrow doorway. In the dim candlelight, she could see a woman sitting beside Pegan holding his hand.

"Averie, I think we should talk," the woman said without looking up.

"Who are you?" Averie whispered, but her voice carried in the darkness.

Lilith looked at Averie. "My name is Lucinda Krauss, but you would know me by my alias, Lilith."

Averie backed away and tried to scream, but no words came, and the door gently closed. Averie looked backward. Her only escape route was now blocked.

"I mean you know harm," Lilith said, "and I care for Pegan every bit as much as you do."

"Get away from him, you heathen," Averie hissed, then reached for her sword, but nothing was there. Her sword remained in the world she left. She was defenseless against this murderer. "I will fight you if I must."

"Nobody is going to fight anyone," Elwrick said as he stepped through the doorway. "I wondered what the outcome would be when you two discovered one another. Surprisingly, I figured Averie would have attacked you by now."

"Why is she here?" Averie screamed. "Why is she not dead?" Everyone knew Lilith was a close associate of Karayan's.

"Lilith is here because Pegan is her son," Elwrick blatantly said.

Averie looked at Elwrick, her golden eyes glowing in the darkness. "What did you say?"

"I am his mother and love him as much as you do. And as his mother, I am here to say he could not have picked a more wonderful woman to love."

"Yet, you would have handed Karayan the knife to cut Robyn out of my stomach."

"Averie," Elwrick compassionately called to her. "You have to understand Lilith's past, and it will all make sense. I think you should sit awhile and listen to her story."

"I want her away from Pegan before she cuts his throat."

"Why would I cut my own son's throat?"

"Don't play me as a fool, I know about the reward offered by Karayan."

"I have no intentions of killing Pegan, or you," Lilith said.

"Why does that heathen have silver eyes?" Averie whispered to Elwrick.

"Because that heathen is a full-blooded Witch," Elwrick answered. "Hopefully, when the man you love awakens, he will bear the same eyes."

"Averie, I would offer my life to save Pegan or you for that matter."

Averie cautiously walked towards Lilith. "Why are you here?" she asked again.

Hearing the commotion, Lady Alenia hobbled from the bed and entered Pegan's room. "Oh no," she whispered. She figured that Averie was gone forever, so she never planned or prepared for this encounter. As Queen of the elves, she had to do something. The elves needed Lilith, needed her fighting abilities. If Lilith fled, it would hamper their chances of victory.

Elwrick sensed the distress in Lady Alenia. "Sit," Elwrick demanded of Averie. "Stop acting like a child and listen to Lilith's tale. You will discover she's a victim the same as you from Karayan's lies."

Lady Alenia held Averie's hand. "If you wish, I will sit with you through its entirety. I believe when you get to know Lilith for who she is, not what she's done, you will understand why she's welcome in Rhunsiire."

Lilith looked into Averie's golden eyes. "If it pleases you, I will abandon the name Lilith and never speak it again. I may as well anyway, that woman is dead to me. I am Lucinda Krauss, she proudly said.

Averie looked to Elwrick for help, then to Lady Alenia. Both of them had her best interest in mind and would never lie to her. "If you both accept her, then I will as well."

Elwrick could tell Averie wasn't too sure about the decision she made, but it was a start. A chance to mend the wound between them. "I believe you should still hear her tale. It will bring you both closer and may help Pegan."

Later that evening as the sunset, the newcomers were escorted to the dining hall by Lady Alenia and Elwrick. In the shadows, Skylar and Miramar followed. Along the way, elves watched them pass before growing brave enough to follow.

"Hello," Ryul said as he greeted each male with the customary handshake and each female with a faint kiss to each cheek. "At this time, I would like to formally welcome you to Rhunsiire, home of the tree elves."

Tom was starving, and it didn't help that the scent of roasted meat lay heavy on the air. "Can we eat now?" he pleaded.

Upon entering, the crowd cheered, stood, clapped their hands, stomped their feet, hooted and hollered. "All of you are the guests of honor and will be dining with Queen Lady Alenia, Elwrick, King Hulradeeh, and his daughter, Saress," Ryul explained. "I took the time to question Averie what food was like on your world so that we could prepare it more to your liking."

At the table, Saress stood then knelt before the newcomers. "I wish to offer my heartfelt gratitude for everything you did to bring Averie safely home. As her protector, you have my approval as a job well done, but I will take it from here."

Tom scratched his head. "It was you who saved us. We should be on our knees thanking you."

Saress shook her head. "Why do you people keep saying that? I never left the Whispering Woods."

"No, it was you," Billy said. "Your bow has the same strange markings as the lizard that saved us."

"Sorry, it wasn't me," Saress explained, then took her place at the table.

Jennifer opened her mouth to speak, stopped, then continued anyway. "How did you learn to speak?"

Saress looked baffled. "That's a silly question, my mother taught me."

"I assume you have no race of reptiles where you're from?" Ryul asked.

"We don't even have a race of elves?" Tom answered.

"Make way, coming through," an elf yelled, carrying something dead on a wooden platter.

Saress licked her lips in anticipation, then scarfed down the animal; hair, skin, teeth, and bones in four bites.

King Hulradeeh looked at his daughter with disgust. "Saress, have you forgotten your manners? We're not in the feeding chamber at home."

"I'm sorry, guess that wasn't very ladylike," she chuckled.

"Is Averie going to join us?" Sarah asked Ryul. "I would like to see her again."

"No, she has decided to remain at Pegan's side. I will see to it she does not go hungry."

"I would like to bring it to her if you don't mind. We kind of bonded and I think she would appreciate seeing me again," Sarah asked.

"I would like to go as well?" Jennifer politely asked.

"I will see to it," Ryul said.

Mike eyed Ryul suspiciously. His years of investigation work told him this man wanted more than to chat about the weather. "You're here for another reason?"

Ryul nodded. "Yes, but I'm not sure how to say it."

Sandy crossed her arms. "I always found it easiest to come right out and say it, then beat the hide off a dead horse."

Ryul agreed. "I don't know how your world was, but here, life is cruel. You have entered a world amid a fierce war, and there is a good chance some, or all of you may not live to see the end of it. Starting tomorrow, you will have no choice but to choose a weapon and begin training."

Jennifer went pale from the thought of having to kill someone. "I can heal the injured. I was a doctor on Earth. I want to be one here as well."

Ryul waved for Gleia to come. "Jennifer says she can heal people, so she falls under your guidance."

Gleia hugged Jennifer. "It seems like everyone wants the glory of killing, but none wants to work in the shadows and heal the wounded. They seem to forget we're the backbone of the army. I'm glad you would rather pick up a bandage than steel. I will get with you in the morning and see where your skills lie."

Ryul felt much better with that out of the way. Raising both hands high he clapped three times. "Let the festivities begin," he yelled.

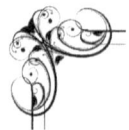
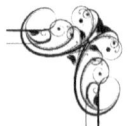

Chapter 108

he following day" Ryul studied the large map splayed out on the table. Using a stick with a forked end, he jockeyed different colored stones into different locations.

A tall, slender elf with flowing hair covered in green leather armor pointed to a ridge on the Ash Mountains. Slung across his back was a longbow and a quiver of arrows. "I will take my team of archers and place them here. We'll draw them away from the Whispering Woods and split their ranks."

"My team of swordsman will break through the opening created by the archers. If we can destroy even half the machines before they reach our borders, it will change the outcome dramatically."

Skylar leaned against the wall listening intently. "I don't think you understand the situation, gentlemen." Skylar took the stick from Ryul and used it to reposition Karayan's troops and their suspected locations. "Even if you place five hundred archers here, which you can't. He could send four times that many to destroy you and still not create an opening. I don't think you grasp the magnitude of the army this man has created."

Ryul took the stick back and used it to slide multiple rows of stones just off the border of the Whispering Woods. "What if we dug trenches here, preventing the machines from reaching us?"

Skylar shook his head in dismay. "Are you not listening to what I said. I walked amongst their ranks, listened to them talk. They've been whipped into a mindless rage and ready to eat their guts. All they want is to destroy the men and enslave the women. We have no choice but to flee while we have time."

"That's a cowards way to talk," Ryul hissed. "You took an oath never to run in the face of death—"

"There is a difference between fighting a battle where the outcome has yet to be determined and this war." Skylar looked around the room at each eye watching him. "I'm telling all of you, this is a war we cannot win."

The door creaked opened and Elwrick entered accompanied by Lady Alenia.

"My lady," Ryul said. "Skylar Nightshade speaks with a blasphemous tongue. He recommends we flee the Whispering Woods. Surrender our homeland to the enemy, run like cowards and hide like vermin."

Lady Alenia eyed Skylar, then Ryul. "And what is his reasoning?"

Skylar explained the situation again.

"I think we should consider it," Lady Alenia said.

"You can't be serious?" Ryul was seething mad.

"I'm only saying it's an option that we should not dismiss so quickly."

"Of course not," Ryul agreed. "Now, let's get back to the seriousness of the situation."

At the table, the elves started discussing different locations where troops should be placed to try and separate Karayan's ranks. "If we can break through and disrupt the supply chain…" an elf started to say.

"Skylar Nightshade is right," Elwrick whispered to Lady Alenia. "If the elves stay here, you might as well order every elf to slice their throats. This way, you know they will not suffer at the hands of Karayan."

"You agree with Skylar?"

"No, but I understand the *Prophecy of Damnation.*"

"What does the prophecy have to do with us?" she asked Elwrick.

At the table the elves began arguing about what the best course of action was to be.

Elwrick watched the elves argue for a minute. "The *Prophecy of Damnation,* if I understand it correctly, explains that all who stand against evil will migrate to *Huelgrawt.*"

"*Huelgrawt?*"

"Yes," Elwrick answered. "It is the birthplace of creation, where it all began."

"And how do you get there?" Lady Alenia asked Elwrick.

Elwrick had a hard time hearing her as the elves arguing had grown obnoxious. "I don't know. My vision is limited to Icearaus. I cannot see beyond these borders."

Ryul slammed his fist down on the desk, catching them all by surprise. "And I am prepared to die—"

"Silence," Elwrick screamed. "This bickering has nothing but stifle our progress. I want everyone out except Ryul and Skylar."

Grumbling and moaning, the others shuffled out.

Elwrick closed then locked the door. "Perhaps now we can make some sense of this."

Ryul crossed his arms knowing Elwrick was going to deliver bad news.

Elwrick made his way to the table and looked at the map. "Skylar has seen the enemy, talked with the enemy, and I have no reason to doubt his word. I believe the seal on the *Prophecy of Damnation* has been broken. If I interpret it correctly, it warns that this war is only the beginning, and is known as the *Time of Sorrows.* It also explains that war will drive all who resist evil to a distant land named *Huelgrawt.* I'm no eschatologist, but from my interpretation of what is to come. Those who don't go to *Huelgrawt* will be destroyed."

Ryul swung his arms madly. "If what Skylar preaches is true, then it must also be true that the Whispering Woods is being watched for any signs of flight. If we leave, we will be exposed and easily slaughtered trying to protect the elderly and the young."

"But one could walk away unnoticed," Elwrick said.

"One, what good is one?" Ryul screamed.

"Because one man could carry all the others inside a strange artifact called the Worlds Stone. The only problem is the only one in existence is located in the Under-Dark, in the City of Österkliġr, and held by an ancient wizard named

Aluneus the Unbeliever. That is if he or the stone still exists."

"Aluneus the Unbeliever?" Ryul mockingly laughed.

"That's not his surname. Aluneus was rightfully given that title because of his disbelief in the Creator. As a stern believer in evolution, he preached that man was born in the salty waters of the ocean from a giant sea turtle. Most believed him to be delusional, neurotic, or out of his blasted mind, but over time; he developed a small following. Ridiculed and harassed, he led his people deep underground, and it was there they settled and built the Pantheon of Acyesis under his guidance."

"So that's it?" Ryul asked. "You're not even going to have the council vote on our future. You're going to have us flee in this so-called Stone we don't have, and may not be able to get."

"I will do my best to recover the artifact," Elwrick said.

"If you do get this stone, where will the man who is designated to carry it go? No place on Icearaus is safe."

"It must be carried beyond our borders into the Wilds and beyond—" Elwrick started to explain.

"And who's going to do that? Nobody knows what lies beyond our borders." Ryul slammed his fist down on the table.

"If not Pegan, Saress would be the best choice," Lady Alenia said. "They found the dwarves, and she knows the way to them. Perhaps they will be willing to help."

Ryul's face was blistering red. To flee was nothing more than a sign of cowardice.

Lady Alenia slowly approached Ryul and took his hand then looked into his eyes. "Why are you so ready for war? Is it because you have never seen war? I have seen war," she whispered. Her eyes had a pasty stare. "I have seen war in the deepest caverns to the highest mountains, in the desert and in the forest. I have seen the wounded knee deep in blood holding their guts screaming from the pain. I have seen elves limping home exhausted. I have seen the mothers crying when their husbands and sons never returned. Even in victory, there are no winners. I hate war."

Ryul stepped back. What Lady Alenia said was true, but he was no rookie. He had seen his fair share of skirmishes.

Elwrick crossed his arms. "I know the word flee isn't in your vocabulary, and you wish for your sword to taste the enemy. Remember though, for each one of your foe's that falls, he takes a little piece of your sanity with him until you're no better off than the fallen."

"I believe it is for the best," Lady Alenia tried to comfort Ryul.

"I will leave first thing in the morning to recover the Worlds Stone. Until then, prepare everybody to flee. Take only what is necessary."

"I'm going with you," Lady Alenia said.

"No," Elwrick firmly said. "Where I'm going is perilous and I don't think you'll survive the ordeal."

"What if you don't survive?" Ryul angrily asked. "We'll be slaughtered without having a chance to defend ourselves."

Skylar rested his hand on Elwrick's shoulder. "I believe you can do it."

"Then it's settled. I see no purpose of me being here any longer." Ryul was fuming mad when he walked from the room.

Lady Alenia watched Ryul exit.

"He will understand in time," Elwrick said. "The war with Karayan is nothing more than a precursor to the *Hour of Reckoning.*"

Lady Alenia held Elwrick's hand. "This evening, I will announce that we must prepare to flee the Whispering Woods."

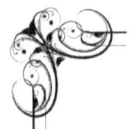
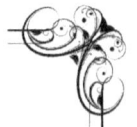

Chapter 109

arayan not only felt old, but he also looked the part. **Deep** wrinkles creased his once flawless face, and his raven black hair had gone to the way of ashen gray. Long forgotten was the thought of joints that moved without pain, and his clothes hung loosely on his deteriorated frame. Hunched slightly at the shoulders, he slowly paced the length of the tent with the aid of a gnarled cane. Malvo had spoken the truth. Time was a vicious, deranged beast bloodthirsty to reclaim what was stolen and attacked with a seething vengeance.

Karayan glanced at his reflection in the shield hanging on the rack. One of his piercing black eyes was milky white, and his vision was no longer clear, but hazy as if looking through a dense fog. Touching his cheek, he thought back to when his eyes were golden, shiny, and sparkled with life. *How did he allow his life to flounder so far out of control? How did he let himself fall to corruption?* Grabbing the shield, he threw it on the ground. There had to be a way to save his soul from eternal torment.

Too tired to make a dedicated alter, he knelt before the brazier and closed his eyes. Pleading to the Dark Master for a chance to redeem himself, he wept. The likelihood of the bearer's child dying before him was now a fallacy. In the embers of the brazier, a tiny flame sparked to life, and it floated to the edge. On it, two little, soulless eyes formed. "Bring me the souls of Lilith and Pegan." The voice was a seething, remorseless, hiss.

Karayan could hear redemption in the Dark Masters voice. It wouldn't restore his immortality, but it would save him from eternal torment.

The runner from God's Perch should have been here by now informing him of the reptiles defeat, but he had heard nothing, but that was no longer a concern. Rhunsiire needed to burn, and it needed to cook now. Releasing a haggard cough, he groaned as the pain went straight to his spine, and he held his chest.

A man entered and knelt, his wet armor glistening in the blood-red light coming off the brazier. "My King. The men are ready. They only wait for your word to begin the march."

Karayan cupped his mouth and released another cough. "I will be there shortly to give my war-speech."

The man nodded, then left.

Karayan stood on the platform overlooking his troops. They were arra-nged in equal teams of one war machine, five carts loaded with wood, three wagons of coal, and two-hundred men. The one hundred groups spread out farther than his eyes could see, and a smile creased his narrow mouth. He had assembled the deadliest army to ever march across Icearaus, and he saw salvation. When Lilith and Pegan burned, his suffering would be nil compared to theirs. No longer was the child even a consideration.

Raising both hands in the air to silence the army, he spoke. "The time to prepare is over; the time to act is now." He coughed again, and a shiver ran up his spine as the rain-soaked clothes chilled his bones.

The army whooped and hollered and pounded their fire-hardened weapons against mirror-polished shields.

"Do not believe the victory has already been achieved because we greatly outnumber the enemy. The elves are cunning, and they fight with a dead man's vengeance." Karayan coughed again, then spit something up. "To make an extended speech only delays the inevitable. The time to march on the Whispering Woods and raze it to the ground is now."

The war machine commanders began barking orders, and the teams rolled out in controlled chaos. It would take the better part of two weeks to cover the distance marching day and night. Three weeks if they stopped to rest.

Karayan made his way back to the tent then wrapped himself in a thick blanket, and stood by the brazier. The heat radiating off the coals eased his aching bones.

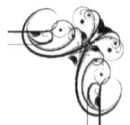

Chapter 110

lwrick woke while Lady Alenia still slept. He didn't need to sleep but knew Lady Alenia did, and she would sleep better with him at her side. After pulling the blanket further up to her neck, he made his way to the window and looked out. The night sky was crystal clear, and a thousand stars twinkled. Soon, he would be going to a world never graced by the light of day, nor a falling star. A world warmed by the core of the planet, not the sun. A world ruled by darkness and governed by brutality—a world rightfully titled the Under-Dark.

Casually strolling across the room he looked down at Lady Alenia. For once, she appeared to be free of the pain brought on by age, by fear, by the unknown. Elwrick knelt beside the bed and ran his fingers through her air and kissed her cheek, which caused her to stir, but not wake. He knew she wouldn't, the herb he placed in her tea that evening to give it a minty flavor had a secondary effect, it was designed to leave her resting peacefully. "May you sleep well until my return," he whispered. Looking back once more as he walked away, there was a mortal moisture in his eyes.

The path glowed like a lit street as he jogged towards his destination on the banks of the Tlumn River. The trail snaked its way through the dense foliage, then climbed to the top of a grassy knoll. From here, he could see the monstrous pile of rocks in the moonlight abandoned here from when the river was a raging monster during the creation of the world. Releasing a ragged sigh, Elwrick continued until arriving at a small cave deep in the rocks. This cave was not here by accident, but by design. It was one of the few remaining locations which allowed access to the Under-Dark from the Mortal Realm. Each time Elwrick returned home, his body went through a metamorphosis. Sometimes this change took weeks to complete depending on how long he stayed in the Mortal Realm. While his body went through this change, he could not return to the Mortal Realm until its completion, so he decided to stay here and travel as an astral gas.

Elwrick's body became vapor-like and slipped through the narrow cracks in the slate ground. Drifting downward, he passed through granite, basalt, quartz, limestone, marble, and a hundred other varieties of stone. Moving at a pace no quicker than the smoke drifting off the bowl of a tobacco pipe, it took days to travel the five leagues before entering a cavern bleak as death and silent as a tomb. Carried on a subterranean breeze, he swirled downward as if caught in a vacuum.

Upon reaching the granite floor, Elwrick formed back into a man and instantly knelt. His eyes were immune to the impenetrable darkness, and he watched as a world built of gray, lifeless stone mixed with depression formed. Remaining there for a spell, he listened intently for the slightest movement. Things lurked here immune to magic, immune to physical attacks, immune to death.

Elwrick motions were quick but controlled as he navigated the darkness. There were no shadows to conceal his movements, so he remained centered in the broad passages created by the sandstone stalagmites and calcium towers. Each step was calculated to avoid ruble as many creatures at this depth were blind, tracking their dinner by sound, smell, or the subtle vibrations made from their heavy footfalls.

Near the back of the cavern buried deep in a forest of impressive crystallized stalagmites, dilapidated huts, and still-water ponds, the Pantheon of Acyesis rose up out of a fractured obsidian mound like some prehistoric beast wearing a crown with many horns. Two, impossibly tall, yet insanely narrow inky black arched windows bore down upon a wing-shaped awning supported by multiple stone pillars of grand proportion. Beneath the canopy, an ever-burning magical lamp recessed inside a stone pillar illuminated the foyer. From the foyer came a narrow staircase of broken and disfigured steps that wound its way down through the upheaved stone to the subterranean floor.

Elwrick stood on the first step, and a shiver crept up his spine as he took in the malevolent structure. Not much was known about Aluneus, the Unbeliever, or his workings as he spent most of his life in solitude. What he did know was the Pantheon of Acyesis—the Temple were Aluneus practiced, and nearly, perfected the arcane arts—was the last known location of his greatest creation, the Worlds Stone.

Elwrick cautiously crept up the nine hundred and ninety-nine remaining steps, occasionally looking back. There were things here that never slept, never stopped searching for a meal. Breaching the rim, he arrived at a full landing decorated with many stone benches. Each bench was positioned to allow those who sat there to look out over the vastness of the cavern. Choosing a seat near the stairs, he looked back the way he had come and down at the small deserted village. *Where had all the wizard's followers gone? What kind of atrocity had occurred?* He wondered, then a strange feeling befell him. Since his arrival, he had heard no sign of life, seen no sign of death. Something very odd occurred in this location.

Back on the move, Elwrick followed the rock-rimmed cobblestone path past multiple broken statues before arriving at two, large, ornately carved, wooden doors edged with engraved steel. Fastened on each door was a large stone knocker carved to resemble the tail of a great serpent.

Elwrick visually examined the door, then ran his hand along the surface. He guessed by the thick layer of dust; the doors had not been opened in a very, very long time. Elwrick twisted one knob, then the other, but both refused his entry. Locks were only a mere inconvenience for a man of his skill, or it should have been, but his Lock Latch Release Spell fizzled. Hmmm, he groaned. A protection ward was in place, which meant someone, or something lived inside. "Well let's see who's home, shall we," he whispered, then looked about making sure his words fell on deaf ears. Lifting the knocker, he let it fall. *BOOM!* The loud noise echoed throughout the cavern and the many wide tunnels and narrow passages that led away.

Elwrick lost track of time as he waited. It could have been ten minutes, an hour, or three days. Elwrick wasn't sure for in the Under-Dark, time was obsolete. Debating if he should knock again, he reached for the knocker the very moment the door flung open and slammed into him. Blindsided by the ferocious attack, he vanished into the darkness as he stumbled backward.

A misty, faint blue haze burst through the opening and snatched the intruder by the foot, jerking him free of the ground. "Who disturbs the Master?" the invisible beast asked with a sultry voice.

Elwrick tried to answer, but the assault was quicker than the blink of an eye, and Elwrick discovered himself dangling upside down near the ceiling. Partially blinded by his robe that covered his face, he caught a brief glimpse of the assailant—and that was all he needed to realize he was in serious trouble. This entity was no wizards spell, or dark arcane magic. This was an ancient life form born in the Great Maelstrom near the center of the Realm of Lucidity.

"Are you a thief, robber… MURDERER?" The cynical voice thundered. "Answer me." The beast violently slammed Elwrick against the ceiling as if he were a club knocking a stalagmite free, sending it falling like a giant tooth into the darkness.

Elwrick's life teetered on the edge of death. One wrong word or movement, and this beast would pulverize him. For the life of him, though, he couldn't understand why she was here. Air elements rarely ventured into the Mortal Realm as the air quality was not conducive to their lifestyle. They preferred the Realm of Lucidity, where the air was more vaporish, thick with moisture, fog-like. "Queen Phecabra, Warlord of Destruction and Lady of the Wind. It is I, Elwrick, Order of the First Flame." His robe muffled his voice. Hopefully, Queen Phecabra would remember him as she occasionally ventured into the Realm of Light when she sought meaningful conversation.

Queen Phecabra thrashed at Elwrick ripping the cloak from his back and sent it fluttering like a wounded bird. "Imposter," Queen Phecabra hissed.

"I am no imposter," Elwrick angrily yelled. "I am here on a mission of diplomacy. I must speak with Aluneus, the Unbeliever immediately," he snarled.

The air element twisted Elwrick as she examined him.

Elwrick grew dizzy from being shifted in a dozen different positions. "The wizard holds the future of mankind," he moaned as his eyes wobbled like marbles in a jar.

Queen Phecabra repositioned Elwrick, so he appeared to be standing on air, then a pair of mesmerizing emerald eyes materialized in the swirling faint-blue mist. "If you're no imposter, then save yourself." Releasing her grip, she watched the man plummet into the darkness.

Elwrick screamed like a frightened cat as the ground rushed toward him. Quickly mumbling a Feather-Light spell, it went into effect seconds before impact, but he still hit with a bone-crushing thud.

Queen Phecabra formed into a translucent woman with crystal hair and stars for eyes. Crossing her arms, she looked down over the man. "Impressive, very impressive."

Elwrick scrambled to his feet. "I have passed your test," he hissed while brushing the dust off his white robe. Afterward, his eyes narrowed; he could see her apprehension. "Besides, if I was not who I said I am, how could I reach this depth knowing that the deep passage has been sealed for all eternity."

Queen Phecabra cocked her head sideways, her color slightly darkened, then she faded nearly from existence. "Sealed—no," she grumbled. "There are ways if you know where to look."

"Then those passages are unknown to me," Elwrick spat back.

Queen Phecabra remained hesitant to accept the man for who he said he was. "What manner of evil on the surface drives a faithful being of the Creator to these depths?"

Elwrick walked to a bench and sat. From here, he looked out over the vast cavern. There was no greenery, no trees or lush forest, no flowing rivers, only gray stone, and stagnant murky pools.

The air elemental followed closely behind.

"The seal has been broken, the *Time of Sorrows* is now," Elwrick whispered.

Queen Phecabra's eyes widened. "Are you positive?" She questioned the intruder, still not sure it was Elwrick.

Elwrick waited a long time before he spoke. "Yes," Elwrick said with a nod. "While I knelt at the Altar of Knowledge, it was revealed to me through a series of visions by Archangel Raziel, the Angel of Knowledge, the *Prophecy of Damnation* HAS been activated."

Queen Phecabra placed her hand on Elwrick's shoulder. "If this is true, then the Hour of Reckoning rides on the horizon."

"Which is why I have come, why I must speak with Aluneus, the Unbeliever. The wizard holds the only device which can save those who resist the darkness. He holds the Worlds Stone."

Queen Phecabra walked to the edge of the stairs and looked out. When she turned, only an outline of her body remained. "The Stone of which you speak has been activated. It is of no use to you. It's of no use to anybody." She kicked a small stone and watched it tumble down the stairs. Each *thwack* created as it hit became fainter than the last as it neared the bottom.

"What manner of creature does Aluneus keep prisoner?" Elwrick suspiciously asked.

"Aluneus, the Unbeliever isn't the keeper. Aluneus and his followers are the kept," she softly spoke.

"How?" Elwrick mumbled? "How do you know this?"

"The few times I'm allowed to visit my daughter, she informs me of what is happening far below."

Elwrick leaped to his feet as if he sat on a cactus. "You need to start making some sense of what in the world is going on down here."

"I don't have the time. If I am caught talking to you, Azmalyn will order my daughter's execution," Queen Phecabra whispered.

Suddenly, the surface world didn't seem so important, even though the love of his life lived there. "Then I guess you're going to have to kill me. I'm not leaving until I have some form of explanation."

Queen Phecabra couldn't kill Elwrick. Not because she couldn't, but because he was her friend. "If I tell you, will you please go?"

"I will, but I won't make a promise never to return."

Queen Phecabra sat on the bench and twiddled her translucent thumbs. "I only know bits and pieces, and even then, it's scarce at best. After the betrayal of the dwarves, the Nendorühl dwarves fled through secretly created tunnels and into the Under-Dark. After many fierce battles, they wound up here and befriended Aluneus, the Unbeliever, who did not know about the incident. Exploiting his generosity, the dwarves convinced him they too were his followers and moved into the Pantheon of Acyesis. Eventually, they took over daily operations. At some point after claiming ownership, a stout dwarf named Azmalyn Alearm, self-proclaimed Queen of the Nendorühl, discovered the Worlds Stone and convinced Aluneus and his followers to enter. Now, she wears the Stone around her neck as a trophy. How did she get them to enter, nobody will ever know as their release seems impossible."

Elwrick sighed. "I assumed the Nendorühl dwarves died, killed by the heathens they aided."

Queen Phecabra shook her head. "They live, and since their flight have become demented."

Elwrick shook his head. "None of this makes any sense. How did the dwarves capture your daughter? They cannot enter the Realm of Lucidity without passing through my Realm."

"They didn't. My daughter came here without my knowledge or permission. You know how children can be. I only found out afterward, but she came here to give Aluneus an elemental tear. I believe it was not Aluneus calling her, but the dwarves. Upon her arrival, she was captured and placed in a cage, a cage which disrupts her magic."

"And you can't free your daughter?"

"If I do not do as Alearm demands, my daughter will be slain. Thus I am a prisoner as well."

Elwrick paced back and forth, mumbling and grumbling. "I don't understand their reasoning. What do they have to gain by keeping you?"

"Elwrick," Queen Phecabra called out. "I am held here to be their protector, and nothing more."

"Protector from what?" Elwrick questioned the Queen. "They already have the protection of the Pantheon of Acyesis."

"The dwarves are not the humanoids you once knew. They are crazy. Their skin has turned pure white, eyes red as flame. The darkness and pressure from the stone above has warped their minds. All they care about now are collecting riches, pillaging the land of all its treasure, collecting anything they see shiny and of value." Queen Phecabra spun in a circle with her arms splayed. "What you see here is nothing. They have a network of tunnels under the ground like the surface has roads. Elwrick, they have broken through into the Nether-Dark." There was fear in her eyes when she spoke the last sentence.

Elwrick slowly shook his head, stunned by what he heard. "They use you to

protect them from what they have unearthed?"

"Yes," she whispered. "Things I have never seen before."

"Things never meant to be disturbed," Elwrick cautiously said. "They must be stopped before what they've unearthed, reaches the surface."

"How?" she asked. "I won't sacrifice my daughter. What she did was foolish, but does not justify death."

Elwrick smiled. He had a plan. "Do you know if Aluneus kept the recipe for the Worlds Stone somewhere besides his mind? On a parchment or inside a tome."

"What are you thinking?" she asked.

"If I can create another Worlds Stone, I could save the greatest underground fighting force alive. I make this promise to you today. Get me that recipe, and I will return and save your daughter."

"It will take some time," she explained. "If anyone knows my daughter would. I will ask her on my next visit."

"Get me those plans, and I will free your daughter," Elwrick slowly hissed as his eyes blazed with anger.

Queen Phecabra smiled for the first time in a long time. "I will get you those plans."

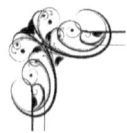
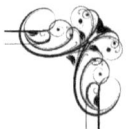

Chapter 111

illy excitedly walked down the aisle, looking at the array of weapons. Now was his chance to live the game he once played. Closely following was Mike, Tom, and Dave. There were scimitars, greatswords, battle axes, a variety of daggers and knives, maces, bows, polearms, and a limited number of shields.

Sandy stood back, visibly shaken as the reality sank in this was not a vacation, but her new life. There was no going home, no waking up from this dream. There was a genuine chance she would die by a weapon similar to the ones she looked at now. "I'm sorry," she said to Ryul, who watched them pick through the weaponry. "I can't do this. I'm a philosopher. I read and study the stars."

"Perhaps then you would be better suited for the Medical Ward," Ryul said.

"I think all of us women would be," Sarah voiced her opinion.

Billy picked up a dagger. It felt good in his hand.

"I don't want Billy fighting," Tom said. "He's only a boy, not a warrior."

Ryul approached Tom. "Do you believe Karayan would not kill him because he is unarmed? Because he is only a boy?"

"I once observed Karayan destroy a homeless child. Beat him until each bone shattered," Lilith said. "Karayan will use your boy to feed off your emotions. Hold him hostage and torture him daily until you surrender with the promise of the child's release, but it will all be a lie. The boy will die, and you will die alongside him."

Sarah looked away. She refused to allow them to see her cry.

"Dad, I want to fight," Billy explained.

Tom sighed. Right before his very eyes, he watched his family fall apart.

Mike selected a longbow. It felt different than the compound bow he hunted with at home. Still, he thought he would quickly adapt to the new style.

Tom selected a curved scimitar with a thin, but deadly sharp blade.

Dave snatched a wooden mace with a knob-covered hardened head with many spikes. To his shock, he discovered it was quite heavy.

"The women will report the Medical Ward, where I'm sure Gleia can teach you to bandage a wound. The men will report to the training grounds and begin training immediately with the weapon's master. May the Creator watch over all of us as we prepare for the inevitable."

"I thought we were going to enter this Worlds Stone?" Sandy asked. "This way, we wouldn't have to fight this man you call Karayan."

Ryul squinted as he looked at Sandy. "Even if we avoid the war with Karayan, sooner or later, we will have to face Malvo in war. There can be no other outcome; it's written in the prophecies."

A ten-day had passed since Karayan gave the orders to begin the march, and the war machines rolled out. In their wake, long nasty scars like stretch marks on the belly of a bloated corpse marred the fertile Plains of Gedeon. It would take years, possibly decades, for the land to heal.

Bermille, a burly man thick with gangly hair and only one eye, whipped the team of horses nearly to exhaustion as they pulled an observation tower that rode on steel axles fed through enormous spiked wheels. Once set in place, Karayan could observe the war, bark commands, or give his victory speech. If things did go sour, it would also afford him enough time to make his escape. Karayan could foresee no problems, though. Between his tower and the Whispering Woods, there would be twenty-thousand bloodthirsty men.

From the east and west came a messenger riding hard. Upon their arrival, they quickly dismounted and performed a gracious bow.

"My King, the war machines heading west will be in place in a handful of days." The soldier informed Karayan of the southern assault team's progress. After he finished, the other man spoke. "The Freihn Sea team will be ready in three. A few war machines sit idle waiting on your word."

"Excellent," Karayan said. "I wish we could begin the siege now, but we must be patient. All the key components must be in place. If we strike early, it allows them the opportunity to counter, or flee—and neither of those sits well with me."

The runner dropped into position unannounced beside Ryul, who stood on a raised platform leaning on the railing. Below him, the newcomers practiced with their perspective experts in a roped-off arena. "We're slowly being surrounded," the runner informed Ryul.

Ryul scrubbed his chin as he intently watched their movements. "Because of Lady Alenia's fear of war, we are now bound to die by it. Had we attacked when I wanted, we may have had a chance. Now, it's too late."

In Ryul's voice, the runner could sense all hope was lost. "There is still time," the runner said.

"Time for what?" Ryul asked. "Even if Elwrick returns with the Stone, how does Saress plan to escape. It's not like she can blend in with Karayan's men. She'll be spotted, chased to exhaustion, strung up and skinned, and the Stone taken. I never dreamed I would die without my blade ever tasting my killer's blood."

"Perhaps Skylar could carry the Stone? Saress could give him directions," the runner said.

"And put our future in the hands of an assassin. What if Skylar delivers us to Malvo? Perhaps this was Malvo's plan from the beginning."

The runner watched them practice for a bit longer. It would take decades to get them ready to face Malvo, decades they didn't have.

"Malvo is going to slaughter them when they finally meet," Ryul said. "Elves are taught to hold a weapon from the minute they can stand, these people, though…" he let his words trail off.

"They come from a different lifestyle," he said. "They have heart, and hope, and combined, they are a deadly combination. Still, I am not giving up on Elwrick and the Stone. Besides, it won't be us fighting Malvo. It will be the Witch and Warlock."

***

Elwrick couldn't wait any longer. He would have to do something soon, or why even bother returning as the war with Karayan would be over. Venturing back to the door, he tried to twist each knob, but they were securely fastened. "Damn," he grumbled, then looked up at the windows. Growing weightless, he floated up to the ledge and positioned himself where he could see inside. The tiny room seemed to have no purpose other than to hold broken furniture or rubbish. On the far wall, he could make out the shape of a broken door hanging from a single rusty hinge. Touching his fingertips against the glass, he could feel no ward, and he briefly smiled. He had discovered a way inside without drawing attention. Elwrick concentrated on the latch while whispering the spell and the lock slowly, silently slid free.

"Where are you going?" a voice from below asked.

Elwrick looked down to see Queen Phecabra waiting at the bottom. Something had gone dreadfully wrong as she favored one side of her body, and at her feet was a translucent puddle of blue blood. Elwrick felt terrible. He knew she was called upon to fight something in the depths.

Elwrick quickly floated down. "You look terrible," he whispered.

Queen Phecabra tried to smile, but the pain was evident in her features. "The dwarves discovered a cavern adjacent to this one. Inside was an unknown species, but they had a cache of gold, silver, jewels, diamonds, and other oddities. The dwarves wanted the booty, so I was sent to destroy them."

Elwrick took her hand and closed his eyes. "Relax," he whispered. Through her, he could see what happened. Hear the drums of war, the music playing, see the viciousness of what she encountered. The creatures were nearly nine feet tall with muscular, horse-like legs that ended with massive black hooves ringed with tufts of gangly hair. They had the bare torso of a giant with extended humanoid arms and swollen hands. A pair of piercing black eyes were sunk back in their goat-shaped, scraggly haired heads. Breaking through the dirty hair were two twisted horns. "The creatures you killed were Satyr's," Elwrick explained. "Not much is known of them except they fought in the Great War beside the minions of hell."

"Satyr's," she slowly whispered.

"Yes," Elwrick whispered back, then his hand begun to glow a faint red.

Queen Phecabra felt her elemental bones mend, and the unseen cuts and slices heal. The aches and pains associated with the assault were nothing more than a distant memory. "I feel honored to heal those who fight beside those who rally against the works of evil."

Queen Phecabra knelt before Elwrick. "I thank you."

"Rise," Elwrick commanded. "You never have to bow to me as I am no king, but a Spiritual Guide who fights for the righteousness of all."

Queen Phecabra held out her hand, and on it formed a thick black tome. "In here, you will find the recipe for the Stone you wish to create." In her other hand, she held a crystal vial. "Inside here is the key component. One elemental tear."

Elwrick took both items. "Continue to perform as required," Elwrick told her. "I will return and free your offspring."

Queen Phecabra bowed again, then quickly vanished back through the doorway.

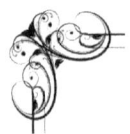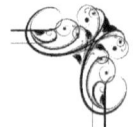

Chapter 112

lwrick returned to discover Rhunsiire in a perpetual state of timorousness. The ground trembled as the War Machines neared. *Boom, boom, boom*—the never-ending drums of doom relentlessly pounded, affording no rest. Karayan ceased to hide his intentions. He wanted them to know he was coming. War was coming, death was coming.

Elwrick ran his fingers through his scraggly beard. It would take time to decipher the intricate writing and gather the components. Luckily, he assumed Queen Phecabra had given him the hardest ingredient to acquire.

"Can you create it?" Lady Alenia asked. She was lying in bed, observing him working at the desk.

"I don't know?" Elwrick truthfully answered. "It seems it can only be made by the hands of a mortal, but the pages are so convoluted it's hard to tell for sure."

A knock at the door caught their attention, and then the uninvited elf barged in without permission. "Lady Alenia," the elf quickly groaned, "The forward scout sends word the War Machines are nearing their designated locations. We must act now while we still have time."

Elwrick looked to the elf, then back at the book. Time was of the essence. He had to discover this formula now, or they were all going to die by flame, smoke, or ash. Flipping through a few pages, he backtracked, read some, then thumbed through a few more and a pattern began to materialize. "It seems Aluneus purposely kept things scrambled to keep an unintended reader baffled."

Lady Alenia laid her head back and covered her eyes. The headache pounding in her brain was louder than the drums, while the fear of burning to death drove tears from her eyes.

Elwrick ripped a few pages from the beginning of the book, then one from the end, and finally a handful from the middle and spread them out on the table. Taking a few minutes to rearrange the pages in chronological order, he slammed his fist against the table. "There, I think I have the formula."

Lady Alenia sat up in bed. "And?"

Elwrick looked at her and smiled. "And all the components are easily obtainable except for the elemental tear, which I possess. All we have to do is get the mold constructed from one solid chunk of pure granite."

Lady Alenia scampered from the bed and grabbed her cane. "Who is going to construct it though?"

"We're going to have no choice but to rescue Aluneus from the dwarves. Hurry, let's get to the Smithy so he can begin constructing the mold while we figure this out."

Birthright

The young apprentice worked the bellows bringing the embers to a glowing, smoldering heap of pure intensity. Sweat dripped from his face staining his soot-covered apron. Elbow-length gloves covered his hands, and thick boots protected his feet from the coals that sputtered and popped from the forge.

The Smithy came out from the small stone building wielding a sword that flickered a faint blue flame. Opposite the building away from anything flammable, he dipped the blade in a ceramic tub filled with yellow oil. "The details in this sword are exquisite," he yelled back to the apprentice. "If you don't mind. I want to wield it when we face Karayan in battle."

Lady Alenia and Elwrick entered. "That won't be necessary. Elwrick is here with the plans for you to construct a mold."

The elf seized up like an ungreased axle. Lady Alenia was not supposed to hear that, no one in the ruling council was. He, like many elves, was having secret meetings on the best way to fight Karayan without the Queen's knowledge. No longer could he hide the truth. "My Lady, have you gone deaf? Karayan is pounding on the door. We've allowed ourselves to become surrounded. It's believed Karayan will start the siege by the end of the week. We must prepare for war. To delay now only ensures our death."

Lady Alenia wiped the sweat from her face. How any elf justified working in this hellish environment defied all logical reasoning. "And he will discover all of his work to be in vain."

The apprentice came from the furnace room, red-faced and exhausted. "Did you get the Worlds Stone?"

Elwrick handed the Smithy the torn-out pages. "Not exactly. The Worlds Stone is unavailable. We have no choice but to make a mold and create one."

The Smithy looked at the plans and grumbled. "I work with metals, not jewelry," he explained, then handed the pages back to Elwrick.

It was apparent Lady Alenia disapproved of the Smithy's lack of interest by the scowl on her face. "You WILL create this Stone," she barked. Snatching the pages from Elwrick's hand, she tossed them at the Smithy. "Every elf in Rhunsiire is counting on this Stone for survival."

The Smithy retrieved the pages from the ash-covered ground, then took a ragged breath as he examined the parchment. "The mold will take a good day, if not longer. The rest of it I cannot do. The heat needed is beyond our capabilities, and the force required to compress the molten metal into the teardrop form..." he allowed his words to trail off. "Is beyond anything imaginable." The Smithy mumbled as he looked away in disgust.

"Create the mold. I will find a way to complete the rest of it."

Later that evening, Elwrick entered the Medical Ward, rubbed Robyn's head, hugged Ellusia, then entered Pegan's private room. To one side of Pegan, Averie sat. To the other, Lilith. They each held one of Pegan's hands. "Has there been any change?" Elwrick whispered upon his approach.

Lilith shook her head, no. "He is as lifeless as the day you left for the Under-Dark."

"I feel like dying—" Averie started to say.

"Don't say that, ever," Elwrick explained. "You don't understand the consequences your words carry."

Averie's eyes opened wide. She had never seen Elwrick so assertive. "I'm sorry. I feel so helpless. The man I love, the man who would sacrifice everything for me is dying, and there is nothing I can do. Nothing none of us can do."

None noticed Lady Alenia enter as they remained focused on Pegan. "The Smithy informed me the mold would be completed by morning as he plans to work through the night."

Elwrick looked to Lady Alenia, then back to Averie, who continued to hold Pegan's hand. "I don't believe he is dying," Elwrick explained. "At least not yet"

Without warning, Pegan released a howl that sounded like a baby tumbling in a dryer, intermittent, muffled, garbled, but none the less distressing and intense.

Lilith wiped away the sweat that dripped down Pegan's face.

"What is happening to him?" Averie screamed at Elwrick.

Pegan arched his back and twisted. The next time he screamed, it forced their blood to run cold.

Pegan went limp, and his breathing was sporadic.

"Look at me," Elwrick softly spoke to Pegan.

Pegan remained lifeless as a corpse.

Elwrick held Pegan's chin while prying the eyelids open. Both eyes were dull gray, lacked pupils, and revealed no signs of functioning.

Averie released Pegan's hand and covered her mouth. "Is he blind?" she asked Elwrick. "I don't care. I will lead him by the hand, bathe and care for him."

Elwrick had a sudden revelation. "No, he is not blind.".

"Then why are his eyes like that?" Averie argued.

Elwrick rubbed his chin "Pegan's eyes look like that because they are still developing."

"What? Explain yourself?" Lilith barked. "Now is not the time to speak in riddles designed to hide the truth."

The look Elwrick shot Lilith sent her reeling backward. *His vision must have come from his father,* he thought. "What we are witnessing here is the rebirth of Pegan outside the womb."

"How is that possible?" Lilith demanded, her face was red as hot coals as she screamed.

"I can't explain it, at least not in a way you would understand."

"You better try," Lady Alenia said. "You have his mother and the woman he loves about to rip you apart if you don't do something."

Elwrick waved his finger at them. "Listen and listen closely. As you know, to be conceived, a child needs a seed from both their mother and father. Take one away, and the child can't exist. When the child is born, it retains attributes from both the mother and the father. For instance, when someone says you have your mother's eyes, that is a trait, an attribute you retained from your mother. As we look at Pegan, the traits, the attributes he received from Malvo are gone so his brain cannot function."

Averie appeared baffled. "Pegan is already alive," Averie said.

"You're correct," Elwrick explained to Averie. "Here is where you get confused. To cure Pegan's infliction, I had to eradicate Malvo's seed "

Lilith went deathly pale when the realization of what Elwrick was explaining came clear. "Pegan is fatherless and shouldn't exist, should have never been born."

"Exactly," Elwrick responded. "I believe the traits of your father are filling the void, or he would have died by now."

"Will he remember me?" Averie asked.

"Yes. Thoughts and abilities are not traits and attributes, but learned skills except for magic, which passes from generation to generation."

"You can heal him, though? Make him better?" Averie looked at Pegan as she spoke.

"No," Elwrick cautiously said. "What is happening falls back to his conception and is beyond anybody's abilities, except the Creators."

Averie sat there with an expressionless look on her face.

"Get some rest. There is nothing we can do but let time play itself out."

"Let time play itself out," Lilith slowly repeated the words, her face scrunched up with anger. "How much time do you believe we have? Karayan is knocking on the door. He won't wait for Pegan to recover so he can enter the Worlds Stone and flee." Lilith gripped Pegan's hand tighter and rested her head on his chest. "I won't abandon my son, not again," she snarled at Elwrick. "Take the elves and flee, Saress knows the way to salvation."

Saress intently watched from the corner where she lay on a bed of hay. Rarely had she left the Medical Ward. If needed, she would do as asked, but it pained her to consider leaving Pegan behind.

Lady Alenia rubbed Lilith's back to comfort the grieving mother. She knew precisely how Lilith felt. She, too, once lost a child. "None of us may be able to escape." Lady Alenia softly spoke as she continued to rub Lilith's back. "Elwrick couldn't recover the Worlds Stone. What he did recover was the book that contained the formula."

Elwrick scowled at Lady Alenia. "This doesn't concern Lilith."

Lilith looked at Lady Alenia, then to Elwrick as the pair argued about the Stones construction. "I can help—"

"NO!" Elwrick hissed. "I will not allow you to help. I will construct the Stone."

"How?" Lady Alenia screamed at Elwrick. "You've already confessed that the Stone can only be constructed by a mortal."

"Why can't Lilith help?" Averie asked Elwrick.

"Because the Stone drains the magic of the one who creates it and infuses it into the Stone."

"And?" Lilith raised her arms looking for an explanation. "I'm a Witch—"

"A young Witch," Elwrick interrupted. "Not long ago you were a Witchling."

"I can do this," Lilith pleaded. "You have to let me try."

Elwrick paced the length of the room. "NO!"

"You can't stop me from trying," Lilith angrily growled.

"I can and I will if I must," Elwrick snarled back.

"What is wrong with you?" Lady Alenia demanded of the Spiritual Guide.

"This isn't like you."

Elwrick looked out the window, and when he turned, he spoke with compassion, not anger. "I can't let her try because the Stone will destroy her."

"Destroy me?" Lilith asked.

"Yes," Elwrick said. "Once the Stone begins draining the magic, it won't stop until either the Stone is complete, or the source of the magic is destroyed. Lilith does not have the strength yet that's required to complete the process."

"I can do this, you have to let me try," Lilith said. "I have faith in myself. All I ask is that you have faith in me as well."

Elwrick shook his head, no. "Why won't you listen to me?" Elwrick pleaded.

"Because—" Lilith started to say.

Averie interrupted Lilith. "If she don't try we're going to die anyway. What's the difference if she dies trying, or she dies by the fires of Karayan?"

Elwrick took an exaggerated breath. "Okay, okay," he mumbled again. "If you feel this is something that you must do, then who am I to stop you."

The sun rose strangely late, painting the sky a dark marmalade. Outside the Medical Ward, Lady Alenia and Lilith waited for the daily scout's update on Karayan's progress. To either side in the shadows, Skylar and Miramar patiently waited.

"Do you believe you can do it?" Lady Alenia asked.

Lilith looked off in the distance watching the scout approach. "I don't know. Aluneus, the Unbeliever succeeded, something inside my soul, a voice, something I can't explain tells me I will succeed as well."

"Excuse me for eavesdropping," Elwrick said as he stepped out onto the landing. "Aluneus, the Unbeliever had thousands of years of experience. You, not so much."

Lady Alenia looked at Elwrick and afforded him a smile. "What Lilith lacks in experience, she makes up in tenacity."

"Lady Alenia," the elf called out as he neared. "The final few machines at the far reaches of the forest are rolling into position. Here soon, I expect the siege to begin."

Lady Alenia looked at Lilith with a smile then rested her arm on the Witches shoulder. "I have complete faith Lilith will create the Worlds Stone and we won't be here to feel the heat, or taste the smoke."

"I hope your right," the scout responded.

Lilith watched Elwrick depart. She could tell he was angry with her decision. "He's upset with me."

Lady Alenia dismissed the scout. "It bothers Elwrick whenever a mortal is willing to sacrifice themselves, even if the cause is just. I will talk to him later. It will be alright, I promise."

Lilith eyed Lady Alenia suspiciously.

"Trust me, Elwrick will be fine."

Together they walked for quite some distance before Lady Alenia spoke. "I wish I would have known you before Malvo. I bet you would have been a wonderful woman."

Lilith stopped Lady Alenia by tugging on her arm. "Even though Averie accepts me, I can feel a serious distrust in her words when we talk. Do you believe she will ever trust me? You know her better than anybody. She looks to you as her mother."

Lady Alenia took a deep breath. "In time, I believe she will. Those of us who care for her are a tiny fraction to those who want to hurt her."

"Can you talk to her for me. I don't want anything coming between Pegan and I, but if it's the only way to make them both happy, I will gracefully leave."

"And go where?" Lady Alenia asked. "The entire world hates you, as much as her."

Lilith nodded in agreement. The rest of the way to the Smithy neither spoke.

Upon their arrival, the Smithy led the two women through a backdoor to a secure area. "I arranged this area exactly as the parchment described." To one side, the mold sat on a perfectly leveled tree stump. Precisely ten steps away to the left, the smelting pot hung from a large iron hook. Below the container, there was no visible source of heat.

Lilith made her way to the mold and ran her fingers over the cold stone frame. "It's perfect." At the bottom of the stone frame, there was a perfect cutout of a teardrop-shaped gem. "I guess our survival now rests on my shoulders."

Elwrick entered the area carrying a handful of items. On the table, he carefully placed each component in order.

Lady Alenia looked at Elwrick and smiled. "She can do this, have some faith."

"I wish I had as much faith as you do," Elwrick admitted.

On the air, you could feel an urgency.

Ignoring the commands from Lady Alenia to stay away, elves gathered. Word spread rapidly across Rhunsiire. The creation of the Worlds Stone had begun.

Lilith carefully walked to the smelting pot and stood there, silently staring at the object. The rough, wide-mouthed smelting pot with a curled lip and iron handle was cold. Down the side, the reminisce of past experiments remained in frozen clumps. The time for questions was at an end. The time for action was now. Taking a deep breath, she closed her eyes and concentrated on nothing but the three bars inside. Two were gold while one was silver.

The Smithy crossed his arms and propped one foot up on a bench. He waited to watch this spectacle unfold.

Lilith faded into a trance, and the air around her crackled with energy, and a dense fog filtered up through the cracks in the stone ground.

With the help of the Smithy, Elwrick repositioned the table closer to the smelting pot in preparation to add the ingredients if Lilith succeeded.

Lilith could see the bars even though her eyes remained shut. Feel the buttery-smooth surface of each, though she had never touched them. Lilith concentrated harder and the outer shell vaporized, and the rough inner-working became visible. To build the heat required, she would need to search deeper, back to the creation of the elements. It would be here where the molecules resided that the heat would need to be applied.

Leaves lifted from the ground as the air around Lilith swirled. Her hair floated like a halo, and her eyes spit spark. Both hands stretched straight out, palms towards the pot, fingers angled at the sky. Faint wisps of smoke drifted from the bars as they slowly heated.

Many elves gathered to watch, and in the shadows, their whispers became chants as they cheered for Lilith's success. Louder and louder it came until it blotted out the war drums.

Lady Alenia spun in a circle with her arms splayed. The crowd approached like an angry mob wanting to pillage and plunder. "Stand back," she demanded. Lady Alenia couldn't risk something happening that may compromise the process.

Lilith wove her hands like two serpents performing a rare mating ritual. Her silver eyes cut through the fog, and strange noises seeped from her curled lips.

Within seconds a blue flame sprouted on one corner of a single bar then quickly spread. Black, oily, smoke swirled from the pot before being swallowed by the mist.

The smelting pot hissed and snarled with displeasure as the heat increased.

Lilith threw her head back and looked skyward. Her face went pale as death, and her screams could bend steel.

From the pot came an eruption as all three bars exploded, then formed at the bottom in a molten puddle.

Elwrick placed his palm on Lilith. Whispering words of encouragement, he could feel the incantations taxing every fiber of her being.

Averie wiggled and squirmed through the crowd and stood beside Elwrick. She didn't know why, but something told her to be here.

Lilith refocused and concentrated on the puddle. She would need more heat to bring the molten metal up to temperature. Searching her soul, she called on her inner-strength and focused on nothing but the bubbling goo.

The gold made a strange, hollow, metallic gurgling sound as it violently churned.

Lady Alenia looked to Elwrick. "How do you know when it reaches the right temperature?"

"The liquid needs to be black as coal and hold a mirror finish."

Lilith levitated from the ground, and her entire body glowed until her bones shown through the skin.

The entire pot shook to the point it threatened to be thrown from the hook.

Lilith's head slumped, and blood seeped from her eyes. The veins in her hands turned black, and her fingernails flaked away and fell like rose petals.

Lady Alenia covered her mouth with both hands. The woman was decaying right before her eyes. "What's happening to her?"

Elwrick lowered his head. "Remember, I told you the Stone drains the magic out of the mortal creating the Stone. It won't be long now until the Stone destroys her."

"Make her stop," Averie screamed to Elwrick.

"The process cannot be stopped. The Stone will continue to drain away her life until there is nothing left but a shriveled-up copse."

The blackened veins leached up Lilith's arms and spread to her neck.

The golden color lost its luster and darkened.

"Look, she's doing it." Screams came from the crowd, followed by cheers of victory.

Lilith slowly lowered to the ground as clumps of hair fell from her head. On her scalp and face ugly black splotches formed and she began to wilt.

The gray succumbed to the gold once more, and its luster returned.

Elwrick sighed. "Lilith did her best, that's all we could ask."

Averie fell to her knees at Lilith's feet, and she gripped the tattered robe. "I can't die without releasing the hate that fills my heart," she whispered. "Not hate for what you've done, but hate because of my selfishness. I didn't want to share Pegan with you. I didn't want to share Pegan with anyone. I was content knowing Pegan never knew his mother as there would be no one to come between us. When I heard your story, I wished Malvo would have killed you." Tears rolled down her cheeks. "Please, save yourself, save Pegan. I will surrender my child to Karayan. It is she who he seeks."

There was a clap of thunder that flattened nearby trees.

"Look," Lady Alenia said. Near the pot, a diaphanous woman with beauty beyond reproach shimmered into existence. She reached out with both hands and stabilized the container, and bowed her head. The very moment her hands made contact, the bubbling molten metal turned black as a starless night and held a mirror sheen.

Elwrick dang near took to flight when he leaped in the air and screamed, "Arabella Krauss." Lilith had called on her mother the same as she did to escape Malvo. The woman appeared unchanged, except she was translucent. Now, the residence of Rhunsiire would get a taste of true power.

Lady Alenia wept as the intense magic made the hair on her body stand erect.

Across the sky, lightning flashed.

Elwrick searched through the components. Somehow in his excitement, he knocked them all into a pile. First, he located the purple tongue from a poison toad and tossed it in. After it dissolved, he added the dehydrated salamander's tail. Stirring the mixture with a spoon made of crystal exactly thirty-seven times, he dumped in four white hairs from an arctic fox. With that complete, he grabbed the magical component and dropped in the elemental tear.

The concoction screamed as the drop made contact and vanished in a puff of blue smoke.

Elwrick began stirring the pot. "It needs to be continually stirred until it turns crystal clear."

Elves formed a line from the smelting pot clear to the dining hall, waiting their turn to stir the dense mixture. As one elf grew exhausted, another took their place. Averie wanted to help, but Elwrick ordered her not to. It was her willingness to sacrifice Robyn to save them all, which made Lilith search her soul for help. Elwrick stood there looking up at the heavens, and his thin lips curled into a smile. Once again, Averie faced a test few would pass, and she succeeded gloriously. Only a woman blessed with the genuine compassion of others would sacrifice their child to save the masses, many of which she had never met.

The elves continued to stir through the night, and when the sky lightened, the contents began to change color. By mid-morning, the materials were crystal clear.

"Now," Elwrick screamed. With the aid of the Smithy, the contents was carefully poured into the mold, making sure not to spill a single drop. The frame popped and hissed from the sudden heat transfer, but remained unbroken.

Lilith focused on the form, spoke in a strange chaotic language, and the puddle began to fold in on itself. With each fold, it reduced in size, slowly compressing into the teardrop shape.

Word spread like fire through dry timbers that Lilith was compressing the molten gold, and elves abandoned their posts to watch.

"Please have the strength," Lady Alenia whispered to Lilith.

"Lilith believes she is doing the work," Elwrick answered Lady Alenia. "But Arabella is now in complete control. Lilith has done all she can, and her mother knows it. For Lilith to continue now, it would destroy her. She is too young to do what was required to make such a potent artifact."

Arabella vanished, then reappeared beside the mold and gripped the frame with both hands. Across from Arabella, a man came to be. He was tremendous in stature with broad shoulders and piercing silver eyes. His hands were enormous and easily covered Arabella's when he placed them on the frame. Inside the structure, the molten metal shrank, filling the cutout.

Elwrick took a step back in shock with what he was observing. Somehow Lilith called her father forward as well.

The *boom* created when the last drop fell into place took them all from their feet except Lilith, who stood on shaking legs. "It is complete," she whispered, then collapsed unconscious.

Averie crawled to Lilith and wrapped her in a hug. "Thank you," she whispered while choking on the tears that streamed down her face.

"We need to get Lilith back to the Medical Ward and healed." Elwrick began barking commands.

The Smithy held a chisel at a predetermined spot and gave it one solid whack with a wooden mallet. The crack sounded like mountains colliding as the mold split perfectly in half. In its wake, a perfectly shaped teardrop gem lay on the table.

Elwrick picked up the Worlds Stone and examined it in the light. No mares were visible in the magnificent jewel, and the light shimmered off the clear surface. Satisfied it was complete, he tucked it safely away in his pocket then looked at Ryul, Skylar, and Miramar. "Spread word tomorrow when the sun rises we will begin the ceremony."

Not too far away sitting on a fallen log, Ruven, the rat smiled, then headed to the celebration clearing.

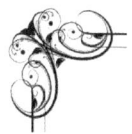 

Chapter 113

 he rider was nearly dead. Through his shoulder, an arrow remained while another jetted from his hip. How he managed to make it this far without dying was remarkable. "The final war machine is in place," he groaned as he leaned. With the aid of another, the man was removed from the mount.

Karayan gripped his sword, but his arm lacked the strength to pull it free. "Ease his suffering," Karayan snarled at his general.

The rider's eyebrows climbed his forehead as his eyes opened wide. He was expecting to be sent to the rear for medical attention, not killed.

The general followed the orders to the letter and forced his blade into the riders back, then drove it up at an angle piercing his heart.

The rider grunted a gurgling scream as the commander jerked the blade free. Looking at Karayan with pleading eyes, he spat up blood and coughed. "Why—" he tried to ask before dying.

Karayan looked east, then west. The silver-rimmed purplish sky warned dawn was quickly approaching. There was a strange pre-war stillness to the air. Both sides had made their choices; all that remained was for the game to begin. "Light the fires, send the signal." he hollered to his generals.

At the nearest war machine, the commander tossed a burning torch into a steel drum loaded with wood painted mossy green. Once fully engulfed, it released plumes of dark green smoke. As each team saw the signal, they lit their drum as well. The process continued until one hundred plumes of smoke filled the air blotting out the young sun. Within minutes, the land fell into an unnatural darkness turning the men into featureless ghastly green shadows.

The crank on the war machine was horrendously large and took a team of four burly men to crank back the massive spring-loaded arm while a fifth set in place a steel lever designed to hold the war machine in a charged position. Up and down the line, the sounds of gears clanking carried on the slight breeze. Each team loaded steel buckets large as wagons first with chunks of coal designed to scatter in flight and ignite everything they impacted. Layered above the coals were logs marinated in lantern oil so that they would burn even in the wettest of weather. Afterward, men drenched the contents with soybean oil. The War Machine commander danced with delight observing his men in action. They worked in perfect unison, and soon the concoction was ready. He added the final component, a burning torch.

For a moment, there was a deathly silence as if the entire world was void of life, then Karayan blew a horn that erupted a ghastly, growling moan.

Standing on the platform, the commander had to reposition himself as the insane heat seared the eyebrows off his face. Raising his gloved fist in the air, he looked up and down the firing line making sure the War Machines to either side of him were prepared. When the signal returned, the commander's hand fell in a chopping motion.

A single man flipped a lever that released the latch allowing the pent-up energy to be released. With nothing holding it back, the arm pivoted upward with tremendous velocity lifting the back half of the War Machine off the ground when it hit the steel stop. One hundred flaming globs of death took to flight. Upon landing, everything the flames touched ignited. Within minutes, the elves were encapsulated in a ring of fire that leaped hundreds of feet into the air. Soon, the smoke would reach Rhunsiire turning the city into a living hell.

The commander raised his fist in the air and cheered. On the ground, his team members did the same. "Ready the War Machine," the commander yelled.

Karayan smiled with glee from the observation tower. "Burn in hell," he whispered.

The elf stood horrified at what he saw from the observation deck located in the center of Rhunsiire. Never in his lifetime could he imagine such destruction was possible as century-old trees went up like kindling. He could hear their screams in the hiss as the water was forced out and vaporized.

In all directions, regardless of which way he turned, flaming balls arced across the hazy sky. Upon crashing, they hit like meteors sending embers shooting straight up hundreds of feet. Oily black smoke billowed as more trees, shrubs, vines, and moss burst into flames and spread to neighboring areas. Luckily, the woodland creatures sensed the danger and evacuated deeper into the woods.

The scout raised the magically imbued silver trumpet adorned with gold trim to his lips then performed a tune that sounded across all Rhunsiire. It was not loud or angry as one might expect when faced with war, but soft and sweet. On it, you could feel the emotion of the trumpeter, and all elves stood still with their eyes closed in prayer. The official signal had been sent, the war had started.

Very few elves remained in their homes as most left earlier for the celebration clearing. Leaving behind family heirlooms, paintings, jewelry, precious stones, items passed on from generation to generation, they each only carried their assigned weapon and a small satchel of food for when they arrived at their destination, wherever that might be.

The elf let the trumpet fall to the deck. The instrument served its purpose and was no longer needed.

Pausing at the stairs, he looked back to see a new round of attacks. More flaming balls filled the sky. Many came apart in mid-air, sending blazing fragments scattering like tiny stars falling from the Heavens. Those that didn't separate reached farther into the woods, making the ground tremble with fear. The sky glowed from the fire, and the smoke swirled in high spires.

The elf looked towards the heavens and said a quick prayer. Hopefully, his mother had arrived safely at the celebration clearing.

Karayan stood in astonishment that a race would rather cower and die in

shame, than die with honor on the field of battle. Not one elf had tried to flee or fight, both to his delight and disgust.

The war machine commander waved his arm in a circular pattern signaling each team to creep forward.

"Faster, load the buckets you maggots," Karayan screamed from the tower. Below him, the workers diligently reloaded the War Machine.

"Fire," the commander screamed and pounded a drum built into the base.

The high-pitched ping of mechanisms breaking free rang in the ears of those nearby, followed by a loud *WOOSH* as flaming globs of material filled the air. Blazing balls of death reached further in finding unburnt wood. Trees splintered at the base and toppled, creating kindling to intensify the fires. Shrubs erupted like cotton balls, and vines hung like burning ropes. Carried on the wind, flaming leaves, grass, and embers brought flames to fresh greenery.

"MOTHER!" Pegan's scream was terrifying. His world nothing more than a silent, bleak abyss of nothingness.

Lilith bolted upright in the bed. Her vision was blurry, and her hearing distorted, but she immediately recognized the cry of her child. "I'm here," she incoherently mumbled, then stumbled out of bed and brushed the tangled mess of hair from her face. Scrambling towards Pegan, Lilith sat on the stool and gripped his hand. "I'm here, son. I'm right here."

Pegan could feel the warm touch of another. "Mama," he cried out, turning his head in all directions. "Where are you? Talk to me?" he cried.

Through him, she could feel his fright. "I'm here, I'm right here," she whispered to him, yet he never acknowledged her voice.

Gleia knew instantly what was wrong with Pegan as he turned his head in all directions. Resting her hand on Lilith's shoulder, Gleia knelt beside the distraught mother. "Pegan is deaf and blind," she whispered.

Buried deep in a dark and silent world, Pegan screamed with his entire body. His eyes were wide with fear, mouth locked open with terror, his face pale as the moon.

Lilith held Pegan tightly to her bosom. "I'm right here," she whispered while stroking his raven black hair. It was now she looked towards Elwrick for help.

Elwrick continually paced the length of the room mumbling spells, which may reduce the gestation period, but there were none. What Pegan was going through was a natural part of life, and it would run its course as nature saw fit.

Pegan wrapped his arms around Lilith. "I can't see, I can't see," he repeated. "Please, talk to me," he begged her.

Averie watched in horror. "How long will this last?" she asked Elwrick.

"I'm not sure," Elwrick answered. "You must remember, a fetus spends nine months in the womb developing."

Pegan gasped and wheezed as if inflicted with a bout of asthma. His chest spasmed, and his teeth gnashed.

The scout burst through the Medical Ward door unannounced. "Lady Alenia. The attack has begun, we must evacuate now."

Lady Alenia looked at Elwrick, then to Pegan.

Averie gripped Pegan's hand. "I won't leave him. You cannot make me."

Elwrick slumped down on a chair. On his face was a distant stare. "We still have time," he whispered. "We cannot abandon Pegan. In his current condition, he cannot enter the Stone."

"How much time do you believe we have?" Lady Alenia asked.

Elwrick looked at Lady Alenia, who now stood by the door. "The war machines are made from wood. The ground will have to cool before he can advance, or he will burn his weapons to the ground. As dense as the forest is, it could take a week or more for the fire to reach Rhunsiire. Pegan needs time to finish the rebirthing process."

"We're not like you," Lady Alenia explained to Elwrick. "It's not the fire that will kill us, but the smoke. Even now, as we speak, the smoke muddles the air. Imagine how it will be tomorrow after it burns all night."

"There must be a way. I need time to think," Elwrick grumbled.

"There is no more time," Lady Alenia said.

Lilith abandoned Pegan to stand before Lady Alenia and placed her hands on the Queen's shoulders. "Go," Lilith whispered. "I will remain with Averie and do what I can to protect us."

Another elf entered the Ward covered in ash and soot. "Another group of machines traveled the bank of the Freihn Sea catching us by surprise. At their rate of travel, Rhunsiire will be within range by nightfall."

"You don't understand—" Elwrick started to say.

"Elwrick, it's okay," Averie said. "My family is at the clearing with Robyn. Please, tell them I love them and to look after Robyn. It's better to let a few perish than an entire race. I've already come to grips with my death. Besides, if Pegan were to die and I live, I might as well be dead as I see no reason to continue living."

"Averie." Elwrick sternly said. "If you want Robyn to live, you must go. The child is too young to concentrate on the Stone. Your thoughts become her thoughts. If you don't go, she'll die in this inferno right alongside you."

Averie wobbled like a newborn fawn, then collapsed at Elwrick's feet.

Lilith knelt beside Averie. "Save your daughter. Pegan and I will be fine. You will always have him in your heart."

Karayan released a sadistic, grossly exaggerated laugh, and then raised his hands to the blackened sky. "Burn, burn you filthy, disgusting animals. Burn in hell, and may your souls be tormented day and night forever and ever," he screamed.

Two hours later, Ryul fitted Saress with a custom made, fire-hardened leather armor then covered her head with a helmet of steel. "The Armorer and the Smithy worked tirelessly constructing this to give you the best chance of success."

Saress ran her hand over the armor. Where her vital parts were, chain mail was woven inside to offer another layer of protection. A normal man could have never carried the weight, but Saress never felt the burden. "I won't fail."

Elwrick watched as the elf buckled the remaining straps. Covered in leather and steel, she didn't look like the same reptile he once knew, but a monster created from discarded scraps of leather and thread stitched together by a blind man.

Saress strapped on an arsenal of weapons, then two elves hoisted a large pack and strapped it to her back. "This contains enough provisions to last a few weeks," the elf said.

Lady Alenia and King Hulradeeh sat in their respected chairs while Elwrick stood between them. Raising his hand, Elwrick drew the crowd's attention. "As you're all aware by now, Karayan has initiated his plans to eradicate the world of all things he deems a threat to his survival. Karayan understands what his future holds and is willing to destroy all that is good to prevent it from coming to fruition. I understand the elves are angry with the thought of fleeing their homeland, but this war is not only foolish, but it is also suicide. Make no mistake with your beliefs. This flight isn't induced by fear because we are weak. This flight is to prove our resilience. The same as the Phoenix appears weak when it bursts into flames and dies. It's reborn stronger from the ashes and a marvel to behold. The same can be said for Rhunsiire as we appear weak in the eyes of Karayan, we will be reborn stronger than he could ever imagine."

The cheers were deafening.

Elwrick raised both hands this time to silence the crowd. "Saress has willingly agreed to carry us to safety, wherever that may be. Do not be scared; do not be frightened. Inside the Stone, you will remain in a state of suspended animation. You will not grow old, weak, or tired, regardless of whether ten minutes or fifty years pass. For those who willingly enter, time for you will no longer exist. Please, let us bow our heads for a moment in silence for Lilith, who has made the tough decision to remain behind with her son who cannot enter the Stone."

"What about my baby?" an ash-covered elf woman screamed.

"I'm going to explain what needs to be done to save your child," Elwrick calmly explained to the distraught elf. "For those with young children or unborn hatchlings, they need to be held by their mother. Her thoughts become the child's thoughts. When you think of the Stone, you must wish to become one with the Stone. Think of nothing but the Stone. Otherwise, you will not be accepted."

A fireball flew across the sky, breaking up over the clearing then rained down tiny chunks of flaming debris.

Men stomped on the fires extinguishing what they could.

"We need to do this now," Lady Alenia said. "That was too close."

Elwrick looked to Saress, who held the Stone. "Hold the Stone straight out and speak the words *Velkommen*. The Stone remains active for only a short duration, then goes dormant and turns baby blue."

"How do I release the people?" Saress asked.

"When you decide it is safe, hold the Stone in your outstretched hand and speak the word *Gratis*."

Averie's face lacked expression as she sat in the ash on the platform steps holding Robyn. "I don't understand any of this. I don't understand why I have to go."

Elwrick sat beside Averie. "I've already explained it to you. A child's mind wanders too much to remain focused on the Stone. The Stone understands this and will accept the mother's thoughts as the child's because they share the same genetics. I'm sorry. I wish there were another way, but that's not how the Stone functions."

Averie stood and faced away, visibly upset. "Why are you lying to me?" Averie hissed. "I think you want Pegan and Lilith to die and for me to be miserable."

The accusations stung like a whip. "Excuse me," Elwrick said. "Now you listen here, young lady. I would offer my life to save Pegan and Lilith, but I cannot. Pegan cannot enter the Stone because his mind is still developing, and to concentrate on the Stone is impossible."

"Why can't Lilith think for him and hold him as I do Robyn?" Averie asked.

"Because Pegan is an adult."

Averie's eyes narrowed. "You said he is like a fetus that is developing outside the womb."

Elwrick started to open his mouth to argue, then quickly changed his mind as his face drained of color. "How can you be so naïve, yet so brilliant. Worse yet, how can I be so stupid?"

Lady Alenia glanced at Elwrick. "Each minute we wait is a minute Saress loses on her chance to escape."

Elwrick pointed at Saress then yelled. "Don't you activate that Stone, don't you dare until my return."

"What are you doing?" Lady Alenia whispered. There was fear in her eyes, and her voice cracked.

Near the clearing, a fireball crashed down spitting oil-infused embers.

"I'm going to save a Witch and Warlock."

"We don't have time. The Medical Ward is to—" Lady Alenia began to say.

Midnight shimmered into existence, and Elwrick hoped on his back before the horse wholly formed. "Ride now," he whispered into the horse's ear. "Ride now as if the flames of hell lick at your hooves."

Midnight didn't need to be told twice. The horse sensed the urgency and bolted away. The pounding of Midnight's hooves sounded like thunder.

Elwrick blew through the smoke and ash. Around him, trees burned, and rope bridges dangled. His only thought was to beat the fire to the Medical Ward. Breaking out onto the main road, he could see the dense leaves which made up the roof of the Medical Ward smoldering, and the stairs that spiraled the tree were on fire. Quickening his pace, Midnight leaped over fallen timber and weaved through flaming bushes.

Midnight skidded to a halt.

Elwrick leaped free and sprinted up the stairs that wound up the trunk. Partway up, he paused to kick away the railing which burned.

BOOM!. Near the base of the tree, a massive fireball landed. The entire tree shook nearly launching Elwrick free. Looking down, the gangly roots that

anchored the tree ignited. "No, no, no," Elwrick screamed as he continued his march up the stairs.

Lilith dipped a cloth in the bucket of water and wiped the sweat from her face. The room felt like a furnace. Everything was hot to the touch, and the air hurt to breathe.

Ka-chink, a faint-blue crack grew the length of the window.

Lilith dipped the rag back in the bucket then wiped Pegan's face. "Not much longer now," she whispered, then laid her head on Pegan's chest.

CRASH, the window threw deadly shards in all directions as it shattered. Smoke blew through the opening filling the room.

WHAM! The door banged open with such force it came clear off the frame and split down the center.

Lilith jerked upright expecting to see Karayan standing in the doorway.

"We need to go, NOW," Elwrick screamed as he bolted inside.

"I told you to leave," she yelled at the Spiritual Guide. "Save yourselves."

Elwrick sprinted past Lilith ignoring the question and grabbed Pegan off the bed and flung him over his shoulder. In Elwrick's eyes, there was a look of sympathy. "Run like you never have before," Elwrick screamed.

BOOM!, somewhere nearby, a fireball crashed down.

Lilith grabbed nothing as she sprinted from the room. Behind her, Elwrick bolted for the opening but stopped only long enough to recover Pegan's weapon's belt. "Can't leave my old friend behind."

Lilith stopped partway down as flames quickly climbed the stairway.

Elwrick never slowed as he zipped passed and grabbed Lilith around the waist and thrust them all over the side.

Lilith screamed, expecting to die. Yet the ground approached slowly, and they touched down beside Midnight, who stomped his hooves with urgency.

Elwrick tossed Pegan across the back of Midnight, then ducked as a flaming ember whizzed past. Behind it, a trail of smoke coiled. "When you get to the clearing, hold Pegan against your chest and wish to enter the Stone—think of nothing but the Stone."

"He can't—"

"Do as your told," Elwrick screamed at her. The ground rumbled as more fireballs crashed down. Behind them, the Medical Ward came crashing down as the roots failed. "Inform Lady Alenia not to fear. I will be with her in the Stone."

Elwrick picked up Lilith and sat her on Midnight's back. "Ride, ride now," he screamed, then slapped Midnight on the rump.

Midnight bolted into action, and Elwrick watched his faithful steed vanish in the swirling haze.

"Activate the stone, Elwrick's not coming back, he's dead," an elf screamed from the crowd.

Saress nervously looked about. Women held their children, and men grabbed their weapons.

"Elwrick had us all gather here to die," another elf screamed.

Saress looked down at the Stone.

Lady Alenia climbed from her seat. "Please don't."

Trolls scattered as a fireball landed where they once stood.

Busting through a wall of flames, Midnight landed then continued tracing the edge of the clearing jumping over or dodging burning timbers.

Lady Alenia pointed at the horse and followed it with her finger as he neared.

Lilith scrambled free when Midnight reached the platform. Her silver eyes were tainted red from the smoke and heat. "Lady Alenia. Elwrick said not to fret. He will be with you in the Stone."

WHAM! A tree collapsed spitting embers and flaming debris into the clearing, nearly killing many elves.

"Where is he?" Lady Alenia asked as she watched the elves scatter as another tree went down.

"He was on the center road when I looked back," Lilith answered. "He loves you too much to lie to you. We must activate the Stone now."

Two elves pulled Pegan free of Midnight and placed him on Lilith's lap as she sat beside Averie.

Lilith looked at Lady Alenia. "Activate the stone."

Lady Alenia looked at Saress. "Do it now."

Saress held the Stone straight out with her closed fist. Throughout the clearing, an untold number of eyes watched her every movement. Every one of these people counted on her success, the future of civilization rested on her shoulders. Saress looked to Lady Alenia, Lilith, who held Pegan, Averie, who kept Robyn, then back to the people of Rhunsiire. "For us," she whispered.

Once Elwrick lost sight of Midnight, he knelt and closed his eyes. First, he focused on the clearing, then Saress. *Think about your route of escape, leave no options unconsidered.* Elwrick sent the words mentally to Saress.

Saress released a dragon's roar as she yelled the activation word, *"Velkommen."* There was no hesitation in her voice, or doubt she was doing the right thing.

The first beams of light came from the platform, and Lady Alenia vanished.

The rock glowed bright pink for a brief second, proof the soul, mind, and body were accepted. Then, from across the clearing, two beams simultaneously fired at the Stone.

A tear leaked from the armor's eye-opening then streaked down the shiny steel as Averie, Robyn, Lilith, Pegan, Ameria, Glorandial, Filaurel, and all the other friends she had made since this adventure began vanished.

Having seen those enter, the rest of the elves, men, reptiles, giants, assassins, and anything living concentrated on the Worlds Stone and the beams came at a blistering pace. The clearing grew brighter than the fires forcing Saress to close her eyes. When she opened them, the meadow was eerily empty of all things living, as if she was the last thing on Icearaus.

Saress stood motionless amid the inferno. Flames leaped hundreds of feet in the air, and the smoke was black as coal. Tucking the light-blue Stone into a protective pouch, she hung the sacred item around her neck then tucked it into her leather armor. There was only one way to escape, and that would be to make it to the Freihn Sea, where she could then turn south and enter the swamp. Once there, she could easily outdistance Karayan's arms.

Sprinting on all fours, she leaped over burning debris and weaved through flaming embers. Most of the town resembled a hellish nightmare where houses where turned to demons with flaming eyes for windows. Evil laughs came from the structures in the form of hisses, pops, and snarls.

The edge of town was still a reasonable distance away, but the heat was impossible to endure. Saress had no choice but to stop and turn back. She would have to head south and try to reach the 'Anor by God's Perch.

Sprinting through the trees, she entered a clearing with a large tree atop a large hill. The grass had long since lost its color and sputtered with flame in various locations. The tree was bare, and many of the smaller branches were already on fire. Above her head, more flaming balls flew past slamming into everything and instantly setting it ablaze. Saress knew it immediately as the room where unusual and undiscovered artifacts were stored. Passing by, she skidded to a halt when the words Elwrick spoke hit her like a fallen tree—*keep all options open*, and her mind drifted back to the Keep. Usually, this room was sealed with a powerful ward to keep all out except Lady Alenia and Elwrick as there were many dangerous items contained within.

Kicking down the door, she entered the gloom. Inside, strange robes hung like angry shadows and dusty boots lay in perfect rows under the robes. Glass orbs with swirling colors inside sat on pedestals, and one wall held a shelf loaded with disheveled looking tomes. Along another wall, a dusty rack littered with potions of different colors which bubbled while beside it was a stack of chests overflowing with undeciphered scrolls. Near the back covered with a heavy blanket was what she sought. Ripping the cover free, she studied the glossy wooden frame and hissed. The images carved into the wood dared her to enter, mocking her actions. Inside, a swirling blue mist weaved a pattern that told of destruction. She knew Karayan used it to travel to the Keep. What she didn't know was where it's twin was stored. If she had to guess though, she assumed somewhere that wasn't on fire.

BOOM, a flaming ball landed outside blowing burning debris inside. Glass shattered as the potions rack crumbled.

WHOOSH, a robe erupted into flames releasing a black, deadly, oil-tainted smoke. From there, it spread to a pair of knee-high black cloth boots.

WHAM, the ground shook, and the tree trembled as more flaming balls landed outside the door.

Saress hesitated. This device was designed by evil for evil. How would it react when the unknown entered. Flames spread up the wall, and the portal frame began to smoke. The time to act was now, or it would be too late. Leaping through the flames, she ran towards the portal. Moments before entering, she slammed her eyes shut and dove in.

Seconds later, the portal erupted into flames, and the twirling blue hue exploded outward, splintering the tree trunk and obliterating everything inside.

Releasing a groan the tree shuttered, then tilted slightly before collapsing.

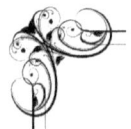

Chapter 114

aress was spat out into pure darkness. Had it not been for her face slamming into the hardwood floor, she would have sworn she was falling into oblivion. Drawing a deep breath, she snorted in a pound of dust then completed a horrendous sneeze, which almost took the helmet from her head. Luckily, she could sense she was alone, so she relaxed for a moment and let the cold, musty air chill her parched throat. Wherever she was, at least it wasn't on fire. Taking a few minutes to clear her mind, she refocused on the task at hand.

"Get up," she whispered at the same time she scrambled to her feet, and her eyes flashed into the thermal spectrum and she viewed her surroundings. The room was more like a hall, long and narrow with a low ceiling. The only exit was at the far end behind a massive door inlaid with steel and large rivets. Beneath the door, a faint light entered through the narrow crack while behind her, an oval framed portal sat undisturbed. Inside the intricate frame the swirling mist was red as flame.

Saress removed the Stone and did a cursory check. The faint blue hue glowed brightly in the darkness told her it survived the journey. "Wish me luck," she whispered, then tucked the Stone safely away then ventured off to see what waited beyond the door.

Staying a few paces away, Saress studied the door for many minutes, searching for the trap. She knew Karayan would not leave something this critical unprotected. Observing nothing out of the ordinary, she remembered the door at the Keep and how the protection ward no longer existed. Perhaps it was the same here, so she took the chance and placed the side of her head against the door, but the helmet prevented her from hearing anything on the other side. She considered removing the helmet, but quickly decided she would be better off with the added protection, then reached for the knob.

The crack of wood splitting caught her attention, and she spun the very moment the portal exploded scattering wooden fragments throughout the room. Had it not been for the armor, a thousand tiny daggers would have pelted her soft underbelly, possibly causing a fatal wound.

No going back now, she thought. Not that she would have anyway, then her attention was drawn back to the door as someone, or something passed.

Saress cracked the door open only far enough to peer out. The narrow aisle ran left to right before abruptly turning at both ends. Directly across from her was a slim hallway that divided a pair of bookshelves. Not seeing anyone, she darted across the aisle and into the narrow passage where she was forced to turn sideways. From here, it was obvious the room was an elegant library from the many rows of shelves, each filled with an odd array of books. There was one wide central aisle that ran the length of the room. In that aisle, many round tables decorated the space, and on each a burning candle gave-off a fresh pine scent. Not far from where she hid, one large section must have been for Karayan's personal use, judging from the plush cushions, ornate rugs, elegant fireplace, and extensive wine rack.

Darting across the wide hall, she entered an adjacent corridor fitted with many windows that looked out over a vacant city. *This must be Lynn Brook*, she thought.

Quietly traveling the corridor, she heard a man's voice heading her direction. Silently removing her sword, she decided it would be best to wait and see who was coming before introducing herself. She was no Pegan Rhoe who could vanish at will, but she did her best with what little shadows there were. As the voice grew louder, the past came rushing back. She had heard this voice before, but where.

Barrett walked down the hall, whistling and singing a tune. How, or why he was promoted to Keeper of the Library remained a mystery. The lie he told Karayan about being abandoned by Jester and tortured by Pegan, plus a few other things to lather up the tale, had paid its dividends many times over.

Now, he had a life of luxury only having to make sure the wine rack remained stocked, fresh logs brought in for the fire, the tables glistened, and the books remained organized, which was never an issue because nobody ever came here.

Saress reached out and snatched the man and drug him back into the shadows. "Well, well, well. Look who we have here," she hissed into his ear.

Barrett tried to look, but a heavily armored hand with lengthy claws covered his face.

"I wondered if I would ever see you again."

Barrett tried to move his head to see his abductor, but the stranger's strength was incredible. "Who are you?" he mumbled through the scaly fingers.

Saress spun him around then raked her claws across his face sending the man stumbling backward, scattering books as he tried to steady himself. "Some things you assumed dead should not have been forgotten," she snarled.

Barrett grabbed at the flap of skin that dangled from his cheek, then looked at the beast clad in leather and steel, which attacked him. "What do you want?" he nervously asked.

Saress slammed the man against the shelf making it wobble.

Barrett squealed, then collapsed at the lizard's feet.

Saress lifted Barrett by his hair with one hand while removing her helmet with the other. "Do you remember me now?"

Barrett nearly fainted. He was positive that day he locked them in Malvo's lair, they were going to die, yet here she stood, holding him by the hair. "Please, I beg you," he cried out. "It wasn't me, I swear on my mother's grave. Jester made me do it. It was all Jester's idea. I wanted to help you with whatever you needed. I promise…" Barrett continued to beg and plead.

Saress walloped Barrett across the head, dropping the man to his knees, then lifted him by his shirt and slammed him against the shelf. All she could think about was him locking them down in that hole to die. "Keep your forked tongue in your filthy mouth, you heathen. Your words are a lie, and you're going to face justice for what you did to us."

Barrett tried to plead his position.

Saress slammed him to the ground and kicked him.

Barrett crawled for the door.

Saress snatched him by his ankle and dragged him back into the shadows of the shelf where muffled grunts and groans grew. When they emerged, Both Barrett's eyes were nearly shut, his tunic was ripped free and used as a gag, and his boot laces bound him at the wrists. "You're going to lead me anywhere I wish to go, or you're going to suffer more than you ever dreamed possible."

Barrett hung his head in shame and limped with each step as he guided Saress from the palace.

Seven days later, the white sails of the *Albatross* came into view as the pair wound their way out of the mountains behind the deserted town of Mill Stone. On the starboard side, she could see Captain Royston patiently waiting. Saress waved with excitement. Something inside, perhaps Pegan speaking to her through the Stone told her the *Albatross* would be here.

"Ahoy mateys," Captain Royston cheered and returned the wave.

"I'm not going on that boat. You may as well kill me now," Barrett hissed.

"I don't think you're in any position to make demands." The voice was deep, and the speaker unknown.

Saress spun jerking her swords free, expecting to discover Malvo was following them.

Two men in white clothing, each carrying a small knife and a handful of pheasants neared."

Saress relaxed and returned her swords. It was the two deckhands of the *Albatross.*

"You look exhausted and starving. Here, eat these." One man handed her the pheasants, which she eagerly accepted. She had barely eaten since fleeing Rhunsiire even though she had a pack loaded with rations. "We'll take him off your hands. The stockade has been ready for his arrival for days."

Saress watched them lead her prisoner away, and she walked rather slowly deep in thought.

Captain Royston met her on the sandy beach. "Something wrong?"

Saress shook her head with confusion. "How did you know I was coming?"

Captain Royston glanced her a crooked smile. "Oh, I don't know, I had a feeling you'd be back. Get aboard. You look famished. The crew is preparing a special dinner—"

"I've already eaten your pheasants. I can't ask for anything more."

"Nonsense," Captain Royston laughed. "Those were only the hors d 'oeuvres. The real meal will be tonight where you'll eat like the Queen you are."

"What of him?" Saress asked as the two men led Barrett below deck.

Captain Royston watched the beat up and exhausted man fade into the darkness of the stairwell. "Let him eat slop."

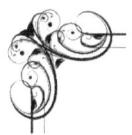

Chapter 115

he Whispering Woods, which once sheltered so many with ancient trees and dense canopies, was nothing more than a graveyard of smoldering husks. The sparkling rivers and fresh streams that carried life to the forest were nothing now but clogged veins of soupy ash, ripe with the raw stench of bloated fish. The dingy light which filtered through the smoky haze did little to brighten the colorless gray environment. Even with the steady rain, it would take months to extinguish the hot spots and even longer to wash away the smell.

Two weeks had passed since the siege ended and the ground cooled enough for Karayan to enter. Sloshing through the ash, he arrived at what he believed to be the center of Rhunsiire. It was here he expected to find a pile of blackened bones partly covered with charred flesh. Frustration filled his sunken eyes, and his pale face creased with anger as he slowly turned in a complete circle. "Find me their bones—NOW!" He screamed at his men.

Doing as instructed, his men set out only to return later that evening with disappointing news. "We've searched the entire area, and the only bones we discovered are those from a cemetery on a grassy knoll."

Karayan curled his fingers inward, forming white-knuckled fists. "I want every inch searched. Somewhere, in one of these charred stumps is the entrance to a tunnel."

The men set out again on a more thorough search but quickly returned with dire news. "My King, we've located a network of caves and determined it was once the home of the cave trolls. There is also evidence of reptiles residing there as well. Unfortunately, the caves are not deep, and no tunnels located. Currently, we have still yet to discover a single bone."

"My King," a young soldier offered his opinion. "Perhaps they slipped between our ranks in the dark of night and fled."

"Negative," the general snarled, then slapped the soldier for his utter insolence. "We had three layers of men, each overlapping the other to prevent that very thing. They're here, somewhere, hiding like cowards."

"They are doing no such thing." A crow-like voice hissed from the shaded interior of a burnt-out home which lay cockeyed from where it fell from a fallen tree.

"Who are you? Step into the light before I have my men drag you out, kicking and screaming," Karayan demanded.

Detaching from the darkness, a cloaked man materialized. "You've failed. Not one has perished, not even a squirrel."

"You lie," the general screamed. "If they live, you aided them and will face the swift punishment of my blade." The sword made a faint hiss as it slid free.

"The words you speak are true. Unknowingly, I did aid them. But I am not alone in my failures. If you wish to kill me for my part in their escape, then you must kill Karayan as well, for he is as guilty as I."

The general looked to Karayan, then quickly reverted his attention to the strange man. "Reveal yourself," the general demanded. "Or I will run you through with my blade."

"I grow tired of your frivolous threats," Malvo cackled, then hissed a quick spell.

The guard suddenly jerked rigid, and his arm popped free of the joint and twisted at a gross angle dislocating the elbow. "No, please no," he cried out and tried to resist, but something with inhuman strength controlled his arm. Slowly, as if enjoying itself, the arm placed the blade against the meaty part of the throat. "Please, NO," the general screamed for the last time as his arm began sawing. At first, only a thin red line appeared until the steel hit both arteries, and the intense pressure of both arteries popped the head free as blood sprayed like a fountain. The corpse should have fallen, yet it wiped the blade clean and slid it back into the sheath before falling at Karayan's feet.

Karayan looked down at his general then up at the stranger. Even though the man remained cloaked, he knew of no other who could complete such a heinous act. "Malvo Necrosyse. I wondered when you were going to rear your ugly head."

"What an ugly thing to say, especially after everything I've done for you."

"What have you done besides allow the bearer to escape. Your pet was worthless—"

"My pet did as I instructed. Had it not been for that filthy Elf Queen, he would still be at my side." Malvo raised his cowl exposing his bone-white face, piercing eyes, and thin black lips.

Karayan's blood ran cold. "You bastard," he snarled, then suddenly changed his demeanor, knowing the power this necromancer possessed. "Since you know they escaped. I assume you know where they fled?"

Malvo shrugged his shoulders. "I have no idea where they fled. Elwrick is cunning, and he now has a Witch under his training. Between the two, the possibilities are endless."

Karayan laughed. "Witches went extinct centuries ago; you're more senile than I imagined. Now, for the last time—"

"You're wrong, one remains, and her name is Lucinda Krauss. I believe you know her quite well as she also goes by the false name of Lilith."

Karayan's eyebrows raised.

"Lilith isn't the woman you believe her to be," Malvo said. "Her history goes much deeper than you can imagine. It took me a long time of searching to find her, but she escaped my control."

Karayan let out a bellowing laugh that echoed through the dismal environment. "You, keep a Witch," Karayan laughed again, "Your powers are child-like compared to a Witch. She would destroy you—"

"I couldn't agree more," Malvo chuckled, then cocked his head slightly to one side. "If I were a necromancer as you believe."

Karayan eyed him suspiciously. "What are you getting at old man?"

"Long before you were born, I sought out Lucinda to be the mother of my child. She fled after she became with child—"

"A Witch cannot carry the child of a necromancer," Karayan sternly explained.

"Lucinda, or Lilith, as you know her is a Witch, there can be no doubt, and she carried my child up until the point she fled."

"If what you speak is true, then where is this bastard child?"

Malvo took a deep breath. "For the longest time, I believed him destroyed. I recently discovered he isn't dead but has been living among us all the time, even working for you at one point. He goes by multiple names, such as Demetrius or Pegan Rhoe. Elwrick performed a banishment removing my seed from him. That is how I discovered the truth, but now I know. Regardless, believing Lucinda killed my child is why you live today. I needed someone who could easily influence the people yet was a fool at heart and easily manipulated. You fit my demands perfectly."

Seconds ago, the crowd focused on Malvo. Now, they turned to Karayan to see his reaction.

Karayan crossed his arms. "My ears have heard enough of your lies and twisted tales. Tell me now where they fled, or I will—"

"You will do what?" Malvo asked. With a simple twitch of his fingers, a flap of thick skin grew over Karayan's mouth. "I grow tired of this conversation, as well. I thought you might want to know what your purpose was before you die, but I guess not."

The skin on Karayan's face flexed as his jaw moved from what appeared to be a scream. Sweat dripped from his face, and both eyes widened until his bushy eyebrows blended in with his disheveled hair.

"Make him kneel," Malvo demanded to Vexacion.

Emerging from the building was several translucent men all wearing black robes. One broke away from the rest and sliced the tendons behind each knee, dropping Karayan.

Even though he was gagged with his own skin, they could hear his cries of pain.

Malvo squatted before Karayan. He could hear the air swishing in and out of each nostril. "Hmmm," he said, then pinched the nose closed until Karayan's face turned three shades of icy blue. "My Father extended his gratitude by offering you a second chance by delivering the souls of Pegan and Lilith to him, and yet you have failed him again."

Karayan fought to fill his lungs with air while attempting to plead.

"I believe the option of another attempt would only delay the inevitable. Good-by Karayan, and may my Father show you some mercy for the souls you have delivered. Somehow though, I find that highly unlikely."

Karayan's face flushed with fright, and his eyes held a distant stare.

Chanting words in a foreign tongue, Malvo raised his hands in the air, and a black mist swirled up from the ash and surrounded Karayan. Thrashing sounds could be heard, and then there was a sudden silence. When the haze faded, there was no blood, no bones, no Karayan. Only the remnants of smoldering clothing and twisted armor.

Each man stood there with their mouths open, not sure exactly what to say or do.

"Come," Malvo said to his men. "It is time to bring chaos to the world and substantially increase our ranks while we prepare for the final destruction of mankind…"

About the Author

J.R. Harris writes action-packed, fast paced, adventure novels where often the main characters are not of human descent. Despite going into the military right after high school then earning his bachelor's degree in Criminal Justice, his love affair with the strange and unusual has always remained strong. An avid reader, gamer, dungeon master, campaign designer, and map creator has left him with a twisted and distorted imagination which propels him to bring to life strange and exotic tales in ways never before imagined possible. Born in Michigan, he now resides in the Greater Pacific Northwest with his wife, dog, and two cats whittling away the days in front of his computer working on his great next novel. **For more information visit him at JRHarris.net and possibly get a sneak peek at his next great adventure.**